ROBINSON CRUSOE

and

A JOURNAL OF
THE PLAGUE YEAR

By DANIEL DEFOE

With an Introduction by
LOUIS KRONENBERGER

THE
MODERN LIBRARY

NEW YORK

THE MODERN LIBRARY
is published by RANDOM HOUSE, INC.

BENNETT CERF • DONALD S. KLOPFER

Manufactured in the United States of America by H. Wolff

CONTENTS

*   *   *

A Journal of the Plague Years   343

INTRODUCTION

by Louis Kronenberger

AMONG the world's great writers, scarcely any has cared so much about expediency, has been so philistine and calculating in his methods as Defoe; and yet none, in a sense, has calculated so badly. For though his works of fiction run to sixteen solid volumes, to the world at large he is simply and solely the author of *Robinson Crusoe*: the rays of that blinding sun have quite extinguished even such brilliant stars as *Moll Flanders* and *Roxana* and *A Journal of the Plague Year*. But that is hardly the worst of it. To the world at large, *Robinson Crusoe*, however celebrated, is not a book for men but a book for boys; lore, not literature. It is something that everybody has read, though perhaps not everybody can remember reading it; it is, or was until recently, as much a part of boyhood as the slingshot and the circus. But it can hardly be said to rank with the indispensable, or with even the most popular, novels for grownups. The reason why—or, better yet, the instinct why—is easy to grasp. If one is not a sentimentalist, one may well wonder whether even the very greatest of boys' books will constitute an exhilarating experience for men. And if one *is* a sentimentalist, one may wonder whether anything one loved so much in childhood should be touched, tampered with, re-examined—how can it help letting one down?

Well, one can only speak for oneself; but when some years ago I went back to *Robinson Crusoe*, I was enthralled. I'm sure it helped that I went back rather expecting to be disappointed, as it may hinder if, after reading this introduction, you expect to be instantly dazzled. But I doubt whether it helped, and I doubt whether it can hinder, much. I can understand (though not easily) anyone quitting the book before Crusoe gets shipwrecked on the island, or again after Crusoe sails away from it. And I can understand (quite easily) anyone who should impatiently toss aside the succeeding volume of Crusoe's adventures—because I have twice done that myself. But in the present book, so long as Robinson is held fast on the island, so long must the reader be too. For just that long, he is in the presence of a masterpiece, and of what might almost be declared a miracle: for a situation that has, in itself, an intense and universal lure is somehow handled exactly as it should be. The only thing that for me has the same kind of magnetism as the island section of *Robinson Crusoe* is the piloting chapters of *Life on the Mississippi.* In both we are offered what might be called a discourse on method; and in the plain utilitarian details of both there is something immensely romantic, something that fires our youth, and then long after rekindles it.

For however grim and disconsolate the situation of a man all alone on an island, who ever saw Crusoe there in any such light? So far from making his hero tragic, Defoe makes us—or at least the eternal boy in us—not pity but envy him. Crusoe is not only monarch of all he surveys; but by virtue of his experiences and his predicament he acquires for us something like the rank of a mighty hunter or a great explorer. What were in truth quite back-breaking obstacles are time and again made to seem like glorious opportunities; he is no realist who pursues *Crusoe* as realism. This is no poor devil who while under sentence, as it were, of solitary confinement must also forage for food and beware of cannibals. This, rather, is a man with a whole island for a toy, who may build him as many residences and pleasuredoms as he fancies, and trek lordlike through his own forests and sail along his coasts and herd his goats and harvest his crops and ransack the ship for plunder. There is something of the morning of the world about it all; yet together with the unspotted opportunities of the first man, Crusoe has all the ingrained skill and knowledge of many generations of Britons. Hence, singlehanded, he converts a rough-hewn Eden into a rough-hewn England. From one point of view, it is odd that we should find all this romantic; for Crusoe's stubborn resistance to the call of the wild is so outside Nature that it could only be believed of something so equally outside Nature as the trueborn Englishman. We can be very glad of this, however. For it would need a rather diseased taste to enjoy watching Robinson sink to the level of the brute and perhaps below it; whereas there is a healthy and creative satisfaction in watching him turn his island into a tidy Little England.

Which brings us to something stranger still—the fact that Crusoe's story is so intensely interesting only because Crusoe himself is so incredibly dull. But then, to do what he did he had to be what he was; to make a second England he had to believe fanatically in the first; not to go mad at the end he had to be a trifle mad from the outset; in the midst of abounding self-pity he had to be sustained by consuming self-interest; even God had to be a sort of Magnate with whom, in effect, a lesser businessman could bargain. Of all the great heroes of fiction Crusoe is surely the one who would have bored us the most in the flesh. With me, indeed, it is a nice point whether I should prefer to be shipwrecked, as he was, alone; or with him alone for company. He has no humor, no charm, no sensibility, no reach of mind, no grace of perception. Dickens truly remarked that *Crusoe* is the one great novel that never calls forth either laughter or tears. Robinson is smug, he is crass, he is—like Defoe himself—hypocritical in grain. But if he contains almost everything that is arid and coarse in the British character, he exemplifies, as well, everything that is admirable. He is plucky, sturdy, self-reliant, practical, imperturbable— the very essence of that race that thinks it unmanly to grumble and ungentlemanly to gloat.

Others have noted how cleverly Defoe allowed Crusoe just enough in the way of equipment and fodder and tools for him at the outset to stay alive, and in the course of time to be made comfortable. And to a nicety too, I would add, Defoe has contrived when total solitude shall cease. For at length the point is reached where Robinson has achieved as much in the way of civilization as he

finds possible, or we find fun; it is the point where, in a
commoner run of novel, the hero after long and arduous
struggle has made his pile and is ready for a mate. Defoe
cannot in the circumstances offer Crusoe a mate; and he
need not—a companion, for the reader at any rate, does
quite as well. So lo! there appears in the sand that single
footprint which is still, after two centuries, more dramatic and thrilling than all the fingerprints in the very
best whodunits; and presently there appears on the
scene that savage who is still, after two centuries, the
most famous of all servants. Once he has Friday to edu-
cate, Crusoe can embark on his great secondary English
role; having contrived all by himself a Little England, he
turns Friday all by himself into a Little India. After that,
and a round of skirmishing with cannibals, it is permitted
to sail for home.

After that, there are further adventures, of course—as
there had been a whole slew of them before the shipwreck. But the picaresque parts of the book, though
lively, are no part of the miracle; the miracle belongs to
the island, where neither Crusoe nor Defoe can go astray,
nor Robinson be ever anywhere but at home. And this
is of enormous help to a teller of stories who is absolutely
incapable of constructing a genuine plot. Defoe can in-
vent endlessly, but hardly integrate at all; one thing does
not come out of another, it merely comes after it. The
artistic shortcomings, the essential discontinuity of such
a method are obvious; and it can be truthfully main-
tained that Defoe's genius most expands where his ge-
ography least does—in the island parts of *Crusoe*, and in
the *Plague Year*. For these two works have something of

the concentration of interest, the intensive force that distinguish the novel from the tale, and the work of art from the mere irruption of talent. On the other hand, by the singularity of their subject-matter, they have had not the slightest influence on the serious novel itself; whereas *Moll Flanders* and *Roxana* have probably had a good deal.

No doubt there is much to say of the exotic fascination of *Robinson Crusoe;* of the oppressive sense of danger and appalling sense of solitude; of the flora and fauna, the parrots and cats. But this side of the story counted much more for me in boyhood than it does now. What lures me on is much less the creepiness of the island noises at midnight than tomorrow's straightforward effort to build a fence or bake a pot; the given A and B, how to contrive C; the given A B and C, how to bring off D— straight on to ampersand. This marvelous resourcefulness on Crusoe's part, this determination to wrest comfort out of chaos, this transforming a wilderness into a one-man state, in which he is both architect and builder, husband-man and housewife, management and labor, commoner and king, awakens in us a very delighted response. But of course *Crusoe* does have much also in the way of thrills and suspense—consider the blood-curdling en-counter with the wolves; and it is the greatest of all boys' books because it is about equally compounded of der-ring-do and *Do and Dare,* the adventure yarn and the Alger story. Accordingly this dullard that one would in real life run screaming from has caught and forever held the imagination of mankind.

A Journal of the Plague Year is, artistically, Defoe's least faulty production. It is the story of just one thing, a plague; and it is confined to just one spot, Greater London. Hence nothing else of Defoe's has a like unity of theme and development; and I think nothing else has quite as much or as marvelous factuality, or knack for making what is fictitious seem genuine.

Of this particular quality Defoe—as who is not aware —had more than any other writer that ever lived; he is by general consent the great master of the convincing detail, the plausible contradiction, the effective irrelevancy, the bright, bland testimony, the true-sounding lie. No one else has ever been so crafty about appearing so honest; one reason why we believe what Defoe tells us is that much of it isn't worth being told; but of course the triviality is the essence of the trick. So again is the extraordinary specificness. Emerson said that Swift—who had much of Defoe's genius for prosaic detail—always described his characters as though for the police: the *Plague Year* impresses you as written for the College of Medicine or the Board of Health. It has the look of something to be used for reference rather than read for pleasure. It is probably the greatest fake document of its length in all literature; and even for a writer who was always trying to make fiction sound like fact, it is a superb tour de force.

To be sure, it gets a great deal of support from history; is, in fact, *very nearly* true. Its account of the plague probably resembles the real plague far more than Crusoe's adventures resemble Selkirk's. There were actual documents for Defoe to draw on, there were his own early recollections and the many first-hand accounts he must have heard from childhood. Even as a document, the *Plague Year* is no doubt a very good guide, true in all essentials and historical in most details. But the point is that Defoe made of his account a seamless whole, and we shall never know just how much of it is fiction and how much is fact.

In any case, the picture it provides is an indelible one; the almost droning clinical manner, the countless statistics, the ceaseless examples all operating in its favor. The effect is the more awful because no effect seems aimed after; as when somebody tells a particularly gruesome story in a particularly flat voice. Furthermore, it is only this flat voice, this matter-of-fact manner, that sustains the length of the book; if it were at all high-pitched, if it used any of the standard devices for being dramatic or pathetic or horrifying, it would soon become a mere melodrama of hideousness, and at length a downright anticlimax of woes. As it is, by making no emotional demands on us, Defoe can pack in an extraordinary amount of physical detail. We are not asked to care deeply about his victims; they die like flies without ever having lived as people. Today, moreover, the horror of the epidemic is somewhat mitigated for us by the remoteness of the disease; and though the awful "tokens" have a fearsome quality still, we can read about the plague with an equanimity we should hardly possess reading about a terrible fictional epidemic of, say, infantile paralysis.

If the personal stories of agony and death, the accounts of entire households and streets and boroughs being laid low, the narratives of frantic and belated migration, the night-lighted pictures of mass burial—if these have not quite the impact of the greatest literature, one and all have the interest of brilliantly graphic journalism. Only in a few places, I think, is one deeply touched; only in a few more truly terrified; but there is hardly a page without something to absorb or appal one, and there are whole stretches—late in the book as well as early—when one is altogether fascinated. That the book as a whole is too long, too loaded with statistics, too studded with examples, too repetitive of facts, too sauntering of movement, may show want of discretion but is yet evidence of art: Defoe gives us more than we need so as to give the book a supreme verisimilitude, an air past all doubt of being a genuine document. I am sure that if we did not know this was fiction we would never suspect it to be. But knowing it, we do tend to find it just a touch too clever for its own good; there are places here, as in almost all Defoe's writing, where we—I am not sure that the metaphor is original—smell out the confidence man in him, and find him so plausible as to be specious. Defoe's marvelous factuality, his wonderful imagination about anything unimaginative, enables him to do superlatively what, in a man of high talent, is not quite, perhaps, worth doing at all. And in the end his very clearsightedness, his 20–20 literary vision, comes to seem a mild form of distortion in itself; we feel that all this is so, but that this is not all. Nobody is better to read than Defoe when one has had one's fill of ecstasy or even emotion; but after a great stretch of him one is glad for the books that do offer laughter and tears.

ROBINSON CRUSOE

Preface

IF EVER the story of any private man's adventures in the world were worth making public, and were acceptable when published, the editor of this account thinks this will be so.

The wonders of this man's life exceed all that (he thinks) is to be found extant; the life of one man being scarce capable of a greater variety.

The story is told with modesty, with seriousness, and with a religious application of events to the uses to which wise men always apply them (viz.) to the instruction of others by this example, and to justify and honor the wisdom of Providence in all the variety of our circumstances, let them happen how they will.

The editor believes the thing to be a just history of fact; neither is there any appearance of fiction in it. And however thinks, because all such things are dispatched, that the improvement of it, as well to the diversion, as to the instruction of the reader, will be the same; and as such, he thinks, without farther compliment to the world, he does them a great service in the publication.

Advice to a Son

I WAS born in the year 1632, in the city of York, of a good family, though not of that country, my father being a foreigner of Bremen who settled first at Hull. He got a good estate by merchandise and, leaving off his trade, lived afterward at York, from whence he had married my mother, whose relations were named Robinson, a very good family in that country, and from whom I was called Robinson Kreutznaer; but by the usual corruption of words in England we are now called, nay, we call ourselves, and write our name "Crusoe," and so my companions always called me.

I had two elder brothers, one of which was lieutenant-colonel to an English regiment of foot in Flanders, formerly commanded by the famous Colonel Lockhart, and was killed at the battle near Dunkirk against the Spaniards; what became of my second brother I never knew, any more than my father or mother did know what was become of me.

Being the third son of the family, and not bred to any trade, my head began to be filled very early with rambling thoughts. My father, who was very ancient, had given me a competent share of learning, as far as house education and a country free school generally goes, and designed me for the law; but I would be satisfied with nothing but going to sea; and my inclination to this led me so strongly against the will, nay, the commands of my father and against all the entreaties and persuasions of my mother and other friends that there seemed to be something fatal in that propension of nature tending directly to the life of misery which was to befall me.

My father, a wise and grave man, gave me serious and excellent counsel against what he foresaw was my design. He called me one morning into his chamber, where he was confined by the gout, and expostulated very warmly with me upon this subject. He asked me what reasons more than a mere wandering inclination I had for leaving my father's house and my native country, where I might be well introduced, and had a prospect of raising my fortune by application and industry, with a life of ease and pleasure. He told me it was for men of desperate fortunes on one hand, or of aspiring, superior fortunes on the other, who went abroad upon adventures, to rise by enterprise, and make themselves famous in undertakings of a nature out of the common road; that these things were all either too far above me, or too far below me; that mine was the middle state, or what might be called the upper station of low life, which he had found by long experience was the best state in the world, the most suited to human happiness, not exposed to the miseries and hardships, the labor and sufferings of the mechanic part of mankind and not embarrassed with the pride, luxury, ambition, and envy of the upper part of mankind. He told me I might judge of the happiness of this state by this one thing, viz., that this was the state of life which all other people envied; that kings have frequently lamented the miserable consequences of being born to great things, and wished they had been placed in the middle of the two extremes, between the mean and the great; that the wise man gave his testimony to this as the just standard of true felicity, when he prayed to have neither poverty or riches.

He bid me observe it, and I should always find, that the calamities of life were shared among the upper and lower part of mankind; but that the middle station had the fewest disasters, and was not exposed to so many vicissitudes as the higher or lower part of mankind; nay, they were not subjected to so many distempers and uneasinesses either of body or mind as those were who, by vicious living, luxury, and extravagances on one hand, or by hard labor, want of necessaries, and mean or insufficient diet on the other hand, bring distempers upon themselves by the natural consequences of their way of living; that the middle station of life was calculated for all kind of virtues and all kinds of enjoyments; that peace and plenty were the handmaids of a middle fortune; that temperance, moderation, quietness, health, society, all agreeable diversions, and all desirable pleasures, were the blessings attending the middle station of life; that this way men went silently and smoothly through the world, and comfortably out of it, not embarrassed with the labors of the hands or of the head, not sold to the life of slavery for daily bread, or harassed with perplexed circumstances, which rob the soul of peace and the body of rest; not enraged with the passion of envy or secret burning lust of ambition for great things; but in easy circumstances sliding gently through the world, and sensibly tasting the sweets of living, without the bitter, feeling that they are happy and learning by every day's experience to know it more sensibly.

After this, he pressed me earnestly, and in the most affectionate manner, not to play the young man, not to precipitate myself into miseries which Nature and the station of life I was born in seemed to have provided against; that I was under no necessity of seeking my bread; that he would do well for me, and endeavor to enter me fairly into the station of life which he had been just recommending to me; and that if I was not very easy and happy in the world, it must be my mere fate or fault that must hinder it, and that he should have nothing to answer for, having thus discharged his duty in warning me against measures which he knew would be to my hurt. In a word, that as he would do very kind things for me if I would stay and settle at home as he directed, so he would not have so much hand in my misfortunes as to give me any encouragement to go away. And to close all, he told me I had my elder brother for an example, to whom he had used the same earnest persuasions to keep him from going into the Low Country wars, but could not prevail, his young desires prompting him to run into the army where he was killed; and though he said he would not cease to pray for me, yet he would venture to say to me that if I did take this foolish step, God would not bless me, and I would have leisure hereafter to reflect upon having neg-lected his counsel when there might be none to assist in my recovery.

I observed in this last part of his discourse, which was truly prophetic, though I suppose my father did not know it to be so himself; I say, I observed the tears run down his face very plentifully, and especially when he spoke of my brother who was killed; and that when he spoke of my having leisure to repent, and none to assist me, he was so moved that he broke off the discourse and told me his heart was so full he could say no more to me.

Bent Upon Seeing the World

I WAS sincerely affected with this discourse, as indeed who could be otherwise? and I resolved not to think of going abroad any more but to settle at home according to my father's desire. But alas! a few days wore it all off;

and in short, to prevent any of my father's farther impor-
tunities, in a few weeks after I resolved to run quite away
from him. However, I did not act so hastily neither as my
first heat of resolution prompted, but I took my mother,
at a time when I thought her a little pleasanter than ordinary, and told her that my thoughts were so entirely bent
upon seeing the world that I should never settle to anything with resolution enough to go through with it, and
my father had better give me his consent than force me
to go without it; that I was now eighteen years old, which
was too late to go apprentice to a trade or clerk to an
attorney; that I was sure, if I did, I should never serve
out my time, and I should certainly run away from my
master before my time was out and go to sea; and if she
would speak to my father to let me go one voyage abroad,
if I came home again and did not like it, I would go no
more, and I would promise by a double diligence to recover that time I had lost.

This put my mother into a great passion. She told me
she knew it would be to no purpose to speak to my father
upon any such subject; that he knew too well what was
my interest to give his consent to anything so much for
my hurt, and that she wondered how I could think of any
such thing after such a discourse as I had had with my
father, and such kind and tender expressions as she knew
my father had used to me; and that, in short, if I would
ruin myself there was no help for me; but I might depend
I should never have their consent to it; that for her part
she would not have so much hand in my destruction; and
I should never have it to say that my mother was willing
when my father was not.

Though my mother refused to move it to my father,
yet as I have heard afterwards, she reported all the discourse to him, and that my father, after shewing a great
concern at it, said to her with a sigh, "That boy might be

happy if he would stay at home, but if he goes abroad he will be the most miserable wretch that was ever born. I can give no consent to it."

It was not till almost a year after this that I broke loose, though in the meantime I continued obstinately deaf to all proposals of settling to business, and frequently expostulating with my father and mother about their being so positively determined against what they knew my inclinations prompted me to. But being one day at Hull, where I went casually, and without any purpose of making an elopement that time; but I say, being there, and one of my companions being going by sea to London in his father's ship and prompting me to go with them, with the common allurement of seafaring men, viz., that it should cost me nothing for my passage, I consulted neither father or mother any more, nor so much as sent them word of it; but leaving them to hear of it as they might, without asking God's blessing, or my father's, without any consideration of circumstances or consequences and in an ill hour, God knows, on the first of September, 1651, I went on board a ship bound for London. Never any young adventurer's misfortunes, I believe, began sooner or continued longer than mine. The ship was no sooner gotten out of the Humber but the wind began to blow and the sea to rise in a most frightful manner; and as I had never been at sea before, I was most inexpressibly sick in body and terrified in my mind. I began now seriously to reflect upon what I had done, and how justly I was overtaken by the judgment of Heaven for my wicked leaving my father's house and abandoning my duty; all the good counsel of my parents, my father's tears and my mother's entreaties came now fresh into my mind, and my conscience, which was not yet come to the pitch of hardness to which it has been since, reproached me with the contempt of advice and the breach of my duty to God and my father.

All this while the storm increased and the sea, which I had never been upon before, went very high, though nothing like what I have seen many times since; no, nor like what I saw a few days after. But it was enough to affect me then, who was but a young sailor and had never known anything of the matter. I expected every wave would have swallowed us up and that every time the ship fell down, as I thought, in the trough or hollow of the sea, we should never rise more; and in this agony of mind I made many vows and resolutions, that if it would please God here to spare my life this one voyage, if ever I got once my foot upon dry land again, I would go directly home to my father and never set it into a ship again while I lived; that I would take his advice and never run myself into such miseries as these any more. Now I saw plainly the goodness of his observations about the middle station of life, how easy, how comfortably he had lived all his days, and never had been exposed to tempests at sea or troubles on shore; and I resolved that I would, like a true repenting prodigal, go home to my father.

These wise and sober thoughts continued all the while the storm continued, and indeed some time after; but the next day the wind was abated and the sea calmer, and I began to be a little inured to it. However, I was very grave for all that day, being also a little seasick still; but towards night the weather cleared up, the wind was quite over, and a charming fine evening followed; the sun went down perfectly clear and rose so the next morning; and having little or no wind and a smooth sea, the sun shining upon it, the sight was, as I thought, the most delightful that ever I saw.

I had slept well in the night and was now no more seasick, but very cheerful, looking with wonder upon the sea that was so rough and terrible the day before and could be so calm and so pleasant in so little time after. And now lest my good resolutions should continue, my companion, who had indeed enticed me away, comes to me. "Well, Bob," says he, clapping me on the shoulder, "how do you do after it? I warrant you were frighted, wa'n't you, last night, when it blew but a capful of wind?" "A capful, d'you call it?" said I, "'twas a terrible storm." "A storm, you fool, you," replies he; "do you call that a storm? why, it was nothing at all; give us but a good ship and sea-room, and we think nothing of such a squall of wind as that; but you're but a fresh-water sailor, Bob; come, let us make a bowl of punch and we'll forget all that; d'ye see what charming weather 'tis now?" To make short this sad part of my story, we went the old way of all sailors; the punch was made, and I was made drunk with it, and in that one night's wickedness I drowned all my repentance, all my reflections upon my past conduct and all my resolutions for my future. In a word, as the sea was returned to its smoothness of surface and settled calmness by the abatement of that storm, so the hurry of my thoughts being over, my fears and apprehensions of being swallowed up by the sea being forgotten, and the current of my former desires returned, I entirely forgot the vows and promises that I made in my distress. I found indeed some intervals of reflection, and the serious thoughts did, as it were, endeavor to return again sometimes; but I shook them off and roused myself from them as it were from a distemper and, applying myself to drink and company, soon mastered the return of those fits, for so I called them, and I had in five or six days got as complete a victory over conscience as any young fellow that resolved not to be troubled with it could desire. But I was to have another trial for it still; and Providence, as in such cases generally it does, resolved to leave me entirely without excuse. For if I would not take this for a deliverance, the next was to be such a one as the worst and most hardened wretch among us would confess both the danger and the mercy.

The sixth day of our being at sea we came into Yarmouth Roads; the wind having been contrary and the weather calm, we had made but little way since the storm. Here we were obliged to come to an anchor, and here we lay, the wind continuing contrary, viz., at southwest, for seven or eight days, during which time a great many ships from Newcastle came into the same Roads, as the common harbor where the ships might wait for a wind for the river.

We had not, however, rid here so long, but should have tided it up the river, but that the wind blew too fresh; and after we had lain four or five days, blew very hard. However, the Roads being reckoned as good as a harbor, the anchorage good, and our ground-tackle very strong, our men were unconcerned and not in the least apprehensive of danger, but spent the time in rest and mirth, after the manner of the sea; but the eighth day in the morning the wind increased, and we had all hands at work to strike our topmasts and make everything snug and close, that the ship might ride as easy as possible. By noon the sea went very high indeed, and our ship rid forecastle in, shipped several seas, and we thought once or twice our anchor had come home; upon which our master ordered out the sheet anchor, so that we rode with two anchors ahead and the cables veered out to the bitter end.

By this time it blew a terrible storm indeed, and now I began to see terror and amazement in the faces even of the seamen themselves. The master, though vigilant to the business of preserving the ship, yet as he went in and out of his cabin by me, I could hear him softly to himself say several times, "Lord, be merciful to us, we shall be all lost, we shall be all undone"; and the like. During these first hurries, I was stupid, lying still in my cabin, which was in the steerage, and cannot describe my temper; I could ill reassume the first penitence, which I had so apparently trampled upon, and hardened myself against. I thought the bitterness of death had been past and that this would be nothing too, like the first. But when the master himself came by me, as I said just now, and said we should be all lost, I was dreadfully frighted. I got up out of my cabin and looked out; but such a dismal sight I never saw: the sea went mountains high and broke upon us every three or four minutes. When I could look about, I could see nothing but distress round us: two ships that rid near us we found had cut their masts by the board, being deep loaden; and our men cried out that a ship which rid about a mile ahead of us was foundered. Two more ships, being driven from their anchors, were run out of the Roads to sea at all adventures, and that with not a mast standing. The light ships fared the best as not so much laboring in the sea; but two or three of them drove and came close by us, running away with only their spritsail out before the wind.

Towards evening the mate and boatswain begged the master of our ship to let them cut away the foremast, which he was very unwilling to do. But the boatswain protesting to him that if he did not the ship would founder, he consented; and when they had cut away the foremast, the mainmast stood so loose and shook the ship so much, they were obliged to cut her away also, and make a clear deck.

Anyone may judge what a condition I must be in at all this, who was but a young sailor, and who had been in such a fright before at but a little. But if I can express at this distance the thoughts I had about me at that time, I was in tenfold more horror of mind upon account of my former convictions, and the having returned from them to the resolutions I had wickedly taken at first, then I was at death itself; and these, added to the terror of the storm, put me into such a condition that I can by no words describe it. But the worst was not come yet; the storm continued with such fury that the seamen themselves acknowledged they had never known a worse. We had a good ship, but she was deep loaden, and wallowed in the sea, that the seamen every now and then cried out she would founder. It was my advantage in one respect that I did not know what they meant by "founder" till I enquired. However, the storm was so violent that I saw what is not often seen; the master, the boatswain, and some others more sensible than the rest, at their prayers and expecting every moment when the ship would go to the bottom. In the middle of the night, and under all the rest of our distresses, one of the men that had been down on purpose to see cried out we had sprung a leak; another said there was four foot water in the hold. Then all hands were called to the pump. At that very word my heart, as I thought, died within me, and I fell backwards upon the side of my bed where I sat into the cabin. However, the men roused me, and told me that I, that was able to do nothing before, was as well able to pump as another; at which I stirred up and went to the pump and worked very heartily. While this was doing, the master, seeing some light colliers, who, not able to ride out the storm, were obliged to slip and run away to sea, and would come near us, ordered to fire a gun as a signal of distress. I, who knew nothing what that meant, was so surprised, that I thought the ship had broke, or some dreadful thing had happened. In a word, I was so surprised that I fell down in a swoon. As this was a time when everybody had his own life to think of, nobody minded me, or what was become of me; but another man stepped up to the pump, and thrusting me aside with his foot, let me lie, thinking I had been dead; and it was a great while before I came to myself.

We worked on, but the water increasing in the hold, it was apparent that the ship would founder, and though the storm began to abate a little, yet as it was not possible she could swim till we might run into a port, so the master continued firing guns for help; and a light ship who had rid it out just ahead of us ventured a boat out to help us. It was with the utmost hazard the boat came near us, but it was impossible for us to get on board, or for the boat to lie near the ship side, till at last the men rowing very heartily and venturing their lives to save ours, our men cast them a rope over the stern with a buoy to it and then veered it out a great length, which they after great labor and hazard took hold of, and we hauled them close under our stern and got all into their boat. It was to no purpose for them or us after we were in the boat to think of reaching to their own ship, so all agreed to let her drive and only to pull her in towards shore as much as we could, and our master promised them, that if the boat was staved upon shore, he would make it good to their master; so, partly rowing and partly driving, our boat went away to the norward, sloping towards the shore almost as far as Winterton Ness.

We were not much more than a quarter of an hour out of our ship but we saw her sink, and then I understood for the first time what was meant by a ship foundering in the sea; I must acknowledge I had hardly eyes to look up when the seamen told me she was sinking; for from that moment they rather put me into the boat than that I might be said to go in, my heart was as it were dead within me, partly with fright, partly with horror of mind and the thoughts of what was yet before me.

While we were in this condition, the men yet laboring at the oar to bring the boat near the shore, we could see, when, our boat mounting the waves, we were able to see the shore, a great many people running along the shore to assist us when we should come near; but we made but slow way towards the shore, nor were we able to reach the shore, till being past the lighthouse at Winterton, the shore falls off to the westward towards Cromer, and so the land broke off a little the violence of the wind. Here we got in, and, though not without much difficulty, got all safe on shore and walked afterwards on foot to Yarmouth, where, as unfortunate men, we were used with great humanity as well by the magistrates of the town, who assigned us good quarters, as by particular merchants and owners of ships, and had money given us sufficient to carry us either to London or back to Hull, as we thought fit.

Had I now had the sense to have gone back to Hull, and have gone home, I had been happy, and my father, an emblem of our blessed Saviour's parable, had even killed the fatted calf for me; for hearing the ship I went away in was cast away in Yarmouth Roads, it was a great while before he had any assurance that I was not drowned.

But my ill fate pushed me on now with an obstinacy that nothing could resist; and though I had several times loud calls from my reason and my more composed judgment to go home, yet I had no power to do it. I know not what to call this, nor will I urge that it is a secret overruling decree that hurries us on to be the instruments of our own destruction, even though it be before us, and that we rush upon it with our eyes open. Certainly nothing but some such decreed unavoidable misery attending, and which it was impossible for me to escape, could have pushed me forward against the calm reasonings and persuasions of my most retired thoughts and against two such visible instructions as I had met with in my first attempt.

My comrade, who had helped to harden me before and who was the master's son, was now less forward than I; the first time he spoke to me after we were at Yarmouth, which was not till two or three days, for we were separated in the town to several quarters; I say, the first time he saw me, it appeared his tone was altered, and looking very melancholy and shaking his head, asked me how I did, and telling his father who I was, and how I had come this voyage only for a trial in order to go farther abroad; his father turning to me with a very grave and concerned tone, "Young man," says he, "you ought never to go to sea any more; you ought to take this for a plain and visible token that you are not to be a seafaring man." "Why, sir," said I, "will you go to sea no more?" "That is another case," said he, "it is my calling and therefore my duty; but as you made this voyage for a trial, you see what a taste Heaven has given you of what you are to expect if you persist; perhaps this is all befallen us on your account, like Jonah in the ship of Tarshish. Pray," continues he, "what are you? and on what account did you go to sea?" Upon that I told him some of my story; at the end of which he burst out with a strange kind of passion, "What had I done," says he, "that such an unhappy wretch should come into my ship? I would not set my foot in the same ship with thee again for a thousand pounds." This indeed was, as I said, an excursion of his spirits, which were yet agitated by the sense of his loss, and was farther than he could have authority to go. However, he afterwards talked very gravely to me, exhorted me to go back to my father and not tempt Providence to my ruin; told me I might see a visible hand of Heaven against me, "And, young man," said he, "depend upon it, if you do not go back, wherever you go, you will meet with nothing but disasters and disappointments, till your father's words are fulfilled upon you."

We parted soon after; for I made him little answer, and I saw him no more; which way he went, I know not. As for me, having some money in my pocket, I traveled to London by land; and there, as well as on the road, had many struggles with myself what course of life I should take, and whether I should go home or go to sea.

As to going home, shame opposed the best motions that offered to my thoughts; and it immediately occurred to me how I should be laughed at among the neighbors and should be ashamed to see not my father and mother only but even everybody else; from whence I have since often observed how incongruous and irrational the common temper of mankind is, especially of youth, to that reason which ought to guide them in such cases, viz., that they are not ashamed to sin, and yet are ashamed to repent; not ashamed of the action for which they ought justly to be esteemed fools but are ashamed of the returning, which only can make them be esteemed wise men.

In this state of life, however, I remained some time, uncertain what measures to take and what course of life to lead. An irresistible reluctance continued to going home; and as I stayed awhile, the remembrance of the distress I had been in wore off; and as that abated, the little motion I had in my desires to a return wore off with it, till at last I quite laid aside the thoughts of it and looked out for a voyage.

The Most Unfortunate of Enterprises

THAT evil influence which carried me first away from my father's house, that hurried me into the wild and in-digested notion of raising my fortune, and that impressed those conceits so forcibly upon me as to make me deaf to all good advice and to the entreaties and even command of my father; I say, the same influence, whatever it was, presented the most unfortunate of all enterprises to my view; and I went on board a vessel bound to the coast of Africa; or, as our sailors vulgarly call it, a voyage to Guinea.

It was my great misfortune that in all these adventures I did not ship myself as a sailor; whereby, though I might indeed have worked a little harder than ordinary, yet at the same time I had learned the duty and office of a foremast man; and in time might have qualified myself for a mate or lieutenant, if not for a master. But as it was always my fate to choose for the worse, so I did here; for having money in my pocket and good clothes upon my back, I would always go on board in the habit of a gentleman; and so I neither had any business in the ship, or learned to do any.

It was my lot first of all to fall into pretty good company in London, which does not always happen to such loose and unguided young fellows as I then was; the devil generally not omitting to lay some snare for them very early. But it was not so with me; I first fell acquainted with the master of a ship who had been on the coast of Guinea; and who having had very good success there was resolved to go again; and who taking a fancy to my conversation, which was not at all disagreeable at that time, hearing me say I had a mind to see the world, told me if I would go the voyage with him I should be at no expense; I should be his messmate and his companion, and if I could carry anything with me, I should have all the advantage of it that the trade would admit; and perhaps I might meet with some encouragement.

I embraced the offer, and, entering into a strict friendship with this captain, who was an honest and plaindealing man, I went the voyage with him and carried a small adventure with me, which, by the disinterested honesty of my friend the captain, I increased very considerably; for I carried about £40 in such toys and trifles as the captain directed me to buy. This £40 I had mustered together by the assistance of some of my relations whom I corresponded with, and who, I believe, got my father, or at least my mother, to contribute so much as that to my first adventure.

This was the only voyage which I may say was successful in all my adventures, and which I owe to the integrity and honesty of my friend the captain, under whom also I got a competent knowledge of the mathematics and the rules of navigation, learned how to keep an account of the ship's course, take an observation, and in short, to understand some things that were needful to be understood by a sailor. For, as he took delight to introduce me, I took delight to learn; and, in a word, this voyage made me both a sailor and a merchant; for I brought home five pounds nine ounces of gold dust for my adventure, which yielded me in London at my return almost £300, and this filled me with those aspiring thoughts which have since so completed my ruin.

Yet even in this voyage I had my misfortunes too; particularly, that I was continually sick, being thrown into a violent calenture [1] by the excessive heat of the climate; our principal trading being upon the coast, from the latitude of fifteen degrees north even to the line itself.

I was now set up for a Guinea trader; and my friend, to my great misfortune, dying soon after his arrival, I resolved to go the same voyage again, and I embarked in the same vessel with one who was his mate in the former voyage and had now got the command of the ship. This was the unhappiest voyage that ever man made; for

[1] *A tropical fever, characterized by delirium.*

though I did not carry quite £100 of my new-gained wealth, so that I had £200 left, and which I lodged with my friend's widow, who was very just to me, yet I fell into terrible misfortunes in this voyage; and the first was this, viz., our ship making her course towards the Canary Islands, or rather between those islands and the African shore, was surprised in the gray of the morning by a Turkish rover of Sallee, who gave chase to us with all the sail she could make. We crowded also as much canvas as our yards would spread, or our masts carry, to have got clear; but finding the pirate gained upon us, and would certainly come up with us in a few hours, we prepared to fight; our ship having twelve guns, and the rogue eighteen. About three in the afternoon he came up with us, and bringing to, by mistake, just athwart our quarter, instead of athwart our stern, as he intended, we brought eight of our guns to bear on that side and poured in a broadside upon him, which made him sheer off again, after returning our fire and pouring in also his small-shot from near 200 men which he had on board. However, we had not a man touched, all our men keeping close. He prepared to attack us again, and we to defend ourselves; but laying us on board the next time upon our other quarter, he entered sixty men upon our decks, who immediately fell to cutting and hacking the decks and rigging. We plied them with small-shot, half-pikes, powder chests, and such like, and cleared our deck of them twice. However, to cut short this melancholy part of our story, our ship being disabled, and three of our men killed and eight wounded, we were obliged to yield, and were carried all prisoners into Sallee, a port belonging to the Moors.

The usage I had there was not so dreadful as at first I apprehended, nor was I carried up the country to the emperor's court, as the rest of our men were, but was kept by the captain of the rover, as his proper prize, and made his slave, being young and nimble and fit for his business. At this surprising change of my circumstances from a merchant to a miserable slave, I was perfectly overwhelmed; and now I looked back upon my father's prophetic discourse to me, that I should be miserable and have none to relieve me, which I thought was now so effectually brought to pass that it could not be worse; that now the hand of Heaven had overtaken me, and I was undone without redemption. But alas! this was but a taste of the misery I was to go through, as will appear in the sequel of this story.

As my new patron or master had taken me home to his house, so I was in hopes that he would take me with him when he went to sea again, believing that it would some time or other be his fate to be taken by a Spanish or Portugal man-of-war; and that then I should be set at liberty. But this hope of mine was soon taken away; for when he went to sea, he left me on shore to look after his little garden and do the common drudgery of slaves about his house; and when he came home again from his cruise, he ordered me to lie in the cabin to look after the ship.

Here I meditated nothing but my escape and what method I might take to effect it, but found no way that had the least probability in it. Nothing presented to make the supposition of it rational; for I had nobody to communicate it to that would embark with me; no fellow-slave, no Englishman, Irishman, or Scotsman there but myself; so that for two years, though I often pleased myself with the imagination, yet I never had the least encouraging prospect of putting it in practice.

After about two years an odd circumstance presented itself, which put the old thought of making some attempt for my liberty again in my head. My patron lying at home longer than usual without fitting out his ship, which, as

I heard, was for want of money, he used constantly, once or twice a week, sometimes oftener if the weather was fair, to take the ship's pinnace and go out into the road a-fishing; and as he always took me and a young Moor with him to row the boat, we made him very merry, and I proved very dexterous in catching fish; insomuch, that sometimes he would send me with a Moor, one of his kinsmen, and the youth, the Moresco, as they called him to catch a dish of fish for him.

It happened one time that, going a-fishing in a stark calm morning, a fog rose so thick, that though we were not half a league from the shore we lost sight of it; and rowing we knew not whither or which way, we labored all day and all the next night, and when the morning came, we found we had pulled off to sea instead of pulling in for the shore; and that we were at least two leagues from the shore. However, we got well in again, though with a great deal of labor and some danger; for the wind began to blow pretty fresh in the morning; but particularly we were all very hungry.

But our patron, warned by this disaster, resolved to take more care of himself for the future; and having lying by him the longboat of our English ship he had taken, he resolved he would not go a-fishing any more without a compass and some provision; so he ordered the carpenter of his ship, who also was an English slave, to build a little stateroom or cabin in the middle of the longboat, like that of a barge, with a place to stand behind it to steer and hale home the main-sheet; and room before for a hand or two to stand and work the sails. She sailed with that we call a shoulder-of-mutton sail; and the boom jibed over the top of the cabin, which lay very snug and low and had in it room for him to lie, with a slave or two, and a table to eat on, with some small lockers to put in some bottles of such liquor as he thought fit to drink; particularly his bread, rice, and coffee.

We went frequently out with this boat a-fishing, and as I was most dexterous to catch fish for him, he never went without me. It happened that he had appointed to go out in this boat, either for pleasure or for fish, with two or three Moors of some distinction in that place, and for whom he had provided extraordinarily; and had therefore sent on board the boat over night, a larger store of provisions than ordinary; and had ordered me to get ready three fusees with powder and shot, which were on board his ship; for that they designed some sport of fowling as well as fishing.

I got all things ready as he had directed, and waited the next morning with the boat washed clean, her ancient [1] and pendants out, and everything to accommodate his guests; when by and by my patron came on board alone and told me his guests had put off going upon some business that fell out, and ordered me with the man and boy, as usual, to go out with the boat and catch them some fish, for that his friends were to sup at his house; and commanded that as soon as I had got some fish I should bring it home to his house; all which I prepared to do.

This moment my former notions of deliverance darted into my thoughts, for now I found I was like to have a little ship at my command; and my master being gone, I prepared to furnish myself, not for a fishing business but for a voyage; though I knew not, neither did I so much as consider whither I should steer; for anywhere to get out of that place was my way.

My first contrivance was to make a pretense to speak to this Moor to get something for our subsistence on board; for I told him we must not presume to eat of our

___
[1] Banner.

patron's bread; he said that was true; so he brought a large basket of rusk or biscuit of their kind and three jars with fresh water into the boat; I knew where my patron's case of bottles stood, which, it was evident by the make, were taken out of some English prize; and I conveyed them into the boat while the Moor was on shore, as if they had been there before, for our master. I conveyed also a great lump of beeswax into the boat, which weighed above half a hundredweight, with a parcel of twine or thread, a hatchet, a saw, and a hammer, all which were of great use to us afterwards; especially the wax to make candles. Another trick I tried upon him, which he innocently came into also. His name was Ismael, who they call Muly, or Moely; so I called to him, "Moely," said I, "our patron's guns are on board the boat; can you not get a little powder and shot? it may be we may kill some alcamies" (a fowl like our curlews) "for ourselves, for I know he keeps the gunner's stores in the ship." "Yes," says he, "I'll bring some"; and accordingly he brought a great leather pouch which held about a pound and a half of powder, or rather more; and another with shot, that had five or six pound, with some bullets; and put all into the boat. At the same time I had found some powder of my master's in the great cabin, with which I filled one of the large bottles in the case, which was almost empty, pouring what was in it into another; and thus furnished with everything needful, we sailed out of the port to fish. The castle, which is at the entrance of the port, knew who we were, and took no notice of us; and we were not above a mile out of the port before we haled in our sail and set us down to fish. The wind blew from the north-northeast, which was contrary to my desire; for had it blown southerly, I had been sure to have made the coast of Spain, and at least reached to the bay of Cadiz; but my resolutions were, blow which way it would, I would be gone from that horrid place where I was, and leave the rest to Fate.

After we had fished some time and catched nothing, for when I had fish on my hook, I would not pull them up, that he might not see them, I said to the Moor, "This will not do, our master will not be thus served, we must stand farther off." He, thinking no harm, agreed and, being in the head of the boat, set the sails; and as I had the helm, I run the boat out near a league farther and then brought her to as if I would fish; when giving the boy the helm, I stepped forward to where the Moor was, and making as if I stooped for something behind him, I took him by surprise with my arm under his twist and tossed him clear overboard into the sea; he rose immediately, for he swam like a cork, and called to me, begged to be taken in, told me he would go all over the world with me. He swam so strong after the boat that he would have reached me very quickly, there being but little wind; upon which I stepped into the cabin, and fetching one of the fowling pieces, I presented it at him and told him I had done him no hurt and, if he would be quiet, I would do him none. "But," said I, "you swim well enough to reach to the shore, and the sea is calm; make the best of your way to shore, and I will do you no harm; but if you come near the boat, I'll shoot you through the head, for I am resolved to have my liberty"; so he turned himself about and swam for the shore, and I make no doubt but he reached it with ease, for he was an excellent swimmer.

I could ha' been content to ha' taken this Moor with me and ha' drowned the boy, but there was no venturing to trust him. When he was gone I turned to the boy, who they called Xury, and said to him, "Xury, if you will be faithful to me I'll make you a great man; but if you will not stroke your face to be true to me," that is, swear by Mahomet and his father's beard, "I must throw you into the sea too." The boy smiled in my face, and spoke so innocently that I could not mistrust him; and swore to be faithful to me and go all over the world with me.

While I was in view of the Moor that was swimming, I stood out directly to sea with the boat, rather stretching to windward, that they might think me gone towards the Straits' mouth (as indeed anyone that had been in their wits must ha' been supposed to do); for who would ha' supposed we were sailed on to the southward to the truly barbarian coast, where whole nations of Negroes were sure to surround us with their canoes, and destroy us; where we could ne'er once go on shore but we should be devoured by savage beasts, or more merciless savages of human kind?

But as soon as it grew dusk in the evening, I changed my course, and steered directly south and by east, bending my course a little toward the east, that I might keep in with the shore; and having a fair, fresh gale of wind and a smooth, quiet sea, I made such sail that I believe by the next day at three o'clock in the afternoon, when I first made the land, I could not be less than 150 miles south of Sallee; quite beyond the Emperor of Morocco's dominions, or indeed of any other king thereabouts, for we saw no people.

Yet such was the fright I had taken at the Moors and the dreadful apprehensions I had of falling into their hands, that I would not stop or go on shore or come to an anchor, the wind continuing fair, till I had sailed in that manner five days: and then the wind shifting to the southward, I concluded also that if any of our vessels were in chase of me, they also would now give over; so I ventured to make to the coast and came to an anchor in the mouth of a little river. I knew not what or where; neither what latitude, what country, what nations or what river. I neither saw, or desired to see, any people; the principal thing I wanted was fresh water. We came into this creek in the evening, resolving to swim on shore as soon as it was dark, and discover the country; but as soon as it was quite dark, we heard such dreadful noises of the barking, roaring, and howling of wild creatures of we knew not what kinds that the poor boy was ready to die with fear and begged of me not to go on shore till day. "Well, Xury," said I, "then I won't; but it may be we may see men by day, who will be as bad to us as those lions." "Then we give them the shoot gun," says Xury, laughing; "make them run wey." Such English Xury spoke by conversing among us slaves. However, I was glad to see the boy so cheerful, and I gave him a dram (out of our patron's case of bottles) to cheer him up. After all, Xury's advice was good, and I took it. We dropped our little anchor and lay still all night; I say still, for we slept none! for in two or three hours we saw vast great creatures (we knew not what to call them) of many sorts come down to the seashore and run into the water, wallowing and washing themselves for the pleasure of cooling themselves; and they made such hideous howlings and yellings that I never indeed heard the like.

Xury was dreadfully frighted, and indeed so was I too; but we were both more frighted when we heard one of these mighty creatures come swimming towards our boat; we could not see him, but we might hear him by his blowing to be a monstrous huge and furious beast. Xury said it was a lion, and it might be so for aught I know; but poor Xury cried to me to weigh the anchor and row away. "No," says I, "Xury, we can slip our cable with the buoy to it and go off to sea; they cannot follow us far." I had no sooner said so but I perceived the creature (whatever it was) within two oars' length, which something surprised me; however, I immediately stepped to the cabin door, and taking up my gun, fired at him; upon which he immediately turned about and swam towards the shore again.

But it is impossible to describe the horrible noises and hideous cries and howlings that were raised, as well upon the edge of the shore as higher within the country, upon the noise or report of the gun, a thing I have some reason to believe those creatures had never heard before. This convinced me that there was no going on shore for us in the night upon that coast; and how to venture on shore in the day was another question too; for to have fallen into the hands of any of the savages had been as bad as to have fallen into the hands of lions and tigers; at least we were equally apprehensive of the danger of it.

Be that as it would, we were obliged to go on shore somewhere or other for water for we had not a pint left in the boat; when or where to get to it was the point. Xury said if I would let him go on shore with one of the jars, he would find if there was any water and bring some to me. I asked him why he would go? Why I should not go and he stay in the boat? They boy answered with so much affection that made me love him ever after. Says he, "If wild mans come, they eat me, you go wey." "Well, Xury," said I, "we will both go, and if the wild mans come, we will kill them; they shall eat neither of us"; so I gave Xury a piece of rusk bread to eat and a dram out of our patron's case of bottles which I mentioned before; and we haled the boat in as near the shore as we thought was proper, and so waded on shore, carrying nothing but our arms and two jars for water.

I did not care to go out of sight of the boat, fearing the coming of canoes with savages down the river; but the boy, seeing a low place about a mile up the country, rambled to it; and by and by I saw him come running towards me. I thought he was pursued by some savage or frighted with some wild beast, and I ran forward towards him to help him; but when I came nearer to him, I saw something hanging over his shoulders, which was a creature that he had shot, like a hare, but different in color and longer legs; however, we were very glad of it, and it was very good meat; but the great joy that poor Xury came with was to tell me he had found good water and seen no wild mans.

But we found afterwards that we need not take such pains for water, for a little higher up the creek where we were, we found the water fresh when the tide was out, which flowed but a little way up; so we filled our jars and feasted on the hare we had killed, and prepared to go on our way, having seen no footsteps of any human creature in that part of the country.

As I had been one voyage to this coast before, I knew very well that the islands of the Canaries and the Cape de Verde Islands also lay not far off from the coast. But as I had no instruments to take an observation to know what latitude we were in and did not exactly know or at least remember what latitude they were in, I knew not where to look for them or when to stand off to sea towards them; otherwise I might now easily have found some of these islands. But my hope was, that if I stood along this coast till I came to that part where the English traded, I should find some of their vessels upon their usual design of trade, that would relieve and take us in.

By the best of my calculation, that place where I now was must be that country, which lying between the Emperor of Morocco's dominions and the Negroes, lies waste and uninhabited, except by wild beasts; the Negroes having abandoned it and gone farther south for fear of the Moors, and the Moors not thinking it worth inhabiting by reason of its barrenness; and indeed both forsaking it because of the prodigious numbers of tigers, lions, leopards, and other furious creatures which harbor there; so that the Moors use it for their hunting only, where they go like an army, two or three thousand men at a time; and indeed for near an hundred miles together upon this coast, we saw nothing but a waste uninhabited country by day and heard nothing but howlings and roarings of wild beasts by night.

Once or twice in the daytime, I thought I saw the Pico of Teneriffe, being the high top of the mountain Teneriffe in the Canaries; and had a great mind to venture out, in hopes of reaching thither; but having tried twice, I was forced in again by contrary winds, the sea also going too high for my little vessel, so I resolved to pursue my first design and keep along the shore.

Several times I was obliged to land for fresh water, after we had left this place; and once in particular, being early in the morning, we came to an anchor under a little point of land which was pretty high, and the tide beginning to flow, we lay still to go farther in. Xury, whose eyes were more about him than it seems mine were, calls softly to me and tells me that we had best go farther off the shore. "For," says he, "look, yonder lies a dreadful monster on the side of that hillock, fast asleep." I looked where he pointed, and saw a dreadful monster indeed, for it was a terrible great lion that lay on the side of the shore, under the shade of a piece of the hill that hung as it were a little over him. "Xury," says I, "you shall go on shore and kill him." Xury looked frightened, and said, "Me kill; he eat me at one mouth"; one mouthful he meant. However, I said no more to the boy, but bade him lie still, and I took our biggest gun, which was almost musket-bore, and loaded it with a good charge of powder and with two slugs, and laid it down; then I loaded another gun with two bullets; and the third, for we had three pieces, I loaded with five smaller bullets. I took the best aim I could with the first piece to have shot him into the head, but he lay so with his leg raised a little above his nose, that the slugs hit his leg about the knee, and broke the bone. He started up growling at first, but finding his leg broke, fell down again, and then got up upon three legs and gave the most hideous roar that ever I heard. I was a little surprised that I had not hit him on the head; however, I took up the second piece immediately and though he began to move off fired again, and shot him into the head, and had the pleasure to see him drop and make but little noise, but lay struggling for life. Then Xury took heart, and would have me let him go on shore. "Well, go," said I, so the boy jumped into the water and, taking a little gun in one hand, swam to shore with the other hand and coming close to the creature, put the muzzle of the piece to his ear and shot him into the head again, which dispatched him quite.

This was game indeed to us but this was no food; and I was very sorry to lose three charges of powder and shot upon a creature that was good for nothing to us. However, Xury said he would have some of him; so he comes on board and asked me to give him the hatchet. "For what, Xury?" said I. "Me cut off his head," said he. However, Xury could not cut off his head, but he cut off a foot and brought it with him, and it was a monstrous great one.

I bethought myself, however, that perhaps the skin of him might one way or other be of some value to us; and I resolved to take off his skin if I could. So Xury and I went to work with him; but Xury was much the better workman at it for I knew very ill how to do it. Indeed it took us both the whole day, but at last we got off the hide of him, and spreading it on the top of our cabin, the sun effectually dried it in two days' time, and it afterwards served me to lie upon.

After this stop we made on to the southward continually for ten or twelve days, living very sparing on our provisions, which began to abate very much, and going no oftener in to the shore than we were obliged to for fresh water; my design in this was to make the river Gambia or Senegal, that is to say, anywhere about the Cape de Verde, where I was in hopes to meet with some European ship, and if I did not, I knew not what course I had to take, but to seek out for the islands, or perish there among the Negroes. I knew that all the ships from Europe which sailed either to the coast of Guinea or to Brazil or to the East Indies made this cape or those islands; and in a word, I put the whole of my fortune upon this single point, either that I must meet with some ship or must perish.

When I had pursued this resolution about ten days longer, as I have said, I began to see that the land was inhabited, and in two or three places, as we sailed by, we saw people stand upon the shore to look at us; we could also perceive they were quite black and stark naked. I was once inclined to ha' gone on shore to them; but Xury was my better counsellor and said to me, "No go, no go." However, I haled in nearer the shore that I might talk to them, and I found they run along the shore by me a good way. I observed they had no weapons in their hands, except one, who had a long slender stick, which Xury said was a lance, and that they would throw them a great way with good aim; so I kept at a distance, but talked with them by signs as well as I could, and particularly made signs for something to eat. They beckoned to me to stop my boat, and that they would fetch me some meat; upon this I lowered the top of my sail and lay by, and two of them run up into the country, and in less than half an hour came back, and brought with them two pieces of dry flesh and some corn, such as is the produce of their country, but we neither knew what the one or the other was; however, we were willing to accept it, but how to come at it was our next dispute, for I was not for venturing on shore to them, and they were as much afraid of us; but they took a safe way for us all, for they brought it to the shore and laid it down, and went and stood a great way off till we fetched it on board and then came close to us again.

We made signs of thanks to them, for we had nothing to make them amends; but an opportunity offered that very instant to oblige them wonderfully, for while we were lying by the shore, came two mighty creatures, one pursuing the other (as we took it) with great fury from the mountains towards the sea; whether it was the male pursuing the female, or whether they were in sport or in rage, we could not tell, any more than we could tell whether it was usual or strange, but I believe it was the latter; because in the first place, those ravenous creatures seldom appear but in the night; and in the second place, we found the people terribly frighted; especially the women. The man that had the lance or dart did not fly from them, but the rest did; however, as the two creatures ran directly into the water, they did not seem to offer to fall upon any of the Negroes, but plunged themselves into the sea and swam about, as if they had come for their diversion; at last one of them began to come nearer our boat than at first I expected; but I lay ready for him, for I had loaded my gun with all possible expedition, and bade Xury load both the other; as soon as he came fairly within my reach, I fired and shot him directly into the head; immediately he sunk down into the water, but rose instantly and plunged up and down as if he was struggling for life, and so indeed he was; he immediately made to the shore; but between the wound, which was his mortal hurt, and the strangling of the water, he died just before he reached the shore.

It is impossible to express the astonishment of these poor creatures at the noise and the fire of my gun; some of them were even ready to die for fear, and fell down as dead with very terror. But when they saw the creature dead and sunk in the water, and that I made signs to them to come to the shore, they took heart and came to the shore, and began to search for the creature. I found him by his blood staining the water, and by the help of a rope which I flung round him and gave the Negroes to haul, they dragged him on shore, and found that it was a most curious leopard, spotted and fine to an admirable degree, and the Negroes held up their hands with admiration to think what it was I had killed him with.

The other creature, frighted with the flash of fire and the noise of the gun, swam on shore, and ran up directly to the mountains from whence they came, nor could I at that distance know what it was. I found quickly the Negroes were for eating the flesh of this creature, so I was willing to have them take it as a favor from me, which, when I made signs to them that they might take him, they were very thankful for. Immediately they fell to work with him, and though they had no knife, yet with a sharpened piece of wood they took off his skin as readily and much more readily than we could have done with a knife; they offered me some of the flesh, which I declined, making as if I would give it them, but made signs for the skin, which they gave me very freely, and brought me a great deal more of their provision, which though I did not understand, yet I accepted; then I made signs to them for some water and held out one of my jars to them, turning it bottom upward, to show that it was empty, and that I wanted to have it filled. They called immediately to some of their friends, and there came two women and brought a great vessel made of earth, and burnt as I suppose in the sun; this they set down for me as before, and I sent Xury on shore with my jars and filled them all three. The women were as stark naked as the men.

I was now furnished with roots and corn, such as it was, and water, and leaving my friendly Negroes, I made forward for about eleven days more without offering to go near the shore, till I saw the land run out a great length into the sea, at about the distance of four or five leagues before me, and the sea being very calm, I kept a large offing to make this point; at length, doubling the point at about two leagues from the land, I saw plainly land on the other side, to seaward; then I concluded, as it was most certain indeed, that this was the Cape de Verde and those the islands, called from thence Cape de Verde Islands. However, they were at a great distance, and I could not well tell what I had best to do; for if I should be taken with a fresh of wind, I might neither reach one or other.

In this dilemma, as I was very pensive, I stepped into the cabin and sat me down, Xury having the helm; when on a sudden the boy cried out, "Master, master, a ship with a sail!" and the foolish boy was frighted out of his wits, thinking it must needs be some of his master's ships sent to pursue us, when I knew we were gotten far enough out of their reach. I jumped out of the cabin, and immediately saw, not only the ship, but what she was, viz., that it was a Portuguese ship, and, as I thought, was bound to the coast of Guinea for Negroes. But when I observed the course she steered, I was soon convinced they were bound some other way, and did not design to come any nearer to the shore; upon which I stretched out to sea as much as I could, resolving to speak with them, if possible.

With all the sail I could make, I found I should not be able to come in their way, but that they would be gone by before I could make any signal to them; but after I had crowded to the utmost and began to despair, they, it seems, saw me by the help of their perspective-glasses, and that it was some European boat, which as they supposed must belong to some ship that was lost, so they shortened sail to let me come up. I was encouraged with this, and as I had my patron's ancient on board, I made a waft of it to them for a signal of distress, and fired a gun, both which they saw, for they told me they saw the smoke, though they did not hear the gun; upon these signals they very kindly brought to and lay by for me, and in about three hours' time I came up with them.

They asked me what I was in Portuguese and in Spanish and in French, but I understood none of them; but at last a Scots sailor who was on board called to me, and I answered him and told him I was an Englishman, that I had made my escape out of slavery from the Moors, at Sallee; then they bade me come on board and very kindly took me in and all my goods.

I Came to the Brazils

IT WAS an inexpressible joy to me, that any one will believe, that I was thus delivered, as I esteemed it, from such a miserable and almost hopeless condition as I was in, and I immediately offered all I had to the captain of the ship as a return for my deliverance; but he generously told me he would take nothing from me, but that all I had should be delivered safe to me when I came to the Brazils. "For," says he, "I have saved your life on no other terms than I would be glad to be saved myself, and it may one time or other be my lot to be taken up in the same condition; besides," said he, "when I carry you to the Brazils, so great a way from your own country, if I should take from you what you have, you will be starved there, and then I only take away that life I have given. No, no, Seignior Inglese," says he [Mr. Englishman], "I will carry you thither in charity, and those things will help you to buy your subsistence there and your passage home again."

As he was charitable in his proposal, so he was just in the performance to a tittle, for he ordered the seamen that none should offer to touch anything I had; then he took everything into his own possession and gave me back an exact inventory of them, that I might have them, even so much as my three earthen jars.

As to my boat, it was a very good one, and that he saw and told me he would buy it of me for the ship's use and asked me what I would have for it. I told him he had been so generous to me in everything that I could not offer to make any price of the boat but left it entirely to him, upon which he told me he would give me a note of his hand to pay me eighty pieces of eight for it at Brazil, and when it came there, if anyone offered to give more, he would make it up; he offered me also sixty pieces of eight more for my boy Xury, which I was loath to take, not that I was not willing to let the captain have him but I was very loath to sell the poor boy's liberty who had assisted me so faithfully in procuring my own. However, when I let him know my reason, he owned it to be just and offered me this medium, that he would give the boy an obligation to set him free in ten years if he turned Christian; upon this, and Xury saying he was willing to go to him, I let the captain have him.

We had a very good voyage to the Brazils and arrived in the Bay de Todos los Santos, or All Saints' Bay, in about twenty-two days after. And now I was once more delivered from the most miserable of all conditions of life, and what to do next with myself I was now to consider.

The generous treatment the captain gave me I can never enough remember; he would take nothing of me for my passage, gave me twenty ducats for the leopard's skin, and forty for the lion's skin which I had in my boat, and caused everything I had in the ship to be punctually delivered me; and what I was willing to sell he bought, such as the case of bottles, two of my guns, and a piece of the lump of beeswax, for I had made candles of the rest; in a word, I made about 220 pieces of eight of all my cargo, and with this stock I went on shore in the Brazils.

I had not been long here, but being recommended to the house of a good honest man like himself, who had an *ingenio* as they call it, that is, a plantation and a sugar-house, I lived with him some time and acquainted myself by that means with the manner of their planting and making of sugar; and seeing how well the planters lived and how they grew rich suddenly, I resolved, if I could get license to settle there, I would turn planter among them, resolving in the meantime to find out some way to get my money which I had left in London remitted to me. To this purpose, getting a kind of a letter of naturalization, I purchased as much land that was uncured as my money would reach and formed a plan for my plantation and settlement, and such a one as might be suitable to the stock which I proposed to myself to receive from England.

I had a neighbor, a Portuguese of Lisbon, but born of English parents, whose name was Wells, and in much such circumstances as I was. I call him my neighbor, because his plantation lay next to mine and we went on very sociably together. My stock was but low, as well as his; and we rather planted for food than anything else for about two years. However, we began to increase, and our land began to come into order; so that the third year we planted some tobacco and made each of us a large piece of ground ready for planting canes in the year to come; but we both wanted help and now I found, more than before, I had done wrong in parting with my boy Xury.

But alas! for me to do wrong that never did right was no great wonder: I had no remedy but to go on; I was gotten into an employment quite remote to my genius and directly contrary to the life I delighted in and for which I forsook my father's house, and broke through all his good advices; nay, I was coming into the very middle station, or upper degree of low life, which my father advised me to before and which, if I resolved to go on with, I might as well ha' stayed at home and never have fatigued myself in the world as I had done; and I used often to say to myself, I could ha' done this as well in England among my friends as ha' gone 5000 miles off to do it among strangers and savages in a wilderness, and at such a distance as never to hear from any part of the world that had the least knowledge of me.

In this manner I used to look upon my condition with the utmost regret. I had nobody to converse with but now and then this neighbor; no work to be done, but by the labor of my hands; and I used to say, I lived just like a man cast away upon some desolate island that had nobody there but himself. But how just has it been, and how should all men reflect, that when they compare their present conditions with others that are worse, Heaven may oblige them to make the exchange and be convinced of their former felicity by their experience; I say, how just has it been, that the truly solitary life I reflected on in an island of mere desolation should be my lot, who had so often unjustly compared it with the life which I then led, in which had I continued, I had in all probability been exceeding prosperous and rich.

I was in some degree settled in my measures for carrying on the plantation, before my kind friend, the captain of the ship that took me up at sea, went back; for the ship remained there in providing his loading, and preparing for his voyage, near three months; when, telling him what little stock I had left behind me in London, he gave me this friendly and sincere advice. "Seignior Inglese," says he, for so he always called me, "if you will give me letters, and a procuration here in form to me, with orders to the person who has your money in London, to send your effects to Lisbon, to such persons as I shall direct, and in such goods as are proper for this country, I will bring you the produce of them, God willing, at my return; but since human affairs are all subject to changes and disasters, I would have you give orders but for one hundred pounds sterling, which you say is half your stock, and let the hazard be run for the first; so that if it come safe, you may order the rest the same way; and if it miscarry, you may have the other half to have recourse to for your supply."

This was so wholesome advice and looked so friendly that I could not but be convinced it was the best course I could take; so I accordingly prepared letters to the gentlewoman with whom I had left my money and a procuration to the Portuguese captain, as he desired.

I wrote the English captain's widow a full account of all my adventures, my slavery, escape, and how I had met with the Portugal captain at sea, the humanity of his behavior and in what condition I was now in, with all other necessary directions for my supply; and when this honest captain came to Lisbon, he found means by some of the English merchants there to send over not the order only, but a full account of my story to a merchant at London, who represented it effectually to her; whereupon she not only delivered the money but out of her own pocket sent the Portugal captain a very handsome present for his humanity and charity to me.

The merchant in London vesting this hundred pounds in English goods, such as the captain had writ for, sent them directly to him at Lisbon, and he brought them all safe to me to the Brazils; among which, without my direction (for I was too young in my business to think of them), he had taken care to have all sorts of tools, ironwork and utensils necessary for my plantation, and which were of great use to me.

When this cargo arrived, I thought my fortunes made, for I was surprised with the joy of it; and my good steward, the captain, had laid out the five pounds which my friend had sent him for a present for himself to purchase and bring me over a servant under bond for six years' service, and would not accept of any consideration, except a little tobacco which I would have him accept, being of my own produce.

Neither was this all; but my goods being all English manufactures, such as cloth, stuffs, baize, and things particularly valuable and desirable in the country, I found means to sell them to a very great advantage; so that I might say I had more than four times the value of my first cargo, and was now infinitely beyond my poor neighbor, I mean in the advancement of my plantation; for the first thing I did, I bought me a Negro slave and an European servant also; I mean another besides that which the captain brought me from Lisbon.

But as abused prosperity is oftentimes made the very means of our greatest adversity, so was it with me. I went on the next year with great success in my plantation. I raised fifty great rolls of tobacco on my own ground, more than I had disposed of for necessaries among my neighbors; and these fifty rolls, being each of above a hundredweight, were well cured and laid by against the return of the fleet from Lisbon. And now increasing in business and in wealth, my head began to be full of projects and undertakings beyond my reach; such as are indeed often the ruin of the best heads in business.

Had I continued in the station I was now in, I had room for all the happy things to have yet befallen me, for which my father so earnestly recommended a quiet, retired life, and of which he had so sensibly described the middle station of life to be full of; but other things attended me, and I was still to be the wilful agent of all my own miseries; and particularly to increase my fault and double the reflections upon myself, which in my future sorrows I should have leisure to make; all these miscarriages were procured by my apparent obstinate adhering to my foolish inclination of wandering abroad and pursuing that inclination, in contradiction to the clearest views of doing myself good in a fair and plain pursuit of those prospects and those measures of life which Nature and Providence concurred to present me with and to make my duty.

As I had once done thus in my breaking away from my parents, so I could not be content now but I must go and leave the happy view I had of being a rich and thriving man in my new plantation only to pursue a rash and immoderate desire of rising faster than the nature of the thing admitted; and thus I cast myself down again into the deepest gulf of human misery that ever man fell into, or perhaps would be consistent with life and a state of health in the world.

To come then, by the just degrees, to the particulars of this part of my story; you may suppose that, having now lived almost four years in the Brazils and beginning to thrive and prosper very well upon my plantation, I had not only learned the language, but had contracted acquaintance and friendship among my fellow-planters, as well as among the merchants at St. Salvadore, which was our port; and that in my discourses among them, I had frequently given them an account of my two voyages to the coast of Guinea, the manner of trading with the Negroes there, and how easy it was to purchase upon the coast, for trifles, such as beads, toys, knives, scissors, hatchets, bits of glass, and the like, not only gold dust,

Guinea grains, elephants' teeth, etc., but Negroes for the service of the Brazils, in great numbers.

They listened always very attentively to my discourses on these heads, but especially to that part which related to the buying Negroes, which was a trade at that time not only not far entered into, but, as far as it was, had been carried on by the *assientos,* or permission of the kings of Spain and Portugal, and engrossed in the public, so that few Negroes were brought, and those excessive dear.

It happened, being in company with some merchants and planters of my acquaintance and talking of those things very earnestly, three of them came to me the next morning and told me they had been musing very much upon what I had discoursed with them of, the last night, and they came to make a secret proposal to me; and after enjoining me secrecy, they told me that they had a mind to fit out a ship to go to Guinea; that they had all planta-tions as well as I, and were straitened for nothing so much as servants; that as it was a trade that could not be carried on, because they could not publicly sell the Negroes when they came home, so they desired to make but one voyage, to bring the Negroes on shore privately, and di-vide them among their own plantations; and in a word, the question was whether I would go their supercargo in the ship to manage the trading part upon the coast of Guinea; and they offered me that I should have my equal share of the Negroes without providing any part of the stock.

This was a fair proposal, it must be confessed, had it been made to any one that had not had a settlement and plantation of his own to look after which was in a fair way of coming to be very considerable and with a good stock upon it. But for me that was thus entered and established and had nothing to do but go on as I had begun for three or four years more, and to have sent for the other hundred pound from England, and who in that time, and with that little addition, could scarce ha' failed of being worth three or four thousand pounds sterling, and that increasing too; for me to think of such a voyage was the most preposterous thing that ever man in such circumstances could be guilty of.

But I that was born to be my own destroyer could no more resist the offer than I could restrain my first rambling designs, when my father's good counsel was lost upon me. In a word, I told them I would go with all my heart, if they would undertake to look after my plantation in my absence and would dispose of it to such as I should direct, if I miscarried. This they all engaged to do, and entered into writings or covenants to do so; and I made a formal will, disposing of my plantation and effects, in case of my death, making the captain of the ship that had saved my life, as before, my universal heir, but obliging him to dispose of my effects as I had directed in my will, one half of the produce being to himself and the other to be shipped to England.

In short, I took all possible caution to preserve my effects and keep up my plantation; had I used half as much prudence to have looked into my own interest and have made a judgment of what I ought to have done and not to have done, I had certainly never gone away from so prosperous an undertaking, leaving all the probable views of a thriving circumstance and gone upon a voyage to sea, attended with all its common hazards; to say nothing of the reasons I had to expect particular misfortunes to myself.

But I was hurried on and obeyed blindly the dictates of my fancy rather than my reason; and accordingly, the ship being fitted out and the cargo furnished, and all things done as by agreement by my partners in the voyage, I went on board in an evil hour, the 1st of September, 1659, being the same day eight years that I went from my father and mother at Hull, in order to act the rebel to their authority and the fool to my own interest.

The Terror of the Storm

OUR SHIP was about 120 ton burden, carried six guns and fourteen men, besides the master, his boy, and myself; we had on board no large cargo of goods, except of such toys as were fit for our trade with the Negroes, such as beads, bits of glass, shells, and odd trifles, especially little looking-glasses, knives, scissors, hatchets, and the like.

The same day I went on board we set sail, standing away to the northward upon our own coast, with design to stretch over for the African coast, when they came about ten or twelve degrees of northern latitude, which it seems was the manner of their course in those days. We had very good weather, only excessive hot, all the way upon our own coast till we came the height of Cape St. Augustino, from whence keeping farther off at sea, we lost sight of land and steered as if we were bound for the Isle Fernand de Noronha, holding our course northeast by north, and leaving those isles on the east; in this course we passed the line in about twelve days' time, and were by our last observation in seven degrees twenty-two minutes northern latitude, when a violent tornado or hurricane took us quite out of our knowledge; it began from the southeast, came about to the northwest, and then settled into the northeast, from whence it blew in such a terrible manner that for twelve days together we could do nothing but drive and, scudding away before it, let it carry us whither ever fate and the fury of the winds directed; and during these twelve days, I need not say, that I expected every day to be swallowed up, nor indeed did any in the ship expect to save their lives.

In this distress we had, besides the terror of the storm, one of our men died of the calenture, and one man and the boy washed overboard. About the twelfth day, the weather abating a little, the master made an observation as well as he could, and found that he was in about eleven degrees north latitude, but that he was twenty-two degrees of longitude difference west from Cape St. Augustino; so that he found he was gotten upon the coast of Guinea, or the north part of Brazil, beyond the river Amazones, toward that of the river Oronoque, commonly called the Great River, and began to consult with me what course he should take, for the ship was leaky and very much disabled and he was going directly back to the coast of Brazil.

I was positively against that, and looking over the charts of the seacoast of America with him, we concluded there was no inhabited country for us to have recourse to till we came within the circle of the Caribbee Islands and therefore resolved to stand away for Barbados, which by keeping off at sea, to avoid the indraft of the Bay or Gulf of Mexico, we might easily perform, as we hoped, in about fifteen days' sail; whereas we could not possibly make our voyage to the coast of Africa without some assistance, both to our ship and to ourselves.

With this design we changed our course and steered away northwest by west in order to reach some of our English islands, where I hoped for relief; but our voyage was otherwise determined, for being in the latitude of twelve degrees eighteen minutes, a second storm came upon us, which carried us away with the same impetuosity westward and drove us so out of the very way of all human commerce, that had all our lives been saved as to the sea, we were rather in danger of being devoured by savages than ever returning to our own country.

In this distress, the wind still blowing very hard, one of our men early in the morning cried out, "Land!" and we had no sooner run out of the cabin to look out in hopes of seeing whereabouts in the world we were but the ship struck upon a sand, and in a moment, her motion being so stopped, the sea broke over her in such a manner that we expected we should all have perished immediately, and we were immediately driven into our close quarters to shelter us from the very foam and spray of the sea.

It is not easy for anyone who has not been in the like condition to describe or conceive the consternation of men in such circumstances; we knew nothing where we were or upon what land it was we were driven, whether an island or the main, whether inhabited or not inhabited; and as the rage of the wind was still great, though rather less than at first, we could not so much as hope to have the ship hold many minutes without breaking in pieces unless the winds by a kind of miracle should turn immediately about. In a word, we sat looking one upon another and expecting death every moment, and every man acting accordingly, as preparing for another world, for there was little or nothing more for us to do in this; that which was our present comfort and all the comfort we had was, that contrary to our expectation, the ship did not break yet and that the master said the wind began to abate.

Now though we thought that the wind did a little abate, yet the ship having thus struck upon the sand, and sticking too fast for us to expect her getting off, we were in a dreadful condition indeed and had nothing to do but to think of saving our lives as well as we could; we had a boat at our stern just before the storm, but she was first staved by dashing against the ship's rudder, and in the next place she broke away and either sunk or was driven off to sea, so there was no hope from her; we had another boat on board, but how to get her off into the sea was a doubtful thing; however, there was no room to debate, for we fancied the ship would break in pieces every minute, and some told us she was actually broken already.

In this distress the mate of our vessel lays hold of the boat, and with the help of the rest of the men, they got her slung over the ship's side and, getting all into her, let go and committed ourselves, being eleven in number, to God's mercy and the wild sea; for though the storm was abated considerably, yet the sea went dreadful high upon the shore, and might well be called *den wild zee,* as the Dutch call the sea in a storm.

And now our case was very dismal indeed; for we all saw plainly that the sea went so high that the boat could not live and that we should be inevitably drowned. As to making sail, we had none; nor, if we had, could we ha' done anything with it; so we worked at the oar towards the land, though with heavy hearts, like men going to execution; for we all knew that when the boat came nearer the shore, she would be dashed in a thousand pieces by the breach of the sea. However, we committed our souls to God in the most earnest manner, and the wind driving us towards the shore, we hastened our destruction with our own hands, pulling as well as we could towards land.

What the shore was, whether rock or sand, whether steep or shoal, we knew not; the only hope that could rationally give us the least shadow of expectation was if we might happen into some bay or gulf, or the mouth of some river, where by great chance we might have run our boat in, or got under the lee of the land, and perhaps made smooth water. But there was nothing of this appeared; but as we made nearer and nearer the shore, the land looked more frightful than the sea.

After we had rowed, or rather driven, about a league and a half, as we reckoned it, a raging wave, mountainlike, came rolling astern of us and plainly bade us expect the *coup de grace*. In a word, it took us with such a fury that it overset the boat at once; and separating us, as well from the boat as from one another, gave us not time hardly to say, "O God!" for we were all swallowed up in a moment.

Nothing can describe the confusion of thought which I felt when I sunk into the water; for though I swam very well, yet I could not deliver myself from the waves so as to draw breath, till that wave having driven me, or rather carried me, a vast way on towards the shore and having spent itself, went back, and left me upon the land almost dry but half dead with the water I took in. I had so much presence of mind as well as breath left, that seeing myself nearer the mainland than I expected, I got upon my feet, and endeavored to make on towards the land as fast as I could, before another wave should return and take me up again. But I soon found it was impossible to avoid it; for I saw the sea come after me as high as a great hill, and as furious as an enemy which I had no means or strength to contend with; my business was to hold my breath and raise myself upon the water, if I could; and so by swimming to preserve my breathing and pilot myself towards the shore, if possible; my greatest concern now being that the sea, as it would carry me a great way towards the shore when it came on, might not carry me back again with it when it gave back towards the sea.

The wave that came upon me again, buried me at once twenty or thirty feet deep in its own body, and I could feel myself carried with a mighty force and swiftness towards the shore a very great way; but I held my breath and assisted myself to swim still forward with all my might. I was ready to burst with holding my breath, when, as I felt myself rising up, so to my immediate relief, I found my head and hands shoot out above the surface of the water; and though it was not two seconds of time that I could keep myself so, yet it relieved me greatly, gave me breath and new courage. I was covered again with water a good while, but not so long but I held it out; and finding the water had spent itself and began to return, I struck forward against the return of the waves, and felt ground again with my feet. I stood still a few moments to recover breath, and till the water went from me, and then took to my heels, and run with what strength I had farther towards the shore. But neither would this deliver me from the fury of the sea, which came pouring in after me again, and twice more I was lifted up by the waves, and carried forwards as before, the shore being very flat.

The last time of these two had well near been fatal to me; for the sea, having hurried me along as before, landed me, or rather dashed me, against a piece of a rock, and that with such force as it left me senseless, and indeed helpless, as to my own deliverance; for the blow, taking my side and breast, beat the breath as it were quite out of my body; and had it returned again immediately, I must have been strangled in the water; but I recovered a little before the return of the waves, and seeing I should be covered again with the water, I resolved to hold fast by a piece of the rock and so to hold my breath, if possible, till the wave went back; now as the waves were not so high as at first, being near land, I held my hold till the wave abated, and then fetched another run, which brought me so near the shore that the next wave, though it went over me, yet did not so swallow me up as to carry me away, and the next run I took, I got to the mainland, where, to my great comfort, I clambered up the clifts of the shore and sat me down upon the grass, free from danger, and quite out of the reach of the water.

A Dreadful Deliverance

I WAS now landed and safe on shore, and began to look up and thank God that my life was saved in a case wherein there was some minutes before scarce any room to hope. I believe it is impossible to express to the life what the ecstasies and transports of the soul are when it is so saved, as I may say, out of the very grave; and I do not wonder now at that custom, viz., that when a male-factor who has the halter about his neck is tied up and just going to be turned off, and has a reprieve brought to him: I say, I do not wonder that they bring a surgeon with it, to let him blood that very moment they tell him of it, that the surprise may not drive the animal spirits from the heart, and overwhelm him:

For sudden joys, like griefs, confound at first.

I walked about on the shore, lifting up my hands, and my whole being, as I may say, wrapt up in the contemplation of my deliverance, making a thousand gestures and motions which I cannot describe, reflecting upon all my comrades that were drowned and that there should not be one soul saved but myself; for, as for them, I never saw them afterwards or any sign of them, except three of their hats, one cap and two shoes that were not fellows.

I cast my eyes to the stranded vessel, when the breach and froth of the sea being so big, I could hardly see it, it lay so far off, and considered, Lord! how was it possible I could get on shore?

After I had solaced my mind with the comfortable part of my condition, I began to look round me to see what kind of place I was in, and what was next to be done, and I soon found my comforts abate, and that, in a word, I had a dreadful deliverance. For I was wet, had no clothes to shift me, nor anything either to eat or drink to comfort me, neither did I see any prospect before me but that of perishing with hunger or being devoured by wild beasts; and that which was particular afflicting to me was that I had no weapon either to hunt and kill any creatures for my sustenance or to defend myself against any other creature that might desire to kill me for theirs. In a word, I had nothing about me but a knife, a tobacco-pipe and a little tobacco in a box; this was all my provision, and this threw me into terrible agonies of mind that for a while I run about like a madman; night coming upon me, I began with a heavy heart to consider what would be my lot if there were any ravenous beasts in that country, seeing at night they always come abroad for their prey.

All the remedy that offered to my thoughts at that time was to get up into a thick bushy tree like a fir, but thorny, which grew near me, and where I resolved to sit all night, and consider the next day what death I should die, for as yet I saw no prospect of life; I walked about a furlong from the shore, to see if I could find any fresh water to drink, which I did, to my great joy; and having drank, and put a little tobacco in my mouth to prevent hunger, I went to the tree, and getting up into it, endeavored to place myself so as that if I should sleep I might not fall; and having cut me a short stick, like a truncheon, for my defense, I took up my lodging, and having been excessively fatigued, I fell fast asleep, and slept as comfortably as, I believe, few could have done in my condition, and found myself the most refreshed with it that I think I ever was on such an occasion.

When I waked it was broad day, the weather clear, and the storm abated, so that the sea did not rage and swell as before. But that which surprised me most was that the ship was lifted off in the night from the sand where she lay by the swelling of the tide, and was driven up almost as far as the rock which I first mentioned, where I had been so bruised by the dashing me against it; this being within about a mile from the shore where I was and the ship seeming to stand upright still, I wished myself on board, that, at least, I might save some necessary things for my use.

When I came down from my apartment in the tree, I looked about me again, and the first thing I found was the boat, which lay as the wind and the sea had tossed her up upon the land, about two miles on my right hand. I walked as far as I could upon the shore to have got to her, but found a neck or inlet of water between me and the boat, which was about half a mile broad, so I came back for the present, being more intent upon getting at the ship, where I hoped to find something for my present subsistence.

A little after noon I found the sea very calm and the tide ebbed so far out that I could come within a quarter of a mile of the ship; and here I found a fresh renewing of my grief, for I saw evidently that if we had kept on board, we had been all safe, that is to say, we had all got safe on shore, and I had not been so miserable as to be left entirely destitute of all comfort and company, as I now was; this forced tears from my eyes again, but as there was little relief in that, I resolved, if possible, to get to the ship; so I pulled off my clothes, for the weather was hot to extremity, and took the water; but when I came to the ship, my difficulty was still greater to know how to get on board, for as she lay aground, and high out of the water, there was nothing within my reach to lay hold of; I swam round her twice, and the second time I spied a small piece of a rope, which I wondered I did not see at first, hang down by the fore-chain so low as that with great difficulty I got hold of it, and by the help of that rope got up into the forecastle of the ship. Here I found that the ship was bulged, and had a great deal of water in her hold, but that she lay so on the side of a bank of hard sand, or rather earth, that her stern lay lifted up upon the bank and her head low almost to the water; by this means all her quarter was free, and all that was in that part was dry; for you may be sure my first work was to search and to see what was spoiled and what was free; and first I found that all the ship's provisions were dry and untouched by the water, and being very well disposed to eat, I went to the bread-room and filled my pockets with biscuit, and eat it as I went about other things, for I had no time to lose; I also found some rum in the great cabin, of which I took a large dram, and which I had indeed enough of to spirit me for what was before me. Now I wanted nothing but a boat, to furnish myself with many things which I foresaw would be very necessary to me.

It was in vain to sit still and wish for what was not to be had, and this extremity roused my application; we had several spare yards and two or three large spars of wood and a spare top mast or two in the ship; I resolved to fall to work with these and flung as many of them overboard as I could manage for their weight, tying every one with a rope that they might not drive away; when this was done I went down the ship's side, and pulling them to me, I tied four of them fast together at both ends as well as I could, in the form of a raft, and laying two or three short pieces of plank upon them crossways, I found I could walk upon it very well, but that it was not able to bear any great weight, the pieces being too light; so I went to work, and with the carpenter's saw I cut a spare top mast into three lengths and added them to my raft, with a great deal of labor and pains; but hope of furnishing myself with necessaries encouraged me to go beyond what I should have been able to have done upon another occasion.

My raft was now strong enough to bear any reasonable weight; my next care was what to load it with and how to preserve what I laid upon it from the surf of the sea; but I was not long considering this; I first laid all the planks or boards upon it that I could get, and having considered well what I most wanted, I first got three of the seamen's chests, which I had broken open and emptied, and lowered them down upon my raft; the first of these I filled with provision, viz., bread, rice, three Dutch cheeses, five pieces of dried goat's flesh, which we lived much upon, and a little remainder of European corn which had been laid by for some fowls which we brought to sea with us, but the fowls were killed; there had been some barley and wheat together, but, to my great disappointment, I found afterwards that the rats had eaten or spoiled it all. As for liquors, I found several cases of bottles belonging to our skipper in which were some cordial waters, and in all about five or six gallons of rack; these I stowed by themselves, there being no need to put them into the chest, nor no room for them. While I was doing this, I found the tide began to flow, though very calm, and I had the mortification to see my coat, shirt, and waistcoat, which I had left on shore upon the sand, swim away; as for my breeches, which were only linen, and open-kneed, I swam on board in them, and my stockings. However, this put me upon rummaging for clothes, of which I found enough but took no more than I wanted for present use, for I had other things which my eye was more upon, as first, tools to work with on shore; and it was after long searching that I found out the carpenter's chest, which was indeed a very useful prize to me, and much more valuable than a ship-loading of gold would have been at that time; I got it down to my raft, even whole as it was, without losing time to look into it for I knew in general what it contained.

My next care was for some ammunition and arms; there were two very good fowling pieces in the great cabin, and two pistols; these I secured first, with some powder-horns, and a small bag of shot, and two old rusty swords; I knew there were three barrels of powder in the ship, but knew not where our gunner had stowed them; but with much search I found them, two of them dry and good, the third had taken water; those two I got to my raft with the arms, and now I thought myself pretty well freighted, and began to think how I should get to shore with them, having neither sail, oar, or rudder; and the least capful of wind would have overset all my navigation.

I had three encouragements: 1. A smooth, calm sea. 2. The tide rising and setting in to the shore. 3. What little wind there was blew me towards the land; and thus, having found two or three broken oars belonging to the boat, and besides the tools which were in the chest, I found two saws, an axe, and a hammer, and with this cargo I put to sea. For a mile or thereabouts my raft went very well, only that I found it drive a little distant from the place where I had landed before, by which I perceived that there was some indraft of the water, and consequently I hoped to find some creek or river there which I might make use of as a port to get to land with my cargo.

As I imagined, so it was; there appeared before me a little opening of the land, and I found a strong current of the tide set into it, so I guided my raft as well as I could to keep in the middle of the stream. But here I had like to have suffered a second shipwreck, which, if I had, I think verily would have broke my heart, for knowing nothing of the coast, my raft run aground at one end of it upon a shoal, and not being aground at the other end, it wanted but a little that all my cargo had slipped off towards that end that was afloat, and so fallen into the water. I did my utmost by setting my back against the chests to keep them in their places, but could not thrust off the raft with all my strength, neither durst I stir from the posture I was in, but holding up the chests with all my might, stood in that manner near half an hour, in which time the rising of the water brought me a little more upon a level; and a little after, the water still rising, my raft floated again, and I thrust her off with the oar I had into the channel and then driving up higher, I at length found myself in the mouth of a little river, with land on both sides, and a strong current or tide running up; I looked on both sides for a proper place to get to shore, for I was not willing to be driven too high up the river, hoping in time to see some ship at sea and therefore resolved to place myself as near the coast as I could.

At length I spied a little cove on the right shore of the creek, to which with great pain and difficulty I guided my raft and at last got so near as that, reaching ground with my oar, I could thrust her directly in; but here I had like to have dipped all my cargo in the sea again; for that shore lying pretty steep, that is to say, sloping, there was no place to land, but where one end of my float, if it run on shore, would lie so high and the other sink lower as before, that it would endanger my cargo again. All that I could do was to wait till the tide was at the highest, keeping the raft with my oar like an anchor to hold the side of it fast to the shore, near a flat piece of ground, which I expected the water would flow over; and so it did. As soon as I found water enough, for my raft drew about a foot of water, I thrust her on upon that flat piece of ground and there fastened or moored her by sticking my two broken oars into the ground, one on one side near one end, and one on the other side near the other end; and thus I lay till the water ebbed away and left my raft and all my cargo safe on shore.

My next work was to view the country, and seek a proper place for my habitation and where to stow my goods to secure them from whatever might happen; where I was I yet knew not, whether on the continent or on an island, whether inhabited or not inhabited, whether in danger of wild beasts or not. There was a hill not above a mile from me, which rose up very steep and high, and which seemed to overtop some other hills which lay as in a ridge from it, northward; I took out one of the fowling pieces, and one of the pistols, and a horn of powder, and thus armed, I traveled for discovery up to the top of that hill, where, after I had with great labor and difficulty got to the top, I saw my fate to my great affliction, viz., that I was in an island environed every way with the sea, no land to be seen, except some rocks which lay a great way off and two small islands less than this, which lay about three leagues to the west.

I found also that the island I was in was barren and, as I saw good reason to believe, uninhabited, except by wild beasts, of whom, however, I saw none, yet I saw abundance of fowls, but knew not their kind; neither when I killed them could I tell what was fit for food, and what not; at my coming back, I shot at a great bird which I saw sitting upon a tree on the side of a great wood. I believe it was the first gun that had been fired there since the creation of the world; I had no sooner fired but from all the parts of the wood there arose an innumerable number of fowls of many sorts, making a confused screaming, and crying every one according to his usual note; but not one of them of any kind that I knew. As for the creature I killed, I took it to be a kind of a hawk, its color and beak resembling it, but had no talons or claws more than common; its flesh was carrion and fit for nothing.

Contented with this discovery, I came back to my raft and fell to work to bring my cargo on shore, which took me up the rest of that day, and what to do with myself at night I knew not, nor indeed where to rest; for I was afraid to lie down on the ground, not knowing but some wild beast might devour me, though, as I afterwards found, there was really no need for those fears.

However, as well as I could, I barricaded myself round with the chests and boards that I had brought on shore and made a kind of a hut for that night's lodging; as for food, I yet saw not which way to supply myself, except that I had seen two or three creatures like hares run out of the wood where I shot the fowl.

I now began to consider that I might yet get a great many things out of the ship, which would be useful to me, and particularly some of the rigging and sails and such other things as might come to land, and I resolved to make another voyage on board the vessel, if possible; and as I knew that the first storm that blew must necessarily break her all in pieces, I resolved to set all other things apart, till I got everything out of the ship that I could get; then I called a council, that is to say, in my thoughts, whether I should take back the raft but this appeared impracticable; so I resolved to go as before, when the tide was down, and I did so, only that I stripped before I went from my hut, having nothing on but a checkered shirt and a pair of linen drawers and a pair of pumps on my feet.

I got on board the ship as before, and prepared a second raft, and having had experience of the first, I neither made this so unwieldy, nor loaded it so hard, but yet I brought away several things very useful to me; as first, in the carpenter's stores I found two or three bags full of nails and spikes, a great screwjack, a dozen or two of hatchets and, above all, that most useful thing called a grindstone; all these I secured together, with several things belonging to the gunner, particularly two or three iron crows and two barrels of musket bullets, seven muskets and another fowling piece, with some small quantity of powder more; a large bag full of small shot and a great roll of sheet lead. But this last was so heavy, I could not hoist it up to get it over the ship's side.

Besides these things, I took all the men's clothes that I could find, and a spare fore topsail, a hammock, and some bedding; and with this I loaded my second raft, and brought them all safe on shore, to my very great comfort.

I was under some apprehensions during my absence from the land, that at least my provisions might be devoured on shore; but when I came back, I found no sign of any visitor, only there sat a creature like a wild cat upon one of the chests, which, when I came towards it, ran away a little distance, and then stood still; she sat very composed and unconcerned and looked full in my face as if she had a mind to be acquainted with me. I presented my gun at her, but as she did not understand it, she was perfectly unconcerned at it, nor did she offer to stir away; upon which I tossed her a bit of biscuit, though, by the way, I was not very free of it, for my store was not great. However, I spared her a bit, I say, and she went to it, smelled of it and ate it and looked (as pleased) for more, but I thanked her and could spare no more; so she marched off.

Having got my second cargo on shore, though I was fain to open the barrels of powder and bring them by parcels, for they were too heavy, being large casks, I went to work to make me a little tent with the sail and some poles which I cut for that purpose, and into this tent I brought everything that I knew would spoil, either with rain or sun, and I piled all the empty chests and casks up in a circle round the tent, to fortify it from any sudden attempt, either from man or beast.

When I had done this I blocked up the door of the tent with some boards within and an empty chest set up on end without, and spreading one of the beds upon the ground, laying my two pistols just at my head and my gun at length by me, I went to bed for the first time, and slept very quietly all night, for I was very weary and heavy, for the night before I had slept little and had labored very hard all day, as well to fetch all those things from the ship, as to get them on shore.

I had the biggest magazine of all kinds now that ever was laid up, I believe, for one man, but I was not satisfied still; for while the ship sat upright in that posture, I thought I ought to get everything out of her that I could; so every day at low water I went on board, and brought away something or other. But particularly the third time I went, I brought away as much of the rigging as I could, as also all the small ropes and rope-twine I could get, with a piece of spare canvas, which was to mend the sails upon occasion, and the barrel of wet gunpowder. In a word, I brought away all the sails first and last, only that I was fain to cut them in pieces, and bring as much at a time as I could; for they were no more useful to be sails but as mere canvas only.

But that which comforted me more still was that at last

of all, after I had made five or six such voyages as these, and thought I had nothing more to expect from the ship that was worth my meddling with; I say, after all this, I found a great hogshead of bread, and three large runlets of rum or spirits, and a box of sugar, and a barrel of fine flour; this was surprising to me, because I had given over expecting any more provisions, except what was spoiled by the water. I soon emptied the hogshead of that bread, and wrapped it up parcel by parcel in pieces of the sails, which I cut out; and in a word, I got all this safe on shore also.

The next day I made another voyage; and now having plundered the ship of what was portable and fit to hand out, I began with the cables; and cutting the great cable into pieces such as I could move, I got two cables and a hawser on shore, with all the ironwork I could get; and having cut down the spritsail yard, and the mizzen yard, and everything I could to make a large raft, I loaded it with all those heavy goods, and came away.

But my good luck began now to leave me; for this raft was so unwieldy and so over-loaden, that after I was entered the little cove, where I had landed the rest of my goods, not being able to guide it so handily as I did the other, it overset, and threw me and all my cargo into the water; as for myself it was no great harm, for I was near the shore; but as to my cargo, it was great part of it lost, especially the iron, which I expected would have been of great use to me. However, when the tide was out, I got most of the pieces of cable ashore, and some of the iron, though with infinite labor; for I was fain to dip for it into the water, a work which fatigued me very much. After this I went every day on board, and brought away what I could get.

I had been now thirteen days on shore, and had been eleven times on board the ship; in which time I had brought away all that one pair of hands could well be supposed capable to bring, though I believe verily, had the calm weather held, I should have brought away the whole ship piece by piece. But preparing the twelfth time to go on board, I found the wind begin to rise; however, at low water I went on board, and though I thought I had rummaged the cabin so effectually, as that nothing more could be found, yet I discovered a locker with drawers in it, in one of which I found two or three razors and one pair of large scissors, with some ten or a dozen of good knives and forks; in another I found about thirty-six pounds value in money, some European coin, some Brazil, some pieces of eight, some gold, some silver.

I smiled to myself at the sight of this money. "O drug!" said I aloud, "what art thou good for? Thou art not worth to me, no, not the taking off of the ground; one of those knives is worth all this heap; I have no manner of use for thee; e'en remain where thou art and go to the bottom as a creature whose life is not worth saving." However, upon second thoughts, I took it away, and wrapping all this in a piece of canvas, I began to think of making another raft; but while I was preparing this, I found the sky overcast, and the wind began to rise, and in a quarter of an hour it blew a fresh gale from the shore; it presently occurred to me that it was in vain to pretend to make a raft with the wind off shore, and that it was my business to be gone before the tide of flood began, otherwise I might not be able to reach the shore at all.

Accordingly I let myself down into the water and swam across the channel, which lay between the ship and the sands, and even that with difficulty enough, partly with the weight of the things I had about me, and partly the roughness of the water, for the wind rose very hastily, and before it was quite high water, it blew a storm.

But I was gotten home to my little tent, where I lay

with all my wealth about me very secure. It blew very hard all that night, and in the morning, when I looked out, behold, no more ship was to be seen; I was a little surprised, but recovered myself with this satisfactory reflection, viz., that I had lost no time, nor abated no diligence to get everything out of her that could be useful to me, and that indeed there was little left in her that I was able to bring away if I had had more time.

Securing Myself Against Savages and Wild Beasts

I NOW gave over any more thoughts of the ship, or of anything out of her, except what might drive on shore from her wreck, as indeed divers pieces of her afterwards did; but those things were of small use to me.

My thoughts were now wholly employed about securing myself against either savages, if any should appear, or wild beasts, if any were in the island; and I had many thoughts of the method how to do this and what kind of dwelling to make, whether I should make me a cave in the earth or a tent upon the earth. And, in short, I resolved upon both, the manner and description of which it may not be improper to give an account of.

I soon found the place I was in was not for my settlement, particularly because it was upon a low moorish ground near the sea, and I believed would not be wholesome, and more particularly because there was no fresh water near it, so I resolved to find a more healthy and more convenient spot of ground.

I consulted several things in my situation, which I found would be proper for me: first, health and fresh water, I just now mentioned; secondly, shelter from the heat of the sun; thirdly, security from ravenous creatures, whether men or beasts; fourthly, a view to the sea, that if God sent any ship in sight, I might not lose any advantage for my deliverance, of which I was not willing to banish all my expectation yet.

In search of a place proper for this I found a little plain on the side of a rising hill, whose front towards this little plain was steep as a house-side so that nothing could come down upon me from the top; on the side of this rock there was a hollow place worn a little way in like the entrance or door of a cave, but there was not really any cave, or way into the rock at all.

On the flat of the green, just before this hollow place, I resolved to pitch my tent. This plain was not above an hundred yards broad and about twice as long, and lay like a green before my door and at the end of it descended irregularly every way down into the low grounds by the seaside. It was on the north-northwest side of the hill, so that I was sheltered from the heat every day, till it came to a west and by south sun, or thereabouts, which in those countries is near the setting.

Before I set up my tent, I drew a half circle before the hollow place, which took in about ten yards in its semi-diameter from the rock and twenty yards in its diameter, from its beginning and ending.

In this half circle I pitched two rows of strong stakes, driving them into the ground till they stood very firm like piles, the biggest end being out of the ground about five foot and a half and sharpened on the top. The two rows did not stand above six inches from one another.

Then I took the pieces of cable which I had cut in the ship, and laid them in rows one upon another, within the circle, between these two rows of stakes, up to the top, placing other stakes in the inside, leaning against them, about two foot and a half high, like a spur to a post; and this fence was so strong that neither man nor beast could get into it or over it. This cost me a great deal of time and labor, especially to cut the piles in the woods, bring them to the place, and drive them into the earth.

The entrance into this place I made to be not by a door, but by a short ladder to go over the top, which ladder, when I was in, I lifted over after me, and so I was completely fenced in, and fortified, as I thought, from all the world, and consequently slept secure in the night, which otherwise I could not have done, though, as it appeared afterward, there was no need of all this caution from the enemies that I apprehended danger from.

Into this fence or fortress, with infinite labor, I carried all my riches, all my provisions, ammunition, and stores, of which you have the account above; and I made me a large tent, which, to preserve me from the rains that in one part of the year are very violent there, I made double, viz., one smaller tent within, and one larger tent above it, and covered the uppermost with a large tarpaulin which I had saved among the sails.

And now I lay no more for a while in the bed which I had brought on shore, but in a hammock, which was indeed a very good one and belonged to the mate of the ship.

Into this tent I brought all my provisions and everything that would spoil by the wet, and having thus enclosed all my goods, I made up the entrance, which till now I had left open, and so passed and repassed, as I said, by a short ladder.

When I had done this, I began to work my way into the rock, and bringing all the earth and stones that I dug down out through my tent, I laid 'em up within my fence in the nature of a terrace, that so it raised the ground within about a foot and a half; and thus I made me a cave just behind my tent, which served me like a cellar to my house.

It cost me much labor and many days before all these things were brought to perfection, and therefore I must go back to some other things which took up some of my thoughts. At the same time it happened, after I had laid my scheme for the setting up my tent and making the cave, that a storm of rain falling from a thick dark cloud, a sudden flash of lightning happened and after that a great clap of thunder, as is naturally the effect of it; I was not so much surprised with the lightning as I was with a thought which darted into my mind as swift as the lightning itself: O my powder! My very heart sunk within me when I thought that at one blast all my powder might be destroyed, on which not my defense only but the providing me food, as I thought, entirely depended; I was nothing near so anxious about my own danger, though had the powder took fire, I had never known who had hurt me.

Such impression did this make upon me that after the storm was over, I laid aside all my works, my building and fortifying, and applied myself to make bags and boxes to separate the powder, and keep it a little and a little in a parcel, in hope that whatever might come it might not all take fire at once, and to keep it so apart that it should not be possible to make one part fire another. I finished this work in about a fortnight, and I think my powder, which in all was about 240 pounds' weight, was divided in not less than a hundred parcels; as to the barrel that had been wet, I did not apprehend any danger from that, so I placed it in my new cave, which in my fancy I called my kitchen, and the rest I hid up and down in holes among the rocks, so that no wet might come to it, marking very carefully where I laid it.

In the interval of time while this was doing, I went out once at least every day with my gun, as well to divert myself as to see if I could kill anything fit for food, and as near as I could to acquaint myself with what the island produced. The first time I went out I presently discovered that there were goats in the island, which was a great satisfaction to me; but then it was attended with this misfortune to me, viz., that they were so shy, so subtile, and so swift of foot that it was the difficultest thing in the world to come at them. But I was not discouraged at this, not doubting but I might now and then shoot one, as it soon happened, for after I had found their haunts a little, I laid wait in this manner for them: I observed if they saw me in the valleys, though they were upon the rocks, they would run away as in a terrible fright; but if they were feeding in the valleys and I was upon the rocks, they took no notice of me, from whence I concluded that, by the position of their optics, their sight was so directed downward that they did not readily see objects that were above them; so afterward I took this method, I always climbed the rocks first to get above them and then had frequently a fair mark. The first shot I made among these creatures, I killed a she-goat which had a little kid by her which she gave suck to, which grieved me heartily; but when the old one fell, the kid stood stock still by her till I came and took her up, and not only so, but when I carried the old one with me upon my shoulders, the kid followed me quite to my enclosure, upon which I laid down the dam and took the kid in my arms and carried it over my pale, in hopes to have bred it up tame, but it would not eat, so I was forced to kill it and eat it myself. These two supplied me with flesh a great while, for I ate sparingly, and saved my provisions (my bread especially) as much as possibly I could.

Having now fixed my habitation, I found it absolutely necessary to provide a place to make a fire in and fuel to burn; and what I did for that, as also how I enlarged my cave, and what conveniences I made, I shall give a full account of in its place. But I must first give some little account of myself and of my thoughts about living, which it may well be supposed were not a few.

I had a dismal prospect of my condition, for as I was not cast away upon that island without being driven, as is said, by a violent storm quite out of the course of our intended voyage and a great way, viz., some hundreds of leagues out of the ordinary course of the trade of mankind, I had great reason to consider it as a determination of Heaven that in this desolate place and in this desolate manner I should end my life; the tears would run plentifully down my face when I made these reflections, and sometimes I would expostulate with myself why Providence should thus completely ruin its creatures and render them so absolutely miserable, so without help abandoned, so entirely depressed that it could hardly be rational to be thankful for such a life.

But something always returned swift upon me to check these thoughts and to reprove me; and particularly one day, walking with my gun in my hand by the seaside, I was very pensive upon the subject of my present condition, when Reason, as it were, expostulated with me t' other way, thus: "Well, you are in a desolate condition, 'tis true, but pray remember, where are the rest of you? Did not you come eleven of you into the boat? Where are the ten? Why were not they saved and you lost? Why were you singled out? Is it better to be here, or there?" And then I pointed to the sea. All evils are to be considered with the good that is in them and with what worse attends them.

Then it occurred to me again how well I was furnished for my subsistence and what would have been my case if it had not happened, which was an hundred thousand to one, that the ship floated from the place where she first struck and was driven so near to the shore that I had time to get all these things out of her. What would have been my case if I had been to have lived in the condition in which I at first came on shore, without necessaries of life, or necessaries to supply and procure them? "Particularly," said I aloud (though to myself), "what should I ha' done without a gun, without ammunition, without any tools to make anything or to work with, without clothes, bedding, a tent, or any manner of covering?" and that now I had all these to a sufficient quantity, and was in a fair way to provide myself in such a manner as to live without my gun when my ammunition was spent; so that I had a tolerable view of subsisting without any want as long as I lived; for I considered from the beginning how I would provide for the accidents that might happen and for the time that was to come, even not only after my ammunition should be spent, but even after my health or strength should decay.

I confess I had not entertained any notion of my ammunition being destroyed at one blast, I mean my powder being blown up by lightning, and this made the thoughts of it so surprising to me when it lightened and thundered, as I observed just now.

And now being to enter into a melancholy relation of a scene of silent life, such perhaps, as was never heard of in the world before, I shall take it from its beginning, and continue it in its order. It was, by my account, the 30th of September when, in the manner as above said, I first set foot upon this horrid island, when the sun, being to us in its autumnal equinox, was almost just over my head, for I reckoned myself, by observation, to be in the latitude of nine degrees twenty-two minutes north of the line.

After I had been there about ten or twelve days, it came into my thoughts that I should lose my reckoning of time for want of books and pen and ink and should even forget the Sabbath days from the working days; but to prevent this I cut it with my knife upon a large post, in capital letters, and making it into a great cross, I set it up on the shore where I first landed, viz., "I came on shore here on the 30th of September 1659." Upon the sides of this square post I cut every day a notch with my knife, and every seventh notch was as long again as the rest, and every first day of the month as long again as that long one; and thus I kept my calendar, or weekly, monthly, and yearly reckoning of time.

In the next place we are to observe that among the many things which I brought out of the ship in the several voyages which, as above mentioned, I made to it, I got several things of less value, but not all less useful to me, which I omitted setting down before; as in particular, pens, ink, and paper, several parcels in the captain's, mate's, gunner's and carpenter's keeping, three or four compasses, some mathematical instruments, dials, perspectives, charts, and books of navigation, all which I huddled together, whether I might want them or no; also I found three very good Bibles, which came to me in my cargo from England, and which I had packed up among my things; some Portuguese books also, and among them two or three Popish prayer-books, and several other books, all which I carefully secured. And I must not forget that we had in the ship a dog and two cats, of whose eminent history I may have occasion to say something in its place; for I carried both the cats with me, and as for the dog, he jumped out of the ship of himself and swam on shore to me the day after I went on shore with my first cargo and was a trusty servant to me many years; I wanted nothing that he could fetch me, nor any company that he could make up to me; I only wanted to have him talk to me, but that would not do. As I observed before, I found pen, ink, and paper, and I husbanded them to the utmost; and I shall show that while my ink lasted, I kept things very exact, but after that was gone, I could not, for I could not make any ink by any means that I could devise.

And this put me in mind that I wanted many things, notwithstanding all that I had amassed together, and of these, this of ink was one, as also spade, pickaxe, and shovel, to dig or remove the earth, needles, pins, and thread; as for linen, I soon learned to want that without much difficulty.

This want of tools made every work I did go on heavily, and it was near a whole year before I had entirely finished my little pale, or surrounded habitation. The piles, or stakes, which were as heavy as I could well lift, were a long time in cutting and preparing in the woods, and more by far in bringing home, so that I spent sometimes two days in cutting and bringing home one of those posts and a third day in driving it into the ground; for which purpose I got a heavy piece of wood at first, but at last bethought myself of one of the iron crows, which, how-ever, though I found it, yet it made driving those posts or piles very laborious and tedious work.

But what need I ha' been concerned at the tediousness of anything I had to do, seeing I had time enough to do it in? Nor had I any other employment, if that had been over, at least that I could foresee, except the ranging the island to seek for food, which I did more or less every day.

My Reason Began to Master My Despondency

I NOW began to consider seriously my condition, and the circumstance I was reduced to, and I drew up the state of my affairs in writing, not so much to leave them to any that were to come after me, for I was like to have but few heirs, as to deliver my thoughts from daily poring upon them, and afflicting my mind; and as my reason began now to master my despondency, I began to comfort myself as well as I could and to set the good against the evil, that I might have something to distinguish my case from worse, and I stated it very impartially, like debtor and creditor, the comforts I enjoyed, against the miseries I suffered, thus:

Evil	Good
I am cast upon a horrible desolate island, void of all hope of recovery.	But I am alive, and not drowned, as all my ship's company was.
I am singled out and separated, as it were, from all the world to be miserable.	But I am singled out, too, from all the ship's crew to be spared from death; and He that miraculously saved me from death can deliver me from this condition.
I am divided from mankind, a solitaire, one banished from human society.	But I am not starved and perishing on a barren place, affording no sustenance.
I have not clothes to cover me.	But I am in a hot climate, where if I had clothes I could hardly wear them.
I am without any defense or means to resist any violence of man or beast.	But I am cast on an island, where I see no wild beasts to hurt me, as I saw on the coast of Africa. And what if I had been shipwrecked there?

Evil	Good
I have no soul to speak to, or relieve me.	But God wonderfully sent the ship in near enough to the shore that I have gotten out so many necessary things as will either supply my wants, or enable me to supply myself even as long as I live.

Upon the whole, here was an undoubted testimony that there was scarce any condition in the world so miserable but there was something negative or something positive to be thankful for in it; and let this stand as a direction from the experience of the most miserable of all conditions in this world, that we may always find in it something to comfort ourselves from and to set in the description of good and evil on the credit side of the account.

Having now brought my mind a little to relish my condition and given over looking out to sea to see if I could spy a ship; I say, giving over these things, I began to apply myself to accommodate my way of living and to make things as easy to me as I could.

I have already described my habitation, which was a tent under the side of a rock, surrounded with a strong pale of posts and cables, but I might now rather call it a wall, for I raised a kind of wall up against it of turfs, about two foot thick on the outside, and after some time, I think it was a year and a half, I raised rafters from it leaning to the rock and thatched or covered it with boughs of trees and such things as I could get to keep out the rain, which I found at some times of the year very violent.

I have already observed how I brought all my goods

into this pale, and into the cave which I had made behind me. But I must observe, too, that at first this was a confused heap of goods, which as they lay in no order, so they took up all my place; I had no room to turn myself; so I set myself to enlarge my cave and works farther into the earth, for it was a loose sandy rock, which yielded easily to the labor I bestowed on it; and so, when I found I was pretty safe as to beasts of prey, I worked sideways to the right hand into the rock, and then turning to the right again, worked quite out, and made me a door to come out on the outside of my pale or fortification.

This gave me not only egress and regress, as it were a back way to my tent and to my storehouse, but gave me room to stow my goods.

And now I began to apply myself to make such necessary things as I found I most wanted, as particularly a chair and a table, for without these I was not able to enjoy the few comforts I had in the world; I could not write, or eat, or do several things with so much pleasure without a table.

So I went to work; and here I must needs observe, that as reason is the substance and original of the mathematics, so by stating and squaring everything by reason and by making the most rational judgment of things, every man may be in time master of every mechanic art. I had never handled a tool in my life, and yet in time, by labor, application, and contrivance, I found at last that I wanted nothing but I could have made it, especially if I had had tools; however, I made abundance of things, even without tools, and some with no more tools than an adze and a hatchet, which perhaps were never made that way before, and that with infinite labor. For example, if I wanted a board, I had no other way but to cut down a tree, set it on an edge before me, and hew it flat on either side with my axe, till I had brought it to be thin as a plank, and then dub it smooth with my adze. It is true, by this method I could make but one board out of a whole tree, but this I had no remedy for but patience, any more than I had for the prodigious deal of time and labor which it took me up to make a plank or board. But my time or labor was little worth, and so it was as well employed one way as another.

However, I made me a table and a chair, as I observed above, in the first place, and this I did out of the shore pieces of boards that I brought on my raft from the ship. But when I had wrought out some boards, as above, I made large shelves of the breadth of a foot and a half one over another, all along one side of my cave, to lay all my tools, nails, and ironwork, and, in a word, to separate everything at large in their places, that I might come easily at them; I knocked pieces into the wall of the rock to hang my guns and all things that would hang up.

So that had my cave been to be seen, it looked like a general magazine of all necessary things, and I had everything so ready at my hand, that it was a great pleasure to me to see all my goods in such order and especially to find my stock of all necessaries so great.

And now it was when I began to keep a journal of every day's employment; for, indeed, at first, I was in too much hurry, and not only hurry as to labor, but in too much discomposure of mind; and my journal would have been full of many dull things. For example, I must have said thus:

September the 30th. After I got to shore and had escaped drowning, instead of being thankful to God for my deliverance, having first vomited with the great quantity of salt water which was gotten into my stomach and recovering myself a little, I ran about the shore, wringing my hands and beating my head and face, exclaiming at my misery and crying out I was undone, undone, till, tired and faint, I was forced to lie down on the ground to repose, but durst not sleep, for fear of being devoured.

Some days after this, and after I had been on board the ship, and got all that I could out of her, yet I could not forbear getting up to the top of a little mountain and looking out to sea in hopes of seeing a ship; then fancy at a vast distance I spied a sail, please myself with the hopes of it and then, after looking steadily till I was almost blind, lose it quite and sit down and weep like a child, and thus increase my misery by my folly.

But having gotten over these things in some measure and having settled my household stuff and habitation, made me a table and a chair, and all as handsome about me as I could, I began to keep my journal, of which I shall here give you the copy (though in it will be told all these particulars over again) as long as it lasted, for having no more ink, I was forced to leave it off.

The Journal

September 30, 1659. I, poor miserable Robinson Crusoe, being shipwrecked during a dreadful storm in the offing, came on shore on this dismal unfortunate island, which I called "the Island of Despair," all the rest of the ship's company being drowned and myself almost dead.

All the rest of that day I spent in afflicting myself at the dismal circumstances I was brought to, viz., I had neither food, house, clothes, weapon, or place to fly to, and in despair of any relief, saw nothing but death before me, either that I should be devoured by wild beasts, murdered by savages, or starved to death for want of

food. At the approach of night, I slept in a tree for fear
of wild creatures, but slept soundly, though it rained all
night.

October 1. In the morning I saw to my great surprise the ship had floated with the high tide and was
driven on shore again much nearer the island, which, as
it was some comfort on one hand, for seeing her sit upright and not broken to pieces, I hoped, if the wind
abated, I might get on board and get some food and
necessaries out of her for my relief; so on the other hand,
it renewed my grief at the loss of my comrades, who, I
imagined, if we had all stayed on board, might have saved
the ship or at least that they would not have been all
drowned as they were; and that had the men been saved,
we might perhaps have built us a boat out of the ruins of
the ship, to have carried us to some other part of the
world. I spent great part of this day in perplexing myself
on these things; but at length seeing the ship almost dry,
I went upon the sand as near as I could, and then swam
on board; this day also it continued raining, though with
no wind at all.

From the *1st of October* to the *24th.* All these
days entirely spent in many several voyages to get all I
could out of the ship, which I brought on shore, every
tide of flood, upon rafts. Much rain also in these days,
though with some intervals of fair weather. But, it seems,
this was the rainy season.

October 20. I overset my raft, and all the goods
I had got upon it, but being in shoal water, and the things
being chiefly heavy, I recovered many of them when the
tide was out.

October 25. It rained all night and all day, with
some gusts of wind, during which time the ship broke in
pieces, the wind blowing a little harder than before,
and was no more to be seen, except the wreck of her, and

that only at low water. I spent this day in covering and securing the goods which I had saved, that the rain might not spoil them.

October 26. I walked about the shore almost all day to find out a place to fix my habitation, greatly concerned to secure myself from an attack in the night, either from wild beasts or men. Towards night I fixed upon a proper place under a rock, and marked out a semicircle for my encampment, which I resolved to strengthen with a work, wall, or fortification made of double piles, lined within with cables, and without with turf.

From the 26th to the 30th I worked very hard in carrying all my goods to my new habitation, though some part of the time it rained exceeding hard.

The 31st in the morning I went out into the island with my gun to seek for some food, and discover the country, when I killed a she-goat, and her kid followed me home, which I afterwards killed also, because it would not feed.

November 1. I set up my tent under a rock, and lay there for the first night, making it as large as I could with stakes driven in to swing my hammock upon.

November 2. I set up all my chests and boards, and the pieces of timber which made my rafts, and with them formed a fence round me, a little within the place I had marked out for my fortification.

November 3. I went out with my gun and killed two fowls like ducks, which were very good food. In the afternoon went to work to make me a table.

November 4. This morning I began to order my times of work, of going out with my gun, time of sleep, and time of diversion, viz., every morning I walked out with my gun for two or three hours if it did not rain, then employed myself to work till about eleven o'clock; then ate what I had to live on and from twelve to two I lay down to sleep, the weather being excessive hot, and then in the evening to work again. The working part of this day and of the next were wholly employed in making my table, for I was yet but a very sorry workman, though time and necessity made me a complete natural mechanic soon after, as I believe it would do anyone else.

November 5. This day went abroad with my gun and my dog, and killed a wild cat; her skin pretty soft, but her flesh good for nothing. Every creature I killed, I took off the skins and preserved them. Coming back by the seashore, I saw many sorts of sea fowls which I did not understand, but was surprised and almost frighted with two or three seals, which, while I was gazing at, not well knowing what they were, got into the sea and escaped me for that time.

November 6. After my morning walk I went to work with my table again, and finished it, though not to my liking; nor was it long before I learned to mend it.

November 7. Now it began to be settled fair weather. The 7th, 8th, 9th, 10th and part of the 12th (for the 11th was Sunday) I took wholly up to make me a chair and with much ado brought it to a tolerable shape, but never to please me, and even in the making, I pulled it in pieces several times. *Note:* I soon neglected my keeping Sundays, for, omitting my mark for them on my post, I forgot which was which.

November 13. This day it rained, which refreshed me exceedingly and cooled the earth, but it was accompanied with terrible thunder and lightning, which frighted me dreadfully, for fear of my powder; as soon as it was over, I resolved to separate my stock of powder into as many little parcels as possible, that it might not be in danger.

November 14, 15, 16. These three days I spent in making little square chests or boxes, which might hold about a pound or two pounds, at most, of powder; and so, putting the powder in, I stowed it in places as secure and remote from one another as possible. On one of these three days I killed a large bird that was good to eat, but I know not what to call it.

November 17. This day I began to dig behind my tent into the rock to make room for my farther conveniency. *Note:* Three things I wanted exceedingly for this work, viz., a pickaxe, a shovel, and a wheelbarrow or basket, so I desisted from my work and began to consider how to supply that want and make me some tools. As for a pickaxe, I made use of the iron crows, which were proper enough, though heavy; but the next thing was a shovel or spade. This was so absolutely necessary, that indeed I could do nothing effectually without it, but what kind of one to make I knew not.

November 18. The next day in searching the woods I found a tree of that wood, or like it, which in the Brazils they call the iron tree, for its exceeding hardness; of this, with great labor, and almost spoiling my axe, I cut a piece and brought it home, too, with difficulty enough, for it was exceeding heavy.

The excessive hardness of the wood, and having no other way, made me a long while upon this machine, for I worked it effectually by little and little into the form of a shovel or spade, the handle exactly shaped like ours in England, only that the broad part having no iron shod upon it at bottom, it would not last me so long; however, it served well enough for the uses which I had occasion to put it to; but never was a shovel, I believe, made after that fashion, or so long a-making.

I was still deficient, for I wanted a basket or a wheelbarrow; a basket I could not make by any means, having no such things as twigs that would bend to make wickerware, at least none yet found out; and as to a wheelbarrow, I fancied I could make all but the wheel, but that

I had no notion of, neither did I know how to go about it; besides, I had no possible way to make the iron gudgeons for the spindle or axis of the wheel to run in, so I gave it over; and so for carrying away the earth which I dug out of the cave, I made me a thing like a hod which the laborers carry mortar in when they serve the brick-layers.

This was not so difficult to me as the making the shovel; and yet this and the shovel and the attempt which I made in vain to make a wheelbarrow took me up no less than four days, I mean always excepting my morning walk with my gun, which I seldom failed, and very seldom failed also bringing home something fit to eat.

November 23. My other work having now stood still because of my making these tools, when they were finished I went on, and working every day, as my strength and time allowed, I spent eighteen days entirely in widening and deepening my cave, that it might hold my goods commodiously.

NOTE: During all this time, I worked to make this room or cave spacious enough to accommodate me as a ware-house or magazine, a kitchen, a dining-room, and a cellar; as for my lodging, I kept to the tent, except that some-times in the wet season of the year it rained so hard that I could not keep myself dry, which caused me afterwards to cover all my place within my pale with long poles, in the form of rafters, leaning against the rock, and load them with flags and large leaves of trees, like a thatch.

December 10. I began now to think my cave or vault finished, when on a sudden (it seems I had made it too large) a great quantity of earth fell down from the top and one side, so much, that, in short, it frighted me, and not without reason too; for if I had been under it I had never wanted a gravedigger. Upon this disaster I had a great deal of work to do over again; for I had the loose earth to carry out; and which was of more importance, I had the ceiling to prop up, so that I might be sure no more would come down.

December 11. This day I went to work with it accordingly and got two shores or posts pitched upright to the top, with two pieces of boards across over each post. This I finished the next day; and setting more posts up with boards, in about a week more I had the roof secured; and the posts, standing in rows, served me for partitions to part of my house.

December 17. From this day to the twentieth I placed shelves and knocked up nails on the posts to hang everything up that could be hung up, and now I began to be in some order within doors.

December 20. Now I carried everything into the cave, and began to furnish my house, and set up some pieces of boards, like a dresser, to order my victuals upon, but boards began to be very scarce with me; also I made me another table.

December 24. Much rain all night and all day; no stirring out.

December 25. Rain all day.

December 26. No rain, and the earth much cooler than before, and pleasanter.

December 27. Killed a young goat, and lamed another, so as that I catched it, and led it home in a string; when I had it home, I bound and splintered up its leg, which was broke. N.B. I took such care of it that it lived, and the leg grew well, and as strong as ever; but by my nursing it so long it grew tame and fed upon the little green at my door and would not go away. This was the first time that I entertained a thought of breeding up some tame creatures, that I might have food when my powder and shot was all spent.

December 28, 29, 30. Great heats and no breeze;

so that there was no stirring abroad, except in the evening for food; this time I spent in putting all my things in order within doors.

January 1. Very hot still, but I went abroad early and late with my gun, and lay still in the middle of the day; this evening going farther into the valleys which lay towards the center of the island, I found there was plenty of goats, though exceeding shy and hard to come at; however, I resolved to try if I could not bring my dog to hunt them down.

January 2. Accordingly, the next day, I went out with my dog, and set him upon the goats; but I was mistaken, for they all faced about upon the dog, and he knew his danger too well, for he would not come near them.

January 3. I began my fence or wall; which, being still jealous of my being attacked by somebody, I resolved to make very thick and strong.

N.B. This wall being described before, I purposely omit what was said in the journal; it is sufficient to observe, that I was no less time than from the 3rd of January to the 14th of April working, finishing and perfecting this wall, though it was no more than about 24 yards in length, being a half circle from one place in the rock to another place about eight yards from it, the door of the cave being in the center behind it.

Managing My Household Affairs

ALL THIS time I worked very hard, the rains hindering me many days, nay, sometimes weeks together; but I thought I should never be perfectly secure till this wall was finished; and it is scarce credible what inexpressible labor everything was done with, especially the bringing piles out of the woods, and driving them into the ground, for I made them much bigger than I need to have done.

When this wall was finished, and the outside double-fenced with a turf wall raised up close to it, I persuaded myself that if any people were to come on shore there, they would not perceive anything like a habitation; and it was very well I did so, as may be observed hereafter upon a very remarkable occasion.

During this time, I made my rounds in the woods for game every day when the rain admitted me and made frequent discoveries in these walks of something or other to my advantage; particularly I found a kind of wild pigeons, who built not as wood pigeons in a tree, but rather as house pigeons, in the holes of the rocks; and taking some young ones, I endeavored to breed them up tame, and did so; but when they grew older they flew all away, which perhaps was at first for want of feeding them, for I had nothing to give them; however, I frequently found their nests and got their young ones, which were very good meat.

And now, in the managing my household affairs, I found myself wanting in many things, which I thought at first it was impossible for me to make, as indeed as to some of them it was; for instance, I could never make a cask to be hooped; I had a small runlet or two, as I observed before, but I could never arrive to the capacity of making one by them, though I spent many weeks about it; I could neither put in the heads, or joint the staves so true to one another, as to make them hold water, so I gave that also over.

In the next place, I was at a great loss for candle; so that as soon as ever it was dark, which was generally by seven o'clock, I was obliged to go to bed. I remembered the lump of beeswax with which I made candles in my African adventure, but I had none of that now; the only remedy I had was, that when I had killed a goat, I saved the tallow, and with a little dish made of clay, which I baked in the sun, to which I added a wick of some oakum, I made me a lamp; and this gave me light, though not a clear steady light like a candle. In the middle of all my labors it happened that, rummaging my things, I found a little bag, which, as I hinted before, had been filled with corn [1] for the feeding of poultry, not for this voyage, but before, as I suppose, when the ship came from Lisbon; what little remained of corn had been in the bag was all devoured with the rats, and I saw nothing in the bag but husks and dust; and being willing to have the bag for some other use, I think it was to put powder in, when I divided it for fear of the lightning, or some such use, I shook the husks of corn out of it on one side of my fortification under the rock.

It was a little before the great rains, just now mentioned, that I threw this stuff away, taking no notice of anything, and not so much as remembering that I had thrown anything there; when about a month after or thereabout I saw some few stalks of something green shooting out of the ground, which I fancied might be some plant I had not seen; but I was surprised and perfectly astonished when after a little longer time I saw about ten or twelve ears come out which were perfect green barley of the same kind as our European, nay, as our English barley.

It is impossible to express the astonishment and confusion of my thoughts on this occasion; I had hitherto acted upon no religious foundation at all; indeed I had very few notions of religion in my head or had entertained any sense of anything that had befallen me otherwise than as a chance, or, as we lightly say, what pleases God; without so much as inquiring into the end of Providence in

[1] *Grain*

these things or His order in governing events in the world. But after I saw barley grow there, in a climate which I know was not proper for corn, and especially that I knew not how it came there, it startled me strangely and I began to suggest that God had miraculously caused this grain to grow without any help of seed sown and that it was so directed purely for my sustenance on that wild miserable place.

This touched my heart a little and brought tears out of my eyes, and I began to bless myself, that such a prodigy of Nature should happen upon my account; and this was the more strange to me because I saw near it still, all along by the side of the rock, some other straggling stalks, which proved to be stalks of rice and which I knew, because I had seen it grow in Africa when I was ashore there.

I not only thought these the pure productions of Providence for my support but not doubting but that there was more in the place, I went all over that part of the island where I had been before, peering in every corner and under every rock, to see for more of it, but I could not find any; at last it occurred to my thoughts that I had shook a bag of chickens' meal out in that place, and then the wonder began to cease; and I must confess, my religious thankfulness to God's Providence began to abate too upon the discovering that all this was nothing but what was common; though I ought to have been as thankful for so strange and unforeseen Providence as if it had been miraculous; for it was really the work of Providence as to me, that should order or appoint, that ten or twelve grains of corn should remain unspoiled (when the rats had destroyed all the rest), as if it had been dropped from Heaven; as also that I should throw it out in that particular place where, it being in the shade of a high rock, it sprang up immediately; whereas, if I had thrown it anywhere else at that time, it had been burnt up and destroyed.

I carefully saved the ears of this corn, you may be sure, in their season, which was about the end of June; and laying up every corn, I resolved to sow them all again, hoping in time to have some quantity sufficient to supply me with bread; but it was not till the fourth year that I could allow myself the least grain of this corn to eat, and even then but sparingly, as I shall say afterwards in its order; for I lost all that I sowed the first season by not observing the proper time; for I sowed it just before the dry season, so that it never came up at all, at least not as it would have done; of which in its place.

Besides this barley, there was, as above, twenty or thirty stalks of rice, which I preserved with the same care, and whose use was of the same kind or to the same purpose, viz., to make me bread, or rather food; for I found ways to cook it up without baking, though I did that also after some time. But to return to my journal.

I worked excessive hard these three or four months to get my wall done; and the 14th of April I closed it up, contriving to go into it, not by a door, but over the wall by a ladder, that there might be no sign in the outside of my habitation.

April 16. I finished the ladder, so I went up with the ladder to the top, and then pulled it up after me, and let it down in the inside. This was a complete enclosure to me; for within I had room enough, and nothing could come at me from without, unless it could first mount my wall.

The very next day after this wall was finished, I had almost had all my labor overthrown at once, and myself killed; the case was thus. As I was busy in the inside of it, behind my tent, just in the entrance into my cave, I was terribly frighted with a most dreadful surprising thing indeed; for all on a sudden I found the earth come crumbling down from the roof of my cave, and from the edge of the hill over my head, and two of the posts I had set up in the cave cracked in a frightful manner; I was heartily scared, but thought nothing of what was really the cause, only thinking that the top of my cave was falling in, as some of it had done before; and for fear I should be buried in it, I ran forward to my ladder, and not thinking myself safe there neither, I got over my wall for fear of the pieces of the hill which I expected might roll down upon me. I was no sooner stepped down upon the firm ground but I plainly saw it was a terrible earthquake, for the ground I stood on shook three times at about eight minutes' distance, with three such shocks as would have overturned the strongest building that could be supposed to have stood on the earth, and a great piece of the top of a rock, which stood about half a mile from me next the sea, fell down with such a terrible noise, as I never heard in all my life. I perceived also the very sea was put into violent motion by it; and I believe the shocks were stronger under the water than on the island.

I was so amazed with the thing itself, having never felt the like or discoursed with anyone that had, that I was like one dead or stupefied; and the motion of the earth made my stomach sick like one that was tossed at sea; but the noise of the falling of the rock awaked me as it were, and rousing me from the stupefied condition I was in, filled me with horror, and I thought of nothing then but the hill falling upon my tent and all my household goods and burying all at once; and this sunk my very soul within me a second time.

After the third shock was over and I felt no more for some time, I began to take courage, and yet I had not heart enough to go over my wall again, for fear of being buried alive, but sat still upon the ground, greatly cast down and disconsolate, not knowing what to do. All this while I had not the least serious religious thought, nothing but the common, "Lord ha' mercy upon me!" and when it was over, that went away too.

While I sat thus, I found the air overcast, and grow cloudy, as if it would rain; soon after that the wind rose by little and little, so that in less than half an hour it blew a most dreadful hurricane. The sea was all on a sudden covered over with foam and froth, the shore was covered with the breach of the water, the trees were torn up by the roots, and a terrible storm it was; and this held about three hours, and then began to abate, and in two hours more it was stark calm, and began to rain very hard.

All this while I sat upon the ground very much terrified and dejected, when on a sudden it came into my thoughts that, these winds and rain being the consequences of the earthquake, the earthquake itself was spent and over, and I might venture into my cave again. With this thought my spirits began to revive, and the rain also helping to persuade me, I went in and sat down in my tent; but the rain was so violent that my tent was ready to be beaten down with it, and I was forced to go into my cave, though very much afraid and uneasy for fear it should fall on my head.

This violent rain forced me to a new work, viz., to cut a hole through my new fortification, like a sink, to let the water go out, which would else have drowned my cave. After I had been in my cave some time, and found still no more shocks of the earthquake follow, I began to be more composed; and now to support my spirits, which indeed wanted it very much, I went to my little store and took a small sup of rum, which, however, I did then and always very sparingly, knowing I could have no more when that was gone.

It continued raining all that night and great part of the

next day, so that I could not stir abroad, but my mind being more composed, I began to think of what I had best do, concluding that if the island was subject to these earthquakes, there would be no living for me in a cave, but I must consider of building me some little hut in an open place which I might surround with a wall, as I had done here, and so make myself secure from wild beasts or men; but concluded, if I stayed where I was, I should certainly, one time or other, be buried alive.

With these thoughts I resolved to remove my tent from the place where it stood, which was just under the hanging precipice of the hill, and which, if it should be shaken again, would certainly fall upon my tent. And I spent the two next days, being the 19th and 20th of April, in contriving where and how to remove my habitation.

The fear of being swallowed up alive made me that I never slept in quiet, and yet the apprehension of lying abroad without any fence was almost equal to it; but still, when I looked about and saw how everything was put in order, how pleasantly concealed I was and how safe from danger, it made me very loath to remove.

In the meantime it occurred to me that it would require a vast deal of time for me to do this, and that I must be contented to run the venture where I was, till I had formed a camp for myself, and had secured it so as to remove to it. So with this resolution I composed myself for a time and resolved that I would go to work with all speed to build me a wall with piles and cables, etc., in a circle as before and set my tent up in it when it was finished, but that I would venture to stay where I was till it was finished and fit to remove. This was the 21st.

April 22. The next morning I began to consider of means to put this resolve in execution, but I was at a great loss about my tools; I had three large axes and abundance of hatchets (for we carried the hatchets for traffic with the Indians), but with much chopping and cutting knotty hard wood, they were all full of notches and dull, and though I had a grindstone, I could not turn it and grind my tools too; this cost me as much thought as a statesman would have bestowed upon a grand point of politics, or a judge upon the life and death of a man. At length I contrived a wheel with a string, to turn it with my foot, that I might have both my hands at liberty. *Note*: I had never seen any such thing in England, or at least not to take notice how it was done, though since I have observed it is very common there; besides that, my grindstone was very large and heavy. This machine cost me a full week's work to bring it to perfection.

April 28, 29. These two whole days I took up in grinding my tools, my machine for turning my grindstone performing very well.

April 30. Having perceived my bread had been low a great while, now I took a survey of it, and reduced myself to one biscuit cake a day, which made my heart very heavy.

May 1. In the morning, looking towards the sea-side, the tide being low, I saw something lie on the shore bigger than ordinary, and it looked like a cask; when I came to it, I found a small barrel and two or three pieces of the wreck of the ship, which were driven on shore by the late hurricane, and looking towards the wreck itself, I thought it seemed to lie higher out of the water than it used to do; I examined the barrel which was driven on shore and soon found it was a barrel of gunpowder, but it had taken water, and the powder was caked as hard as a stone; however, I rolled it farther on shore for the present and went on upon the sands as near as I could to the wreck of the ship to look for more.

When I came down to the ship I found it strangely removed. The forecastle, which lay before buried in sand, was heaved up at least six foot, and the stern, which was broke to pieces and parted from the rest by the force of the sea soon after I had left rummaging her, was tossed, as it were, up, and cast on one side, and the sand was thrown so high on that side next her stern that whereas there was a great place of water before, so that I could not come within a quarter of a mile of the wreck without swimming, I could now walk quite up to her when the tide was out; I was surprised with this at first, but soon concluded it must be done by the earthquake, and as by this violence the ship was more broken open than formerly, so many things came daily on shore, which the sea had loosened and which the winds and water rolled by degrees to the land.

This wholly diverted my thoughts from the design of removing my habitation; and I busied myself mightily that day especially in searching whether I could make any way into the ship, but I found nothing was to be expected of that kind, for that all the inside of the ship was choked up with sand. However, as I had learned not to despair of anything, I resolved to pull everything to pieces that I could of the ship, concluding that everything I could get from her would be of some use or other to me.

May 3. I began with my saw, and cut a piece of a beam through, which I thought held some of the upper part or quarter-deck together, and when I had cut it through, I cleared away the sand as well as I could from the side which lay highest; but the tide coming in, I was obliged to give over for that time.

May 4. I went a-fishing, but caught not one fish that I durst eat of, till I was weary of my sport, when, just going to leave off, I caught a young dolphin. I had made me a long line of some rope yarn, but I had no hooks, yet I frequently caught fish enough, as much as I cared to eat; all which I dried in the sun and eat them dry.

May 5. Worked on the wreck, cut another beam asunder, and brought three great fir planks off from the decks, which I tied together and made swim on shore when the tide of flood came on.

May 6. Worked on the wreck, got several iron bolts out of her and other pieces of ironwork; worked very hard and came home very much tired and had thoughts of giving it over.

May 7. Went to the wreck again, but with an intent not to work, but found the weight of the wreck had broke itself down, the beams being cut, that several pieces of the ship seemed to lie loose, and the inside of the hold lay so open that I could see into it, but almost full of water and sand.

May 8. Went to the wreck, and carried an iron crow to wrench up the deck, which lay now quite clear of the water or sand; I wrenched open two planks and brought them on shore also with the tide. I left the iron crow in the wreck for next day.

May 9. Went to the wreck and with the crow made way into the body of the wreck and felt several casks and loosened them with the crow, but could not break them up; I felt also the roll of English lead and could stir it, but it was too heavy to remove.

May 10, 11, 12, 13, 14. Went every day to the wreck, and got a great deal of pieces of timber and boards, or plank, and two or three hundredweight of iron.

May 15. I carried two hatchets to try if I could not cut a piece off of the roll of lead, by placing the edge of one hatchet and driving it with the other; but as it lay about a foot and a half in the water, I could not make any blow to drive the hatchet.

May 16. It had blowed hard in the night, and the wreck appeared more broken by the force of the water; but I stayed so long in the woods to get pigeons for food that the tide prevented me going to the wreck that day.

May 17. I saw some pieces of the wreck blown on shore, at a great distance, near two miles off me, but resolved to see what they were and found it was a piece of the head, but too heavy for me to bring away.

May 24. Every day to this day I worked on the wreck, and with hard labor I loosened some things so much with the crow, that with the first blowing tide several casks floated out and two of the seamen's chests; but the wind blowing from the shore, nothing came to land that day but pieces of timber and a hogshead which had some Brazil pork in it, but the salt water and the sand had spoiled it.

I continued this work every day to the 15th of June, except the time necessary to get food, which I always appointed, during this part of my employment, to be when the tide was up, that I might be ready when it was ebbed out, and by this time I had gotten timber and plank and ironwork enough to have builded a good boat, if I had known how; and also, I got at several times and in several pieces near one hundredweight of the sheet lead.

June 16. Going down to the seaside, I found a large tortoise, or turtle; this was the first I had seen, which it seems was only my misfortune, not any defect of the place, or scarcity; for had I happened to be on the other side of the island, I might have had hundreds of them every day, as I found afterwards; but perhaps had paid dear enough for them.

June 17. I spent in cooking the turtle; I found in her threescore eggs; and her flesh was to me at that time the most savory and pleasant that ever I tasted in my life, having had no flesh but of goats and fowls since I landed in this horrid place.

June 18. Rained all day, and I stayed within. I thought at this time the rain felt cold, and I was something chilly, which I knew was not usual in that latitude.

Delivered Wonderfully from Sickness

June 19. Very ill, and shivering, as if the weather had been cold.

June 20. No rest all night; violent pains in my head, and feverish.

June 21. Very ill, frighted almost to death with the apprehensions of my sad condition, to be sick and no help. Prayed to God for the first time since the storm off of Hull, but scarce knew what I said, or why; my thoughts being all confused.

June 22. A little better, but under dreadful apprehensions of sickness.

June 23. Very bad again; cold and shivering, and then a violent headache.

June 24. Much better.

June 25. An ague very violent; the fit held me seven hours, cold fit and hot, with faint sweats after it.

June 26. Better; and having no victuals to eat, took my gun, but found myself very weak; however, I killed a she-goat and with much difficulty got it home and broiled some of it and eat; I would fain have stewed it and made some broth, but had no pot.

June 27. The ague again so violent that I lay abed all day and neither eat nor drank. I was ready to perish for thirst. but so weak I had not strength to stand up or to get myself any water to drink. Prayed to God again, but was lightheaded; and when I was not, I was so ignorant that I knew not what to say; only I lay and cried, "Lord, look upon me! Lord, pity me! Lord, have mercy upon me!" I suppose I did nothing else for two or three hours till, the fit wearing off, I fell asleep and did not wake till far in the night; when I waked, I found myself much refreshed, but weak and exceeding thirsty. However, as I had no water in my whole habitation, I was forced to lie till morning and went to sleep again. In this second sleep I had this terrible dream.

I thought that I was sitting on the ground, on the outside of my wall, where I sat when the storm blew after the earthquake, and that I saw a man descend from a great black cloud, in a bright flame of fire, and light upon the ground. He was all over as bright as a flame, so that I could but just bear to look towards him; his countenance was most inexpressibly dreadful, impossible for words to describe; when he stepped upon the ground with his feet, I thought the earth trembled, just as it had done before in the earthquake, and all the air looked, to my apprehension, as if it had been filled with flashes of fire.

He was no sooner landed upon the earth but he moved forward towards me, with a long spear or weapon in his hand, to kill me; and when he came to a rising ground, at some distance, he spoke to me, or I heard a voice so terrible, that it is impossible to express the terror of it; all that I can say I understood was this: "Seeing all these things have not brought thee to repentance, now thou shalt die." At which words, I thought he lifted up the spear that was in his hand, to kill me.

No one that shall ever read this account will expect that I should be able to describe the horrors of my soul at this terrible vision; I mean, that even while it was a dream, I even dreamed of those horrors; nor is it any more possible to describe the impression that remained upon my mind when I awaked and found it was but a dream.

I had, alas! no divine knowledge; what I had received by the good instruction of my father was then worn out by an uninterrupted series, for eight years, of seafaring wickedness and a constant conversation with nothing but such as were, like myself, wicked and profane to the last degree. I do not remember that I had in all that time one thought that so much as tended either to looking upwards toward God or inwards towards a reflection upon my own ways. But a certain stupidity of soul, without desire of good or conscience of evil, had entirely overwhelmed me, and I was all that the most hardened, unthinking, wicked creature among our common sailors can be supposed to be, not having the least sense either of the fear of God in danger or of thankfulness to God in deliverances.

In the relating what is already past of my story, this will be the more easily believed, when I shall add, that through all the variety of miseries that had to this day befallen me, I never had so much as one thought of it being the hand of God or that it was a just punishment for my sin: my rebellious behavior against my father, or my present sins, which were great; or so much as a punishment for the general course of my wicked life. When I was on the desperate expedition on the desert shores of Africa, I never had so much as one thought of what would become of me; or one wish to God to direct me whither I should go or to keep me from the danger which apparently surrounded me, as well from voracious creatures as cruel savages. But I was merely thoughtless of a God, or a Providence; acted like a mere brute from the principles of Nature and by the dictates of common sense only, and indeed hardly that.

When I was delivered and taken up at sea by the

Portugal captain, well used and dealt justly and honorably with, as well as charitably, I had not the least thankfulness in my thoughts. When again I was shipwrecked, ruined, and in danger of drowning on this island, I was as far from remorse or looking on it as a judgment; I only said to myself often that I was an unfortunate dog and born to be always miserable.

It is true, when I got on shore first here and found all my ship's crew drowned and myself spared, I was surprised with a kind of ecstasy and some transports of soul which, had the grace of God assisted, might have come up to true thankfulness; but it ended where it begun, in a mere common flight of joy, or, as I may say, *being glad I was alive*, without the least reflection upon the distinguishing goodness of the hand which had preserved me and had singled me out to be preserved when all the rest were destroyed; or an inquiry why Providence had been thus merciful to me; even just the same common sort of joy which seamen generally have after they are got safe ashore from a shipwreck, which they drown all in the next bowl of punch and forget almost as soon as it is over; and all the rest of my life was like it.

Even when I was afterwards, on due consideration, made sensible of my condition, how I was cast on this dreadful place, out of the reach of human kind, out of all hope of relief or prospect of redemption, as soon as I saw but a prospect of living and that I should not starve and perish for hunger, all the sense of my affliction wore off, and I began to be very easy, applied myself to the works proper for my preservation and supply and was far enough from being afflicted at my condition, as a judgment from Heaven, or as the hand of God against me; these were thoughts which very seldom entered into my head.

The growing up of the corn, as is hinted in my journal,

had at first some little influence upon me, and began to affect me with seriousness, as long as I thought it had something miraculous in it; but as soon as ever that part of the thought was removed, all the impression which was raised from it wore off also, as I have noted already.

Even the earthquake, though nothing could be more terrible in its nature or more immediately directing to the invisible Power which alone directs such things, yet no sooner was the first fright over but the impression it had made went off also. I had no more sense of God or His judgments, much less of the present affliction of my circumstances being from His hand, than if I had been in the most prosperous condition of life.

But now, when I began to be sick and a leisurely view of the miseries of death came to place itself before me; when my spirits began to sink under the burden of a strong distemper and nature was exhausted with the violence of the fever; conscience that had slept so long began to awake, and I began to reproach myself with my past life, in which I had so evidently, by uncommon wickedness, provoked the justice of God to lay me under uncommon strokes and to deal with me in so vindictive a manner.

These reflections oppressed me for the second or third day of my distemper, and in the violence as well of the fever as of the dreadful reproaches of my conscience extorted some words from me, like praying to God, though I cannot say they were either a prayer attended with desires or with hopes; it was rather the voice of mere fright and distress; my thoughts were confused, the convictions great upon my mind, and the horror of dying in such a miserable condition raised vapors into my head with the mere apprehensions; and in these hurries of my soul I know not what my tongue might express; but it was rather exclamation, such as, "Lord! what a miserable creature am I! If I should be sick, I shall certainly die for want of help, and what will become of me?" Then the tears burst out of my eyes, and I could say no more for a good while.

In this interval, the good advice of my father came to my mind, and presently his prediction, which I mentioned at the beginning of this story, viz., that if I did take this foolish step, God would not bless me, and I would have leisure hereafter to reflect upon having neglected his counsel, when there might be none to assist in my recovery. "Now," said I aloud, "my dear father's words are come to pass. God's justice has overtaken me, and I have none to help or hear me. I rejected the voice of Providence, which had mercifully put me in a posture or station of life wherein I might have been happy and easy; but I would neither see it myself or learn to know the blessing of it from my parents; I left them to mourn over my folly, and now I am left to mourn under the consequences of it. I refused their help and assistance who would have lifted me into the world and would have made everything easy to me, and now I have difficulties to struggle with, too great for even nature itself to support, and no assistance, no help, no comfort, no advice." Then I cried out, "Lord, be my help, for I am in great distress."

This was the first prayer, if I may call it so, that I had made for many years. But I return to my journal.

June 28. Having been somewhat refreshed with the sleep I had had, and the fit being entirely off, I got up; and though the fright and terror of my dream was very great, yet I considered that the fit of the ague would return again the next day, and now was my time to get something to refresh and support myself when I should be ill; and the first thing I did, I filled a large square case-bottle with water, and set it upon my table, in reach of my bed; and to take off the chill or aguish disposition of the water, I put about a quarter of a pint of rum into it and mixed them together; then I got me a piece of the goat's flesh, and broiled it on the coals, but could eat very little; I walked about, but was very weak and withal very sad and heavy-hearted in the sense of my miserable condition, dreading the return of my distemper the next day. At night I made my supper of three of the turtle's eggs, which I roasted in the ashes, and eat, as we call it, in the shell; and this was the first bit of meat I had ever asked God's blessing to, even as I could remember, in my whole life.

After I had eaten, I tried to walk, but found myself so weak that I could hardly carry the gun (for I never went out without that); so I went but a little way, and sat down upon the ground, looking out upon the sea, which was just before me and very calm and smooth. As I sat here, some thoughts as these occurred to me.

What is this earth and sea, of which I have seen so much? Whence is it produced? And what am I and all the other creatures, wild and tame, human and brutal, whence are we?

Sure we are all made by some secret Power who formed the earth and sea, the air and sky; and who is that?

Then it followed most naturally, It is God that has made it all. Well, but then, it came on strangely, if God has made all these things, He guides and governs them all and all things that concern them; for the Power that could make all things must certainly have power to guide and direct them.

If so, nothing can happen in the great circuit of His works either without His knowledge or appointment.

And if nothing happens without His knowledge, He knows that I am here and am in this dreadful condition, and if nothing happens without His appointment, He has appointed all this to befall me.

Nothing occurred to my thoughts to contradict any of these conclusions; and therefore it rested upon me with the greater force that it must needs be that God had appointed all this to befall me; that I was brought to this miserable circumstance by His direction, He having the sole power, not of me only, but of everything that happened in the world. Immediately it followed:

Why has God done this to me? What have I done to be thus used?

My conscience presently checked me in that inquiry, as if I had blasphemed, and methought it spoke to me like a voice: "WRETCH! dost thou ask what thou hast done? Look back upon a dreadful misspent life and ask thyself what thou hast not done; ask, why is it that thou wert not long ago destroyed? Why wert thou not drowned in Yarmouth Roads? killed in the fight when the ship was taken by the Sallee man-of-war? devoured by the wild beasts on the coast of Africa? or drowned here, when all the crew perished but thyself? Dost thou ask, What have I done?"

I was struck dumb with these reflections, as one astonished, and had not a word to say, no, not to answer to myself, but rose up pensive and sad, walked back to my retreat, and went up over my wall, as if I had been going to bed, but my thoughts were sadly disturbed and I had no inclination to sleep; so I sat down in my chair and lighted my lamp, for it began to be dark. Now as the apprehension of the return of my distemper terrified me very much, it occurred to my thought that the Brazilians take no physic but their tobacco, for almost all distempers; and I had a piece of a roll of tobacco in one of the chests which was quite cured and some also that was green and not quite cured.

I went, directed by Heaven no doubt; for in this chest I found a cure both for soul and body. I opened the chest, and found what I looked for, viz., the tobacco; and as the

few books I had saved lay there too, I took out one of
the Bibles which I mentioned before and which to this
time I had not found leisure, or so much as inclination, to
look into; I say, I took it out, and brought both that and
the tobacco with me to the table.

What use to make of the tobacco I knew not, as to my
distemper, or whether it was good for it or no; but I tried
several experiments with it as if I was resolved it should
hit one way or other. I first took a piece of a leaf, and
chewed it in my mouth, which indeed at first almost stupefied my brain, the tobacco being green and strong and
that I had not been much used to it; then I took some
and steeped it an hour or two in some rum, and resolved
to take a dose of it when I lay down; and lastly, I burnt
some upon a pan of coals and held my nose close over
the smoke of it, as long as I could bear it as well for the
heat as almost for suffocation.

In the interval of this operation, I took up the Bible
and began to read, but my head was too much disturbed
with the tobacco to bear reading, at least that time; only
having opened the book casually, the first words that occurred to me were these, "Call on Me in the day of trouble, and I will deliver, and thou shalt glorify Me."

The words were very apt to my case, and made some
impression upon my thoughts at the time of reading them,
though not so much as they did afterwards; for as for being delivered, the word had no sound, as I may say, to
me; the thing was so remote, so impossible in my apprehension of things that I began to say, as the children of
Israel did when they were promised flesh to eat, "Can
God spread a table in the wilderness?"; so I began to say,
"Can God Himself deliver me from this place?" and as it
was not for many years that any hope appeared, this prevailed very often upon my thoughts. But however, the
words made a great impression upon me, and I mused

upon them very often. It grew now late, and the tobacco had, as I said, dozed my head so much that I inclined to sleep; so I left my lamp burning in the cave lest I should want anything in the night and went to bed; but before I lay down, I did what I never had done in all my life; I kneeled down and prayed to God to fulfill the promise to me, that if I called upon Him in the day of trouble, He would deliver me. After my broken and imperfect prayer was over, I drank the rum in which I had steeped the tobacco, which was so strong and rank of the tobacco that indeed I could scarce get it down; immediately upon this I went to bed; I found presently it flew up in my head violently, but I fell into a sound sleep and waked no more till by the sun it must necessarily be near three o'clock in the afternoon the next day; nay, to this hour I'm partly of the opinion that I slept all the next day and night, and till almost three that day after; for otherwise I knew not how I should lose a day out of my reckoning in the days of the week, as it appeared some years after I had done; for if I had lost it by crossing and re-crossing the line, I should have lost more than one day. But certainly I lost a day in my account and never knew which way.

Be that, however, one way or the other, when I awaked I found myself exceedingly refreshed and my spirits lively and cheerful; when I got up, I was stronger than I was the day before and my stomach better, for I was hungry; and in short, I had no fit the next day, but continued much altered for the better; this was the 29th.

The 30th was my well day, of course, and I went abroad with my gun but did not care to travel too far. I killed a seafowl or two, something like a brand goose, and brought them home, but was not very forward to eat them; so I ate some more of the turtle's eggs, which were very good. This evening I renewed the medicine, which

I had supposed did me good the day before, viz., the tobacco steeped in rum, only I did not take so much as before, nor did I chew any of the leaf or hold my head over the smoke. However, I was not so well the next day, which was the first of July, as I hoped I should have been; for I had a little spice of the cold fit, but it was not much.

July 2. I renewed the medicine all the three ways, and dosed myself with it as at first; and doubled the quantity which I drank.

July 3. I missed the fit for good and all, though I did not recover my full strength for some weeks after; while I was gathering strength, my thoughts ran exceedingly upon this Scripture, "I will deliver thee," and the impossibility of my deliverance lay much upon my mind, in bar of my ever expecting it. But as I was discouraging myself with such thoughts, it occurred to my mind, that I pored so much upon my deliverance from the main affliction that I disregarded the deliverance I had received; and I was, as it were, made to ask myself such questions as these, viz.: Have I not been delivered, and wonderfully, too, from sickness? from the most distressed condition that could be and that was so frightful to me? And what notice had I taken of it? Had I done my part? God had delivered me, but I had not glorified Him; that is to say, I had not owned and been thankful for that as a deliverance, and how could I expect greater deliverance?

This touched my heart very much, and immediately I kneeled down and gave God thanks aloud for my recovery from my sickness.

July 4. In the morning I took the Bible, and beginning at the New Testament, I began seriously to read it, and imposed upon myself to read a while every morning and every night, not tying myself to the number of chapters, but as long as my thoughts should engage me. It was not long after I set seriously to this work, but I found my heart more deeply and sincerely affected with the wickedness of my past life. The impression of my dream revived, and the words, "All these things have not brought thee to repentance," ran seriously in my thought. I was earnestly begging of God to give me repentance, when it happened providentially the very day that reading the Scripture, I came to these words, "He is exalted a Prince and a Saviour, to give repentance, and to give remission." I threw down the book, and with my heart as well as my hands lifted up to Heaven, in a kind of ecstasy of joy, I cried out aloud, "Jesus, Thou Son of David, Jesus, Thou exalted Prince and Saviour, give me repentance!"

This was the first time that I could say, in the true sense of the words, that I prayed in all my life; for now I prayed with a sense of my condition and with a true Scripture view of hope founded on the encouragement of the Word of God; and from this time, I may say, I began to have hope that God would hear me.

Now I began to construe the words mentioned above, "Call on Me, and I will deliver you," in a different sense from what I had ever done before; for then I had no notion of anything being called deliverance but my being delivered from the captivity I was in; for though I was indeed at large in the place, yet the island was certainly a prison to me, and that in the worst sense in the world; but now I learned to take it in another sense. Now I looked back upon my past life with such horror, and my sins appeared so dreadful, that my soul sought nothing of God but deliverance from the load of guilt that bore down all my comfort. As for my solitary life, it was nothing; I did not so much as pray to be delivered from it or think of it; it was all of no consideration in comparison to this. And I add this part here, to hint to whoever shall read it, that whenever they come to a true sense of things, they will find deliverance from sin a much greater blessing than deliverance from affliction.

But, leaving this part, I return to my journal.

My condition began now to be, though not less miserable as to my way of living, yet much easier to my mind; and my thoughts being directed by a constant reading the Scripture and praying to God to things of a higher nature, I had a great deal of comfort within which till now I knew nothing of; also, as my health and strength returned, I bestirred myself to furnish myself with everything that I wanted and make my way of living as regular as I could.

From the 4th of July to the 14th I was chiefly employed in walking about with my gun in my hand, a little and a little at a time, as a man that was gathering up his strength after a fit of sickness. For it is hardly to be imagined how low I was, and to what weakness I was reduced. The application which I made use of was perfectly new and perhaps what had never cured an ague before; neither can I recommend it to anyone to practice, by this experiment; and though it did carry off the fit, yet it rather contributed to weakening me; for I had frequent convulsions in my nerves and limbs for some time.

I learned from it also this in particular, that being abroad in the rainy season was the most pernicious thing to my health that could be, especially in those rains which came attended with storms and hurricanes of wind; for as the rain which came in the dry season was always most accompanied with such storms, so I found that rain was much more dangerous than the rain which fell in September and October.

A More Perfect Discovery of the Island

I HAD been now in this unhappy island above ten months; all possibility of deliverance from this condition seemed to be entirely taken from me; and I firmly believed that no human shape had ever set foot upon that place. Having now secured my habitation, as I thought, fully to my mind, I had a great desire to make a more perfect discovery of the island and to see what other productions I might find, which I yet knew nothing of.

It was the 15th July that I began to take a more particular survey of the island itself. I went up the creek first, where, as I hinted, I brought my rafts on shore; I found after I came about two miles up that the tide did not flow any higher and that it was no more than a little brook of running water, and very fresh and good; but this being the dry season, there was hardly any water in some parts of it, at least, not enough to run in any stream so as it could be perceived.

On the bank of this brook I found many pleasant savannas, or meadows, plain, smooth, and covered with grass; and on the rising parts of them next to the higher grounds, where the water, as it might be supposed, never overflowed, I found a great deal of tobacco, green and growing to a great and very strong stalk; there were divers other plants, which I had no notion of, or understanding about, and might perhaps have virtues of their own, which I could not find out.

I searched for the cassava root, which the Indians in all that climate make their bread of, but I could find none. I saw large plants of aloes, but did not then understand them. I saw several sugar-canes, but wild and, for want of cultivation, imperfect. I contented myself with these discoveries for this time, and came back musing with myself what course I might take to know the virtue and goodness of any of the fruits or plants which I should discover; but could bring it to no conclusion; for in short, I had made so little observation while I was in the Brazils that I knew little of the plants in the field, at least very little that might serve me to any purpose now in my distress.

The next day, the 16th, I went up the same way again, and after going something farther than I had gone the day before, I found the brook and the savannas began to cease, and the country became more woody than before; in this part I found different fruits, and particularly I found melons upon the ground in great abundance and grapes upon the trees; the vines had spread indeed over the trees, and the clusters of grapes were just now in their prime, very ripe and rich. This was a surprising discovery, and I was exceeding glad of them; but I was warned by my experience to eat sparingly of them, remembering that when I was ashore in Barbary the eating of grapes killed several of our Englishmen who were slaves there, by throwing them into fluxes and fevers. But I found an excellent use for these grapes, and that was to cure or dry them in the sun and keep them as dried grapes or raisins are kept, which I thought would be, as indeed they were, as wholesome as agreeable to eat when no grapes might be to be had.

I spent all that evening there, and went not back to my habitation, which by the way was the first night, as I might say, I had lain from home. In the night I took my first contrivance and got up into a tree, where I slept well; and the next morning proceeded upon my discovery, traveling near four miles, as I might judge by the length of the valley, keeping still due north, with a ridge of hills on the south and north side of me.

At the end of this march I came to an opening, where the country seemed to descend to the west, and a little spring of fresh water, which issued out of the side of the hill by me, run the other way, that is, due east; and the country appeared so fresh, so green, so flourishing, everything being in a constant verdure, or flourish of spring, that it looked like a planted garden.

I descended a little on the side of that delicious vale, surveying it with a secret kind of pleasure (though mixed with my other afflicting thoughts), to think that this was all my own, that I was king and lord of all this country indefeasibly and had a right of possession; and if I could convey it, I might have it in inheritance, as completely as any lord of a manor in England. I saw here abundance of cocoa trees, orange and lemon and citron trees; but all wild and very few bearing any fruit, at least not then. However, the green limes that I gathered were not only pleasant to eat but very wholesome; and I mixed their juice afterwards with water, which made it very wholesome and very cool and refreshing.

I found now I had business enough to gather and carry home; and I resolved to lay up a store as well of grapes as limes and lemons, to furnish myself for the wet season, which I knew was approaching.

In order to do this, I gathered a great heap of grapes in one place and a lesser heap in another place, and a great parcel of limes and lemons in another place; and taking a few of each with me, I traveled homeward and resolved to come again and bring a bag or sack, or what I could make, to carry the rest home.

Accordingly, having spent three days in this journey, I came home, so I must now call my tent and my cave. But before I got thither, the grapes were spoiled; the richness of the fruits and the weight of the juice having broken them and bruised them, they were good for little or nothing; as to the limes, they were good, but I could bring but a few.

The next day, being the 19th, I went back, having made me two small bags to bring home my harvest. But I was surprised, when coming to my heap of grapes, which were so rich and fine when I gathered them, I found them all spread about, trod to pieces and dragged about, some here, some there, and abundance eaten and devoured. By this I concluded there were some wild creatures thereabouts which had done this; but what they were I knew not.

However, as I found that there was no laying them up in heaps, and no carrying them away in a sack, but that one way they would be destroyed, and the other way they would be crushed with their own weight, I took another course; for I gathered a large quantity of the grapes, and hung them up upon the out-branches of the trees, that they might cure and dry in the sun; and as for the limes and lemons, I carried as many back as I could well stand under.

When I came home from this journey, I contemplated with great pleasure the fruitfulness of that valley and the pleasantness of the situation, the security from storms on that side the water and the wood, and concluded that I had pitched upon a place to fix my abode which was by far the worst part of the country. Upon the whole, I began to consider of removing my habitation; and to look out for a place equally safe as where I now was situate, if possible, in that pleasant fruitful part of the island.

This thought ran long in my head, and I was exceeding fond of it for some time, the pleasantness of the place tempting me; but when I came to a nearer view of it and to consider that I was now by the seaside, where it was at least possible that something might happen to my advantage, and by the same ill fate that brought me hither might bring some other unhappy wretches to the same place; and though it was scarce probable that any such thing should ever happen, yet to enclose myself among the hills and woods, in the center of the island, was to anticipate my bondage and to render such an affair not only improbable but impossible; and that therefore I ought not by any means to remove.

However, I was so enamored of this place that I spent

much of my time there, for the whole remaining part of the month of July; and though upon second thoughts I resolved as above not to remove, yet I built me a little kind of a bower and surrounded it at a distance with a strong fence, being a double hedge as high as I could reach, well staked and filled between with brushwood; and here I lay very secure, sometimes two or three nights together, always going over it with a ladder, as before; so that I fancied now I had my country house and my sea-coast house. And this work took me up to the beginning of August.

I had but newly finished my fence and began to enjoy my labor, but the rains came on and made me stick close to my first habitation! for though I had made me a tent like the other with a piece of a sail and spread it very well, yet I had not the shelter of a hill to keep me from storms, not a cave behind me to retreat into, when the rains were extraordinary.

About the beginning of August, as I said, I had finished my bower and began to enjoy myself. The 3rd of August I found the grapes I had hung up were perfectly dried and, indeed, were excellent good raisins of the sun; so I began to take them down from the trees, and it was very happy that I did so; for the rains which followed would have spoiled them and I had lost the best part of my winter food; for I had above two hundred large bunches of them. No sooner had I taken them all down and carried most of them home to my cave but it began to rain, and from hence, which was the 14th of August, it rained more or less, every day, till the middle of October, and sometimes so violently that I could not stir out of my cave for several days.

In this season I was much surprised with the increase of my family; I had been concerned for the loss of one of my cats, who run away from me, or, as I thought, had been dead, and I heard no more tale or tidings of her till, to my astonishment, she came home about the end of August, with three kittens; this was the more strange to me, because, though I had killed a wild cat, as I called it, with my gun, yet I thought it was a quite different kind from our European cats; yet the young cats were the same kind of house breed like the old one; and both my cats being females, I thought it very strange. But from these three cats, I afterwards came to be so pestered with cats that I was forced to kill them like vermin or wild beasts and to drive them from my house as much as possible.

From the 14th of August to the 26th, incessant rain, so that I could not stir and was now very careful not to be much wet. In this confinement I began to be straitened for food, but venturing out twice, I one day killed a goat and the last day, which was the 26th, found a very large tortoise, which was a treat to me, and my food was regulated thus: I eat a bunch of raisins for my breakfast, a piece of the goat's flesh or of the turtle for my dinner, broiled; for to my great misfortune I had no vessel to boil or stew anything; and two or three of the turtle's eggs for my supper.

During this confinement in my cover by the rain, I worked daily two or three hours at enlarging my cave, and by degrees worked it on towards one side, till I came to the outside of the hill, and made a door or way out, which came beyond my fence or wall, and so I came in and out this way; but I was not perfectly easy at lying so open; for as I had managed myself before, I was in a perfect enclosure, whereas now I thought I lay exposed and open for anything to come in upon me; and yet I could not perceive that there was any living thing to fear, the biggest creature that I had yet seen upon the island being a goat.

September 30. I was now come to the unhappy

anniversary of my landing. I cast up the notches on my post, and found I had been on shore three hundred and sixty-five days. I kept this day as a solemn fast, setting it apart to religious exercise, prostrating myself on the ground with the most serious humiliation, confessing my sins to God, acknowledging His righteous judgments upon me and praying to Him to have mercy on me through Jesus Christ; and having not tasted the least refreshment for twelve hours, even till the going down of the sun, I then eat a biscuit cake and a bunch of grapes and went to bed, finishing the day as I began it.

I had all this time observed no Sabbath day; for as at first I had no sense of religion upon my mind, I had after some time omitted to distinguish the weeks by making a longer notch than ordinary for the Sabbath day, and so did not really know what any of the days were; but now having cast up the days, as above, I found I had been there a year; so I divided it into weeks, and set apart every seventh day for a Sabbath; though I found at the end of my account I had lost a day or two in my reckoning.

A little after this my ink began to fail me, and so I contented myself to use it more sparingly, and to write down only the most remarkable events of my life, without continuing a daily memorandum of other things.

The rainy season and the dry season began now to appear regular to me, and I learned to divide them so as to provide for them accordingly. But I bought all my experience before I had it; and this I am going to relate was one of the most discouraging experiments that I made at all. I have mentioned that I had saved the few ears of barley and rice, which I had so surprisingly found spring up, as I thought, of themselves, and believe there was about thirty stalks of rice and about twenty of barley; and now I thought it a proper time to sow it after the rains, the sun being in its southern position, going from me.

Accordingly I dug up a piece of ground as well as I could with my wooden spade, and dividing it into two parts, I sowed my grain; but as I was sowing, it casually occurred to my thoughts that I would not sow it all at first, because I did not know when was the proper time for it; so I sowed about two-thirds of the seed, leaving about a handful of each.

It was a great comfort to me afterwards that I did so, for not one grain of that I sowed this time came to anything; for the dry months following, the earth having had no rain after the seed was sown, it had no moisture to assist its growth, and never came up at all till the wet season had come again, and then it grew as if it had been but newly sown.

Finding my first seed did not grow, which I easily imagined was by the drought, I sought for a moister piece of ground to make another trial in, and I dug up a piece of ground near my new bower and sowed the rest of my seed in February, a little before the vernal equinox; and this, having the rainy months of March and April to water it, sprung up very pleasantly and yielded a very good crop; but having part of the seed left only, and not daring to sow all that I had, I had but a small quantity at last, my whole crop not amounting to above half a peck of each kind.

But by this experiment I was made master of my business, and knew exactly when the proper season was to sow; and that I might expect two seed times, and two harvests every year.

While this corn was growing, I made a little discovery which was of use to me afterwards. As soon as the rains were over and the weather began to settle, which was about the month of November, I made a visit up the country to my bower, where, though I had not been some months, yet I found all things just as I left them. The circle or double hedge that I had made was not only firm and entire, but the stakes which I had cut out of some trees that grew thereabouts were all shot out and grown with long branches, as much as a willow-tree usually shoots the first year after lopping its head. I could not tell what tree to call it, that these stakes were cut from. I was surprised, and yet very well pleased, to see the young trees grow; and I pruned them, and led them up to grow as much alike as I could; and it is scarce credible how beautiful a figure they grew into in three years; so that though the hedge made a circle of about twenty-five yards in diameter, yet the trees, for such I might now call them, soon covered it; and it was a complete shade, sufficient to lodge under all the dry season.

This made me resolve to cut some more stakes, and make me a hedge like this, in a semicircle round my wall (I mean that of my first dwelling), which I did; and placing the trees or stakes in a double row, at about eight yards' distance from my first fence, they grew presently and were at first a fine cover to my habitation and afterward served for a defense also, as I shall observe in its order.

I found now that the seasons of the year might generally be divided, not into summer and winter, as in Europe, but into the rainy seasons and the dry seasons, which were generally thus:

Half *February,* *March,* Half *April,*	Rainy, the sun being then on or near the equinox.

Half *April.*
    May.
    June,
    July,
Half *August,*
	Dry, the sun being then to the north of the line.

| Half *August,* September, Half *October,* | Rainy, the sun being then come back. |

| Half *October,* November, December, *January,* Half *February,* | Dry, the sun being then to the south of the line. |

The rainy season sometimes held longer or shorter, as the winds happened to blow; but this was the general observation I made. After I had found by experience the ill consequence of being abroad in the rain, I took care to furnish myself with provisions beforehand, that I might not be obliged to go out; and I sat within doors as much as possible during the wet months.

This time I found much employment (and very suitable also to the time), for I found great occasion of many things which I had no way to furnish myself with but by hard labor and constant application; particularly, I tried many ways to make myself a basket, but all the twigs I could get for the purpose proved so brittle that they would do nothing. It proved of excellent advantage to me now, that when I was a boy, I used to take great delight in standing at a basket maker's, in the town where my father lived, to see them make their wickerware; and being, as boys usually are, very officious to help and a great observer of the manner how they worked those things and sometimes lending a hand, I had by this means full knowledge of the methods of it, that I wanted nothing but the materials; when it came into my mind that the twigs of that tree from whence I cut my stakes that grew might possibly be as tough as the sallows and willows and osiers in England, and I resolved to try.

Accordingly, the next day I went to my country house,

as I called it, and cutting some of the smaller twigs, I found them to my purpose as much as I could desire; whereupon I came the next time prepared with a hatchet to cut down a quantity, which I soon found, for there was great plenty of them; these I set up to dry within my circle or hedge, and when they were fit for use, I carried them to my cave, and here during the next season I employed myself in making, as well as I could, a great many baskets, both to carry earth or to carry or lay up anything as I had occasion; and though I did not finish them very handsomely, yet I made them sufficiently serviceable for my purpose; and thus afterwards I took care never to be without them; and as my wickerware decayed, I made more; especially, I made strong deep baskets to place my corn in, instead of sacks, when I should come to have any quantity of it.

Having mastered this difficulty, and employed a world of time about it, I bestirred myself to see if possible how to supply two wants. I had no vessels to hold anything that was liquid, except two runlets which were almost full of rum and some glass bottles, some of the common size, and others which were case bottles, square, for the holding of waters, spirits, etc. I had not so much as a pot to boil anything, except a great kettle, which I saved out of the ship and which was too big for such use as I desired it, viz., to make broth and stew a bit of meat by itself. The second thing I would fain have had was a tobacco-pipe; but it was impossible to me to make one; however, I found a contrivance for that, too, at last.

I employed myself in planting my second rows of stakes, or piles, and in this wicker-working all the summer, or dry season, when another business took me up more time than it could be imagined I could spare.

I mentioned before that I had a great mind to see the whole island and that I had traveled up the brook and so on to where I built my bower and where I had an opening quite to the sea, on the other side of the island; I now resolved to travel quite cross to the seashore on that side; so taking my gun, a hatchet, and my dog, and a larger quantity of powder and shot than usual, with two biscuit cakes and a great bunch of raisins in my pouch for my store, I began my journey. When I had passed the vale where my bower stood, as above, I came within view of the sea to the west, and it being a very clear day, I fairly descried land, whether an island or a continent I could not tell; but it lay very high, extending from the west to the west-southwest, at a very great distance; by my guess it could not be less than fifteen or twenty leagues off.

I could not tell what part of the world this might be, otherwise than that I knew it must be part of America and, as I concluded by all my observations, must be near the Spanish dominions and perhaps was all inhabited by savages, where if I should have landed, I had been in a worse condition than I was now; and therefore I acquiesced in the dispositions of Providence, which, I began now to own and to believe, ordered everything for the best; I say, I quieted my mind with this, and left afflicting myself with fruitless wishes of being there.

Besides, after some pause upon this affair, I considered that if this land was the Spanish coast, I should certainly, one time or other, see some vessel pass or repass one way or other; but if not, then it was the savage coast between the Spanish country and Brazils, which are indeed the worst of savages; for they are cannibals, or men-eaters, and fail not to murder and devour all the human bodies that fall into their hands.

With these considerations I walked very leisurely forward. I found that side of the island, where I now was, much pleasanter than mine, the open or savanna fields sweet, adorned with flowers and grass and full of very fine woods. I saw abundance of parrots, and fain I would have caught one, if possible, to have kept it to be tame and taught it to speak to me. I did, after some painstaking, catch a young parrot, for I knocked it down with a stick, and having recovered it, I brought it home; but it was some years before I could make him speak. However, at last I taught him to call me by my name very familiarly. But the accident that followed, though it be a trifle, will be very diverting in its place.

I was exceedingly diverted with this journey. I found in the low grounds hares, as I thought them to be, and foxes, but they differed greatly from all the other kinds I had met with; nor could I satisfy myself to eat them, though I killed several. But I had no need to be venturous; for I had no want of food, and of that which was very good too; especially these three sorts, viz., goats, pigeons, and turtle or tortoise; which, added to my grapes, Leadenhall Market could not have furnished a table better than I, in proportion to the company; and though my case was deplorable enough, yet I had great cause for thankfulness, and that I was not driven to any extremities for food; but rather plenty, even to dainties.

I never traveled in this journey above two miles outright in a day, or thereabouts; but I took so many turns and returns, to see what discoveries I could make, that I came weary enough to the place where I resolved to sit down for all night; and then I either reposed myself in a tree, or surrounded myself with a row of stakes set upright in the ground, either from one tree to another, or so as no wild creature could come at me without waking me.

As soon as I came to the seashore, I was surprised to see that I had taken up my lot on the worst side of the island; for here indeed the shore was covered with innumerable turtles, whereas on the other side I had found but three in a year and a half. Here was also an infinite number of fowls of many kinds, some which I had seen, and some which I had not seen of before, and many of them very good meat; but such as I knew not the names of, except those called penguins.

I could have shot as many as I pleased, but was very sparing of my powder and shot; and therefore had more mind to kill a she-goat, if I could, which I could better feed on; and though there were many goats here, more than on my side the island, yet it was with much more difficulty that I could come near them, the country being flat and even, and they saw me much sooner than when I was on the hill.

I confess this side of the country was much pleasanter than mine, but yet I had not the least inclination to remove; for as I was fixed in my habitation, it became natural to me, and I seemed all the while I was here to be, as it were, upon a journey and from home. However, I traveled along the shore of the sea towards the east, I suppose about twelve miles; and then setting up a great pole upon the shore for a mark, I concluded I would go home again; and that the next journey I took should be on the other side of the island, east from my dwelling, and so round till I came to my post again. Of which in its place.

I took another way to come back than that I went, thinking I could easily keep all the island so much in my view that I could not miss finding my first dwelling by viewing the country. But I found myself mistaken; for being come about two or three miles, I found myself descended into a very large valley, but so surrounded with hills, and those hills covered with wood, that I could not see which was my way by any direction but that of the sun, nor even then, unless I knew very well the position of the sun at that time of the day.

It happened to my farther misfortune that the weather proved hazy for three or four days while I was in this valley; and not being able to see the sun, I wandered about very uncomfortably and at last was obliged to find out the seaside, look for my post, and come back the same way I went; and then by easy journeys I turned homeward, the weather being exceeding hot and my gun, ammunition, hatchet, and other things very heavy.

In this journey my dog surprised a young kid, and seized upon it, and I, running in to take hold of it, caught it and saved it alive from the dog. I had a great mind to bring it home if I could; for I had often been musing whether it might not be possible to get a kid or two and so raise a breed of tame goats, which might supply me when my powder and shot should be all spent.

I made a collar to this little creature, and with a string which I made of some rope-yarn, which I always carried about me, I led him along, though with some difficulty, till I came to my bower, and there I enclosed him and left him; for I was very impatient to be at home from whence I had been absent above a month.

I cannot express what a satisfaction it was to me to come into my old hutch and lie down in my hammock-bed. This little wandering journey, without settled place of abode, had been so unpleasant to me that my own house, as I called it to myself, was a perfect settlement to me compared to that; and it rendered everything about me so comfortable that I resolved I would never go a great way from it again while it should be my lot to stay on the island.

I reposed myself here a week, to rest and regale myself after my long journey; during which most of the time was taken up in the weighty affair of making a cage for my Poll, who began now to be a mere domestic and to be mighty well acquainted with me. Then I began to think of the poor kid, which I had penned in within my little circle, and resolved to go and fetch it home, or give it some food; accordingly I went, and found it where I left it; for indeed it could not get out, but almost starved for want of food. I went and cut boughs of trees, and branches of such shrubs as I could find and threw it over, and having fed it, I tied it as I did before to lead it away; but it was so tame with being hungry that I had no need to have tied it, for it followed me like a dog; and as I continually fed it, the creature became so loving, so gentle, and so fond, that it became from that time one of my domestics also, and would never leave me afterwards.

I Began My Third Year

THE rainy season of the autumnal equinox was now come, and I kept the 30th of September in the same solemn manner as before, being the anniversary of my landing on the island, having now been there two years, and no more prospect of being delivered than the first day I came there. I spent the whole day in humble and thankful acknowledgments of the many wonderful mercies which my solitary condition was attended with and without which it might have been infinitely more miserable. I gave humble and hearty thanks that God had been pleased to discover to me even that it was possible I might be more happy in this solitary condition than I should have been in a liberty of society and in all the pleasures of the world; that He could fully make up to me the deficiencies of my solitary state and the want of human society by His presence and the communications of His grace to my soul, supporting, comforting, and encouraging me to depend upon His Providence here and hope for His eternal presence hereafter.

It was now that I began sensibly to feel how much more happy this life I now led was, with all its miserable circumstances, than the wicked, cursed, abominable life I led all the past part of my days; and now I changed both my sorrows and my joys; my very desires altered, my affections changed their gusts and my delights were perfectly new, from what they were at my first coming, or indeed for the two years past.

Before, as I walked about, either on my hunting or for viewing the country, the anguish of my soul at my condition would break out upon me on a sudden, and my very heart would die within me to think of the woods, the mountains, the deserts I was in; and how I was a prisoner locked up with the eternal bars and bolts of the ocean in an uninhabited wilderness, without redemption. In the midst of the greatest composures of my mind, this would break out upon me like a storm and make me wring my hands and weep like a child. Sometimes it would take me in the middle of my work, and I would immediately sit down and sigh and look upon the ground for an hour or two together; and this was still worse to me, for if I could burst out into tears or vent myself by words, it would go off, and the grief having exhausted itself would abate.

But now I began to exercise myself with new thoughts; I daily read the Word of God and applied all the comforts of it to my present state. One morning, being very sad, I opened the Bible upon these words, "I will never, never leave thee, nor forsake thee"; immediately it occurred that these words were to me; why else should they be directed in such a manner, just at the moment when I was mourning over my condition, as one forsaken of God and man? "Well then," said I, "if God does not forsake me, of what ill consequence can it be or what matters it though the world should all forsake me, seeing on the other hand, if I had all the world and should lose the favor and blessing of God, there would be no comparison in the loss?"

From this moment I began to conclude in my mind that it was possible for me to be more happy in this forsaken solitary condition than it was probable I should ever have been in any other particular state in the world; and with this thought I was going to give thanks to God for bringing me to this place.

I know not what it was but something shocked my mind at that thought and I durst not speak the words. "How canst thou be such a hypocrite," said I, even audibly, "to pretend to be thankful for a condition which however thou may'st endeavor to be contented with, thou would'st rather pray heartily to be delivered from?" So I stopped there. But though I could not say I thanked God for being there, yet I sincerely gave thanks to God for opening my eyes, by whatever afflicting providences, to see the former condition of my life and to mourn for my wickedness and repent. I never opened the Bible or shut it, but my very soul within me blessed God for directing my friend in England, without any order of mine, to pack it up among my goods and for assisting me afterwards to save it out of the wreck of the ship.

Thus, and in this disposition of mind, I began my third year; and though I have not given the reader the trouble of so particular account of my works this year as the first, yet in general it may be observed that I was very seldom idle; but having regularly divided my time, according to the several daily employments that were before me, such as, first, my duty to God and the reading the Scriptures, which I constantly set apart some time for thrice every day; secondly, the going abroad with my gun for food, which generally took me up three hours in every morning, when it did not rain; thirdly, the ordering, curing, preserving, and cooking what I had killed or catched for my supply; these took up great part of the day; also it is to be considered that the middle of the day when the sun was in the zenith, the violence of the heat was too great to stir out; so that about four hours in the evening was all the time I could be supposed to work in; with this exception, that sometimes I changed my hours of hunting and working and went to work in the morning and abroad with my gun in the afternoon.

To this short time allowed for labor, I desire may be added the exceeding laboriousness of my work; the many hours which for want of tools, want of help, and want of skill everything I did took up out of my time. For example, I was full two and forty days making me a board for a long shelf, which I wanted in my cave; whereas two sawyers with their tools and a saw-pit would have cut six of them out of the same tree in half a day.

My case was this: it was to be a large tree which was to be cut down, because my board was to be a broad one. This tree I was three days a-cutting down, and two more cutting off the boughs, and reducing it to a log, or piece of timber. With inexpressible hacking and hewing, I reduced both the sides of it into chips till it began to be light enough to move; then I turned it and made one side of it smooth and flat as a board from end to end; then turning that side downward, cut the other side, till I brought the plank to be about three inches thick and smooth on both sides. Anyone may judge the labor of my hands in such a piece of work; but labor and patience carried me through that and many other things. I only observe this in particular, to show the reason why so much of my time went away with so little work, viz., that what might be a little to be done with help and tools was a vast labor and required a prodigious time to do alone and by hand.

But notwithstanding this, with patience and labor I went through many things; and indeed everything that my circumstances made necessary to me to do, as will appear by what follows.

I was now, in the months of November and December, expecting my crop of barley and rice. The ground I had manured or dug up for them was not great; for as I observed, my seed of each was not above the quantity of half a peck; for I had lost one whole crop by sowing in the dry season; but now my crop promised very well, when on a sudden I found I was in danger of losing it all again by enemies of several sorts, which it was scarce possible to keep from it; at first, the goats, and wild creatures which I called hares, who, tasting the sweetness of the blade, lay in it night and day, as soon as it came up, and eat it so close that it could get no time to shoot up into stalk.

This I saw no remedy for, but by making an enclosure about it with a hedge, which I did with a great deal of toil; and the more, because it required speed. However, as my arable land was but small, suited to my crop, I got it totally well fenced in about three weeks' time; and shooting some of the creatures in the daytime, I set my dog to guard it in the night, tying him up to a stake at the gate, where he would stand and bark all night long; so in a little time the enemies forsook the place, and the corn grew very strong and well, and began to ripen apace.

But as the beasts ruined me before, while my corn was in the blade, so the birds were as likely to ruin me now, when it was in the ear; for going along by the place to see how it throve, I saw my little crop surrounded with fowls of I know not how many sorts, who stood, as it were, watching till I should be gone. I immediately let fly among them (for I always had my gun with me). I had no sooner shot, but there rose up a little cloud of fowls, which I had not seen at all, from among the corn itself.

This touched me sensibly, for I foresaw that in a few days they would devour all my hopes, that I should be starved and never be able to raise a crop at all, and what to do I could not tell. However, I resolved not to lose my corn, if possible, though I should watch it night and day. In the first place, I went among it to see what damage was already done and found they had spoiled a good deal of it, but that as it was yet too green for them, the loss was not so great, but that the remainder was like to be a good crop if it could be saved.

I stayed by it to load my gun, and then coming away I could easily see the thieves sitting upon all the trees about me, as if they only waited till I was gone away, and the event proved it to be so; for as I walked off as if I was gone, I was no sooner out of their sight but they dropped down one by one into the corn again. I was so provoked that I could not have patience to stay till more came on, knowing that every grain that they eat now was, as it might be said, a peck-loaf to me in the consequence; but coming up to the hedge, I fired again, and killed three of them. This was what I wished for; so I took them up and served them as we serve notorious thieves in England, viz., hanged them in chains for a terror to others; it is impossible to imagine, almost, that this should have such an effect as it had; for the fowls would not only not come at the corn but, in short, they forsook all that part of the island and I could never see a bird near the place as long as my scarecrows hung there.

This I was very glad of, you may be sure, and about the latter end of December, which was our second harvest of the year, I reaped my crop.

I was sadly put to it for a scythe or a sickle to cut it down, and all I could do was to make one as well as I could out of one of the broadswords, or cutlasses, which

I saved among the arms out of the ship. However, as my first crop was but small, I had no great difficulty to cut it down; in short, I reaped it my way, for I cut nothing off but the ears, and carried it away in a great basket which I had made, and so rubbed it out with my hands; and at the end of all my harvesting, I found that out of my half peck of seed I had near two bushels of rice and above two bushels and a half of barley, that is to say, by my guess, for I had no measure at that time.

However, this was a great encouragement to me, and I foresaw that in time it would please God to supply me with bread. And yet here I was perplexed again, for I neither knew how to grind or make meal of my corn, or indeed how to clean it and part it; nor if made into meal, how to make bread of it; and if how to make it, yet I knew not how to bake it; these things being added to my desire of having a good quantity for store, and to secure a constant supply, I resolved not to taste any of this crop, but to preserve it all for seed against the next season, and in the meantime to employ all my study and hours of working to accomplish this great work of providing myself with corn and bread.

It might be truly said that now I worked for my bread; 'tis a little wonderful, and what I believe few people have thought much upon, viz., the strange multitude of little things necessary in the providing, producing, curing, dressing, making, and finishing this one article of bread.

I, that was reduced to a mere state of nature, found this to my daily discouragement and was made more and more sensible of it every hour, even after I had got the first handful of seed-corn, which, as I have said, came up unexpectedly and indeed to a surprise.

First, I had no plough to turn up the earth, no spade or shovel to dig it. Well, this I conquered by making a wooden spade, as I observed before; but this did my work in but a wooden manner, and though it cost me a great many days to make it, yet for want of iron it not only wore out the sooner, but made my work the harder and made it be performed much worse.

However, this I bore with, and was content to work it out with patience and bear with the badness of the performance. When the corn was sowed, I had no harrow but was forced to go over it myself and drag a great heavy bough of a tree over it, to scratch it, as it may be called, rather than rake or harrow it.

When it was growing and grown, I have observed already how many things I wanted, to fence it, secure it, mow or reap it, cure and carry it home, thrash, part it from the chaff and save it. Then I wanted a mill to grind it, sieves to dress it, yeast and salt to make it into bread and an oven to bake it; and yet all these things I did without, as shall be observed; and yet the corn was an inestimable comfort and advantage to me too. All this, as I said, made everything laborious and tedious to me, but that there was no help for; neither was my time so much loss to me, because, as I had divided it, a certain part of it was every day appointed to these works; and as I resolved to use none of the corn for bread till I had a greater quantity by me, I had the next six months to apply myself wholly by labor and invention to furnish myself with utensils proper for the performing all the operations necessary for the making the corn (when I had it) fit for my use.

But first I was to prepare more land, for I had now seed enough to sow above an acre of ground. Before I did this, I had a week's work at least to make me a spade, which when it was done was but a sorry one indeed, and very heavy, and required double labor to work with it; however, I went through that and sowed my seed in two large flat pieces of ground, as near my house as I could find them to my mind, and fenced them in with a good hedge, the stakes of which were all cut of that wood which I had set before, and knew it would grow; so that in one year's time I knew I should have a quick or living hedge that would want but little repair. This work was not so little as to take me up less than three months, because great part of that time was of the wet season, when I could not go abroad.

Within doors, that is, when it rained, and I could not go out, I found employment on the following occasions; always observing, that all the while I was at work I diverted myself with talking to my parrot and teaching him to speak, and I quickly learned him to know his own name and at last to speak it out pretty loud, "Poll," which was the first word I ever heard spoken in the island by any mouth but my own. This therefore was not my work, but an assistant to my work, for now, as I said, I had a great employment upon my hand, as follows, viz., I had long studied, by some means or other, to make myself some earthen vessels, which indeed I wanted sorely, but knew not where to come at them. However, considering the heat of the climate, I did not doubt but if I could find out any such clay, I might botch up some such pot, as might, being dried in the sun, be hard enough and strong enough to bear handling, and to hold anything that was dry, and required to be kept so; and as this was necessary in the preparing corn, meal, etc., which was the thing I was upon, I resolved to make some as large as I could and fit only to stand like jars, to hold what should be put into them.

It would make the reader pity me, or rather laugh at me, to tell how many awkward ways I took to raise this paste; what odd, misshapen, ugly things I made; how many of them fell in, and how many fell out, the clay not being stiff enough to bear its own weight; how many cracked by the over-violent heat of the sun, being set out too hastily; and how many fell in pieces with only removing, as well before as after they were dried; and in a word, how after having labored hard to find the clay, to dig it, to temper it, to bring it home and work it, I could not make above two large earthen ugly things, I cannot call them jars, in about two months' labor.

However, as the sun baked these two very dry and hard, I lifted them very gently up, and set them down again in two great wicker baskets, which I had made on purpose for them, that they might not break, and as between the pot and the basket there was a little room to spare, I stuffed it full of the rice and barley straw, and these two pots being to stand always dry, I thought would hold my dry corn and perhaps the meal, when the corn was bruised.

Though I miscarried so much in my design for large pots, yet I made several smaller things with better success; such as little round pots, flat dishes, pitchers, and pipkins, and any things my hand turned to; and the heat of the sun baked them strangely hard.

But all this would not answer my end, which was to get an earthen pot to hold what was liquid and bear the fire, which none of these could do. It happened after some time, making a pretty large fire for cooking my meat, when I went to put it out after I had done with it, I found a broken piece of one of my earthenware vessels in the fire, burnt as hard as a stone, and red as a tile. I was agreeably surprised to see it and said to myself that certainly they might be made to burn whole, if they would burn broken.

This set me to studying how to order my fire, so as to make it burn me some pots. I had no notion of a kiln such as the potters burn in or of glazing them with lead, though I had some lead to do it with; but I placed three large pipkins and two or three pots in a pile one upon another and placed my firewood all round it with a great heap of embers under them; I plied the fire with fresh fuel round the outside and upon the top, till I saw the pots in the inside red hot quite through, and observed that they did not crack at all; when I saw them clear red, I let them stand in that heat about five or six hours, till I found one of them, though it did not crack, did melt or run, for the sand which was mixed with the clay melted by the violence of the heat, and would have run into glass if I had gone on; so I slacked my fire gradually till the pots began to abate of the red color; and watching them all night that I might not let the fire abate too fast, in the morning I had three very good, I will not say handsome, pipkins and two other earthen pots, as hard burnt as could be desired; and one of them perfectly glazed with the running of the sand.

After this experiment, I need not say that I wanted no sort of earthenware for my use; but I must needs say, as to the shapes of them, they were very indifferent, as anyone may suppose, when I had no way of making them but as the children make dirt pies or as a woman would make pies that never learned to raise paste.

No joy at a thing of so mean a nature was ever equal to mine, when I found I had made an earthen pot that would bear the fire; and I had hardly patience to stay till they were cold, before I set one upon the fire again, with some water in it, to boil me some meat, which it did admirably well; and with a piece of a kid I made some very good broth, though I wanted oatmeal and several other ingredients requisite to make it so good as I would have had it been.

My next concern was to get me a stone mortar to stamp or beat some corn in; for as to the mill, there was no thought at arriving to that perfection of art with one pair of hands. To supply this want I was at a great loss; for of all trades in the world I was as perfectly unqualified for a stone-cutter as for any whatever; neither had I any tools to go about it with. I spent many a day to find out a great stone big enough to cut hollow and make fit for a mortar, and could find none at all, except what was in the solid rock, and which I had no way to dig or cut out; nor indeed were the rocks in the island of hardness sufficient, but were all of a sandy crumbling stone, which neither would bear the weight of a heavy pestle or would break the corn without filling it with sand; so after a great deal of time lost in searching for a stone, I gave it over, and resolved to look out for a great block of hard wood, which I found indeed much easier; and getting one as big as I had strength to stir, I rounded it, and formed it in the outside with my axe and hatchet, and then with the help of fire, and infinite labor, made a hollow place in it, as the Indians in Brazil make their canoes. After this, I made a great heavy pestle, or beater, of the wood called the iron-wood, and this I prepared and laid by against I had my next crop of corn, when I proposed to myself to grind, or rather pound, my corn into meal, to make my bread.

My next difficulty was to make a sieve, or searce, to dress my meal and to part it from the bran and the husk, without which I did not see is possible I could have any bread. This was a most difficult thing, so much as but to think on; for to be sure, I had nothing like the necessary thing to make it; I mean fine thin canvas or stuff, to searce the meal through. And here I was at a full stop for many months, nor did I really know what to do; linen I had none left, but what was mere rags; I had goats' hair, but neither knew I how to weave it or spin it; and had I known how, here was no tools to work it with; all the remedy that I found for this was that at last I did remember I had among the seamen's clothes which were saved out of the ship, some neckcloths of calico or muslin; and with some pieces of these, I made three small sieves, but proper enough for the work; and thus I made shift for some years. How I did afterwards, I shall show in its place.

The baking part was the next thing to be considered and how I should make bread when I came to have corn; for, first, I had no yeast; as to that part, as there was no supplying the want, so I did not concern myself much about it; but for an oven I was indeed in great pain; at length I found out an experiment for that also, which was this; I made some earthen vessels very broad, but not deep; that is to say, about two feet diameter, and not above nine inches deep; these I burnt in the fire, as I had done the other, and laid them by; and when I wanted to bake, I made a great fire upon my hearth, which I had paved with some square tiles of my own making and burning also; but I should not call them square.

When the firewood was burnt pretty much into embers, or live coals, I drew them forward upon this hearth, so as to cover it all over, and there I let them lie, till the hearth was very hot; then sweeping away all the embers, I set down my loaf, or loaves, and whelming down the earthen pot upon them, drew the embers all round the outside of the pot, to keep in and add to the heat; and thus, as well as in the best oven in the world, I baked my barley loaves, and became in little time a mere pastry-cook into the bargain; for I made myself several cakes of the rice and puddings; indeed I made no pies, neither had I anything to put into them, supposing I had, except the flesh either of fowls or goats.

It need not be wondered at, if all these things took me up most part of the third year of my abode here; for it is to be observed that in the intervals of these things I had my new harvest and husbandry to manage; for I reaped my corn in its season and carried it home as well as I could and laid it up in the ear, in my large baskets, till I had time to rub it out; for I had no floor to thrash it on or instrument to thrash it with.

And now indeed my stock of corn increasing, I really wanted to build my barns bigger. I wanted a place to lay it up in; for the increase of the corn now yielded me so much that I had of the barley about twenty bushels and of the rice as much or more; insomuch that now I resolved to begin to use it freely, for my bread had been quite gone a great while; also I resolved to see what quantity would be sufficient for me a whole year, and to sow but once a year.

Upon the whole, I found that the forty bushels of barley and rice was much more than I could consume in a year; so I resolved to sow just the same quantity every year that I sowed the last, in hopes that such a quantity would fully provide me with bread, etc.

My Desire to Venture Over the Main

ALL the while these things were doing, you may be sure my thoughts run many times upon the prospect of land which I had seen from the other side of the island, and I was not without secret wishes that I were on shore there, fancying that seeing the mainland and an inhabited country, I might find some way or other to convey myself farther, and perhaps at last find some means of escape.

But all this while I made no allowance for the dangers of such a condition, and how I might fall into the hands of savages, and perhaps such as I might have reason to think far worse than the lions and tigers of Africa. That if I once came into their power, I should run a hazard more than a thousand to one of being killed and perhaps of being eaten; for I had heard that the people of the Caribbean coasts were cannibals, or man-eaters, and I knew by the latitude that I could not be far off from that shore. That suppose they were not cannibals, yet that they might kill me, as many Europeans who had fallen into their hands had been served, even when they had been ten or twenty together; much more I, that was but one, and could make little or no defense. All these things, I say, which I ought to have considered well of and did cast up in my thoughts afterwards yet took up none of my apprehensions at first; but my head run mightily upon the thought of getting over to the shore.

Now I wished for my boy Xury and the longboat with the shoulder-of-mutton sail with which I sailed above a thousand miles on the coast of Africa; but this was in vain. Then I thought I would go and look at our ship's boat, which, as I have said, was blown up upon the shore a great way in the storm, when we were first cast away. She lay almost where she did at first, but not quite; and was turned by the force of the waves and the winds almost bottom upward against a high ridge of beachy rough sand; but no water about her as before.

If I had had hands to have refitted her and to have launched her into the water, the boat would have done well enough, and I might have gone back into the Brazils with her easily enough; but I might have foreseen that I could no more turn her and set her upright upon her bottom than I could remove the island. However, I went to the woods and cut levers and rollers and brought them to the boat, resolved to try what I could do, suggesting to myself that if I could but turn her down, I might easily repair the damage she had received, and she would be a very good boat, and I might go to sea in her very easily.

I spared no pains, indeed, in this piece of fruitless toil and spent, I think, three or four weeks about it; at last finding it impossible to heave it up with my little strength, I fell to digging away the sand, to undermine it and so to make it fall down, setting pieces of wood to thrust and guide it right in the fall.

But when I had done this, I was unable to stir it up again, or to get under it, much less to move it forward towards the water; so I was forced to give it over; and yet, though I gave over the hopes of the boat, my desire to venture over for the main increased, rather than decreased, as the means for it seemed impossible.

This at length put me upon thinking whether it was not possible to make myself a canoe, or *periagua*, such as the natives of those climates make, even without tools, or, as I might say, without hands, viz., of the trunk of a great tree. This I not only thought possible but easy, and pleased myself extremely with the thoughts of making it and with my having much more convenience for it than any of the Negroes or Indians; but not at all considering the particular inconveniences which I lay under, more than the Indians did, viz., want of hands to move it, when it was made, into the water, a difficulty much harder for me to surmount than all the consequences of want of tools could be to them; for what was it to me, that when I had chosen a vast tree in the woods, I might with much trouble cut it down, if after I might be able with my tools to hew and dub the outside into the proper shape of a boat, and burn or cut out the inside to make it hollow, so to make a boat of it—if after all this, I must leave it just there where I found it, and was not able to launch it into the water?

One would have thought I could not have had the least reflection upon my mind of my circumstance, while I was making this boat; but I should have immediately thought how I should get it into the sea; but my thoughts were so intent upon my voyage over the sea in it that I never once considered how I should get it off of the land; and was really in its own nature more easy for me to guide it over forty-five miles of sea than about forty-five fathoms of land, where it lay, to set it afloat in the water.

I went to work upon this boat the most like a fool that ever man did, who had any of his senses awake. I pleased myself with the design, without determining whether I was ever able to undertake it; not but that the difficulty of launching my boat came often into my head; but I put a stop to my own inquiries into it, by this foolish answer which I gave myself, "Let's first make it; I'll warrant I'll find some way or other to get it along, when 'tis done."

This was a most preposterous method; but the eagerness of my fancy prevailed, and to work I went. I felled a cedar tree. I question much whether Solomon ever had such a one for the building of the Temple at Jerusalem. It was five foot ten inches diameter at the lower part next the stump and four foot eleven inches diameter at the end of twenty-two foot, after which it lessened for a while, and then parted into branches. It was not without infinite labor that I felled this tree. I was twenty days hacking and hewing at it at the bottom. I was fourteen more getting the branches and limbs, and the vast spreading head of it cut off, which I hacked and hewed through with axe and hatchet and inexpressible labor. After this, it cost me a month to shape it and dub it to a proportion, and to something like the bottom of a boat, that it might swim upright as it ought to do. It cost me near three months more to clear the inside, and work it so as to make an exact boat of it. This I did indeed without fire, by mere mallet and chisel, and by the dint of hard labor, till I had brought it to be a very handsome *periagua* and big enough to have carried six and twenty men, and consequently big enough to have carried me and all my cargo.

When I had gone through this work, I was extremely delighted with it. The boat was really much bigger than I ever saw a canoe, or *periagua,* that was made of one tree, in my life. Many a weary stroke it had cost, you may be sure; and there remained nothing but to get it into the water; and had I gotten it into the water, I make no question but I should have begun the maddest voyage and the most unlikely to be performed that ever was undertaken.

But all my devices to get it into the water failed me; though they cost me infinite labor, too. It lay about one hundred yards from the water, and not more. But the first inconvenience was, it was uphill towards the creek; well, to take away this discouragement, I resolved to dig into the surface of the earth, and so make a declivity. This I begun, and it cost me a prodigious deal of pains; but who grudges pains, that have their deliverance in view? But when this was worked through, and this difficulty managed, it was still much at one; for I could no more stir the canoe than I could the other boat.

Then I measured the distance of ground, and resolved to cut a dock, or canal, to bring the water up to the canoe, seeing I could not bring the canoe down to the water. Well, I began this work; and when I began to enter into it and calculate how deep it was to be dug, how broad, how the stuff to be thrown out, I found that by the number of hands I had, being none but my own, it must have been ten or twelve years before I should have gone through with it; for the shore lay high, so that at the upper end it must have been at least twenty foot deep: so at length, though with great reluctancy, I gave this attempt over also.

This grieved me heartily, and now I saw, though too late, the folly of beginning a work before we count the cost and before we judge rightly of our own strength to go through with it.

In the middle of this work I finished my fourth year in this place, and kept my anniversary with the same devotion and with as much comfort as ever before; for by a constant study, and serious application of the Word of God, and by the assistance of His grace, I gained a different knowledge from what I had before. I entertained different notions of things. I looked now upon the world as a thing remote, which I had nothing to do with, no expectation from, and, indeed, no desires about. In a word, I had nothing indeed to do with it, nor was ever like to have; so, I thought, it looked as we may perhaps look upon it hereafter, viz., as a place I had lived in but was come out of it; and well might I say, as Father Abraham to Dives, "Between me and thee is a great gulf fixed."

In the first place, I was removed from all the wickedness of the world here. I had neither the lust of the flesh, the lust of the eye or the pride of life. I had nothing to covet; for I had all that I was now capable of enjoying. I was lord of the whole manor; or if I pleased, I might call myself king, or emperor over the whole country which I had possession of. There were no rivals. I had no competitor, none to dispute sovereignty or command with me. I might have raised shiploadings of corn; but I had no use for it; so I let as little grow as I thought enough for my occasion. I had tortoise or turtles enough; but now and then one was as much as I could put to any use. I had timber enough to have built a fleet of ships. I had grapes enough to have made wine, or to have cured into raisins, to have loaded that fleet, when they had been built.

But all I could make use of was all that was valuable. I had enough to eat, and to supply my wants, and what was all the rest to me? If I killed more flesh than I could eat, the dog must eat it, or the vermin. If I sowed more corn than I could eat, it must be spoiled. The trees that I cut down were lying to rot on the ground. I could make no more use of them than for fuel; and that I had no occasion for but to dress my food.

In a word, the nature and experience of things dictated to me upon just reflection that all the good things of this world are no farther good to us than they are for our use; and that whatever we may heap up indeed to give others, we enjoy just as much as we can use, and no more. The most covetous griping miser in the world would have been cured of the vice of covetousness, if he had been in my case; for I posessed infinitely more than I knew what to do with. I had not room for desire, except it was of things which I had not, and they were but trifles, though indeed of great use to me. I had, as I hinted before, a parcel of money, as well gold as silver, about thirty-six pounds sterling. Alas! There the nasty, sorry, useless stuff lay; I had no manner of business for it; and I often thought with myself that I would have given a handful of it for a gross of tobacco-pipes or for a hand-mill to grind my corn; nay, I would have given it all for sixpenny-worth of turnip and carrot seed out of England or for a handful of peas and beans and a bottle of ink. As it was, I had not the least advantage by it or benefit from it; but there it lay in a drawer and grew moldy with the damp of the cave in the wet season; and if I had had the drawer full of diamonds, it had been the same case; and they had been of no manner of value to me because of no use.

I had now brought my state of life to be much easier in itself than it was at first and much easier to my mind, as well as to my body. I frequently sat down to my meat with thankfulness and admired the hand of God's providence, which had thus spread my table in the wilderness. I learned to look more upon the bright side of my condition and less upon the dark side and to consider what I enjoyed rather than what I wanted; and this gave me sometimes such secret comforts that I cannot express them; and which I take notice of here, to put those discontented people in mind of it who cannot enjoy comfortable what God had given them because they see and covet something that He has not given them. All our discontents about what we want appeared to me to spring from the want of thankfulness for what we have.

Another reflection was of great use to me and doubtless would be so to anyone that should fall into such distress as mine was; and this was to compare my present condition with what I at first expected it should be; nay, with what it would certainly have been, if the good providence of God had not wonderfully ordered the ship to be cast up nearer to the shore, where I not only could come at her but could bring what I got out of her to the shore for my relief and comfort; without which, I had wanted for tools to work, weapons for defense, or gunpowder and shot for getting my food.

I spent whole hours, I may say whole days, in representing to myself, in the most lively colors, how I must have acted if I had got nothing out of the ship. How I could not have so much as got any food, except fish and turtles; and that, as it was long before I found any of them, I must have perished first. That I should have lived, if I had not perished, like a mere savage. That if I had killed a goat, or a fowl, by any contrivance, I had no way to flay or open them, or part the flesh from the skin and the bowels, or to cut it up; but must gnaw it with my teeth and pull it with my claws like a beast.

These reflections made me very sensible of the goodness of Providence to me and very thankful for my present condition, with all its hardships and misfortunes. And this part also I cannot but recommend to the reflection of those who are apt in their misery to say, "Is any affliction like mine?" Let them consider how much worse the cases of some people are and their case might have been, if Providence had thought fit.

I had another reflection which assisted me also to comfort my mind with hopes; and this was comparing my present condition with what I had deserved and had therefore reason to expect from the hand of Providence. I had lived a dreadful life, perfectly destitute of the knowledge and fear of God. I had been well instructed by father and mother; neither had they been wanting to me in their early endeavors to infuse a religious awe of God into my mind, a sense of my duty and of what the nature and end of my being required of me. But alas! falling early into the seafaring life, which of all the lives is the most destitute of the fear of God, though His terrors are always before them; I say, falling early into the seafaring life and into seafaring company, all that little sense of religion which I had entertained was laughed out of me by my messmates; by a hardened despising of dangers and the views of death, which grew habitual to me; by my long absence from all manner of opportunities to converse with anything but what was like myself or to hear anything that was good or tended towards it.

So void was I of everything that was good, or of the least sense of what I was or was to be, that in the greatest deliverances I enjoyed, such as my escape from Sallee, my being taken up by the Portuguese master of the ship, my being planted so well in the Brazils, my receiving the cargo from England and the like, I never had once the words, "Thank God," as much as on my mind or in my mouth; nor in the greatest distress had I so much a thought to pray to Him or so much as to say, "Lord, have mercy upon me"; no, nor to mention the name of God, unless it was to swear by and blaspheme it.

I had terrible reflections upon my mind for many months, as I have already observed, on the account of my wicked and hardened life past; and when I looked about me and considered what particular providences had attended me since my coming into this place, and how God had dealt bountifully with me; had not only punished me less than my iniquity had deserved, but had so plentifully provided for me; this gave me great hopes that my repentance was accepted, and that God had yet mercy in store for me.

With these reflections I worked my mind up not only to resignation to the will of God in the present disposition of my circumstances but even to a sincere thankfulness for my condition; and that I, who was yet a living man, ought not to complain, seeing I had not the due punishment of my sins; that I enjoyed so many mercies which I had no reason to have expected in that place; that I ought never more to repine at my condition but to rejoice and to give daily thanks for that daily bread, which nothing but a crowd of wonders could have brought. That I ought to consider I had been fed even by miracle, even as great as that of feeding Elijah by ravens; nay, by a long series of miracles; and that I could hardly have named a place in the unhabitable part of the world where I could have been cast more to my advantage. A place, where as I had no society, which was my affliction on one hand, so I found no ravenous beast, no furious wolves or tigers to threaten my life, no venomous creatures or poisonous which I might feed on to my hurt, no savages to murder and devour me.

In a word, as my life was a life of sorrow one way, so it was a life of mercy another; and I wanted nothing to make it a life of comfort but to be able to make my sense of God's goodness to me, and care over me in this condition, be my daily consolation; and after I did make a just improvement of these things, I went away and was no more sad.

I had now been here so long that many things which I brought on shore for my help were either quite gone, or very much wasted and near spent.

My ink, as I observed, had been gone for some time, all but a very little, which I eked out with water, a little and a little, till it was so pale it scarce left any appearance of black upon the paper. As long as it lasted, I made use of it to minute down the days of the month on which any remarkable thing happened to me; and first, by casting up times past, I remember that there was a strange concurrence of days in the various providences which befell me and which, if I had been superstitiously inclined to observe days as fatal or fortunate, I might have had reason to have looked upon with a great deal of curiosity.

First, I had observed that the same day that I broke away from my father and my friends and ran away to Hull in order to go to sea, the same day afterwards I was taken by the Sallee man-of-war and made a slave.

The same day of the year that I escaped out of the wreck of that ship in Yarmouth Roads, that same day-year afterwards I made my escape from Sallee in the boat.

The same day of the year I was born on, viz., the 30th of September, that same day I had my life so miraculously saved twenty-six years after, when I was cast on shore in this island; so that my wicked life and my solitary life begun both on a day.

The next thing to my ink's being wasted was that of my bread, I mean the biscuit which I brought out of the ship. This I had husbanded to the last degree, allowing myself but one cake of bread a day for above a year, and yet I was quite without bread for near a year before I got any corn of my own, and great reason I had to be thankful that I had any at all, the getting it being. as has been already observed, next to miraculous.

My clothes began to decay, too, mightily. As to linen, I had none a good while, except some checkered shirts which I found in the chests of the other seamen, and which I carefully preserved, because many times I could bear no other clothes on but a shirt; and it was a very great help to me that I had among all the men's clothes of the ship almost three dozen of shirts. There were also several thick watch coats of the seamen's, which were left indeed, but they were too hot to wear; and though it is true that the weather was so violent hot that there was no need of clothes, yet I could not go quite naked; no, though I had been inclined to it, which I was not, nor could abide the thoughts of it, though I was all alone.

The reason why I could not go quite naked was, I could not bear the heat of the sun so well when quite naked, as with some clothes on; nay, the very heat frequently blistered my skin; whereas with a shirt on, the air itself made some motion and, whistling under that shirt, was twofold cooler than without it. No more could I ever bring myself to go out in the heat of the sun without a cap or a hat; the heat of the sun, beating with such violence as it does in that place, would give me the headache presently, by darting so directly on my head, without a cap or hat on, so that I could not bear it; whereas, if I put on my hat, it would presently go away.

Upon those views I began to consider about putting the few rags I had, which I called clothes, into some order; I had worn out all the waistcoats I had, and my business was now to try if I could not make jackets out of the great watch coats which I had by me, and with such other materials as I had; so I set to work a-tailoring, or rather indeed a-botching, for I made most piteous work of it.

However, I made shift to make two or three new waist-coats, which I hoped would serve me a great while; as for breeches or drawers, I made but a very sorry shift indeed till afterward.

I have mentioned that I saved the skins of all the creatures that I killed, I mean four-footed ones, and I had hung them up stretched out with sticks in the sun, by which means some of them were so dry and hard that they were fit for little, but others it seems were very useful. The first thing I made of these was a great cap for my head, with the hair on the outside, to shoot off the rain; and this I performed so well, that after this I made me a suit of clothes wholly of these skins, that is to say, a waistcoat, and breeches open at knees, and both loose, for they were rather wanting to keep me cool than to keep me warm. I must not omit to acknowledge that they were wretchedly made; for if I was a bad carpenter, I was a worse tailor. However, they were such as I made very good shift with; and when I was abroad, if it happened to rain, the hair of my waistcoat and cap being outermost, I was kept very dry.

After this I spent a great deal of time and pains to make me an umbrella; I was indeed in great want of one, and had a great mind to make one; I had seen them made in the Brazils, where they are very useful in the great heats which are there. And I felt the heats every jot as great here, and greater too, being nearer the equinox; besides as I was obliged to be much abroad, it was a most useful thing to me, as well for the rains as the heats. I took a world of pains at it, and was a great while before I could make anything likely to hold; nay, after I thought I had hit the way, I spoiled two or three before I made one to my mind; but at last I made one that answered indifferently well. The main difficulty I found was to make it to let down. I could make it to spread, but if it did not let down too and draw in, it was not portable for me any way but just over my head, which would not do. However, at last, as I said, I made one to answer and covered it with skins, the hair upwards, so that it cast off the rains like a penthouse and kept off the sun so effectually, that I could walk out in the hottest of the weather with greater advantage than I could before in the coolest, and when I had no need of it, could close it and carry it under my arm.

Sailing Round the Island

THUS I lived mighty comfortably, my mind being entirely composed by resigning to the will of God and throwing myself wholly upon the disposal of His Providence. This made my life better than sociable, for when I began to regret the want of conversation, I would ask myself whether thus conversing mutually with my own thoughts and, as I hope I may say, with even God Himself, by ejaculations, was not better than the utmost enjoyment ot human society in the world.

I cannot say that after this, for five years, any extraordinary thing happened to me, but I lived on in the same course, in the same posture and place, just as before; the chief thing I was employed in, besides my yearly labor of planting my barley and rice and curing my raisins, of both which I always kept up just enough to have sufficient stock of one year's provisions beforehand; I say, besides this yearly labor and my daily labor of going out with my gun, I had one labor, to make me a canoe, which at last I finished. So that by digging a canal to it of six foot wide, and four foot deep, I brought it into the creek, almost half a mile. As for the first, which was so vastly

big, as I made it without considering beforehand, as I
ought to do, how I should be able to launch it; so, never
being able to bring it to the water, or bring the water to
it, I was obliged to let it lie where it was, as a memorandum to teach me to be wiser next time. Indeed, the
next time, though I could not get a tree proper for it, and
in a place where I could not get the water to it at any less
distance than, as I have said, near half a mile, yet as I
saw it was practicable at last, I never gave it over; and
though I was near two years about it, yet I never grudged
my labor, in hopes of having a boat to go off to sea at
last.

However, though my little *periagua* was finished, yet
the size of it was not at all answerable to the design which
I had in view, when I made the first; I mean, of venturing
over to the *terra firma*, where it was above forty miles
broad; accordingly, the smallness of my boat assisted to
put an end to that design, and now I thought no more of
it. But as I had a boat, my next design was to make a tour
round the island; for as I had been on the other side in
one place, crossing, as I have already described it, over
the land, so the discoveries I made in that little journey
made me very eager to see other parts of the coast; and
now I had a boat, I thought of nothing but sailing round
the island.

For this purpose, that I might do everything with discretion and consideration, I fitted up a little mast to my
boat, and made a sail to it out of some of the pieces of
the ship's sail, which lay in store, and of which I had a
great stock by me.

Having fitted my mast and sail and tried the boat, I
found she would sail very well. Then I made little lockers,
or boxes, at either end of my boat, to put provisions, necessaries and ammunition, etc., into, to be kept dry, either

from rain or the spray of the sea; and a little long hollow place I cut in the inside of the boat, where I could lay my gun, making a flap to hang down over it to keep it dry.

I fixed my umbrella also in a step at the stern, like a mast, to stand over my head, and keep the heat of the sun off of me like an awning; and thus I every now and then took a little voyage upon the sea but never went far out, nor far from the little creek; but at last being eager to view the circumference of my little kingdom, I resolved upon my tour and accordingly I victualed my ship for the voyage, putting in two dozen of my loaves (cakes I should rather call them) of barley bread, an earthen pot full of parched rice, a food I eat a great deal of, a little bottle of rum, half a goat and powder and shot for killing more, and two large watch coats, of those which, as I mentioned before, I had saved out of the seamen's chests; these I took, one to lie upon, and the other to cover me in the night.

It was the 6th of November, in the sixth year of my reign, or my captivity, which you please, that I set out on this voyage, and I found it much longer than I expected; for though the island itself was not very large, yet when I came to the east side of it, I found a great ledge of rocks lie out above two leagues into the sea, some above water, some under it, and beyond that, a shoal of sand lying dry half a league more; so that I was obliged to go a great way out to sea to double the point.

When first I discovered them, I was going to give over my enterprise, and come back again, not knowing how far it might oblige me to go out to sea; and above all, doubting how I should get back again; so I came to an anchor; for I had made me a kind of an anchor with a piece of a broken grappling, which I got out of the ship.

Having secured my boat, I took my gun and went on shore, climbing up upon a hill, which seemed to overlook that point, where I saw the full extent of it, and resolved to venture.

In my viewing the sea from that hill where I stood, I perceived a strong, and indeed a most furious current, which run to the east, and even came close to the point; and I took the more notice of it, because I saw there might be some danger that when I came into it, I might be carried out to sea by the strength of it and not be able to make the island again; and indeed, had I not gotten first up upon this hill, I believe it would have been so; for there was the same current on the other side the island, only that it set off at a farther distance; and I saw there was a strong eddy under the shore; so I had nothing to do but to get in out of the first current, and I should presently be in an eddy.

I lay here, however, two days; because the wind blowing pretty fresh at east-southeast, and that being just contrary to the said current, made a great breach of the sea upon the point; so that it was not safe for me to keep too close to the shore for the breach, nor to go too far off because of the stream.

The third day in the morning, the wind having abated overnight, the sea was calm, and I ventured; but I am a warning piece again to all rash and ignorant pilots; for no sooner was I come to the point, when even I was not my boat's length from the shore, but I found myself in a great depth of water, and a current like the sluice of a mill. It carried my boat along with it with such violence that all I could do could not keep her so much as on the edge of it; but I found it hurried me farther and farther out from the eddy, which was on my left hand. There was no wind stirring to help me, and all I could do with my paddles signified nothing; and now I began to give myself over for lost; for as the current was on both sides of the island, I knew in a few leagues' distance they must join again, and then I was irrecoverably gone; nor did I see any possibility of avoiding it; so that I had no prospect before me but of perishing; not by the sea, for that was calm enough, but of starving for hunger. I had indeed found a tortoise on the shore, as big almost as I could lift, and had tossed it into the boat; and I had a great jar of fresh water, that is to say, one of my earthen pots; but what was all this to being driven into the vast ocean, where, to be sure, there was no shore, no mainland or island, for a thousand leagues at least?

And now I saw how easy it was for the Providence of God to make the most miserable condition mankind could be in worse. Now I looked back upon my desolate solitary island as the most pleasant place in the world, and all the happiness my heart could wish for was to be but there again. I stretched out my hands to it, with eager wishes. "O happy desert!" said I, "I shall never see thee more. O miserable creature," said I, "whither am I going?" Then I reproached myself with my unthankful temper and how I had repined at my solitary condition; and now what would I give to be on shore there again! Thus we never see the true state of our condition till it is illustrated to us by its contraries; nor know how to value what we enjoy, but by the want of it. It is scarce possible to imagine the consternation I was now in, being driven from my beloved island (for so it appeared to me now to be) into the wide ocean almost two leagues, and in the utmost despair of ever recovering it again. However, I worked hard, till indeed my strength was almost exhausted, and kept my boat as much to the northward, that is, towards the side of the current which the eddy lay on, as possibly I could; when about noon, as the sun passed the meridian, I thought I felt a little breeze of wind in my face, springing up from the south-southeast. This cheered my heart a little and especially when, in about half an hour more, it blew a pretty small gentle gale. By this time I was gotten at a frightful distance from the island, and had the least cloud or hazy weather intervened, I had been undone another way too; for I had no compass on board, and should never have known how to have steered towards the island, if I had but once lost sight of it; but the weather continuing clear, I applied myself to get up my mast again and spread my sail, standing away to the north as much as possible, to get out of the current.

Just as I had set my mast and sail, and the boat began to stretch away, I saw even by the clearness of the water some alteration of the current was near; for where the current was so strong, the water was foul; but perceiving the water clear, I found the current abate, and presently I found to the east, at about half a mile, a breach of the sea upon some rocks; these rocks I found caused the current to part again, and as the main stress of it ran away more southerly, leaving the rocks to the northeast, so the other returned by the repulse of the rocks and made a strong eddy, which run back again to the northwest, with a very sharp stream.

They who know what it is to have a reprieve brought to them upon the ladder or to be rescued from thieves just a-going to murder them, or who have been in such like extremities, may guess what my present surprise of joy was and how gladly I put my boat into the stream of this eddy, and the wind also freshening, how gladly I spread my sail to it, running cheerfully before the wind and with a strong tide or eddy under foot.

This eddy carried me about a league in my way back again, directly towards the island, but about two leagues more to the northward than the current which carried me away at first; so that when I came near the island, I found myself open to the northern shore of it, that is to say, the other end of the island, opposite to that which I went out from.

When I had made something more than a league of way by the help of this current or eddy, I found it was spent and served me no farther. However, I found that being between the two great currents, viz., that on the south side, which had hurried me away, and that on the north, which lay about a league on the other side: I say, between these two, in the wake of the island, I found the water at least still and running no way, and having still a breeze of wind fair for me, I kept on steering directly for the island, though not making such fresh way as I did before.

About four o'clock in the evening, being then within about a league of the island, I found the point of the rocks which occasioned this disaster stretching out, as is described before, to the southward, and casting off the current more southwardly, had of course made another eddy to the north, and this I found very strong, but not directly setting the way my course lay, which was due west, but almost full north. However, having a fresh gale, I stretched across this eddy, slanting northwest, and in about an hour came within about a mile of the shore, where, it being smooth water, I soon got to land.

When I was on shore, I fell on my knees, and gave God thanks for my deliverance, resolving to lay aside all thoughts of my deliverance by my boat; and refreshing myself with such things as I had, I brought my boat close to the shore in a little cove that I had spied under some trees and laid me down to sleep, being quite spent with the labor and fatigue of the voyage.

I was now at a great loss which way to get home with my boat. I had run so much hazard, and knew too much the case, to think of attempting it by the way I went out, and what might be at the other side (I mean the west side) I knew not, nor had I any mind to run any more ventures; so I only resolved in the morning to make my way westward along the shore and to see if there was no creek where I might lay up my frigate in safety, so as to have her again if I wanted her; in about three miles, or there about, coasting the shore, I came to a very good inlet or bay about a mile over, which narrowed till it came to a very little rivulet or brook, where I found a very convenient harbor for my boat and where she lay as if she had been in a little dock made on purpose for her. Here I put in, and having stowed my boat very safe, I went on shore to look about me and see where I was.

I soon found I had but a little passed by the place where I had been before, when I traveled on foot to that shore; so taking nothing out of my boat but my gun and my umbrella, for it was exceedingly hot, I began my march. The way was comfortable enough after such a voyage as I had been upon, and I reached my old bower in the evening, where I found everything standing as I left it; for I always kept it in good order, being, as I said before, my country house.

I got over the fence and laid me down in the shade to rest my limbs, for I was very weary, and fell asleep. But judge you, if you can, that read my story, what a surprise I must be in, when I was waked out of my sleep by a voice calling me by my name several times, "Robin, Robin, Robin Crusoe, poor Robin Crusoe! Where are you, Robin Crusoe? Where are you? Where have you been?"

I was so dead asleep at first, being fatigued with rowing, or paddling, as it is called, the first part of the day and with walking the latter part that I did not wake thoroughly, but dozing between sleeping and waking, thought I dreamed that somebody spoke to me. But as the voice continued to repeat "Robin Crusoe, Robin Crusoe," at last I began to wake more perfectly and was at first dreadfully frighted and started up in the utmost consternation. But no sooner were my eyes open, but I saw my Poll sitting on the top of the hedge; and immediately knew that it was he that spoke to me; for just in such bemoaning language I had used to talk to him, and teach him; and he had learned it so perfectly that he would sit upon my finger and lay his bill close to my face, and cry, "Poor Robin Crusoe! Where are you? Where have you been? How come you here?" and such things as I had taught him.

However, even though I knew it was the parrot, and that indeed it could be nobody else, it was a good while before I could compose myself. First, I was amazed how the creature got thither and then, how he should just keep about the place and nowhere else. But as I was well satisfied it could be nobody but honest Poll, I got it over; and holding out my hand, and calling him by his name, "Poll," the sociable creature came to me, and sat upon my thumb, as he used to do, and continued talking to me, "Poor Robin Crusoe!" and how did I come here? and where had I been? just as if he had been overjoyed to see me again; and so I carried him home along with me.

I had now had enough of rambling to sea for some time and had enough to do for many days to sit still and reflect upon the danger I had been in. I would have been very glad to have had my boat again on my side of the island; but I knew not how it was practicable to get it about. As to the east side of the island, which I had gone round, I knew well enough there was no venturing that way; my very heart would shrink and my very blood run chill but to think of it. And as to the other side of the island, I did not know how it might be there; but supposing the current ran with the same force against the shore at the east as it passed by it on the other, I might run the same risk of being driven down the stream, and carried by the island, as I had been before of being carried away from it; so, with these thoughts, I contented myself to be without any boat, though it had been the product of so many months' labor to make it, and of so many more to get it unto the sea.

A Very Sedate Retired Life

IN THIS government of my temper I remained near a year, lived a very sedate, retired life, as you may well suppose; and my thoughts being very much composed as to my condition and fully comforted in resigning myself to the dispositions of Providence, I thought I lived really very happily in all things, except that of society.

I improved myself in this time in all the mechanic exercises which my necessities put me upon applying myself to and I believe could, upon occasion, make a very good carpenter, especially considering how few tools I had.

Besides this, I arrived at an unexpected perfection in my earthenware, and contrived well enough to make them with a wheel, which I found infinitely easier and better; because I made things round and shapable which before were filthy things indeed to look on. But I think I was never more vain of my own performance, or more joyful for anything I found out, than for my being able to make a tobacco-pipe. And though it was a very ugly, clumsy thing when it was done, and only burnt red, like other earthenware, yet as it was hard and firm, and would draw the smoke, I was exceedingly comforted with it, for I had been always used to smoke and there were pipes in the ship, but I forgot them at first, not knowing that there was tobacco in the island; and afterwards, when I searched the ship again, I could not come at any pipes at all.

In my wickerware also I improved much and made abundance of necessary baskets, as well as my invention showed me; though not very handsome, yet they were such as were very handy and convenient for my laying things up in, or fetching things home in. For example, if I killed a goat abroad, I could hang it up in a tree, flay it and dress it and cut it in pieces and bring it home in a basket; and the like by a turtle, I could cut it up, take out the eggs, and a piece or two of the flesh, which was enough for me, and bring them home in a basket, and leave the rest behind me. Also large deep baskets were my receivers for my corn, which I always rubbed out as soon as it was dry and cured and kept it in great baskets.

I began now to perceive my powder abated considerably, and this was a want which it was impossible for me to supply; and I began seriously to consider what I must do when I should have no more powder; that is to say, how I should do to kill any goat. I had, as is observed in the third year of my being here, kept a young kid, and bred her up tame, and I was in hope of getting a he-goat; but I could not by any means bring it to pass, till my kid grew an old goat; and I could never find in my heart to kill her, till she died at last of mere age.

But being now in the eleventh year of my residence, and, as I have said, my ammunition growing low, I set myself to study some art to trap and snare the goats, to see whether I could not catch some of them alive, and particularly, I wanted a she-goat great with young.

To this purpose I made snares to hamper them, and I do believe they were more than once taken in them, but my tackle was not good, for I had no wire, and I always found them broken and my bait devoured.

At length I resolved to try a pitfall, so I dug several large pits in the earth, in places where I had observed the goats used to feed, and over these pits I placed hurdles, of my own making too, with a great weight upon them; and several times I put ears of barley and dry rice, without setting the trap, and I could easily perceive that the goats had gone in and eaten up the corn, for I could see the mark of their feet. At length I set three traps in one night, and going the next morning, I found them all standing, and yet the bait eaten and gone. This was very discouraging. However, I altered my trap, and, not to trouble you with particulars, going one morning to see my trap, I found in one of them a large old he-goat, and in one of the other, three kids, a male and two females.

As to the old one, I knew not what to do with him, he was so fierce I durst not go into the pit to him; that is to say, to go about to bring him away alive, which was what I wanted. I could have killed him, but that was not my business, nor would it answer my end. So I e'en let him out, and he ran away, as if he had been frighted out of his wits. But I had forgot then what I learned afterwards, that hunger will tame a lion. If I had let him stay there three or four days without food and then have carried him some water to drink, and then a little corn, he would have been as tame as one of the kids, for they are mighty sagacious, tractable creatures where they are well used.

However, for the present I let him go, knowing no better at that time; then I went to the three kids, and taking them one by one, I tied them with strings together and with some difficulty brought them all home.

It was a good while before they would feed, but throwing them some sweet corn, it tempted them and they began to be tame; and now I found that if I expected to supply myself with goat-flesh when I had no powder or shot left, breeding some up tame was my only way, when perhaps I might have them about my house like a flock of sheep.

But then it presently occurred to me that I must keep the tame from the wild, or else they would always run wild when they grew up, and the only way for this was to have some enclosed piece of ground, well fenced either with hedge or pale, to keep them in so effectually that those within might not break out, or those without break in.

This was a great undertaking for one pair of hands, yet as I saw there was an absolute necessity of doing it, my first piece of work was to find a proper piece of ground, viz., where there was likely to be herbage for them to eat, water for them to drink, and cover to keep them from the sun.

Those who understand such enclosures will think I had very little contrivance, when I pitched upon a place very proper for all these, being a plain open piece of meadow land, or savanna (as our people call it in the western colonies), which had two or three little drills of fresh water in it and at one end was very woody. I say, they will smile at my forecast, when I shall tell them I began my enclosing of this piece or ground in such a manner that my hedge or pale must have been at least two mile about. Nor was the madness of it so great as to the compass, for if it was ten mile about, I was like to have time enough to do it in. But I did not consider that my goats would be as wild in so much compass as if they had had the whole island, and I should have so much room to chase them in that I should never catch them.

My hedge was begun and carried on, I believe, about fifty yards, when this thought occurred to me, so I presently stopped short and for the first beginning I resolved to enclose a piece of about 150 yards in length, and 100 yards in breadth, which, as it would maintain as many as I should have in any reasonable time, so, as my flock increased, I could add more ground to my enclosure.

This was acting with some prudence, and I went to work with courage. I was about three months hedging in the first piece, and till I had done it I tethered the three kids in the best part of it and used them to feed as near me as possible to make them familiar; and very often I would go and carry them some ears of barley or a handful of rice and feed them out of my hand; so that after my enclosure was finished and I let them loose, they would follow me up and down, bleating after me for a handful of corn.

This answered my end, and in about a year and a half I had a flock of about twelve goats, kids and all; and in two years more I had three and forty, besides several that I took and killed for my food. And after that I enclosed five several pieces of ground to feed them in, with little pens to drive them into, to take them as I wanted, and gates out of one piece of ground into another.

But this was not all, for now I not only had goat's flesh to feed on when I pleased, but milk too, a thing which indeed in my beginning I did not so much as think of, and which, when it came into my thoughts, was really an agreeable surprise. For now I set up my dairy and had sometimes a gallon or two of milk in a day. And as Nature, who gives supplies of food to every creature, dictates even naturally how to make use of it, so I that had never milked a cow, much less a goat, or seen butter or cheese made, very readily and handily, though after a great many essays and miscarriages, made me both butter and cheese at last and never wanted it afterwards.

How mercifully can our great Creator treat His creatures, even in those conditions in which they seemed to be overwhelmed in destruction! How can He sweeten the bitterest providences and give us cause to praise Him for dungeons and prisons! What a table was here spread for me in a wilderness, where I saw nothing at first but to perish for hunger!

It would have made a stoic smile to have seen me and my little family sit down to dinner; there was my majesty, the prince and lord of the whole island; I had the lives of all my subjects at my absolute command. I could hang, draw, give liberty, and take it away, and no rebels among all my subjects.

Then to see how like a king I dined, too, all alone, attended by my servants; Poll, as if he had been my favorite, was the only person permitted to talk to me. My dog, who was now grown very old and crazy and had found no species to multiply his kind upon, sat always at my right hand, and two cats, one on one side the table and one on the other, expecting now and then a bit from my hand, as a mark of special favor.

But these were not the two cats which I brought on shore at first, for they were both of them dead and had been interred near my habitation by my own hand; but one of them having multiplied by I know not what kind of creature, these were two which I had preserved tame, whereas the rest run wild in the woods and became indeed troublesome to me at last; for they would often come into my house and plunder me too, till at last I was obliged to shoot them, and did kill a great many; at length they left me with this attendance, and in this plentiful manner, I lived; neither could I be said to want anything but society, and of that in some time after this, I was like to have too much.

I was something impatient, as I have observed, to have the use of my boat, though very loath to run any more hazards; and therefore sometimes I sat contriving ways

to get her about the island, and at other times I sat myself down contented enough without her. But I had a
strange uneasiness in my mind to go down to the point
of the island where, as I have said, in my last ramble I
went up the hill to see how the shore lay and how the
current set that I might see what I had to do. This inclination increased upon me every day, and at length I resolved to travel thither by land; following the edge of the
shore I did so. But had anyone in England been to meet
such a man as I was, it must either have frighted them or
raised a great deal of laughter; and as I frequently stood
still to look at myself, I could not but smile at the notion
of my traveling through Yorkshire with such an equipage
and in such a dress. Be pleased to take a sketch of my
figure as follows:

I had a great high shapeless cap, made of a goatskin,
with a flap hanging down behind, as well to keep the
sun from me as to shoot the rain off from running into
my neck; nothing being so hurtful in these climates as
the rain upon the flesh under the clothes.

I had a short jacket of goatskin, the skirts coming down
to about the middle of my thighs; and a pair of open-
kneed breeches of the same; the breeches were made of
the skin of an old he-goat, whose hair hung down such a
length on either side that, like pantaloons, it reached to
the middle of my legs; stockings and shoes I had none,
but had made me a pair of somethings, I scarce know
what to call them, like buskins, to flap over my legs, and
lace on either side like spatterdashes; but of a most barbarous shape, as indeed were all the rest of my clothes.

I had on a broad belt of goatskin dried, which I drew
together with two thongs of the same, instead of buckles;
and in a kind of a frog on either side of this, instead of a
sword and a dagger, hung a little saw and a hatchet, one
on one side, one on the other. I had another belt, not so

broad and fastened in the same manner, which hung over my shoulder; and at the end of it, under my left arm, hung two pouches, both made of goatskin too; in one of which hung my powder, in the other my shot. At my back I carried my basket, on my shoulder my gun, and over my head a great clumsy ugly goatskin umbrella, but which, after all, was the most necessary thing I had about me, next to my gun. As for my face, the color of it was really not so Mulatto like as one might expect from a man not at all careful of it and living within nineteen degrees of the equinox. My beard I had once suffered to grow till it was about a quarter of a yard long; but as I had both scissors and razors sufficient, I had cut it pretty short, except what grew on my upper lip, which I had trimmed into a large pair of Mahometan whiskers, such as I had seen worn by some Turks who I saw at Sallee; for the Moors did not wear such, though the Turks did; of these mustachios or whiskers, I will not say they were long enough to hang my hat upon them, but they were of a length and shape monstrous enough and such as in England would have passed for frightful.

But all this is by the bye; for as to my figure, I had so few to observe me that it was of no manner of consequence; so I say no more to that part. In this kind of figure I went my new journey, and was out five or six days. I traveled first along the seashore, directly to the place where I first brought my boat to an anchor, to get up upon the rocks; and having no boat now to take care of, I went over the land a nearer way to the same height that I was upon before, when, looking forward to the point of the rocks which lay out, and which I was obliged to double with my boat, as is said above, I was surprised to see the sea all smooth and quiet, no rippling, no motion, no current, any more there than in other places.

I was at a strange loss to understand this, and resolved

to spend some time in the observing it, to see if nothing from the sets of the tide had occasioned it; but I was presently convinced how it was, viz., that the tide of ebb setting from the west and joining with the current of waters from some great river on the shore must be the occasion of this current; and that according as the wind blew more forcibly from the west or from the north, this current came near, or went farther from the shore; for waiting there abouts till evening, I went up to the rock again, and then the tide of the ebb being made, I plainly saw the current again as before, only that it run farther off, being near half a league from the shore; whereas in my case it set close upon the shore, and hurried me and my canoe along with it, which at another time it would not have done.

This observation convinced me that I had nothing to do but to observe the ebbing and the flowing of the tide, and I might very easily bring my boat about the island again. But when I began to think of putting it in practice, I had such a terror upon my spirits at the remembrance of the danger I had been in that I could not think of it again with any patience; but on the contrary, I took up another resolution, which was more safe, though more laborious; and this was that I would build, or rather make me another *periagua*, or canoe; and so have one for one side of the island and one for the other.

You are to understand that now I had, as I may call it, two plantations in the island; one my little fortification or tent, with the wall about it under the rock, with the cave behind me, which by this time I had enlarged into several apartments, or caves, one within another. One of these, which was the driest and largest, and had a door out beyond my wall or fortification, that is to say, beyond where my wall joined to the rock, was all filled up with the large earthen pots, of which I have given an account, and with fourteen or fifteen great baskets, which would hold five or six bushels each, where I laid up my stores of provision, especially my corn, some in the ear cut off short from the straw, and the other rubbed out with my hand.

As for my wall, made, as before, with long stakes, or piles, those piles grew all like trees and were by this time grown so big and spread so very much that there was not the least appearance to any one's view of any habitation behind them.

Near this dwelling of mine but a little farther within the land and upon lower ground, lay my two pieces of corn ground, which I kept duly cultivated and sowed, and which duly yielded me their harvest in its season; and whenever I had occasion for more corn, I had more land adjoining as fit as that.

Besides this, I had my country seat, and I had now a tolerable plantation there also; for first, I had my little bower, as I called it, which I kept in repair; that is to say, I kept the hedge which circled it in constantly fitted up to its usual height, the ladder standing always in the inside; I kept the trees, which at first were no more than my stakes, but were now grown very firm and tall, I kept them always so cut that they might spread and grow thick and wild, and make the more agreeable shade, which they did effectually to my mind. In the middle of this I had my tent always standing, being a piece of a sail spread over poles set up for that purpose, and which never wanted any repair or renewing; and under this I had made me a squab, or couch, with the skins of the creatures I had killed and with other soft things, and a blanket laid on them such as belong to our seabedding, which I had saved, and a great watch coat to cover me; and here, whenever I had occasion to be absent from my chief seat, I took up my country habitation.

Adjoining to this I had my enclosures for my cattle, that

is to say, my goats. And as I had taken an inconceivable deal of pains to fence and enclose this ground, so I was so uneasy to see it kept entire, lest the goats should break through, that 1 never left off till with infinite labor I had struck the outside of the hedge so full of small stakes, and so near to one another, that it was rather a pale than a hedge, and there was scarce room to put a hand through between them; which afterwards, when those stakes grew, as they all did in the next rainy season, made the enclosure strong like a wall, indeed, stronger than any wall.

This will testify for me that I was not idle and that I spared no pains to bring to pass whatever appeared necessary for my comfortable support; for I considered the keeping up a breed of tame creatures thus at my hand would be a living magazine of flesh, milk, butter, and cheese for me as long as I lived in the place, if it were to be forty years; and that keeping them in my reach depended entirely upon my perfecting my enclosures to such a degree that I might be sure of keeping them together; which by this method indeed, I so effectually secured that when these little stakes began to grow, I had planted them so very thick I was forced to pull some of them up again.

In this place also I had my grapes growing, which I principally depended on for my winter store of raisins and which I never failed to preserve very carefully, as the best and most agreeable dainty of my whole diet; and indeed they were not agreeable only, but physical, wholesome, nourishing, and refreshing to the last degree.

As this was also about halfway between my other habitation and the place where I had laid up my boat, I generally stayed and lay here in my way thither; for I used frequently to visit my boat, and I kept all things about or belonging to her in very good order; sometimes

I went out in her to divert myself, but no more hazardous voyages would I go nor scarce ever above a stone's cast or two from the shore, I was so apprehensive of being hurried out of my knowledge again by the currents, or winds, or any other accident. But now I come to a new scene of my life.

The Print of a Man's Naked Foot

IT HAPPENED one day about noon going towards my boat, I was exceedingly surprised with the print of a man's naked foot on the shore, which was very plain to be seen in the sand. I stood like one thunderstruck, or as if I had seen an apparition; I listened, I looked round me; I could hear nothing, nor see anything; I went up to a rising ground to look farther, I went up the shore and down the shore, but it was all one, I could see no other impression but that one. I went to it again to see if there were any more and to observe if it might not be my fancy; but there was no room for that; for there was exactly the very print of a foot, toes, heel, and every part of a foot; how it came thither I knew not, nor could in the least imagine. But after innumerable fluttering thoughts, like a man perfectly confused and out of myself, I came home to my fortification, not feeling, as we say, the ground I went on but terrified to the last degree, looking behind me at every two or three steps, mistaking every bush and tree, and fancying every stump at a distance to be a man; nor is it possible to describe how many various shapes affrighted imagination represented things to me in, how many wild ideas were found every moment in my fancy, and what strange, unaccountable whimsies came into my thoughts by the way.

When I came to my castle, for so I think I called it ever

after this, I fled into it like one pursued; whether I went over by the ladder as first contrived, or went in at the hole in the rock, which I called a door, I cannot remember; no, nor could I remember the next morning; for never frighted hare fled to cover, or fox to earth, with more terror of mind than I to this retreat.

I slept none that night; the farther I was from the occasion of my fright, the greater my apprehensions were, which is something contrary to the nature of such things and especially to the usual practice of all creatures in fear. But I was so embarrassed with my own frightful ideas of the thing that I formed nothing but dismal imaginations to myself, even though I was now a great way off of it. Sometimes I fancied it must be the Devil; and reason joined in with me upon this supposition. For how should any other thing in human shape come into the place? Where was the vessel that brought them? What marks were there of any other footsteps? And how was it possible a man should come there? But then to think that Satan should take human shape upon him in such a place where there could be no manner of occasion for it, but to leave the print of his foot behind him, and that even for no purpose too, for he could not be sure I should see it; this was an amusement the other way. I considered that the Devil might have found out abundance of other ways to have terrified me than this of the single print of a foot. That as I lived quite on the other side of the island, he would never have been so simple to leave a mark in a place where 'twas ten thousand to one whether I should ever see it or not, and in the sand too, which the first surge of the sea upon a high wind would have defaced entirely. All this seemed inconsistent with the thing itself, and with all the notions we usually entertain of the subtilty of the Devil.

Abundance of such things as these assisted to argue me

out of all apprehensions of its being the Devil. And I presently concluded then that it must be some more dangerous creature, viz., that it must be some of the savages of the mainland over against me, who had wandered out to sea in their canoes and either driven by the currents or by contrary winds had made the island; and had been on shore, but were gone away again to sea, being as loath, perhaps, to have stayed in this desolate island as I would have been to have had them.

While these reflections were rolling upon my mind, I was very thankful in my thoughts that I was so happy as not to be thereabouts at that time or that they did not see my boat, by which they would have concluded that some inhabitants had been in the place, and perhaps have searched farther for me. Then terrible thoughts racked my imagination about their having found my boat, and that there were people here; and that if so, I should certainly have them come again in great numbers, and devour me; that if it should happen so that they should not find me, yet they would find my enclosure, destroy all my corn, carry away all my flock of tame goats, and I should perish at last for mere want.

Thus my fear banished all my religious hope; all that former confidence in God, which was founded upon such wonderful experience as I had had of His goodness, now vanished, as if He that had fed me by miracle hitherto could not preserve by His power the provision which He had made for me by His goodness. I reproached myself with my easiness, that would not sow any more corn one year than would just serve me till the next season, as if no accident could intervene to prevent my enjoying the crop that was upon the ground; and this I thought so just a reproof that I resolved for the future to have two or three years' corn beforehand, so that whatever might come, I might not perish for want of bread.

How strange a checker-work of Providence is the life
of man! and by what secret differing springs are the affections hurried about as differing circumstances present?
Today we love what tomorrow we hate; today we seek
what tomorrow we shun; today we desire what tomorrow
we fear; nay, even tremble at the apprehensions of; this
was exemplified in me at this time. in the most lively
manner imaginable; for I, whose only affliction was that
I seemed banished from human society, that I was alone,
circumscribed by the boundless ocean, cut off from mankind, and condemned to what I called silent life; that
I was as one who Heaven thought not worthy to be numbered among the living, or to appear among the rest of
His creatures; that to have seen one of my own species
would have seemed to me a raising me from death to life,
and the greatest blessing that Heaven itself, next to the
supreme blessing of salvation, could bestow; I say, that I
should now tremble at the very apprehensions of seeing
a man, and was ready to sink into the ground at but the
shadow or silent appearance of a man's having set his
foot in the island.

Such is the uneven state of human life. And it afforded
me a great many curious speculations afterwards, when
I had a little recovered my first surprise; I considered that
this was the station of life the infinitely wise and good
providence of God had determined for me; that as I
could not foresee what the ends of Divine wisdom might
be in all this, so I was not to dispute His sovereignty,
who, as I was His creature, had an undoubted right by
creation to govern and dispose of me absolutely as He
thought fit; and who, as I was a creature who had offended Him, had likewise a judicial right to condemn me
to what punishment He thought fit; and that it was my
part to submit to bear His indignation, because I had
sinned against Him.

I then reflected that God, who was not only righteous but omnipotent, as He had thought fit thus to punish and afflict me, so He was able to deliver me; that if He did not think fit to do it, 'twas my unquestioned duty to resign myself absolutely and entirely to His will; and on the other hand, it was my duty also to hope in Him, pray to Him, and quietly to attend the dictates and directions of His daily providence.

These thoughts took me up many hours, days, nay, I may say, weeks and months; and one particular effect of my cogitations on this occasion I cannot omit, viz., one morning early, lying in my bed, and filled with thought about my danger from the appearance of savages, I found it discomposed me very much, upon which those words of the Scripture came into my thoughts, "Call upon Me in the day of trouble, and I will deliver, and thou shalt glorify Me."

Upon this, rising cheerfully out of my bed, my heart was not only comforted but I was guided and encouraged to pray earnestly to God for deliverance. When I had done praying, I took up my Bible, and opening it to read, the first words that presented to me were, "Wait on the Lord, and be of good cheer, and He shall strengthen thy heart; wait, I say, on the Lord." It is impossible to express the comfort this gave me. In answer, I thankfully laid down the book, and was no more sad, at least not on that occasion.

In the middle of these cogitations, apprehensions, and reflections, it came into my thought one day that all this might be a mere chimera of my own; and that this foot might be the print of my own foot, when I came on shore from my boat. This cheered me up a little too, and I began to persuade myself it was all a delusion; that it was nothing else but my own foot; and why might not I come that way from the boat, as well as I was going that way to the boat? Again, I considered also that I could by no means tell for certain where I had trod, and where I had not; and that if at last this was only the print of my own foot, I had played the part of those fools who strive to make stories of specters and apparitions, and then are frighted at them more than anybody.

Now I began to take courage and to peep abroad again, for I had not stirred out of my castle for three days and nights, so that I began to starve for provision; for I had little or nothing within doors, but some barley-cakes and water. Then I knew that my goats wanted to be milked too, which usually was my evening diversion; and the poor creatures were in great pain and inconvenience for want of it; and indeed, it almost spoiled some of them, and almost dried up their milk.

Heartening myself, therefore, with the belief that this was nothing but the print of one of my own feet, and so I might be truly said to start at my own shadow, I began to go abroad again, and went to my country house to milk my flock; but to see with what fear I went forward, how often I looked behind me, how I was ready every now and then to lay down my basket, and run for my life, it would have made anyone have thought I was haunted with an evil conscience, or that I had been lately most terribly frighted; and so indeed I had.

However, as I went down thus two or three days, and having seen nothing, I began to be a little bolder, and to think there was really nothing in it but my own imagination. But I could not persuade myself fully of this, till I should go down to the shore again, and see this print of a foot, and measure it by my own, and see if there was any similitude or fitness, that I might be assured it was my own foot. But when I came to the place, first, it appeared evidently to me, that when I laid up my boat, I could not possibly be on shore anywhere thereabout;

secondly, when I came to measure the mark with my own foot, I found my foot not so large by a great deal. Both these things filled my head with new imaginations, and gave me the vapors again to the highest degree; so that I shook with cold, like one in an ague. And I went home again, filled with the belief that some man or men had been on shore there; or in short, that the island was inhabited, and I might be surprised before I was aware; and what course to take for my security, I knew not.

O what ridiculous resolution men take when possessed with fear! It deprives them of the use of those means which reason offers for their relief. The first thing I proposed to myself was to throw down my enclosures, and turn all my tame cattle wild into the woods, that the enemy might not find them and then frequent the island in prospect of the same or the like booty: then to the simple thing of digging up my two cornfields, that they might not find such a grain there and still be prompted to frequent the island; then to demolish my bower and tent, that they might not see any vestiges of habitation, and be prompted to look farther, in order to find out the persons inhabiting.

These were the subject of the first night's cogitation, after I was come home again, while the apprehensions which had so overrun my mind were fresh upon me, and my head was full of vapors, as above. Thus fear of danger is ten thousand times more terrifying than danger itself, when apparent to the eyes; and we find the burden of anxiety greater, by much, than the evil which we are anxious about; and which was worse than all this, I had not that relief in this trouble from the resignation I used to practice, that I hoped to have. I looked, I thought, like Saul, who complained not only that the Philistines were upon him but that God had forsaken him; for I did not now take due ways to compose my mind, by crying to

God in my distress, and resting upon His providence, as I had done before, for my defense and deliverance; which if I had done, I had, at least, been more cheerfully supported under this new surprise and perhaps carried through it with more resolution.

This confusion of my thoughts kept me waking all night; but in the morning I fell asleep, and having by the amusement of my mind, been, as it were, tired, and my spirits exhausted, I slept very soundly, and waked much better composed than I had ever been before; and now I began to think sedately; and upon the utmost debate with myself, I concluded that this island, which was so exceeding pleasant, fruitful, and no farther from the mainland than as I had seen, was not so entirely abandoned as I might imagine. That although there were no stated inhabitants who lived on the spot, yet that there might sometimes come boats off from the shore, who either with design, or perhaps never but when they were driven by cross winds, might come to this place. That I had lived here fifteen years now, and had not met with the least shadow or figure of any people yet; and that if at any time they should be driven here, it was probable they went way again as soon as ever they could, seeing they had never thought fit to fix there upon any occasion to this time.

That the most I could suggest any danger from was from any such casual accidental landing of straggling people from the main, who, as it was likely if they were driven hither, were here against their wills; so they made no stay here, but went off again with all possible speed, seldom staying one night on shore, lest they should not have the help of the tides and daylight back again; and that therefore I had nothing to do but to consider of some safe retreat, in case I should see any savages land upon the spot.

Now I began sorely to repent that I had dug my cave so large as to bring a door through again, which door, as I said, came out beyond where my fortification joined to the rock; upon maturely considering this therefore, I resolved to draw me a second fortification, in the same manner of a semicircle, at a distance from my wall, just where I had planted a double row of trees about twelve years before, of which I made mention. These trees having been planted so thick before, they wanted but a few piles to be driven between them, that they should be thicker and stronger, and my wall would be soon finished.

So that I had now a double wall, and my outer wall was thickened with pieces of timber, old cables, and everything I could think of to make it strong; having in it seven little holes, about as big as I might put my arm out at. In the inside of this, I thickened my wall to above ten foot thick, with continual bringing earth out of my cave, and laying it at the foot of the wall, and walking upon it; and through the seven holes I contrived to plant the muskets, of which I took notice that I got seven on shore out of the ship; these, I say, I planted like my cannon, and fitted them into frames that held them like a carriage, that so I could fire all the seven guns in two minutes' time. This wall I was many a weary month a-finishing, and yet never thought myself safe till it was done.

When this was done, I stuck all the ground without my wall, for a great way every way, as full with stakes or sticks, of the osier-like wood, which I found so apt to grow, as they could well stand; insomuch, that I believe I might set in near twenty thousand of them, leaving a pretty large space between them and my wall, that I might have room to see an enemy, and they might have no shelter from the young trees, if they attempted to approach my outer wall.

Thus in two years' time I had a thick grove, and in five or six years' time I had a wood before my dwelling, growing so monstrous thick and strong that it was indeed perfectly impassable; and no men of what kind soever would ever imagine that there was anything beyond it, much less a habitation. As for the way which I proposed to myself to go in and out, for I left no avenue, it was by setting two ladders, one to a part of the rock which was below, and then broke in, and left room to place another ladder upon that; so when the two ladders were taken down, no man living could come down to me without mischieving himself; and if they had come down, they were still on the outside of my outer wall.

Thus I took all the measures human prudence could suggest for my own preservation; and it will be seen at length that they were not altogether without just reason; though I foresaw nothing at that time more than my mere fear suggested to me.

While this was doing, I was not altogether careless of my other affairs; for I had a great concern upon me for my little herd of goats; they were not only a present supply to me upon every occasion, and began to be sufficient to me, without the expense of powder and shot, but also without the fatigue of hunting after the wild ones; and I was loath to lose the advantage of them, and to have them all to nurse up over again.

To this purpose, after long consideration, I could think of but two ways to preserve them; one was to find another convenient place to dig a cave underground, and to drive them into it every night; and the other was to enclose two or three little bits of land, remote from one another and as much concealed as I could, where I might keep about half a dozen young goats in each place; so that if any disaster happened to the flock in general, I might be able to raise them again with little trouble and time.

And this, though it would require a great deal of time and labor, I thought was the most rational design.

Accordingly, I spent some time to find out the most retired parts of the island; and I pitched upon one which was as private indeed as my heart could wish for; it was a little damp piece of ground in the middle of the hollow and thick woods, where, as is observed, I almost lost myself once before, endeavoring to come back that way from the eastern part of the island. Here I found a clear piece of land, near three acres, so surrounded with woods that it was almost an enclosure by Nature, at least it did not want near so much labor to make it so as the other pieces of ground I had worked so hard at.

I immediately went to work with this piece of ground, and in less than a month's time I had so fenced it round that my flock or herd, call it which you please, who were not so wild now as at first they might be supposed to be, were well enough secured in it. So, without any farther delay, I removed ten young she-goats and two he-goats to this piece; and when they were there, I continued to perfect the fence, till I had made it as secure as the other, which, however, I did at more leisure, and it took me up more time by a great deal.

Cannibals!

ALL this labor I was at the expense of purely from my apprehensions on the account of the print of a man's foot which I had seen; for as yet I never saw any human creature come near the island; and I had now lived two years under these uneasinesses, which indeed made my life much less comfortable than it was before; as may well be imagined by any who know what it is to live in the constant snare of the fear of man; and this I must observe with grief too, that the discomposure of my mind had too great impressions also upon the religious part of my thoughts, for the dread and terror of falling into the hands of savages and cannibals lay so upon my spirits that I seldom found myself in a due temper for application to my Maker, at least not with the sedate calmness and resignation of soul which I was wont to do; I rather prayed to God as under great affliction and pressure of mind, surrounded with danger, and in expectation every night of being murdered and devoured before morning; and I must testify from my experience that a temper of peace, thankfulness, love, and affection is much more the proper frame for prayer than that of terror and discomposure; and that under the dread of mischief impending, a man is no more fit for a comforting performance of the duty of praying to God than he is for repentance on a sickbed. For these discomposures affect the mind, as the others do the body; and the discomposure of the mind must necessarily be as great a disability as that of the body, and much greater, praying to God being properly an act of the mind, not of the body.

But to go on. After I had thus secured one part of my little living stock, I went about the whole island searching for another private place to make such another deposit; when wandering more to the west point of the island than I had ever done yet, and looking out to sea, I thought I saw a boat upon the sea, at a great distance; I had found a perspective-glass or two, in one of the seamen's chests which I saved out of our ship; but I had it not about me, and this was so remote that I could not tell what to make of it, though I looked at it till my eyes were not able to hold to look any longer; whether it was a boat or not, I do not know; but as I descended from the hill, I could see no more of it, so I gave it over; only I resolved to go no more out without a perspective-glass in my pocket.

When I was come down the hill to the end of the island, where indeed I had never been before, I was presently convinced that the seeing the print of a man's foot was not such a strange thing in the island as I imagined; and but that it was a special providence that I was cast upon the side of the island where the savages never came, I should easily have known that nothing was more frequent than for the canoes from the main, when they happened to be a little too far out at sea, to shoot over to that side of the island for harbor; likewise, as they often met and fought in their canoes, the victors, having taken any prisoners, would bring them over to this shore, where, according to their dreadful customs, being all cannibals, they would kill and eat them; of which hereafter.

When I was come down the hill to the shore, as I said above, being the southwest point of the island, I was perfectly confounded and amazed; nor is it possible for me to express the horror of my mind at seeing the shore spread with skulls, hands, feet, and other bones of human bodies; and particularly, I observed a place where there had been a fire made, and a circle dug in the earth, like a cockpit, where it is supposed the savage wretches had sat down to their inhuman feastings upon the bodies of their fellow creatures.

I was so astonished with the sight of these things that I entertained no notions of any danger to myself from it for a long while; all my apprehensions were buried in the thoughts of such a pitch of inhuman, hellish brutality, and the horror of the degeneracy of human nature; which though I had heard of often, yet I never had so near a view of before; in short, I turned away my face from the horrid spectacle; my stomach grew sick, and I was just at the point of fainting, when Nature discharged the disorder from my stomach; and having vomited with an uncommon violence, I was a little relieved but could not bear to stay in the place a moment; so I gat me up the hill again, with all the speed I could, and walked on towards my own habitation.

When I came a little out of that part of the island, I stood still a while as amazed; and then recovering myself, I looked up with the utmost affection of my soul, and with a flood of tears in my eyes, gave God thanks that had cast my first lot in a part of the world where I was distinguished from such dreadful creatures as these; and that though I had esteemed my present condition very miserable, had yet given me so many comforts in it that I had still more to give thanks for than to complain of; and this above all, that I had even in this miserable condition been comforted with the knowledge of Himself and the hope of His blessing, which was a felicity more than sufficiently equivalent to all the misery which I had suffered or could suffer.

In this frame of thankfulness I went home to my castle, and began to be much easier now, as to the safety of my circumstances, than ever I was before; for I observed that these wretches never came to this island in search of what they could get; perhaps not seeking, not wanting, or not expecting anything here; and having often, no doubt, been up in the covered, woody part of it, without finding anything to their purpose. I knew I had been here now almost eighteen years, and never saw the least footsteps of human creature there before; and I might be here eighteen more as entirely concealed as I was now, if I did not discover myself to them, which I had no manner of occasion to do, it being my only business to keep myself entirely concealed where I was, unless I found a better sort of creatures than cannibals to make myself known to.

Yet I entertained such an abhorrence of the savage wretches that I have been speaking of and of the wretched, inhuman custom of their devouring and eating one another up that I continued pensive and sad, and kept close within my own circle for almost two years after this. When I say my own circle, I mean by it my three plantations, viz., my castle, my country seat, which I called my bower, and my enclosure in the woods; nor did I look after this for any other use than as an enclosure for my goats; for the aversion which Nature gave me to these hellish wretches was such that I was fearful of seeing them as of seeing the Devil himself; nor did I so much as go to look after my boat in all this time, but began rather to think of making me another; for I could not think of ever making any more attempts to bring the other boat round the island to me, lest I should meet with some of these creatures at sea, in which, if I had happened to have fallen into their hands, I knew what would have been my lot.

Time, however, and the satisfaction I had that I was in no danger of being discovered by these people began to wear off my uneasiness about them; and I began to live just in the same composed manner as before; only with this difference, that I used more caution and kept my eyes more about me than I did before, lest I should happen to be seen by any of them; and particularly, I was more cautious of firing my gun, lest any of them, being on the island, should happen to hear of it; and it was therefore a very good providence to me that I had furnished myself with a tame breed of goats, that I needed not hunt any more about the woods, or shoot at them; and if I did catch any of them after this, it was by traps and snares, as I had done before; so that for two years after this, I believe I never fired my gun once off, though I never went out without it; and which was more, as I had saved three pistols out of the ship, I always carried them out with me, or at least two of them, sticking them in my goatskin belt; also I furbished up one of the great cutlasses that I had out of the ship, and made me a belt to put it on also; so that I was now a most formidable fellow to look at when I went abroad, if you add to the former description of myself the particular of two pistols and a great broadsword. hanging at my side in a belt, but without a scabbard.

Things going on thus, as I have said, for some time, I seemed, excepting these cautions, to be reduced to my former calm, sedate way of living; all these things tended to showing me more and more how far my condition was from being miserable, compared to some others; nay, to many other particulars of life which it might have pleased God to have made my lot. It put me upon reflecting how little repining there would be among mankind at any condition of life, if people would rather compare their condition with those that are worse, in order to be thankful, than be always comparing them with those which are better, to assist their murmurings and complainings.

As in my present condition there were not really many things which I wanted, so indeed I thought that the frights I had been in about these savage wretches and the concern I had been in for my own preservation had taken off the edge of my invention for my own conveniences; and I had dropped a good design, which I had once bent my thoughts too much upon; and that was to try if I could not make some of my barley into malt and then try to brew myself some beer. This was really a whimsical thought, and I reproved myself often for the simplicity of it; for I presently saw there would be the want of several things necessary to the making my beer that it would be impossible for me to supply; as first, casks to preserve it in, which was a thing that, as I have observed already, I could never compass; no, though I spent not many days, but weeks, nay, months, in attempting it but to no purpose. In the next place, I had no hops to make it keep, no yeast to make it work, no copper or kettle to make it boil; and yet all these things notwithstanding, I verily believe, had not these things intervened, I mean the frights and terrors I was in about the savages, I had undertaken it and perhaps brought it to pass too, for I seldom gave anything over without accomplishing it, when I once had it in my head enough to begin it.

But my invention now ran quite another way; for night and day I could think of nothing but how I might destroy some of these monsters in their cruel, bloody entertainment and, if possible, save the victim they should bring hither to destroy. It would take up a larger volume than this whole work is intended to be, to set down all the contrivances I hatched, or rather brooded upon in my thought, for the destroying these creatures, or at least frightening them so as to prevent their coming hither any more; but all was abortive, nothing could be possible to take effect, unless I was to be there to do it myself; and what could one man do among them, when perhaps there might be twenty or thirty of them together, with their darts, or their bows and arrows, with which they could shoot as true to a mark as I could with my gun?

Sometimes I contrived to dig a hole under the place where they made their fire and put in five or six pound of gunpowder, which, when they kindled their fire, would consequently take fire and blow up all that was near it; but as in the first place I should be very loath to waste so much powder upon them, my store being now within the quantity of one barrel, so neither could I be sure of its going off at any certain time, when it might surprise them; and at best, that it would do little more than just blow the fire about their ears and fright them, but not sufficient to make them forsake the place; so I laid it aside, and then proposed that I would place myself in ambush, in some convenient place, with my three guns all double-loaded; and in the middle of their bloody ceremony, let fly at them, when I should be sure to kill or wound perhaps two or three at every shoot; and then falling in upon them with my three pistols and my sword, I made no doubt but that if there was twenty I should kill them all. This fancy pleased my thoughts for some weeks, and I was so full of it that I often dreamed of it; and sometimes that I was just going to let fly at them in my sleep.

I went so far with it in my imagination that I employed myself several days to find out proper places to put myself in ambuscade, as I said, to watch for them; and I went frequently to the place itself, which was now grown more familiar to me; and especially while my mind was thus filled with thoughts of revenge and of a bloody putting twenty or thirty of them to the sword, as I may call it, the horror I had at the place and at the signals of the barbarous wretches devouring one another abated my malice.

Well, at length I found a place in the side of the hill where I was satisfied I might securely wait till I saw any of their boats coming, and might then, even before they would be ready to come on shore, convey myself unseen into thickets of trees, in one of which there was a hollow large enough to conceal me entirely; and where I might sit and observe all their bloody doings, and take my full aim at their heads, when they were so close together as that it would be next to impossible that I should miss my shoot or that I could fail wounding three or four of them at the first shoot.

In this place, then, I resolved to fix my design, and accordingly I prepared two muskets and my ordinary fowling piece. The two muskets I loaded with a brace of slugs each, and four or five smaller bullets, about the size of pistol bullets; and the fowling piece I loaded with near a handful of swan shot, of the largest size; I also loaded my pistols with about four bullets each, and in this posture, well provided with ammunition for a second and third charge, I prepared myself for my expedition.

After I had thus laid the scheme of my design, and in my imagination put it in practice, I continually made my tour every morning up to the top of the hill, which was from my castle, as I called it, about three miles, or more, to see if I could observe any boats upon the sea, coming near the island, or standing over towards it; but I began to tire of this hard duty, after I had for two or three months constantly kept my watch; but came always back without any discovery, there having not, in all that time, been the least appearance, not only on or near the shore, but not on the whole ocean, so far as my eyes or glasses could reach every way.

As long as I kept up my daily tour to the hill to look out, so long also I kept up the vigor of my design, and my spirits seemed to be all the while in a suitable form for so outrageous an execution as the killing twenty or thirty naked savages for an offense which I had not at all entered into a discussion of in my thoughts, any farther than my passions were at first fired by the horror I conceived at the unnatural custom of that people of the country, who it seems had been suffered by Providence, in His wise disposition of the world, to have no other guide than that of their own abominable and vitiated passions; and consequently were left, and perhaps had been so for some ages, to act such horrid things and receive such dreadful customs, as nothing but nature entirely abandoned of Heaven and acted by some hellish degeneracy could have run them into. But now, when as I have said, I began to be weary of the fruitless excursion which I had made so long, and so far every morning in vain, so my opinion of the action itself began to alter, and I began with cooler and calmer thoughts to consider what it was

I was going to engage in. What authority or call I had to pretend to be judge and executioner upon these men as criminals, whom Heaven had thought fit for so many ages to suffer unpunished to go on and to be, as it were, the executioners of His judgments one upon another? How far these people were offenders against me, and what right I had to engage in the quarrel of that blood, which they shed promiscuously one upon another? I debated this very often with myself thus: "How do I know what God Himself judges in this particular case? It is certain these people either do not commit this as a crime; it is not against their own consciences' reproving or their light reproaching them. They do not know it to be an offense, and then commit it in defiance of Divine justice, as we do in almost all the sins we commit. They think it no more a crime to kill a captive taken in war than we do to kill an ox; nor to eat human flesh, than we do to eat mutton."

When I had considered this a little, it followed necessarily that I was certainly in the wrong in it; that these people were not murderers in the sense that I had before condemned them in my thoughts; any more than those Christians were murderers, who often put to death the prisoners taken in battle; or more frequently, upon many occasions, put whole troops of men to the sword, without giving quarter, though they threw down their arms and submitted.

In the next place it occurred to me that albeit the usage they thus gave one another was thus brutish and inhuman, yet it was really nothing to me. These people had done me no injury. That if they attempted me, or I saw it necessary for my immediate preservation to fall upon them, something might be said of it; but that I was yet out of their power and they had really no knowledge of me, and consequently no design upon me, and therefore

it could not be just for me to fall upon them. That this
would justify the conduct of the Spaniards in all their
barbarities practiced in America, and where they destroyed millions of these people, who, however they were
idolaters and barbarians and had several bloody and
barbarous rites in their customs, such as sacrificing human
bodies to their idols, were yet, as to the Spaniards, very
innocent people; and that the rooting them out of the
country is spoken of with the utmost abhorrence and
detestation by even the Spaniards themselves, at this
time, and by all other Christian nations of Europe as a
mere butchery, a bloody and unnatural piece of cruelty,
unjustifiable either to God or man; and such as for which
the very name of a Spaniard is reckoned to be frightful
and terrible to all people of humanity or of Christian
compassion; as if the kingdom of Spain were particularly
eminent for the product of a race of men who were without principles of tenderness, or the common bowels of
pity to the miserable, which is reckoned to be a mark of
generous temper in the mind.

These considerations really put me to a pause and to a
kind of a full stop; and I began by little and little to be
off of my design and to conclude I had taken wrong measures in my resolutions to attack the savages; that it was
not my business to meddle with them unless they first
attacked me; and this it was my business if possible to
prevent; but that if I were discovered and attacked, then
I knew my duty.

On the other hand, I argued with myself that this really
was the way not to deliver myself, but entirely to ruin
and destroy myself; for unless I was sure to kill every one
that not only should be on shore at that time, but that
should ever come on shore afterwards, if but one of them
escaped to tell their country people what had happened,
they would come over again by thousands to revenge the

death of their fellows, and I should only bring upon myself a certain destruction, which at present I had no
manner of occasion for.

Upon the whole I concluded that neither in principle
or in policy I ought one way or other to concern myself
in this affair. That my busines was by all possible means
to conceal myself from them and not to leave the least
signal to them to guess by that there were any living
creatures upon the island; I mean of human shape.

Religion joined in with this prudential, and I was convinced now, many ways, that I was perfectly out of my
duty, when I was laying all my bloody schemes for the
destruction of innocent creatures, I mean innocent as to
me. As to the crimes they were guilty of towards one
another, I had nothing to do with them; they were national, and I ought to leave them to the justice of God,
who is the Governor of nations and knows how by national punishments to make a just retribution for national
offenses; and to bring public judgments upon those who
offend in a public manner, by such ways as best pleases
Him.

This appeared so clear to me now that nothing was a
greater satisfaction to me than that I had not been suffered to do a thing which I now saw so much reason to
believe would have been no less a sin than that of willful
murder, if I had committed it; and I gave most humble
thanks on my knees to God, that had thus delivered me
from blood-guiltiness; beseeching Him to grant me the
protection of His Providence, that I might not fall into
the hands of the barbarians; or that I might not lay my
hands upon them, unless I had a more clear call from
Heaven to do it, in defense of my own life.

In this disposition I continued for near a year after
this; and so far was I from desiring an occasion for falling
upon these wretches, that in all that time I never once

went up the hill to see whether there were any of them
in sight, or to know whether any of them had been on
shore there or not, that I might not be tempted to renew
any of my contrivances against them, or be provoked by
any advantage which might present itself to fall upon
them; only this I did: I went and removed my boat, which
I had on the other side the island, and carried it down to
the east end of the whole island, where I ran it into a little
cove which I found under some high rocks, and where I
knew, by reason of the currents, the savages durst not, at
least would not, come with their boats upon any account
whatsoever.

With my boat I carried away everything that I had left
there belonging to her, though not necessary for the bare
going thither, viz., a mast and sail which I had made for
her, and a thing like an anchor, but indeed which could
not be called either anchor or grappling; however, it was
the best I could make of its kind. All these I removed, that
there might not be the least shadow of any discovery, or
any appearance of any boat or of any human habitation
upon the island.

Besides this, I kept myself, as I said, more retired than
ever, and seldom went from my cell, other than upon my
constant employment, viz., to milk my she-goats and
manage my little flock in the wood, which, as it was quite
on the other part of the island, was quite out of danger;
for certain it is, that these savage people who sometimes
haunted this island never came with any thoughts of
finding anything here; and consequently never wandered
off from the coast; and I doubt not but they might have
been several times on shore, after my apprehensions of
them had made me cautious, as well as before; and indeed, I looked back with some horror upon the thoughts
of what my condition would have been, if I had chopped [1]
upon them and been discovered before that, when naked

[1] *Come quickly.*

and unarmed, except with one gun, and that loaden often only with small shot, I walked everywhere, peeping and peeping about the island to see what I could get; what a surprise should I have been in, if when I discovered the print of a man's foot, I had instead of that seen fifteen or twenty savages and found them pursuing me, and by the swiftness of their running, no possibility of my escaping them!

The thoughts of this sometimes sunk my very soul within me, and distressed my mind so much that I could not soon recover it, to think what I should have done, and how I not only should not have been able to resist them but even should not have had presence of mind enough to do what I might have done, much less what now, after so much consideration and preparation, I might be able to do. Indeed, after serious thinking of these things, I should be very melancholy, and sometimes it would last a great while; but I resolved it at last all into thankfulness to that Providence which had delivered me from so many unseen dangers and had kept me from those mischiefs which I could no way have been the agent in delivering myself from, because I had not the least notion of any such thing depending, or the least supposition of it being possible.

This renewed a contemplation which often had come to my thoughts in former time, when first I began to see the merciful dispositions of Heaven in the dangers we run through in this life. How wonderfully we are delivered, when we know nothing of it. How, when we are in a quandary (as we call it), a doubt or hesitation, whether to go this way, or that way, a secret hint shall direct us this way, when we intended to go that way; nay, when sense, our own inclination, and perhaps business has called to go the other way, yet a strange impression upon the mind, from we know not what strings and by we know not what power, shall overrule us to go this way; and it shall afterwards appear that had we gone that way which we should have gone, and even to our imagination ought to have gone, we should have been ruined and lost. Upon these, and many like reflections, I afterwards made it a certain rule with me that whenever I found those secret hints, or pressings of my mind, to doing or not doing anything that presented, or to going this way or that way, I never failed to obey the secret dictate; though I knew no other reason for it than that such a pressure, or such a hint, hung upon my mind. I could give many examples of the success of this conduct in the course of my life; but more especially in the latter part of my inhabiting this unhappy island; besides many occasions which it is very likely I might have taken notice of, if I had seen with the same eyes then that I saw with now. But 'tis never too late to be wise; and I cannot but advise all considering men, whose lives are attended with such extraordinary incidents as mine, or even though not so extraordinary, not to slight such secret intimations of Providence, let them come from what invisible intelligence they will, that I shall not discuss and perhaps cannot account for; but certainly they are a proof of the converse of spirits and the secret communication between those embodied and those unembodied; and such a proof as can never be withstood. Of which I shall have occasion to give some very remarkable instances in the remainder of my solitary residence in this dismal place.

The Care of My Safety

I BELIEVE the reader of this will not think strange if I confess that these anxieties, these constant dangers I lived in and the concern that was now upon me, put an end to all invention and to all the contrivances that I had laid

for my future accommodations and conveniences. I had
the care of my safety more now upon my hands than that
of my food. I cared not to drive a nail or chop a stick of
wood now for fear the noise I should make should be
heard; much less would I fire a gun, for the same reason;
and above all, I was intolerably uneasy at making any
fire, lest the smoke, which is visible at a great distance in
the day, should betray me; and for this reason I removed
that part of my business which required fire, such as
burning of pots and pipes, etc., into my new apartment in
the woods, where after I had been some time, I found,
to my unspeakable consolation, a mere natural cave in the
earth, which went in a vast way, and where, I dare say,
no savage, had he been at the mouth of it, would be so
hardy as to venture in, nor indeed, would any man else
but one who, like me, wanted nothing so much as a safe
retreat.

The mouth of this hollow was at the bottom of a great
rock, where, by mere accident (I would say, if I did not
see abundant reason to ascribe all such things now to
Providence), I was cutting down some thick branches of
trees to make charcoal; and before I go on, I must observe the reason of my making this charcoal, which was
thus:

I was afraid of making a smoke about my habitation,
as I said before; and yet I could not live there without
baking my bread, cooking my meat, etc.; so I contrived
to burn some wood here, as I had seen done in England,
under turf, till it became chark, or dry coal; and then putting the fire out, I preserved the coal to carry home and
perform the other services which fire was wanting for at
home, without danger of smoke.

But this is by the bye. While I was cutting down some
wood here, I perceived that behind a very thick branch
of low brushwood, or underwood, there was a kind of

hollow place; I was curious to look into it, and getting with difficulty into the mouth of it, I found it was pretty large; that is to say, sufficient for me to stand upright in it, and perhaps another with me; but I must confess to you I made more haste out than I did in, when looking farther into the place, and which was perfectly dark, I saw two broad shining eyes of some creature, whether devil or man I knew not, which twinkled like two stars, the dim light from the cave's mouth shining directly in and making the reflection.

However, after some pause, I recovered myself, and began to call myself a thousand fools, and tell myself that he that was afraid to see the Devil was not fit to live twenty years in an island all alone; and that I durst to believe there was nothing in this cave that was more frightful than myself; upon this, plucking up my courage, I took up a great firebrand, and in I rushed again with the stick flaming in my hand; I had not gone three steps in but I was almost as much frighted as I was before; for I heard a very loud sigh, like that of a man in some pain, and it was followed by a broken noise, as if of words half expressed, and then a deep sigh again. I stepped back and was indeed struck with such a surprise that it put me into a cold sweat; and if I had had a hat on my head, I will not answer for it that my hair might not have lifted it off. But still plucking up my spirits as well as I could, and encouraging myself a little with considering that the power and presence of God was everywhere and was able to protect me, upon this I stepped forward again, and by the light of the firebrand, holding it up a little over my head, I saw lying on the ground a most monstrous, frightful old he-goat, just making his will, as we say, and gasping for life and dying indeed of mere old age.

I stirred him a little to see if I could get him out, and he essayed to get up, but was not able to raise himself;

and I thought with myself, he might even lie there; for if he had frighted me so, he would certainly fright any of the savages, if any of them should be so hardy as to come in there while he had any life in him.

I was now recovered from my surprise and began to look round me, when I found the cave was but very small, that is to say, it might be about twelve foot over, but in no manner of shape, either round or square, no hands having ever been employed in making it but those of mere Nature. I observed also that there was a place at the farther side of it that went in farther but was so low that it required me to creep upon my hands and knees to go into it, and whither I went I knew not; so having no candle, I gave it over for some time but resolved to come again the next day, provided with candles and a tinder-box, which I had made of the lock of one of the muskets, with some wild-fire in the pan.

Accordingly, the next day I came provided with six large candles of my own making, for I made very good candles now of goat's tallow; and going into this low place, I was obliged to creep upon all fours, as I have said, almost ten yards; which, by the way, I thought was a venture bold enough, considering that I knew not how far it might go, nor what was beyond it. When I was got through the strait, I found the roof rose higher up, I believe near twenty foot; but never was such a glorious sight seen in the island, I dare say, as it was to look round the sides and roof of this vault, or cave; the walls reflected one hundred thousand lights to me from my two candles; what it was in the rock, whether diamonds or any other precious stones or gold, which I rather supposed it to be, I knew not.

The place I was in was a most delightful cavity or grotto of its kind, as could be expected, though perfectly dark; the floor was dry and level and had a sort of small loose gravel upon it, so that there was no nauseous or venomous creature to be seen, neither was there any damp or wet on the sides or roof. The only difficulty in it was the entrance, which, however, as it was a place of security, and such a retreat as I wanted, I thought that was a convenience; so that I was really rejoiced at the discovery and resolved, without any delay, to bring some of those things which I was most anxious about to this place; particularly, I resolved to bring hither my magazine of powder, and all my spare arms, viz., two fowling pieces, for I had three in all; and three muskets, for of them I had eight in all; so I kept at my castle only five, which stood ready mounted, like pieces of cannon, on my outmost fence; and were ready also to take out upon any expedition.

Upon this occasion of removing my ammunition, I took occasion to open the barrel of powder which I took up out of the sea, and which had been wet; and I found that the water had penetrated about three or four inches into the powder on every side, which, caking and growing hard, had preserved the inside like a kernel in a shell; so that I had near sixty pound of very good powder in the center of the cask, and this was an agreeable discovery to me at that time; so I carried all away thither, never keeping above two or three pound of powder with me in my castle, for fear of a surprise of any kind. I also carried thither all the lead I had left for bullets.

I fancied myself now like one of the ancient giants, which were said to live in caves and holes in the rocks, where none could come at them; for I persuaded myself, while I was here, if five hundred savages were to hunt me, they could never find me out; or, if they did, they would not venture to attack me here.

The old goat who I found expiring died in the mouth of the cave the next day after I made this discovery; and

I found it much easier to dig a great hole there and throw him in and cover him with earth than to drag him out; so I interred him there, to prevent the offense to my nose.

I was now in my twenty-third year of residence in this island and was so naturalized to the place and to the manner of living that could I have but enjoyed the certainty that no savages would come to the place to disturb me, I could have been content to have capitulated for spending the rest of my time there, even to the last moment, till I had laid me down and died, like the old goat in the cave. I had also arrived to some little diversions and amusements, which made the time pass more pleasantly with me a great deal than it did before; as, first, I had taught my Poll, as I noted before, to speak; and he did it so familiarly, and talked so articulately and plain, that it was very pleasant to me; and he lived with me no less than six and twenty years. How long he might live afterwards I know not; though I know they have a notion in the Brazils that they live a hundred years; perhaps poor Poll may be alive there still, calling after poor Robin Crusoe to this day. I wish no Englishman the ill luck to come there and hear him; but if he did, he would certainly believe it was the Devil. My dog was a very pleasant and loving companion to me for no less than sixteen years of my time, and then died of mere old age; as for my cats, they multiplied, as I have observed, to that degree, that I was obliged to shoot several of them at first to keep them from devouring me and all I had; but at length, when the two old ones I brought with me were gone, and after some time continually driving them from me and letting them have no provision with me, they all ran wild into the woods, except two or three favorites, which I kept tame and whose young, when they had any, I always drowned; and these were part of my family. Besides these, I always kept two or three household kids about me, who I taught to feed out of my hand; and I had two more parrots, which talked pretty well and would all call "Robin Crusoe"; but none like my first; nor indeed did I take the pains with any of them that I had done with him. I had also several tame seafowls, whose names I know not, who I caught upon the shore, and cut their wings; and the little stakes which I had planted before my castle wall being now grown up to a good thick grove, these fowls all lived among these low trees and bred there, which was very agreeable to me; so that, as I said above, I began to be very well contented with the life I led, if it might but have been secured from the dread of the savages.

But it was otherwise directed; and it may not be amiss for all people who shall meet with my story to make this just observation from it, viz., how frequently in the course of our lives, the evil which in itself we seek most to shun, and which, when we are fallen into it, is the most dreadful to us, is oftentimes the very means or door of our deliverance, by which alone we can be raised again from the affliction we are fallen into. I could give many examples of this in the course of my unaccountable life; but in nothing was it more particularly remarkable than in the circumstances of my last years of solitary residence in this island.

It was now the month of December, as I said above, in my twenty-third year; and this being the southern solstice, for winter I cannot call it, was the particular time of my harvest and required my being pretty much abroad in the fields, when, going out pretty early in the morning, even before it was thorough daylight, I was surprised with seeing a light of some fire upon the shore, at a distance from me of about two mile, towards the end of the island, where I had observed some savages had been, as before; but not on the other side; but to my great affliction, it was on my side of the island.

I was indeed terribly surprised at the sight and stopped short within my grove, not daring to go out, lest I might be surprised; and yet I had no more peace within, from the apprehensions I had that if these savages, in rambling over the island, should find my corn standing or cut, or any of my works and improvements, they would immediately conclude that there were people in the place and would then never give over till they had found me out. In this extremity I went back directly to my castle, pulled up the ladder after me, and made all things without look as wild and natural as I could.

Then I prepared myself within, putting myself in a posture of defense; I loaded all my cannon, as I called them; that is to say, my muskets, which were mounted upon my new fortification, and all my pistols, and resolved to defend myself to the last gasp, not forgetting seriously to commend myself to the Divine protection and earnestly to pray to God to deliver me out of the hands of the barbarians; and in this posture I continued about two hours; but began to be mighty impatient for intelligence abroad, for I had no spies to send out.

After sitting a while longer and musing what I should do in this case, I was not able to bear sitting in ignorance any longer; so setting up my ladder to the side of the hill where there was a flat place, as I observed before, and then pulling the ladder up after me, I set it up again and mounted to the top of the hill; and pulling out my perspective-glass, which I had taken on purpose, I laid me down flat on my belly on the ground and began to look for the place; I presently found there was no less than nine naked savages sitting round a small fire they had made, not to warm them, for they had no need of that, the weather being extreme hot; but, as I supposed, to dress some of their barbarous diet of human flesh, which they had brought with them, whether alive or dead I could not know.

They had two canoes with them, which they had haled up upon the shore; and as it was then tide of ebb, they seemed to me to wait for the return of the flood to go away again; it is not easy to imagine what confusion this sight put me into, especially seeing them come on my side the island, and so near me too; but when I observed their coming must be always with the current of the ebb, I began afterwards to be more sedate in my mind, being satisfied that I might go abroad with safety all the time of the tide of flood, if they were not on shore before. And having made this observation, I went abroad about my harvest work with the more composure.

As I expected, so it proved; for as soon as the tide made to the westward, I saw them all take boat, and row (or paddle, as we call it) all away. I should have observed that, for an hour and more before they went off, they went to dancing, and I could easily discern their postures and gestures by my glasses. I could not perceive, by my nicest observation, but that they were stark naked and had not the least covering upon them; but whether they were men or women, that I could not distinguish.

As soon as I saw them shipped and gone, I took two guns upon my shoulders and two pistols at my girdle and my great sword by my side, without a scabbard, and with all the speed I was able to make, I went away to the hill where I had discovered the first appearance of all; and as soon as I gat thither, which was not less than two hours, for I could not go apace, being so loaden with arms as I was, I perceived there had been three canoes more of savages on that place; and looking out farther, I saw they were all at sea together, making over for the main.

This was a dreadful sight to me, especially when going down to the shore, I could see the marks of horror which the dismal work they had been about had left behind it, viz., the blood, the bones, and part of the flesh of human bodies, eaten and devoured by those wretches, with merriment and sport. I was so filled with indignation at the sight that I began now to premeditate the destruction of the next that I saw there, let them be who or how many soever.

It seemed evident to me that the visits which they thus made to this island are not very frequent; for it was above fifteen months before any more of them came on shore there again; that is to say, I neither saw them, or any footsteps, or signals of them, in all that time; for as to the rainy seasons, then they are sure not to come abroad, at least not so far; yet all this while I lived uncomfortably, by reason of the constant apprehensions I was in of their coming upon me by surprise; from whence I observe that the expectation of evil is more bitter than the suffering, especially if there is no room to shake off that expectation, or those apprehensions.

During all this time, I was in the murdering humor, and took up most of my hours, which should have been better employed, in contriving how to circumvent and fall upon them the very next time I should see them; especially if they should be divided, as they were the last time, into two parties; nor did I consider at all that if I killed one party, suppose ten or a dozen, I was still the next day, or week, or month, to kill another, and so another, even *ad infinitum*, till I should be at length no less a murderer than they were in being man-eaters; and perhaps much more so.

I spent my days now in great perplexity and anxiety of

mind, expecting that I should one day or other fall into the hands of these merciless creatures; and if I did at any time venture abroad, it was not without looking round me with the greatest care and caution imaginable; and now I found to my great comfort how happy it was that I provided for a tame flock or herd of goats; for I durst not upon any account fire my gun, especially near that side of the island where they usually came, lest I should alarm the savages; and if they had fled from me now, I was sure to have them come back again, with perhaps two or three hundred canoes with them, in a few days, and then I knew what to expect.

However, I wore out a year and three months more before I ever saw any more of these savages, and then I found them again, as I shall soon observe. It is true they might have been there once or twice; but either they made no stay, or at least I did not hear them; but in the month of May, as near as I could calculate, and in my four and twentieth year, I had a very strange encounter with them, of which in its place.

The perturbation of my mind, during this fifteen or sixteen months' interval, was very great; I slept unquiet, dreamed always frightful dreams, and often started out of my sleep in the night. In the day great troubles overwhelmed my mind, and in the night I dreamed often of killing the savages, and of the reasons why I might justify the doing of it; but to waive all this for a while; it was in the middle of May, on the sixteenth day, I think, as well as my poor wooden calendar would reckon; for I marked all upon the post still; I say, it was the sixteenth of May that it blew a very great storm of wind all day, with a great deal of lightning and thunder, and a very foul night it was after it; I know not what was the particular occasion of it; but as I was reading in the Bible, and taken up with very serious thoughts about my present condition, I was surprised with a noise of a gun, as I thought, fired at sea.

Ship in Distress

THIS was to be sure a surprise of a quite different nature from any I had met with before; for the notions this put into my thoughts were quite of another kind. I started up in the greatest haste imaginable, and in a trice clapped my ladder to the middle place of the rock, and pulled it after me, and mounting it the second time, got to the top of the hill the very moment that a flash of fire bid me listen for a second gun, which accordingly, in about half a minute I heard; and by the sound, knew that it was from that part of the sea where I was driven down the current in my boat.

I immediately considered that this must be some ship in distress, and that they had some comrade, or some other ship in company, and fired these guns for signals of distress and to obtain help. I had this presence of mind at that minute as to think that though I could not help them, it may be they might help me; so I brought together all the dry wood I could get at hand, and making a good handsome pile, I set it on fire upon the hill; the wood was dry and blazed freely; and though the wind blew very hard, yet it burnt fairly out; that I was certain, if there was any such thing as a ship, they must needs see it, and no doubt they did; for as soon as ever my fire blazed up, I heard another gun, and after that several others, all from the same quarter; I plied my fire all night long, till day broke; and when it was broad day, and the air cleared up, I saw something at a great distance at sea, full east of the island, whether a sail or a hull I could not distinguish, no, not with my glasses, the distance was so great, and the weather still something hazy also; at least it was so out at sea.

I looked frequently at it all that day, and soon perceived that it did not move; so I presently concluded that it was a ship at an anchor, and being eager, you may be sure, to be satisfied, I took my gun in my hand, and run toward the south side of the island, to the rocks where I had formerly been carried away with the current, and getting up there, the weather by this time being perfectly clear, I could plainly see, to my great sorrow, the wreck of a ship cast away in the night upon those concealed rocks which I found when I was out in my boat; and which rocks, as they checked the violence of the stream, and made a kind of counter-stream or eddy, were the occasion of my recovering from the most desperate, hopeless condition that ever I had been in, in all my life.

Thus what is one man's safety is another man's destruction; for it seems these men, whoever they were, being out of their knowledge, and the rocks being wholly under water, had been driven upon them in the night, the wind blowing hard at east and east-northeast. Had they seen the island, as I must necessarily suppose they did not, they must, as I thought, have endeavored to have saved themselves on shore by the help of their boat; but their firing of guns for help, especially when they saw, as I imagined, my fire, filled me with many thoughts. First, I imagined that upon seeing my light, they might have put themselves into their boat and having endeavored to make the shore; but that the sea going very high, they might have been cast away; other times I imagined that they might have lost their boat before, as might be the case many ways; as particularly by the breaking of the sea upon their ship, which many times obliges men to stave, or take in pieces their boat; and sometimes to throw it overboard with their own hands. Other times I imagined they had some other ship, or ships in company, who, upon the signals of distress they had made, had taken them up, and carried them off. Other whiles I fancied they were all gone off to sea in their boat, and being hurried away by the current that I had been formerly in, were carried out into the great ocean, where there was nothing but misery and perishing; and that perhaps they might by this time think of starving and of being in a condition to eat one another.

As all these were but conjectures at best, so, in the condition I was in, I could do no more than look on upon the misery of the poor men and pity them; which had still this good effect on my side, that it gave me more and more cause to give thanks to God, who had so happily and comfortably provided for me in my desolate condition; and that of two ships' companies who were now cast away upon this part of the world, not one life should be spared but mine. I learned here again to observe that it is very rare that the providence of God casts us into any condition of life so low, or any misery so great, but we may see something or other to be thankful for; and may see others in worse circumstances than our own.

Such certainly was the case of these men, of whom I could not so much as see room to suppose any of them were saved; nothing could make it rational; so much as to wish or expect that they did not all perish there; except the possibility only of their being taken up by another ship in company, and this was but mere possibility indeed; for I saw not the least signal or appearance of any such thing.

I cannot explain by any possible energy of words what a strange longing or hankering of desires I felt in my soul upon this sight, breaking out sometimes thus: "O that there had been but one or two, nay, or but one soul, saved out of this ship, to have escaped to me, that I might but have had one companion, one fellow-creature to have spoken to me and to have conversed with!" In all the time of my solitary life, I never felt so earnest, so strong a desire after the society of my fellow-creatures, or so deep a regret at the want of it.

There are some secret moving springs in the affections, which when they are set a-going by some object in view, or be it some object, though not in view, yet rendered present to the mind by the power of imagination, that motion carries out the soul by its impetuosity to such violent eager embracings of the object that the absence of it is insupportable.

Such were these earnest wishings that but one man had been saved! "O that it had been but one!" I believe I repeated the words, "O that it had been one!" a thousand times; and the desires were so moved by it that when I spoke the words my hands would clinch together and my fingers press the palms of my hands, that if I had had any soft thing in my hand, it would have crushed it involuntarily; and my teeth in my head would strike together and set against one another so strong that for some time I could not part them again.

Let the naturalists explain these things, and the reason and manner of them; all I can say to them is to describe the fact, which was even surprising to me when I found it, though I knew not from what it should proceed; it was doubtless the effect of ardent wishes and of strong ideas formed in my mind, realizing the comfort which the conversation of one of my fellow Christians would have been to me.

But it was not to be; either their fate or mine, or both, forbid it; for till the last year of my being on this island, I never knew whether any were saved out of that ship or no; and had only the affliction some days after to see the corpse of a drowned boy come on shore at the end of the island which was next the shipwreck. He had on no clothes but a seaman's waistcoat, a pair of open-kneed linen drawers, and a blue linen shirt; but nothing to direct me so much as to guess what nation he was of. He had nothing in his pocket but two pieces of eight and a tobacco-pipe; the last was to me of ten times more value than the first.

It was now calm, and I had a great mind to venture out in my boat to this wreck, not doubting but I might find something on board that might be useful to me; but that did not altogether press me so much as the possibility that there might be yet some living creature on board, whose life I might not only save but might, by saving that life, comfort my own to the last degree; and this thought clung so to my heart that I could not be quiet night or day, but I must venture out in my boat on board this wreck; and committing the rest to God's providence, I thought the impression was so strong upon my mind that it could not be resisted, that it must come from some invisible direction, and that I should be wanting to myself if I did not go.

Under the power of this impression, I hastened back to my castle, prepared everything for my voyage, took a quantity of bread, a great pot for fresh water, a compass to steer by, a bottle of rum; for I had still a great deal of that left; a basket full of raisins. And thus loading myself with everything necessary, I went down to my boat, got the water out of her, and got her afloat, loaded all my cargo in her, and then went home again for more; my second cargo was a great bag full of rice, the umbrella to set up over my head for shade, another large pot full of fresh water, and about two dozen of my small loaves, or barley-cakes, more than before, with a bottle of goat's milk and a cheese; all which, with great labor and sweat, I brought to my boat; and praying to God to direct my voyage, I put out, and rowing or paddling the canoe along the shore, I came at last to the utmost point of the island on that side, viz., northeast. And now I was to launch out into the ocean, and either to venture or not to venture. I looked on the rapid currents which ran constantly on both sides of the island at a distance and which were very terrible to me, from the remembrance of the hazard I had been in before, and my heart began to fail me; for I foresaw that if I was driven into either of those currents, I should be carried a vast way out to sea, and perhaps out of my reach or sight of the island again; and that then, as my boat was but small, if any little gale of wind should rise, I should be inevitably lost.

These thoughts so oppressed my mind that I began to give over my enterprise, and having haled my boat into a little creek on the shore, I stepped out and sat me down upon a little rising bit of ground, very pensive and anxious, between fear and desire, about my voyage; when, as I was musing, I could perceive that the tide was turned and the flood come on, upon which my going was for so many hours impracticable; upon this, presently it occurred to me that I should go up to the highest piece of ground I could find, and observe, if I could, how the sets of the tide or currents lay, when the flood came in, that I might judge whether, if I was driven one way out, I might not expect to be driven another way home, with the same rapidness of the currents. This thought was no sooner in my head, but I cast my eye upon a little hill, which sufficiently overlooked the sea both ways and from whence I had a clear view of the currents, or sets of the tide, and which way I was to guide myself in my return; here I found that as the current of the ebb set out close by the south point of the island, so the current of the flood set in close by the shore of the north side, and that I had nothing to do but to keep to the north of the island in my return, and I should do well enough.

Encouraged with this observation, I resolved the next morning to set out with the first of the tide; and reposing myself for the night in the canoe, under the great watch coat I mentioned, I launched out. I made first a little out to sea, full north, till I began to feel the benefit of the current, which set eastward and which carried me at a great rate, and yet did not so hurry me as the southern side current had done before, and so as to take from me all government of the boat; but having a strong steerage with my paddle, I went at a great rate, directly for the wreck, and in less than two hours I came up to it.

It was a dismal sight to look at. The ship, which by its building was Spanish, stuck fast, jammed in between two rocks; all the stern and quarter of her was beaten to pieces with the sea; and as her forecastle, which stuck in the rocks, had run on with great violence, her mainmast and foremast were brought by the board; that is to say, broken short off; but her bowsprit was sound, and the head and bow appeared firm. When I came close to her, a dog appeared upon her, who, seeing me coming, yelped and cried; and as soon as I called him, jumped into the sea to come to me, and I took him into the boat; but found him almost dead for hunger and thirst. I gave him a cake of my bread, and he eat it like a ravenous wolf that had been starving a fortnight in the snow. I then gave the poor creature some fresh water, with which, if I would have let him, he would have burst himself.

After this I went on board; but the first sight I met with was two men drowned in the cook-room, or forecastle of the ship, with their arms fast about one another. I concluded, as is indeed probable, that when the ship struck, it being in a storm, the sea broke so high and so continually over her that the men were not able to bear it and were strangled with the constant rushing in of the water, as much as if they had been under water. Besides the dog, there was nothing left in the ship that had life;

nor any goods that I could see but what were spoiled by the water. There were some casks of liquor, whether wine or brandy, I knew not, which lay lower in the hold; and which, the water being ebbed out, I could see; but they were too big to meddle with. I saw several chests, which I believed belonged to some of the seamen; and I got two of them into the boat, without examining what was in them.

Had the stern of the ship been fixed and the forepart broken off, I am persuaded I might have made a good voyage; for by what I found in these two chests, I had room to suppose the ship had a great deal of wealth on board; and if I may guess by the course she steered, she must have been bound from the Buenos Ayres, or the Rio de la Plata, in the south part of America, beyond the Brazils, to the Havana, in the Gulf of Mexico, and so perhaps to Spain. She had, no doubt, a great treasure in her; but of no use at that time to anybody; and what became of the rest of her people, I then knew not.

I found, besides these chests, a little cask full of liquor, of about twenty gallons, which I got into my boat with much difficulty; there were several muskets in a cabin and a great powder horn, with about four pounds of powder in it; as for the muskets, I had no occasion for them; so I left them, but took the powder horn. I took a fire shovel and tongs, which I wanted extremely; as also two little brass kettles, a copper pot to make chocolate, and a gridiron; and with this cargo and the dog I came away, the tide beginning to make home again; and the same evening, about an hour within night, I reached the island again, weary and fatigued to the last degree.

I reposed that night in the boat, and in the morning I resolved to harbor what I had gotten in my new cave, not to carry it home to my castle. After refreshing myself, I got all my cargo on shore, and began to examine the particulars. The cask of liquor I found to be a kind of rum, but not such as we had at the Brazils; and in a word, not at all good; but when I came to open the chests, I found several things of great use to me. For example, I found in one a fine case of bottles, of an extraordinary kind and filled with cordial waters, fine and very good; the bottles held about three pints each and were tipped with silver. I found two pots of very good succades, or sweetmeats, so fastened also on top that the salt water had not hurt them; and two more of the same, which the water had spoiled. I found some very good shirts, which were very welcome to me; and about a dozen and a half of linen white handkerchiefs and colored neckcloths; the former were also very welcome, being exceeding refreshing to wipe my face in a hot day; besides this, when I came to the till in the chest, I found there three great bags of pieces of eight, which held out about eleven hundred pieces in all; and in one of them, wrapped up in a paper, six doubloons of gold and some small bars or wedges of gold; I suppose they might all weigh near a pound.

The other chest I found had some clothes in it, but of little value; but by the circumstances it must have belonged to the gunner's mate; though there was no powder in it but about two pound of fine glazed powder, in three small flasks, kept, I suppose, for charging their fowling pieces on occasion. Upon the whole, I got very little by this voyage that was of any use to me; for as to the money, I had no manner of occasion for it. 'Twas to me as the dirt under my feet; and I would have given it all for three or four pair of English shoes and stockings, which were things I greatly wanted but had not had on my feet now for many years. I had indeed gotten two pair of shoes now, which I took off of the feet of the two drowned men, who I saw in the wreck; and I found two pair more in one of the chests, which were very welcome to me;

but they were not like our English shoes, either for ease or service, being rather what we call pumps than shoes. I found in this seaman's chest about fifty pieces of eight in royals but no gold; I suppose this belonged to a poorer man than the other, which seemed to belong to some officer.

Well, however, I lugged this money home to my cave and laid it up, as I had done that before which I brought from our own ship; but it was great pity, as I said, that the other part of this ship had not come to my share; for I am satisfied I might have loaded my canoe several times over with money, which, if I had ever escaped to England, would have lain here safe enough till I might have come again and fetched it.

Having now brought all my things on shore and secured them, I went back to my boat and rowed or paddled her along the shore to her old harbor, where I laid her up, and made the best of my way to my old habitation, where I found everything safe and quiet; so I began to repose myself, live after my old fashion, and take care of my family affairs; and, for a while, I lived easy enough, only that I was more vigilant than I used to be, looked out oftener, and did not go abroad so much; and if at any time I did stir with any freedom, it was always to the east part of the island, where I was pretty well satisfied the savages never came, and where I could go without so many precautions and such a load of arms and ammunition as I always carried with me if I went the other way.

Time to Get Me a Servant

I LIVED in this condition near two years more; but my unlucky head, that was always to let me know it was born to make my body miserable, was all this two years filled with projects and designs, how, if it were possible, I might get away from this island; for sometimes I was for making another voyage to the wreck, though my reason told me that there was nothing left there worth the hazard of my voyage; sometimes for a ramble one way, sometimes another; and I believe verily, if I had had the boat that I went from Sallee in, I should have ventured to sea, bound anywhere, I knew not whither.

I have been in all my circumstances a *memento* to those who are touched with the general plague of mankind, whence, for aught I know, one half of their miseries flow; I mean, that of not being satisfied with the station wherein God and Nature had placed them; for, not to look back upon my primitive condition and the excellent advice of my father, the opposition to which was, as I may call it, my *original sin,* my subsequent mistakes of the same kind had been the means of my coming into this miserable condition; for had that Providence, which so happily had seated me at the Brazils as a planter, blessed me with confined desires, and I could have been contented to have gone on gradually, I might have been, by this time, I mean in the time of my being in this island, one of the most considerable planters in the Brazils; nay, I am persuaded that by the improvements I had made in that little time I lived there and the increase I should probably have made if I had stayed, I might have been worth an hundred thousand moidores; and what business had I to leave a settled fortune, a well-stocked plantation, improving and increasing, to turn supercargo to Guinea, to fetch Negroes, when patience and time would have so increased our stock at home that we could have bought them at our own door from those whose business it was to fetch them? And though it had cost us something more, yet the difference of that price was by no means worth saving at so great a hazard.

But as this is ordinarily the fate of young heads, so reflection upon the folly of it is as ordinarily the exercise
of more years or of the dear bought experience of time;
and so it was with me now; and yet so deep had the mistake taken root in my temper that I could not satisfy
myself in my station but was continually poring upon the
means and possibility of my escape from this place; and
that I may, with the greater pleasure to the reader, bring
on the remaining part of my story, it may not be improper to give some account of my first conceptions on
the subject of this foolish scheme for my escape, and how,
and upon what foundation, I acted.

I am now to be supposed retired into my castle, after
my late voyage to the wreck, my frigate laid up and secured under water, as usual, and my condition restored
to what it was before. I had more wealth, indeed, than
I had before, but was not at all the richer; for I had no
more use for it than the Indians of Peru had before the
Spaniards came there.

It was one of the nights in the rainy season in March,
the four and twentieth year of my first setting foot in this
island of solitariness; I was lying in my bed, or hammock,
awake, very well in health, had no pain, no distemper, no
uneasiness of body; no, nor any uneasiness of mind, more
than ordinary; but could by no means close my eyes; that
is, so as to sleep; no, not a wink all night long, otherwise
than as follows:

It is as impossible as needless to set down the innumerable crowd of thoughts that whirled through that
great thoroughfare of the brain, the memory, in this
night's time. I run over the whole history of my life in
miniature, or by abridgment, as I may call it, to my coming to this island; and also of the part of my life since I
came to this island. In my reflections upon the state of
my case since I came on shore on this island, I was com-

paring the happy posture of my affairs in the first years of my habitation here, compared to the life of anxiety, fear, and care, which I had lived ever since I had seen the print of a foot in the sand; not that I did not believe the savages had frequented the island even all the while and might have been several hundreds of them at times on shore there; but I had never known it and was incapable of any apprehensions about it; my satisfaction was perfect, though my danger was the same; and I was as happy in not knowing my danger as if I had never really been exposed to it. This furnished my thoughts with many very profitable reflections, and particularly this one: how infinitely good that Providence is which has provided in its government of mankind such narrow bounds to his sight and knowledge of things; and though he walks in the midst of so many thousand dangers, the sight of which, if discovered to him, would distract his mind and sink his spirits, he is kept serene and calm by having the events of things hid from his eyes and knowing nothing of the dangers which surround him.

After these thoughts had for some time entertained me, I came to reflect seriously upon the real danger I had been in for so many years in this very island; and how I had walked about in the greatest security and with all possible tranquillity even when perhaps nothing but a brow of a hill, a great tree, or the casual approach of night, had been between me and the worst kind of destruction, viz., that of falling into the hands of cannibals and savages, who would have seized on me with the same view as I did of a goat, or a turtle; and have thought it no more a crime to kill and devour me than I did of a pigeon or a curlew. I would unjustly slander myself if I should say I was not sincerely thankful to my great Preserver, to whose singular protection I acknowledged, with great humility, that all these unknown deliverances were due;

and without which I must inevitably have fallen into their merciless hands.

When these thoughts were over, my head was for some time taken up in considering the nature of these wretched creatures, I mean the savages; and how it came to pass in the world that the wise Governor of all things should give up any of His creatures to such inhumanity; nay, to something so much below even brutality itself as to devour its own kind; but as this ended in some (at that time fruitless) speculations, it occurred to me to inquire what part of the world these wretches lived in; how far off the coast was from whence they came; what they ventured over so far from home for; what kind of boats they had; and why I might not order myself and my business so that I might be as able to go over thither as they were to come to me.

I never so much as troubled myself to consider what I should do with myself when I came thither; what would become of me, if I fell into the hands of the savages; or how I should escape from them, if they attempted me; no, nor so much as how it was possible for me to reach the coast and not be attempted by some or other of them, without any possibility of delivering myself; and if I should not fall into their hands, what I should do for provision, or whither I should bend my course; none of these thoughts, I say, so much as came in my way; but my mind was wholly bent upon the notion of my passing over in my boat to the mainland. I looked back upon my present condition as the most miserable that could possibly be; that I was not able to throw myself into anything but death that could be called worse; that if I reached the shore of the main, I might perhaps meet with relief, or I might coast along, as I did on the shore of Africa, till I came to some inhabited country, and where I might find some relief; and after all, perhaps I might fall in with some Christian ship that might take me in; and if the worse came to the worst, I could but die, which would put an end to all these miseries at once. Pray note, all this was the fruit of a disturbed mind, an impatient temper, made, as it were, desperate by the long continuance of my troubles and the disappointments I had met in the wreck I had been on board of, and where I had been so near the obtaining what I so earnestly longed for, viz., somebody to speak to and to learn some knowledge from of the place where I was and of the probable means of my deliverance; I say, I was agitated wholly by these thoughts. All my calm of mind in my resignation to Providence, and waiting the issue of the dispositions of Heaven, seemed to be suspended; and I had, as it were, no power to turn my thoughts to anything but to the project of a voyage to the main, which came upon me with such force and such an impetuosity of desire that it was not to be resisted.

When this had agitated my thoughts for two hours or more, with such violence that it set my very blood into a ferment, and my pulse beat as high as if I had been in a fever merely with the extraordinary fervor of my mind about it, Nature, as if I had been fatigued and exhausted with the very thought of it, threw me into a sound sleep. One would have thought I should have dreamed of it; but I did not, nor of anything relating to it; but I dreamed that as I was going out in the morning as usual from my castle, I saw upon the shore two canoes and eleven savages coming to land, and that they brought with them another savage, whom they were going to kill, in order to eat him; when on a sudden, the savage that they were going to kill jumped away, and ran for his life; and I thought in my sleep that he came running into my little thick grove, before my fortification, to hide himself; and that I, seeing him alone and not perceiving that the other sought him that way, showed myself to him, and smiling upon him, encouraged him; that he kneeled down to me, seeming to pray me to assist him; upon which I showed my ladder, made him go up, and carried him into my cave, and he became my servant; and that as soon as I had gotten this man, I said to myself, "Now I may certainly venture to the mainland; for this fellow will serve me as a pilot, and will tell me what to do and whither to go for provisions; and whither not to go for fear of being devoured; what places to venture into, and what to escape." I waked with this thought and was under such inexpressible impressions of joy at the prospect of my escape in my dream that the disappointments which I felt upon coming to myself and finding it was no more than a dream were equally extravagant the other way, and threw me into a very great dejection of spirit.

Upon this, however, I made this conclusion, that my only way to go about an attempt for an escape was, if possible, to get a savage into my possession; and if possible, it should be one of their prisoners who they had condemned to be eaten and should bring hither to kill; but these thoughts still were attended with this difficulty, that it was impossible to effect this without attacking a whole caravan of them and killing them all; and this was not only a very desperate attempt and might miscarry, but on the other hand, I had greatly scrupled the lawfulness of it to me; and my heart trembled at the thoughts of shedding so much blood, though it was for my deliverance. I need not repeat the arguments which occurred to me against this, they being the same mentioned before; but though I had other reasons to offer now, viz., that those men were enemies to my life and would devour me if they could; that it was self-preservation, in the highest degree, to deliver myself from this death of a life, and was acting in my own defense as much as if they were actually assaulting me, and the like; I say, though these things argued for it, yet the thoughts of shedding human blood for my deliverance were very terrible to me, and such as I could by no means reconcile myself to a great while.

However, at last, after many secret disputes with myself and after great perplexities about it, for all these arguments, one way and another, struggled in my head a long time, the eager prevailing desire of deliverance at length mastered all the rest, and I resolved, if possible, to get one of those savages into my hands, cost what it would. My next thing then was to contrive how to do it, and this indeed was very difficult to resolve on. But as I could pitch upon no probable means for it, so I resolved to put myself upon the watch, to see them when they came on shore, and leave the rest to the event, taking such measures as the opportunity should present, let be what would be.

With these resolutions in my thoughts, I set myself upon the scout, as often as possible, and indeed so often till I was heartily tired of it; for it was above a year and half that I waited, and for a great part of that time went out to the west end and to the southwest corner of the island almost every day to see for canoes, but none appeared. This was very discouraging, and began to trouble me much; though I cannot say that it did in this case, as it had done some time before that, viz., wear off the edge of my desire to the thing. But the longer it seemed to be delayed, the more eager I was for it; in a word, I was not at first so careful to shun the sight of these savages and avoid being seen by them as I was now eager to be upon them.

Besides, I fancied myself able to manage one, nay, two or three savages, if I had them, so as to make them entirely slaves to me, to do whatever I should direct them and to prevent their being able at any time to do me any hurt. It was a great while that I pleased myself with this affair, but nothing still presented; all my fancies and schemes came to nothing, for no savages came near me for a great while.

About a year and half after I had entertained these notions and, by long musing, had as it were resolved them all into nothing, for want of an occasion to put them in execution, I was surprised one morning early with seeing no less than five canoes all on shore together on my side the island; and the people who belonged to them all landed, and out of my sight. The number of them broke all my measures, for seeing so many and knowing that they always came four or six, or sometimes more in a boat, I could not tell what to think of it, or how to take my measures, to attack twenty or thirty men singlehanded; so I lay still in my castle, perplexed and discomforted. However, I put myself into all the same postures for an attack that I had formerly provided and was just ready for action if anything had presented; having waited a good while, listening to hear if they made any noise, at length being very impatient, I set my guns at the foot of my ladder and clambered up to the top of the hill by my two stages as usual; standing so, however, that my head did not appear above the hill, so that they could not perceive me by any means; here I observed by the help of my perspective-glass that they were no less than thirty in number, that they had a fire kindled, that they had had meat dressed. How they had cooked it, that I knew not, or what it was; but they were all dancing in I know not how many barbarous gestures and figures, their own way, round the fire.

While I was thus looking on them, I perceived by my perspective two miserable wretches dragged from the boats, where, it seems, they were laid by, and were now brought out for the slaughter, I perceived one of them immediately fell, being knocked down, I suppose, with a club or wooden sword, for that was their way, and two or three others were at work immediately, cutting him open for their cookery, while the other victim was left standing by himself, till they should be ready for him. In that very moment, this poor wretch seeing himself a little at liberty, Nature inspired him with hopes of life, and he started away from them, and ran with incredible swiftness along the sands directly towards me, I mean towards that part of the coast where my habitation was.

I was dreadfully frighted (that I must acknowledge) when I perceived him to run my way; and especially, when, as I thought, I saw him pursued by the whole body; and now I expected that part of my dream was coming to pass, and that he would certainly take shelter in my grove; but I could not depend by any means upon my dream for the rest of it, viz., that the other savages would not pursue him thither, and find him there. However, I kept my station, and my spirits began to recover when I found that there was not above three men that followed him; and still more was I encouraged when I found that he outstripped them exceedingly in running and gained ground of them; so that if he could but hold it for half an hour, I saw easily he would fairly get away from them all.

There was between them and my castle the creek which I mentioned often at the first part of my story, when I landed my cargoes out of the ship; and this I saw plainly he must necessarily swim over, or the poor wretch would be taken there. But when the savage escaping came thither, he made nothing of it, though the tide was then up, but plunging in, swam through in about thirty strokes or thereabouts, landed, and ran on with exceeding strength and swiftness; when the three persons came to the creek, I found that two of them could swim, but the third could not, and that standing on the other side, he looked at the other, but went no further; and soon after went softly back again; which, as it happened, was very well for him in the main.

I observed that the two who swam were yet more than twice as long swimming over the creek as the fellow was that fled from them. It came now very warmly upon my thoughts, and indeed irresistibly, that now was my time to get me a servant, and perhaps a companion, or assistant; and that I was called plainly by Providence to save this poor creature's life; I immediately run down the ladders with all possible expedition, fetched my two guns, for they were both but at the foot of the ladders, as I observed above; and getting up again, with the same haste, to the top of the hill, I crossed toward the sea; and having a very short cut, and all down hill, clapped myself in the way between the pursuers and the pursued; hallooing aloud to him that fled, who, looking back, was at first perhaps as much frighted at me as at them; but I beckoned with my hand to him to come back; and in the meantime, I slowly advanced towards the two that followed; then rushing at once upon the foremost, I knocked him down with the stock of my piece; I was loath to fire, because I would not have the rest hear; though at that distance, it would not have been easily heard, and being out of sight of the smoke too, they would not have easily known what to make of it. Having knocked this fellow down, the other who pursued with him stopped, as if he had been frighted; and I advanced apace towards him; but as I came nearer, I perceived presently he had a bow and arrow and was fitting it to shoot at me; so I was then necessitated to shoot at him first, which I did, and killed him at the first shoot; the poor savage who fled, but had stopped, though he saw both his enemies fallen and killed, as he thought, yet was so frighted with the fire and noise of my piece, that he stood stock still and neither came forward or went backward, though he seemed rather inclined to fly still than to come on; I hallooed again to him, and made signs to come forward, which he easily understood and came a little way, then stopped again and then a little further and stopped again, and I could then perceive that he stood trembling, as if he had been taken prisoner, and had just been to be killed, as his two enemies were; I beckoned him again to come to me and gave him all the signs of encouragement that I could think of, and he came nearer and nearer, kneeling down every ten or twelve steps in token of acknowledgment for my saving his life. I smiled at him and looked pleasantly and beckoned to him to come still nearer; at length he came close to me, and then he kneeled down again, kissed the ground, and laid his head upon the ground, and, taking me by the foot, set my foot upon his head; this, it seems, was in token of swearing to be my slave forever; I took him up, and made much of him, and encouraged him all I could. But there was more work to do yet, for I perceived the savage who I knocked down was not killed, but stunned with the blow, and began to come to himself; so I pointed to him, and showing him the savage, that he was not dead; upon this he spoke some words to me, and though I could not understand them, yet I thought they were pleasant to hear, for they were the first sound of a man's voice that I had heard, my own excepted, for about twenty-five years. But there was no time for such reflections now; the savage who was knocked down recovered himself so far as to sit up upon the ground, and I perceived that my savage began to be afraid; but when I saw that, I presented my other piece at the man as if I would shoot him; upon this my savage, for so I call him now, made·a motion to me to lend him my sword, which hung naked in a belt by my side; so I did. He no sooner had it, but he runs to his enemy, and at one blow cut off his head as cleverly, no executioner in Germany could have done it sooner or better; which I thought very strange for one who I had reason to believe never saw a sword in his life before, except their own wooden swords; however, it seems, as I learned afterwards, they make their wooden swords so sharp, so heavy, and the wood is so hard, that they will cut off heads even with them, ay, and arms, and that at one blow too; when he had done this, he comes laughing to me in sign of triumph and brought me the sword again, and with abundance of gestures which I did not understand, laid it down, with the head of the savage that he had killed, just before me.

But that which astonished him most was to know how I had killed the other Indian so far off; so pointing to him, he made signs to me to let him go to him; so I bade him go, as well as I could; when he came to him, he stood like one amazed, looking at him, turned him first on one side, then on t' other, looked at the wound the bullet had made, which, it seems, was just in his breast, where it had made a hole, and no great quantity of blood had followed, but he had bled inwardly, for he was quite dead. He took up his bow and arrows, and came back; so I turned to go away and beckoned to him to follow me, making signs to him that more might come after them.

Upon this he signed to me that he should bury them with sand, that they might not be seen by the rest if they followed; and so I made signs again to him to do so; he fell to work, and in an instant he had scraped a hole in the sand with his hands big enough to bury the first in, and then dragged him into it and covered him and did so also by the other; I believe he had buried them both in a quarter of an hour; then calling him away, I carried him, not to my castle, but quite away to my cave, on the farther part of the island; so I did not let my dream come to pass in that part, viz., that he came into my grove for shelter.

Here I gave him bread and a bunch of raisins to eat, and a draught of water, which I found he was indeed in great distress for, by his running; and having refreshed him, I made signs for him to go lie down and sleep, pointing to a place where I had laid a great parcel of rice-straw and a blanket upon it, which I used to sleep upon myself sometimes; so the poor creature laid down and went to sleep.

My Man Friday

HE WAS a comely, handsome fellow, perfectly well made, with straight strong limbs, not too large; tall and well-shaped, and, as I reckon, about twenty-six years of age. He had a very good countenance, not a fierce and surly aspect; but seemed to have something very manly in his face, and yet he had all the sweetness and softness of an European in his countenance too, especially when he smiled. His hair was long and black, not curled like wool; his forehead very high and large; and a great vivacity and sparkling sharpness in his eyes. The color of his skin was not quite black, but very tawny; and yet not of an ugly, yellow, nauseous tawny, as the Brazilians and Virginians, and other natives of America are; but of a bright kind of a dun olive color that had in it something very agreeable, though not very easy to describe. His face was round and plump; his nose small, not flat like the Negroes; a very good mouth, thin lips, and his fine teeth well set, and white as ivory. After he had slumbered, rather than slept, about half an hour, he waked again, and comes out of the cave to me; for I had been milking my goats, which I had in the enclosure just by. When he espied me, he came running to me, laying himself down again upon the ground, with all the possible signs of an humble, thankful disposition, making a many antic gestures to show it. At last he lays his head flat upon the ground, close to my foot, and sets my other foot upon his head, as he had done before; and after this, made all the signs to me of subjection, servitude, and submission imaginable, to let me know how he would serve me as long as he lived; I understood him in many things and let him know I was very well pleased with him; in a little time I began to speak to him and teach him to speak to me; and first, I made him know his name should be *Friday*, which was the day I saved his life; I called him so for the memory of the time; I likewise taught him to say *Master*, and then let him know that was to be my name; I likewise taught him to say *Yes* and *No* and to know the meaning of them; I gave him some milk in an earthen pot and let him see me drink it before him and sop my bread in it; and I gave him a cake of bread to do the like, which he quickly complied with, and made signs that it was very good for him.

I kept there with him all that night; but as soon as it was day, I beckoned to him to come with me, and let him know I would give him some clothes, at which he seemed very glad, for he was stark naked. As we went by the place where he had buried the two men, he pointed exactly to the place and showed me the marks that he had made to find them again, making signs to me that we should dig them up again and eat them; at this I appeared very angry, expressed my abhorrence of it, made as if I would vomit at the thoughts of it, and beckoned with my hand to him to come away, which he did immediately, with great submission. I then led him up to the top of the hill, to see if his enemies were gone; and pulling out my glass, I looked, and saw plainly the place where they had been, but no appearance of them or of their canoes; so that it was plain they were gone and had left their two comrades behind them, without any search after them.

But I was not content with this discovery; but having now more courage, and consequently more curiosity, I takes my man Friday with me, giving him the sword in his hand, with the bow and arrows at his back, which I found he could use very dexterously, making him carry one gun for me, and I two for myself, and away we marched to the place where these creatures had been; for I had a mind now to get some fuller intelligence of them. When I came to the place, my very blood ran chill in my veins and my heart sunk within me at the horror of the spectacle. Indeed it was a dreadful sight, at least it was so to me, though Friday made nothing of it. The place was covered with human bones, the ground dyed with their blood, great pieces of flesh left here and there, half eaten, mangled and scorched; and in short, of all the tokens of the triumphant feast they had been making there, after a victory over their enemies. I saw three skulls, five hands, and the bones of three or four legs and feet, and abundance of other parts of the bodies; and Friday, by his signs, made me understand that they brought over four prisoners to feast upon; that three of them were eaten up and that he, pointing to himself, was the fourth; that there had been a great battle between them and their next king, whose subjects it seems he had been one of; and that they had taken a great number of prisoners, all which were carried to several places by those that had taken them in the fight, in order to feast upon them, as was done here by these wretches upon those they brought hither.

I caused Friday to gather all the skulls, bones, flesh,

and whatever remained, and lay them together on a heap and make a great fire upon it and burn them all to ashes. I found Friday had still a hankering stomach after some of the flesh, and was still a cannibal in his nature; but I discovered so much abhorrence at the very thoughts of it and at the least appearance of it that he durst not discover it; for I had by some means let him know that I would kill him if he offered it.

When we had done this, we came back to our castle, and there I fell to work for my man Friday; and first of all, I gave him a pair of linen drawers, which I had out of the poor gunner's chest I mentioned, and which I found in the wreck; and which with a little alteration fitted him very well; then I made him a jerkin of goat's skin, as well as my skill would allow, and I was now grown a tolerable good tailor; and I gave him a cap, which I had made of a hare-skin, very convenient and fashionable enough; and thus he was clothed for the present tolerably well; and was mighty well pleased to see himself almost as well clothed as his master. It is true, he went awkwardly in these things at first; wearing the drawers was very awkward to him, and the sleeves of the waistcoat galled his shoulders and the inside of his arms; but a little easing them where he complained they hurt him and using himself to them, at length he took to them very well.

The next day after I came home to my hutch with him, I began to consider where I should lodge him; and that I might do well for him and yet be perfectly easy myself, I made a little tent for him in the vacant place between my two fortifications, in the inside of the last and in the outside of the first; and as there was a door or entrance there into my cave, I made a formal framed door-case, and a door to it of boards, and set it up in the passage, a little within the entrance; and causing the door to open on the inside, I barred it up in the night, taking in my ladders too; so that Friday could no way come at me in the inside of my innermost wall without making so much noise in getting over that it must needs waken me; for my first wall had now a complete roof over it of long poles, covering all my tent and leaning up to the side of the hill, which was again laid across with smaller sticks instead of laths, and then thatched over a great thickness with the rice-straw, which was strong like reeds; and at the hole or place which was left to go in or out by the ladder I had placed a kind of trapdoor, which, if it had been attempted on the outside, would not have opened at all, but would have fallen down and made a great noise; and as to weapons, I took them all into my side every night.

But I needed none of all this precaution; for never man had a more faithful, loving, sincere servant than Friday was to me; without passions, sullenness, or designs, perfectly obliged and engaged; his very affections were tied to me, like those of a child to a father; and I dare say he would have sacrificed his life for the saving mine upon any occasion whatsoever; the many testimonies he gave me of this put it out of doubt and soon convinced me that I needed to use no precautions as to my safety on his account.

This frequently gave me occasion to observe, and that with wonder, that however it had pleased God, in His providence, and in the government of the works of His hands, to take from so great a part of the world of His creatures the best uses to which their faculties and the powers of their souls are adapted, yet that He has bestowed upon them the same powers, the same reason, the same affections, the same sentiments of kindness and obligation, the same passions and resentments of wrongs, the same sense of gratitude, sincerity, fidelity, and all the capacities of doing good and receiving good that He has given to us; and that when He pleases to offer to them occasions of exerting these, they are as ready, nay, more ready to apply them to the right uses for which they were bestowed than we are. And this made me very melancholy sometimes, in reflecting, as the several occasions presented, how mean a use we make of all these, even though we have these powers enlightened by the great lamp of instruction, the Spirit of God, and by the knowledge of His Word, added to our understanding; and why it has pleased God to hide the like saving knowledge from so many millions of souls, who, if I might judge by this poor savage, would make a much better use of it than we did.

From hence, I sometimes was led too far to invade the sovereignty of Providence and, as it were, arraign the justice of so arbitrary a disposition of things that should hide that light from some and reveal it to others, and yet expect a like duty from both. But I shut it up and checked my thoughts with this conclusion; first, that we did not know by what light and law these should be condemned; but that as God was necessarily, and by the nature of His being, infinitely holy and just, so it could not be but that if these creatures were all sentenced to absence from Himself, it was on account of sinning against that light which, as the Scripture says, was a law to themselves, and by such rules as their consciences would acknowledge to be just, though the foundation was not discovered to us. And second, that still, as we are all the clay in the hand of the Potter, no vessel could say to Him, "Why hast Thou formed me thus?"

But to return to my new companion: I was greatly delighted with him and made it my business to teach him everything that was proper to make him useful, handy, and helpful; but especially to make him speak and understand me when I spake; and he was the aptest scholar that ever was, and particularly was so merry, so constantly diligent, and so pleased when he could but understand me or make me understand him that it was very pleasant to me to talk to him; and now my life began to be so easy that I began to say to myself that could I but have been safe from more savages, I cared not if I was never to remove from the place while I lived.

After I had been two or three days returned to my castle, I thought that, in order to bring Friday off from his horrid way of feeding and from the relish of a cannibal's stomach, I ought to let him taste other flesh; so I took him out with me one morning to the woods. I went, indeed, intending to kill a kid out of my own flock and bring him home and dress it. But as I was going, I saw a she-goat lying down in the shade and two young kids sitting by her; I catched hold of Friday. "Hold," says I, "stand still"; and made signs to him not to stir; immediately I presented my piece, shot and killed one of the kids. The poor creature, who had at a distance, indeed, seen me kill the savage, his enemy, but did not know or could imagine how it was done, was sensibly surprised, trembled and shook, and looked so amazed that I thought he would have sunk down. He did not see the kid I had shot at, or perceive I had killed it, but ripped up his waistcoat to feel if he was not wounded, and, as I found presently, thought I was resolved to kill him; for he came and kneeled down to me and, embracing my knees, said a great many things I did not understand; but I could easily see that the meaning was to pray me not to kill him.

I soon found a way to convince him that I would do him no harm and, taking him up by the hand, laughed at him and pointed to the kid which I had killed, beckoned to him to run and fetch it, which he did; and while he was wondering and looking to see how the creature was killed, I loaded my gun again, and by and by I saw a great fowl, like a hawk, sit upon a tree, within shot; so, *o let Friday understand a little what I would do, I called him to me again, pointed at the fowl, which was indeed a parrot, though I thought it had been a hawk; I say, pointing to the parrot and to my gun and to the ground under the parrot, to let him see I would make it fall, I made him understand that I would shoot and kill that bird; accordingly I fired and bade him look, and immediately he saw the parrot fall, he stood like one frighted again, notwithstanding all I had said to him; and I found he was the more amazed because he did not see me put anything into the gun; but thought that there must be some wonderful fund of death and destruction in that thing, able to kill man, beast, bird, or anything near or far off; and the astonishment this created in him was such as could not wear off for a long time; and I believe, if I would have let him, he would have worshiped me and my gun. As for the gun itself, he would not so much as touch it for several days after; but would speak to it and talk to it as if it had answered him, when he was by himself; which, as I afterwards learned of him, was to desire it not to kill him.

Well, after his astonishment was a little over at this, I pointed to him to run and fetch the bird I had shot, which he did, but stayed some time; for the parrot, not being quite dead, was fluttered away a good way off from the place where she fell; however, he found her, took her up, and brought her to me; and as I had perceived his ignorance about the gun before, I took this advantage to charge the gun again and not let him see me do it, that I might be ready for any other mark that might present; but nothing more offered at that time; so I brought home the kid, and the same evening I took the skin off and cut it out as well as I could; and having a pot for that purpose, I boiled, or stewed, some of the flesh, and made some very good broth; and after I had begun to eat some, I gave some to my man, who seemed very glad of it and liked it very well; but that which was strangest to him was to see me eat salt with it; he made a sign to me that the salt was not good to eat, and putting a little into his own mouth, he seemed to nauseate it, and would spit and sputter at it, washing his mouth with fresh water after it; on the other hand, I took some meat in my mouth without salt, and I pretended to spit and sputter for want of salt, as fast as he had done at the salt; but it would not do; he would never care for salt with his meat or in his broth; at least, not a great while, and then but a very little.

Having thus fed him with boiled meat and broth, I was resolved to feast him the next day with roasting a piece of the kid; this I did by hanging it before the fire in a string, as I had seen many people do in England, setting two poles up, one on each side the fire, and one cross on the top, and tying the string to the cross-stick, letting the meat turn continually. This Friday admired very much; but when he came to taste the flesh, he took so many ways to tell me how well he liked it that I could not but understand him; and at last he told me he would never eat man's flesh any more, which I was very glad to hear.

The next day I set him to work to beating some corn out, and sifting it in the manner I used to do, as I observed before, and he soon understood how to do it as well as I, especially after he had seen what the meaning of it was, and that it was to make bread of; for after that I let him see me make my bread and bake it too, and in a little time Friday was able to do all the work for me, as well as I could do it myself.

I began now to consider that having two mouths to feed instead of one, I must provide more ground for my harvest and plant a larger quantity of corn than I used to do; so I marked out a larger piece of land and began the fence in the same manner as before, in which Friday not only worked very willingly and very hard but did it very cheerfully; and I told him what it was for, that it was for corn to make more bread, because he was now with me, and that I might have enough for him and myself too. He appeared very sensible of that part and let me know that he thought I had much more labor upon me on his account than I had for myself; and that he would work the harder for me, if I would tell him what to do.

Some Hopes That I Might Escape

THIS was the pleasantest year of all the life I led in this place; Friday began to talk pretty well and understand the names of almost everything I had occasion to call for, and of every place I had to send him to, and talk a great deal to me; so that, in short, I began now to have some use for my tongue again, which indeed I had very little occasion for before; that is to say, about speech; besides the pleasure of talking to him, I had a singular satisfaction in the fellow himself; his simple, unfeigned honesty appeared to me more and more every day, and I began really to love the creature; and, on his side, I believe he loved me more than it was possible for him ever to love anything before.

I had a mind once to try if he had any hankering inclination to his own country again, and having learned him English so well that he could answer me almost any questions, I asked him whether the nation that he belonged to never conquered in battle. At which he smiled, and said, "Yes, yes, we always fight the better"; that is, he meant, always get the better in fight; and so we began the following discourse: "You always fight the better," said I, "how came you to be taken prisoner then, Friday?"

FRIDAY: My nation beat much, for all that.

MASTER: How beat? If your nation beat them, how come you to be taken?

FRIDAY: They more many than my nation in the place where me was; they take one, two, three, and me; my nation overbeat them in the yonder place, where me no was; there my nation take one, two, great thousand.

MASTER: But why did not your side recover you from the hands of your enemies then?

FRIDAY: They run one, two, three, and me, and make go in the canoe; my nation have no canoe that time.

MASTER: Well, Friday, and what does your nation do with the men they take? Do they carry them away, and eat them, as these did?

FRIDAY: Yes, my nation eat mans too, eat all up.

MASTER: Where do they carry them?

FRIDAY: Go to other place, where they think.

MASTER: Do they come hither?

FRIDAY: Yes, yes, they come hither; come other else place.

MASTER: Have you been here with them?

FRIDAY: Yes, I been here. [Points to the northwest side of the island, which it seems was their side.]

By this I understood that my man Friday had formerly been among the savages who used to come on shore on the farther part of the island, on the same man-eating occasions that he was now brought for; and some time after, when I took the courage to carry him to that side, being the same I formerly mentioned, he presently knew the place and told me he was there once when they eat up twenty men, two women, and one child; he could not tell twenty in English, but he numbered them by laying so many stones on a row and pointing to me to tell them over.

I have told this passage because it introduces what follows; that after I had had this discourse with him, I asked him how far it was from our island to the shore, and whether the canoes were not often lost; he told me there was no danger, no canoes ever lost; but that after a little way out to the sea, there was a current and a wind, always one way in the morning, the other in the afternoon.

This I understood to be no more than the sets of the tide, as going out or coming in; but I afterwards understood it was occasioned by the great draft and reflux of the mighty river Oroonoko, in the mouth, or the gulf, of which river, as I found afterwards, our island lay; and this land which I perceived to the west and northwest was the great island Trinidad, on the north point of the mouth of the river. I asked Friday a thousand questions about the country, the inhabitants, the sea, the coast, and what nation were near; he told me all he knew with the greatest openness imaginable; I asked him the names of the several nations of his sort of people, but could get no other name than Caribs; from whence I easily understood that these were the Caribbees, which our maps place on the part of America which reaches from the mouth of the river Oroonoko to Guiana, and onwards to St. Martha. He told me that up a great way beyond the moon, that was, beyond the setting of the moon, which must be west from their country, there dwelt white-bearded men, like me, and pointed to my great whiskers, which I mentioned before; and that they had killed *much Mans*, that was his word; by all which I understood he meant the Spaniards, whose cruelties in America had been spread over the whole countries and was remembered by all the nations from father to son.

I inquired if he could tell me how I might come from this island and get among those white men; he told me, "Yes, yes, I might go in two canoe"; I could not understand what he meant, or make him describe to me what he meant by "two canoe," till at last, with great difficulty,

I found he meant it must be in a large great boat, as big as two canoes.

This part of Friday's discourse began to relish with me very well and from this time I entertained some hopes that, one time or other, I might find an opportunity to make my escape from this place and that this poor savage might be a means to help me to do it.

During the long time that Friday had now been with me, and that he began to speak to me, and understand me, I was not wanting to lay a foundation of religious knowledge in his mind; particularly I asked him one time, who made him? The poor creature did not understand me at all, but thought I had asked who was his father; but I took it by another handle and asked him who made the sea, the ground we walked on, and the hills and woods; he told me it was one old Benamuckee, that lived beyond all. He could describe nothing of this great person but that he was very old; much older, he said, than the sea or the land, than the moon or the stars. I asked him then, if this old person had made all things, why did not all things worship him. He looked very grave, and with a perfect look of innocence, said, "All things do say 'O!' to him." I asked him if the people who die in his country went away anywhere; he said, yes, they all went to Benamuckee; then I asked him whether these they eat up went thither too. He said, "Yes."

From these things I began to instruct him in the knowledge of the true God. I told him that the great Maker of all things lived up there, pointing up towards Heaven. That He governs the world by the same Power and Providence by which He made it. That He was omnipotent, could do everything for us, give everything to us, take everything from us; and thus by degrees I opened his eyes. He listened with great attention, and received with pleasure the notion of Jesus Christ being sent to redeem us, and of the manner of making our prayers to God, and His being able to hear us, even into Heaven; he told me one day that if our God could hear us up beyond the sun, He must needs be a greater God than their Benamuckee, who lived but a little way off, and yet could not hear till they went up to the great mountains where he dwelt, to speak to him; I asked him if he ever went thither to speak to him; he said, no; they never went that were young men; none went thither but the old men, who he called their Oowokakee, that is, as I made him explain it to me, their religious, or clergy; and that they went to say O (so he called saying prayers), and then came back and told them what Benamuckee said. By this I observed, that there is priestcraft even amongst the most blinded, ignorant pagans in the world; and the policy of making a secret religion, in order to preserve the veneration of the people to the clergy, is not only to be found in the Roman but perhaps among all religions in the world, even among the most brutish and barbarous savages.

I endeavored to clear up this fraud to my man Friday, and told him that the pretense of their old men going up the mountains to say O to their god Benamuckee was a cheat, and their bringing word from thence what he said was much more so; that if they met with any answer or spake with anyone there, it must be with an evil spirit. And then I entered into a long discourse with him about the Devil, the original of him, his rebellion against God, his enmity to man, the reason of it, his setting himself up in the dark parts of the world to be worshipped instead of God, and as God, and the many stratagems he made use of to delude mankind to his ruin; how he had a secret access to our passions and to our affections, to adapt his snares so to our inclinations as to cause us even to be our own tempters and to run upon our destruction by our own choice.

I found it was not so easy to imprint right notions in his mind about the Devil, as it was about the being of a God. Nature assisted all my arguments to evidence to him even the necessity of a great First Cause and overruling, governing Power, a secret directing Providence, and of the equity and justice of paying homage to Him that made us, and the like. But there appeared nothing of all this in the notion of an evil spirit, of his original, his being, his nature, and above all, of his inclination to do evil, and to draw us in to do so too; and the poor creature puzzled me once in such a manner, by a question merely natural and innocent, that I scarce knew what to say to him. I had been talking a great deal to him of the power of God, His omnipotence, His dreadful nature to sin, His being a consuming fire to the workers of iniquity; how, as He had made us all, He could destroy us and all the world in a moment; and he listened with great seriousness to me all the while.

After this, I had been telling him how the Devil was God's enemy in the hearts of men and used all his malice and skill to defeat the good designs of Providence and to ruin the kingdom of Christ in the world, and the like. "Well," says Friday, "but you say, God is so strong, so great; is He not much strong, much might as the Devil?" "Yes, yes," says I, "Friday, God is stronger than the Devil, God is above the Devil, and therefore we pray to God to tread him down under our feet and enable us to resist his temptations and quench his fiery darts." "But," says he again, "if God much strong, much might as the Devil, why God no kill the Devil, so make him no more do wicked?"

I was strangely surprised at his question, and after all, though I was now an old man, yet I was but a young doctor, and ill enough qualified for a casuist, or a solver of difficulties. And at first I could not tell what to say, so I pretended not to hear him, and asked him what he said. But he was too earnest for an answer to forget his question; so that he repeated it in the very same broken words as above. By this time I had recovered myself a little, and I said, "God will at last punish him severely; he is reserved for the judgment and is to be cast into the bottomless pit, to dwell with everlasting fire." This did not satisfy Friday, but he returns upon me, repeating my words, " 'Reserve at last,' me no understand; but why not kill the Devil now, not kill great ago?" "You may as well ask me," said I, "why God does not kill you and I, when we do wicked things here that offend Him. We are preserved to repent and be pardoned." He muses awhile at this. "Well, well," says he, mighty affectionately, "that well; so you, I, Devil, all wicked, all preserve, repent, God pardon all." Here I was run down again by him to the last degree, and it was a testimony to me how the mere notions of nature, though they will guide reasonable creatures to the knowledge of a God, and of a worship or homage due to the supreme being of God, as the consequence of our nature, yet nothing but Divine revelation can form the knowledge of Jesus Christ and of a redemption purchased for us, of a Mediator of the new covenant, and of an Intercessor at the footstool of God's throne; I say, nothing but a revelation from Heaven can form these in the soul; and that therefore the Gospel of our Lord and Saviour Jesus Christ, I mean, the Word of God and the Spirit of God promised for the guide and sanctifier of His people are the absolutely necessary instructors of the souls of men, in the saving knowledge of God, and the means of salvation.

I therefore diverted the present discourse between me and my man, rising up hastily, as upon some sudden occasion of going out; then sending him for something a good way off, I seriously prayed to God that He would enable me to instruct savingly this poor savage, assisting by His Spirit the heart of the poor ignorant creature to receive the light of the knowledge of God in Christ, reconciling him to Himself, and would guide me to speak so to him from the Word of God as his conscience might be convinced, his eyes opened, and his soul saved. When he came again to me, I entered into a long discourse with him upon the subject of the redemption of man by the Saviour of the world, and of the doctrine of the Gospel preached from Heaven, viz., of repentance towards God, and faith in our blessed Lord Jesus. I then explained to him, as well as I could, why our blessed Redeemer took not on Him the nature of angels but the seed of Abraham, and how for that reason the fallen angels had no share in the redemption; that He came only to the lost sheep of the House of Israel, and the like.

I had, God knows, more sincerity than knowledge in all the methods I took for this poor creature's instruction and must acknowledge what I believe all that act upon the same principle will find, that in laying things open to him, I really informed and instructed myself in many things, that either I did not know or had not fully considered before, but which occurred naturally to my mind upon my searching into them for the information of this poor savage; and I had more affection in my inquiry after things upon this occasion than ever I felt before; so that whether this poor wild wretch was the better for me, or no, I had great reason to be thankful that ever he came to me. My grief set lighter upon me, my habitation grew comfortable to me beyond measure; and when I reflected that in this solitary life which I had been confined to I had not only been moved myself to look up to Heaven and to seek to the Hand that had brought me there; but was now to be made an instrument under Providence to save the life and, for aught I knew, the

soul of a poor savage, and bring him to the true knowledge of religion, and of the Christian doctrine, that he
might know Christ Jesus, to know whom is life eternal;
I say, when I reflected upon all these things, a secret joy
run through every part of my soul, and I frequently rejoiced that ever I was brought to this place, which I had
so often thought the most dreadful of all afflictions that
could possibly have befallen me.

In this thankful frame I continued all the remainder of
my time, and the conversation which employed the hours
between Friday and I was such as made the three years
which we lived there together perfectly and completely
happy, if any such thing as complete happiness can be
formed in a sublunary state. The savage was now a good
Christian, a much better than I; though I have reason
to hope, and bless God for it, that we were equally
penitent, and comforted, restored penitents; we had here
the Word of God to read and no farther off from His
Spirit to instruct than if we had been in England.

I always applied myself in reading the Scripture to let
him know, as well as I could, the meaning of what I
read; and he again, by his serious inquiries and ques-
tionings, made me, as I said before, a much better scholar
in the Scripture knowledge than I should ever have been
by my own private mere reading. Another thing I cannot
refrain from observing here also, from experience in this
retired part of my life, viz., how infinite and inexpressible
a blessing it is that the knowledge of God and of the
doctrine of salvation by Christ Jesus is so plainly laid
down in the Word of God, so easy to be received and understood, that as the bare reading the Scripture made me
capable of understanding enough of my duty to carry me
directly on to the great work of sincere repentance for
my sins, and laying hold of a Saviour for life and salvation, to a stated reformation in practice, and obedience to

all God's commands, and this without any teacher or instructor, I mean, human; so the same plain instruction
sufficiently served to the enlightening this savage creature
and bringing him to be such a Christian as I have known
few equal to him in my life.

As to all the disputes, wranglings, strife, and contention
which has happened in the world about religion, whether
niceties in doctrines, or schemes of church government,
they were all perfectly useless to us; as for aught I can
yet see, they have been to all the rest in the world. We
had the sure guide to Heaven, viz., the Word of God;
and we had, blessed be God, comfortable views of the
Spirit of God teaching and instructing us by His Word,
leading us into all truth, and making us both willing and
obedient to the instruction of His Word; and I cannot
see the last use that the greatest knowledge of the disputed points in religion, which have made such confusions in the world, would have been to us, if we could
have obtained it; but I must go on with the historical
part of things, and take every part in its order.

After Friday and I became more intimately acquainted,
and that he could understand almost all I said to him and
speak fluently, though in broken English, to me, I acquainted him with my own story, or at least so much of
it as related to my coming into the place; how I had
lived there, and how long. I let him into the mystery, for
such it was to him, of gunpowder and bullet, and taught
him how to shoot. I gave him a knife, which he was
wonderfully delighted with, and I made him a belt, with
a frog hanging to it, such as in England we wear hangers
in; and in the frog, instead of a hanger, I gave him a
hatchet, which was not only as good a weapon, in some
cases, but much more useful upon other occasions.

I described to him the country of Europe, and particularly England, which I came from: how we lived, how

we worshipped God, how we behaved to one another; and how we traded in ships to all parts of the world. I gave him an account of the wreck which I had been on board of and showed him as near as I could the place where she lay; but she was all beaten in pieces before, and gone.

I showed him the ruins of our boat, which we lost when we escaped, and which I could not stir with my whole strength then, but was now fallen almost all to pieces. Upon seeing this boat, Friday stood musing a great while, and said nothing; I asked him what it was he studied upon; at last says he, "Me see such boat like come to place at my nation."

I did not understand him a good while; but at last, when I had examined farther into it, I understood by him that a boat, such as that had been, came on shore upon the country where he lived; that is, as he explained it, was driven thither by stress of weather. I presently imagined that some European ship must have been cast away upon their coast, and the boat might get loose and drive ashore; but was so dull that I never once thought of men making escape from a wreck thither, much less whence they might come; so I only inquired after a description of the boat.

Friday described the boat to me well enough; but brought me better to understand him when he added with some warmth, "We save the white mans from drown." Then I presently asked him if there was any white mans, as he called them, in the boat. "Yes," he said, "the boat full of white mans." I asked him how many; he told upon his fingers seventeen. I asked him then what become of them; he told me, "They live, they dwell at my nation."

This put new thoughts into my head; for I presently imagined that these might be the men belonging to the ship that was cast away in sight of my island, as I now call it; and who, after the ship was struck on the rock and they saw her inevitably lost, had saved themselves in their boat and were landed upon that wild shore among the savages.

Upon this I inquired of him more critically what was become of them. He assured me they lived still there; that they had been there about four years; that the savages let them alone, and gave them victuals to live. I asked him how it came to pass they did not kill them and eat them. He said, "No, they make brother with them"; that is, as I understood him, a truce. And then he added, "They no eat mans but when make the war fight"; that is to say, they never eat any men but such as come to fight with them and are taken in battle.

It was after this some considerable time that being on the top of the hill, at the east side of the island from whence, as I have said, I had in a clear day discovered the main, or continent of America, Friday, the weather being very serene, looks very earnestly towards the mainland and, in a kind of surprise, falls a-jumping and dancing, and calls out to me, for I was at some distance from him. I asked him what was the matter. "O joy!" says he, "O glad! There see my country, there my nation!"

I observed an extraordinary sense of pleasure appeared in his face, and his eyes sparkled, and his countenance discovered a strange eagerness, as if he had a mind to be in his own country again; and this observation of mine put a great many thoughts into me, which made me at first not so easy about my new man Friday as I was before; and I made no doubt but that if Friday could get back to his own nation again, he would not only forget all his religion but all his obligation to me; and would be forward enough to give his countrymen an account of me and come back, perhaps with a hundred or two of them, and make a feast upon me, at which he might be as merry as he used to be with those of his enemies, when they were taken in war.

But I wronged the poor honest creature very much, for which I was very sorry afterwards. However, as my jealousy increased, and held me some weeks, I was a little more circumspect, and not so familiar and kind to him as before; in which I was certainly in the wrong too, the honest grateful creature having no thought about it but what consisted with the best principles, both as a religious Christian and as a grateful friend, as appeared afterwards to my full satisfaction.

While my jealousy of him lasted, you may be sure I was every day pumping him to see if he would discover any of the new thoughts which I suspected were in him; but I found everything he said was so honest and so innocent that I could find nothing to nourish my suspicion; and in spite of all my uneasiness he made me at last entirely his own again, nor did he in the least perceive that I was uneasy, and therefore I could not suspect him of deceit.

One day, walking up the same hill, but the weather being hazy at sea so that we could not see the continent, I called to him, and said, "Friday, do not you wish yourself in your own country, your own nation?" "Yes," he said, he be much O glad to be at his own nation. "What would you do there?" said I; "would you turn wild again, eat men's flesh again, and be a savage as you were before?" He looked full of concern, and shaking his head, said, "No, no; Friday tell them to live good, tell them to pray God, tell them to eat corn-bread, cattle-flesh, milk, no eat man again." "Why then," said I to him, "they will kill you." He looked grave at that, and then said, "No, they no kill me, they willing love learn." He meant by this, they would be willing to learn. He added, they learned much of the bearded mans that come in the boat. Then I asked him if he would go back to them. He smiled at that and told me he could not swim so far. I told him I would make a canoe for him. He told me he would go, if I would go with him. "I go!" says I; "why, they will eat me if I come there." "No, no," says he, "me make they no eat you; me make they much love you." He meant he would tell them how I had killed his enemies and saved his life, and so he would make them love me; then he told me as well as he could how kind they were to seventeen white men, or bearded men, as he called them, who came on shore there in distress.

From this time I confess I had a mind to venture over, and see if I could possibly join with these bearded men, who, I made no doubt, were Spaniards or Portuguese; not doubting but, if I could, we might find some method to escape from thence, being upon the continent, and a good company together, better than I could from an island forty miles off the shore, and alone without help. So after some days I took Friday to work again, by way of discourse, and told him I would give him a boat to go back to his own nation; and accordingly I carried him to my frigate, which lay on the other side of the island, and having cleared it of water, for I always kept it sunk in the water, I brought it out, showed it him, and we both went into it.

I found he was a most dexterous fellow at managing it, would make it go almost as swift and fast again as I could; so when he was in, I said to him, "Well, now, Friday, shall we go to your nation?" He looked very dull at my saying so, which it seems was because he thought the boat too small to go so far. I told him then I had a bigger; so the next day I went to the place where the first boat lay which I had made, but which I could not get into water. He said that was big enough; but then, as I had taken no care of it, and it had lain two or three and twenty years there, the sun had split and dried it, that it was in a manner rotten. Friday told me such a boat would do very well and would carry "much enough victual, drink, bread"; that was his way of talking.

Upon the whole, I was by this time so fixed upon my design of going over with him to the continent, that I told him we would go and make one as big as that, and he should go home in it. He answered not one word, but looked very grave and sad. I asked him what was the matter with him. He asked me again thus, "Why you angry mad with Friday? what me done?" I asked him what he meant; I told him I was not angry with him at all. "No angry! no angry!" says he, repeating the words several times, "Why send Friday home away to my nation?" "Why," says I, "Friday, did you not say you wished you were there?" "Yes, yes," says he, "wish be both there, no wish Friday there, no master there." In a word, he would not think of going there without me. "I go there, Friday!" says I, "what shall I do there?" He turned very quick upon me at this: "You do great deal much good," says he, "you teach wild mans be good sober tame mans; you tell them know God, pray God, and live new life." "Alas! Friday," says I, "thou knowest not what thou sayest; I am but an ignorant man myself." "Yes, yes," says he, "you teachee me good, you teachee them good." "No, no, Friday," says I, "you shall go without me; leave me here to live by myself, as I did before." He looked confused again at that word, and running to one of the hatchets which he used to wear, he takes it up hastily, comes and gives it me. "What must I do with this?" says I to him. "You take, kill Friday," says he. "What must I kill you for?" said I again. He returns very quick, "What you send Friday away for? Take, kill Friday, no send Friday away." This he spoke so earnestly that I saw tears stand in his eyes. In a word, I so plainly discovered the utmost affection in him to me, and a firm resolution in him, that I told him then, and often after, that I would never send him away from me if he was willing to stay with me.

Upon the whole, as I found by all his discourse a settled affection to me, and that nothing should part him from me, so I found all the foundation of his desire to go to his own country was laid in his ardent affection to the people and his hopes of my doing them good; a thing which, as I had no notion of myself, so I had not the least thought or intention or desire of undertaking it. But still I found a strong inclination to my attempting an escape as above, founded on the supposition gathered from the discourse, viz., that there were seventeen bearded men there; and therefore, without any more delay, I went to work with Friday to find out a great tree proper to fell, and make a large *periagua* or canoe to undertake the voyage. There were trees enough in the island to have built a little fleet, not of *periaguas* and canoes, but even of good large vessels. But the main thing I looked at was to get one so near the water that we might launch it when it was made, to avoid the mistake I committed at first.

At last, Friday pitched upon a tree, for I found he knew much better than I what kind of wood was fittest for it, nor can I tell to this day what wood to call the tree we cut down, except that it was very like the tree we call *fustic*, or between that and the Nicaragua wood, for it was much of the same color and smell. Friday was for burning the hollow or cavity of this tree out, to make it for a boat. But I showed him how rather to cut it out with tools, which, after I had showed him how to use, he did very handily; and in about a month's hard labor, we finished it and made it very handsome, especially when with our axes, which I showed him how to handle, we cut and hewed the outside into the true shape of a boat; after this, however, it cost us near a fortnight's time to get her along, as it were inch by inch, upon great rollers into the water. But when she was in, she would have carried twenty men with great ease.

When she was in the water, and though she was so big, it amazed me to see with what dexterity and how swift my man Friday would manage her, turn her, and paddle her along; so I asked him if he would, and if we might venture over in her. "Yes," he said, "he venture over in her very well, though great blow wind." However, I had a farther design that he knew nothing of, and that was to make a mast and sail, and to fit her with an anchor and cable. As to a mast, that was easy enough to get; so I pitched upon a straight young cedar-tree, which I found near the place, and which there was great plenty of in the island, and I set Friday to work to cut it down, and gave him directions how to shape and order it. But as to the sail, that was my particular care; I knew I had old sails, or rather pieces of old sails, enough; but as I had had them now six and twenty years by me and had not been very careful to preserve them, not imagining that I should ever have this kind of use for them, I did not doubt but they were all rotten, and indeed most of them were so; however, I found two pieces which appeared pretty good, and with these I went to work, and with a great deal of pains, and awkward tedious stitching (you may be sure) for want of needles, I at length made a three-cornered ugly thing, like what we call in England a shoulder-of-mutton sail, to go with a boom at bottom, and a little short sprit at the top, such as usually our ships' longboats sail with, and such as I best knew how to manage; because it was such a one as I had to the boat in which I made my escape from Barbary, as related in the first part of my story.

I was near two months performing this last work, viz., rigging and fitting my mast and sails; for I finished them very complete, making a small stay and a sail, or foresail to it, to assist, if we should turn to windward; and which was more than all, I fixed a rudder to the stern of her, to steer with; and though I was but a bungling shipwright, yet as I knew the usefulness, and even necessity of such a thing, I applied myself with so much pains to do it that at last I brought it to pass; though considering the many dull contrivances I had for it that failed, I think it cost me almost as much labor as making the boat.

After all this was done too, I had my man Friday to teach as to what belonged to the navigation of my boat; for though he knew very well how to paddle a canoe, he knew nothing what belonged to a sail and a rudder; and was the most amazed when he saw me work the boat to and again in the sea by the rudder, and how the sail jibed, and filled this way, or that way, as the course we sailed changed; I say, when he saw this, he stood like one astonished and amazed. However, with a little use I made all these things familiar to him; and he became an expert sailor, except that as to the compass, I could make him understand very little of that. On the other hand, as there was very little cloudy weather, and seldom or never any fogs in those parts, there was the less occasion for a compass, seeing the stars were always to be seen by night and the shore by day, except in the rainy seasons, and then nobody cared to stir abroad, either by land or sea.

I was now entered on the seven and twentieth year of my captivity in this place; though the three last years that I had this creature with me ought rather to be left out of the account, my habitation being quite of another kind than in all the rest of the time. I kept the anniversary of my landing here with the same thankfulness to God for His mercies as at first; and if I had such cause of acknowl·edgment at first, I had much more so now, having such additional testimonies of the care of Providence over me,

and the great hopes I had of being effectually and speedily delivered; for I had an invincible impression upon my
thoughts that my deliverance was at hand, and that I
should not be another year in this place. However, I went
on with my husbandry, digging, planting, fencing, as
usual; I gathered and cured my grapes, and did every
necessary thing as before.

The rainy season was in the meantime upon us, when
I kept more within doors than at other times; so I had
stowed our new vessel as secure as we could, bringing her
up into the creek, where, as I said in the beginning, I
landed my rafts from the ship and, hauling her up to the
shore, at high water mark, I made my man Friday dig a
little dock, just big enough to hold her, and just deep
enough to give her water enough to fleet in; and then
when the tide was out, we made a strong dam cross the
end of it, to keep the water out; and so she lay dry, as to
the tide from the sea; and to keep the rain off, we laid a
great many boughs of trees, so thick that she was as well
thatched as a house; and thus we waited for the months
of November and December, in which I designed to make
my adventure.

I Dip My Hands in Blood

WHEN the settled season began to come in, as the
thought of my design returned with the fair weather, I
was preparing daily for the voyage; and the first thing
I did was to lay by a certain quantity of provisions, being
the stores for our voyage; and intended, in a week or a
fortnight's time, to open the dock, and launch out our
boat. I was busy one morning upon something of this
kind, when I called to Friday, and bid him go to the
seashore, and see if he could find a turtle, or tortoise, a

thing which we generally got once a week, for the sake of the eggs as well as the flesh. Friday had not been long gone when he came running back and flew over my outer wall, or fence, like one that felt not the ground or the steps he set his feet on; and before I had time to speak to him, he cries out to me, "O master! O master! O sorrow! O bad!" "What's the matter, Friday?" says I. "O yonder, there," says he, "one, two, three canoe! one, two, three!" By his way of speaking, I concluded there were six; but on inquiry I found it was but three. "Well, Friday," says I, "do not be frighted"; so I heartened him up as well as I could. However, I saw the poor fellow was most terribly scared; for nothing ran in his head but that they were come to look for him and would cut him in pieces and eat him; and the poor fellow trembled so that I scarce knew what to do with him. I comforted him as well as I could, and told him I was in as much danger as he, and that they would eat me as well as him; "but," says I, "Friday, we must resolve to fight them; can you fight, Friday?" "Me shoot," says he, "but there come many great number." "No matter for that," said I again, "our guns will fright them that we do not kill"; so I asked him, whether if I resolved to defend him, he would defend me and stand by me and do just as I bid him. He said, "Me die when you bid die, master"; so I went and fetched a good dram of rum and gave him; for I had been so good a husband of my rum, that I had a great deal left. When he had drank it, I made him take the two fowling pieces, which we always carried, and load them with large swan-shot, as big as small pistol bullets; then I took four muskets, and loaded them with two slugs and five small bullets each; and my two pistols I loaded with a brace of bullets each; I hung my great sword, as usual, naked by my side, and gave Friday his hatchet.

When I had thus prepared myself, I took my perspective-glass and went up to the side of the hill, to see what I could discover; and I found quickly, by my glass, that there were one-and-twenty savages, three prisoners, and three canoes; and that their whole business seemed to be the triumphant banquet upon these three human bodies, a barbarous feast indeed, but nothing else more than, as I had observed, was usual with them.

I observed also that they were landed, not where they had done when Friday made his escape, but nearer to my creek, where the shore was low, and where a thick wood came close almost down to the sea. This, with the abhorrence of the inhuman errand these wretches came about, filled me with such indignation that I came down again to Friday, and told him I was resolved to go down to them, and kill them all; and asked him if he would stand by me. He was now gotten over his fright, and his spirits being a little raised with the dram I had given him, he was very cheerful and told me, as before, he would die when I bid die.

In this fit of fury, I took first and divided the arms which I had charged, as before, between us; I gave Friday one pistol to stick in his girdle, and three guns upon his shoulder; and I took one pistol, and the other three myself; and in this posture we marched out. I took a small bottle of rum in my pocket and gave Friday a large bag with more powder and bullets; and as to orders, I charged him to keep close behind me, and not to stir or shoot or do anything till I bid him and in the meantime not to speak a word. In this posture I fetched a compass to my right hand of near a mile, as well to get over the creek, as to get into the wood; so that I might come within shoot of them before I should be discovered, which I had seen by my glass, it was easy to do.

While I was making this march, my former thoughts returning, I began to abate my resolution; I do not mean that I entertained any fear of their number; for as they were naked, unarmed wretches, 'tis certain I was superior to them; nay, though I had been alone; but it occurred to my thoughts what call, what occasion, much less what necessity, I was in to go and dip my hands in blood, to attack people who had neither done or intended me any wrong; who, as to me, were innocent and whose barbarous customs were their own disaster, being in them a token indeed of God's having left them, with the other nations of that part of the world, to such stupidity and to such inhuman courses, but did not call me to take upon me to be a judge of their actions, much less an executioneer of His Justice; that whenever He thought fit, He would take the cause into His own hands and by national vengeance punish them as a people for national crimes; but that, in the meantime, it was none of my business; that it was true, Friday might justify it, because he was a declared enemy and in a state of war with those very particular people; and it was lawful for him to attack them; but I could not say the same with respect to me. These things were so warmly pressed upon my thoughts all the way as I went that I resolved I would only go and place myself near them, that I might observe their barbarous feast and that I would act then as God should direct; but that unless something offered that was more a call to me than yet I knew of, I would not meddle with them.

With this resolution I entered the wood, and, with all possible wariness and silence, Friday following close at my heels, I marched till I came to the skirt of the wood, on the side which was next to them; only that one corner of the wood lay between me and them; here I called softly to Friday, and showing him a great tree, which was just at the corner of the wood, I bade him go to the tree, and bring me word if he would see there plainly what they were doing; he did so and came immediately back to me and told me they might be plainly viewed there; that they were all about their fire, eating the flesh of one of their prisoners; and that another lay bound upon the sand, a little from them, which he said they would kill next; and which fired all the very soul within me, he told me it was not one of their nation but one of the bearded men, who he had told me of that came to their country in the boat. I was filled with horror at the very naming the white bearded man, and going to the tree, I saw plainly by my glass a white man who lay upon the beach of the sea, with his hands and his feet tied with flags, or things like rushes, and that he was an European and had clothes on.

There was another tree and a little thicket beyond it, about fifty yards nearer to them than the place where I was, which by going a little way about, I saw I might come at undiscovered, and that then I should be within half shot of them; so I withheld my passion, though I was indeed enraged to the highest degree, and going back about twenty paces, I got behind some bushes, which held all the way, till I came to the other tree; and then I came to a little rising ground, which gave me a full view of them, at the distance of about eighty yards.

I had now not a moment to lose; for nineteen of the dreadful wretches sat upon the ground, all close huddled together, and had just sent the other two to butcher the poor Christian and bring him, perhaps limb by limb, to their fire, and they were stooped down to untie the bands at his feet. I turned to Friday. "Now, Friday," said I, "do as I bid thee." Friday said he would. "Then, Friday," says I, "do exactly as you see me do; fail in nothing." So I set down one of the muskets and the fowling piece upon the ground, and Friday did the like by his; and with the other musket I took my aim at the savages, bidding him do the like; then asking him if he was ready, he said, "Yes."

"Then fire at them," said I; and the same moment I fired also.

Friday took his aim so much better than I that on the side that he shot he killed two of them and wounded three more; and on my side, I killed one and wounded two. They were, you may be sure, in a dreadful consternation; and all of them, who were not hurt, jumped up upon their feet, but did not immediately know which way to run or which way to look; for they knew not from whence their destruction came. Friday kept his eyes close upon me, that, as I had bid him, he might observe what I did; so, as soon as the first shot was made, I threw down the piece, and took up the fowling piece, and Friday did the like; he sees me cock and present; he did the same again. "Are you ready, Friday?" said I. "Yes," says he. "Let fly, then," says I, "in the name of God!" and with that I fired again among the amazed wretches, and so did Friday; and as our pieces were now loaden with what I called swan-shot, or small pistol bullets, we found only two drop, but so many were wounded that they run about yelling and screaming like mad creatures, all bloody, and miserably wounded most of them; whereof three more fell quickly after, though not quite dead.

"Now, Friday," says I, laying down the discharged pieces and taking up the musket which was yet loaded; "follow me," says I, which he did with a great deal of courage; upon which I rushed out of the wood and showed myself, and Friday close at my foot; as soon as I perceived they saw me, I shouted as loud as I could and bade Friday do so too; and running as fast as I could, which, by the way, was not very fast, being loaden with arms as I was, I made directly towards the poor victim, who was, as I said, lying upon the beach, or shore, between the place where they sat and the sea; the two butchers who were just going to work with him had left him at the surprise of our first fire and fled in a terrible fright to the sea-side and had jumped into a canoe, and three more of the rest made the same way; I turned to Friday and bid him step forwards and fire at them. He understood me immediately, and running about forty yards, to be near them, he shot at them, and I thought he had killed them all; for I see them all fall of a heap into the boat; though I saw two of them up again quickly. However, he killed two of them and wounded the third, so that he lay down in the bottom of the boat, as if he had been dead.

While my man Friday fired at them, I pulled out my knife and cut the flags that bound the poor victim, and, loosing his hands and feet, I lifted him up and asked him in the Portuguese tongue what he was. He answered in Latin, "Christianus"; but was so weak and faint that he could scarce stand or speak; I took my bottle out of my pocket and gave it him, making signs that he should drink, which he did; and I gave him a piece of bread, which he eat; then I asked him what countryman he was. And he said "Espagniole"; and being a little recovered, let me know by all the signs he could possibly make how much he was in my debt for his deliverance. "Seignior," said I, with as much Spanish as I could make up, "we will talk afterwards, but we must fight now; if you have any strength left, take this pistol and sword and lay about you." He took them very thankfully, and no sooner had he the arms in his hands, but as if they had put new vigor into him, he flew upon his murderers like a fury and had cut two of them in pieces in an instant; for the truth is, as the whole was a surprise to them, so the poor creatures were so much frighted with the noise of our pieces that they fell down for mere amazement and fear and had no more power to attempt their own escape than their flesh had to resist our shot; and that was the case of those five that Friday shot at in the boat; for as three of them fell with the hurt they received, so the other two fell with the fright.

I kept my piece in my hand still, without firing, being willing to keep my charge ready, because I had given the Spaniard my pistol and sword; so I called to Friday and bade him run up to the tree from whence we first fired and fetch the arms which lay there that had been discharged, which he did with great swiftness; and then giving him my musket, I sat down myself to load all the rest again, and bade them come to me when they wanted. While I was loading these pieces, there happened a fierce engagement between the Spaniard and one of the savages, who made at him with one of their great wooden swords, the same weapon that was to have killed him before, if I had not prevented it. The Spaniard, who was as bold and as brave as could be imagined, though weak, had fought this Indian a good while and had cut him two great wounds on his head; but the savage being a stout lusty fellow, closing in with him, had thrown him down, being faint, and was wringing my sword out of his hand, when the Spaniard, though undermost, wisely quitting the sword, drew the pistol from his girdle, shot the savage through the body and killed him upon the spot, before I, who was running to help him, could come near him.

Friday being now left to his liberty, pursued the flying wretches with no weapon in his hand but his hatchet; and with that he dispatched those three, who, as I said before, were wounded at first and fallen, and all the rest he could come up with; and the Spaniard coming to me for a gun, I gave him one of the fowling pieces, with which he pursued two of the savages, and wounded them both; but as he was not able to run, they both got from him into the wood, where Friday pursued them and killed one of them; but the other was too nimble for him, and though he was wounded, yet had plunged himself into the sea and swam with all his might off to those two who were left in the canoe; which three in the canoe, with one wounded, who we know not whether he died or no, were all that escaped our hands of one-and-twenty. The account of the rest is as follows:

3 killed at our first shot from the tree.
2 killed at the next shot.
2 killed by Friday in the boat.
2 killed by ditto, of those at first wounded.
1 killed by ditto in the wood.
3 killed by the Spaniard.
4 killed, being found dropped here and there of their wounds, or killed by Friday in his chase of them.
4 escaped in the boat, whereof one wounded, if not dead.

21 in all.

Those that were in the canoe worked hard to get out of gunshot; and though Friday made two or three shot at them, I did not find that he hit any of them. Friday would fain have had me took one of their canoes and pursued them; and indeed I was very anxious about their escape, lest, carrying the news home to their people, they should come back perhaps with two or three hundred of their canoes and devour us by mere multitude; so I consented to pursue them by sea, and running to one of their canoes, I jumped in and bade Friday follow me; but when I was in the canoe, I was surprised to find another poor creature lie there alive, bound hand and foot, as the Spaniard was, for the slaughter, and almost dead with fear, not knowing what the matter was; for he had not been able to look up over the side of the boat, he was tied so hard, neck and heels, and had been tied so long that he had really but little life in him.

I immediately cut the twisted flags, or rushes, which

they had bound him with, and would have helped him up; but he could not stand or speak, but groaned most piteously, believing, it seems, still that he was only unbound in order to be killed.

When Friday came to him, I bade him speak to him and tell him of his deliverance, and pulling out my bottle, made him give the poor wretch a dram, which, with the news of his being delivered, revived him, and he sat up in the boat; but when Friday came to hear him speak, and look in his face, it would have moved any one to tears, to have seen how Friday kissed him, embraced him, hugged him, cried, laughed, hallooed, jumped about, danced, sung, then cried again, wrung his hands, beat his own face and head, and then sung and jumped about again, like a distracted creature. It was a good while before I could make him speak to me, or tell me what was the matter; but when he came a little to himself he told me that it was his father.

It is not easy for me to express how it moved me to see what ecstasy and filial affection had worked in this poor savage, at the sight of his father and of his being delivered from death; nor indeed can I describe half the extravagances of his affection after this; for he went into the boat and out of the boat a great many times. When he went in to him, he would sit down by him, open his breast, and hold his father's head close to his bosom, half an hour together, to nourish it; then he took his arms and ankles, which were numbed and stiff with the binding, and chafed and rubbed them with his hands; and I, perceiving what the case was, gave him some rum out of my bottle to rub them with, which did them a great deal of good.

This action put an end to our pursuit of the canoe with the other savages, who were now gotten almost out of sight; and it was happy for us that we did not; for it blew so hard within two hours after, and before they could be gotten a quarter of their way, and continued blowing so hard all night, and that from the northwest, which was against them, that I could not suppose their boat could live, or that they ever reached to their own coast.

But to return to Friday; he was so busy about his father that I could not find in my heart to take him off for some time. But after I thought he could leave him a little, I called him to me, and he came jumping and laughing, and pleased to the highest extreme; then I asked him if he had given his father any bread. He shook his head and said, "None; ugly dog eat all up self." So I gave him a cake of bread out of a little pouch I carried on purpose; I also gave him a dram for himself, but he would not taste it but carried it to his father. I had in my pocket also two or three bunches of my raisins, so I gave him a handful of them for his father. He had no sooner given his father these raisins but I saw him come out of the boat and run away, as if he had been bewitched, he ran at such a rate; for he was the swiftest fellow of his foot that ever I saw; I say, he run at such a rate that he was out of sight, as it were, in an instant; and though I called, and hallooed, too, after him, it was all one, away he went, and in a quarter of an hour I saw him come back again, though not so fast as he went; and as he came nearer, I found his pace was slacker because he had something in his hand.

When he came up to me, I found he had been quite home for an earthen jug or pot to bring his father some fresh water, and that he had got two more cakes or loaves of bread. The bread he gave me, but the water he carried to his father. However, as I was very thirsty too, I took a little sup of it. This water revived his father more than all the rum or spirits I had given him, for he was just fainting with thirst.

When his father had drank, I called to him to know if

there was any water left; he said "Yes"; and I bade him
give it to the poor Spaniard, who was in as much want
of it as his father; and I sent one of the cakes that Friday
brought to the Spaniard too, who was indeed very weak,
and was reposing himself upon a green place under the
shade of a tree; and whose limbs were also very stiff, and
very much swelled with the rude bandage he had been
tied with. When I saw that, upon Friday's coming to him
with the water, he sat up and drank, and took the bread
and began to eat, I went to him and gave him a handful
of raisins; he looked up in my face with all the tokens of
gratitude and thankfulness that could appear in any
countenance; but was so weak, notwithstanding he had so
exerted himself in the fight that he could not stand up
upon his feet; he tried to do it two or three times, but was
really not able, his ankles were so swelled and so painful
to him; so I bade him sit still, and caused Friday to rub
his ankles and bathe them with rum, as he had done his
father's.

I observed the poor affectionate creature, every two
minutes or perhaps less, all the while he was here, turned
his head about to see if his father was in the same place
and posture as he left him sitting; and at last he found he
was not to be seen; at which he started up and without
speaking a word flew with that swiftness to him, that one
could scarce perceive his feet to touch the ground as he
went. But when he came, he only found he had laid himself down to ease his limbs; so Friday came back to me
presently, and I then spoke to the Spaniard to let Friday
help him up if he could and lead him to the boat, and
then he should carry him to our dwelling, where I would
take care of him. But Friday, a lusty strong fellow, took
the Spaniard quite up upon his back and carried him
away to the boat and set him down softly upon the side,
or gunnel, of the canoe, with his feet in the inside of it,
and then lifted him quite in and set him close to his

father, and presently stepping out again, launched the boat off, and paddled it along the shore faster than I could walk, though the wind blew pretty hard too; so he brought them both safe into our creek; and leaving them in the boat, runs away to fetch the other canoe. As he passed me, I spoke to him, and asked him whither he went; he told me, "Go fetch more boat"; so away he went like the wind; for sure never man or horse run like him, and he had the other canoe in the creek almost as soon as I got to it by land; so he wafted me over, and then went to help our new guests out of the boat, which he did; but they were neither of them able to walk; so that poor Friday knew not what to do.

To remedy this, I went to work in my thought, and calling to Friday to bid them sit down on the bank while he came to me, I soon made a kind of hand-barrow to lay them on, and Friday and I carried them up both together upon it between us. But when we got them to the outside of our wall or fortification, we were at a worse loss than before; for it was impossible to get them over, and I was resolved not to break it down. So I set to work again; and Friday and I, in about two hours' time, made a very handsome tent, covered with old sails, and above that with boughs of trees, being in the space without our outward fence, and between that and the grove of young wood which I had planted. And here we made them two beds of such things as I had, viz., of good rice-straw, with blankets laid upon it to lie on, and another to cover them, on each bed.

My Island Was Now Peopled

MY ISLAND was now peopled, and I thought myself very rich in subjects; and it was a merry reflection, which I frequently made, how like a king I looked. First of all, the whole country was my own mere property, so that I had an undoubted right of dominion. Secondly, my people were perfectly subjected. I was absolute lord and lawgiver; they all owed their lives to me, and were ready to lay down their lives, if there had been occasion of it, for me. It was remarkable, too, we had but three subjects, and they were of three different religions. My man Friday was a Protestant, his father was a Pagan and a cannibal, and the Spaniard was a Papist. However, I allowed liberty of conscience throughout my dominions. But this is by the way.

As soon as I had secured my two weak rescued prisoners, and given them shelter and a place to rest them upon, I began to think of making some provision for them. And the first thing I did, I ordered Friday to take a yearling goat, betwixt a kid and a goat, out of my particular flock, to be killed; when I cut off the hinder quarter, and chopping it into small pieces, I set Friday to work to boiling and stewing, and made them a very good dish, I assure you, of flesh and broth, having put some barley and rice also into the broth; and as I cooked it without doors, for I made no fire within my inner wall, so I carried it all into the new tent; and having set a table there for them, I sat down and eat my own dinner also with them, and, as well as I could, cheered them and encouraged them; Friday being my interpreter, especially to his father, and indeed to the Spaniard too; for the Spaniard spoke the language of the savages pretty well.

After we had dined, or rather supped, I ordered Friday to take one of the canoes, and go and fetch our muskets and other firearms, which for want of time we had left upon the place of battle; and the next day I ordered him to go and bury the dead bodies of the savages, which lay open to the sun, and would presently be offensive; and

I also ordered him to bury the horrid remains of their barbarous feast, which I knew were pretty much, and which I could not think of doing myself; nay, I could not bear to see them, if I went that way. All of which he punctually performed, and defaced the very appearance of the savages being there, so that when I went again I could scarce know where it was, otherwise than by the corner of the wood pointing to the place.

I then began to enter into a little conversation with my two new subjects; and first I set Friday to inquire of his father what he thought of the escape of the savages in that canoe, and whether we might expect a return of them with a power too great for us to resist. His first opinion was that the savages in the boat never could live out the storm which blew that night they went off but must of necessity be drowned or driven south to those other shores, where they were as sure to be devoured as they were to be drowned if they were cast away; but as to what they would do if they came safe on shore, he said he knew not; but it was his opinion that they were so dreadfully frighted with the manner of their being attacked, the noise and the fire, that he believed they would tell their people they were all killed by thunder and lightning, not by the hand of man, and that the two which appeared, viz., Friday and me, were two heavenly spirits or furies, come down to destroy them, and not men with weapons. This he said he knew, because he heard them all cry out so in their language to one another, for it was impossible to them to conceive that a man could dart fire and speak thunder and kill at a distance without lifting up the hand, as was done now. And this old savage was in the right; for, as I understood since by other hands, the savages never attempted to go over to the island afterwards; they were so terrified with the accounts given by those four men (for it seems they did escape the sea) that they believed whoever went to that enchanted island would be destroyed with fire from the gods.

This, however, I knew not, and therefore was under continual apprehensions for a good while and kept always upon my guard, me and all my army; for as we were now four of us, I would have ventured upon a hundred of them fairly in the open field at any time.

In a little time, however, no more canoes appearing, the fear of their coming wore off, and I began to take my former thoughts of a voyage to the main into consideration; being likewise assured by Friday's father that I might depend upon good usage from their nation on his account, if I would go.

But my thoughts were a little suspended when I had a serious discourse with the Spaniard and when I understood that there were sixteen more of his countrymen and Portuguese, who, having been cast away and made their escape to that side, lived there at peace indeed with the savages but were very sore put to it for necessaries, and indeed for life. I asked him all the particulars of their voyage and found they were a Spanish ship bound from the Rio de la Plata to the Havana, being directed to leave their loading there, which was chiefly hides and silver, and to bring back what European goods they could meet with there; that they had five Portuguese seamen on board, who they took out of another wreck; that five of their own men were drowned when the first ship was lost, and that these escaped, through infinite dangers and hazards, and arrived, almost starved, on the cannibal coast, where they expected to have been devoured every moment.

He told me they had some arms with them, but they were perfectly useless, for that they had neither powder or ball, the washing of the sea having spoiled all their powder but a little, which they used at their first landing to provide themselves some food.

I asked him what he thought would become of them there, and if they had formed no design of making any escape. He said they had many consultations about it, but that having neither vessel, or tools to build one, or provisions of any kind, their councils always ended in tears and despair.

I asked him how he thought they would receive a proposal from me, which might tend towards an escape; and whether, if they were all here, it might not be done. I told him with freedom, I feared mostly their treachery and ill usage of me, if I put my life in their hands; for that gratitude was no inherent virtue in the nature of man; nor did men always square their dealings by the obligations they had received so much as they did by the advantages they expected. I told him it would be very hard that I should be the instrument of their deliverance and that they should afterwards make me their prisoner in New Spain, where an Englishman was certain to be made a sacrifice, what necessity or what accident soever brought him thither. And that I had rather be delivered up to the savages and be devoured alive than fall into the merciless claws of the priests and be carried into the Inquisition. I added that otherwise I was persuaded, if they were all here, we might, with so many hands, build a bark large enough to carry us all away, either to the Brazils southward, or to the islands or Spanish coast northward. But that if in requital they should, when I had put weapons into their hands, carry me by force among their own people, I might be ill used for my kindness to them and make my case worse than it was before.

He answered with a great deal of candor and ingenuity

that their condition was so miserable and they were so sensible of it that he believed they would abhor the thought of using any man unkindly that should contribute to their deliverance; and that, if I pleased, he would go to them with the old man and discourse with them about it, and return again and bring me their answer. That he would make conditions with them upon their solemn oath, that they should be absolutely under my leading, as their commander and captain; and that they should swear upon the Holy Sacraments and the Gospel to be true to me and to go to such Christian country as that I should agree to, and no other; and to be directed wholly and absolutely by my orders, till they were landed safely in such country as I intended; and that he would bring a contract from them, under their hands, for that purpose.

Then he told me he would first swear to me himself that he would never stir from me as long as he lived, till I gave him orders; and that he would take my side to the last drop of his blood, if there should happen the least breach of faith among his countrymen.

He told me they were all of them very civil honest men, and they were under the greatest distress imaginable, having neither weapons or clothes, nor any food, but at the mercy and discretion of the savages; out of all hopes of ever returning to their own country; and that he was sure, if I would undertake their relief, they would live and die by me.

Upon these assurances, I resolved to venture to relieve them, if possible, and to send the old savage and this Spaniard over to them to treat. But when we had gotten all things in a readiness to go, the Spaniard himself started an objection, which had so much prudence in it on one hand, and so much sincerity on the other hand, that I could not but be very well satisfied in it; and, by his advice, put off the deliverance of his comrades for at least half a year. The case was thus:

He had been with us now about a month, during which time I had let him see in what manner I had provided, with the assistance of Providence, for my support; and he saw evidently what stock of corn and rice I had laid up; which, as it was more than sufficient for myself, so it was not sufficient, at least without good husbandry, for my family, now it was increased to number four. But much less would it be sufficient, if his countrymen, who were, as he said, fourteen still alive, should come over. And least of all would it be sufficient to victual our vessel, if we should build one, for a voyage to any of the Christian colonies of America. So he told me he thought it would be more advisable to let him and the two others dig and cultivate some more land, as much as I could spare seed to sow; and that we should wait another harvest, that we might have a supply of corn for his countrymen when they should come; for want might be a temptation to them to disagree, or not to think themselves delivered, otherwise than out of one difficulty into another. "You know," says he, "the Children of Israel, though they rejoiced at first for their being delivered out of Egypt, yet rebelled even again God Himself that delivered them, when they came to want bread in the wilderness."

His caution was so seasonable, and his advice so good, that I could not but be very well pleased with his proposal, as well as I was satisfied with his fidelity. So we fell to digging, all four of us, as well as the wooden tools we were furnished with permitted; and in about a month's time, by the end of which it was seed time, we had gotten as much land cured and trimmed up as we sowed twenty-two bushels of barley on, and sixteen jars of rice, which was, in short, all the seed we had to spare; nor indeed did we leave ourselves barley sufficient for our own food for the six months that we had to expect our crop, that is to say, reckoning from the time we set our seed aside for sowing; for it is not to be supposed it is six months in the ground in the country.

Having now society enough, and our number being sufficient to put us out of fear of the savages, if they had come, unless their number had been very great, we went freely all over the island, wherever we found occasion; and as here we had our escape or deliverance upon our thoughts, it was impossible, at least for me, to have the means of it out of mine; to this purpose, I marked out several trees which I thought fit for our work, and I set Friday and his father to cutting them down; and then I caused the Spaniard, to whom I imparted my thought on that affair, to oversee and direct their work. I showed them with what indefatigable pains I had hewed a large tree into single planks, and I caused them to do the like, till they had made about a dozen large planks of good oak, near two foot broad, thirty-five foot long, and from two inches to four inches thick. What prodigious labor it took up, anyone may imagine.

At the same time I contrived to increase my little flock of tame goats as much as I could; and to this purpose I made Friday and the Spaniard go out one day, and myself with Friday the next day, for we took our turns, and by this means we got above twenty young kids to breed up with the rest; for whenever we shot the dam, we saved the kids, and added them to our flock. But above all, the season for curing the grapes coming on, I caused such a prodigious quantity to be hung up in the sun, that I believe, had we been at Alicante, where the raisins of the sun are cured, we could have filled sixty or eighty barrels; and these with our bread was a great part of our food, and very good living too, I assure you; for it is an exceeding nourishing food.

It was now harvest, and our crop in good order; it was not the most plentiful increase I had seen in the island, but, however, it was enough to answer our end; for from our twenty-two bushels of barley we brought in and thrashed out above 220 bushels; and the like in proportion of the rice, which was store enough for our food to the next harvest, though all the sixteen Spaniards had been on shore with me; or if we had been ready for a voyage, it would very plentifully have victualed our ship, to have carried us to any part of the world, that is to say, of America.

When we had thus housed and secured our magazine of corn, we fell to work to make more wicker-work, viz., great baskets in which we kept it; and the Spaniard was very handy and dexterous at this part, and often blamed me that I did not make some things for defense of this kind of work; but I saw no need of it.

And now having a full supply of food for all the guests I expected, I gave the Spaniard leave to go over to the main, to see what he could do with those he had left behind him there. I gave him a strict charge in writing not to bring any man with him who would not first swear in the presence of himself and of the old savage that he would no way injure, fight with, or attack the person he should find in the island, who was so kind to send for them in order to their deliverance; but that they would stand by and defend him against all such attempts, and wherever they went, would be entirely under and sub-jected to his commands; and that this should be put in writing and signed with their hands. How we were to have this done, when I knew they had neither pen or ink, that indeed was a question which we never asked.

Under these instructions, the Spaniard and the old

savage, the father of Friday, went away in one of the canoes which they might be said to come in, or rather were brought in, when they came as prisoners to be devoured by the savages.

I gave each of them a musket with a firelock on it and about eight charges of powder and ball, charging them to be very good husbands of both and not to use either of them but upon urgent occasion.

This was a cheerful work, being the first measures used by me, in view of my deliverance, for now twenty-seven years and some days. I gave them provisions of bread and of dried grapes sufficient for themselves for many days, and sufficient for all their countrymen for about eight days' time; and wishing them a good voyage, I see them go, agreeing with them about a signal they should hang out at their return, by which I should know them again when they came back, at a distance, before they came on shore.

They went away with a fair gale on the day that the moon was at full; by my account, in the month of October; but as for an exact reckoning of days, after I had once lost it, I could never recover it again; nor had I kept even the number of years so punctually as to be sure that I was right, though as it proved, when I afterwards examined my account, I found I had kept a true reckoning of years.

An English Ship

IT WAS no less than eight days I had waited for them, when a strange and unforeseen accident intervened, of which the like has not perhaps been heard of in history. I was fast asleep in my hutch one morning, when my man Friday came running in to me and called aloud, "Master, master, they are come, they are come!"

I jumped up, and regardless of danger I went out, as soon as I could get my clothes on, through my little grove, which, by the way, was by this time grown to be a very thick wood; I say, regardless of danger, I went without my arms, which was not my custom to do. But I was surprised when turning my eyes to the sea, I presently saw a boat at about a league and half's distance, standing in for the shore, with a shoulder-of-mutton sail, as they call it, and the wind blowing pretty fair to bring them in; also I observed presently that they did not come from that side which the shore lay on, but from the southermost end of the island. Upon this I called Friday in, and bid him lie close, for these were not the people we looked for, and that we might not know yet whether they were friends or enemies.

In the next place, I went in to fetch my perspective-glass, to see what I could make of them; and having taken the ladder out, I climbed up to the top of the hill, as I used to do when I was apprehensive of anything, and to take my view the plainer without being discovered.

I had scarce set my foot on the hill, when my eye plainly discovered a ship lying at an anchor at about two leagues and a half's distance from me, south-southeast, but not above a league and a half from the shore. By my observation it appeared plainly to be an English ship, and the boat appeared to be an English longboat.

I cannot express the confusion I was in, though the joy of seeing a ship, and one who I had reason to believe was manned by my own countrymen, and consequently friends, was such as I cannot describe; but yet I had some secret doubts hung about me, I cannot tell from whence they came, bidding me keep upon my guard. In the first place, it occurred to me to consider what business an English ship could have in that part of the world, since it was not the way to or from any part of the world where the English had any traffic; and I knew there had been no storms to drive them in there, as in distress; and that if they were English really, it was most probable that they were here upon no good design; and that I had better continue as I was than fall into the hands of thieves and murderers.

Let no man despise the secret hints and notices of danger, which sometimes are given him, when he may think there is no possibility of its being real. That such hints and notices are given us, I believe few that have made any observations of things can deny; that they are certain discoveries of an invisible world, and a converse of spirits, we cannot doubt; and if the tendency of them seems to be to warn us of danger, why should we not suppose they are from some friendly agent, whether supreme, or inferior and subordinate, is not the question; and that they are given for our good?

The present question abundantly confirms me in the justice of this reasoning; for had I not been made cautious by this secret admonition, come it from whence it will, I had been undone inevitably, and in a far worse condition than before, as you will see presently.

I had not kept myself long in this posture but I saw the boat draw near the shore, as if they looked for a creek to thrust in at for the convenience of landing; however, as they did not come quite far enough, they did not see the little inlet where I formerly landed my rafts; but run their boat on shore upon the beach, at about half a mile from me, which was very happy for me, for otherwise they would have landed just, as I may say, at my door, and would soon have beaten me out of my castle and perhaps have plundered me of all I had.

When they were on shore, I was fully satisfied that they were Englishmen, at least most of them; one or two I thought were Dutch, but it did not prove so. There were in all eleven men, whereof three of them, I found, were unarmed, and, as I thought, bound; and when the first four or five of them were jumped on shore, they took those three out of the boat as prisoners. One of the three I could perceive using the most passionate gestures of entreaty, affliction, and despair, even to a kind of extravagance; the other two I could perceive lifted up their hands sometimes, and appeared concerned indeed, but not to such a degree as the first.

I was perfectly confounded at the sight, and knew not what the meaning of it should be. Friday called out to me in English as well as he could, "O master! you see English mans eat prisoner as well as savage mans." "Why," says I, "Friday, do you think they are a-going to eat them then?" "Yes," says Friday, "they will eat them." "No, no," says I, "Friday, I am afraid they will murder them indeed, but you may be sure they will not eat them."

All this while I had no thought of what the matter really was; but stood trembling with the horror of the sight, expecting every moment when the three prisoners should be killed; nay, once I saw one of the villains lift up his arm with a great cutlass, as the seamen call it, or sword, to strike one of the poor men; and I expected to see him fall every moment, at which all the blood in my body seemed to run chill in my veins.

I wished heartily now for my Spaniard, and the savage that was gone with him; or that I had any way to have come undiscovered within shot of them, that I might have rescued the three men, for I saw no firearms they had among them; but it fell out to my mind another way.

After I had observed the outrageous usage of the three men by the insolent seamen, I observed the fellows run scattering about the land, as if they wanted to see the country. I observed that the three other men had liberty to go also where they pleased; but they sat down all three upon the ground, very pensive, and looked like men in despair.

This put me in mind of the first time when I came on shore, and began to look about me; how I gave myself over for lost; how wildly I looked round me; what dreadful apprehensions I had; and how I lodged in the tree all night for fear of being devoured by wild beasts.

As I knew nothing that night of the supply I was to receive by the providential driving of the ship nearer the land by the storms and tide, by which I have since been so long nourished and supported; so these three poor desolate men knew nothing how certain of deliverance and supply they were, how near it was to them, and how effectually and really they were in a condition of safety at the same time that they thought themselves lost and their case desperate.

So little do we see before us in the world and so much reason have we to depend cheerfully upon the great Maker of the world, that He does not leave His creatures so absolutely destitute but that in the worst circumstances they have always something to be thankful for, and sometimes are nearer their deliverance than they imagine; nay, are even brought to their deliverance by the means by which they seem to be brought to their destruction.

It was just at the top of high water when these people came on shore, and while partly they stood parleying with the prisoners they brought, and partly while they rambled about to see what kind of a place they were in, they had carelessly stayed till the tide was spent, and the water was ebbed considerably away, leaving their boat aground.

They had left two men in the boat, who, as I found afterwards, having drank a little too much brandy, fell asleep; however, one of them waking sooner than the other, and finding the boat too fast aground for him to stir it, hallooed for the rest, who were straggling about, upon which they all soon came to the boat; but it was past all their strength to launch her, the boat being very heavy, and the shore on that side being a soft oozy sand, almost like a quicksand.

In this condition, like true seamen, who are perhaps the least of all mankind given to forethought, they gave it over, and away they strolled about the country again; and I heard one of them say aloud to another, calling them off from the boat, "Why, let her alone, Jack, can't ye? she will float next tide"; by which I was fully confirmed in the main inquiry of what countrymen they were.

All this while I kept myself very close, not once daring to stir out of my castle, any farther than to my place of observation near the top of the hill; and very glad I was to think how well it was fortified. I knew it was no less than ten hours before the boat could be on float again, and by that time it would be dark, and I might be at more liberty to see their motions, and to hear their discourse, if they had any.

In the meantime I fitted myself up for a battle, as before; though with more caution, knowing I had to do with another kind of enemy than I had at first. I ordered Friday also, who I had made an excellent marksman with his gun, to load himself with arms. I took myself two fowling pieces, and I gave him three muskets; my figure, indeed, was very fierce; I had my formidable goatskin coat on, with the great cap I have mentioned, a naked sword by my side, two pistols in my belt, and a gun upon each shoulder.

It was my design, as I said above, not to have made any attempt till it was dark. But about two o'clock being the heat of the day, I found that, in short, they were all gone straggling into the woods and, as I thought, were laid down to sleep. The three poor distressed men, too anxious for their condition to get any sleep, were, however, set down under the shelter of a great tree, at about a quarter of a mile from me, and, as I thought, out of sight of any of the rest.

Upon this I resolved to discover myself to them and learn something of their condition. Immediately I marched in the figure as above, my man Friday at a good distance behind me, as formidable for his arms as I, but not making quite so staring a specter-like figure as I did.

I came as near them undiscovered as I could, and then before any of them saw me, I called aloud to them in Spanish, "What are ye, gentlemen?"

They started up at the noise, but were ten times more confounded when they saw me, and the uncouth figure that I made. They made no answer at all, but I thought I perceived them just going to fly from me, when I spoke to them in English: "Gentlemen," said I, "do not be surprised at me; perhaps you may have a friend near you, when you did not expect it." "He must be sent directly from Heaven then," said one of them very gravely to me, and pulling off his hat at the same time to me, "for our condition is past the help of man." "All help is from Heaven, sir," said I. "But can you put a stranger in the way how to help you, for you seem to me to be in some great distress? I saw you when you landed, and when you seemed to make applications to the brutes that came with you, I saw one of them lift up his sword to kill you."

The poor man, with tears running down his face, and trembling, looking like one astonished, returned, "Am I talking to God, or man? Is it a real man, or an angel?" "Be in no fear about that, sir," said I, "if God had sent an angel to relieve you, he would have come better clothed, and armed after another manner than you see me in; pray lay aside your fears; I am a man, an Englishman, and disposed to assist you, you see; I have one servant only; we have arms and ammunition; tell us freely, can we serve you? What is your case?"

"Our case," said he, "sir, is too long to tell you, while our murderers are so near; but in short, sir, I was commander of that ship; my men have mutinied against me, they have been hardly prevailed on not to murder me, and at last have set me on shore in this desolate place, with these two men with me, one my mate, the other a passenger, where we expected to perish, believing the place to be uninhabited, and know not yet what to think of it."

"Where are those brutes, your enemies?" said I. "Do you know where they are gone?" "There they lie, sir," said he, pointing to a thicket of trees; "my heart trembles for fear they have seen us and heard you speak; if they have, they will certainly murder us all."

"Have they any firearms?" said I. He answered they had only two pieces, and one which they left in the boat. "Well then," said I, "leave the rest to me; I see they are all asleep; it is an easy thing to kill them all; but shall we rather take them prisoners?" He told me there were two desperate villains among them that it was scarce safe to show any mercy to; but if they were secured, he believed all the rest would return to their duty. I asked him which they were. He told me he could not at that distance describe them, but he would obey my orders in anything I would direct. "Well," says I, "let us retreat out of their view or hearing, lest they awake, and we will resolve further"; so they willingly went back with me, till the woods covered us from them.

"Look you, sir," said I, "if I venture upon your deliverance, are you willing to make two conditions with me?" He anticipated my proposals by telling me that both he and the ship, if recovered, should be wholly directed and commanded by me in everything; and if the ship was not recovered, he would live and die with me in what part of the world soever I would send him; and the two other men said the same.

"Well," says I, "my conditions are but two. 1. That while you stay on this island with me, you will not pretend to any authority here; and if I put arms into your hands, you will upon all occasions give them up to me and do no prejudice to me or mine upon this island, and in the meantime, be governed by my orders. 2. That if the ship is or may be recovered, you will carry me and my man to England, passage free."

He gave me all the assurances that the invention and faith of man could devise that he would comply with these most reasonable demands and besides would owe his life to me and acknowledge it upon all occasions as long as he lived.

"Well then," said I, "here are three muskets for you, with powder and ball; tell me next what you think is proper to be done." He showed all the testimony of his gratitude that he was able, but offered to be wholly guided by me. I told him I thought it was hard venturing anything; but the best method I could think of was to fire upon them at once, as they lay; and if any was not killed at the first volley, and offered to submit, we might save them, and so put it wholly upon God's Providence to direct the shot.

He said very modestly that he was loath to kill them, if he could help it, but that those two were incorrigible villains and had been the authors of all the mutiny in the ship, and if they escaped, we should be undone still; for they would go on board and bring the whole ship's company, and destroy us all. "Well then," says I, "necessity legitimates my advice; for it is the only way to save our lives." However, seeing him still cautious of shedding blood, I told him they should go themselves and manage as they found convenient.

In the middle of this discourse we heard some of them awake, and soon after, we saw two of them on their feet. I asked him if either of them were of the men who he had said were the heads of the mutiny. He said, "No." "Well then," said I, "you may let them escape; and Providence seems to have wakened them on purpose to save themselves. Now," says I, "if the rest escape you, it is your fault."

Animated with this, he took the musket I had given him in his hand, and a pistol in his belt, and his two comrades with him, with each man a piece in his hand. The two men who were with him, going first, made some noise, at which one of the seamen, who was awake turned about, and seeing them coming cried out to the rest; but it was too late then, for the moment he cried out they fired; I mean the two men, the captain wisely reserving his own piece. They had so well aimed their shot at the men they knew that one of them was killed on the spot, and the other very much wounded; but not being dead, he started up upon his feet, and called eagerly for help to the other; but the captain, stepping to him, told him 'twas too late to cry for help, he should call upon God to forgive his villainy, and with that word knocked him down with the stock of his musket, so that he never spoke more. There were three more in the company, and one of them was also slightly wounded. By this time I was come, and when they saw their danger and that it was in vain to resist, they begged for mercy. The captain told them he would spare their lives, if they would give him any assurance of their abhorrence of the treachery they had been guilty of and would swear to be faithful to him in recovering the ship and afterwards in carrying her back to Jamaica, from whence they came. They gave him all the protestations of their sincerity that could be desired, and he was willing to believe them, and spare their lives, which I was not against, only I obliged him to keep them bound hand and foot while they were upon the island.

While this was doing, I sent Friday with the captain's mate to the boat, with orders to secure her and bring away the oars and sail, which they did; and by and by, three straggling men, that were (happily for them) parted from the rest, came back upon hearing the guns fired, and seeing their captain, who before was their prisoner, now their conqueror, they submitted to be bound also; and so our victory was complete.

It now remained that the captain and I should inquire into one another's circumstances. I began first, and told him my whole history, which he heard with an attention even to amazement; and particularly at the wonderful manner of my being furnished with provisions and ammunition; and, indeed, as my story is a whole collection of wonders, it affected him deeply; but when he reflected from thence upon himself and how I seemed to have been preserved there on purpose to save his life, the tears ran down his face, and he could not speak a word more.

After this communication was at an end, I carried him and his two men into my apartment, leading them in just where I came out, viz., at the top of the house, where I refreshed them with such provisions as I had, and showed them all the contrivances I had made during my long, long inhabiting that place.

Our Business Was to Recover the Ship

ALL I showed them, all I said to them, was perfectly amazing; but above all, the captain admired my fortification and how perfectly I had concealed my retreat with a grove of trees, which having been now planted near twenty years, and the trees growing must faster than in England, was become a little wood, and so thick, that it was unpassable in any part of it, but at that one side, where I had reserved my little winding passage into it. I told him this was my castle and my residence, but that I had a seat in the country, as most princes have, whither I could retreat upon occasion, and I would show him that too another time; but at present our business was to consider how to recover the ship. He agreed with me as to that; but told me he was perfectly at a loss what measures to take; for that there were still six-and-twenty hands on board, who, having entered into a cursed conspiracy, by which they had all forfeited their lives to the law, would be hardened in it now by desperation; and would carry it on, knowing that if they were reduced, they should be brought to the gallows as soon as they came to England or to any of the English colonies; and that therefore there would be no attacking them with so small a number as we were.

I mused for some time upon what he said, and found it was a very rational conclusion, and that therefore something was to be resolved on very speedily, as well to draw the men on board into some snare for their surprise, as to prevent their landing upon us, and destroying us; upon this it presently occurred to me that in a little while the ship's crew, wondering what was become of their comrades and of the boat, would certainly come on shore in their other boat to see for them, and that then perhaps they might come armed and be too strong for us; this he allowed was rational.

Upon this, I told him the first thing we had to do was to stave the boat, which lay upon the beach, so that they might not carry her off; and taking everything out of her, leave her so far useless as not to be fit to swim; accordingly we went on board, took the arms which were left on board out of her and whatever else we found there, which was a bottle of brandy, and another of rum, a few biscuit cakes, a horn of powder, and a great lump of sugar in a piece of canvas; the sugar was five or six pounds; all which was very welcome to me, especially the brandy and sugar, of which I had had none left for many years.

When we had carried all these things on shore (the oars, mast, sail, and rudder of the boat were carried away before, as above), we knocked a great hole in her bottom, that if they had come strong enough to master us, yet they could not carry off the boat.

Indeed, it was not much in my thoughts that we could be able to recover the ship; but my view was that if they went away without the boat, I did not much question to make her fit again to carry us away to the Leeward Islands and call upon our friends, the Spaniards, in my way, for I had them still in my thoughts.

While we were thus preparing our designs and had first by main strength heaved the boat up upon the beach so high that the tide would not fleet her off at high-water mark, and besides had broke a hole in her bottom too big to be quickly stopped and were sat down musing what we should do, we heard the ship fire a gun and saw her make a waft with her ancient as a signal for the boat to come on board; but no boat stirred; and they fired several times, making other signals for the boat.

At last, when all their signals and firings proved fruitless, and they found the boat did not stir, we saw them, by the help of my glasses, hoist another boat out, and row towards the shore; and we found, as they approached, that there was no less than ten men in her, and that they had firearms with them.

As the ship lay almost two leagues from the shore, we

had a full view of them as they came, and a plain sight of the men, even of their faces, because the tide having set them a little to the east of the other boat, they rowed up under shore, to come to the same place where the other had landed, and where the boat lay.

By this means, I say, we had a full view of them and the captain knew the persons and characters of all the men in the boat, of whom he said that there were three very honest fellows, who, he was sure, were led into this conspiracy by the rest, being overpowered and frighted. But that as for the boatswain, who, it seems, was the chief officer among them, and all the rest, they were as outrageous as any of the ship's crew, and were no doubt made desperate in their new enterprise; and terribly apprehensive he was that they would be too powerful for us.

I smiled at him and told him that men in our circumstances were past the operation of fear. That seeing almost every condition that could be was better than that which we were supposed to be in, we ought to expect that the consequence, whether death or life, would be sure to be a deliverance. I asked him what he thought of the circumstances of my life and whether a deliverance were not worth venturing for. "And where, sir," said I, "is your belief of my being preserved here on purpose to save your life, which elevated you a little while ago? For my part," said I, "there seems to be but one thing amiss in all the prospects of it." "What's that?" says he. "Why," said I, " 'tis that, as you say, there are three or four honest fellows among them, which should be spared; had they been all of the wicked part of the crew I should have thought God's Providence had signaled them out to deliver them into your hands; for depend upon it, every man of them that comes ashore are our own and shall die or live as they behave to us."

As I spoke this with a raised voice and cheerful countenance, I found it greatly encouraged him; so we set vigorously to our business. We had, upon the first appearance of the boat's coming from the ship, considered of separating our prisoners, and had indeed secured them effectually.

Two of them, of whom the captain was less assured than ordinary, I sent with Friday and one of the three delivered men to my cave, where they were remote enough and out of danger of being heard or discovered, or of finding their way out of the woods, if they could have delivered themselves. Here they left them bound, but gave them provisions, and promised them, if they continue there quietly, to give them their liberty in a day or two; but that if they attempted their escape, they should be put to death without mercy. They promised faithfully to bear their confinement with patience and were very thankful that they had such good usage as to have provisions and a light left them; for Friday gave them candles (such as we made ourselves) for their comfort; and they did not know but that he stood sentinel over them at the entrance.

The other prisoners had better usage; two of them were kept pinioned indeed, because the captain was not free to trust them; but the other two were taken into my service upon their captain's recommendation and upon their solemnly engaging to live and die with us; so with them and the three honest men we were seven men, well armed; and I made no doubt we should be able to deal well enough with the ten that were a-coming, considering that the captain had said there were three or four honest men among them also.

As soon as they got to the place where their other boat lay, they ran their boat into the beach, and came all on shore, hauling the boat up after them, which I was glad to see; for I was afraid they would rather have left the boat at an anchor, some distance from the shore, with some hands in her, to guard her; and so we should not be able to seize the boat.

Being on shore, the first thing they did, they ran all to their other boat; and it was easy to see that they were under a great surprise to find her stripped, as above, of all that was in her, and a great hole in her bottom.

After they had mused a while upon this, they set up two or three great shouts, hallooing with all their might, to try if they could make their companions hear; but all was to no purpose. Then they came all close in a ring, and fired a volley of their small arms, which indeed we heard, and the echoes made the woods ring; but it was all one; those in the cave we were sure could not hear, and those in our keeping, though they heard it well enough, yet durst give no answer to them.

They were so astonished at the surprise of this that, as they told us afterwards, they resolved to go all on board again, to their ship, and let them know that the men were all murdered and the longboat staved; accordingly, they immediately launched their boat again, and gat all of them on board.

The captin was terribly amazed and even confounded at this, believing they would go on board the ship again and set sail, giving their comrades for lost, and so he should still lose the ship, which he was in hopes we should have recovered; but he was quickly as much frighted the other way.

They had not been long put off with the boat, but we perceived them all coming on shore again; but with this new measure in their conduct, which it seems they consulted together upon, viz., to leave three men in the boat, and the rest to go on shore, and go up into the country to look for their fellows.

This was a great disappointment to us; for now we were

at a loss what to do; for our seizing those seven men on shore would be no advantage to us, if we let the boat escape; because they would then row away to the ship, and then the rest of them would be sure to weigh and set sail, and so our recovering the ship would be lost.

However, we had no remedy but to wait and see what the issue of things might present; the seven men came on shore, and the three who remained in the boat put her off to a good distance from the shore, and came to an anchor to wait for them; so that it was impossible for us to come at them in the boat.

Those that came on shore kept close together, marching towards the top of the little hill under which my habitation lay; and we could see them plainly, though they could not perceive us. We could have been very glad they would have come nearer to us, so that we might have fired at them, or that they would have gone farther off, that we might have come abroad.

But when they were come to the brow of the hill, where they could see a great way into the valleys and woods, which lay towards the northeast part, and where the island lay lowest, they shouted and hallooed till they were weary; and not caring, it seems, to venture far from the shore, nor far from one another, they sat down together under a tree, to consider of it. Had they thought fit to have gone to sleep here, as the other party of them had done, they had done the job for us; but they were too full of apprehensions of danger to venture to go to sleep, though they could not tell what the danger was they had to fear neither.

The captain made a very just proposal to me, upon this consultation of theirs, viz., that perhaps they would all fire a volley again, to endeavor to make their fellows hear, and that we should all sally upon them, just at the juncture when their pieces were all discharged, and they

would certainly yield and we should have them without
bloodshed. I liked the proposal, provided it was done
while we were near enough to come up to them before
they could load their pieces again.

But this event did not happen, and we lay still a long
time, very irresolute what course to take; at length I told
them there would be nothing to be done in my opinion
till night, and then, if they did not return to the boat,
perhaps we might find a way to get between them and
the shore, and so might use some stratagem with them in
the boat, to get them on shore.

We waited a great while, though very impatient for
their removing; and were very uneasy, when, after long
consultations, we saw them start all up and march down
towards the sea. It seems they had such dreadful apprehensions upon them of the danger of the place that they
resolved to go on board the ship again, give their companions over for lost, and so go on with their intended
voyage with the ship.

As soon as I perceived them go towards the shore, I
imagined it to be as it really was, that they had given over
their search, and were for going back again; and the
captain, as soon as I told him my thoughts, was ready to
sink at the apprehensions of it; but I presently thought
of a stratagem to fetch them back again, and which answered my end to a tittle.

I ordered Friday and the captain's mate to go over the
little creek westward, towards the place where the savages came on shore when Friday was rescued; and as soon
as they came to a little rising ground, at about half a mile
distance, I bade them halloo as loud as they could and
wait till they found the seamen heard them; that as soon
as ever they heard the seamen answer them, they should
return it again, and then keeping out of sight, take a
round. always answering when the other hallooed, to

draw them as far into the island and among the woods as possible and then wheel about again to me, by such ways as I directed them.

They were just going into the boat, when Friday and the mate hallooed; and they presently heard them, and answering, run along the shore westward towards the voices they heard, when they were presently stopped by the creek, where, the water being up, they could not get over, and called for the boat to come up and set them over, as indeed I expected.

When they had set themselves over, I observed that the boat being gone up a good way into the creek, and, as it were, in a harbor within the land, they took one of the three men out of her to go along with them, and left only two in the boat, having fastened her to the stump of a little tree on the shore.

This was what I wished for, and immediately leaving Friday and the captain's mate to their business, I took the rest with me, and crossing the creek out of their sight, we surprised the two men before they were aware; one of them lying on shore, and the other being in the boat; the fellow on shore was between sleeping and waking and going to start up; the captain, who was foremost, ran in upon him, and knocked him down, and then called out to him in the boat to yield, or he was a dead man.

There needed very few arguments to persuade a single man to yield, when he saw five men upon him and his comrade knocked down; besides, this was, it seems, one of the three who were not so hearty in the mutiny as the rest of the crew, and therefore was easily persuaded not only to yield but afterwards to join very sincere with us.

In the meantime, Friday and the captain's mate so well managed their business with the rest that they drew them by hallooing and answering from one hill to another, and from one wood to another, till they not only heartily tired them but left them, where they were very sure they could not reach back to the boat before it was dark; and indeed they were heartily tired themselves also by the time they came back to us.

We had nothing now to do but to watch for them in the dark and to fall upon them, so as to make sure work with them.

It was several hours after Friday came back to me before they came back to their boat; and we could hear the foremost of them, long before they came quite up, calling to those behind to come along, and could also hear them answer and complain how lame and tired they were and not able to come any faster, which was very welcome news to us.

At length they came up to the boat; but 'tis impossible to express their confusion, when they found the boat fast aground in the creek, the tide ebbed out, and their two men gone. We could hear them call to one another in a most lamentable manner, telling one another they were gotten into an enchanted island; that either there were inhabitants in it, and they should all be murdered, or else there were devils and spirits in it, and they should be all carried away and devoured.

They hallooed again, and called their two comrades by their names a great many times, but no answer. After some time, we could see them, by the little light there was, run about, wringing their hands like men in despair; and that sometimes they would go and sit down in the boat to rest themselves, then come ashore again, and walk about again, and so over the same thing again.

My men would fain have me given them leave to fall upon them at once in the dark; but I was willing to take them at some advantage, so to spare them, and kill as few of them as I could; and especially I was unwilling to hazard the killing any of our own men, knowing the other were very well armed. I resolved to wait to see if they did not separate; and therefore to make sure of them, I drew my ambuscade nearer and ordered Friday and the captain to creep upon their hands and feet, as close to the ground as they could, that they might not be discovered, and get as near them as they could possibly before they offered to fire.

They had not been long in that posture, but that the boatswain, who was the principal ringleader of the mutiny and had now shown himself the most dejected and dispirited of all the rest, came walking towards them, with two more of their crew; the captain was so eager, as having this principal rogue so much in his power, that he could hardly have patience to let him come so near as to be sure of him; for they only heard his tongue before. But when they came nearer, the captain and Friday, starting up on their feet, let fly at them.

The boatswain was killed upon the spot; the next man was shot into the body, and fell just by him, though he did not die till an hour or two after; and the third run for it.

At the noise of the fire, I immediately advanced with my whole army, which was now eight men, viz., myself, generalissimo, Friday, my lieutenant-general, the captain and his two men, and the three prisoners of war, who we had trusted with arms.

We came upon them indeed in the dark, so that they could not see our number; and I made the man they had left in the boat, who was now one of us, call to them by name, to try if I could bring them to a parley and so might perhaps reduce them to terms, which fell out just as we desired. For indeed it was easy to think, as their condition then was, they would be very willing to capitulate; so he calls out as loud as he could to one of them, "Tom Smith! Tom Smith!" Tom Smith answered immediately,

"Who's that? Robinson?" for it seems he knew his voice. T' other answered, "Ay, ay; for God's sake, Tom Smith, throw down your arms and yield, or you are all dead men this moment."

"Who must we yield to? Where are they?" says Smith again. "Here they are," says he; "here's our captain, and fifty men with him, have been hunting you this two hours; the boatswain is killed, Will Frye is wounded, and I am a prisoner; and if you do not yield, you are all lost."

"Will they give us quarter then," says Tom Smith, "and we will yield?" "I'll go and ask, if you promise to yield," says Robinson; so he asked the captain, and the captain then calls himself out, "You, Smith, you know my voice. If you lay down your arms immediately and submit, you shall have your lives, all but Will Atkins."

Upon this Will Atkins cried out, "For God's sake, captain, give me quarter; what have I done? They have been all as bad as I"; which, by the way, was not true neither; for it seems this Will Atkins was the first man that laid hold of the captain, when they first mutinied, and used him barbarously, in tying his hands and giving him injurious language. However, the captain told him he must lay down his arms at discretion and trust to the governor's mercy; by which he meant me, for they all called me governor.

In a word, they all laid down their arms and begged their lives; and I sent the man that had parleyed with them and two more, who bound them all; and then my great army of fifty men, which, particularly with those three, were all but eight, came up and seized upon them all and upon their boat; only that I kept myself and one more out of sight, for reasons of state.

Our next work was to repair the boat and think of seizing the ship; and as for the captain, now he had leisure to parley with them. He expostulated with them upon the villainy of their practices with him, and at length upon the farther wickedness of their design, and how certainly it must bring them to misery and distress in the end, and perhaps to the gallows.

They all appeared very penitent and begged hard for their lives; as for that, he told them they were none of his prisoners, but the commander of the island; that they thought they had set him on shore in a barren uninhabited island, but it had pleased God so to direct them that the island was inhabited, and that the governor was an Englishman; that he might hang them all there, if he pleased; but as he had given them all quarter, he supposed he would send them to England, to be dealt with there as justice required, except Atkins, who he was commanded by the governor to advise to prepare for death; for that he would be hanged in the morning.

Though this was all a fiction of his own, yet it had its desired effect; Atkins fell upon his knees to beg the captain to intercede with the governor for his life; and all the rest begged of him, for God's sake, that they might not be sent to England.

It now occurred to me that the time of our deliverance was come, and that it would be a most easy thing to bring these fellows in to be hearty in getting possession of the ship; so I retired in the dark from them, that they might not see what kind of a governor they had, and called the captain to me; when I called, as at a great distance, one of the men was ordered to speak again and say to the captain, "Captain, the commander calls for you"; and presently the captain replied, "Tell his excellency, I am just a-coming." This more perfectly amused them, and they all believed that the commander was just by with his fifty men.

Deliverance Put in My Hands

UPON the captain's coming to me, I told him my project for seizing the ship, which he liked of wonderfully well, and resolved to put it in execution the next morning.

But in order to execute it with more art, and secure of success, I told him we must divide the prisoners, and that he should go and take Atkins and two more of the worst of them, and send them pinioned to the cave where the others lay. This was committed to Friday and the two men who came on shore with the captain.

They conveyed them to the cave, as to a prison; and it was indeed a dismal place, especially to men in their condition.

The other I ordered to my bower, as I called it, of which I have given a full description; and as it was fenced in, and they pinioned, the place was secure enough, considering they were upon their behavior.

To these in the morning I sent the captain, who was to enter into a parley with them; in a word, to try them, and tell me, whether he thought they might be trusted or no, to go on board and surprise the ship. He talked to them of the injury done him, of the condition they were brought to; and that though the governor had given them quarter for their lives, as to the present action, yet that if they were sent to England, they would all be hanged in chains, to be sure; but that if they would join in so just an attempt as to recover the ship, he would have the governor's engagement for their pardon.

Anyone may guess how readily such a proposal would be accepted by men in their condition; they fell down on their knees to the captain and promised with the deepest imprecations that they would be faithful to him to the last drop, and that they should owe their lives to him and would go with hir. all over the world; that they would own him for a father to them as long as they lived.

"Well," says the captain, "I must go and tell the governor what you say, and see what I can do to bring him to consent to it." So he brought me an account of the temper he found them in; and that he verily believed they would be faithful.

However, that we might be very secure, I told him he should go back again and choose out five of them, and tell them they might see that he did not want them, that he would take out those five to be his assistants, and that the governor would keep the other two and the three that were sent prisoners to the castle (my cave) as hostages, for the fidelity of those five; and that if they proved unfaithful in the execution, the five hostages should be hanged in chains alive upon the shore.

This looked severe, and convinced them that the governor was in earnest; however, they had no way left them but to accept it; and it was now the business of the prisoners, as much as of the captain, to persuade the other five to do their duty.

Our strength was now thus ordered for the expedition. 1. The captain, his mate, and passenger. 2. Then the two prisoners of the first gang, to whom, having their characters from the captain, I had given their liberty, and trusted them with arms. 3. The other two who I had kept till now in my apartment, pinioned; but upon the captain's motion, had now released. 4. The single man taken in the boat. 5. These five released at last. So that they were thirteen in all, besides five we kept prisoners in the cave, and the two hostages.

I asked the captain if he was willing to venture with these hands on board the ship; for as for me and my man Friday, I did not think it was proper for us to stir, having

seven men left behind, and it was employment enough
for us to keep them asunder, and supply them with
victuals.

As to the five in the cave, I resolved to keep them fast;
but Friday went in twice a day to them, to supply them
with necessaries; and I made the other two carry provisions to a certain distance, where Friday was to take it.

When I showed myself to the two hostages, it was with
the captain, who told them I was the person the governor
had ordered to look after them, and that it was the governor's pleasure they should not stir anywhere but by my
direction; that if they did, they should be fetched into
the castle, and be laid in irons; so that as we never suffered them to see me as governor, so I now appeared as
another person, and spoke of the governor, the garrison,
the castle, and the like, upon all occasions.

The captain now had no difficulty before him, but to
furnish his two boats, stop the breach of one, and man
them. He made his passenger captain of one, with four
other men; and himself and his mate and six more went
in the other. And they contrived their business very well;
for they came up to the ship about midnight. As soon as
they came within call of the ship, he made Robinson hail
them and tell them they had brought off the men and the
boat, but that it was a long time before they had found
them, and the like; holding them in a chat till they came
to the ship's side; when the captain and the mate entering
first with their arms, immediately knocked down the second mate and carpenter with the butt-end of their
muskets. Being very faithfully seconded by their men,
they secured all the rest that were upon the main and
quarter decks and began to fasten the hatches to keep
them down who were below, when the other boat and
their men entering at the fore chains, secured the forecastle of the ship and the scuttle which went down into

the cook room, making three men they found there prisoners.

When this was done, and all safe upon deck, the captain ordered the mate with three men to break into the roundhouse, where the new rebel captain lay, and having taken the alarm, was gotten up, and with two men and a boy had gotten firearms in their hands; and when the mate with a crow split open the door, the new captain and his men fired boldly among them and wounded the mate with a musket ball, which broke his arm and wounded two more of the men, but killed nobody.

The mate, calling for help, rushed however into the roundhouse, wounded as he was, and with his pistol shot the new captain through the head, the bullet entering at his mouth, and came out again behind one of his ears, so that he never spoke a word; upon which the rest yielded, and the ship was taken effectually, without any more lives lost.

As soon as the ship was thus secured, the captain ordered seven guns to be fired, which was the signal agreed upon with me, to give me notice of his success, which you may be sure I was very glad to hear, having sat watching upon the shore for it till near two of the clock in the morning.

Having thus heard the signal plainly, I laid me down; and it having been a day of great fatigue to me, I slept very sound, till I was something surprised with the noise of a gun; and presently starting up, I heard a man call me by the name of "Governor, Governor," and presently I knew the captain's voice; when, climbing up to the top of the hill, there he stood, and pointing to the ship, he embraced me in his arms. "My dear friend and deliverer," says he, "there's your ship, for she is all yours, and so are we and all that belong to her." I cast my eyes to the ship, and there she rode within little more than half a mile of the shore; for they had weighed her anchor as soon as they were masters of her; and the weather being fair, had brought her to an anchor just against the mouth of the little creek; and the tide being up, the captain had brought the pinnace in near the place where I at first landed my rafts, and so landed just at my door.

I was at first ready to sink down with the surprise. For I saw my deliverance indeed visibly put into my hands, all things easy, and a large ship just ready to carry me away whither I pleased to go. At first, for some time, I was not able to answer him one word; but as he had taken me in his arms, I held fast by him or I should have fallen to the ground.

He perceived the surprise, and immediately pulls a bottle out of his pocket, and gave me a dram of cordial, which he had brought on purpose for me; after I had drank it, I sat down upon the ground; and though it brought me to myself, yet it was a good while before I could speak a word to him.

All this while the poor man was in as great an ecstasy as I, only not under any surprise, as I was; and he said a thousand kind tender things to me, to compose me and bring me to myself; but such was the flood of joy in my breast that it put all my spirits into confusion; at last it broke out into tears, and in a little while after I recovered my speech.

Then I took my turn and embraced him as my deliverer, and we rejoiced together. I told him I looked upon him as a man sent from Heaven to deliver me, and that the whole transaction seemed to be a chain of wonders; that such things as these were the testimonies we had of a secret hand of Providence governing the world, and an evidence that the eyes of an infinite Power could search into the remotest corner of the world, and send help to the miserable whenever He pleased.

I forgot not to lift up my heart in thankfulness to Heaven; and what heart could forbear to bless Him, who had not only in a miraculous manner provided for one in such a wilderness and in such a desolate condition, but from whom every deliverance must always be acknowledged to proceed.

When we had talked a while, the captain told me he had brought me some little refreshment, such as the ship afforded, and such as the wretches that had been so long his masters had not plundered him of. Upon this he called aloud to the boat, and bid his men bring the things ashore that were for the governor; and indeed it was a present, as if I had been one, not that was to be carried away along with them, but as if I had been to dwell upon the island still and they were to go without me.

First, he had brought me a case of bottles full of excellent cordial waters, six large bottles of madeira wine (the bottles held two quarts apiece), two pound of excellent good tobacco, twelve good pieces of the ship's beef, and six pieces of pork, with a bag of peas, and about a hundredweight of biscuit.

He brought me also a box of sugar, a box of flour, a bag full of lemons, and two bottles of lime-juice, and abundance of other things. But besides these, and what was a thousand times more useful to me, he brought me six clean new shirts, six very good neckcloths, two pair of gloves, one pair of shoes, a hat, and one pair of stockings, and a very good suit of clothes of his own, which had been worn but very little. In a word, he clothed me from head to foot.

It was a very kind and agreeable present, as anyone may imagine, to one in my circumstances. But never was anything in the world of that kind so unpleasant, awkward, and uneasy as it was to me to wear such clothes at their first putting on.

After these ceremonies passed, and after all his good things were brought into my little apartment, we began to consult what was to be done with the prisoners we had; for it was worth considering whether we might venture to take them away with us or no, especially two of them, who we knew to be incorrigible and refractory to the last degree; and the captain said, he knew they were such rogues that there was no obliging them, and if he did carry them away, it must be in irons, as malefactors, to be delivered over to justice at the first English colony he could come at; and I found that the captain himself was very anxious about it.

Upon this, I told him, that if he desired it, I durst undertake to bring the two men he spoke of to make it their own request that he should leave them upon the island. "I should be very glad of that," says the captain, "with all my heart."

"Well," says I, "I will send for them up, and talk with them for you"; so I caused Friday and the two hostages, for they were now discharged, their comrades having performed their promise; I say, I caused them to go to the cave and bring up the five men, pinioned as they were, to the bower, and keep them there till I came.

After some time I came thither dressed in my new habit, and now I was called governor again; being all met, and the captain with me, I caused the men to be brought before me, and I told them, I had had a full account of their villainous behavior to the captain, and how they had run away with the ship and were preparing to commit farther robberies, but that Providence had ensnared them in their own ways and that they were fallen into the pit which they had digged for others.

I let them know that by my direction the ship had been seized, that she lay now in the road; and they might see by and by that their new captain had received the reward of his villainy; for that they might see him hanging at the yardarm.

That as to them, I wanted to know what they had to say, why I should not execute them as pirates taken in the fact, as by my commission they could not doubt I had authority to do.

One of them answered in the name of the rest that they had nothing to say but this, that when they were taken, the captain promised them their lives, and they humbly implored my mercy. But I told them, I knew not what mercy to show them; for as for myself, I had resolved to quit the island with all my men, and had taken passage with the captain to go for England. And as for the captain, he could not carry them to England other than as prisoners in irons, to be tried for mutiny and running away with the ship; the consequence of which, they must needs know, would be the gallows; so that I could not tell which was best for them, unless they had a mind to take their fate in the island; if they desired that, I did not care, as I had liberty to leave it; I had some inclination to give them their lives, if they thought they could shift on shore.

They seemed very thankful for it, said they would much rather venture to stay there than to be carried to England to be hanged; so I left it on that issue.

However, the captain seemed to make some difficulty of it, as if he durst not leave them there. Upon this I seemed a little angry with the captain, and told him that they were my prisoners, not his; and that seeing I had offered them so much favor, I would be as good as my word; and that if he did not think fit to consent to it, I would set them at liberty, as I found them; and if he did not like it, he might take them again if he could catch them.

Upon this they appeared very thankful, and I accordingly set them at liberty, and bade them retire into the woods to the place whence they came, and I would leave them some firearms, some ammunition, and some directions how they should live very well, if they thought fit.

Upon this I prepared to go on board the ship, but told the captain that I would stay that night to prepare my things, and desired him to go on board in the meantime, and keep all right in the ship, and send the boat on shore the next day for me; ordering him in the meantime to cause the new captain who was killed to be hanged at the yardarm, that these men might see him.

When the captain was gone, I sent for the men up to me to my apartment and entered seriously into discourse with them of their circumstances. I told them I thought they had made a right choice; that if the captain carried them away, they would certainly be hanged. I showed them the new captain hanging at the yardarm of the ship, and told them they had nothing less to expect.

When they had all declared their willingness to stay, I then told them I would let them into the story of my living there, and put them into the way of making it easy to them. Accordingly I gave them the whole history of the place and of my coming to it; showed them my fortifications, the way I made my bread, planted my corn, cured my grapes; and in a word, all that was necessary to make them easy. I told them the story also of the sixteen Spaniards that were to be expected; for whom I left a letter, and made them promise to treat them in common with themselves.

I left them my firearms, viz., five muskets, three fowling pieces, and three swords. I had above a barrel and half of powder left; for after the first year or two I used but little, and wasted none. I gave them a description of the way I managed the goats, and directions to milk and fatten them, and to make both butter and cheese.

In a word, I gave them every part of my own story; and I told them I would prevail with the captain to leave them two barrels of gunpowder more and some garden seeds, which I told them I would have been very glad of; also I gave them the bag of peas which the captain had brought me to eat, and bade them be sure to sow and increase them.

Having done all this, I left them the next day and went on board the ship. We prepared immediately to sail, but did not weigh that night. The next morning early, two of the five men came swimming to the ship's side, and making a most lamentable complaint of the other three, begged to be taken into the ship, for God's sake, for they should be murdered and begged the captain to take them on board, though he hanged them immediately.

Upon this the captain pretended to have no power without me; but after some difficulty, and after their solemn promises of amendment, they were taken on board, and were some time after soundly whipped and pickled; after which, they proved very honest and quiet fellows.

Some time after this, the boat was ordered on shore, the tide being up, with the things promised to the men, to which the captain, at my intercession, caused their chests and clothes to be added, which they took and were very thankful for; I also encouraged them by telling them that if it lay in my way to send any vessel to take them in, I would not forget them.

When I took leave of this island, I carried on board for relics, the great goatskin cap I had made, my umbrella, and my parrot; also I forgot not to take the money I formerly mentioned, which had lain by me so long useless that it was grown rusty, or tarnished, and could hardly pass for silver, till it had been a little rubbed and handled; as also the money I found in the wreck of the Spanish ship.

And thus I left the island, the 19th of December, as I found by the ship's account, in the year 1686, after I had been upon it eight-and-twenty years, two months, and nineteen days; being delivered from this second captivity the same day of the month that I first made my escape in the *barco-longo*, from among the Moors of Sallee.

In this vessel, after a long voyage, I arrived in England, the 11th of June, in the year 1687, having been thirty-and-five years absent.

Settling in the World

WHEN I came to England, I was as perfect a stranger to all the world as if I had never been known there. My benefactor and faithful steward, who I had left in trust with my money, was alive; but had had great misfortunes in the world; was become a widow the second time, and very low in the world. I made her easy as to what she owed me, assuring her I would give her no trouble; but on the contrary, in gratitude to her former care and faithfulness to me, I relieved her as my little stock would afford, which, at that time, would indeed allow me to do but little for her; but I assured her, I would never forget her former kindness to me nor did I forget her, when I had sufficient to help her, as shall be observed in its place.

I went down afterwards into Yorkshire; but my father was dead, and my mother and all the family extinct, except that I found two sisters, and two of the children of one of my brothers; and as I had been long ago given over for dead, there had been no provision made for me; so that in a word, I found nothing to relieve or assist me; and that little money I had would not do much for me as to settling in the world.

I met with one piece of gratitude indeed, which I did

not expect; and this was that the master of the ship, whom I had so happily delivered, and by the same means saved the ship and cargo, having given a very handsome account to the owners of the manner how I had saved the lives of the men and the ship, they invited me to meet them, and some other merchants concerned, and all together made me a very handsome compliment upon the subject, and a present of almost two hundred pounds sterling.

But after making several reflections upon the circumstances of my life, and how little way this would go toward settling me in the world, I resolved to go to Lisbon and see if I might not come by some information of the state of my plantation in the Brazils, and of what was become of my partner, who I had reason to suppose had some years now given me over for dead.

With this view I took shipping for Lisbon, where I arrived in April following; my man Friday accompanying me very honestly in all these ramblings and proving a most faithful servant upon all occasions.

When I came to Lisbon, I found out by inquiry, and to my particular satisfaction, my old friend the captain of the ship, who first took me up at sea off of the shore of Africa. He was now grown old and had left off the sea, having put his son, who was far from a young man, into his ship; and who still used the Brazil trade. The old man did not know me, and, indeed, I hardly knew him; but I soon brought him to my remembrance, and as soon brought myself to his remembrance, when I told him who I was.

After some passionate expressions of the old acquaintance, I inquired, you may be sure, after my plantation and my partner. The old man told me he had not been in the Brazils for about nine years; but that he could assure me that when he came away my partner was living, but

the trustees, who I had joined with him to take cogni-
zance of my part, were both dead; that however, he believed that I would have a very good account of the
improvement of the plantation; for that, upon the general
belief of my being cast away and drowned, my trustees
had given in the account of the produce of my part of the
plantation to the procurator fiscal, who had appropriated
it, in case I never came to claim it, one third to the king,
and two thirds to the monastery of St. Augustine, to be
expended for the benefit of the poor and for the conver-
sion of the Indians to the Catholic faith; but that if I
appeared, or anyone for me, to claim the inheritance, it
should be restored; only that the improvement, or annual
production, being distributed to charitable uses, could
not be restored; but he assured me that the steward of
the king's revenue (from lands) and the *proviedore*, or
steward of the monastery, had taken great care all along
that the incumbent, that is to say, my partner, gave every
year a faithful account of the produce, of which they received duly my moiety.

I asked him if he knew to what height of improvement
he had brought the plantation, and whether he thought
it might be worth looking after; or whether, on my going
thither, I should meet with no obstruction to my possess-
ing my just right in the moiety.

He told me, he could not tell exactly to what degree
the plantation was improved; but this he knew, that my
partner was growing exceeding rich upon the enjoying
but one half of it; and that to the best of his remembrance, he had heard that the king's third of my part,
which was, it seems, granted away to some other monastery, or religious house, amounted to above two hundred moidores a year; that as to my being restored to a
quiet possession of it, there was no question to be made

of that, my partner being alive to witness my title, and my name being also enrolled in the register of the country; also he told me that the survivors of my two trustees were very fair, honest people, and very wealthy; and he believed I would not only have their assistance for putting me in possession but would find a very considerable sum of money in their hands for my account, being the produce of the farm while their fathers held the trust, and before it was given up as above, which, as he remembered, was for about twelve years.

I showed myself a little concerned and uneasy at this account and inquired of the old captain how it came to pass that the trustees should thus dispose my effects, when he knew that I had made my will and had made him, the Portuguese captain, my universal heir, etc.

He told me that was true; but that as there was no proof of my being dead, he could not act as executor until some certain account should come of my death; and that besides, he was not willing to intermeddle with a thing so remote; that it was true he had registered my will and put in his claim; and could he have given any account of my being dead or alive, he would have acted by procuration, and taken possession of the *ingenio,* so they called the sugar-house, and had given his son, who was now at the Brazils, order to do it.

"But," says the old man, "I have one piece of news to tell you, which perhaps may not be so acceptable to you as the rest, and that is, that believing you were lost, and all the world believing so also, your partner and trustees did offer to account to me, in your name, for six or eight of the first years of profits, which I received; but there being at the time," says he, "great disbursements for increasing the works, building an *ingenio,* and buying slaves, it did not amount to near so much as afterwards it produced. However," says the old man, "I shall give you a true account of what I have received in all, and how I have disposed of it."

After a few days' farther conference with this ancient friend, he brought me an account of the six first years' income of my plantation, signed by my partner and the merchant trustees, being always delivered in goods, viz., tobacco in roll, and sugar in chests, besides rum, molasses, etc., which is the consequence of a sugar work; and I found by this account, that every year the income considerably increased; but as above, the disbursement being large, the sum at first was small. However, the old man let me see, that he was debtor to me 470 moidores of gold, besides sixty chests of sugar, and fifteen double rolls of tobacco, which were lost in his ship; he having been shipwrecked coming home to Lisbon, about eleven years after my leaving the place.

The good man then began to complain of his misfortunes, and how he had been obliged to make use of my money to recover his losses, and buy him a share in a new ship. "However, my old friend," says he, "you shall not want a supply in your necessity; and as soon as my son returns, you shall be fully satisfied."

Upon this, he pulls out an old pouch, and gives me 160 Portugal moidores in gold; and giving me the writing of his title to the ship, which his son was gone to the Brazils in, of which he was a quarter part owner, and his son another, he puts them both into my hands for security of the rest.

I was too much moved with the honesty and kindness of the poor man to be able to bear this; and remembering what he had done for me, how he had taken me up at sea, and how generously he had used me on all occasions, and particularly how sincere a friend he was now to me, I could hardly refrain weeping at what he said to me.

Therefore, first I asked him, if his circumstances admitted him to spare so much money at that time, and if it would not straiten him. He told me he could not say but it might straiten him a little; but however, it was my money, and I might want it more than he.

Everything the good man said was full of affection, and I could hardly refrain from tears while he spoke. In short, I took 100 of the moidores and called for a pen and ink to give him a receipt for them; then I returned him the rest, and told him if ever I had possession of the plantation, I would return the other to him also, as indeed I afterwards did; and that as to the bill of sale of his part in his son's ship, I would not take it by any means; but that if I wanted the money, I found he was honest enough to pay me; and if I did not, but came to receive what he gave me reason to expect, I would never have a penny more from him.

When this was passed, the old man began to ask me if he should put me into a method to make my claim to my plantation. I told him I thought to go over to it myself. He said I might do so if I pleased; but that if I did not, there were ways enough to secure my right, and immediately to appropriate the profits to my use; and as there were ships in the river of Lisbon just ready to go away to Brazil, he made me enter my name in a public register, with his affidavit, affirming upon oath that I was alive, and that I was the same person who took up the land for the planting the said plantation at first.

This being regularly attested by a notary, and a procuration affixed, he directed me to send it, with a letter of his writing, to a merchant of his acquaintance at the place, and then proposed my staying with him till an account came of the return.

Never anything was more honorable than the proceedings upon this procuration; for in less than seven months

I received a large packet from the survivors of my trustees, the merchants, for whose account I went to sea, in
which were the following particular letters and papers
enclosed.

First, there was the account current of the produce of
my farm, or plantation, from the year when their fathers
had balanced with my old Portugal captain, being for
six years; the balance appeared to be 1174 moidores in
my favor.

Secondly, there was the account of four years more,
while they kept the effects in their hands, before the
government claimed the administration, as being the effects of a person not to be found, which they called civil
death; and the balance of this, the value of the plantation increasing, amounted to [38,892] crusadoes, which
made 3241 moidores.

Thirdly, there was the Prior of the Augustines' account,
who had received the profits for above fourteen years;
but not being to account for what was disposed to the
hospital, very honestly declared he had 872 moidores not
distributed, which he acknowledged to my account; as
to the king's part, that refunded nothing.

There was a letter of my partner's, congratulating me
very affectionately upon my being alive, giving me an
account how the estate was improved, and what it produced a year, with a particular of the number of squares
or acres that it contained; how planted, how many slaves
there were upon it, and making two-and-twenty crosses
for blessings, told me he had said so many *Ave Marias* to
thank the Blessed Virgin that I was alive; inviting me
very passionately to come over and take possession of my
own; and in the meantime to give him orders to whom
he should deliver my effects, if I did not come myself;
concluding with a hearty tender of his friendship, and
that of his family; and sent me, as a present, seven fine

leopards' skins, which he had it seems received from Africa, by some other ship which he had sent thither, and who it seems had made a better voyage than I. He sent me also five chests of excellent sweetmeats, and an hundred pieces of gold uncoined, not quite so large as moidores.

By the same fleet, my two merchant trustees shipped me 1200 chests of sugar, 800 rolls of tobacco, and the rest of the whole account in gold.

I might well say now indeed that the latter end of Job was better than the beginning. It is impossible to express here the flutterings of my very heart when I looked over these letters, and especially when I found all my wealth about me; for as the Brazil ships come all in fleets, the same ships which brought my letters brought my goods; and the effects were safe in the river before the letters came to my hand. In a word, I turned pale, and grew sick; and had not the old man run and fetched me a cordial, I believe the sudden surprise of joy had overset Nature, and I had died upon the spot.

Nay after that, I continued very ill, and was so some hours, till a physician being sent for, and something of the real cause of my illness being known, he ordered me to be let blood; after which I had relief and grew well. But I verily believe, if it had not been eased by a vent given in that manner to the spirits, I should have died.

I was now master, all on a sudden, of above £5000 sterling in money, and had an estate, as I might well call it, in the Brazils, of above a thousand pounds a year, as sure as an estate of lands in England. And in a word, I was in a condition which I scarce knew how to understand, or how to compose myself for the enjoyment of it.

The first thing I did was to recompense my original benefactor, my good old captain, who had been first charitable to me in my distress, kind to me in my beginning, and honest to me at the end. I showed him all that was sent me; I told him that next to the Providence of Heaven, which disposes all things, it was owing to him; and that it now lay on me to reward him, which I would do a hundredfold. So I first returned to him the hundred moidores I had received of him; then I sent for a notary, and caused him to draw up a general release or discharge for the 470 moidores, which he had acknowledged he owed me, in the fullest and firmest manner possible; after which, I caused a procuration to be drawn, empowering him to be my receiver of the annual profits of my plantation, and appointing my partner to account to him and make the return by the usual fleets to him in my name; and a clause in the end, being a grant of one hundred moidores a year to him, during his life, out of the effects, and fifty moidores a year to his son after him, for his life. And thus I requited my old man.

I was now to consider which way to steer my course next, and what to do with the estate that Providence had thus put into my hands; and indeed I had more care upon my head now, than I had in my silent state of life in the island, where I wanted nothing but what I had, and had nothing but what I wanted; whereas I had now a great charge upon me, and my business was how to secure it. I had ne'er a cave now to hide my money in, or a place where it might lie without lock or key, till it grew moldy and tarnished before anybody would meddle with it. On the contrary, I knew not where to put it, or whom to trust with it. My old patron, the captain, indeed was honest, and that was the only refuge I had.

In the next place, my interest in the Brazils seemed to summon me thither, but now I could not tell how to think of going thither till I had settled my affairs and left my effects in some safe hands behind me. At first I thought of my old friend the widow, who I knew was honest, and would be just to me; but then she was in years, and but poor, and for aught I knew, might be in debt; so that in a word, I had no way but to go back to England myself, and take my effects with me.

It was some months, however, before I resolved upon this; and therefore, as I had rewarded the old captain fully, and to his satisfaction, who had been my former benefactor, so I began to think of my poor widow, whose husband had been my first benefactor, and she, while it was in her power, my faithful steward and instructor. So the first thing I did, I got a merchant in Lisbon to write to his correspondent in London, not only to pay a bill, but to go find her out and carry her in money a hundred pounds from me and to talk with her and comfort her in her poverty, by telling her she should, if I lived, have a further supply. At the same time I sent my two sisters in the country each of them a hundred pounds, they being, though not in want, yet not in very good circumstances; one having been married and left a widow; and the other having a husband not so kind to her as he should be.

But among all my relations, or acquaintances, I could not yet pitch upon one to whom I durst commit the gross of my stock, that I might go away to the Brazils and leave things safe behind me; and this greatly perplexed me.

I had once a mind to have gone to the Brazils, and have settled myself there, for I was, as it were, naturalized to the place; but I had some little scruple in my mind about religion, which insensibly drew me back, of which I shall say more presently. However, it was not religion that kept me from going there for the present; and as I had made no scruple of being openly of the religion of the country, all the while I was among them, so neither did I yet; only that now and then having of late thought more of it than formerly, when I began to think of living and dying among them, I began to regret my having professed myself a Papist, and thought it might not be the best religion to die with.

But, as I have said, this was not the main thing that kept me from going to the Brazils, but that really I did not know with whom to leave my effects behind me; so I resolved at last to go to England with it, where, if I arrived, I concluded I should make some acquaintance, or find some relations that would be faithful to me; and accordingly I prepared to go for England with all my wealth.

In order to prepare things for my going home, I first, the Brazil fleet being just going away, resolved to give answers suitable to the just and faithful account of things I had from thence; and first, to the Prior of St. Augustine I wrote a letter full of thanks for their just dealings, and the offer of the 872 moidores which was indisposed of, which I desired might be given, 500 to the monastery, and 372 to the poor, as the Prior should direct, desiring the good padre's prayers for me, and the like.

I wrote next a letter of thanks to my two trustees, with all the acknowledgment that so much justice and honesty called for; as for sending them any present, they were far above having any occasion of it.

Lastly, I wrote to my partner, acknowledging his industry in the improving the plantation and his integrity in increasing the stock of the works, giving him instructions for his future government of my part, according to the powers I had left with my old patron, to whom I desired him to send whatever became due to me, till he should hear from me more particularly; assuring him that it was my intention not only to come to him, but to settle myself there for the remainder of my life. To this I added a very handsome present of some Italian silks for his wife and two daughters, for such the captain's son informed me he had; with two pieces of fine English broadcloth, the best I could get in Lisbon, five pieces of black baize, and some Flanders lace of a good value.

Over the Mountains

HAVING thus settled my affairs, sold my cargo, and turned all my effects into good bills of exchange, my next difficulty was, which way to go to England. I had been accustomed enough to the sea, and yet I had a strange aversion to going to England by sea at that time; and though I could give no reason for it, yet the difficulty increased upon me so much, that though I had once shipped my baggage, in order to go, yet I altered my mind, and that not once but two or three times.

It is true I had been very unfortunate by sea, and this might be some of the reason. But let no man slight the strong impulses of his own thoughts in cases of such moment. Two of the ships which I had singled out to go in, I mean more particularly singled out than any other, that is to say, so as in one of them to put my things on board and in the other to have agreed with the captain; I say, two of these ships miscarried, viz., one was taken by the Algerines, and the other was cast away on the Start, near Torbay, and all the people drowned except three; so that in either of those vessels I had been made miserable; and in which most, it was hard to say.

Having been thus harassed in my thoughts, my old pilot, to whom I communicated everything, pressed me earnestly not to go by sea, but either to go by land to the Groyne, and cross over the Bay of Biscay to Rochelle, from whence it was but an easy and safe journey by land to Paris, and so to Calais and Dover; or to go up to Madrid, and so all the way by land through France.

In a word, I was so prepossessed against my going by

sea at all, except from Calais to Dover, that I resolved to
travel all the way by land; which, as I was not in haste,
and did not value the charge, was by much the pleasanter
way; and to make it more so, my old captain brought an
English gentleman, the son of a merchant in Lisbon, who
was willing to travel with me. After which, we picked up
two more English merchants also, and two young Portuguese gentlemen, the last going to Paris only; so that we
were in all six of us, and five servants; the two merchants
and the two Portuguese contenting themselves with one
servant between two, to save the charge; and as for me,
I got an English sailor to travel with me as a servant, besides my man Friday, who was too much a stranger to be
capable of supplying the place of a servant on the road.

In this manner I set out from Lisbon; and our company
being all very well mounted and armed, we made a little
troop, whereof they did me the honor to call me captain,
as well because I was the oldest man as because I had two
servants, and indeed was the original of the whole journey.

As I have troubled you with none of my sea journals,
so I shall trouble you now with none of my land journal;
but some adventures that happened to us in this tedious
and difficult journey I must not omit.

When we came to Madrid, we, being all of us strangers
to Spain, were willing to stay some time to see the court
of Spain, and to see what was worth observing; but it
being the latter part of the summer, we hastened away,
and set out from Madrid about the middle of October.
But when we came to the edge of Navarre, we were
alarmed at several towns on the way with an account that
so much snow was fallen on the French side of the mountains, that several travelers were obliged to come back to
Pampeluna, after having attempted, at an extreme hazard,
to pass on.

When we came to Pampeluna itself, we found it so indeed; and to me that had been always used to a hot climate, and indeed to countries where we could scarce bear any clothes on, the cold was insufferable; nor indeed was it more painful than it was surprising to come but ten days before out of the Old Castile, where the weather was not only warm, but very hot, and immediately to feel a wind from the Pyrenean mountains so very keen, so severely cold as to be intolerable and to endanger benumbing and perishing of our fingers and toes.

Poor Friday was really frighted when he saw the mountains all covered with snow, and felt cold weather, which he had never seen or felt before in his life.

To mend the matter, when we came to Pampeluna, it continued snowing with so much violence and so long that the people said winter was come before its time; and the roads which were difficult before were now quite impassable. For, in a word, the snow lay in some places too thick for us to travel; and being not hard frozen, as is the case in northern countries, there was no going without being in danger of being buried alive every step. We stayed no less than twenty days at Pampeluna; when seeing the winter coming on, and no likelihood of its being better, for it was the severest winter all over Europe that had been known in the memory of man, I proposed that we should all go away to Fontarabia, and there take shipping for Bordeaux, which was a very little voyage.

But while we were considering this, there came in four French gentlemen, who, having been stopped on the French side of the passes, as we were on the Spanish, had found out a guide, who, traversing the country near the head of Languedoc, had brought them over the mountains by such ways that they were not much incommoded with the snow; and where they met with snow in any quantity, they said it was frozen hard enough to bear them and their horses.

We sent for this guide, who told us he would undertake

to carry us the same way with no hazard from the snow, provided we were armed sufficiently to protect us from wild beasts; for, he said, upon these great snows it was frequent for some wolves to show themselves at the foot of the mountains, being made ravenous for want of food, the ground being covered with snow. We told him we were well enough prepared for such creatures as they were, if he would ensure us from a kind of two-legged wolves, which we were told, we were in most danger from, especially on the French side of the mountains.

He satisfied us there was no danger of that kind in the way that we were to go; so we readily agreed to follow him, as did also twelve other gentlemen, with their servants, some French, some Spanish, who, as I said, had attempted to go, and were obliged to come back again.

Accordingly, we all set out from Pampeluna, with our guide, on the 15th of November; and indeed, I was surprised, when instead of going forward, he came directly back with us, on the same road that we came from Madrid, above twenty miles; when being passed two rivers and come into the plain country, we found ourselves in a warm climate again, where the country was pleasant, and no snow to be seen; but on a sudden, turning to his left, he approached the mountains another way; and though it is true the hills and precipices looked dreadful, yet he made so many tours, such meanders, and led us by such winding ways, that we were insensibly passed the height of the mountains without being much encumbered with the snow; and all on a sudden, he showed us the pleasant fruitful provinces of Languedoc and Gascoigne, all green and flourishing, though indeed it was at a great distance, and we had some rough way to pass yet.

We were a little uneasy however, when we found it snowed one whole day and a night so fast that we could not travel; but he bid us be easy, we should soon be past it all. We found indeed that we began to descend every day, and to come more north than before; and so depending upon our guide, we went on.

It was about two hours before night, when our guide being something before us, and not just in sight, out rushed three monstrous wolves, and after them a bear, out of a hollow way, adjoining to a thick wood; two of the wolves flew upon the guide, and had he been half a mile before us, he had been devoured indeed before we would have helped him. One of them fastened upon his horse, and the other attacked the man with that violence that he had not time, or not presence of mind enough to draw his pistol, but hallooed and cried out to us most lustily; my man Friday being next to me, I bid him ride up and see what was the matter; as soon as Friday came in sight of the man, he hallooed as loud as t'other, "O master! O master!" but like a bold fellow, rode directly up to the poor man and with his pistol shot the wolf that attacked him into the head.

It was happy for the poor man that it was my man Friday; for he having been used to that kind of creature in his country, had no fear upon him, but went close up to him and shot him, as above; whereas any of us would have fired at a farther distance, and have perhaps either missed the wolf, or endangered shooting the man.

But it was enough to have terrified a bolder man than I; and indeed it alarmed all our company, when, with the noise of Friday's pistol, we heard on both sides the dismalest howling of wolves, and the noise redoubled by the echo of the mountains, that it was to us as if there had been a prodigious multitude of them; and perhaps indeed there was such a few as that we had no cause of apprehensions.

However, as Friday had killed this wolf, the other that had fastened upon the horse left him immediately and fled; having happily fastened upon his head, where the bosses of the bridle had stuck in his teeth; so that he had not done him much hurt. The man indeed was most hurt; for the raging creature had bit him twice, once on the arm, and the other time a little above his knee; and he was just as it were tumbling down by the disorder of his horse, when Friday came up and shot the wolf.

It is easy to suppose that at the noise of Friday's pistol we all mended our pace and rid up as fast as the way (which was very difficult) would give us leave, to see what was the matter; as soon as we came clear of the trees, which blinded us before, we saw clearly what had been the case, and how Friday had disengaged the poor guide; though we did not presently discern what kind of creature it was he had killed.

But never was a fight managed so hardily, and in such a surprising manner, as that which followed between Friday and the bear, which gave us all (though at first we were surprised and afraid for him) the greatest diversion imaginable. As the bear is a heavy, clumsy creature, and does not gallop as the wolf does, who is swift and light, so he has two particular qualities, which generally are the rule of his actions; first, as to men, who are not his proper prey; I say, not his proper prey, because though I cannot say what excessive hunger might do, which was now their case, the ground being all covered with snow; but as to men, he does not usually attempt them, unless they first attack him. On the contrary, if you meet him in the woods, if you don't meddle with him, he won't meddle with you; but then you must take care to be very civil to him, and give him the road; for he is a very nice gentle man, he won't go a step out of his way for a prince; nay, if you are really afraid, your best way is to look another way and keep going on; for sometimes if you stop, and stand still, and look steadily at him, he takes it for an affront; but if you throw or toss anything at him, and it hits him, though it were but a bit of a stick as big as your finger, he takes it for an affront and sets all his other business aside to pursue his revenge; for he will have satisfaction in point of honor; that is his first quality. The next is, that if he be once affronted, he will never leave you, night or day, till he has his revenge; but follows at a good round rate till he overtakes you.

My man Friday had delivered our guide, and when we came up to him, he was helping him off from his horse; for the man was both hurt and frighted, and indeed, the last more than the first; when on the sudden, we spied the bear come out of the wood, and a vast monstrous one it was, the biggest by far that ever I saw. We were all a little surprised, when we saw him; but when Friday saw him, it was easy to see joy and courage in the fellow's countenance. "O! O! O!" says Friday, three times, pointing to him; "O master! You give me te leave! Me shakee te hand with him. Me make you good laugh."

I was surprised to see the fellow so pleased. "You fool you," says I, "he will eat you up." "Eatee me up! Eatee me up!" says Friday, twice over again; "me eatee him up. Me make you good laugh. You all stay here, me show you good laugh!" So down he sits, and gets his boots off in a moment, and put on a pair of pumps (as we call the flat shoes they wear) and which he had in his pocket, gives my other servant his horse, and with his gun away he flew, swift like the wind.

The bear was walking softly on, and offered to meddle with nobody till Friday coming pretty near, calls to him, as if the bear could understand him. "Hark ye, hark ye," says Friday, "me speakee wit you." We followed at a distance; for now being come down on the Gascoigne side

of the mountains, we were entered a vast great forest,
where the country was plain and pretty open, though
many trees in it scattered here and there.

Friday, who had, as we say, the heels of the bear, came
up with him quickly and takes up a great stone, and
throws at him, and hit him just on the head, but did him
no more harm than if he had thrown it against a wall; but
it answered Friday's end, for the rogue was so void of
fear, that he did it purely to make the bear follow him
and show us "some laugh," as he called it.

As soon as the bear felt the stone, and saw him, he turns
about, and comes after him, taking devilish long strides,
and shuffling along at a strange rate, so as would have put
a horse to a middling gallop; away runs Friday, and takes
his course, as if he run toward us for help; so we all resolved to fire at once upon the bear, and deliver my man;
though I was angry at him heartily for bringing the bear
back upon us, when he was going about his own business another way; and especially I was angry that he had
turned the bear upon us, and then run away; and I called
out, "You dog," said I, "is this your making us laugh?
Come away, and take your horse, that we may shoot the
creature." He hears me, and cries out, "No shoot, no
shoot; stand still, you get much laugh." And as the nimble
creature run two foot for the beast's one, he turned on a
sudden, on one side of us, and seeing a great oak tree fit
for his purpose, he beckoned to us to follow; and doubling his pace, he gets nimbly up the tree, laying his gun
down upon the ground, at about five or six yards from the
bottom of the tree.

The bear soon came to the tree, and we followed at a
distance; the first thing he did, he stopped at the gun,
smelt to it, but let it lie, and up he scrambles into the tree,
climbing like a cat, though so monstrously heavy. I was
amazed at the folly, as I thought it, of my man and could

not for my life see anything to laugh at yet, till seeing the bear get up the tree, we all rode nearer to him.

When we came to the tree, there was Friday got out to the small end of a large limb of the tree, and the bear got about half way to him; as soon as the bear got out to that part where the limb of the tree was weaker, "Ha!" says he to us, "now you see me teachee the bear dance"; so he falls a-jumping and shaking the bough, at which the bear began to totter, but stood still and begun to look behind him, to see how he should get back; then, indeed, we did laugh heartily. But Friday had not done with him by a great deal; when he sees him stand still, he calls out to him again, as if he had supposed the bear could speak English, "What, you no come farther? pray you come farther"; so he left jumping and shaking the tree; and the bear, just as if he had understood what he said, did come a little further; then he fell a-jumping again, and the bear stopped again.

We thought now was a good time to knock him on the head, and I called to Friday to stand still, and we would shoot the bear; but he cried out earnestly, "O pray! O pray! No shoot, me shoot, by and then"; he would have said "by and by." However, to shorten the story, Friday danced so much, and the bear stood so ticklish, that we had laughing enough indeed, but still could not imagine what the fellow would do; for first we thought he depended upon shaking the bear off; and we found the bear was too cunning for that too; for he would not go out far enough to be thrown down, but clings fast with his great broad claws and feet, so that we could not imagine what would be the end of it and where the jest would be at last.

But Friday put us out of doubt quickly; for seeing the bear cling fast to the bough, and that he would not be persuaded to come any farther, "Well, well," says Friday, "you no come farther, me go, me go; you no come to me, me go come to you"; and upon this, he goes out to the smallest end of the bough, where it would bend with his weight, and gently lets himself down by it, sliding down the bough, till he came near enough to jump down on his feet, and away he run to his gun, takes it up, and stands still.

"Well," said I to him, "Friday, what will you do now? Why don't you shoot him?" "No shoot," says Friday, "no yet; me shoot now, me no kill; me stay, give you one more laugh"; and indeed so he did, as you will see presently; for when the bear see his enemy gone, he comes back from the bough where he stood, but did it mighty leisurely, looking behind him every step and coming backward till he got into the body of the tree; then with the same hinder end foremost, he came down the tree, grasping it with his claws, and moving one foot at a time, very leisurely; at this juncture, and just before he could set his hind feet upon the ground, Friday stepped up close to him, clapped the muzzle of his piece into his ear, and shot him dead as a stone.

Then the rogue turned about to see if we did not laugh; and when he saw we were pleased by our looks, he falls a-laughing himself very loud. "So we kill bear in my country," says Friday. "So you kill them?" says I; "why, you have no guns." "No," says he, "no gun, but shoot, great much long arrow."

This was indeed a good diversion to us; but we were still in a wild place, and our guide very much hurt, and what to do we hardly knew; the howling of wolves run much in my head; and indeed, except the noise I once heard on the shore of Africa, of which I have said something already, I never heard anything that filled me with so much horror.

These things and the approach of night called us off,

or else, as Friday would have had us, we should certainly
have taken the skin of this monstrous creature off, which
was worth saving; but we had three leagues to go, and
our guide hastened us; so we left him and went forward
on our journey.

The ground was still covered with snow, though not so
deep and dangerous as on the mountains; and the ravenous creatures, as we heard afterwards, were come down
into the forest and plain country, pressed by hunger to
seek for food; and had done a great deal of mischief in
the villages, where they surprised the country people,
killed a great many of their sheep and horses, and some
people too.

We had one dangerous place to pass, which our guide
told us, if there were any more wolves in the country, we
should find them there; and this was in a small plain, surrounded with woods on every side, and a long narrow
defile or lane, which we were to pass to get through the
wood, and then we should come to the village where we
were to lodge.

It was within half an hour of sunset when we entered
the first wood; and a little after sunset when we came
into the plain. We met with nothing in the first wood,
except that in a little plain within the wood, which was
not above two furlongs over, we saw five great wolves
cross the road, full speed one after another, as if they had
been in chase of some prey, and had it in view; they took
no notice of us, and were gone and out of our sight in a
few moments.

Upon this our guide, who, by the way, was a wretched
faint-hearted fellow, bid us keep in a ready posture; for
he believed there were more wolves a-coming.

We kept our arms ready, and our eyes about us, but
we saw no more wolves, till we came through that wood
which was near half a league, and entered the plain; as

soon as we came into the plain, we had occasion enough
to look about us. The first object we met with was a dead
horse; that is to say, a poor horse which the wolves had
killed, and at least a dozen of them at work; we could
not say eating of him, but picking of his bones rather; for
they had eaten up all the flesh before.

We did not think fit to disturb them at their feast,
neither did they take much notice of us. Friday would
have let fly at them, but I would not suffer him by any
means; for I found we were like to have more business
upon our hands than we were aware of. We were not
gone half over the plain, but we began to hear the wolves
howl in the wood on our left in a frightful manner, and
presently after, we saw about a hundred coming on directly toward us, all in a body, and most of them in a
line, as regularly as an army drawn up by experienced
officers. I scarce knew in what manner to receive them;
but found to draw ourselves in a close line was the only
way. So we formed in a moment. But that we might not
have too much interval, I ordered that only every other
man should fire, and that the others who had not fired
should stand ready to give them a second volley immediately, if they continued to advance upon us, and that then
those who had fired at first should not pretend to load
their fusees again, but stand ready with every one a
pistol; for we were all armed with a fusee and a pair of
pistols each man; so we were by this method able to fire
six volleys, half of us at a time; however, at present we
had no necessity; for upon firing the first volley, the enemy made a full stop, being terrified as well with the
noise as with the fire; four of them being shot into the
head, dropped, several others were wounded, and went
bleeding off, as we could see by the snow. I found they
stopped, but did not immediately retreat; whereupon, remembering that I had been told that the fiercest creatures

were terrified at the voice of a man, I caused all our company to halloo as loud as we could; and I found the notion not altogether mistaken, for upon our shout they began to retire and turn about; then I ordered a second volley to be fired in their rear, which put them to the gallop, and away they went to the woods.

This gave us leisure to charge our pieces again, and that we might lose no time, we kept going; but we had but little more than loaded our fusees, and put ourselves into a readiness, when we heard a terrible noise in the same wood on our left, only that it was farther onward the same way we were to go.

The night was coming on, and the light began to be dusky, which made it worse on our side; but the noise increasing, we could easily perceive that it was the howling and yelling of those hellish creatures; and on a sudden, we perceived two or three troops of wolves, one on our left, one behind us, and one on our front, so that we seemed to be surrounded with 'em; however, as they did not fall upon us, we kept our way forward, as fast as we could make our horses go, which, the way being very rough, was only a good large trot; and in this manner we came in view of the entrance of a wood, through which we were to pass, at the farther side of the plain; but we were greatly surprised when coming nearer the lane, or pass, we saw a confused number of wolves standing just at the entrance.

On a sudden, at another opening of the wood, we heard the noise of a gun; and looking that way, out rushed a horse, with a saddle and a bridle on him, flying like the wind, and sixteen or seventeen wolves after him, full speed; indeed, the horse had the heels of them; but as we supposed that he could not hold it at that rate, we doubted not but they would get up with him at last, and no question but they did.

But here we had a most horrible sight; for riding up to the entrance where the horse came out, we found the carcass of another horse, and of two men, devoured by the ravenous creatures, and one of the men was no doubt the same who we heard fire the gun; for there lay a gun just by him, fired off; but as to the man, his head and the upper part of his body was eaten up.

This filled us with horror and we knew not what course to take, but the creatures resolved us soon; for they gathered about us presently in hopes of prey; and I verily believe there were three hundred of them. It happened very much to our advantage, that at the entrance into the wood, but a little way from it, there lay some large timber trees, which had been cut down the summer before, and I suppose lay there for carriage; I drew my little troop in among those trees, and placing ourselves in a line, behind one long tree, I advised them all to light, and keeping that tree before us, for a breastwork, to stand in a triangle, or three fronts, enclosing our horses in the center.

We did so, and it was well we did; for never was a more furious charge than the creatures made upon us in the place; they came on us with a growling kind of a noise, and mounted the piece of timber, which, as I said, was our breastwork, as if they were only rushing upon their prey; and this fury of theirs, it seems, was principally occasioned by their seeing our horses behind us, which was the prey they aimed it. I ordered our men to fire as before, every other man; and they took their aim so sure, that indeed they killed several of the wolves at the first volley; but there was a necessity to keep a continual firing; for they came on like devils, those behind pushing on those before.

When we had fired our second volley of our fusees, we thought they stopped a little, and I hoped they would have gone off, but it was but a moment, for others came

forward again; so we fired two volleys of our pistols, and
I believe in these four firings we had killed seventeen or
eighteen of them, and lamed twice as many; yet they
came on again.

I was loath to spend our last shot too hastily; so I called
my servant, not my man Friday, for he was better employed; for with the greatest dexterity imaginable, he had
charged my fusee and his own, while we were engaged;
but as I said, I called my other man, and giving him a
horn of powder, I bade him lay a train all along the piece
of timber, and let it be a large train; he did so, and had
but just time to get away, when the wolves came up to
it, and some were got up upon it, when I, snapping an un-
charged pistol close to the powder, set it on fire; those
that were upon the timber were scorched with it, and six
or seven of them fell, or rather jumped in among us, with
the force and fright of the fire; we dispatched these in an
instant, and the rest were so frighted with the light, which
the night, for it was now very near dark, made more terrible, that they drew back a little.

Upon which I ordered our last pistols to be fired off in
one volley, and after that we gave a shout; upon this, the
wolves turned tail, and we sallied immediately upon near
twenty lame ones, who we found struggling on the
ground, and fell a-cutting them with our swords, which
answered our expectation; for the crying and howling
they made was better understood by their fellows, so
that they all fled and left us.

We had, first and last, killed about threescore of them;
and had it been daylight, we had killed many more. The
field of battle being thus cleared, we made forward again;
for we had still near a league to go. We heard the ravenous creatures howl and yell in the woods as we went
several times; and sometimes we fancied we saw some of
them, but the snow dazzling our eyes, we were not cer-

tain; so in about an hour more, we came to the town where we were to lodge, which we found in a terrible fright, and all in arms; for it seems that the night before the wolves and some bears had broke into the village in the night and put them in a terrible fright, and they were obliged to keep guard night and day, but especially in the night, to preserve their cattle and indeed their people.

The next morning our guide was so ill, and his limbs swelled with the rankling of his two wounds that he could go no farther; so we were obliged to take a new guide there, and go to Toulouse, where we found a warm climate, a fruitful pleasant country, and no snow, no wolves, or anything like them; but when we told our story at Toulouse, they told us it was nothing but what was ordinary in the great forest at the foot of the mountains, especially when the snow lay on the ground. But they inquired much what kind of a guide we had gotten, that would venture to bring us that way in such a severe season; and told us it was very much we were not all devoured. When we told them how we placed ourselves, and the horses in the middle, they blamed us exceedingly, and told us it was fifty to one but we had been all destroyed; for it was the sight of the horses which made the wolves so furious, seeing their prey; and that at other times they are really afraid of a gun; but they being excessive hungry, and raging on that account, the eagerness to come at the horses had made them senseless of danger; and that if we had not by the continued fire, and at last by the stratagem of the train of powder, mastered them, it had been great odds but that we had been torn to pieces; whereas, had we been content to have sat still on horseback, and fired as horsemen, they would not have taken the horses for so much their own, when men were on their backs, as otherwise; and withal, they told us, that at last, if we had stood all together, and left our horses, they would have been so eager to have devoured them, that we might have come off safe, especially having our firearms in our hands, and being so many in number.

For my part, I was never so sensible of danger in my life; for seeing above three hundred devils come roaring and open-mouthed to devour us, and having nothing to shelter us, or retreat to, I gave myself over for lost; and as it was, I believe I shall never care to cross those mountains again; I think I would much rather go a thousand leagues by sea, though I were sure to meet with a storm once a week.

I have nothing uncommon to take notice of in my passage through France; nothing but what other travelers have given an account of, with much more advantage than I can. I traveled from Toulouse to Paris, and without any considerable stay came to Calais and landed safe at Dover the fourteenth of January, after having had a severe cold season to travel in.

I was now come to the center of my travels, and had in a little time all my new discovered estate safe about me, the bills of exchange which I brought with me having been very currently paid.

My principal guide and privy councilor was my good ancient widow; who, in gratitude for the money I had sent her, thought no pains too much, or care too great, to employ for me; and I trusted her so entirely with everything that I was perfectly easy as to the security of my effects; and indeed, I was very happy from my beginning, and now to the end, in the unspotted integrity of this good gentlewoman.

And now I began to think of leaving my effects with this woman and setting out for Lisbon, and so to the Brazils; but now another scruple came in my way, and that was religion; for as I had entertained some doubts about the Roman religion, even while I was abroad, especially in my state of solitude, so I knew there was no going to the Brazils for me, much less going to settle there, unless I resolved to embrace the Roman Catholic religion without any reserve; unless on the other hand, I resolved to be a sacrifice to my principles, be a martyr for religion, and die in the Inquisition; so I resolved to stay at home, and if I could find means for it, to dispose of my plantation.

To this purpose I wrote to my old friend at Lisbon, who in return gave me notice that he could easily dispose of it there. But that if I thought fit to give him leave to offer it in my name to the two merchants, the survivors of my trustees, who lived in the Brazils, who must fully understand the value of it, who lived just upon the spot, and who I knew were very rich, so that he believed they would be fond of buying it, he did not doubt but I should make 4 or 4,000 pieces of eight the more of it.

Accordingly I agreed, gave him order to offer it to them, and he did so; and in about eight months more, the ship being then returned, he sent me account, that they had accepted the offer, and had remitted 33,000 pieces of eight to a correspondent of theirs at Lisbon to pay for it.

In return, I signed the instrument of sale in the form which they sent from Lisbon, and sent it to my old man, who sent me bills of exchange for 32,800 pieces of eight to me, for the estate; reserving the payment of 100 moidores a year to him, the old man, during his life, and 50 moidores afterwards to his son for his life, which I had promised them, which the plantation was to make good as a rent-charge. And thus I have given the first part of a life of fortune and adventure, a life of Providence's checker-work, and of a variety which the world will seldom be able to show the like of. Beginning foolishly, but closing much more happily than any part of it ever gave me leave so much as to hope for.

Anyone would think that in this state of complicated good fortune, I was past running any more hazards; and so indeed I had been, if other circumstances had concurred, but I was inured to a wandering life, had no family, not many relations, nor, however rich, had I contracted much acquaintance; and though I had sold my estate in the Brazils, yet I could not keep the country out of my head, and had a great mind to be upon the wing again; especially I could not resist the strong inclination I had to see my island, and to know if the poor Spaniards were in being there, and how the rogues I left there had used them.

My true friend, the widow, earnestly dissuaded me from it, and so far prevailed with me that for almost seven years she prevented my running abroad; during which time, I took my two nephews, the children of one of my brothers, into my care. The eldest having something of his own, I bred up as a gentleman, and gave him a settlement of some addition to his estate, after my decease; the other I put out to a captain of a ship; and after five years, finding him a sensible, bold, enterprising young fellow, I put him into a good ship, and sent him to sea. And this young fellow afterwards drew me in, as old as I was, to farther adventures myself.

In the meantime, I in part settled myself here; for first of all I married, and that not either to my disadvantage or dissatisfaction, and had three children, two sons and one daughter. But my wife dying, and my nephew coming home with good success from a voyage to Spain, my inclination to go abroad and his importunity prevailed and engaged me to go in his ship, as a private trader to the East Indies. This was in the year 1694.

In this voyage I visited my new colony in the island, saw my successors the Spaniards, had the whole story of their lives, and of the villains I left there; how at first they insulted the poor Spaniards, how they afterwards agreed, disagreed, united, separated, and how at last the Spaniards were obliged to use violence with them, how they were subjected to the Spaniards, how honestly the Spaniards used them; a history, if it were entered into, as full of variety and wonderful accidents as my own part; particularly also as to their battles with the Caribbeans, who landed several times upon the island, and as to the improvement they made upon the island itself, and how five of them made an attempt upon the mainland, and brought away eleven men and five women prisoners, by which, at my coming, I found about twenty young children on the island.

Here I stayed about twenty days, left them supplies of all necessary things, and particularly of arms, powder, shot, clothes, tools, and two workmen, which I brought from England with me, viz., a carpenter and a smith.

Besides this, I shared the island into parts with 'em, reserved to myself the property of the whole, but gave them such parts respectively as they agreed on; and having settled all things with them, and engaged them not to leave the place, I left them there.

From thence I touched at the Brazils, from whence I sent a bark, which I bought there, with more people to the island; and in it, besides other supplies, I sent seven women, being such as I found proper for service, or for wives to such as would take them. As to the Englishmen, I promised them to send them some women from England, with a good cargo of necessaries, if they would apply themselves to planting, which I afterwards performed. And the fellows proved very honest and diligent after they were mastered and had their properties set apart for them. I sent them also from the Brazils five cows, three of them being big with calf, some sheep, and some hogs, which, when I came again, were considerably increased.

But all these things, with an account how 300 Caribbees came and invaded them, and ruined their plantations, and how they fought with that whole number twice, and were at first defeated, and three of them killed; but at last, a storm destroying their enemies' canoes, they famished or destroyed almost all the rest, and renewed and recovered the possession of their plantation, and still lived upon the island.

All these things, with some very surprising incidents in some new adventures of my own, for ten years more, I may perhaps give a farther account of hereafter.

A JOURNAL OF
THE PLAGUE YEAR

IT WAS about the beginning of September 1664, that I, among the rest of my neighbours, heard, in ordinary discourse, that the plague was returned again in Holland; for it had been very violent there, and particularly at Amsterdam and Rotterdam, in the year 1663, whither, they say, it was brought, some said from Italy, others from the Levant, among some goods, which were brought home by their Turkey fleet; others said it was brought from Candia; others from Cyprus. It mattered not from whence it came; but all agreed it was come into Holland again.

We had no such thing as printed newspapers in those days to spread rumours and reports of things, and to improve them by the invention of men, as I have lived to see practised since. But such things as those were gathered from the letters of merchants and others who corresponded abroad, and from them was handed about by word of mouth only; so that things did not spread instantly over the whole nation, as they do now. But it seems that the Government had a true account of it, and several councils were held about ways to prevent its coming over; but all was kept very private. Hence it was that this rumour died off again, and people began to forget it, as a thing we were very little concerned in, and that we hoped was not true, till the latter end of November or the beginning of December 1664, when two men, said to be Frenchmen, died of the plague in Long Acre, or rather at the upper end of Drury Lane. The family they were in endeavoured to conceal it as much as possible, but as it had gotten some vent in the discourse of the neighbourhood, the Secretaries of State got knowledge of it, and concerning themselves to inquire about it, in order to be certain of the truth, two physicians and a surgeon were ordered to go to the house and make inspection. This they did; and finding evident tokens of the sickness upon both the bodies that were dead, they gave their opinions publicly that they died of the plague. Whereupon it was given in to the parish clerk, and he also returned them to the Hall; and it was printed in the weekly bill of mortality in the usual manner, thus—

Plague, 2. Parishes infected, 1.

The people showed a great concern at this, and began to be alarmed all over the town, and the more, because in the last week in December 1664 another man died in the same house, and of the same distemper. And then we were easy again for about six weeks, when none having died with any marks of infection, it was said the distemper was gone; but after that, I think it was about the 12th of February, another died in another house, but in the same parish and in the same manner.

This turned the people's eyes pretty much towards that end of the town, and the weekly bills showing an increase of burials in St. Giles's parish more than usual, it began to be suspected that the plague was among the people at that end of the town, and that many had died of it, though they had taken care to keep it as much from the knowledge of the public as possible. This possessed the heads of the people very much, and few cared to go through Drury Lane, or the other streets suspected, unless they had extraordinary business, that obliged them to it.

This increase of the bills stood thus: the usual number of burials in a week, in the parishes of St. Giles-in-the-Fields and St. Andrew, Holborn, were from twelve to seventeen or nineteen each, few more or less; but from the time that the plague first began in St. Giles's parish, it was observed that the ordinary burials increased in number considerably. For example:—

From December 27 to January 3 .	St. Giles's . . .	16
	St. Andrew's. . .	17
" January 3 " " 10 .	St. Giles's . . .	12
	St. Andrew's. . .	25
" January 10 " " 17 .	St. Giles's . . .	18
	St. Andrew's. . .	18
" January 17 " " 24 .	St. Giles's . . .	23
	St. Andrew's. . .	16
" January 24 " " 31 .	St. Giles's . . .	24
	St. Andrew's. . .	15
" January 30 " February 7. .	St. Giles's . . .	21
	St. Andrew's. . .	23
" February 7 " " 14 .	St. Giles's . . .	24

Whereof one of the plague.

The like increase of the bills was observed in the parishes of St. Bride, adjoining on one side of Holborn parish, and in the parish of St. James, Clerkenwell, adjoining on the other side of Holborn; in both which parishes the usual numbers that died weekly were from four to six or eight, whereas at that time they were increased as follows:—

From December 20 to December 27 .	St. Bride's . .	0
	St. James's . .	8
" December 27 to January 3 .	St. Bride's . .	6
	St. James's . .	9

					St. Bride's	. .	11
"	January 3	"	"	10 . .	St. James's	. .	7
"	January 10	"	"	17 . .	St. Bride's	. .	12
					St. James's	. .	9
From January 17 to January 24 . .					St. Bride's	. .	9
					St. James's	. .	15
"	January 24 "	"	31 . .		St. Bride's	. .	8
					St. James's	. .	12
"	January 31 " February 7 . .				St. Bride's	. .	13
					St. James's	. .	5
"	February 7 "	"	14 . .		St. Bride's	. .	12
					St. James's	. .	6

Besides this, it was observed with great uneasiness by the people that the weekly bills in general increased very much during these weeks, although it was at a time of the year when usually the bills are very moderate.

The usual number of burials within the bills of mortality for a week was from about 240 or thereabouts to 300. The last was esteemed a pretty high bill; but after this we found the bills successively increasing, as follows:—

	Buried.	Increased.
December the 20th to the 27th	291	..
" 27th " 3rd January . .	349	58
January the 3rd " 10th " . .	394	45
" 10th " 17th " . .	415	21
" 17th " 24th " . .	474	59

This last bill was really frightful, being a higher number than had been known to have been buried in one week since the preceding visitation of 1656.

However, all this went off again, and the weather proving cold, and the frost, which began in December, still continuing very severe, even till near the end of February, attended with sharp though moderate winds, the bills decreased again, and the city grew healthy, and everybody began to look upon the danger as good as over; only that still the burials in St. Giles's continued high. From the beginning of April especially they stood at twenty-five each week, till the week from the 18th to the 25th, when there was buried in St. Giles's parish thirty, whereof two of the plague and eight of the spotted-fever, which was looked upon as the same thing; likewise the number that died of the spotted-fever in the whole increased, being eight the week before, and twelve the week above named.

This alarmed us all again, and terrible apprehensions were among the people, especially the weather being now changed and growing warm, and the summer being at hand. However, the next week there seemed to be some hopes again; the bills were low, the number of the dead in all was but 388, there was none of the plague, and but four of the spotted-fever.

But the following week it returned again, and the distemper was spread into two or three other parishes, viz., St. Andrew's, Holborn; St. Clement Danes; and, to the great affliction of the city, one died within the walls, in the parish of St. Mary Woolchurch, that is to say, in Bearbinder Lane, near Stocks Market; in all there were nine of the plague and six of the spotted-fever. It was, however, upon inquiry, found that this Frenchman who died in Bearbinder Lane was one who, having lived in Long Acre, near the infected houses, had removed for fear of the distemper, not knowing that he was already infected.

This was the beginning of May, yet the weather was temperate, variable, and cool enough, and people had still some hopes. That which encouraged them was, that the city was healthy, the whole ninety-seven parishes buried but fifty-four, and we began to hope, that as it was chiefly among the people at that end of the town, it might go no farther; and the rather, because the next week, which was from the 9th of May to the 16th, there died but three, of which not one within the whole city or liberties; and St. Andrew's buried but fifteen, which was very low. 'T is true St. Giles's buried two-and-thirty, but still, as there was but one of the plague, people began to be easy. The whole bill also was very low, for the week before the bill was but 347, and the week above mentioned but 343. We continued in these hopes for a few days, but it was but for a few, for the people were no more to be deceived thus; they searched the houses, and found that the plague was really spread every way, and that many died of it every day. So that now all our extenuations abated, and it was no more to be concealed; nay, it quickly appeared that the infection had spread itself beyond all hopes of abatement; that in the parish of St. Giles it was gotten into several streets, and several families lay all sick together; and, accordingly, in the weekly bill for the next week the thing began to show itself. There was indeed but fourteen set down of the plague, but this was all knavery and collusion, for in St. Giles's parish they buried forty in all, whereof it was certain most of them died of the plague, though they were set down of other distempers; and though the number of all the burials were not increased above thirty-two, and the whole bill being but 385, yet there was fourteen of the spotted-fever, as well as fourteen of the plague; and we took it for granted upon the whole that there were fifty died that week of the plague.

The next bill was from the 23rd of May to the 30th, when the number of the plague was seventeen. But the burials in St. Giles's were fifty-three—a frightful number! —of whom they set down but nine of the plague; but on an examination more strictly by the justices of the peace, and at the Lord Mayor's request, it was found there were twenty more who were really dead of the plague in that parish, but had been set down of the spotted-fever or other distempers, besides others concealed.

But those were trifling things to what followed immediately after; for now the weather set in hot, and from the first week in June the infection spread in a dreadful manner, and the bills rose high; the articles of the fever, spotted-fever, and teeth began to swell; for all that could conceal their distempers did it, to prevent their neighbours shunning and refusing to converse with them, and also to prevent authority shutting up their houses, which though it was not yet practised, yet was threatened, and people were extremely terrified at the thoughts of it.

The second week in June, the parish of St. Giles, where still the weight of the infection lay, buried 120, whereof, though the bills said but sixty-eight of the plague, everybody said there had been 100 at least, calculating it from the usual number of funerals in that parish, as above.

Till this week the city continued free, there having never any died, except that one Frenchman whom I mentioned before, within the whole ninety-seven parishes. Now there died four within the city, one in Wood Street, one in Fenchurch Street, and two in Crooked Lane. Southwark was entirely free, having not one yet died on that side of the water.

I lived without Aldgate, about midway between Aldgate Church and Whitechapel Bars, on the left hand or north side of the street; and as the distemper had not reached to that side of the city, our neighbourhood continued very easy. But at the other end of the town their consternation was very great; and the richer sort of people, especially the nobility and gentry from the west part of the city, thronged out of town with their families and servants in an unusual manner; and this was more particularly seen in Whitechapel; that is to say, the Broad Street where I lived; indeed, nothing was to be seen but waggons and carts, with goods, women, servants, children, &c.; coaches filled with people of the better sort, and horsemen attending them, and all hurrying away; then empty waggons and carts appeared, and spare horses with servants, who, it was apparent, were returning or sent from the countries to fetch more people; besides innumerable numbers of men on horseback, some alone, others with servants, and, generally speaking, all loaded with baggage and fitted out for travelling, as any one might perceive by their appearance.

This was a very terrible and melancholy thing to see, and as it was a sight which I could not but look on from morning to night, for indeed there was nothing else of moment to be seen, it filled me with very serious thoughts of the misery that was coming upon the city, and the unhappy condition of those that would be left in it.

This hurry of the people was such for some weeks that there was no getting at the Lord Mayor's door without exceeding difficulty; there was such pressing and crowding there to get passes and certificates of health for such as travelled abroad, for without these there was no being admitted to pass through the towns upon the road, or to lodge in any inn. Now, as there had none died in the city for all this time, my Lord Mayor gave certificates of health without any difficulty to all those who lived in the ninety-seven parishes, and to those within the liberties too for a while.

This hurry, I say, continued some weeks, that is to say, all the month of May and June, and the more because it was rumoured that an order of the Government was to be issued out to place turnpikes and barriers on the road to prevent people travelling, and that the towns on the road would not suffer people from London to pass for fear of bringing the infection along with them, though neither of these rumours had any foundation but in the imagination, especially at first.

I now began to consider seriously with myself concerning my own case, and how I should dispose of myself; that is to say, whether I should resolve to stay in London or shut up my house and flee, as many of my neighbours did. I have set this particular down so fully, because I know not but it may be of moment to those who come after me, if they come to be brought to the same distress, and to the same manner of making their choice; and therefore I desire this account may pass with them rather for a direction to themselves to act by than a history of my actings, seeing it may not be of one farthing value to them to note what became of me.

I had two important things before me: the one was the carrying on my business and shop, which was considerable, and in which was embarked all my effects in the world; and the other was the preservation of my life in so dismal a calamity as I saw apparently was coming upon the whole city, and which, however great it was, my fears perhaps, as well as other people's, represented to be much greater than it could be.

The first consideration was of great moment to me; my trade was a sadler, and as my dealings were chiefly not by a shop or chance trade, but among the merchants trading to the English colonies in America, so my effects lay very much in the hands of such. I was a single man, 't is true, but I had a family of servants whom I kept at my business; had a house, shop, and warehouses filled with goods; and, in short, to leave them all as things in such a case must be left, that is to say, without any overseer or person fit to be trusted with them, had been to hazard the loss not only of my trade, but of my goods, and indeed of all I had in the world.

I had an elder brother at the same time in London, and not many years before come over from Portugal, and advising with him, his answer was in three words, the same that was given in another case quite different, viz., "Master, save thyself." In a word, he was for my retiring into the country, as he resolved to do himself with his family; telling me, what he had, it seems, heard abroad, that the best preparation for the plague was to run away from it. As to my argument of losing my trade, my goods, or debts, he quite confuted me. He told me the same thing which I argued for my staying, viz., that I would trust God with my safety and health, was the strongest repulse to my pretensions of losing my trade and my goods; "for," says he, "is it not as reasonable that you should trust God with the chance or risk of losing your trade, as that you should stay in so eminent a point of danger, and trust Him with your life?"

I could not argue that I was in any strait as to a place where to go, having several friends and relations in Northamptonshire, whence our family first came from; and particularly, I had an only sister in Lincolnshire, very willing to receive and entertain me.

My brother, who had already sent his wife and two children into Bedfordshire, and resolved to follow them, pressed my going very earnestly; and I had once resolved to comply with his desires, but at that time could get no horse; for though it is true all the people did not go out of the city of London, yet I may venture to say, that in a manner all the horses did; for there was hardly a horse to be bought or hired in the whole city for some weeks. Once I resolved to travel on foot with one servant, and, as many did, lie at no inn, but carry a soldier's tent with us, and so lie in the fields, the weather being very warm, and no danger from taking cold. I say, as many did, because several did so at last, especially those who had been in the armies in the war which had not been many years past; and I must needs say that, speaking of second causes, had most of the people that travelled done so, the plague had not been carried into so many country towns and houses as it was, to the great damage, and indeed to the ruin, of abundance of people.

But then my servant, whom I had intended to take down with me, deceived me; and being frighted at the increase of the distemper, and not knowing when I should go, he took other measures, and left me, so I was put off for that time; and, one way or other, I always found that to appoint to go away was always crossed by some accident or other, so as to disappoint and put it off again; and this brings in a story which otherwise might be thought a needless digression, viz., about these disappointments being from Heaven.

I mention this story also as the best method I can advise any person to take in such a case, especially if he be one that makes conscience of his duty, and would be directed what to do in it, namely, that he should keep his eye upon the particular providences which occur at that time, and look upon them complexly, as they regard one another, and as all together regard the question before him, and then, I think, he may safely take them for intimations from Heaven of what is his unquestioned duty to do in such a case; I mean as to going away from or staying in the place where we dwell, when visited with an infectious distemper.

It came very warmly into my mind one morning, as I was musing on this particular thing, that as nothing attended us without the direction or permission of Divine Power, so these disappointments must have something in them extraordinary; and I ought to consider whether it did not evidently point out, or intimate to me, that it was the will of Heaven I should not go. It immediately followed in my thoughts, that if it really was from God that I should stay, He was able effectually to preserve me in the midst of all the death and danger that would surround me; and that if I attempted to secure myself by fleeing from my habitation, and acted contrary to these intimations, which I believed to be Divine, it was a kind of flying from God, and that He could cause His justice to overtake me when and where He thought fit.

These thoughts quite turned my resolutions again, and when I came to discourse with my brother again, I told him that I inclined to stay and take my lot in that station in which God had placed me, and that it seemed to be made more especially my duty, on the account of what I have said.

My brother, though a very religious man himself, laughed at all I had suggested about its being an intimation from Heaven, and told me several stories of such foolhardy people, as he called them, as I was; that I ought indeed to submit to it as a work of Heaven if I had been any way disabled by distempers or diseases, and that then not being able to go, I ought to acquiesce in the direction of Him, who, having been my Maker, had an undisputed right of sovereignty in disposing of me, and that then there had been no difficulty to determine which was the call of His providence and which was not; but that I should take it as an intimation from Heaven that I should not go out of town, only because I could not hire a horse to go, or my fellow was run away that was to attend me, was ridiculous, since at the same time I had my health and limbs, and other servants, and might with ease travel a day or two on foot, and having a good certificate of being in perfect health, might either hire a horse or take post on the road, as I thought fit.

Then he proceeded to tell me of the mischievous consequences which attended the presumption of the Turks and Mahometans in Asia and in other places where he had been (for my brother, being a merchant, was a few years before, as I have already observed, returned from abroad, coming last from Lisbon), and how, presuming upon their professed predestinating notions, and of every man's end being predetermined and unalterably before-hand decreed, they would go unconcerned into infected places and converse with infected persons, by which means they died at the rate of ten or fifteen thousand a week, whereas the Europeans or Christian merchants, who kept themselves retired and reserved, generally escaped the contagion.

Upon these arguments my brother changed my resolutions again, and I began to resolve to go, and accordingly made all things ready; for, in short, the infection increased round me, and the bills were risen to almost seven hundred a week, and my brother told me he would venture to stay no longer. I desired him to let me consider of it but till the next day, and I would resolve; and as I had already prepared everything as well as I could as to my business, and whom to entrust my affairs with, I had little to do but to resolve.

I went home that evening greatly oppressed in my mind, irresolute, and not knowing what to do. I had set the evening wholly apart to consider seriously about it, and was all alone; for already people had, as it were by a general consent, taken up the custom of not going out of doors after sunset; the reasons I shall have occasion to say more of by-and-by.

In the retirement of this evening I endeavoured to re-solve, first, what was my duty to do, and I stated the arguments with which my brother had pressed me to go into the country, and I set against them the strong impressions which I had on my mind for staying; the visible call I seemed to have from the particular circumstance of my calling, and the care due from me for the preservation of my effects, which were, as I might say, my estate; also the intimations which I thought I had from Heaven, that to me signified a kind of direction to venture; and it occurred to me, that if I had what I might call a direction to stay, I ought to suppose it contained a promise of being preserved if I obeyed.

This lay close to me, and my mind seemed more and more encouraged to stay than ever, and supported with a secret satisfaction that I should be kept. Add to this, that, turning over the Bible which lay before me, and while my thoughts were more than ordinarily serious upon the question, I cried out, "Well, I know not what to do; Lord, direct me!" and the like; and at that juncture I happened to stop turning over the book at the 91st Psalm, and casting my eye on the second verse, I read on to the seventh verse exclusive, and after that included the tenth, as follows: "I will say of the Lord, He is my refuge and my fortress: my God, in Him will I trust. Surely He shall deliver thee from the snare of the fowler, and from the noisome pestilence. He shall cover thee with His feathers, and under His wings shalt thou trust: His truth shall be thy shield and buckler. Thou shalt not be afraid for the terror by night; nor for the arrow that flieth by day; nor for the pestilence that walketh in darkness; nor for the destruction that wasteth at noonday. A thousand shall fall at thy side, and ten thousand at thy right hand; but it shall not come nigh thee. Only with thine eyes shalt thou behold and see the reward of the wicked. Because thou hast made the Lord, which is my refuge, even the most High, thy habitation; there shall no evil befall thee, neither shall any plague come nigh thy dwelling," &c.

I scarce need tell the reader that from that moment I resolved that I would stay in the town, and casting myself entirely upon the goodness and protection of the

Almighty, would not seek any other shelter whatever; and that, as my times were in His hands, He was as able to keep me in a time of the infection as in a time of health; and if He did not think fit to deliver me, still I was in His hands, and it was meet He should do with me as should seem good to Him.

With this resolution I went to bed; and I was further confirmed in it the next day by the woman being taken ill with whom I had intended to entrust my house and all my affairs. But I had a further obligation laid on me on the same side, for the next day I found myself very much out of order also, so that if I would have gone away, I could not; and I continued ill three or four days, and this entirely determined my stay; so I took my leave of my brother, who went away to Dorking, in Surrey, and afterwards fetched a round farther into Buckinghamshire or Bedfordshire, to a retreat he had found out there for his family.

It was a very ill time to be sick in, for if any one complained, it was immediately said he had the plague; and though I had indeed no symptoms of that distemper, yet being very ill, both in my head and in my stomach, I was not without apprehension that I really was infected; but in about three days I grew better; the third night I rested well, sweated a little, and was much refreshed. The apprehensions of its being the infection went also quite away with my illness, and I went about my business as usual.

These things, however, put off all my thoughts of going into the country; and my brother also being gone, I had no more debate either with him or with myself on that subject.

It was now mid-July, and the plague, which had chiefly raged at the other end of the town, and, as I said before, in the parishes of St. Giles, St. Andrew, Holborn, and towards Westminster, began to now come eastward towards the part where I lived. It was to be observed, indeed, that it did not come straight on towards us; for the city, that is to say, within the walls, was indifferently healthy still; nor was it got then very much over the water into Southwark; for though there died that week 1268 of all distempers, whereof it might be supposed above 900 died of the plague, yet there was but twenty-eight in the whole city, within the walls, and but nineteen in Southwark, Lambeth parish included; whereas in the parishes of St. Giles and St. Martin-in-the-Fields alone there died 421.

But we perceived the infection kept chiefly in the out-parishes, which being very populous, and fuller also of poor, the distemper found more to prey upon than in the city, as I shall observe afterwards. We perceived, I say, the distemper to draw our way, viz., by the parishes of Clerkenwell, Cripplegate, Shoreditch, and Bishopsgate; which last two parishes joining to Aldgate, Whitechapel, and Stepney, the infection came at length to spread its utmost rage and violence in those parts, even when it abated at the western parishes where it began.

It was very strange to observe that in this particular week, from the 4th to the 11th of July, when, as I have observed, there died near 400 of the plague in the two parishes of St. Martin and St. Giles-in-the-Fields only, there died in the parish of Aldgate but four, in the parish of Whitechapel three, in the parish of Stepney but one.

Likewise in the next week, from the 11th of July to the 18th, when the week's bill was 1761, yet there died no more of the plague, on the whole Southwark side of the water, than sixteen.

But this face of things soon changed, and it began to thicken in Cripplegate parish especially, and in Clerkenwell; so that by the second week in August, Cripplegate parish alone buried 886, and Clerkenwell 155. Of the first, 850 might well be reckoned to die of the plague; and of the last, the bill itself said 145 were of the plague.

During the month of July, and while, as I have observed, our part of the town seemed to be spared in comparison of the west part, I went ordinarily about the streets, as my business required, and particularly went generally once in a day, or in two days, into the city, to my brother's house, which he had given me charge of, and to see if it was safe; and having the key in my pocket, I used to go into the house, and over most of the rooms, to see that all was well; for though it be something wonderful to tell, that any should have hearts so hardened in the midst of such a calamity as to rob and steal, yet certain it is that all sorts of villainies, and even levities and debaucheries, were then practised in the town as openly as ever—I will not say quite as frequently, because the numbers of people were many ways lessened.

But the city itself began now to be visited too, I mean within the walls; but the number of people there were indeed extremely lessened by so great a multitude having been gone into the country; and even all this month of July they continued to flee, though not in such multitudes as formerly. In August, indeed, they fled in such a manner that I began to think there would be really none but magistrates and servants left in the city.

As they fled now out of the city, so I should observe that the Court removed early, viz., in the month of June, and went to Oxford, where it pleased God to preserve them; and the distemper did not, as I heard of, so much as touch them, for which I cannot say that I ever saw they showed any great token of thankfulness, and hardly anything of reformation, though they did not want being told that their crying vices might, without breach of charity, be said to have gone far in bringing that terrible judgment upon the whole nation.

The face of London was now indeed strangely altered, I mean the whole mass of buildings, city, liberties, suburbs, Westminster, Southwark, and altogether; for as to the particular part called the city, or within the walls, that was not yet much infected. But in the whole the face of things, I say, was much altered; sorrow and sadness sat upon every face; and though some parts were not yet overwhelmed, yet all looked deeply concerned; and as we saw it apparently coming on, so every one looked on himself and his family as in the utmost danger. Were it possible to represent those times exactly to those that did not see them, and give the reader due ideas of the horror that everywhere presented itself, it must make just impressions upon their minds and fill them with surprise. London might well be said to be all in tears; the mourners did not go about the streets indeed, for nobody put on black or made a formal dress of mourning for their nearest friends; but the voice of mourning was truly heard in the streets. The shrieks of women and children at the windows and doors of their houses, where their dearest relations were perhaps dying, or just dead, were so frequent to be heard as we passed the streets, that it was enough to pierce the stoutest heart in the world to hear them. Tears and lamentations were seen almost in every house, especially in the first part of the visitation; for towards the latter end men's hearts were hardened, and death was so always before their eyes, that they did not so much concern themselves for the loss of their friends, expecting that themselves should be summoned the next hour.

Business led me out sometimes to the other end of the town, even when the sickness was chiefly there; and as the thing was new to me, as well as to everybody else, it was a most surprising thing to see those streets which were usually so thronged now grown desolate, and so few people to be seen in them, that if I had been a stranger and at a loss for my way, I might sometimes have gone the length of a whole street, I mean of the by-streets, and seen nobody to direct me except watchmen set at the doors of such houses as were shut up, of which I shall speak presently.

One day, being at that part of the town on some special business, curiosity led me to observe things more than usually, and indeed I walked a great way where I had no business. I went up Holborn, and there the street was full of people, but they walked in the middle of the great street, neither on one side or other, because, as I suppose, they would not mingle with anybody that came out of houses, or meet with smells and scents from houses that might be infected.

The Inns of Court were all shut up; nor were very many of the lawyers in the Temple, or Lincoln's Inn, or Gray's Inn, to be seen there. Everybody was at peace; there was no occasion for lawyers; besides, it being in the time of the vacation too, they were generally gone into the country. Whole rows of houses in some places were shut close up, the inhabitants all fled, and only a watchman or two left.

When I speak of rows of houses being shut up, I do not mean shut up by the magistrates, but that great numbers of persons followed the Court, by the necessity of their employments and other dependences; and as others retired, really frighted with the distemper, it was a mere desolating of some of the streets. But the fright was not yet near so great in the city, abstractly so called, and particularly because, though they were at first in a most inexpressible consternation, yet as I have observed that the distemper intermitted often at first, so they were, as it were, alarmed and unalarmed again, and this several times, till it began to be familiar to them; and that even when it appeared violent, yet seeing it did not presently spread into the city, or the east and south parts, the people began to take courage, and to be, as I may say, a little hardened. It is true a vast many people fled, as I have observed, yet they were chiefly from the west end of the town, and from that we call the heart of the city, that is to say, among the wealthiest of the people, and such people as were unencumbered with trades and business. But of the rest, the generality stayed, and seemed to abide the worst; so that in the place we call the Liberties, and in the suburbs, in Southwark, and in the east part, such as Wapping, Ratcliff, Stepney, Rotherhithe, and the like, the people generally stayed, except here and there a few wealthy families, who, as above, did not depend upon their business.

It must not be forgot here that the city and suburbs were prodigiously full of people at the time of this visitation, I mean at the time that it began; for though I have lived to see a further increase, and mighty throngs of people settling in London more than ever, yet we had always a notion that the numbers of people which, the wars being over, the armies disbanded, and the royal family and the monarchy being restored, had flocked to London to settle in business, or to depend upon and attend the Court for rewards of services, preferments, and the like, was such that the town was computed to have in it above a hundred thousand people more than ever it held before; nay, some took upon them to say it had twice as many, because all the ruined families of the royal party flocked hither. All the old soldiers set up trades here, and abundance of families settled here. Again, the Court brought with them a great flux of pride and new fashions.

All people were grown gay and luxurious, and the joy of the Restoration had brought a vast many families to London.

I often thought that as Jerusalem was besieged by the Romans when the Jews were assembled together to celebrate the Passover, by which means an incredible number of people were surprised there who would otherwise have been in other countries; so the plague entered London when an incredible increase of people had happened occasionally, by the particular circumstances above named. As this conflux of the people to a youthful and gay Court made a great trade in the city, especially in everything that belonged to fashion and finery, so it drew by consequence a great number of workmen, manufacturers, and the like, being mostly poor people who depended upon their labour. And I remember in particular, that in a representation to my Lord Mayor of the condition of the poor, it was estimated that there were no less than an hundred thousand riband-weavers in and about the city, the chiefest number of whom lived then in the parishes of Shoreditch, Stepney, Whitechapel, and Bishopsgate, that, namely, about Spitalfields; that is to say, as Spitalfields was then, for it was not so large as now by one fifth part.

By this, however, the number of people in the whole may be judged of; and, indeed, I often wondered that, after the prodigious numbers of people that went away at first, there was yet so great a multitude left as it appeared there was.

But I must go back again to the beginning of this surprising time. While the fears of the people were young, they were increased strangely by several odd accidents, which put altogether, it was really a wonder the whole body of the people did not rise as one man and abandon their dwellings, leaving the place as a space of ground designed by Heaven for an Aceldama, doomed to be destroyed from the face of the earth, and that all that would be found in it would perish with it. I shall name but a few of these things; but sure they were so many, and so many wizards and cunning people propagating them, that I have often wondered there was any (women especially) left behind.

In the first place, a blazing star or comet appeared for several months before the plague, as there did the year after another, a little before the fire. The old women and the phlegmatic hypochondriac part of the other sex, whom I could almost call old women too, remarked (especially afterward, though not till both those judgments were over) that those two comets passed directly over the city, and that so very near the houses that it was plain they imported something peculiar to the city alone; that the comet before the pestilence was of a faint, dull, languid colour, and its motion very heavy, solemn, and slow; but that the comet before the fire was bright and sparkling, or, as others said, flaming, and its motion swift and furious; and that accordingly one foretold a heavy judgment, slow but severe, terrible and frightful, as was the plague; but the other foretold a stroke, sudden, swift, and fiery as the conflagration. Nay, so particular some people were, that as they looked upon that comet preceding the fire, they fancied that they not only saw it pass swiftly and fiercely, and could perceive the motion with their eye, but even they heard it; that it made a rushing, mighty noise, fierce and terrible, though at a distance, and but just perceivable.

I saw both these stars, and, I must confess, had so much of the common notion of such things in my head, that I was apt to look upon them as the forerunners and warnings of God's judgments; and especially when, after the plague had followed the first, I yet saw another of the like kind, I could not but say God had not yet sufficiently scourged the city.

But I could not at the same time carry these things to the height that others did, knowing, too, that natural causes are assigned by the astronomers for such things and that their motions and even their revolutions are calculated, or pretended to be calculated, so that they cannot be so perfectly called the forerunners or foretellers, much less the procurers, of such events as pestilence, war, fire, and the like.

But let my thoughts and the thoughts of the philosophers be, or have been, what they will, these things had a more than ordinary influence upon the minds of the common people, and they had almost universal melancholy apprehensions of some dreadful calamity and judgment coming upon the city; and this principally from the sight of this comet, and the little alarm that was given in December by two people dying at St. Giles's, as above.

The apprehensions of the people were likewise strangely increased by the error of the times, in which, I think, the people, from what principle I cannot imagine, were more addicted to prophecies and astrological conjurations, dreams, and old wives' tales than ever they were before or since. Whether this unhappy temper was originally raised by the follies of some people who got money by it, that is to say, by printing predictions and prognostications, I know not; but certain it is, books frighted them terribly, such as Lilly's Almanack, Gadbury's Astrological Predictions, Poor Robin's Almanack, and the like; also several pretended religious books, one entitled, "Come out of her, my People, lest you be Partaker of her Plagues;" another called, "Fair Warning;" another, "Britain's Remembrancer;" and many such, all, or most part of which, foretold, directly or covertly, the ruin of the city. Nay, some were so enthusiastically bold as to run about the streets with their oral predictions, pretending they were sent to preach to the city; and one in particular, who, like Jonah to Nineveh, cried in the streets, "Yet forty days, and London shall be destroyed." I will not be positive whether he said yet forty days or yet a few days. Another ran about naked, except a pair of drawers about his waist, crying day and night, like a man that Josephus mentions, who cried, "Woe to Jerusalem!" a little before the destruction of that city. So this poor naked creature cried, "Oh, the great and the dreadful God!" and said no more, but repeated those words continually, with a voice and countenance full of horror, a swift pace; and nobody could ever find him to stop or rest, or take any sustenance, at least that ever I could hear of. I met this poor creature several times in the streets, and would have spoke to him, but he would not enter into speech with me or any one else, but held on his dismal cries continually.

These things terrified the people to the last degree, and especially when two or three times, as I have mentioned already, they found one or two in the bills dead of the plague at St. Giles's.

Next to these public things were the dreams of old women, or, I should say, the interpretation of old women upon other people's dreams; and these put abundance of people even out of their wits. Some heard voices warning them to be gone, for that there would be such a plague in London, so that the living would not be able to bury the dead. Others saw apparitions in the air; and I must be allowed to say of both, I hope without breach of charity, that they heard voices that never spake, and saw sights that never appeared, but the imagination of the people was really turned wayward and possessed. And no wonder, if they who were poring continually at the clouds saw shapes and figures, representations and appearances, which had nothing in them but air and vapour. Here they told us they saw a flaming sword held in a hand coming out of a cloud, with a point hanging directly over the city; there they saw hearses and coffins in the air carrying to be buried; and there again, heaps of dead bodies lying unburied, and the like, just as the imagination of the poor terrified people furnished them with matter to work upon.

> "So hypochondriac fancies represent
> Ships, armies, battles in the firmament;
> Till steady eyes the exhalations solve,
> And all to its first matter, cloud, resolve."

I could fill this account with the strange relations such people gave every day of what they had seen; and every one was so positive of their having seen what they pretended to see, that there was no contradicting them without breach of friendship, or being accounted rude and unmannerly on the one hand, and profane and impenetrable on the other. One time before the plague was begun (otherwise than as I have said in St. Giles's), I think it was in March, seeing a crowd of people in the street, I joined with them to satisfy my curiosity, and found them all staring up into the air to see what a woman told them appeared plain to her, which was an angel clothed in white, with a fiery sword in his hand, waving it or brandishing it over his head. She described every part of the figure to the life, showed them the motion and the form, and the poor people came into it so eagerly, and with so much readiness; "Yes, I see it all plainly," says one; "there's the sword as plain as can be." Another saw the angel. One saw his very face, and cried out what a glorious creature he was! One saw one thing, and one another. I looked as earnestly as the rest, but perhaps not with so much willingness to be imposed upon; and I said, indeed, that I could see nothing but a white cloud, bright on one side by the shining of the sun upon the other part. The woman endeavoured to show it me, but could not make me confess that I saw it, which, indeed, if I had I must have lied. But the woman, turning upon me, looked in my face, and fancied I laughed, in which her imagination deceived her too, for I really did not laugh, but was very seriously reflecting how the poor people were terrified by the force of their own imagination. However, she turned from me, called me profane fellow, and a scoffer; told me that it was a time of God's anger, and dreadful judgments were approaching, and that despisers such as I should wander and perish.

The people about her seemed disgusted as well as she; and I found there was no persuading them that I did not laugh at them, and that I should be rather mobbed by them than be able to undeceive them. So I left them; and this appearance passed for as real as the blazing star itself.

Another encounter I had in the open day also; and this was in going through a narrow passage from Petty France into Bishopsgate Churchyard, by a row of alms-houses. There are two churchyards to Bishopsgate church or parish; one we go over to pass from the place called Petty France into Bishopsgate Street, coming out just by the church door; the other is on the side of the narrow passage where the alms-houses are on the left; and a dwarf-wall with a palisado on it on the right hand, and the city wall on the other side more to the right.

In this narrow passage stands a man looking through between the palisadoes into the burying-place, and as many people as the narrowness of the passage would admit to stop, without hindering the passage of others, and he was talking mighty eagerly to them, and pointing now to one place, then to another, and affirming that he saw

a ghost walking upon such a gravestone there. He described the shape, the posture, and the movement of it so
exactly that it was the greatest matter of amazement to
him in the world that everybody did not see it as well as
he. On a sudden he would cry, "There it is; now it comes
this way." Then, "'T is turned back;" till at length he
persuaded the people into so firm a belief of it, that one
fancied he saw it, and another fancied he saw it; and
thus he came every day making a strange hubbub, considering it was in so narrow a passage, till Bishopsgate
clock struck eleven, and then the ghost would seem to
start, and, as if he were called away, disappeared on a
sudden.

I looked earnestly every way, and at the very moment
that this man directed, but could not see the least appearance of anything; but so positive was this poor man,
that he gave the people the vapours in abundance, and
sent them away trembling and frighted, till at length few
people that knew of it cared to go through that passage,
and hardly anybody by night on any account whatever.

This ghost, as the poor man affirmed, made signs to the
houses, and to the ground, and to the people, plainly intimating, or else they so understanding it, that abundance
of the people should come to be buried in that churchyard, as indeed happened; but that he saw such aspects I
must acknowledge I never believed, nor could I see anything of it myself, though I looked most earnestly to see
it, if possible.

These things serve to show how far the people were
really overcome with delusions; and as they had a notion
of the approach of a visitation, all their predictions ran
upon a most dreadful plague, which should lay the whole
city, and even the kingdom, waste, and should destroy
almost all the nation, both man and beast.

To this, as I said before, the astrologers added stories

of the conjunctions of planets in a malignant manner and with a mischievous influence, one of which conjunctions was to happen, and did happen, in October, and the other in November; and they filled the people's heads with predictions on these signs of the heavens, intimating that those conjunctions foretold drought, famine, and pestilence. In the two first of them, however, they were entirely mistaken, for we had no droughty season, but in the beginning of the year a hard frost, which lasted from December almost to March, and after that moderate weather, rather warm than hot, with refreshing winds, and, in short, very seasonable weather, and also several very great rains.

Some endeavours were used to suppress the printing of such books as terrified the people, and to frighten the dispersers of them, some of whom were taken up; but nothing was done in it, as I am informed, the Government being unwilling to exasperate the people, who were, as I may say, all out of their wits already.

Neither can I acquit those ministers that in their sermons rather sank than lifted up the hearts of their hearers. Many of them no doubt did it for the strengthening the resolution of the people, and especially for quickening them to repentance, but it certainly answered not their end, at least not in proportion to the injury it did another way; and indeed, as God Himself through the whole Scriptures rather draws to Him by invitations and calls to turn to Him and live, than drives us by terror and amazement, so I must confess I thought the ministers should have done also, imitating our blessed Lord and Master in this, that His whole Gospel is full of declarations from heaven of God's mercy, and His readiness to receive penitents and forgive them, complaining, "Ye will not come unto Me that ye may have life," and that therefore His Gospel is called the Gospel of Peace and the Gospel of Grace.

But we had some good men, and that of all persuasions and opinions, whose discourses were full of terror, who spoke nothing but dismal things; and as they brought the people together with a kind of horror, sent them away in tears, prophesying nothing but evil tidings, terrifying the people with the apprehensions of being utterly destroyed, not guiding them, at least not enough, to cry to heaven for mercy.

It was, indeed, a time of very unhappy breaches among us in matters of religion. Innumerable sects and divisions and separate opinions prevailed among the people. The Church of England was restored, indeed, with the restoration of the monarchy, about four years before, but the ministers and preachers of the Presbyterians and Independents, and of all the other sorts of professions, had begun to gather separate societies and erect altar against altar, and all those had their meetings for worship apart, as they have now, but not so many then, the Dissenters being not thoroughly formed into a body as they are since; and those congregations, which were thus gathered together were yet but few. And even those that were the Government did not allow, but endeavoured to suppress them and shut up their meetings.

But the visitation reconciled them again, at least for a time, and many of the best and most valuable ministers and preachers of the Dissenters were suffered to go into the churches where the incumbents were fled away, as many were, not being able to stand it; and the people flocked without distinction to hear them preach, not much inquiring who or what opinion they were of. But after the sickness was over, that spirit of charity abated; and every church being again supplied with their own ministers, or others presented where the minister was dead, things returned to their old channel again.

One mischief always introduces another. These terrors and apprehensions of the people led them into a thousand weak, foolish, and wicked things, which they wanted not a sort of people really wicked to encourage them to, and this was running about to fortune-tellers, cunning-men, and astrologers to know their fortune, or, as it is vulgarly expressed, to have their fortunes told them, their nativities calculated, and the like; and this folly presently made the town swarm with a wicked generation of pretenders to magic, to the black art, as they called it, and I know not what; nay, to a thousand worse dealings with the devil than they were really guilty of. And this trade grew so open and so generally practised that it became common to have signs and inscriptions set up at doors: "Here lives a fortune-teller," "Here lives an astrologer," "Here you may have your nativity calculated," and the like; and Friar Bacon's brazen-head, which was the usual sign of these people's dwellings, was to be seen almost in every street, or else the sign of Mother Shipton, or of Merlin's head, and the like.

With what blind, absurd, and ridiculous stuff these oracles of the devil pleased and satisfied the people I really know not, but certain it is that innumerable attendants crowded about their doors every day. And if but a grave fellow in a velvet jacket, a band, and a black cloak, which was the habit those quack-conjurers generally went in, was but seen in the streets the people would follow them in crowds, and ask them questions as they went along.

I need not mention what a horrid delusion this was, or what it tended to; but there was no remedy for it till the plague itself put an end to it all, and, I suppose, cleared the town of most of those calculators themselves.

One mischief was, that if the poor people asked these mock astrologers whether there would be a plague or no, they all agreed in general to answer "Yes," for that kept up their trade. And had the people not been kept in a fright about that, the wizards would presently have been rendered useless, and their craft had been at an end. But they always talked to them of such-and-such influences of the stars, of the conjunctions of such-and-such planets, which must necessarily bring sickness and distempers, and consequently the plague. And some had the assurance to tell them the plague was begun already, which was too true, though they that said so knew nothing of the matter. The ministers, to do them justice, and preachers of most sorts that were serious and understanding persons, thundered against these and other wicked practices, and exposed the folly as well as the wickedness of them together, and the most sober and judicious people despised and abhorred them. But it was impossible to make any impression upon the middling people and the working labouring poor. Their fears were predominant over all their passions, and they threw away their money in a most distracted manner upon those whimsies. Maid-servants especially, and men-servants, were the chief of their customers, and their question generally was, after the first demand of "Will there be a plague?" I say, the next question was, "Oh, sir! for the Lord's sake, what will become of me? Will my mistress keep me, or will she turn me off? Will she stay here, or will she go into the country? And if she goes into the country, will she take me with her, or leave me here to be starved and undone?" And the like of men-servants.

The truth is, the case of poor servants was very dismal, as I shall have occasion to mention again by-and-by, for it was apparent a prodigious number of them would be turned away, and it was so. And of them abundance perished, and particularly of those that these false prophets had flattered with hopes that they should be continued in their services, and carried with their masters and mistresses into the country; and had not public charity provided for these poor creatures, whose number was exceeding great, and in all cases of this nature must be so, they would have been in the worst condition of any people in the city.

These things agitated the minds of the common people for many months, while the first apprehensions were upon them, and while the plague was not, as I may say, yet broken out. But I must also not forget that the more serious part of the inhabitants behaved after another manner. The Government encouraged their devotion, and appointed public prayers and days of fasting and humiliation, to make public confession of sin and implore the mercy of God to avert the dreadful judgment which hung over their heads; and it is not to be expressed with what alacrity the people of all persuasions embraced the occasion; how they flocked to the churches and meetings, and they were all so thronged that there was often no coming near, no, not to the very doors of the largest churches. Also there were daily prayers appointed morning and evening at several churches, and days of private praying at other places; at all which the people attended, I say, with an uncommon devotion. Several private families also, as well as one opinion as of another, kept family fasts, to which they admitted their near relations only. So that, in a word, those people who were really serious and religious applied themselves in a truly Christian manner to the proper work of repentance and humiliation, as a Christian people ought to do.

Again, the public showed that they would bear their share in these things; the very Court, which was then gay and luxurious, put on a face of just concern for the public danger. All the plays and interludes which, after the manner of the French Court, had been set up, and began to increase among us, were forbid to act; the gaming-tables, public dancing-rooms, and music-houses, which multiplied and began to debauch the manners of the people, were shut up and suppressed; and the jack-puddings, merry-andrews, puppet-shows, rope-dancers, and such-like doings, which had bewitched the poor common people, shut up their shops, finding indeed no trade; for the minds of the people were agitated with other things, and a kind of sadness and horror at these things sat upon the countenances even of the common people. Death was before their eyes, and everybody began to think of their graves, not of mirth and diversions.

But even those wholesome reflections, which, rightly managed, would have most happily led the people to fall upon their knees, make confession of their sins, and look up to their merciful Saviour for pardon, imploring His compassion on them in such a time of their distress, by which we might have been as a second Nineveh, had a quite contrary extreme in the common people, who, ignorant and stupid in their reflections, as they were brutishly wicked and thoughtless before, were now led by their fright to extremes of folly; and, as I have said before that they ran to conjurers and witches, and all sorts of deceivers, to know what should become of them (who fed their fears, and kept them always alarmed and awake on purpose to delude them and pick their pockets), so they were as mad upon their running after quacks and mountebanks, and every practising old woman, for medicines and remedies; storing themselves with such multitudes of pills, potions, and preservatives, as they were called, that they not only spent their money, but even poisoned themselves beforehand, for fear of the poison of the infection, and prepared their bodies for the plague, instead of preserving them against it. On the other hand, it is incredible, and scarce to be imagined, how the posts of houses and corners of streets were plastered over with doctors' bills and papers of ignorant fellows, quacking and tampering in physic, and inviting the people to come to them for remedies, which was generally set off with such flourishes as these, viz.: "Infallible preventive pills against the plague." "Never-failing preservatives against the infection." "Sovereign cordials against the corruption of the air." "Exact regulations for the conduct of the body in case of an infection." "Anti-pestilential pills." "Incomparable drink against the plague, never found out before." "An universal remedy for the plague." "The only true plague water." "The royal antidote against all kinds of infection;" and such a number more that I cannot reckon up; and if I could, would fill a book of themselves to set them down.

Others set up bills to summon people to their lodgings for directions and advice in the case of infection. These had specious titles also, such as these:

"An eminent High Dutch physician, newly come over from Holland, where he resided during all the time of the great plague last year in Amsterdam, and cured multitudes of people that actually had the plague upon them."

"An Italian gentlewoman just arrived from Naples, having a choice secret to prevent infection, which she found out by her great experience, and did wonderful cures with it in the late plague there, wherein there died 20,000 in one day."

"An ancient gentlewoman, having practised with great success in the late plague in this city, anno 1636, gives her advice only to the female sex. To be spoke with," &c.

"An experienced physician, who has long studied the doctrine of antidotes against all sorts of poison and infection, has, after forty years' practice, arrived to such skill as may, with God's blessing, direct persons how to prevent their being touched by any contagious distemper whatsoever. He directs the poor gratis."

I take notice of these by way of specimen. I could give you two or three dozen of the like and yet have abundance left behind. 'T is sufficient from these to apprise any one of the humour of those times, and how a set of thieves and pickpockets not only robbed and cheated the poor people of their money, but poisoned their bodies with odious and fatal preparations; some with mercury, and some with other things as bad, perfectly remote from the thing pretended to, and rather hurtful than serviceable to the body in case an infection followed.

I cannot omit a subtilty of one of those quack operators, with which he gulled the poor people to crowd about him, but did nothing for them without money. He had, it seems, added to his bills, which he gave about the streets, this advertisement in capital letters, viz., "He gives advice to the poor for nothing."

Abundance of poor people came to him accordingly, to whom he made a great many fine speeches, examined them of the state of their health and of the constitution of their bodies, and told them many good things for them to do, which were of no great moment. But the issue and conclusion of all was, that he had a preparation which if they took such a quantity of every morning, he would pawn his life they should never have the plague; no, though they lived in the house with people that were infected. This made the people all resolve to have it; but then the price of that was so much, I think 't was half-a-crown. "But, sir," says one poor woman, "I am a poor alms-woman, and am kept by the parish, and your bills say you give the poor your help for nothing." "Ay, good woman," says the doctor, "so I do, as I published there.

I give my advice to the poor for nothing, but not my physic." "Alas, sir!" says she, "that is a snare laid for the poor, then; for you give them your advice for nothing; that is to say, you advise them gratis, to buy your physic for their money; so does every shopkeeper with his wares." Here the woman began to give him ill words, and stood at his door all that day, telling her tale to all the people that came, till the doctor finding she turned away his customers, was obliged to call her upstairs again, and give her his box of physic for nothing, which perhaps, too, was good for nothing when she had it.

But to return to the people, whose confusions fitted them to be imposed upon by all sorts of pretenders and by every mountebank. There is no doubt but these quacking sort of fellows raised great gains out of the miserable people, for we daily found the crowds that ran after them were infinitely greater, and their doors were more thronged than those of Dr. Brooks, Dr. Upton, Dr. Hodges, Dr. Berwick, or any, though the most famous men of the time. And I was told that some of them got five pounds a day by their physic.

But there was still another madness beyond all this, which may serve to give an idea of the distracted humour of the poor people at that time, and this was their following a worse sort of deceivers than any of these; for these petty thieves only deluded them to pick their pockets and get their money, in which their wickedness, whatever it was, lay chiefly on the side of the deceivers deceiving, not upon the deceived. But in this part I am going to mention it lay chiefly in the people deceived, or equally in both, and this was in wearing charms, philtres, exorcisms, amulets, and I know not what preparations, to fortify the body with them against the plague; as if the plague was not the hand of God, but a kind of a possession of an evil spirit, and that it was to be kept off with crossings, signs of the zodiac, papers tied up with so many knots, and certain words of figures written on them, as particularly the word Abracadabra, formed in triangle or pyramid, thus:—

ABRACADABRA
ABRACADABR
ABRACADAB
ABRACADA
ABRACAD
ABRACA
ABRAC
ABRA
ABR
AB
A

Others had the Jesuits'
mark in a cross:
I H
S.
Others nothing but this
mark, thus:

✳

I might spend a great deal of time in my exclamations against the follies, and indeed the wickedness, of those things, in a time of such danger, in a matter of such consequences as this, of a national infection. But my memorandums of these things relate rather to take notice only of the fact, and mention only that it was so. How the poor people found the insufficiency of those things, and how many of them were afterwards carried away in the dead-carts and thrown into the common graves of every parish with these hellish charms and trumpery hanging about their necks, remains to be spoken of as we go along.

All this was the effect of the hurry the people were in, after the first notion of the plague being at hand was among them, and which may be said to be from about Michaelmas 1664, but more particularly after the two men died in St. Giles's, in the beginning of December; and again, after another alarm in February. For when the plague evidently spread itself, they soon began to see the folly of trusting to those unperforming creatures who had gulled them of their money; and then their fears worked another way, namely, to amazement and stupidity, not knowing what course to take or what to do either to help or relieve themselves. But they ran about from one neighbour's house to another, and even in the streets, from one door to another, with repeated cries of, "Lord, have mercy upon us! What shall we do?"

Indeed, the poor people were to be pitied in one particular thing, in which they had little or no relief, and which I desire to mention with a serious awe and reflection, which perhaps every one that reads this may not relish, namely, that whereas death now began not, as we may say, to hover over every one's head only, but to look into their houses and chambers, and stare in their faces. Though there might be some stupidity and dulness of the mind, and there was so, a great deal, yet there was a great deal of just alarm sounded into the very inmost soul, if I may so say, of others. Many consciences were awakened; many hard hearts melted into tears; many a penitent confession was made of crimes long concealed. It would wound the soul of any Christian to have heard the dying groans of many a despairing creature, and none durst come near to comfort them. Many a robbery, many a murder, was then confessed aloud, and nobody surviving to record the accounts of it. People might be heard, even into the streets as we passed along, calling upon God for mercy, through Jesus Christ, and saying, "I have been a thief," "I have been an adulterer," "I have been a murderer," and the like, and none durst stop to make the least inquiry into such things or to administer comfort to the poor creatures, that in the anguish both of soul and body thus cried out. Some of the ministers did visit the sick at first and for a little while, but it was not to be done. It would have been present death to have gone into some houses. The very buriers of the dead, who were the hardenedest creatures in town, were sometimes beaten back and so terrified that they durst not go into houses where the whole families were swept away together, and where the circumstances were more particularly horrible, as some were; but this was, indeed, at the first heat of the distemper.

Time inured them to it all, and they ventured everywhere afterwards without hesitation, as I shall have occasion to mention at large hereafter.

I am supposing now the plague to be begun, as I have said, and that the magistrates began to take the condition of the people into their serious consideration. What they did as to the regulation of the inhabitants and of infected families I shall speak to by itself; but as to the affair of health, it is proper to mention it here, that, having seen the foolish humour of the people in running after quacks and mountebanks, wizards and fortune-tellers, which they did as above, even to madness, the Lord Mayor, a very sober and religious gentleman, appointed physicians and surgeons for relief of the poor—I mean the diseased poor —and in particular ordered the College of Physicians to publish directions for cheap remedies for the poor, in all the circumstances of the distemper. This, indeed, was one of the most charitable and judicious things that could be done at that time, for this drove the people from haunting the doors of every disperser of bills, and from taking down blindly, and without consideration, poison for physic and death instead of life.

This direction of the physicians was done by a consultation of the whole College, and as it was particularly calculated for the use of the poor and for cheap medicines, it was made public, so that everybody might see it, and copies were given gratis to all that desired it. But as it is public, and to be seen on all occasions, I need not give the reader of this the trouble of it.

I shall not be supposed to lessen the authority or capacity of the physicians when I say that the violence of the distemper, when it came to its extremity, was like the fire the next year. The fire, which consumed what the plague could not touch, defied all the application of remedies; the fire-engines were broken, the buckets thrown away, and the power of man was baffled and brought to an end. So the plague defied all medicines; the very physicians were seized with it, with their preservatives in their mouths; and men went about prescribing to others and telling them what to do, till the tokens were upon them, and they dropped down dead, destroyed by that very enemy they directed others to oppose. This was the case of several physicians, even some of them the most eminent, and of several of the most skilful surgeons. Abundance of quacks too died, who had the folly to trust to their own medicines, which they must needs be conscious to themselves were good for nothing, and who rather ought, like other sorts of thieves, to have run away, sensible of their guilt, from the justice that they could not but expect should punish them as they knew they had deserved.

Not that it is any derogation from the labour or application of the physicians to say they fell in the common calamity; nor is it so intended by me; it rather is to their praise that they ventured their lives so far as even to lose them in the service of mankind. They endeavoured to do good, and to save the lives of others. But we were not to expect that the physicians could stop God's judgments, or prevent a distemper eminently armed from heaven from executing the errand it was sent about.

Doubtless, the physicians assisted many by their skill, and by their prudence and applications, to the saving of their lives and restoring their health. But it is not lessening their character or their skill, to say they could not cure those that had the tokens upon them, or those who were mortally infected before the physicians were sent for, as was frequently the case.

It remains to mention now what public measures were taken by the magistrates for the general safety, and to prevent the spreading of the distemper, when it first broke out. I shall have frequent occasion to speak of the prudence of the magistrates, their charity, their vigilance for the poor, and for preserving good order, furnishing provisions, and the like, when the plague was increased, as it afterwards was. But I am now upon the order and regulations they published for the government of infected families.

I mentioned above shutting of houses up; and it is needful to say something particularly to that, for this part of the history of the plague is very melancholy, but the most grievous story must be told.

About June the Lord Mayor of London and the Court of Aldermen, as I have said, began more particularly to concern themselves for the regulation of the city.

The Justices of Peace for Middlesex, by direction of the Secretary of State, had begun to shut up houses in the parishes of St. Giles-in-the-Fields, St. Martin, St. Clement Danes, &c., and it was with good success; for in several streets where the plague broke out, upon strict guarding the houses that were infected, and taking care to bury those that died immediately after they were known to be dead, the plague ceased in those streets. It was also observed that the plague decreased sooner in those parishes after they had been visited to the full than it did in the parishes of Bishopsgate, Shoreditch, Aldgate, Whitechapel, Stepney, and others, the early care taken in that manner being a great means to the putting a check to it.

This shutting up of houses was a method first taken, as I understand, in the plague which happened in 1603, at the coming of King James the First to the crown; and the power of shutting people up in their own houses was granted by Act of Parliament, entitled, "An Act for the charitable Relief and Ordering of Persons infected with the Plague;" on which Act of Parliament the Lord Mayor and aldermen of the city of London founded the order they made at this time, and which took place the 1st of July 1665, when the numbers infected within the city were but few, the last bill for the ninety-two parishes being but four; and some houses having been shut up in the city, and some people being removed to the pest-house beyond Bunhill Fields, in the way to Islington,—I say, by these means, when there died near one thousand a week in the whole, the number in the city was but twenty-eight, and the city was preserved more healthy in proportion than any other place all the time of the infection.

These orders of my Lord Mayor's were published, as I have said, the latter end of June, and took place from the 1st of July, and were as follows, viz.:—

ORDERS CONCEIVED AND PUBLISHED BY THE LORD MAYOR AND ALDERMEN OF THE CITY OF LONDON CONCERNING THE INFECTION OF THE PLAGUE, 1665.

"WHEREAS in the reign of our late sovereign King James, of happy memory, an Act was made for the charitable relief and ordering of persons infected with the plague, whereby authority was given to justices of the peace, mayors, bailiffs, and other head-officers to appoint within their several limits examiners, searchers, watchmen, keepers, and buriers for the persons and places infected, and to minister unto them oaths for the performance of their offices. And the same statute did also authorise the giving of other directions, as unto them for the present necessity should seem good in their discretions. It is now, upon special consideration, thought very expedient for preventing and avoiding of infection of sickness (if it shall so please Almighty God) that these officers following be appointed, and these orders hereafter duly observed.

Examiners to be appointed in every Parish.

"First, it is thought requisite, and so ordered, that in every parish there be one, two, or more persons of good sort and credit chosen and appointed by the alderman, his deputy, and common council of every ward, by the name of examiners, to continue in that office the space of two months at least. And if any fit person so appointed shall refuse to undertake the same, the said parties so refusing to be committed to prison until they shall conform themselves accordingly.

The Examiners' Office.

"That these examiners be sworn by the aldermen to inquire and learn from time to time what houses in every parish be visited, and what persons be sick, and of what diseases, as near as they can inform themselves; and upon doubt in that case, to command restraint of access until it appear what the disease shall prove. And if they find any person sick of the infection, to give order to the constable that the house be shut up; and if the constable shall be found remiss or negligent, to give present notice thereof to the alderman of the ward.

Watchmen.

"That to every infected house there be appointed two watchmen, one for every day, and the other for the night; and that these watchmen have a special care that no person go in or out of such infected houses whereof they have the charge, upon pain of severe punishment. And the said watchmen to do such further offices as the sick house shall need and require; and if the watchman be sent upon any business, to lock up the house and take the key with him; and the watchman by day to attend until ten of the clock at night, and the watchman by night until six in the morning.

Searchers.

"That there be a special care to appoint women searchers in every parish, such as are of honest reputation, and of the best sort as can be got in this kind; and these to be sworn to make due search and true report to the utmost of their knowledge whether the persons whose bodies they are appointed to search do die of the infection, or of what other diseases, as near as they can. And that the physicians who shall be appointed for cure and prevention of the infection do call before them the said searchers who are, or shall be, appointed for the several parishes under their respective cares, to the end they may consider whether they are fitly qualified for that employment, and charge them from time to time as they shall see cause, if they appear defective in their duties.

"That no searcher during this time of visitation be permitted to use any public work or employment, or keep any shop or stall, or be employed as a laundress, or in any other common employment whatsoever.

Chirurgeons.

"For better assistance of the searchers, forasmuch as there hath been heretofore great abuse in misreporting the disease, to the further spreading of the infection, it is therefore ordered that there be chosen and appointed able and discreet chirurgeons, besides those that do already belong to the pest-house, amongst whom the city and Liberties to be quartered as the places lie most apt and convenient; and every of these to have one quarter for his limit; and the said chirurgeons in every of their limits to join with the searchers for the view of the body, to the end there may be a true report made of the disease.

"And further, that the said chirurgeons shall visit and search such-like persons as shall either send for them or be named and directed unto them by the examiners of every parish, and inform themselves of the disease of the said parties.

"And forasmuch as the said chirurgeons are to be sequestered from all other cures, and kept only to this disease of the infection, it is ordered that every of the said chirurgeons shall have twelvepence a body searched by them, to be paid out of the goods of the party searched, if he be able, or otherwise by the parish.

Nurse-keepers.

"If any nurse-keeper shall remove herself out of any infected house before twenty-eight days after the decease of any person dying of the infection, the house to which the said nurse-keeper doth so remove herself shall be shut up until the said twenty-eight days be expired."

ORDERS CONCERNING INFECTED HOUSES AND PERSONS SICK OF THE PLAGUE

Notice to be given of the Sickness.

"The master of every house, as soon as any one in his house complaineth, either of blotch or purple, or swelling in any part of his body, or falleth otherwise dangerously sick, without apparent cause of some other disease, shall give knowledge thereof to the examiner of health within two hours after the said sign shall appear.

Sequestration of the Sick.

"As soon as any man shall be found by this examiner, chirurgeon, or searcher to be sick of the plague, he shall the same night be sequestered in the same house; and in case he be so sequestered, then, though he afterwards die not, the house wherein he sickened should be shut up for a month, after the use of the due preservatives taken by the rest.

Airing the Stuff.

"For sequestration of the goods and stuff of the infection, their bedding and apparel and hangings of chambers must be well aired with fire and such perfumes as are requisite within the infected house before they be taken again to use. This to be done by the appointment of the examiner.

Shutting up of the House.

"If any person shall have visited any man known to be infected of the plague, or entered willingly into any known infected house, being not allowed, the house wherein he inhabiteth shall be shut up for certain days by the examiner's direction.

None to be removed out of infected Houses, but, &c.

"Item, that none be removed out of the house where he falleth sick of the infection into any other house in the city (except it be to the pest-house or a tent, or unto some such house which the owner of the said visited house holdeth in his own hands and occupieth by his own servants); and so as security be given to the parish whither such remove is made, that the attendance and charge about the said visited persons shall be observed and charged in all the particularities before expressed, without any cost of that parish to which any such remove shall happen to be made, and this remove to be done by night. And it shall be lawful to any person that hath two houses to remove either his sound or his infected people to his spare house at his choice, so as, if he sent away first his sound, he not after send thither the sick, nor again unto the sick the sound; and that the same which he sendeth be for one week at the least shut up and secluded from company, for fear of some infection at the first not appearing.

Burial of the Dead.

"That the burial of the dead by this visitation be at most convenient hours, always either before sun-rising or after sun-setting, with the privity of the church-wardens or constable, and not otherwise; and that no neighbours nor friends be suffered to accompany the corpse to church, or to enter the house visited, upon pain of having his house shut up or be imprisoned.

"And that no corpse dying of infection shall be buried, or remain in any church in time of common prayer, sermon, or lecture. And that no children be suffered at time of burial of any corpse in any church, churchyard, or burying-place to come near the corpse, coffin, or grave. And that all the graves shall be at least six feet deep.

"And further, all public assemblies at other burials are to be forborne during the continuance of this visitation.

No infected Stuff to be uttered.

"That no clothes, stuff, bedding, or garments be suffered to be carried or conveyed out of any infected houses, and that the criers and carriers abroad of bedding or old apparel to be sold or pawned be utterly prohibited and restrained, and no brokers of bedding or old apparel be permitted to make any outward show, or hang forth on their stalls, shop-boards, or windows, towards any street, lane, common way, or passage, any old bedding or apparel to be sold, upon pain of imprisonment. And if any broker or other person shall buy any bedding, apparel, or other stuff out of any infected house within two months after the infection hath been there, his house shall be shut up as infected, and so shall continue shut up twenty days at the least.

No Person to be conveyed out of any infected House.

"If any person visited do fortune by negligent looking unto, or by any other means, to come or be conveyed from a place infected to any other place, the parish from whence such party hath come or been conveyed, upon notice thereof given, shall at their charge cause the said party so visited and escaped to be carried and brought back again by night, and the parties in this case offending to be punished at the direction of the alderman of the ward, and the house of the receiver of such visited person to be shut up for twenty days.

Every visited House to be marked.

"That every house visited be marked with a red cross of a foot long in the middle of the door, evident to be seen, and with these usual printed words, that is to say, 'Lord, have mercy upon us,' to be set close over the same cross, there to continue until lawful opening of the same house.

Every visited House to be watched.

"That the constables see every house shut up, and to be attended with watchmen, which may keep them in, and minister necessaries unto them at their own charges, if they be able, or at the common charge, if they be unable; the shutting up to be for the space of four weeks after all be whole.

"That precise order be taken that the searchers, chirurgeons, keepers, and buriers are not to pass the streets without holding a red rod or wand of three feet in length in their hands, open and evident to be seen, and are not to go into any other house than into their own, or into that whereunto they are directed or sent for; but to forbear and abstain from company, especially when they have been lately used in any such business or attendance.

Inmates.

"That where several inmates are in one and the same house, and any person in that house happens to be infected, no other person or family of such house shall be suffered to remove him or themselves without a certificate from the examiners of health of that parish; or in default thereof, the house whither he or they so remove shall be shut up as in case of visitation.

Hackney-coaches.

"That care be taken of hackney-coachmen, that they may not (as some of them have been observed to do after carrying of infected persons to the pest-house and other places) be admitted to common use till their coaches be well aired, and have stood unemployed by the space of five or six days after such service."

ORDERS FOR CLEANSING AND KEEPING OF THE STREETS SWEET.

The Streets to be kept Clean.

"First, it is thought necessary, and so ordered, that every householder do cause the street to be daily prepared before his door, and so to keep it clean swept all the week long.

That Rakers take it from out the Houses.

"That the sweeping and filth of houses be daily carried away by the rakers, and that the raker shall give notice of his coming by the blowing of a horn, as hitherto hath been done.

Laystalls to be made far off from the City.

"That the laystalls be removed as far as may be out of the city and common passages, and that no nightman or other be suffered to empty a vault into any garden near about the city.

Care to be had of unwholesome Fish or Flesh, and of musty Corn.

"That special care be taken that no stinking fish, or unwholesome flesh, or musty corn, or other corrupt fruits of what sort soever, be suffered to be sold about the city, or any part of the same.

"That the brewers and tippling-houses be looked unto for musty and unwholesome casks.

"That no hogs, dogs, or cats, or tame pigeons, or conies, be suffered to be kept within any part of the city, or any swine to be or stray in the streets or lanes, but that such swine be impounded by the beadle or any other officer, and the owner punished according to Act of Common Council, and that the dogs be killed by the dog-killers appointed for that purpose."

ORDERS CONCERNING LOOSE PERSONS AND IDLE ASSEMBLIES.

Beggars.

"Forasmuch as nothing is more complained of than the multitude of rogues and wandering beggars that swarm in every place about the city, being a great cause of the spreading of the infection, and will not be avoided, notwithstanding any orders that have been given to the contrary: It is therefore now ordered, that such constables, and others whom this matter may any way concern, take special care that no wandering beggars be suffered in the streets of this city in any fashion or manner whatsoever, upon the penalty provided by the law, to be duly and severely executed upon them.

Plays.

"That all plays, bear-baitings, games, singing of ballads, buckler-play, or such-like causes of assemblies of people be utterly prohibited, and the parties offending severely punished by every alderman in his ward.

Feasting prohibited.

"That all public feastings, and particularly by the companies of this city, and dinners at taverns, ale-houses, and other places of common entertainment, be forborne till further order and allowance; and that the money thereby spared be preserved and employed for the benefit and relief of the poor visited with the infection.

Tippling-houses.

"That disorderly tippling in taverns, ale-houses, coffee-houses, and cellars be severely looked unto, as the common sin of this time and the greatest occasion of dispersing the plague. And that no company or person be suffered to remain or come into any tavern, ale-house, or coffee-house to drink after nine of the clock in the evening, according to the ancient law and custom of this city, upon the penalties ordained in that behalf.

"And for the better execution of these orders, and such other rules and directions as, upon further consideration, shall be found needful: It is ordered and enjoined that the aldermen, deputies, and common councilmen shall meet together weekly, once, twice, thrice or oftener (as cause shall require), at some one general place accustomed in their respective wards (being clear from infection of the plague), to consult how the said orders may be duly put in execution; not intending that any dwelling in or near places infected shall come to the said meeting while their coming may be doubtful. And the said aldermen, and deputies, and common councilmen in their several wards may put in execution any other good orders that by them at their said meetings shall be conceived and devised for preservation of his Majesty's subjects from the infection.

"Sir JOHN LAWRENCE, *Lord Mayor.*
Sir GEORGE WATERMAN, *Sheriffs.*"
Sir CHARLES DOE,

I need not say that these orders extended only to such places as were within the Lord Mayor's jurisdiction, so it is requisite to observe that the Justices of Peace within those parishes and places as were called the Hamlets and out-parts took the same method. As I remember, the orders for shutting up of houses did not take place so soon on our side, because, as I said before, the plague did not reach to these eastern parts of the town at least, nor begin to be very violent, till the beginning of August. For example, the whole bill from the 11th to the 18th of July

was 1761, yet there died but 71 of the plague in all those
parishes we call the Tower Hamlets, and they were as
follows:—

		The next week was thus:	And to the 1st of Aug. thus:
Aldgate	14	34	65
Stepney	33	58	76
Whitechapel	21	48	79
St. Catherine, Tower . . .	2	4	4
Trinity, Minories	1	1	4
	71	145	228

It was indeed coming on amain, for the burials that
same week were in the next adjoining parishes thus:—

		The next week prodigiously increased, as:	To the 1st of Aug. thus:
St. Leonard's, Shoreditch .	64	84	110
St. Botolph's, Bishopsgate	65	105	116
St. Giles's, Cripplegate .	213	421	554
	342	610	780

This shutting up of houses was at first counted a very
cruel and unchristian method, and the poor people so
confined made bitter lamentations. Complaints of the
severity of it were also daily brought to my Lord Mayor,
of houses causelessly (and some maliciously) shut up. I
cannot say; but upon inquiry many that complained so
loudly were found in a condition to be continued; and
others again, inspection being made upon the sick person, and the sickness not appearing infectious, or if uncertain, yet on his being content to be carried to the
pest-house, were released.

It is true that the locking up the doors of people's

houses, and setting a watchman there night and day to prevent their stirring out or any coming to them, when perhaps the sound people in the family might have escaped if they had been removed from the sick, looked very hard and cruel; and many people perished in these miserable confinements which, 't is reasonable to believe, would not have been distempered if they had had liberty, though the plague was in the house; at which the people were very clamorous and uneasy at first, and several violences were committed and injuries offered to the men who were set to watch the houses so shut up; also several people broke out by force in many places, as I shall observe by-and-by. But it was a public good that justified the private mischief, and there was no obtaining the least mitigation by any application to magistrates or government at that time, at least not that I heard of. This put the people upon all manner of stratagem in order, if possible, to get out; and it would fill a little volume to set down the arts used by the people of such houses to shut the eyes of the watchmen who were employed, to deceive them, and to escape or break out from them, in which frequent scuffles and some mischief happened; of which by itself.

As I went along Houndsditch one morning about eight o'clock there was a great noise. It is true, indeed, there was not much crowd, because people were not very free to gather together, or to stay long together when they were there; nor did I stay long there. But the outcry was loud enough to prompt my curiosity, and I called to one that looked out of a window, and asked what was the matter.

A watchman, it seems, had been employed to keep his post at the door of a house which was infected, or said to be infected, and was shut up. He had been there all night for two nights together, as he told his story, and the day-watchman had been there one day, and was now come to relieve him. All this while no noise had been heard in the house, no light had been seen; they called for nothing, sent him of no errands, which used to be the chief business of the watchmen; neither had they given him any disturbance, as he said, from the Monday afternoon, when he heard great crying and screaming in the house, which, as he supposed, was occasioned by some of the family dying just at that time. It seems, the night before, the dead-cart, as it was called, had been stopped there, and a servant-maid had been brought down to the door dead, and the buriers or bearers, as they were called, put her into the cart, wrapt only in a green rug, and carried her away.

The watchman had knocked at the door, it seems, when he heard that noise and crying, as above, and nobody answered a great while; but at last one looked out and said with an angry, quick tone, and yet a kind of crying voice, or a voice of one that was crying, "What d'ye want, that ye make such a knocking?" He answered, "I am the watchman! How do you do? What is the matter?" The person answered, "What is that to you? Stop the dead-cart." This, it seems, was about one o'clock. Soon after, as the fellow said, he stopped the dead-cart, and then knocked again, but nobody answered. He continued knocking, and the bellman called out several times, "Bring out your dead;" but nobody answered, till the man that drove the cart, being called to other houses, would stay no longer, and drove away.

The watchman knew not what to make of all this, so he let them alone till the morning-man or day-watchman, as they called him, came to relieve him. Giving him an account of the particulars, they knocked at the door a great while, but nobody answered; and they observed that the window or casement at which the person had looked out who had answered before continued open, being up two pairs of stairs.

Upon this the two men, to satisfy their curiosity, got a long ladder, and one of them went up to the window and looked into the room, where he saw a woman lying dead upon the floor in a dismal manner, having no clothes on but her shift. But though he called aloud, and putting in his long staff, knocked hard on the floor, yet nobody stirred or answered; neither could he hear any noise in the house.

He came down again upon this, and acquainted his fellow, who went up also; and finding it just so, they resolved to acquaint either the Lord Mayor or some other magistrate of it, but did not offer to go in at the window. The magistrate, it seems, upon the information of the two men, ordered the house to be broke open, a constable and other persons being appointed to be present, that nothing might be plundered; and accordingly it was so done, when nobody was found in the house but that young woman, who having been infected and past recovery, the rest had left her to die by herself, and were every one gone, having found some way to delude the watchman, and to get open the door, or get out at some back door, or over the tops of the houses, so that he knew nothing of it; and as to those cries and shrieks which he heard, it was supposed they were the passionate cries of the family at the bitter parting, which, to be sure, it was to them all, this being the sister to the mistress of the family. The man of the house, his wife, several children, and servants, being all gone and fled, whether sick or sound, that I could never learn; nor, indeed, did I make much inquiry after it.

Many such escapes were made out of infected houses, as particularly when the watchman was sent of some errand; for it was his business to go of any errand that the family sent him of; that is to say, for necessaries, such as food and physic; to fetch physicians, if they would come, or surgeons, or nurses, or to order the dead-cart, and the like; but with this condition, too, that when he went he was to lock up the outer door of the house and take the key away with him. To evade this, and cheat the watchmen, people got two or three keys made to their locks, or they found ways to unscrew the locks such as were screwed on, and so take off the lock, being in the inside of the house, and while they sent away the watch-man to the market, to the bake-house, or for one trifle or another, open the door and go out as often as they pleased. But this being found out, the officers afterwards had orders to padlock up the doors on the outside, and place bolts on them as they thought fit.

At another house, as I was informed, in the street next within Aldgate, a whole family was shut up and locked in because the maid-servant was taken sick. The master of the house had complained by his friends to the next alderman and to the Lord Mayor, and had consented to have the maid carried to the pest-house, but was refused; so the door was marked with a red cross, a padlock on the outside, as above, and a watchman set to keep the door, according to public order.

After the master of the house found there was no remedy, but that he, his wife, and his children were to be locked up with this poor distempered servant, he called to the watchman, and told him he must go then and fetch a nurse for them to attend this poor girl, for that it would be certain death to them all to oblige them to nurse her; and told him plainly that if he would not do this, the maid must perish either of the distemper or be starved for want of food, for he was resolved none of his family should go near her; and she lay in the garret four storey high, where she could not cry out, or call to anybody for help.

The watchman consented to that, and went and fetched a nurse, as he was appointed, and brought her to them the same evening. During this interval the master of the house took his opportunity to break a large hole through his shop into a bulk or stall, where formerly a cobbler had sat, before or under his shop-window; but the tenant, as may be supposed at such a dismal time as that, was dead or removed, and so he had the key in his own keeping. Having made his way into this stall, which he could not have done if the man had been at the door, the noise he was obliged to make being such as would have alarmed the watchman; I say, having made his way into this stall, he sat still till the watchman returned with the nurse, and all the next day also. But the night following, having contrived to send the watchman on another trifling errand, which, as I take it, was to an apothecary's for a plaister for the maid, which he was to stay for the making up, or some other such errand that might secure his staying some time; in that time he conveyed himself and all his family out of the house, and left the nurse and the watchman to bury the poor wench—that is, throw her into the cart—and take care of the house.

I could give a great many such stories as these, diverting enough, which in the long course of that dismal year I met with—that is, heard of—and which are very certain to be true, or very near the truth; that is to say, true in the general, for no man could at such a time learn all the particulars. There was likewise violence used with the watchman, as was reported, in abundance of places; and I believe that from the beginning of the visitation to the end, there was not less than eighteen or twenty of them killed, or so wounded as to be taken up for dead, which was supposed to be done by the people in the infected houses which were shut up, and where they attempted to come out, and were opposed.

Nor, indeed, could less be expected, for here were so many prisons in the town as there were houses shut up; and as the people shut up or imprisoned so were guilty of no crime, only shut up because miserable, it was really the more intolerable to them.

It had also this difference, that every prison, as we may call it, had but one jailer, and as he had the whole house to guard, and that many houses were so situated as that they had several ways out, some more, some less, and some into several streets, it was impossible for one man so to guard all the passages as to prevent the escape of people made desperate by the fright of their circumstances, by the resentment of their usage, or by the raging of the distemper itself; so that they would talk to the watchman on one side of the house, while the family made their escape at another.

For example, in Coleman Street there are abundance of alleys, as appears still. A house was shut up in that they call White's Alley, and this house had a back-window, not a door, into a court, which had a passage into Bell Alley. A watchman was set by the constable at the door of this house, and there he stood, or his comrade, night and day, while the family went all away in the evening out at that window into the court, and left the poor fellows warding and watching for near a fortnight.

Not far from the same place they blew up a watchman with gunpowder, and burned the poor fellow dreadfully; and while he made hideous cries, and nobody would venture to come near to help him, the whole family that were able to stir got out at the windows one storey high, two that were left sick calling out for help. Care was taken to give them nurses to look after them, but the persons fled were never found, till after the plague was abated they returned; but as nothing could be proved, so nothing could be done to them.

It is to be considered, too, that as these were prisons without bars and bolts, which our common prisons are furnished with, so the people let themselves down out of their windows, even in the face of the watchman, bringing swords or pistols in their hands, and threatening the poor wretch to shoot him if he stirred or called for help.

In other cases, some had gardens, and walls or pales, between them and their neighbours, or yards and back-houses; and these, by friendship and entreaties, would get leave to get over those walls or pales, and so go out at their neighbours' doors; or, by giving money to their servants, get them to let them through in the night; so that, in short, the shutting up of houses was in no wise to be depended upon. Neither did it answer the end at all, serving more to make the people desperate, and drive them to such extremities as that they would break out at all adventures.

And that which was still worse, those that did thus break out spread the infection farther by their wandering about with the distemper upon them, in their desperate circumstances, than they would otherwise have done; for whoever considers all the particulars in such cases must acknowledge, and we cannot doubt but the severity of those confinements made many people desperate, and made them run out of their houses at all hazards, and with the plague visibly upon them, not knowing either whither to go or what to do, or, indeed, what they did; and many that did so were driven to dreadful exigencies and extremities, and perished in the streets or fields for mere want, or dropped down by the raging violence of the fever upon them. Others wandered into the country, and went forward any way, as their desperation guided them, not knowing whither they went or would go, till faint and tired, and not getting any relief, the houses and villages on the road refusing to admit them to lodge, whether infected or no, they have perished by the road-side, or gotten into barns and died there, none daring to come to them or relieve them, though perhaps not infected, for nobody would believe them.

On the other hand, when the plague at first seized a family, that is to say, when any one body of the family had gone out and unwarily or otherwise catched the distemper and brought it home, it was certainly known by the family before it was known to the officers, who, as you will see by the order, were appointed to examine into the circumstances of all sick persons when they heard of their being sick.

In this interval between their being taken sick and the examiners coming, the master of the house had leisure and liberty to remove himself or all his family, if he knew whither to go, and many did so. But the great disaster was, that many did thus after they were really infected themselves, and so carried the disease into the houses of those who were so hospitable as to receive them, which, it must be confessed, was very cruel and ungrateful.

And this was, in part, the reason of the general notion, or scandal rather, which went about of the temper of people infected, namely, that they did not take the least care or make any scruple of infecting others, though I cannot say but there might be some truth in it too, but not so general as was reported. What natural reason could be given for so wicked a thing at a time when they might conclude themselves just going to appear at the bar of Divine Justice I know not. I am very well satisfied that it cannot be reconciled to religion and principle any more than it can be to generosity and humanity, but I may speak of that again.

I am speaking now of people made desperate by the

apprehensions of their being shut up, and their breaking out by stratagem or force, either before or after they were shut up, whose misery was not lessened when they were out, but sadly increased. On the other hand, many that thus got away had retreats to go to and other houses, where they locked themselves up and kept hid till the plague was over; and many families, foreseeing the approach of the distemper, laid up stores of provisions sufficient for their whole families, and shut themselves up, and that so entirely that they were neither seen or heard of till the infection was quite ceased, and then came abroad sound and well. I might recollect several such as these, and give you the particulars of their management; for, doubtless, it was the most effectual secure step that could be taken for such whose circumstances would not admit them to remove, or who had not retreats abroad proper for the case; for, in being thus shut up, they were as if they had been a hundred miles off. Nor do I remember that any of those families miscarried. Among these several Dutch merchants were particularly remarkable, who kept their houses like little garrisons besieged, suffering none to go in or out or come near them, particularly one in a court in Throgmorton Street, whose house looked into Draper's Garden.

But I come back to the case of families infected, and shut up by the magistrates. The misery of those families is not to be expressed; and it was generally in such houses that we heard the most dismal shrieks and outcries of the poor people, terrified and even frighted to death by the sight of the condition of their dearest relations, and by the terror of being imprisoned as they were.

I remember, and while I am writing this story I think I hear the very sound of it, a certain lady had an only daughter, a young maiden about nineteen years old, and who was possessed of a very considerable fortune. They were only lodgers in the house where they were. The young woman, her mother, and the maid had been abroad on some occasion, I do not remember what, for the house was not shut up; but about two hours after they came home the young lady complained she was not well; in a quarter of an hour more she vomited and had a violent pain in her head. "Pray God," says her mother, in a terrible fright, "my child has not the distemper!" The pain in her head increasing, her mother ordered the bed to be warmed, and resolved to put her to bed, and prepared to give her things to sweat, which was the ordinary remedy to be taken when the first apprehensions of the distemper began.

While the bed was airing the mother undressed the young woman, and just as she was laid down in the bed, she, looking upon her body with a candle, immediately discovered the fatal tokens on the inside of her thighs. Her mother, not being able to contain herself, threw down her candle and screeched out in such a frightful manner that it was enough to place horror upon the stoutest heart in the world; nor was it one scream or one cry, but the fright having seized her spirits, she fainted first, then recovered, then ran all over the house, up the stairs and down the stairs, like one distracted, and indeed really was distracted, and continued screeching and crying out for several hours void of all sense, or, at least, government of her senses, and, as I was told, never came thoroughly to herself again. As to the young maiden, she was a dead corpse from that moment, for the gangrene which occasions the spots had spread [over] her whole body, and she died in less than two hours. But still the mother continued crying out, not knowing anything more of her child, several hours after she was dead. It is so long ago that I am not certain, but I think the mother never recovered, but died in two or three weeks after.

This was an extraordinary case, and I am therefore the more particular in it, because I came so much to the knowledge of it; but there were innumerable such-like cases, and it was seldom that the weekly bill came in but there were two or three put in frighted; that is, that may well be called frighted to death. But besides those who were so frighted as to die upon the spot, there were great numbers frighted to other extremes, some frighted out of their senses, some out of their memory, and some out of their understanding. But I return to the shutting up of houses.

As several people, I say, got out of their houses by stratagem after they were shut up, so others got out by bribing the watchmen, and giving them money to let them go privately out in the night. I must confess I thought it at that time the most innocent corruption or bribery that any man could be guilty of, and therefore could not but pity the poor men, and think it was hard when three of those watchmen were publicly whipped through the streets for suffering people to go out of houses shut up.

But notwithstanding that severity, money prevailed with the poor men, and many families found means to make sallies out, and escape that way after they had been shut up; but these were generally such as had some places to retire to; and though there was no easy passing the roads any whither after the 1st of August, yet there were many ways of retreat, and particularly, as I hinted, some got tents and set them up in the fields, carrying beds or straw to lie on, and provisions to eat, and so lived in them as hermits in a cell, for nobody would venture to come near them; and several stories were told of such, some comical, some tragical, some who lived like wandering pilgrims in the deserts, and escaped by making themselves exiles in such a manner as is scarce to be credited, and who yet enjoyed more liberty than was to be expected in such cases.

I have by me a story of two brothers and their kinsman, who being single men, but that had stayed in the city too long to get away, and indeed not knowing where to go to have any retreat, nor having wherewith to travel far, took a course for their own preservation, which though in itself at first desperate, yet was so natural that it may be wondered that no more did so at that time. They were but of mean condition, and yet not so very poor as that they could not furnish themselves with some little conveniences such as might serve to keep life and soul together; and finding the distemper increasing in a terrible manner, they resolved to shift as well as they could, and to be gone.

One of them had been a soldier in the late wars, and before that in the Low Countries, and having been bred to no particular employment but his arms, and besides being wounded, and not able to work very hard, had for some time been employed at a baker's of sea-biscuit in Wapping.

The brother of this man was a seaman too, but somehow or other had been hurt of one leg, that he could not go to sea, but had worked for his living at a sailmaker's in Wapping, or thereabouts; and being a good husband, had laid up some money, and was the richest of the three.

The third man was a joiner or carpenter by trade, a handy fellow, and he had no wealth but his box or basket of tools, with the help of which he could at any time get his living, such a time as this excepted, wherever he went, and he lived near Shadwell.

They all lived in Stepney parish, which, as I have said, being the last that was infected, or at least violently, they stayed there till they evidently saw the plague was abating at the west part of the town, and coming towards the east, where they lived.

The story of those three men, if the reader will be content to have me give it in their own persons, without taking upon me to either vouch the particulars or answer for any mistakes, I shall give as distinctly as I can, believing the history will be a very good pattern for any poor man to follow, in case the like public desolation should happen here; and if there may be no such occasion, which God of His infinite mercy grant us, still the story may have its uses so many ways as that it will, I hope, never be said that the relating has been unprofitable.

I say all this previous to the history, having yet, for the present, much more to say before I quit my own part.

I went all the first part of the time freely about the streets, though not so freely as to run myself into apparent danger, except when they dug the great pit in the churchyard of our parish of Aldgate. A terrible pit it was, and I could not resist my curiosity to go and see it. As near as I may judge, it was about forty feet in length, and about fifteen or sixteen feet broad, and, at the time I first looked at it, about nine feet deep; but it was said they dug it near twenty feet deep afterwards in one part of it, till they could go no deeper for the water; for they had, it seems, dug several large pits before this. For though the plague was long a-coming to our parish, yet, when it did come, there was no parish in or about London where it raged with such violence as in the two parishes of Aldgate and Whitechapel.

I say they had dug several pits in another ground, when the distemper began to spread in our parish, and especially when the dead-carts began to go about, which was not, in our parish, till the beginning of August. Into these pits they had put perhaps fifty or sixty bodies each; then they made larger holes, wherein they buried all that the cart brought in a week, which, by the middle to the end of August, came to from 200 to 400 a week; and they could not well dig them larger, because of the order of the magistrates confining them to leave no bodies within six feet of the surface; and the water coming on at about seventeen or eighteen feet, they could not well, I say, put more in one pit. But now, at the beginning of September, the plague raging in a dreadful manner, and the number of burials in our parish increasing to more than was ever buried in any parish about London of no larger extent, they ordered this dreadful gulf to be dug, for such it was rather than a pit.

They had supposed this pit would have supplied them for a month or more when they dug it, and some blamed the churchwardens for suffering such a frightful thing, telling them they were making preparations to bury the whole parish, and the like; but time made it appear the churchwardens knew the condition of the parish better than they did, for the pit being finished the 4th of September, I think, they began to bury in it the 6th, and by the 20th, which was just two weeks, they had thrown into it 1114 bodies, when they were obliged to fill it up, the bodies being then come to lie within six feet of the surface. I doubt not but there may be some ancient persons alive in the parish who can justify the fact of this, and are able to show even in what place of the churchyard the pit lay better than I can. The mark of it also was many years to be seen in the churchyard on the surface, lying in length parallel with the passage which goes by the west wall of the churchyard out of Houndsditch, and turns east again into Whitechapel, coming out near the Three Nuns' Inn.

It was about the 10th of September that my curiosity

led, or rather drove, me to go and see this pit again, when there had been near 400 people buried in it; and I was not content to see it in the day-time, as I had done before, for then there would have been nothing to have been seen but the loose earth; for all the bodies that were thrown in were immediately covered with earth by those they called the buriers, which at other times were called bearers; but I resolved to go in the night and see some of them thrown in.

There was a strict order to prevent people coming to those pits, and that was only to prevent infection. But after some time that order was more necessary, for people that were infected and near their end, and delirious also, would run to those pits, wrapt in blankets or rugs, and throw themselves in, and, as they said, bury themselves. I cannot say that the officers suffered any willingly to lie there; but I have heard that in a great pit in Finsbury, in the parish of Cripplegate, it lying open then to the fields, for it was not then walled about, [some] came and threw themselves in, and expired there, before they threw any earth upon them; and that when they came to bury others, and found them there, they were quite dead, though not cold.

This may serve a little to describe the dreadful condition of that day, though it is impossible to say anything that is able to give a true idea of it to those who did not see it, other than this, that it was indeed very, very, very dreadful, and such as no tongue can express.

I got admittance into the churchyard by being acquainted with the sexton who attended, who though he did not refuse me at all, yet earnestly persuaded me not to go, telling me very seriously, for he was a good, religious, and sensible man, that it was indeed their business and duty to venture, and to run all hazards, and that in it they might hope to be preserved; but that I had no apparent call to it but my own curiosity, which, he said, he believed I would not pretend was sufficient to justify my running that hazard. I told him I had been pressed in my mind to go, and that perhaps it might be an instructing sight, that might not be without its uses. "Nay," says the good man, "if you will venture upon that score, name of God go in; for, depend upon it, 't will be a sermon to you, it may be, the best that ever you heard in your life. 'T is a speaking sight," says he, "and has a voice with it, and a loud one, to call us all to repentance;" and with that he opened the door and said, "Go, if you will."

His discourse had shocked my resolution a little, and I stood wavering for a good while, but just at that interval I saw two links come over from the end of the Minories, and heard the bellman, and then appeared a dead-cart, as they called it, coming over the streets; so I could no longer resist my desire of seeing it, and went in. There was nobody, as I could perceive at first, in the church-yard, or going into it, but the buriers and the fellow that drove the cart, or rather led the horse and cart; but when they came up to the pit they saw a man go to and again, muffled up in a brown cloak, and making motions with his hands under his cloak, as if he was in a great agony, and the buriers immediately gathered about him, supposing he was one of those poor delirious or desperate creatures that used to pretend, as I have said, to bury themselves. He said nothing as he walked about, but two or three times groaned very deeply and loud, and sighed as he would break his heart.

When the buriers came up to him they soon found he was neither a person infected and desperate, as I have observed above, or a person distempered in mind, but one oppressed with a dreadful weight of grief indeed, having his wife and several of his children all in the cart that was just come in with him, and he followed in an agony and excess of sorrow. He mourned heartily, as it was easy to see, but with a kind of masculine grief that could not give itself vent by tears; and calmly defying the buriers to let him alone, said he would only see the bodies thrown in and go away, so they left importuning him. But no sooner was the cart turned round and the bodies shot into the pit promiscuously, which was a surprise to him, for he at least expected they would have been decently laid in, though indeed he was afterwards convinced that was impracticable; I say, no sooner did he see the sight but he cried out aloud, unable to contain himself. I could not hear what he said, but he went backwards two or three steps and fell down in a swoon. The buriers ran to him and took him up, and in a little while he came to himself, and they led him away to the Pie Tavern over against the end of Houndsditch, where, it seems, the man was known, and where they took care of him. He looked into the pit again as he went away, but the buriers had covered the bodies so immediately with throwing in earth, that though there was light enough, for there were lanterns, and candles in them, placed all night round the sides of the pit, upon heaps of earth, seven or eight, or perhaps more, yet nothing could be seen.

This was a mournful scene indeed, and affected me almost as much as the rest; but the other was awful and full of terror. The cart had in it sixteen or seventeen bodies; some were wrapt up in linen sheets, some in rags, some little other than naked, or so loose that what covering they had fell from them in the shooting out of the cart, and they fell quite naked among the rest; but the matter was not much to them, or the indecency much to any one else, seeing they were all dead, and were to be huddled together into the common grave of mankind, as we may call it, for here was no difference made, but poor and rich went together; there was no other way of burials, neither was it possible there should, for coffins were not to be had for the prodigious numbers that fell in such a calamity as this.

It was reported by way of scandal upon the buriers, that if any corpse was delivered to them decently wound up, as we called it then, in a winding-sheet tied over the head and feet, which some did, and which was generally of good linen; I say, it was reported that the buriers were so wicked as to strip them in the cart and carry them quite naked to the ground. But as I cannot easily credit any-thing so vile among Christians, and at a time so filled with terrors as that was, I can only relate it and leave it un-determined.

Innumerable stories also went about of the cruel be-haviours and practices of nurses who tended the sick, and of their hastening on the fate of those they tended in their sickness. But I shall say more of this in its place.

I was indeed shocked with this sight; it almost over-whelmed me, and I went away with my heart most af-flicted, and full of the afflicting thoughts, such as I can-not describe. Just at my going out of the church, and turning up the street towards my own house, I saw an-other cart with links, and a bellman going before, coming out of Harrow Alley in the Butcher Row, on the other side of the way, and being, as I perceived, very full of dead bodies, it went directly over the street also toward the church. I stood a while, but I had no stomach to go back again to see the same dismal scene over again, so I went directly home, where I could not but consider with thankfulness the risk I had run, believing I had gotten no injury, as indeed I had not.

Here the poor unhappy gentleman's grief came into my head again, and indeed I could not but shed tears in the reflection upon it, perhaps more than he did himself; but his case lay so heavy upon my mind that I could not prevail with myself, but that I must go out again into the street, and go to the Pie Tavern, resolving to inquire what became of him.

It was by this time one o'clock in the morning, and yet the poor gentleman was there. The truth was, the people of the house, knowing him, had entertained him, and kept him there all the night, notwithstanding the danger of being infected by him, though it appeared the man was perfectly sound himself.

It is with regret that I take notice of this tavern. The people were civil, mannerly, and an obliging sort of folks enough, and had till this time kept their house open and their trade going on, though not so very publicly as formerly; but there was a dreadful set of fellows that used their house, and who, in the middle of all this horror, met there every night, behaved with all the revelling and roaring extravagances as is usual for such people to do at other times, and, indeed, to such an offensive degree that the very master and mistress of the house grew first ashamed and then terrified at them.

They sat generally in a room next the street, and as they always kept late hours, so when the dead-cart came across the street-end to go into Houndsditch, which was in view of the tavern windows, they would frequently open the windows as soon as they heard the bell and look out at them; and as they might often hear sad lamentations of people in the streets or at their windows as the carts went along, they would make their impudent mocks and jeers at them, especially if they heard the poor people call upon God to have mercy upon them, as many would do at those times in their ordinary passing along the streets.

These gentlemen, being something disturbed with the clutter of bringing the poor gentleman into the house, as above, were first angry and very high with the master of the house for suffering such a fellow, as they called him, to be brought out of the grave into their house; but being answered that the man was a neighbour, and that he was sound, but overwhelmed with the calamity of his family, and the like, they turned their anger into ridiculing the man and his sorrow for his wife and children, taunted him with want of courage to leap into the great pit and go to heaven, as they jeeringly expressed it, along with them, adding some very profane and even blasphemous expressions.

They were at this vile work when I came back to the house, and, as far as I could see, though the man sat still, mute and disconsolate, and their affronts could not divert his sorrow, yet he was both grieved and offended at their discourse. Upon this I gently reproved them, being well enough acquainted with their characters, and not unknown in person to two of them.

They immediately fell upon me with ill language and oaths, asked me what I did out of my grave at such a time when so many honester men were carried into the church-yard, and why I was not at home saying my prayers against the dead-cart coming for me, and the like.

I was indeed astonished at the impudence of the men, though not at all discomposed at their treatment of me. However, I kept my temper. I told them that though I defied them or any man in the world to tax me with any dishonesty, yet I acknowledged that in this terrible judgment of God many better than I were swept away and carried to their grave. But to answer their question directly, the case was, that I was mercifully preserved by that great God whose name they had blasphemed and taken in vain by cursing and swearing in a dreadful manner, and that I believed I was preserved in particular, among other ends of His goodness, that I might reprove them for their audacious boldness in behaving in such a

manner and in such an awful time as this was, especially
for their jeering and mocking at an honest gentleman and
a neighbour (for some of them knew him), who, they
saw, was overwhelmed with sorrow for the breaches
which it had pleased God to make upon his family.

I cannot call exactly to mind the hellish, abominable
raillery which was the return they made to that talk of
mine, being provoked, it seems, that I was not at all
afraid to be free with them; nor, if I could remember,
would I fill my account with any of the words, the horrid
oaths, curses, and vile expressions, such as, at that time
of the day, even the worst and ordinariest people in the
street would not use; for, except such hardened creatures
as these, the most wicked wretches that could be found
had at that time some terror upon their minds of the
hand of that Power which could thus in a moment destroy
them.

But that which was the worst in all their devilish
language was, that they were not afraid to blaspheme
God and talk atheistically, making a jest of my calling
the plague the hand of God; mocking, and even laughing, at the word judgment, as if the providence of God
had no concern in the inflicting such a desolating stroke,
and that the people calling upon God as they saw the
carts carrying away the dead bodies was all enthusiastic,
absurd, and impertinent.

I made them some reply, such as I thought proper,
but which I found was so far from putting a check to
their horrid way of speaking that it made them rail the
more, so that I confess it filled me with horror and a kind
of rage, and I came away, as I told them, lest the hand of
that Judgment which had visited the whole city should
glorify His vengeance upon them, and all that were near
them.

They received all reproof with the utmost contempt,

and made the greatest mockery that was possible for them to do at me, giving me all the opprobrious, insolent scoffs that they could think of for preaching to them, as they called it, which indeed grieved me, rather than angered me; and I went away, blessing God, however, in my mind that I had not spared them, though they had insulted me so much.

They continued this wretched course three or four days after this, continually mocking and jeering at all that showed themselves religious or serious, or that were any way touched with the sense of the terrible judgment of God upon us; and I was informed they flouted in the same manner at the good people who, notwithstanding the contagion, met at the church, fasted, and prayed to God to remove His hand from them.

I say, they continued this dreadful course three of four days—I think it was no more—when one of them, particularly he who asked the poor gentleman what he did out of his grave, was struck from Heaven with the plague, and died in the most deplorable manner; and, in a word, they were every one of them carried into the great pit which I have mentioned above, before it was quite filled up, which was not above a fortnight or thereabout.

These men were guilty of many extravagances, such as one would think human nature should have trembled at the thoughts of at such a time of general terror as was then upon us, and particularly scoffing and mocking at everything which they happened to see that was religious among the people, especially at their thronging zealously to the place of public worship to implore mercy from Heaven in such a time of distress; and this tavern where they held their club being within view of the church-door, they had the more particular occasion for their atheistical profane mirth.

But this began to abate a little with them before the

accident which I have related happened, for the infection increased so violently at this part of the town now, that people began to be afraid to come to the church; at least such numbers did not resort thither as was usual. Many of the clergymen likewise were dead, and others gone into the country; for it really required a steady courage and a strong faith for a man not only to venture being in town at such a time as this, but likewise to venture to come to church and perform the office of a minister to a congregation, of whom he had reason to believe many of them were actually infected with the plague, and to do this every day, or twice a day, as in some places was done.

It is true the people showed an extraordinary zeal in these religious exercises and as the church-doors were always open, people would go in single at all times, whether the minister was officiating or no, and locking themselves into separate pews, would be praying to God with great fervency and devotion.

Others assembled at meeting-houses, every one as their different opinions in such things guided, but all were promiscuously the subject of these men's drollery, especially at the beginning of the visitation.

It seems they had been checked for their open insulting religion in this manner by several good people of every persuasion, and that, and the violent raging of the infection, I suppose, was the occasion that they had abated much of their rudeness for some time before, and were only roused by the spirit of ribaldry and atheism at the clamour which was made when the gentleman was first brought in there, and perhaps were agitated by the same devil, when I took upon me to reprove them; though I did it at first with all the calmness, temper, and good manners that I could, which for a while they insulted me the more for, thinking it had been in fear of their resentment, though afterwards they found the contrary.

I went home, indeed, grieved and afflicted in my mind at the abominable wickedness of those men, not doubting, however, that they would be made dreadful examples of God's justice; for I looked upon this dismal time to be a particular season of Divine vengeance, and that God would on this occasion single out the proper objects of His displeasure in a more especial and remarkable manner than at another time; and that though I did believe that many good people would, and did, fall in the common calamity, and that it was no certain rule to judge of the eternal state of any one by their being distinguished in such a time of general destruction neither one way or other, yet, I say, it could not but seem reasonable to believe that God would not think fit to spare by His mercy such open declared enemies, that should insult His name and Being, defy His vengeance, and mock at His worship and worshippers at such a time; no, not though His mercy had thought fit to bear with and spare them at other times; that this was a day of visitation, a day of God's anger, and those words came into my thought, Jer. v. 9: "Shall I not visit for these things? saith the Lord: and shall not My soul be avenged of such a nation as this!"

These things, I say, lay upon my mind, and I went home very much grieved and oppressed with the horror of these men's wickedness, and to think that anything could be so vile, so hardened, and so notoriously wicked as to insult God, and His servants, and His worship in such a manner, and at such a time as this was, when He had, as it were, His sword drawn in His hand on purpose to take vengeance, not on them only, but on the whole nation.

I had, indeed, been in some passion at first with them, though it was really raised, not by any affront they had offered me personally, but by the horror their blaspheming tongues filled me with. However, I was doubtful in my thoughts whether the resentment I retained was not all upon my own private account, for they had given me a great deal of ill language too—I mean personally; but after some pause, and having a weight of grief upon my mind, I retired myself as soon as I came home, for I slept not that night; and giving God most humble thanks for my preservation in the eminent danger I had been in, I set my mind seriously and with the utmost earnestness to pray for those desperate wretches, that God would pardon them, open their eyes, and effectually humble them.

By this I not only did my duty, namely, to pray for those who despitefully used me, but I fully tried my own heart, to my full satisfaction, that it was not filled with any spirit of resentment as they had offended me in particular; and I humbly recommended the method to all those that would know, or be certain, how to distinguish between their real zeal for the honour of God and the effects of their private passions and resentment.

But I must go back here to the particular incidents which occur to my thoughts of the time of the visitation, and particularly to the time of their shutting up houses, in the first part of their sickness; for before the sickness was come to its height people had more room to make their observations than they had afterward; but when it was in the extremity there was no such thing as communication with one another, as before.

During the shutting up of houses, as I have said, some violence was offered to the watchmen. As to soldiers, there were none to be found; the few guards which the king then had, which were nothing like the number entertained since, were dispersed, either at Oxford with the Court, or in quarters in the remoter parts of the country, small detachments excepted, who did duty at the Tower and at Whitehall, and these but very few. Neither am I positive that there was any other guard at the Tower than the warders, as they called them, who stand at the gate with gowns and caps, the same as the yeomen of the guard, except the ordinary gunners, who were twenty-four, and the officers appointed to look after the magazine, who were called armourers. As to trained bands, there was no possibility of raising any; neither, if the Lieutenancy, either of London or Middlesex, had ordered the drums to beat for the militia, would any of the companies, I believe, have drawn together, whatever risk they had run.

This made the watchmen be the less regarded, and perhaps occasioned the greater violence to be used against them. I mention it on this score to observe that the setting watchmen thus to keep the people in was, first of all, not effectual, but that the people broke out, whether by force or by stratagem, even almost as often as they pleased; and, second, that those that did thus break out were generally people infected, who, in their desperation, running about from one place to another, valued not whom they injured, and which perhaps, as I have said, might give birth to report that it was natural to the infected people to desire to infect others, which report was really false.

And I know it so well, and in so many several cases, that I could give several relations of good, pious, and religious people who, when they have had the distemper, have been so far from being forward to infect others that they have forbid their own family to come near them, in hopes of their being preserved, and have even died with-out seeing their nearest relations, lest they should be instrumental to give them the distemper, and infect or endanger them. If, then, there were cases wherein the infected people were careless of the injury they did to others, this was certainly one of them, if not the chief, namely, when people who had the distemper had broken out from houses which were so shut up, and having been driven to extremities for provision or for entertainment, had endeavoured to conceal their condition, and have been thereby instrumental involuntarily to infect others who have been ignorant and unwary.

This is one of the reasons why I believed then, and do believe still, that the shutting up houses thus by force, and restraining, or rather imprisoning, people in their own houses, as I said above, was of little or no service in the whole. Nay, I am of opinion it was rather hurtful, having forced those desperate people to wander abroad with the plague upon them, who would otherwise have died quietly in their beds.

I remember one citizen who, having thus broken out of his house in Aldersgate Street or thereabout, went along the road to Islington; he attempted to have gone in at the Angel Inn, and after that at the White Horse, two inns known still by the same signs, but was refused; after which he came to the Pied Bull, an inn also still continuing the same sign. He asked them for lodging for one night only, pretending to be going into Lincolnshire, and assuring them of his being very sound and free from the infection, which also at that time had not reached much that way.

They told him they had no lodging that they could spare but one bed up in the garret, and that they could spare that bed but for one night, some drovers being expected the next day with cattle; so, if he would accept of that lodging, he might have it, which he did. So a servant was sent up with a candle with him to show him the room. He was very well dressed, and looked like a person not used to lie in a garret; and when he came to the room he fetched a deep sigh, and said to the servant, "I have seldom lain in such a lodging as this." However, the servant assuring him again that they had no better, "Well," says he, "I must make shift; this is a dreadful time; but it is but for one night." So he sat down upon the bedside, and bade the maid, I think it was, fetch him up a pint of warm ale. Accordingly the servant went for the ale, but some hurry in the house, which perhaps employed her other ways, put it out of her head, and she went up no more to him.

The next morning, seeing no appearance of the gentleman, somebody in the house asked the servant that had showed him upstairs what was become of him. She started. "Alas!" says she, "I never thought more of him. He bade me carry him some warm ale, but I forgot." Upon which, not the maid, but some other person was sent up to see after him, who, coming into the room, found him stark dead and almost cold, stretched out across the bed. His clothes were pulled off, his jaw fallen, his eyes open in a most frightful posture, the rug of the bed being grasped hard in one of his hands, so that it was plain he died soon after the maid left him; and 't is probable, had she gone up with the ale, she had found him dead in a few minutes after he sat down upon the bed. The alarm was great in the house, as any one may suppose, they having been free from the distemper till that disaster, which, bringing the infection to the house, spread it immediately to other houses round about it. I do not remember how many died in the house itself, but I think the maid-servant who went up first with him fell presently ill by the fright, and several others; for, whereas there died but two in Islington of the plague the week before, there died seventeen the week after, whereof fourteen were of the plague. This was in the week from the 11th of July to the 18th.

There was one shift that some families had, and that not a few, when their houses happened to be infected, and that was this: the families who, in the first breaking out of the distemper, fled away into the country and had retreats among their friends, generally found some or other of their neighbours or relations to commit the charge of those houses to for the safety of the goods and the like. Some houses were, indeed, entirely locked up, the doors padlocked, the windows and doors having deal boards nailed over them, and only the inspection of them committed to the ordinary watchmen and parish officers; but these were but few.

It was thought that there were not less than 10,000 houses forsaken of the inhabitants in the city and suburbs, including what was in the outparishes and in Surrey, or the side of the water they called Southwark. This was besides the numbers of lodgers, and of particular persons who were fled out of other families; so that in all it was computed that about 200,000 people were fled and gone. But of this I shall speak again. But I mention it here on this account, namely, that it was a rule with those who had thus two houses in their keeping or care, that if anybody was taken sick in a family, before the master of the family let the examiners or any other officer know of it, he immediately would send all the rest of his family, whether children or servants, as it fell out to be, to such other house which he had so in charge, and then giving notice of the sick person to the examiner, have a nurse or nurses appointed, and have another person to be shut up in the house with them (which many for money would do), so to take charge of the house in case the person should die.

This was, in many cases, the saving a whole family,

who, if they had been shut up with the sick person, would inevitably have perished. But, on the other hand, this was another of the inconveniences of shutting up houses; for the apprehensions and terror of being shut up made many run away with the rest of the family, who, though it was not publicly known, and they were not quite sick, had yet the distemper upon them; and who, by having an uninterrupted liberty to go about, but being obliged still to conceal their circumstances, or perhaps not knowing it themselves, gave the distemper to others, and spread the infection in a dreadful manner, as I shall explain further hereafter.

And here I may be able to make an observation or two of my own, which may be of use hereafter to those into whose hands these may come, if they should ever see the like dreadful visitation. (1.) The infection generally came into the houses of the citizens by the means of their servants, whom they were obliged to send up and down the streets for necessaries; that is to say, for food or physic, to bake-houses, brew-houses, shops, &c.; and who going necessarily through the streets into shops, markets, and the like, it was impossible but that they should, one way or other, meet with distempered people, who conveyed the fatal breath into them, and they brought it home to the families to which they belonged. (2.) It was a great mistake that such a great city as this had but one pest-house; for had there been, instead of one pest-house— viz., beyond Bunhill Fields, where, at most, they could receive, perhaps, two hundred or three hundred people —I say, had there, instead of that one, been several pest-houses, every one able to contain a thousand people, without lying two in a bed, or two beds in a room; and had every master of a family, as soon as any servant especially had been taken sick in his house, been obliged to send them to the next pest-house, if they were willing, as many were, and had the examiners done the like among the poor people when any had been stricken with the infection; I say, had this been done where the people were willing (not otherwise), and the houses not been shut, I am persuaded, and was all the while of that opinion, that not so many, by several thousands, had died; for it was observed, and I could give several instances within the compass of my own knowledge, where a servant had been taken sick, and the family had either time to send him out or retire from the house and leave the sick person, as I have said above, they had all been preserved; whereas when, upon one or more sickening in a family, the house has been shut up, the whole family have perished, and the bearers been obliged to go in to fetch out the dead bodies, not being able to bring them to the door, and at last none left to do it.

(3.) This put it out of question to me, that the calamity was spread by infection; that is to say, by some certain steams or fumes, which the physicians call effluvia, by the breath, or by the sweat, or by the stench of the sores of the sick persons, or some other way, perhaps, beyond even the reach of the physicians themselves, which effluvia affected the sound who came within certain distances of the sick, immediately penetrating the vital parts of the said sound persons, putting their blood into an immediate ferment, and agitating their spirits to that degree which it was found they were agitated; and so those newly infected persons communicated it in the same manner to others. And this I shall give some instances of, that cannot but convince those who seriously consider it; and I cannot but with some wonder find some people, now the contagion is over, talk of its being an immediate stroke from Heaven, without the agency of means, having commission to strike this and that particular person, and none other, which I look upon with contempt as the effect of manifest ignorance and enthusiasm; likewise the opinion of others, who talk of infection being carried on by the air only, by carrying with it vast numbers of insects and invisible creatures, who enter into the body with the breath, or even at the pores with the air, and there generate or emit most acute poisons, or poisonous ovæ or eggs, which mingle themselves with the blood, and so infect the body: a discourse full of learned simplicity, and manifested to be so by universal experience; but I shall say more to this case in its order.

I must here take further notice that nothing was more fatal to the inhabitants of this city than the supine negligence of the people themselves, who, during the long notice or warning they had of the visitation, made no provision for it, by laying in store of provisions, or of other necessaries, by which they might have lived retired, and within their own houses, as I have observed others did, and who were in a great measure preserved by that caution; nor were they, after they were a little hardened to it, so shy of conversing with one another, when actually infected, as they were at first, no, though they knew it.

I acknowledge I was one of those thoughtless ones that had made so little provision that my servants were obliged to go out of doors to buy every trifle by penny and halfpenny, just as before it began, even till my experience showing me the folly, I began to be wiser so late that I had scarce time to store myself sufficient for our common subsistence for a month.

I had in family only an ancient woman that managed the house, a maid-servant, two apprentices, and myself; and the plague beginning to increase about us, I had many sad thoughts about what course I should take, and how I should act. The many dismal objects, which happened everywhere as I went about the streets, had filled my mind with a great deal of horror, for fear of the distemper, which was, indeed, very horrible in itself, and in some more than in others. The swellings, which were generally in the neck or groin, when they grew hard and would not break, grew so painful that it was equal to the most exquisite torture; and some, not able to bear the torment, threw themselves out at windows or shot themselves, or otherwise made themselves away, and I saw several dismal objects of that kind. Others, unable to contain themselves, vented their pain by incessant roarings, and such loud and lamentable cries were to be heard as we walked along the streets that would pierce the very heart to think of, especially when it was to be considered that the same dreadful scourge might be expected every moment to seize upon ourselves.

I cannot say but that now I began to faint in my resolutions; my heart failed me very much, and sorely I repented of my rashness. When I had been out, and met with such terrible things as these I have talked of, I say I repented my rashness in venturing to abide in town. I wished often that I had not taken upon me to stay, but had gone away with my brother and his family.

Terrified by those frightful objects, I would retire home sometimes, and resolve to go out no more; and perhaps I would keep those resolutions for three or four days, which time I spent in the most serious thankfulness for my preservation and the preservation of my family, and the constant confession of my sins, giving myself up to God every day, and applying to Him with fasting, humiliation, and meditation. Such intervals as I had I employed in reading books and in writing down my memorandums of what occurred to me every day, and out of which, afterwards, I took most of this work, as it relates to my observations without doors. What I wrote of my private meditations I reserve for private use, and desire it may not be made public on any account whatever.

I also wrote other meditations upon divine subjects, such as occurred to me at that time and were profitable to myself, but not fit for any other view, and therefore I say no more of that.

I had a very good friend, a physician, whose name was Heath, whom I frequently visited during this dismal time, and to whose advice I was very much obliged for many things which he directed me to take, by way of preventing the infection when I went out, as he found I frequently did, and to hold in my mouth when I was in the streets. He also came very often to see me, and as he was a good Christian as well as a good physician, his agreeable conversation was a very great support to me in the worst of this terrible time.

It was now the beginning of August, and the plague grew very violent and terrible in the place where I lived, and Dr. Heath coming to visit me, and finding that I ventured so often out in the streets, earnestly persuaded me to lock myself up and my family, and not to suffer any of us to go out of doors; to keep all our windows fast, shutters and curtains close, and never to open them; but first, to make a very strong smoke in the room where the window or door was to be opened, with rosin and pitch, brimstone or gunpowder, and the like; and we did this for some time; but as I had not laid in a store of provision for such a retreat, it was impossible that we could keep within doors entirely. However, I attempted, though it was so very late, to do something towards it; and first, as I had convenience both for brewing and baking, I went and bought two sacks of meal, and for several weeks, having an oven, we baked all our own bread; also I bought malt, and brewed as much beer as all the casks I had would hold, and which seemed enough to serve my house for five or six weeks; also I laid in a quantity of salt butter and Cheshire cheese; but I had no flesh-meat, and the plague raged so violently among the butchers and slaughter-houses on the other side of our street, where they are known to dwell in great numbers, that it was not advisable so much as to go over the street among them.

And here I must observe again, that this necessity of going out of our houses to buy provisions was in a great measure the ruin of the whole city, for the people catched the distemper on these occasions one of another, and even the provisions themselves were often tainted; at least I have great reason to believe so; and therefore I cannot say with satisfaction what I know is repeated with great assurance, that the market-people and such as brought provisions to town were never infected. I am certain the butchers of Whitechapel, where the greatest part of the flesh-meat was killed, were dreadfully visited, and that at least to such a degree that few of their shops were kept open, and those that remained of them killed their meat at Mile End and that way, and brought it to market upon horses.

However, the poor people could not lay up provisions, and there was a necessity that they must go to market to buy, and others to send servants or their children; and as this was a necessity which renewed itself daily, it brought abundance of unsound people to the markets, and a great many that went thither sound brought death home with them.

It is true people used all possible precaution. When any one bought a joint of meat in the market they would not take it off the butcher's hand, but took it off the hooks themselves. On the other hand, the butcher would not touch the money, but have it put into a pot full of vinegar, which he kept for that purpose. The buyer carried always small money to make up any odd sum, that they might take no change. They carried bottles of scents and perfumes in their hands, and all the means that could be used were used; but then the poor could not do even these things, and they went at all hazards.

Innumerable dismal stories we heard every day on this very account. Sometimes a man or woman dropped down dead in the very markets, for many people that had the plague upon them knew nothing of it till the inward gangrene had affected their vitals, and they died in a few moments. This caused that many died frequently in that manner in the streets suddenly, without any warning; others perhaps had time to go to the next bulk or stall, or to any door-porch, and just sit down and die, as I have said before.

These objects were so frequent in the streets that when the plague came to be very raging on one side, there was scarce any passing by the streets but that several dead bodies would be lying here and there upon the ground. On the other hand, it is observable, that though at first the people would stop as they went along and call to the neighbours to come out on such an occasion, yet afterward no notice was taken of them; but that, if at any time we found a corpse lying, go across the way and not come near it; or, if in a narrow lane or passage, go back again and seek some other way to go on the business we were upon; and in those cases the corpse was always left till the officers had notice to come and take them away, or till night, when the bearers attending the dead-cart would take them up and carry them away. Nor did those undaunted creatures who performed these offices fail to search their pockets, and sometimes strip off their clothes if they were well dressed, as sometimes they were, and carry off what they could get.

But to return to the markets. The butchers took that care that if any person died in the market they had the officers always at hand to take them up upon hand-barrows and carry them to the next churchyard; and this was so frequent that such were not entered in the weekly bill, "Found dead in the streets or fields," as is the case now, but they went into the general articles of the great distemper.

But now the fury of the distemper increased to such a degree that even the markets were but very thinly furnished with provisions or frequented with buyers compared to what they were before; and the Lord Mayor caused the country people who brought provisions to be stopped in the streets leading into the town, and to sit down there with their goods, where they sold what they brought, and went immediately away; and this encouraged the country people greatly to do so, for they sold their provisions at the very entrances into the town, and even in the fields, as particularly in the fields beyond Whitechapel, in Spitalfields; * also in St. George's Fields in Southwark, in Bunhill Fields, and in a great field called Wood's Close, near Islington. Thither the Lord Mayor, aldermen, and magistrates sent their officers and servants to buy for their families, themselves keeping within doors as much as possible, and the like did many other people; and after this method was taken the country people came with great cheerfulness, and brought provisions of all sorts, and very seldom got any harm, which, I suppose, added also to that report of their being miraculously preserved.

As for my little family, having thus, as I have said, laid in a store of bread, butter, cheese, and beer, I took my friend and physician's advice, and locked myself up, and my family, and resolved to suffer the hardship of living a few months without flesh-meat, rather than to purchase it at the hazard of our lives.

* *Those streets now called Spitalfields were then indeed open fields. [1754 edition.]*

But though I confined my family, I could not prevail upon my unsatisfied curiosity to stay within entirely myself; and though I generally came frighted and terrified home, yet I could not restrain; only that indeed I did not do it so frequently as at first.

I had some little obligations, indeed, upon me to go to my brother's house, which was in Coleman Street parish, and which he had left to my care, and I went at first every day, but afterwards only once or twice a week.

In these walks I had many dismal scenes before my eyes, as particularly of persons falling dead in the streets, terrible shrieks and screechings of women, who, in their agonies, would throw open their chamber windows and cry out in a dismal, surprising manner. It is impossible to describe the variety of postures in which the passions of the poor people would express themselves.

Passing through Tokenhouse Yard, in Lothbury, of a sudden a casement violently opened just over my head, and a woman gave three frightful screeches, and then cried, "Oh! death, death, death!" in a most inimitable tone, and which struck me with horror and a chillness in my very blood. There was nobody to be seen in the whole street, neither did any other window open, for people had no curiosity now in any case, nor could anybody help one another, so I went on to pass into Bell Alley.

Just in Bell Alley, on the right hand of the passage, there was a more terrible cry than that, though it was not so directed out at the window; but the whole family was in a terrible fright, and I could hear women and children run screaming about the rooms like distracted, when a garret-window opened, and somebody from a window on the other side the alley called and asked, "What is the matter?" upon which, from the first window it was answered, "O Lord, my old master has hanged himself!" The other asked again, "Is he quite dead?" and the first answered, "Ay, ay, quite dead; quite dead and cold!" This person was a merchant and a deputy alderman, and very rich. I care not to mention the name, though I knew his name too, but that would be an hardship to the family, which is now flourishing again.

But this is but one; it is scarce credible what dreadful cases happened in particular families every day. People in the rage of the distemper, or in the torment of their swellings, which was indeed intolerable, running out of their own government, raving and distracted, and often-times laying violent hands upon themselves, throwing themselves out at their windows, shooting themselves, &c.; mothers murdering their own children in their lun-acy, some dying of mere grief as a passion, some of mere fright and surprise without any infection at all, others frighted into idiotism and foolish distractions, some into despair and lunacy, others into melancholy madness.

The pain of the swelling was in particular very violent, and to some intolerable; the physicians and surgeons may be said to have tortured many poor creatures even to death. The swellings in some grew hard, and they applied violent drawing-plaisters or poultices to break them, and if these did not do they cut and scarified them in a terrible manner. In some those swellings were made hard partly by the force of the distemper and partly by their being too violently drawn, and were so hard that no instrument could cut them, and then they burnt them with caustics, so that many died raving mad with the torment, and some in the very operation. In these distresses, some, for want of help to hold them down in their beds, or to look to them, laid hands upon themselves, as above. Some broke out into the streets, perhaps naked, and would run di-rectly down to the river, if they were not stopped by the watchmen or other officers, and plunge themselves into the water wherever they found it.

It often pierced my very soul to hear the groans and cries of those who were thus tormented, but of the two this was counted the most promising particular in the whole infection, for, if these swellings could be brought to a head, and to break and run, or, as the surgeons call it, to digest, the patient generally recovered; whereas those who, like the gentlewoman's daughter, were struck with death at the beginning, and had the tokens come out upon them, often went about indifferent easy till a little before they died, and some till the moment they dropped down, as in apoplexies and epilepsies is often the case. Such would be taken suddenly very sick, and would run to a bench or bulk, or any convenient place that offered itself, or to their own houses if possible, as I mentioned before, and there sit down, grow faint, and die. This kind of dying was much the same as it was with those who die of common mortifications, who die swooning, and, as it were, go away in a dream. Such as died thus had very little notice of their being infected at all till the gangrene was spread through their whole body; nor could physicians themselves know certainly how it was with them, till they opened their breasts or other parts of their body, and saw the tokens.

We had at this time a great many frightful stories told us of nurses and watchmen who looked after the dying people; that is to say, hired nurses, who attended infected people, using them barbarously, starving them, smothering them, or by other wicked means hastening their end, that is to say, murdering of them; and watchmen, being set to guard houses that were shut up when there has been but one person left, and perhaps that one lying sick, that they have broke in and murdered that body, and immediately thrown them out into the dead-cart! and so they have gone scarce cold to the grave.

I cannot say but that some such murders were committed, and I think two were sent to prison for it, but died before they could be tried; and I have heard that three others, at several times, were excused for murders of that kind; but I must say I believe nothing of its being so common a crime as some have since been pleased to say, nor did it seem to be so rational where the people were brought so low as not to be able to help themselves, for such seldom recovered, and there was no temptation to commit a murder, at least none equal to the fact, where they were sure persons would die in so short a time, and could not live.

That there were a great many robberies and wicked practices committed even in this dreadful time I do not deny. The power of avarice was so strong in some that they would run any hazard to steal and to plunder; and particularly in houses where all the families or inhabitants have been dead and carried out, they would break in at all hazards, and without regard to the danger of infection, take even the clothes off the dead bodies and the bed-clothes from others where they lay dead.

This, I suppose, must be the case of a family in Houndsditch, where a man and his daughter, the rest of the family being, as I suppose, carried away before by the dead-cart, were found stark naked, one in one chamber and one in another, lying dead on the floor, and the clothes of the beds, from whence 't is supposed they were rolled off by thieves, stolen and carried quite away.

It is indeed to be observed that the women were in all this calamity the most rash, fearless, and desperate creatures, and as there were vast numbers that went about as nurses to tend those that were sick, they committed a great many petty thieveries in the houses where they were employed; and some of them were publicly whipped for it, when perhaps they ought rather to have been hanged for examples, for numbers of houses were robbed on these occasions, till at length the parish officers were sent to recommend nurses to the sick, and always took an account whom it was they sent, so as that they might call them to account if the house had been abused where they were placed.

But these robberies extended chiefly to wearing-clothes, linen, and what rings or money they could come at when the person died who was under their care, but not to a general plunder of the houses; and I could give you an account of one of these nurses, who, several years after, being on her death-bed, confessed with the utmost horror the robberies she had committed at the time of her being a nurse, and by which she had enriched herself to a great degree. But as for murders, I do not find that there was ever any proof of the facts in the manner as it has been reported, except as above.

They did tell me, indeed, of a nurse in one place that laid a wet cloth upon the face of a dying patient whom she tended, and so put an end to this life, who was just expiring before; and another that smothered a young woman she was looking to when she was in a fainting fit, and would have come to herself; some that killed them by giving them one thing, some another, and some starved them by giving them nothing at all. But these stories had two marks of suspicion that always attended them, which caused me always to slight them, and to look on them as mere stories, that people continually frighted one another with. First, that wherever it was that we heard it, they always placed the scene at the farther end of the town, opposite or most remote from where you were to hear it. If you heard it in Whitechapel, it had happened at St. Giles's, or at Westminster, or Holborn, or that end of the town. If you heard of it at that end of the town, then it was done in Whitechapel, or the Minories, or about Cripplegate parish. If you heard of it in the city, why, then it happened in Southwark; and if you heard of it in Southwark, then it was done in the city, and the like.

In the next place, of what part soever you heard the story, the particulars were always the same, especially that of laying a wet double clout on a dying man's face, and that of smothering a young gentlewoman; so that it was apparent, at least to my judgment, that there was more of tale than of truth in those things.

However, I cannot say but it had some effect upon the people, and particularly that, as I said before, they grew more cautious whom they took into their houses, and whom they trusted their lives with, and had them always recommended if they could; and where they could not find such, for they were not very plenty, they applied to the parish officers.

But here again the misery of that time lay upon the poor, who, being infected, had neither food or physic, neither physician or apothecary to assist them, or nurse to attend them. Many of those died calling for help, and even for sustenance, out at their windows, in a most miserable and deplorable manner; but it must be added that whenever the cases of such persons or families were represented to my Lord Mayor they always were relieved.

It is true, in some houses where the people were not very poor, yet where they had sent perhaps their wives and children away, and if they had any servants they had been dismissed;—I say, it is true, that to save the expenses, many such as these shut themselves in, and not having help, died alone.

A neighbour and acquaintance of mine, having some money owing to him from a shopkeeper in Whitecross Street or thereabouts, sent his apprentice, a youth about eighteen years of age, to endeavour to get the money. He came to the door, and finding it shut, knocked pretty hard, and, as he thought, heard somebody answer within, but was not sure, so he waited, and after some stay knocked again, and then a third time, when he heard somebody coming downstairs.

At length the man of the house came to the door; he had on his breeches or drawers, and a yellow flannel waistcoat, no stockings, a pair of slipped-shoes, a white cap on his head, and, as the young man said, "death in his face."

When he opened the door, says he, "What do you disturb me thus for?" The boy, though a little surprised, replied, "I come from such a one, and my master sent me for the money which he says you know of." "Very well, child," returns the living ghost; "call as you go by at Cripplegate Church, and bid them ring the bell:" and with these words shut the door again, and went up again, and died the same day; nay, perhaps the same hour. This the young man told me himself, and I have reason to believe it. This was while the plague was not come to a height: I think it was in June, towards the latter end of the month; it must be before the dead-carts came about, and while they used the ceremony of ringing the bell for the dead, which was over for certain, in that parish at least, before the month of July, for by the 25th of July there died 550 and upwards in a week, and then they could no more bury in form, rich or poor.

I have mentioned above that notwithstanding this dreadful calamity, yet the numbers of thieves were abroad upon all occasions, where they had found any prey, and that these were generally women. It was one morning about eleven o'clock, I had walked out to my brother's house in Coleman Street parish, as I often did, to see that all was safe.

My brother's house had a little court before it, and a brick wall and a gate in it, and within that several warehouses where his goods of several sorts lay. It happened that in one of these warehouses were several packs of women's high-crowned hats, which came out of the country, and were, as I suppose, for exportation, whither I know not.

I was surprised that when I came near my brother's door, which was in a place they called Swan Alley, I met three or four women with high-crowned hats on their heads; and, as I remembered afterwards, one, if not more, had some hats likewise in their hands; but as I did not see them come out at my brother's door, and not knowing that my brother had any such goods in his warehouse, I did not offer to say anything to them, but went across the way to shun meeting them, as was usual to do at that time, for fear of the plague. But when I came nearer to the gate, I met another woman with more hats come out of the gate. "What business, mistress," said I, "have you had there?" "There are more people there," said she; "I have had no more business there than they." I was hasty to get to the gate then, and said no more to her, by which means she got away. But just as I came to the gate, I saw two more coming across the yard to come out with hats also on their heads and under their arms, at which I threw the gate to behind me, which having a spring lock fastened itself; and turning to the women, "Forsooth," said I, "what are you doing here?" and seized upon the hats, and took them from them. One of them, who, I confess, did not look like a thief—"Indeed," says she, "we are wrong, but we were told they were goods that had no owner. Be pleased to take them again; and look yonder, there are more such customers as we." She cried and looked pitifully, so I took the hats from her, and opened the gate, and bade them be gone, for I pitied the women indeed; but when I looked towards the warehouse, as she directed, there were six or seven more, all women, fitting themselves with hats, as unconcerned and quiet as if they had been at a hatter's shop buying for their money.

I was surprised, not at the sight of so many thieves only, but at the circumstances I was in; being now to thrust myself in among so many people, who for some weeks had been so shy of myself, that if I met anybody in the street I would cross the way from them.

They were equally surprised, though on another account. They all told me they were neighbours, that they had heard any one might take them, that they were nobody's goods, and the like. I talked big to them at first, went back to the gate and took out the key, so that they were all my prisoners, threatened to lock them all into the warehouse, and go and fetch my Lord Mayor's officers for them.

They begged heartily, protested they found the gate open, and the warehouse door open; and that it had no doubt been broken open by some who expected to find goods of greater value, which indeed was reasonable to believe, because the lock was broke, and a padlock that hung to the door on the outside also loose, and not abundance of the hats carried away.

At length I considered that this was not a time to be cruel and rigorous; and besides that, it would necessarily oblige me to go much about, to have several people come to me, and I go to several whose circumstances of health I knew nothing of; and that even at this time the plague was so high as that there died 4000 a week; so that in showing my resentment, or even in seeking justice for my brother's goods, I might lose my own life; so I contented myself with taking the names and places where some of them lived, who were really inhabitants in the neighbourhood, and threatening that my brother should call them to an account for it when he returned to his habitation.

Then I talked a little upon another foot with them, and asked them how they could do such things as these in a time of such general calamity, and, as it were, in the face of God's most dreadful judgments, when the plague was at their very doors, and, it may be, in their very houses, and they did not know but that the dead-cart might stop at their doors in a few hours, to carry them to their graves.

I could not perceive that my discourse made much impression upon them all that while, till it happened that there came two men of the neighbourhood, hearing of the disturbance, and knowing my brother, for they had been both dependents upon his family, and they came to my assistance. These being, as I said, neighbours, presently knew three of the women, and told me who they were, and where they lived; and, it seems, they had given me a true account of themselves before.

This brings these two men to a further remembrance. The name of one was John Hayward, who was at that time under-sexton of the parish of St. Stephen, Coleman Street. By under-sexton was understood at that time gravedigger and bearer of the dead. This man carried, or assisted to carry, all the dead to their graves which were buried in that large parish, and who were carried in form, and after that form of burying was stopped, went with the dead-cart and the bell to fetch the dead bodies from the houses where they lay, and fetched many of them out of the chambers and houses; for the parish was, and is still, remarkable particularly, above all the parishes in London, for a great number of alleys and thoroughfares, very long, into which no carts could come, and where they were obliged to go and fetch the bodies a very long way; which alleys now remain to witness it, such as White's Alley, Cross Key Court, Swan Alley, Bell Alley, White Horse Alley, and many more. Here they went with a kind of hand-barrow and laid the dead bodies on it, and carried them out to the carts; which work he performed and never had the distemper at all, but lived about twenty years after it, and was sexton of the parish to the time of his death. His wife at the same time was a nurse to infected people, and tended many that died in the parish, being for her honesty recommended by the parish officers, yet she never was infected neither.

He never used any preservative against the infection, other than holding garlic and rue in his mouth, and smoking tobacco. This I also had from his own mouth. And his wife's remedy was washing her head in vinegar, and sprinkling her head-clothes so with vinegar as to keep them always moist; and if the smell of any of those she waited on was more than ordinary offensive, she snuffed vinegar up her nose and sprinkled vinegar upon her head-clothes, and held a handkerchief wetted with vinegar to her mouth.

It must be confessed that though the plague was chiefly among the poor, yet were the poor the most venturous and fearless of it, and went about their employment with a sort of brutal courage; I must call it so, for it was founded neither on religion nor prudence; scarce did they use any caution, but ran into any business which they could get employment in, though it was the most hazardous. Such was that of tending the sick, watching houses shut up, carrying infected persons to the pest-house, and, which was still worse, carrying the dead away to their graves.

It was under this John Hayward's care, and within his bounds, that the story of the piper, with which people have made themselves so merry, happened, and he assured me that it was true. It is said that it was a blind piper; but, as John told me, the fellow was not blind, but an ignorant, weak, poor man, and usually walked his rounds about ten o'clock at night and went piping along from door to door, and the people usually took him in at public-houses where they knew him, and would give him drink and victuals, and sometimes farthings; and he in return would pipe and sing and talk simply, which diverted the people; and thus he lived. It was but a very bad time for this diversion while things were as I have told, yet the poor fellow went about as usual, but was almost starved; and when anybody asked how he did he would answer, the dead-cart had not taken him yet, but that they had promised to call for him next week.

It happened one night that this poor fellow, whether somebody had given him too much drink or no—John Hayward said he had not drink in his house, but that they had given him a little more victuals than ordinary at a public-house in Coleman Street—and the poor fellow, having not usually had a bellyful for perhaps not a good while, was laid all along upon the top of a bulk or stall, and fast asleep, at a door in the street near London Wall, towards Cripplegate, and that upon the same bulk or stall the people of some house, in the alley of which the house was a corner, hearing a bell, which they always rang before the cart came, had laid a body really dead of the plague just by him, thinking, too, that this poor fellow had been a dead body, as the other was, and laid there by some of the neighbours.

Accordingly, when John Hayward with his bell and the cart came along, finding two dead bodies lie upon the stall, they took them up with the instrument they used and threw them into the cart, and all this while the piper slept soundly.

From hence they passed along and took in other dead bodies, till, as honest John Hayward told me, they almost buried him alive in the cart; yet all this while he slept soundly. At length the cart came to the place where the bodies were to be thrown into the ground, which, as I do remember, was at Mount Mill; and as the cart usually stopped some time before they were ready to shoot out the melancholy load they had in it, as soon as the cart stopped the fellow awaked and struggled a little to get his head out from among the dead bodies, when, raising himself up in the cart, he called out, "Hey! where am I?" This frighted the fellow that attended about the work; but after some pause John Hayward, recovering himself, said, "Lord, bless us! There's somebody in the cart not quite dead!" So another called to him and said, "Who are you?" The fellow answered, "I am the poor piper. Where am I?" "Where are you?" says Hayward. "Why, you are in the dead-cart, and we are going to bury you." "But I an't dead though, am I?" says the piper, which made them laugh a little, though, as John said, they were heartily frighted at first; so they helped the poor fellow down, and he went about his business.

I know the story goes he set up his pipes in the cart and frighted the bearers and others so that they ran away; but John Hayward did not tell the story so, nor say anything of his piping at all; but that he was a poor piper, and that he was carried away as above I am fully satisfied of the truth of.

It is to be noted here that the dead-carts in the city were not confined to particular parishes, but one cart went through several parishes, according as the number of dead presented; nor were they tied to carry the dead to their respective parishes, but many of the dead taken up in the city were carried to the burying-ground in the out-parts for want of room.

I have already mentioned the surprise that this judgment was at first among the people. I must be allowed to give some of my observations on the more serious and religious part. Surely never city, at least of this bulk and magnitude, was taken in a condition so perfectly unprepared for such a dreadful visitation, whether I am to speak of the civil preparations or religious. They were, indeed, as if they had had no warning, no expectation, no apprehensions, and consequently the least provision imaginable was made for it in a public way. For example, the Lord Mayor and sheriffs had made no provision as magistrates for the regulations which were to be observed. They had gone into no measures for relief of the poor. The citizens had no public magazines or store-houses for corn or meal for the subsistence of the poor, which if they had provided themselves, as in such cases is done abroad, many miserable families, who were now reduced to the utmost distress, would have been relieved, and that in a better manner than now could be done.

The stock of the city's money I can say but little to. The Chamber of London was said to be exceeding rich, and it may be concluded that they were so, by the vast sums of money issued from thence in the rebuilding the public edifices after the fire of London, and in building new works, such as, for the first part, the Guildhall, Blackwell Hall, part of Leadenhall, half the Exchange, the Session House, the Compter, the prisons of Ludgate, Newgate &c., several of the wharfs and stairs and landing-places on the river; all which were either burned down or damaged by the great fire of London, the next year after the plague; and of the second sort, the Monument, Fleet Ditch with its bridges, and the Hospital of Bethlehem or Bedlam, &c. But possibly the managers of the city's credit at that time made more conscience of breaking in upon the orphan's money to show charity to the distressed citizens than the managers in the following years did to beautify the city and re-edify the buildings, though, in the first case, the losers would have thought their fortunes better bestowed, and the public faith of the city have been less subjected to scandal and reproach.

It must be acknowledged that the absent citizens, who, though they were fled for safety into the country, were yet greatly interested in the welfare of those whom they left behind, forgot not to contribute liberally to the relief of the poor, and large sums were also collected among trading towns in the remotest parts of England; and, as I have heard also, the nobility and the gentry in all parts of England took the deplorable condition of the city into their consideration, and sent up large sums of money in charity to the Lord Mayor and magistrates for the relief of the poor. The king also, as I was told, ordered a thousand pounds a week to be distributed in four parts: one quarter to the city and liberty of Westminster; one quarter or part among the inhabitants of the Southwark side of the water; one quarter to the liberty and parts within of the city, exclusive of the city within the walls; and one-fourth part to the suburbs in the county of Middlesex, and the east and north parts of the city. But this latter I only speak of as a report.

Certain it is, the greatest part of the poor or families who formerly lived by their labour, or by retail trade, lived now on charity; and had there not been prodigious sums of money given by charitable, well-minded Christians for the support of such, the city could never have subsisted. There were, no question, accounts kept of their charity, and of the just distribution of it by the magistrates. But as such multitudes of those very officers died through whose hands it was distributed, and also that, as I have been told, most of the accounts of those things were lost in the great fire which happened in the very next year, and which burnt even the chamberlain's office and many of their papers, so I could never come at the particular account, which I used great endeavours to have seen.

It may, however, be a direction in case of the approach

of a like visitation, which God keep the city from;—I say, it may be of use to observe that by the care of the Lord Mayor and aldermen at that time in distributing weekly great sums of money for relief of the poor, a multitude of people, who would otherwise have perished, were relieved, and their lives preserved. And here let me enter into a brief state of the case of the poor at that time, and what way apprehended from them, from whence may be judged hereafter what may be expected if the like distress should come upon the city.

At the beginning of the plague, when there was now no more hope but that the whole city would be visited; when, as I have said, all that had friends or estates in the country retired with their families; and when, indeed, one would have thought the very city itself was running out of the gates, and that there would be nobody left behind; you may be sure from that hour all trade, except such as related to immediate subsistence, was, as it were, at a full stop.

This is so lively a case, and contains in it so much of the real condition of the people, that I think I cannot be too particular in it, and therefore I descend to the several arrangements or classes of people who fell into immediate distress upon this occasion. For example:—

1. All master-workmen in manufactures, especially such as belonged to ornament, and the less necessary parts of the people's dress, clothes, and furniture for houses, such as riband-weavers and other weavers, gold and silver lace makers, and gold and silver wire drawers, sempstresses, milliners, shoemakers, hatmakers, and glovemakers; also upholsterers, joiners, cabinet-makers, looking-glass makers, and innumerable trades which depend upon such as these;—I say, the master-workmen in such stopped their work, dismissed their journeymen and workmen, and all their dependents.

2. As merchandising was at a full stop, for very few ships ventured to come up the river, and none at all went out, so

all the extraordinary officers of the customs, likewise the watermen, carmen, porters, and all the poor, whose labour depended upon the merchants, were at once dismissed, and put out of business.

3. All the tradesmen usually employed in building or repairing of houses were at a full stop, for the people were far from wanting to build houses when so many thousand houses were at once stripped of their inhabitants; so that this one article turned all the ordinary workmen of that kind out of business, such as bricklayers, masons, carpenters, joiners, plasterers, painters, glaziers, smiths, plumbers, and all the labourers depending on such.

4. As navigation was at a stop, our ships neither coming in or going out as before, so the seamen were all out of employment, and many of them in the last and lowest degree of distress; and with the seamen were all the several tradesmen and workmen belonging to and depending upon the building and fitting out of ships, such as ship-carpenters, caulkers, ropemakers, dry coopers, sailmakers, anchorsmiths, and other smiths; blockmakers, carvers, gunsmiths, ship-chandlers, ship-carvers, and the like. The masters of those perhaps might live upon their substance, but the traders were universally at a stop, and consequently all their workmen discharged. Add to these that the river was in a manner without boats, and all or most part of the watermen, lightermen, boat-builders, and lighter-builders, in like manner idle and laid by.

5. All families retrenched their living as much as possible, as well those that fled as those that stayed; so that an innumerable multitude of footmen, serving-men, shopkeepers, journeymen, merchants' bookkeepers, and such sort of people, and especially poor maid-servants, were turned off, and left friendless and helpless, without employment and without habitation, and this was really a dismal article.

I might be more particular as to this part, but it may suffice to mention in general, all trades being stopped, employment ceased, the labour, and by that the bread, of the poor were cut off; and at first indeed the cries of the poor were most lamentable to hear, though by the distribution of charity their misery that way was greatly abated. Many indeed fled into the counties, but thousands of them having stayed in London till nothing but desperation sent them away, death overtook them on the road, and they served for no better than the messengers of death; indeed, others carrying the infection along with them, spread it very unhappily into the remotest parts of the kingdom.

Many of these were the miserable objects of despair which I have mentioned before, and were removed by the destruction which followed. These might be said to perish, not by the infection itself, but by the consequence of it; indeed, namely, by hunger and distress, and the want of all things, being without lodging, without money, without friends, without means to get their bread, or without any one to give it them; for many of them were without what we call legal settlements, and so could not claim of the parishes, and all the support they had was by application to the magistrates for relief, which relief was (to give the magistrates their due) carefully and cheerfully administered, as they found it necessary, and those that stayed behind never felt the want and distress of that kind, which they felt who went away in the manner above noted.

Let any one who is acquainted with what multitudes of people get their daily bread in this city by their labour, whether artificers or mere workmen—I say, let any man consider what must be the miserable condition of this town if, on a sudden, they should be all turned out of employment, that labour should cease, and wages for work be no more.

This was the case with us at that time; and had not the sums of money contributed in charity by well-disposed people of every kind, as well abroad as at home, been prodigiously great, it had not been in the power of the

Lord Mayor and sheriffs to have kept the public peace. Nor were they without apprehensions, as it was, that desperation should push the people upon tumults, and cause them to rifle the houses of rich men and plunder the markets of provisions; in which case the country people, who brought provisions very freely and boldly to town, would have been terrified from coming any more, and the town would have sunk under an unavoidable famine.

But the prudence of my Lord Mayor and the Court of Aldermen within the city, and of the justices of peace in the out-parts, was such, and they were supported with money from all parts so well, that the poor people were kept quiet, and their wants everywhere relieved, as far as was possible to be done.

Two things besides this contributed to prevent the mob doing any mischief. One was, that really the rich themselves had not laid up stores of provisions in their houses, as indeed they ought to have done, and which if they had been wise enough to have done, and locked themselves entirely up, as some few did, they had perhaps escaped the disease better. But as it appeared they had not, so the mob had no notion of finding stores of provisions there if they had broken in, as it is plain they were sometimes very near doing, and which, if they had, they had finished the ruin of the whole city, for there were no regular troops to have withstood them, nor could the trained bands have been brought together to defend the city, no men being to be found to bear arms.

But the vigilance of the Lord Mayor and such magistrates as could be had (for some, even of the aldermen, were dead, and some absent) prevented this; and they did it by the most kind and gentle methods they could think of, as particularly by relieving the most desperate with money, and putting others into business, and par-

ticularly that employment of watching houses that were
infected and shut up. And as the number of these were
very great, for it was said there was at one time ten thousand houses shut up, and every house had two watchmen
to guard it, viz., one by night and the other by day, this
gave opportunity to employ a very great number of poor
men at a time.

The women and servants that were turned off from
their places were likewise employed as nurses to tend the
sick in all places, and this took off a very great number
of them.

And, which though a melancholy article in itself, yet
was a deliverance in its kind, namely, the plague, which
raged in a dreadful manner from the middle of August to
the middle of October, carried off in that time thirty or
forty thousand of these very people, which, had they been
left, would certainly have been an insufferable burden
by their poverty; that is to say, the whole city could not
have supported the expense of them, or have provided
food for them; and they would in time have been even
driven to the necessity of plundering either the city itself
or the country adjacent, to have subsisted themselves,
which would, first or last, have put the whole nation, as
well as the city, into the utmost terror and confusion.

It was observable, then, that this calamity of the people
made them very humble; for now for about nine weeks
together there died near a thousand a day, one day with
another, even by the account of the weekly bills, which
yet, I have reason to be assured, never gave a full account, by many thousands, the confusion being such, and
the carts working in the dark when they carried the dead,
that in some places no account at all was kept, but they
worked on, the clerks and sextons not attending for weeks
together, and not knowing what number they carried.

This account is verified by the following bills of mortality:—

		OF ALL DISEASES	OF THE PLAGUE
From August	8 to August 15	5319	3880
" "	15 " 22	5568	4237
" "	22 " 29	7496	6102
" "	29 to September 5 . . .	8252	6988
" September	5 " 12 . . .	7690	6544
" "	12 " 19 . . .	8297	7165
" "	19 " 26 . . .	6460	5533
" "	26 to October 3 . . .	5720	4929
" October	3 " 10 . . .	5068	4327
		59,870	49,705

So that the gross of the people were carried off in these two months; for, as the whole number which was brought in to die of the plague was but 68,590, here is 50,000 of them, within a trifle, in two months; I say 50,000, because, as there wants 295 in the number above, so there wants two days [*sic*] of two months in the account of time.

Now, when I say that the parish officers did not give in a full account, or were not to be depended upon for their account, let any one but consider how men could be exact in such a time of dreadful distress, and when many of them were taken sick themselves, and perhaps died in the very time when their accounts were to be given in; I mean the parish clerks, besides inferior officers; for though these poor men ventured at all hazards, yet they were far from being exempt from the common calamity, especially if it be true that the parish of Stepney had, within the year, 116 sextons, gravediggers, and their assistants; that is to say, bearers, bellmen, and drivers of carts for carrying off the dead bodies.

Indeed the work was not of a nature to allow them leisure to take an exact tale of the dead bodies, which were all huddled together in the dark into a pit; which pit or trench no man could come nigh but at the utmost peril. I observed often that in the parishes of Aldgate and Cripplegate, Whitechapel and Stepney, there were five, six, seven, and eight hundred in a week in the bills, whereas, if we may believe the opinion of those that lived in the city all the time as well as I, there died sometimes 2000 a week in those parishes; and I saw it under the hand of one that made as strict an examination into that part as he could, that there really died an hundred thousand people of the plague in that one year, whereas in the bills, the articles of the plague, it was but 68,590.

If I may be allowed to give my opinion, by what I saw with my eyes and heard from other people that were eye-witnesses, I do verily believe the same, viz., that there died at least 100,000 of the plague only, besides other distempers, and besides those which died in the fields and highways and secret places out of the compass of the communication, as it was called, and who were not put down in the bills, though they really belonged to the body of the inhabitants. It was known to us all that abundance of poor despairing creatures who had the distemper upon them, and were grown stupid or melancholy by their misery, as many were, wandered away into the fields and woods, and into secret, uncouth places, almost anywhere, to creep into a bush or hedge and die.

The inhabitants of the villages adjacent would, in pity, carry them food, and set it at a distance, that they might fetch it, if they were able; and sometimes they were not able, and the next time they went they should find the poor wretches lie dead and the food untouched. The number of these miserable objects were many, and I know so many that perished thus, and so exactly where, that I believe I could go to the very place and dig their bones up still; for the country people would go and dig a hole at a distance from them, and then with long poles, and hooks at the end of them, drag the bodies into these pits, and then throw the earth in from as far as they could cast it, to cover them, taking notice how the wind blew, and so coming on that side which the seamen call to windward, that the scent of the bodies might blow from them; and thus great numbers went out of the world, who were never known, or any account of them taken, as well within the bills of mortality as without.

This, indeed, I had in the main only from the relation of others, for I seldom walked into the fields, except towards Bethnal Green and Hackney, or as hereafter. But when I did walk, I always saw a great many poor wanderers at a distance; but I could know little of their cases, for whether it were in the street or in the fields, if we had seen anybody coming, it was a general method to walk away; yet I believe the account is exactly true.

As this puts me upon mentioning my walking the streets and fields, I cannot omit taking notice what a desolate place the city was at that time. The great street I lived in, which is known to be one of the broadest of all the streets of London, I mean of the suburbs as well as the liberties, all the side where the butchers lived, especially without the bars, was more like a green field than a paved street, and the people generally went in the middle with the horses and carts. It is true that the farthest end towards Whitechapel Church was not all paved, but even the part that was paved was full of grass also; but this need not seem strange, since the great streets within the city, such as Leadenhall Street, Bishopsgate Street, Cornhill, and even the Exchange itself, had grass growing in them in several places; neither cart or coach were seen in the streets from morning to evening, except some country carts to bring roots and beans, or peas, hay, and straw, to the market, and those but very few compared to what was usual. As for coaches, they were scarce used but to carry sick people to the pest-house, and to other hospitals, and some few to carry physicians to such places as they thought fit to venture to visit; for really coaches were dangerous things, and people did not care to venture into them, because they did not know who might have been carried in them last, and sick, infected people were, as I have said, ordinarily carried in them to the pest-houses, and sometimes people expired in them as they went along.

It is true, when the infection came to such a height as I have now mentioned, there were very few physicians which cared to stir abroad to sick houses, and very many of the most eminent of the faculty were dead, as well as the surgeons also; for now it was indeed a dismal time, and for about a month together, not taking any notice of the bills of mortality, I believed there did not die less than 1500 or 1700 a day, one day with another.

One of the worst days we had in the whole time, as I thought, was in the beginning of September, when, indeed, good people began to think that God was resolved to make a full end of the people in this miserable city. This was at that time when the plague was fully come into the eastern parishes. The parish of Aldgate, if I may give my opinion, buried above a thousand a week for two weeks, though the bills did not say so many;—but it surrounded me at so dismal a rate that there was not a house in twenty uninfected in the Minories, in Houndsditch, and in those parts of Aldgate parish about the Butcher Row and the alleys over against me. I say, in those places death reigned in every corner. Whitechapel parish was in the same condition, and though much less than the parish I lived in, yet buried near 600 a week by the bills, and in my opinion near twice as many. Whole families, and indeed whole streets of families, were swept away together; insomuch that it was frequent for neighbours to call to the bellman to go to such-and-such houses and fetch out the people, for that they were all dead.

And, indeed, the work of removing the dead bodies by carts was now grown so very odious and dangerous that it was complained of that the bearers did not take care to clear such houses where all the inhabitants were dead, but that sometimes the bodies lay several days unburied, till the neighbouring families were offended with the stench, and consequently infected; and this neglect of the officers was such that the churchwardens and constables were summoned to look after it, and even the justices of the Hamlets were obliged to venture their lives among them to quicken and encourage them, for innumerable of the bearers died of the distemper, infected by the bodies they were obliged to come so near. And had it not been that the number of poor people who wanted employment and wanted bread (as I have said before) was so great that necessity drove them to undertake anything and venture anything, they would never have found people to be employed. And then the bodies of the dead would have lain above ground, and have perished and rotted in a dreadful manner.

But the magistrates cannot be enough commended in this, that they kept such good order for the burying of the dead, that as fast as any of those they employed to carry off and bury the dead fell sick or died, as was many times the case, they immediately supplied the places with others, which, by reason of the great number of poor that was left out of business, as above, was not hard to do. This occasioned, that notwithstanding the infinite number of people which died and were sick, almost all together, yet they were always cleared away and carried off every night, so that it was never to be said of London that the living were not able to bury the dead.

As the desolation was greater during those terrible times, so the amazement of the people increased, and a thousand unaccountable things they would do in the violence of their fright, as others did the same in the agonies of their distemper, and this part was very affecting. Some went roaring and crying and wringing their hands along the street; some would go praying and lifting up their hands to heaven, calling upon God for mercy. I cannot say, indeed, whether this was not in their distraction, but, be it so, it was still an indication of a more serious mind, when they had the use of their senses, and was much better, even as it was, than the frightful yellings and cryings that every day, and especially in the evenings, were heard in some streets. I suppose the world has heard of the famous Solomon Eagle, an enthusiast. He, though not infected at all but in his head, went about denouncing of judgment upon the city in a frightful manner, sometimes quite naked, and with a pan of burning charcoal on his head. What he said, or pretended, indeed I could not learn.

I will not say whether that clergyman was distracted or not, or whether he did it in pure zeal for the poor people, who went every evening through the streets of Whitechapel, and, with his hands lifted up, repeated that part of the Liturgy of the Church continually, "Spare us, good Lord; spare Thy people, whom Thou hast redeemed with Thy most precious blood." I say, I cannot speak positively of these things, because these were only the dismal objects which represented themselves to me as I looked through my chamber windows (for I seldom opened the casements), while I confined myself within doors during that most violent raging of the pestilence; when, indeed, as I have said, many began to think, and even to say, that there would none escape; and indeed I began to think so too, and therefore kept within doors for about a fortnight, and never stirred out. But I could not hold it. Besides, there were some people who, notwithstanding the danger, did not omit publicly to attend the worship of God, even in the most dangerous times; and though it is true that a great many clergymen did shut up their churches, and fled, as other people did, for the safety of their lives, yet all did not do so. Some ventured to officiate and to keep up the assemblies of the people by constant prayers, and sometimes sermons or brief exhortations to repentance and reformation, and this as long as any would come to hear them. And Dissenters did the like also, and even in the very churches where the parish ministers were either dead or fled; nor was there any room for making difference at such a time as this was.

It was indeed a lamentable thing to hear the miserable lamentations of poor dying creatures calling out for ministers to comfort them and pray with them, to counsel them and to direct them, calling out to God for pardon and mercy, and confessing aloud their past sins. It would make the stoutest heart bleed to hear how many warnings were then given by dying penitents to others not to put off and delay their repentance to the day of distress; that such a time of calamity as this was no time for repentance, was no time to call upon God. I wish I could repeat the very sound of those groans and of those exclamations that I heard from some poor dying creatures when in the height of their agonies and distress, and that I could make him that reads this hear, as I imagine I now hear them, for the sound seems still to ring in my ears.

If I could but tell this part in such moving accents as should alarm the very soul of the reader, I should rejoice that I recorded those things, however short and imperfect.

It pleased God that I was still spared, and very hearty and sound in health, but very impatient of being pent up within doors without air, as I have been for fourteen days or thereabouts, and I could not restrain myself, but I would go to carry a letter for my brother to the post-house. Then it was indeed that I observed a profound silence in the streets. When I came to the post-house, as I went to put in my letter, I saw a man standing in one corner of the yard and talking to another at a window, and a third had opened a door belonging to the office. In the middle of the yard lay a small leather purse with two keys hanging at it, with money in it, but nobody would meddle with it. I asked how long it had lain there; the man at the window said it had lain almost an hour, but that they had not meddled with it, because they did not know but the person who dropped it might come back to look for it. I had no such need of money, nor was the sum so big that I had any inclination to meddle with it, or to get the money at the hazard it might be attended with; so I seemed to go away, when the man who had opened the door said he would take it up, but so that if the right owner came for it he should be sure to have it. So he went in and fetched a pail of water, and set it down hard by the purse, then went again and fetched some gunpowder, and cast a good deal of powder upon the purse, and then made a train from that which he had thrown loose upon the purse. The train reached about two yards. After this he goes in a third time and fetches out a pair of tongs red hot, and which he had prepared, I suppose, on purpose, and first setting fire to the train of powder, that signed the purse, and also smoked the air sufficiently. But he was not content with that, but he then takes up the purse with the tongs, holding it so long till the tongs burnt through the purse, and then he shook the money out into the pail of water, so he carried it in. The money, as I remember, was about thirteen shillings and some smooth groats and brass farthings.

There might perhaps have been several poor people, as I have observed above, that would have been hardy enough to have ventured for the sake of the money; but you may easily see by what I have observed that the few people who were spared were very careful of themselves at that time when the distress was so exceeding great.

Much about the same time I walked out into the fields towards Bow; for I had a great mind to see how things were managed in the river and among the ships; and as I had some concern in shipping, I had a notion that it had been one of the best ways of securing one's self from the infection to have retired into a ship; and musing how to satisfy my curiosity in that point, I turned away over the fields from Bow to Bromley, and down to Blackwall to the stairs, which are there for landing or taking water.

Here I saw a poor man walking on the bank, or sea-wall, as they call it, by himself. I walked a while also about, seeing the houses all shut up. At last I fell into some talk, at a distance, with this poor man; first I asked him how people did thereabouts. "Alas, sir!" says he, "almost desolate; all dead or sick. Here are very few families in this part, or in that village" (pointing at Poplar), "where half of them are not dead already, and the rest sick." Then he pointing to one house, "There they are all dead," said he, "and the house stands open; nobody dares go into it. A poor thief," says he, "ventured in to steal something, but he paid dear for his theft, for he was carried to the churchyard too last night." Then he pointed to several other houses. "There," says he, "they are all dead, the man and his wife, and five children. There," says he, "they are shut up; you see a watchman at the door;" and so of other houses. "Why," says I, "what do you here all alone?" "Why," says he, "I am a poor, desolate man; it has pleased God I am not yet visited, though my family is, and one of my children dead." "How do you mean, then," said I, "that you are not visited?" "Why," says he, "that's my house" (pointing to a very little, low-boarded house), "and there my poor wife and two children live," said he, "if they may be said to live, for my wife and one of the children are visited, but I do not come at them." And with that word I saw the tears run very plentifully down his face; and so they did down mine too, I assure you.

"But," said I, "why do you not come at them? How can you abandon your own flesh and blood?" "Oh, sir," says he, "the Lord forbid! I do not abandon them; I work for them as much as I am able; and, blessed be the Lord, I keep them from want;" and with that I observed he lifted up his eyes to heaven, with a countenance that presently told me I had happened on a man that was no hypocrite, but a serious, religious, good man, and his ejaculation was an expression of thankfulness that, in such a condition as he was in, he should be able to say his family did not want. "Well," says I, "honest man, that is a great mercy as things go now with the poor. But how do you live, then, and how are you kept from the dreadful calamity that is now upon us all?" "Why, sir," says he, "I am a watchman, and there's my boat," says he, "and the boat serves me for a house. I work in it in the day, and I sleep in it in the night; and what I get I lay down upon that stone," says he, showing me a broad stone on the other side of the street, a good way from his house; "and then," says he, "I halloo, and call to them till I make them hear; and they come and fetch it."

"Well, friend," says I, "but how can you get any money as a waterman? Does anybody go by water these times?" "Yes, sir," says he, "in the way I am employed there does. Do you see there," says he, "five ships lie at anchor" (pointing down the river a good way below the town), "and do you see," says he, "eight or ten ships lie at the chain there, and at anchor yonder?" (pointing above the town). "All those ships have families on board, of their merchants and owners, and such-like, who have locked themselves up and live on board, close shut in, for fear of the infection; and I tend on them to fetch things for them, carry letters, and do what is absolutely necessary, that they may not be obliged to come on shore; and every night I fasten my boat on board one of the ship's boats, and there I sleep by myself, and, blessed be God, I am preserved hitherto."

"Well," said I, "friend, but will they let you come on board after you have been on shore here, when this is such a terrible place, and so infected as it is?"

"Why, as to that," said he, "I very seldom go up the ship-side, but deliver what I bring to their boat, or lie by the side, and they hoist it on board. If I did, I think they are in no danger from me, for I never go into any house on shore, or touch anybody, no, not of my own family; but I fetch provisions for them."

"Nay," says I, "but that may be worse, for you must have those provisions of somebody or other; and since all this part of the town is so infected, it is dangerous so much as to speak with anybody, for the village," said I, "is, as it were, the beginning of London, though it be at some distance from it."

"That is true," added he; "but you do not understand me right; I do not buy provisions for them here. I row up to Greenwich and buy fresh meat there, and some- times I row down the river to Woolwich and buy there; then I go to single farm-houses on the Kentish side, where I am known, and buy fowls and eggs and butter, and bring to the ships, as they direct me, sometimes one, sometimes the other. I seldom come on shore here, and I came now only to call to my wife and hear how my little family do, and give them a little money, which I received last night."

"Poor man!" said I; "and how much hast thou gotten for them?"

"I have gotten four shillings," said he, "which is a great sum, as things go now with poor men; but they have given me a bag of bread too, and a salt fish and some flesh; so all helps out."

"Well," said I, "and have you given it them yet?"

"No," said he; "but I have called, and my wife has answered that she cannot come out yet, but in half-an-hour she hopes to come, and I am waiting for her. Poor woman!" says he, "she is brought sadly down. She has a swelling, and it is broke, and I hope she will recover; but I fear the child will die, but it is the Lord——"

Here he stopped, and wept very much.

"Well, honest friend," said I, "thou hast a sure Comforter, if thou hast brought thyself to be resigned to the will of God; He is dealing with us all in judgment."

"Oh, sir!" says he, "it is infinite mercy if any of us are spared, and who am I to repine!"

"Sayest thou so?" said I, "and how much less is my faith than thine?" And here my heart smote me, suggesting how much better this poor man's foundation was on which he stayed in the danger than mine; that he had nowhere to fly; that he had a family to bind him to attendance, which I had not; and mine was mere presumption, his a true dependence, and a courage resting on God; and yet that he used all possible caution for his safety.

I turned a little way from the man while these thoughts engaged me, for, indeed, I could no more refrain from tears than he.

At length, after some further talk, the poor woman

opened the door and called, "Robert, Robert." He an-swered, and bid her stay a few moments and he would come; so he ran down the common stairs to his boat and fetched up a sack, in which was the provisions he had brought from the ships; and when he returned he hal-looed again. Then he went to the great stone which he showed me and emptied the sack, and laid all out, every-thing by themselves, and then retired; and his wife came with a little boy to fetch them away, and he called and said such a captain had sent such a thing, and such a cap-tain such a thing, and at the end adds, "God has sent it all; give thanks to Him." When the poor woman had taken up all, she was so weak she could not carry it at once in, though the weight was not much neither; so she left the biscuit which was in a little bag, and left a little boy to watch it till she came again.

"Well, but," says I to him, "did you leave her the four shillings too, which you said was your week's pay?"

"Yes, yes," says he; "you shall hear her own it." So he calls again, "Rachel, Rachel," which, it seems, was her name, "did you take up the money?" "Yes," said she. "How much was it?" said he. "Four shillings and a groat," said she. "Well, well," says he, "the Lord keep you all;" and so he turned to go away.

As I could not refrain contributing tears to this man's story, so neither could I refrain my charity for his assist-ance. So I called him, "Hark thee, friend," said I, "come hither, for I believe thou art in health, that I may venture thee;" so I pulled out my hand, which was in my pocket before, "Here," says I, "go and call thy Rachel once more, and give her a little more comfort from me. God will never forsake a family that trust in Him as thou dost." So I gave him four other shillings, and bid him go lay them on the stone and call his wife.

I had not words to express the poor man's thankfulness,

neither could he express it himself but by tears running down his face. He called his wife, and told her God had moved the heart of a stranger, upon hearing their condition, to give them all that money, and a great deal more such as that he said to her. The woman, too, made signs of the like thankfulness, as well to Heaven as to me, and joyfully picked it up; and I parted with no money all that year that I thought better bestowed.

I then asked the poor man if the distemper had not reached to Greenwich. He said it had not till about a fortnight before; but that then he feared it had, but that it was only at that end of the town which lay south towards Deptford Bridge; that he went only to a butcher's shop and a grocer's, where he generally bought such things as they sent him for, but was very careful.

I asked him then how it came to pass that those people who had so shut themselves up in the ships had not laid in sufficient stores of all things necessary. He said some of them had, but, on the other hand, some did not come on board till they were frighted into it, and till it was too dangerous for them to go to the proper people to lay in quantities of things, and that he waited on two ships, which he showed me, that had laid in little or nothing but biscuit bread and ship beer, and that he had bought everything else almost for them. I asked him if there was any more ships that had separated themselves as those had done. He told me yes, all the way up from the point, right against Greenwich, to within the shore of Limehouse and Redriff, all the ships that could have room rid two and two in the middle of the stream, and that some of them had several families on board. I asked him if the distemper had not reached them. He said he believed it had not, except two or three ships, whose people had not been so watchful to keep the seamen from going on shore,

as others had been, and he said it was a very fine sight to
see how the ships lay up the Pool.

When he said he was going over to Greenwich as soon
as the tide began to come in, I asked if he would let me
go with him, and bring me back, for that I had a great
mind to see how the ships were ranged, as he had told
me. He told me, if I would assure him on the word of a
Christian and of an honest man, that I had not the distemper, he would. I assured him that I had not; that it
had pleased God to preserve me; that I lived in Whitechapel, but was too impatient of being so long within
doors, and that I had ventured out so far for the refreshment of a little air, but that none in my house had so
much as been touched with it.

"Well, sir," says he, "as your charity has been moved to
pity me and my poor family, sure you cannot have so
little pity left as to put yourself into my boat if you were
not sound in health, which would be nothing less than
killing me, and ruining my whole family." The poor man
troubled me so much when he spoke of his family with
such a sensible concern, and in such an affectionate manner, that I could not satisfy myself at first to go at all. I
told him I would lay aside my curiosity rather than make
him uneasy, though I was sure, and very thankful for it,
that I had no more distemper upon me than the freshest
man in the world. Well, he would not have me put it off
neither, but, to let me see how confident he was that I
was just to him, now importuned me to go; so when the
tide came up to his boat I went in, and he carried me to
Greenwich. While he bought the things which he had in
his charge to buy, I walked up to the top of the hill under
which the town stands, and on the east side of the town,
to get a prospect of the river. But it was a surprising sight
to see the number of ships which lay in rows, two and

two, and some places two or three such lines in the breadth of the river, and this not only up quite to the town, between the houses which we call Ratcliff and Redriff, which they name the Pool, but even down the whole river, as far as the head of Long Reach, which is as far as the hills give us leave to see it.

I cannot guess at the number of ships, but I think there must be several hundreds of sail; and I could not but applaud the contrivance, for ten thousand people, and more, who attended ship affairs were certainly sheltered here from the violence of the contagion, and lived very safe and very easy.

I returned to my own dwelling very well satisfied with my day's journey, and particularly with the poor man; also, I rejoiced to see that such little sanctuaries were provided for so many families in a time of such desolation. I observed also, that as the violence of the plague had increased, so the ships which had families on board removed and went farther off, till, as I was told, some went quite away to sea, and put into such harbours and safe roads on the north coast as they could best come at.

But it was also true that all the people who thus left the land and lived on board the ships were not entirely safe from the infection, for many died and were thrown overboard into the river, some in coffins, and some, as I heard, without coffins, whose bodies were seen sometimes to drive up and down with the tide in the river.

But I believe I may venture to say that in those ships which were thus infected it either happened where the people had recourse to them too late, and did not fly to the ship till they had stayed too long on shore and had the distemper upon them, though perhaps they might not perceive it, and so the distemper did not come to them on board the ships, but they really carried it with them;

or it was in these ships where the poor waterman said they had not had time to furnish themselves with provisions, but were obliged to send often on shore to buy what they had occasion for, or suffered boats to come to them from the shore. And so the distemper was brought insensibly among them.

And here I cannot but take notice that the strange temper of the people of London at that time contributed extremely to their own destruction. The plague began, as I have observed, at the other end of the town, namely, in Long Acre, Drury Lane, &c., and came on towards the city very gradually and slowly. It was felt at first in December, then again in February, then again in April, and always but a very little at a time; then it stopped till May, and even the last week in May there was but seventeen, and all at that end of the town; and all this while, even so long as till there died above 3000 a week, yet had the people in Redriff, and in Wapping and Ratcliff, on both sides the river, and almost all Southwark side, a mighty fancy that they should not be visited, or at least that it would not be so violent among them. Some people fancied the smell of the pitch and tar, and such other things as oil and rosin and brimstone, which is so much used by all trades relating to shipping, would preserve them. Others argued it, because it was in its extremest violence in Westminster and the parish of St. Giles and St. Andrew, &c., and began to abate again before it came among them, which was true indeed, in part. For example——

From the 8th to the 15th August—

St. Giles-in-the-Fields	242
Cripplegate	886
Stepney	197
St. Margaret, Bermondsey	24
Rotherhithe	3
Total this week	4030

From the 15th to the 22nd August—

St. Giles-in-the-Fields	175
Cripplegate	847
Stepney	273
St. Margaret, Bermondsey	36
Rotherhithe	2
Total this week	5319

N.B.—That it was observed the numbers mentioned in Stepney parish at that time were generally all on that side where Stepney parish joined to Shoreditch, which we now call Spitalfields, where the parish of Stepney comes up to the very wall of Shoreditch Churchyard, and the plague at this time was abated at St. Giles-in-the-Fields, and raged most violently in Cripplegate,. Bishopsgate, and Shoreditch parishes; but there was not ten people a week that died of it in all that part of Stepney parish which takes in Limehouse, Ratcliff Highway, and which are now the parishes of Shadwell and Wapping, even to St. Catherine's by the Tower, till after the whole month of August was expired. But they paid for it afterwards, as I shall observe by-and-by.

This, I say, made the people of Redriff and Wapping, Ratcliff and Limehouse, so secure, and flatter themselves so much with the plague's going off without reaching them, that they took no care either to fly into the country or shut themselves up. Nay, so far were they from stirring that they rather received their friends and relations from the city into their houses, and several from other places really took sanctuary in that part of the town as a place of safety, and as a place which they thought God would pass over, and not visit as the rest was visited.

And this was the reason that when it came upon them they were more surprised, more unprovided, and more at a loss what to do than they were in other places; for when it came among them really and with violence, as it did indeed in September and October, there was then no stirring out into the country, nobody would suffer a stranger to come near them, no, nor near the towns where they dwelt; and, as I have been told, several that wandered into the country on Surrey side were found starved to death in the woods and commons, that country being more open and more woody than any other part so near London, especially about Norwood and the parishes of Camberwell, Dulwich, and Lusum, where, it seems, nobody durst relieve the poor distressed people for fear of the infection.

This notion having, as I said, prevailed with the people in that part of the town, was in part the occasion, as I said before, that they had recourse to ships for their retreat; and where they did this early and with prudence, furnishing themselves so with provisions that they had no need to go on shore for supplies or suffer boats to come on board to bring them,—I say, where they did so they had certainly the safest retreat of any people whatsover; but the distress was such that people ran on board, in their fright, without bread to eat, and some into ships that had no men on board to remove them farther off, or to take the boat and go down the river to buy provisions where it might be done safely, and these often suffered and were infected on board as much as on shore.

As the richer sort got into ships, so the lower rank got into hoys, smacks, lighters, and fishing-boats; and many, especially watermen, lay in their boats; but those made sad work of it, especially the latter, for, going about for provision, and perhaps to get their subsistence, the infection got in among them and made a fearful havoc; many of the watermen died alone in their wherries as they rid at their roads, as well above bridge as below, and were not found sometimes till they were not in condition for anybody to touch or come near them.

Indeed, the distress of the people at this seafaring end of the town was very deplorable, and deserved the greatest commiseration. But, alas! this was a time when every one's private safety lay so near them that they had no room to pity the distresses of others; for every one had death, as it were, at his door, and many even in their families, and knew not what to do or whither to fly.

This, I say, took away all compassion; self-preservation, indeed, appeared here to be the first law. For the children ran away from their parents as they languished in the utmost distress. And in some places, though not so frequent as the other, parents did the like to their children; nay, some dreadful examples there were, and particularly two in one week, of distressed mothers, raving and distracted, killing their own children; one whereof was not far off from where I dwelt, the poor lunatic creature not living herself long enough to be sensible of the sin of what she had done, much less to be punished for it.

It is not, indeed, to be wondered at, for the danger of immediate death to ourselves took away all bowels of love, all concern for one another. I speak in general, for there were many instances of immovable affection, pity, and duty in many, and some that came to my knowledge, that is to say, by hearsay; for I shall not take upon me to vouch the truth of the particulars.

To introduce one, let me first mention that one of the most deplorable cases in all the present calamity was that of women with child, who, when they came to the hour of their sorrows and their pains come upon them, could neither have help of one kind or another; neither midwife or neighbouring women to come near them. Most of the midwives were dead, especially of such as served the poor; and many, if not all the midwives of note, were fled into the country; so that it was next to impossible for a poor woman that could not pay an immoderate price to get any midwife to come to her, and if they did, those they could get were generally unskilful and ignorant creatures; and the consequence of this was, that a most unusual and incredible number of women were reduced to the utmost distress. Some were delivered and spoiled by the rashness and ignorance of those who pretended to lay them. Children without number were, I might say, murdered by the same, but a more justifiable ignorance, pretending they would save the mother, whatever became of the child; and many times both mother and child were lost in the same manner; and especially where the mother had the distemper, there nobody would come near them, and both sometimes perished. Sometimes the mother has died of the plague, and the infant, it may be, half born, or born but not parted from the mother. Some died in the very pains of their travail, and not delivered at all; and so many were the cases of this kind that it is hard to judge of them.

Something of it will appear in the unusual numbers which are put into the weekly bills (though I am far from allowing them to be able to give anything of a full account) under the articles of——

Child-bed.
Abortive and Still-born.
Chrisoms and Infants.

Take the weeks in which the plague was most violent, and compare them with the weeks before the distemper began, even in the same year. For example:——

	Child-bed.	Abor-tive.	Still-born.
From January 3 to January 10 . .	7	1	13
" " 10 " 17 . .	8	6	11
" " 17 " 24 . .	9	5	15
" " 24 " 31 . .	3	2	9
" " 31 to February 7 . .	3	3	8
" February 7 " 14 . .	6	2	11
" " 14 " 21 . .	5	2	13
" " 21 " 28 . .	2	2	10
" " 28 to March 7 . .	5	1	10
	48	24	100

From August	1 to August	8	. . 25	5	11
" "	8 "	15	. . 23	6	8
" "	15 "	22	. . 28	4	4
" "	22 "	29	. . 40	6	10
" "	29 to September	5	. 38	2	11
" September	5 to "	12	. 39	23	. .
" "	12 "	19	. 42	5	17
" "	19 "	26	. 42	6	10
" "	26 to October	3	. 14	4	9
			291	61	80

To the disparity of these numbers is to be considered and allowed for, that, according to our usual opinion who were then upon the spot, there were not one-third of the people in the town during the months of August and September as were in the months of January and February. In a word, the usual number that used to die of these three articles, and, as I hear, did die of them the year before, was thus:——

1664.		1665.	
Child-bed	189	Child-bed . . .	625
Abortive and still-born .	458	Abortive and still-born .	617
	647		1242

This inequality, I say, is exceedingly augmented when the numbers of people are considered. I pretend not to make any exact calculation of the numbers of people which were at this time in the city, but I shall make a probable conjecture at that part by-and-by. What I have said now is to explain the misery of those poor creatures Woe be to those who are with child, and to those which above, so that it might well be said, as in the Scripture, give suck in that day. For, indeed, it was a woe to them in particular.

I was not conversant in many particular families where these things happened, but the outcries of the miserable were heard afar off. As to those who were with child, we have seen some calculation made; 291 women dead in child-bed in nine weeks, out of one-third part of the number of whom there usually died in that time but eighty-four of the same disaster. Let the reader calculate the proportion.

There is no room to doubt but the misery of those that gave suck was in proportion as great. Our bills of mortality could give but little light in this, yet some it did. There were several more than usual starved at nurse, but this was nothing. The misery was where they were, first, starved for want of a nurse, the mother dying, and all the family and the infants found dead by them, merely for want; and, if I may speak my opinion, I do believe that many hundreds of poor helpless infants perished in this manner. Secondly, not starved, but poisoned by the nurse. Nay, even where the mother has been nurse, and having received the infection, has poisoned, that is, infected the infant with her milk, even before they knew they were infected themselves; nay, and the infant has died in such a case before the mother. I cannot but remember to leave this admonition upon record, if ever such another dreadful visitation should happen in this city, that all women that are with child or that give suck should be gone, if they have any possible means, out of the place, because their misery, if infected, will so much exceed all other people's.

I could tell here dismal stories of living infants being found sucking the breasts of their mothers, or nurses, after they have been dead of the plague. Of a mother in the parish where I lived, who, having a child that was not well, sent for an apothecary to view the child; and when he came, as the relation goes, was giving the child suck at her breast, and to all appearance was herself very well; but when the apothecary came close to her he saw the tokens upon that breast with which she was suckling the child. He was surprised enough, to be sure, but, not willing to fright the poor woman too much, he desired she would give the child into his hand; so he takes the child, and going to a cradle in the room, lays it in, and opening its cloths, found the tokens upon the child too, and both died before he could get home to send a preventive medicine to the father of the child, to whom he had told their condition. Whether the child infected the nurse-mother or the mother the child was not certain, but the last most likely. Likewise of a child brought home to the parents from a nurse that had died of the plague, yet the tender mother would not refuse to take in her child, and laid it in her bosom, by which she was infected, and died with the child in her arms dead also.

It would make the hardest heart move at the instances that were frequently found of tender mothers tending and watching with their dear children, and even dying before them, and sometimes taking the distemper from them and dying, when the child for whom the affectionate heart had been sacrificed has got over it and escaped.

The like of a tradesman in East Smithfield, whose wife was big with child of her first child, and fell in labour, having the plague upon her. He could neither get midwife to assist her or nurse to tend her, and two servants which he kept fled both from her. He ran from house to house like one distracted, but could get no help; the utmost he could get was, that a watchman, who attended at an infected house shut up, promised to send a nurse in the morning. The poor man, with his heart broke, went back, assisted his wife what he could, acted the part of the midwife, brought the child dead into the world, and his wife in about an hour died in his arms, where he held her dead body fast till the morning, when the watchman came and brought the nurse as he had promised; and coming up the stairs, for he had left the door open, or only latched, they found the man sitting with his dead wife in his arms, and so over-whelmed with grief that he died in a few hours after, without any sign of the infection upon him, but merely sank under the weight of his grief.

I have heard also of some who, on the death of their relations, have grown stupid with the insupportable sorrow, and of one in particular, who was so absolutely overcome with the pressure upon his spirits that by degrees his head sank into his body, so between his shoulders, that the crown of his head was very little seen above the bone of his shoulders; and by degrees, losing both voice and sense, his face, looking forward, lay against his collarbone, and could not be kept up any otherwise, unless held up by the hands of other people; and the poor man never came to himself again, but languished near a year in that condition, and died. Nor was he ever once seen to lift up his eyes or to look upon any particular object.

I cannot undertake to give any other than a summary of such passages as these, because it was not possible to come at the particulars, where sometimes the whole families where such things happened were carried off by the distemper. But there were innumerable cases of this kind which presented to the eye and the ear, even in passing along the streets, as I have hinted above. Nor is it easy to give any story of this or that family which there was not divers parallel stories to be met with of the same kind.

But as I am now talking of the time when the plague raged at the easternmost part of the town, how for a long time the people of those parts had flattered themselves that they should escape, and how they were surprised when it came upon them as it did; for, indeed, it came upon them like an armed man when it did come;—I say, this brings me back to the three poor men who wandered from Wapping, not knowing whither to go or what to do, and whom I mentioned before; one a biscuit-baker, one a sail-maker, and the other a joiner, all of Wapping or thereabouts.

The sleepiness and security of that part, as I have observed, was such that they not only did not shift for themselves as others did, but they boasted of being safe, and of safety being with them; and many people fled out of the city, and out of the infected suburbs, to Wapping, Ratcliff, Limehouse, Poplar, and such places, as to places of security; and it is not at all unlikely that their doing this helped to bring the plague that way faster than it might otherwise have come. For though I am much for people flying away, and emptying such a town as this, upon the first appearance of a like visitation, and that all people who have any possible retreat should make use of it in time, and be gone, yet I must say, when all that will fly are gone, those that are left, and must stand it, should stand stock-still where they are, and not shift from one end of the town or one part of the town to the other; for that is the bane and mischief of the whole, and they carry the plague from house to house in their very clothes.

Wherefore were we ordered to kill all the dogs and cats, but because as they were domestic animals, and are apt to run from house to house, and from street to street, so they are capable of carrying the effluvia or infectious steams of bodies infected even in their furs and hair. And therefore it was that, in the beginning of the infection, an order was published by the Lord Mayor, and by the magistrates, according to the advice of the physicians, that all the dogs and cats should be immediately killed, and an officer was appointed for the execution.

It is incredible, if their account is to be depended upon,

what a prodigious number of those creatures were destroyed. I think they talked of forty thousand dogs, and
five times as many cats, few houses being without a cat,
some having several, sometimes five or six in a house. All
possible endeavours were used, also, to destroy the mice
and rats, especially the latter, by laying ratsbane and
other poisons for them, and a prodigious multitude of
them were also destroyed.

I often reflected upon the unprovided condition that
the whole body of the people were in at the first coming
of this calamity upon them, and how it was for want of
timely entering into measures and managements, as well
public as private, that all the confusions that followed
were brought upon us, and that such a prodigious number
of people sank in that disaster, which, if proper steps had
been taken, might, Providence concurring, have been
avoided, and which, if posterity think fit, they may take a
caution and warning from. But I shall come to this part
again.

I come back to my three men. Their story has a moral
in every part of it, and their whole conduct, and that of
some whom they joined with, is a pattern for all poor men
to follow, or women either, if ever such a time comes
again; and if there was no other end in recording it, I
think this a very just one, whether my account be exactly
according to fact or no.

Two of them are said to be brothers, the one an old
soldier, but now a biscuit-baker; the other a lame sailor,
but now a sailmaker; the third a joiner. Says John the
biscuit-baker one day to Thomas his brother, the sailmaker, "Brother Tom, what will become of us? The
plague grows hot in the city, and increases this way.
What shall we do?"

"Truly," says Thomas, "I am at a great loss what to do,
for I find if it comes down into Wapping I shall be turned

out of my lodging." And thus they began to talk of it beforehand.

JOHN: Turned out of your lodging, Tom! If you are, I don't know who will take you in; for people are so afraid of one another now, there's no getting a lodging anywhere.

THOMAS: Why, the people where I lodge are good, civil people, and have kindness enough for me too; but they say I go abroad every day to my work, and it will be dangerous; and they talk of locking themselves up and letting nobody come near them.

JOHN: Why, they are in the right, to be sure, if they resolve to venture staying in town.

THOMAS: Nay, I might even resolve to stay within doors too, for, except a suit of sails that my master has in hand, and which I am just finishing, I am like to get no more work a great while. There's no trade stirs now. Workmen and servants are turned off everywhere, so that I might be glad to be locked up too; but I do not see they will be willing to consent to that, any more than to the other.

JOHN: Why, what will you do then, brother? And what shall I do? for I am almost as bad as you. The people where I lodge are all gone into the country but a maid, and she is to go next week, and to shut the house quite up, so that I shall be turned adrift to the wide world before you, and I am resolved to go away too, if I knew but where to go.

THOMAS: We were both distracted we did not go away at first; then we might have travelled anywhere. There's no stirring now; we shall be starved if we pretend to go out of town. They won't let us have victuals, no, not for our money, nor let us come into the towns, much less into their houses.

JOHN: And that which is almost as bad, I have but little money to help myself with neither.

THOMAS: As to that, we might make shift. I have a little, though not much; but I tell you there's no stirring on the road. I know a couple of poor honest men in our street have attempted to travel, and at Barnet, or Whetstone, or thereabout, the people offered to fire at them if they pretended to go forward, so they are come back again quite discouraged.

JOHN: I would have ventured their fire if I had been there. If I had been denied food for my money they should have seen me take it before their faces, and if I had tendered money for it they could not have taken any course with me by law.

THOMAS: You talk your old soldier's language, as if you were in the Low Countries now, but this is a serious thing. The people have good reason to keep anybody off that they are not satisfied are sound, at such a time as this, and we must not plunder them.

JOHN: No, brother, you mistake the case, and mistake me too. I would plunder nobody; but for any town upon the road to deny me leave to pass through the town in the open highway, and deny me provisions for my money, is to say the town has a right to starve me to death, which cannot be true.

THOMAS: But they do not deny you liberty to go back again from whence you came, and therefore they do not starve you.

JOHN: But the next town behind me will, by the same rule, deny me leave to go back, and so they do starve me between them. Besides, there is no law to prohibit my travelling wherever I will on the road.

THOMAS: But there will be so much difficulty in disputing with them at every town on the road that it is not for poor men to do it or undertake it, at such a time as this is especially.

JOHN: Why, brother, our condition at this rate is worse than anybody else's, for we can neither go away nor stay here. I am of the same mind with the lepers of Samaria. If we stay here we are sure to die; I mean especially as you and I are stated, without a dwelling-house of our own, and without lodging in anybody else's. There is no lying in the street at such a time as this; we had as good go into the dead-cart at once. Therefore I say, if we stay here we are sure to die, and if we go away we can but die; I am resolved to be gone.

THOMAS: You will go away. Whither will you go, and what can you do? I would as willingly go away as you, if I knew whither. But we have no acquaintance, no friends. Here we were born, and here we must die.

JOHN: Look you, Tom, the whole kingdom is my native country as well as this town. You may as well say I must not go out of my house if it is on fire as that I must not go out of the town I was born in when it is infected with the plague. I was born in England, and have a right to live in it if I can.

THOMAS: But you know every vagrant person may, by the laws of England, be taken up, and passed back to their last legal settlement.

JOHN: But how shall they make me vagrant? I desire only to travel on, upon my lawful occasions.

THOMAS: What lawful occasions can we pretend to travel, or rather wander upon? They will not be put off with words.

JOHN: Is not flying to save our lives a lawful occasion? And do they not all know that the fact is true? We cannot be said to dissemble.

THOMAS: But suppose they let us pass, whither shall we go?

JOHN: Anywhere to save our lives; it is time enough to consider that when we are got out of this town. If I am once out of this dreadful place, I care not where I go.

THOMAS: We shall be driven to great extremities. I know not what to think of it.

JOHN: Well, Tom, consider of it a little.

This was about the beginning of July; and though the plague was come forward in the west and north parts of the town, yet all Wapping, as I have observed before, and Redriff, and Ratcliff, and Limehouse, and Poplar, in short, Deptford and Greenwich, all both sides of the river from the Hermitage, and from over against it, quite down to Blackwall, was entirely free; there had not one person died of the plague in all Stepney parish, and not one on the south side of Whitechapel Road, no, not in any parish; and yet the weekly bill was that very week risen up to 1006.

It was a fortnight after this before the two brothers met again, and then the case was a little altered, and the plague was exceedingly advanced and the number greatly increased; the bill was up at 2785, and prodigiously increasing, though still both sides of the river, as below, kept pretty well. But some began to die in Redriff, and about five or six in Ratcliff Highway, when the sailmaker came to his brother John express, and in some fright; for he was absolutely warned out of his lodging, and had only a week to provide himself. His brother John was in as bad a case, for he was quiet out, and had only begged leave of his master, the biscuit-baker, to lodge in an outhouse belonging to his work-house, where he only lay upon stray, with some biscuit-sacks, or bread-sacks, as they called them, laid upon it, and some of the same sacks to cover him.

Here they resolved, seeing all employment being at an end, and no work or wages to be had, they would make the best of their way to get out of the reach of the dreadful infection, and, being as good husbands as they could, would endeavour to live upon what they had as long as it would last, and then work for more, if they could get work anywhere, of any kind, let it be what it would.

While they were considering to put this resolution in practice in the best manner they could, the third man, who was acquainted very well with the sailmaker, came to know of the design, and got leave to be one of the number; and thus they prepared to set out.

It happened that they had not an equal share of money, but as the sailmaker, who had the best stock, was, besides his being lame, the most unfit to expect to get anything by working in the country, so he was content that what money they had should all go into one public stock, on condition that whatever any one of them could gain more than another, it should, without any grudging, be all added to the public stock.

They resolved to load themselves with as little baggage as possible, because they resolved at first to travel on foot, and to go a great way, that they might, if possible, be effectually safe; and a great many consultations they had with themselves before they could agree about what way they should travel, which they were so far from adjusting that even to the morning they set out they were not resolved on it.

At last the seaman put in a hint that determined it. "First," says he, "the weather is very hot, and therefore I am for travelling north, that we may not have the sun upon our faces and beating on our breasts, which will heat and suffocate us; and I have been told," says he, "that it is not good to overheat our blood at a time when, for aught we know, the infection may be in the very air. In the next place," says he, "I am for going the way that may be contrary to the wind, as it may blow when we set out, that we may not have the wind blow the air of the city on our backs as we go." These two cautions were approved of, if it could be brought so to hit that the wind might not be in the south when they set out to go north.

John the baker, who had been a soldier, then put in his opinion. "First," says he, "we none of us expect to get any lodging on the road, and it will be a little too hard to lie just in the open air. Though it be warm weather, yet it may be wet and damp, and we have a double reason to take care of our healths at such a time as this; and therefore," says he, "you, brother Tom, that are a sailmaker, might easily make us a little tent, and I will undertake to set it up every night, and take it down, and a fig for all the inns in England; if we have a good tent over our heads we shall do well enough."

The joiner opposed this, and told them, let them leave that to him; he would undertake to build them a house every night with his hatchet and mallet, though he had no other tools, which should be fully to their satisfaction, and as good as a tent.

The soldier and the joiner disputed that point some time, but at last the soldier carried it for a tent. The only objection against it was, that it must be carried with them, and that would increase their baggage too much, the weather being hot; but the sailmaker had a piece of good hap fell in which made that easy, for his master whom he worked for, having a rope-walk as well as sail-making trade, had a little, poor horse that he made no use of then, and being willing to assist the three honest men, he gave them the horse for the carrying their baggage; also for a small matter of three days' work that his man did for him before he went, he let him have an old top-gallant sail that was worn out, but was sufficient and more than enough to make a very good tent. The soldier showed how to shape it, and they soon by his direction made their tent, and fitted it with poles or staves for the purpose; and thus they were furnished for their journey, viz., three men, one tent, one horse, one gun, for the soldier would not go without arms, for now he said he was no more a biscuit-baker, but a trooper.

The joiner had a small bag of tools, such as might be useful if he should get any work abroad, as well for their subsistence as his own. What money they had they brought all into one public stock, and thus they began their journey. It seems that in the morning when they set out the wind blew, as the sailor said, by his pocket-compass, at N.W. by W. So they directed, or rather resolved to direct, their course N.W.

But then a difficulty came in their way, that, as they set out from the hither end of Wapping, near the Hermitage, and that the plague was now very violent, especially on the north side of the city, as in Shoreditch and Cripplegate parish, they did not think it safe for them to go near those parts; so they went away east through Ratcliff Highway as far as Ratcliff Cross, and leaving Stepney Church still on their left hand, being afraid to come up from Ratcliff Cross to Mile End, because they must come just by the churchyard, and because the wind, that seemed to blow more from the west, blew directly from the side of the city where the plague was hottest. So I say, leaving Stepney, they fetched a long compass, and going to Poplar and Bromley, came into the great road just at Bow.

Here the watch placed upon Bow Bridge would have questioned them, but they, crossing the road into a narrow way that turns out of the hither end of the town of Bow to Old Ford, avoided any inquiry there, and travelled to Old Ford. The constables everywhere were upon their guard, not so much, it seems, to stop people passing by as to stop them from taking up their abode in their towns, and withal because of a report that was newly raised at that time, and that, indeed, was not very improbable, viz., that the poor people in London, being distressed and starved for want of work, and by that means for want of bread, were up in arms and had raised a tumult, and that they would come out to all the towns round to plunder for bread. This, I say, was only a rumour, and it was very well it was no more. But it was not so far off from being a reality as it has been thought, for in a few weeks more the poor people became so desperate by the calamity they suffered that they were with great difficulty kept from running out into the fields and towns, and tearing all in pieces wherever they came; and, as I have observed before, nothing hindered them but that the plague raged so violently, and fell in upon them so furiously, that they rather went to the grave by thousands than into the fields in mobs by thousands; for, in the parts about the parishes of St. Sepulchre, Clerkenwell, Cripplegate, Bishopsgate, and Shoreditch, which were the places where the mob began to threaten, the distemper came on so furiously that there died in those few parishes even then, before the plague was come to its height, no less than 5361 people in the first three weeks in August, when, at the same time, the parts about Wapping, Ratcliff, and Rotherhithe were, as before described, hardly touched, or but very lightly; so that, in a word, though, as I said before, the good management of the Lord Mayor and justices did much to prevent the rage and desperation of the people from breaking out in rabbles and tumults, and, in short, from the poor plundering the rich,—I say, though they did much, the dead-carts did more, for as I have said that in five parishes only there died about 5000 in twenty days, so there might be probably three times that number sick all that time, for some recovered, and great numbers fell sick every day and died afterwards. Besides, I must still be allowed to say that if the bills of mortality said five thousand, I always believed it was near twice as many in reality, there being no room to believe that the account they gave was right, or that, indeed, they were, among such confusions as I saw them in, in any condition to keep an exact account.

But to return to my travellers. Here they were only examined, and as they seemed rather coming from the country than from the city, they found the people the easier with them; that they talked to them, let them come into a public-house where the constable and his warders were, and gave them drink and some victuals, which greatly refreshed and encouraged them; and here it came into their heads to say, when they should be inquired of afterwards, not that they came from London, but that they came out of Essex.

To forward this little fraud, they obtained so much favour of the constable at Old Ford as to give them a certificate of their passing from Essex through that village, and that they had not been at London, which, though false in the common acceptation of London in the county, yet was literally true, Wapping or Ratcliff being no part either of the city or liberty.

This certificate directed to the next constable that was at Homerton, one of the hamlets of the parish of Hackney, was so serviceable to them that it procured them, not a free passage there only, but a full certificate of health from a justice of the peace, who, upon the constable's application, granted it without much difficulty; and thus they passed through the long divided town of Hackney (for it lay then in several separated hamlets), and travelled on till they came into the great north road on the top of Stamford Hill.

By this time they began to be weary, and so in the back-road from Hackney, a little before it opened into the said great road, they resolved to set up their tent and encamp for the first night, which they did accordingly, with this addition, that finding a barn, or a building like a barn, and first searching as well as they could to be sure there was nobody in it, they set up their tent, with the head of it against the barn. This they did also because the wind blew that night very high, and they were but young at such a way of lodging, as well as at the managing their tent.

Here they went to sleep; but the joiner, a grave and sober man, and not pleased with their lying at this loose rate the first night, could not sleep, and resolved, after trying to sleep to no purpose, that he would get out, and, taking the gun in his hand, stand sentinel and guard his companions. So, with the gun in his hand, he walked to and again before the barn, for that stood in the field near the road, but within the hedge. He had not been long upon the scout but he heard a noise of people coming on, as if it had been a great number, and they came on, as he thought, directly towards the barn. He did not presently awake his companions, but in a few minutes more, their noise growing louder and louder, the biscuit-baker called to him and asked him what was the matter, and quickly started out too. The other, being the lame sailmaker and most weary, lay still in the tent.

As they expected, so the people whom they had heard came on directly to the barn, when one of our travellers challenged, like soldiers upon the guard, with "Who comes there?" The people did not answer immediately, but one of them speaking to another that was behind him, "Alas! alas! we are all disappointed," says he. "Here are some people before us; the barn is taken up."

They all stopped upon that, as under some surprise, and it seems there was about thirteen of them in all, and some women among them. They consulted together what they should do, and by their discourse our travellers soon found they were poor, distressed people too, like themselves, seeking shelter and safety; and besides, our travellers had no need to be afraid of their coming up to disturb them, for as soon as they heard the words, "Who comes there?" these could hear the women say, as if frighted, "Do not go near them. How do you know but they may have the plague?" And when one of the men said, "Let us but speak to them," the women said, "No, don't by any means. We have escaped thus far by the goodness of God; do not let us run into danger now, we beseech you."

Our travellers found by this that they were a good, sober sort of people, and flying for their lives, as they were; and, as they were encouraged by it, so John said to the joiner, his comrade, "Let us encourage them too as much as we can;" so he called to them, "Hark ye, good people," say the joiner, "we find by your talk that you are flying from the same dreadful enemy as we are. Do not be afraid of us; we are only three poor men of us. If you are free from the distemper you shall not be hurt by us. We are not in the barn, but in a little tent here in the outside, and we will remove for you; we can set up our tent again immediately anywhere else;" and upon this a parley began between the joiner, whose name was Richard, and one of their men, who said his name was Ford.

FORD: And do you assure us that you are all sound men?

RICHARD: Nay, we are concerned to tell you of it, that you may not be uneasy or think yourselves in danger; but you see we do not desire you should put yourselves into any danger, and therefore I tell you that we have not made use of the barn, so we will remove from it, that you may be safe and we also.

FORD: That is very kind and charitable; but if we have reason to be satisfied that you are sound and free from the visitation, why should we make you remove now you are settled in your lodging, and, it may be, are laid down to rest? We will go into the barn, if you please, to rest ourselves a while, and we need not disturb you.

RICHARD: Well, but you are more than we are. I hope you will assure us that you are all of you sound too, for the danger is as great from you to us as from us to you.

FORD: Blessed be God that some do escape, though it is but few; what may be our portion still we know not, but hitherto we are preserved.

RICHARD: What part of the town do you come from? Was the plague come to the places where you lived?

FORD: Ay, ay, in a most frightful and terrible manner, or else we had not fled away as we do; but we believe there will be very few left alive behind us.

RICHARD: What part do you come from?

FORD: We are most of us of Cripplegate parish, only two or three of Clerkenwell parish, but on the hither side.

RICHARD: How then was it that you came away no sooner?

FORD: We have been away some time, and kept together as well as we could at the hither end of Islington, where we got leave to lie in an old uninhabited house, and had some bedding and conveniences of our own that we brought with us; but the plague is come up into Islington too, and a house next door to our poor dwelling was infected and shut up, and we are come away in a fright.

RICHARD: And what way are you going?

FORD: As our lot shall cast us; we know not whither, but God will guide those that look up to Him.

They parleyed no further at that time, but came all up

to the barn, and with some difficulty got into it. There was nothing but hay in the barn, but it was almost full of that, and they accommodated themselves as well as they could, and went to rest; but our travellers observed that before they went to sleep an ancient man, who, it seems, was father of one of the women, went to prayer with all the company, recommending themselves to the blessing and direction of Providence, before they went to sleep.

It was soon day at that time of the year, and as Richard the joiner had kept guard the first part of the night, so John the soldier relieved him, and he had the post in the morning, and they began to be acquainted with one another. It seems when they left Islington they intended to have gone north, away to Highgate, but were stopped at Holloway, and there they would not let them pass; so they crossed over the fields and hills to the eastward, and came out at the Boarded River, and so avoiding the towns, they left Hornsey on the left hand and Newington on the right hand, and came into the great road about Stamford Hill on that side, as the three travellers had done on the other side. And now they had thoughts of going over the river in the marshes, and make forwards to Epping Forest, where they hoped they should get leave to rest. It seems they were not poor, at least not so poor as to be in want; at least they had enough to subsist them moderately for two or three months, when, as they said, they were in hopes the cold weather would check the infection, or at least the violence of it would have spent itself, and would abate, if it were only for want of people left alive to be infected.

This was much the fate of our three travellers, only that they seemed to be the better furnished for travelling, and had it in their view to go farther off; for as to the first, they did not propose to go farther than one day's journey, that so they might have intelligence every two or three days how things were at London.

But here our travellers found themselves under an unexpected inconvenience, namely, that of their horse, for by means of the horse to carry their baggage they were obliged to keep in the road, whereas the people of this other band went over the fields or roads, path or no path, way or no way, as they pleased; neither had they any occasion to pass through any town, or come near any town, other than to buy such things as they wanted for their necessary subsistence, and in that indeed they were put to much difficulty; of which in its place.

But our three travellers were obliged to keep the road, or else they must commit spoil, and do the country a great deal of damage in breaking down fences and gates to go over enclosed fields, which they were loath to do if they could help it.

Our three travellers, however, had a great mind to join themselves to this company and take their lot with them; and after some discourse they laid aside their first design which looked northward, and resolved to follow the other into Essex; so in the morning they took up their tent and loaded their horse, and away they travelled all together.

They had some difficulty in passing the ferry at the river-side, the ferryman being afraid of them; but after some parley at a distance, the ferryman was content to bring his boat to a place distant from the usual ferry, and leave it there for them to take it; so putting themselves over, he directed them to leave the boat, and he, having another boat, said he would fetch it again, which it seems, however, he did not do for above eight days.

Here giving the ferryman money beforehand, they had a supply of victuals and drink, which he brought and left in the boat for them, but not without, as I said, having received the money beforehand. But now our travellers were at a great loss and difficulty how to get the horse over, the boat being small and not fit for it, and at last could not do it without unloading the baggage and making him swim over.

From the river they travelled towards the forest, but when they came to Walthamstow the people of that town denied to admit them, as was the case everywhere. The constables and their watchmen kept them off at a distance and parleyed with them. They gave the same account of themselves as before, but these gave no credit to what they said, giving it for a reason that two or three companies had already come that way and made the like pretences, but that they had given several people the distemper in the towns where they had passed, and had been afterwards so hardly used by the country, though with justice too, as they had deserved, that about Brentwood, or that way, several of them perished in the fields, whether of the plague or of mere want and distress they could not tell.

This was a good reason indeed why the people of Walthamstow should be very cautious, and why they should resolve not to entertain anybody that they were not well satisfied of. But, as Richard the joiner and one of the other men who parleyed with them told them, it was no reason why they should block up the roads and refuse to let people pass through the town, and who asked nothing of them but to go through the street; that if their people were afraid of them, they might go into their houses and shut their doors; they would neither show them civility nor incivility, but go on about their business.

The constables and attendants, not to be persuaded by reason, continued obstinate, and would hearken to nothing, so the two men that talked with them went back to their fellows to consult what was to be done. It was very discouraging in the whole, and they knew not what to do for a good while; but at last John the soldier and biscuit-baker, considering a while, "Come," says he, "leave the rest of the parley to me." He had not appeared yet, so he sets the joiner, Richard, to work to cut some poles out of the trees and shape them as like guns as he could, and in a little time he had five or six fair muskets, which at a distance would not be known; and about the part where the lock of a gun is he caused them to wrap cloth and rags such as they had, as soldiers do in wet weather to preserve the locks of their pieces from rust; the rest was discoloured with clay or mud, such as they could get; and all this while the rest of them sat under the trees by his direction, in two or three bodies, where they made fires at a good distance from one another.

While this was doing he advanced himself and two or three with him, and set up their tent in the lane within sight of the barrier which the town's men had made, and set a sentinel just by it with the real gun, the only one they had, and who walked to and fro with the gun on his shoulder, so as that the people of the town might see them. Also, he tied the horse to a gate in the hedge just by, and got some dry sticks together and kindled a fire on the other side of the tent, so that the people of the town could see the fire and the smoke, but could not see what they were doing at it.

After the country people had looked upon them very earnestly a great while, and, by all that they could see, could not but suppose that they were a great many in company, they began to be uneasy, not for their going away, but for staying where they were; and above all, perceiving they had horses and arms, for they had seen one horse and one gun at the tent, and they had seen others of them walk about the field on the inside of the hedge by the side of the lane with their muskets, as they took them to be, shouldered; I say, upon such a sight as this, you may be assured they were alarmed and terribly frighted, and it seems they went to a justice of the peace to know what they should do. What the justice advised them to I know not, but towards the evening they called from the barrier, as above, to the sentinel at the tent.

"What do you want?" says John.[1]

"Why, what do you intend to do?" says the constable.

"To do," says John; "what would you have us to do?"

CONSTABLE: Why don't you be gone? What do you stay there for?

JOHN: Why do you stop us on the king's highway, and pretend to refuse us leave to go on our way?

CONSTABLE: We are not bound to tell you our reason, though we did let you know it was because of the plague.

JOHN: We told you we were all sound and free from the plague, which we were not bound to have satisfied you of, and yet you pretend to stop us on the highway.

CONSTABLE: We have a right to stop it up, and our own safety obliges us to it. Besides, this is not the king's highway; 't is a way upon sufferance. You see here is a gate, and if we do let people pass here, we make them pay toll.

JOHN: We have a right to seek our own safety as well as you, and you may see we are flying for our lives, and 't is very unchristian and unjust to stop us.

CONSTABLE: You may go back from whence you came; we do not hinder you from that.

JOHN: No; it is a stronger enemy than you that keeps us from doing that, or else we should not have come hither.

---

[1] *It seems John was in the tent, but hearing them call, he steps out, and taking the gun upon his shoulder, talked to them as if he had been the sentinel placed there upon the guard by some officer that was his superior.*

CONSTABLE: Well, you may go any other way, then.

JOHN: No, no; I suppose you see we are able to send you going, and all the people of your parish, and come through your town when we will; but since you have stopped us here, we are content. You see we have encamped here, and here we will live. We hope you will furnish us with victuals.

CONSTABLE: We furnish you! What mean you by that?

JOHN: Why, you would not have us starve, would you? If you stop us here, you must keep us.

CONSTABLE: You will be ill kept at our maintenance.

JOHN: If you stint us, we shall make ourselves the better allowance.

CONSTABLE: Why, you will not pretend to quarter upon us by force, will you?

JOHN: We have offered no violence to you yet. Why do you seem to oblige us to it? I am an old soldier, and cannot starve, and if you think that we shall be obliged to go back for want of provisions, you are mistaken.

CONSTABLE: Since you threaten us, we shall take care to be strong enough for you. I have orders to raise the county upon you.

JOHN: It is you that threaten, not we. And since you are for mischief, you cannot blame us if we do not give you time for it; we shall begin our march in a few minutes.[1]

CONSTABLE: What is it you demand of us?

JOHN: At first we desired nothing of you but leave to go through the town; we should have offered no injury to any of you, neither would you have had any injury or loss by us. We are not thieves, but poor people in distress, and flying from the dreadful plague in London, which devours thousands every week. We wonder how you could be so unmerciful!

[1] *This frighted the constable and the people that were with him, that they immediately changed their note.*

CONSTABLE: Self-preservation obliges us.

JOHN: What! To shut up your compassion in a case of such distress as this?

CONSTABLE: Well, if you will pass over the fields on your left hand, and behind that part of the town, I will endeavour to have gates opened for you.

JOHN: Our horsemen [1] cannot pass with our baggage that way; it does not lead into the road that we want to go, and why should you force us out of the road? Besides, you have kept us here all day without any provisions but such as we brought with us. I think you ought to send us some provisions for our relief.

CONSTABLE: If you will go another way we will send you some provisions.

JOHN: That is the way to have all the towns in the county stop up the ways against us.

CONSTABLE: If they all furnish you with food, what will you be the worse? I see you have tents; you want no lodging.

JOHN: Well, what quantity of provisions will you send us?

CONSTABLE: How many are you?

JOHN: Nay, we do not ask enough for all our company; we are in three companies. If you will send us bread for twenty men and about six or seven women for three days, and show us the way over the field you speak of, we desire not to put your people into any fear for us; we will go out of our way to oblige you, though we are as free from infection as you are. [2]

CONSTABLE: And will you assure us that your other people shall offer us no new disturbance?

JOHN: No, no, you may depend on it.

[1] *They had but one horse among them.*
[2] *Here he called to one of his men, and bade him order Captain Richard and his people to march the lower way on the side of the marches, and meet them in the forest; which was all a sham, for they had no Captain Richard, or any such company.*

CONSTABLE: You must oblige yourself, too, that none of your people shall come a step nearer than where the provisions we send you shall be set down.

JOHN: I answer for it we will not.

Accordingly they sent to the place twenty loaves of bread and three or four large pieces of good beef, and opened some gates, through which they passed; but none of them had courage so much as to look out to see them go, and, as it was evening, if they had looked they could not have seen them so as to know how few they were.

This was John the soldier's management. But this gave such an alarm to the county, that had they really been two or three hundred the whole county would have been raised upon them, and they would have been sent to prison, or perhaps knocked on the head.

They were soon made sensible of this, for two days afterwards they found several parties of horsemen and footmen also about, in pursuit of three companies of men, armed, as they said, with muskets, who were broke out from London, and had the plague upon them, and that were not only spreading the distemper among the people, but plundering the country.

As they saw now the consequence of their case, they soon saw the danger they were in, so they resolved, by the advice also of the old soldier, to divide themselves again. John and his two comrades, with the horse, went away as if towards Waltham; the other in two companies, but all a little asunder, and went towards Epping.

The first night they encamped all in the forest, and not far off of one another, but not setting up the tent, lest that should discover them. On the other hand, Richard went to work with his axe and his hatchet, and cutting down branches of trees, he built three tents or hovels, in which they all encamped with as much convenience as they could expect.

The provisions they had at Walthamstow served them

very plentifully this night; and as for the next, they left it to Providence. They had fared so well with the old soldier's conduct that they now willingly made him their leader, and the first of his conduct appeared to be very good. He told them that they were now at a proper distance enough from London; that as they need not be immediately beholden to the country for relief, so they ought to be as careful the country did not infect them as that they did not infect the country; that what little money they had, they must be as frugal of as they could; that as he would not have them think of offering the country any violence, so they must endeavour to make the sense of their condition go as far with the country as it could. They all referred themselves to his direction, so they left their three houses standing, and the next day went away towards Epping. The captain also, for so they now called him, and his two fellow-travellers laid aside their design of going to Waltham, and all went together.

When they came near Epping they halted, choosing out a proper place in the open forest, not very near the highway, but not far out of it on the north side, under a little cluster of low pollard-trees. Here they pitched their little camp, which consisted of three large tents or huts made of poles, which their carpenter, and such as were his assistants, cut down and fixed in the ground in a circle, binding all the small ends together at the top, and thickening the sides with boughs of trees and bushes, so that they were completely close and warm. They had, besides this, a little tent, where the women lay by themselves, and a hut to put the horse in.

It happened that the next day, or next but one, was market-day at Epping, when Captain John and one of the other men went to market and bought some provisions; that is to say, bread, and some mutton and beef; and two of the women went separately, as if they had not belonged to the rest, and bought more. John took the horse to bring it home, and the sack which the carpenter carried his tools in to put it in. The carpenter went to work and made them benches and stools to sit on, such as the wood he could get would afford, and a kind of table to dine on.

They were taken no notice of for two or three days, but after that abundance of people ran out of the town to look at them, and all the country was alarmed about them. The people at first seemed afraid to come near them; and, on the other hand, they desired the people to keep off, for there was a rumour that the plague was at Waltham, and that it had been in Epping two or three days; so John called out to them not to come to them, "for," says he, "we are all whole and sound people here, and we would not have you bring the plague among us, nor pretend we brought it among you."

After this the parish officers came up to them and parleyed with them at a distance, and desired to know who they were, and by what authority they pretended to fix their stand at that place. John answered very frankly, they were poor distressed people from London, who, foreseeing the misery they should be reduced to if the plague spread into the city, had fled out in time for their lives, and, having no acquaintance or relations to fly to, had first taken up at Islington, but, the plague being come into that town, were fled farther; and as they supposed that the people of Epping might have refused them coming into their town, they had pitched their tents thus in the open field and in the forest, being willing to bear all the hardships of such a disconsolate lodging rather than have any one think or be afraid that they should receive injury by them.

At first the Epping people talked roughly to them, and told them they must remove; that this was no place for them; and that they pretended to be sound and well, but that they might be infected with the plague for aught they knew, and might infect the whole country, and they could not suffer them there.

John argued very calmly with them a great while, and told them that London was the place by which they, that is, the townsmen of Epping and all the country round them, subsisted; to whom they sold the produce of their lands, and out of whom they made their rent of their farms; and to be so cruel to the inhabitants of London, or to any of those by whom they gained so much, was very hard, and they would be loth to have it remembered hereafter, and have it told how barbarous, how inhospitable, and how unkind they were to the people of London when they fled from the face of the most terrible enemy in the world; that it would be enough to make the name of an Epping man hateful through all the city, and to have the rabble stone them in the very streets whenever they came so much as to market; that they were not yet secure from being visited themselves, and that, as he heard, Waltham was already; that they would think it very hard that when any of them fled for fear before they were touched, they should be denied the liberty of lying so much as in the open fields.

The Epping men told them again that they, indeed, said they were sound and free from the infection, but that they had no assurance of it; and that it was reported that there had been a great rabble of people at Walthamstow, who made such pretences of being sound as they did, but that they threatened to plunder the town and force their way, whether the parish officers would or no; that there were near two hundred of them, and had arms and tents like Low Country soldiers; that they extorted provisions from the town, by threatening them with living upon them at free quarter, showing their arms, and talking in the language of soldiers; and that several of them being gone away towards Romford and Brentwood, the country had been infected by them, and the plague spread into both those large towns, so that the people durst not go to market there as usual; that it was very likely they were some of that party; and if so, they deserved to be sent to the county jail, and be secured till they had made satisfaction for the damage they had done, and for the terror and fright they had put the country into.

John answered that what other people had done was nothing to them; that they assured them they were all of one company; that they had never been more in number than they saw them at that time (which, by the way, was very true); that they came out in two separate companies, but joined by the way, their cases being the same; that they were ready to give what account of themselves anybody could desire of them and to give in their names and places of abode, that so they might be called to an account for any disorder that they might be guilty of; that the townsmen might see they were content to live hardly, and only desired a little room to breathe in on the forest where it was wholesome; for where it was not they could not stay, and would decamp if they found it otherwise there.

"But," said the townsmen, "we have a great charge of poor upon our hands already, and we must take care not to increase it; we suppose you can give us no security against your being chargeable to our parish and to the inhabitants, any more than you can of being dangerous to us as to the infection."

"Why, look you," says John, "as to being chargeable to you, we hope we shall not. If you will relieve us with provisions for our present necessity, we will be very thankful; as we all lived without charity when we were at home, so we will oblige ourselves fully to repay you, if God please to bring us back to our own families and houses in safety, and to restore health to the people of London.

"As to our dying here, we assure you, if any of us die, we that survive will bury them, and put you to no expense, except it should be that we should all die, and then, indeed, the last man not being able to bury himself, would put you to that single expense, which, I am persuaded," says John, "he would leave enough behind him to pay you for the expense of.

"On the other hand," says John, "if you will shut up all bowels of compassion, and not relieve us at all, we shall not extort anything by violence or steal from any one; but when what little we have is spent, if we perish for want, God's will be done."

John wrought so up the townsmen, by talking thus rationally and smoothly to them, that they went away; and though they did not give any consent to their staying there, yet they did not molest them; and the poor people continued there three or four days longer without any disturbance. In this time they had got some remote acquaintance with a victualling-house at the outskirts of the town, to whom they called at a distance to bring some little things that they wanted, and which they caused to be set down at a distance, and always paid for very honestly.

During this time the younger people of the town came frequently pretty near them, and would stand and look at them, and sometimes talk with them at some space between; and particularly it was observed that the first Sabbath-day the poor people kept retired, worshipped God together, and were heard to sing psalms.

These things, and a quiet, inoffensive behaviour, began to get them the good opinion of the country, and people began to pity them and speak very well of them; the consequence of which was, that upon the occasion of a very wet, rainy night, a certain gentleman who lived in the neighbourhood sent them a little cart with twelve trusses or bundles of straw, as well for them to lodge upon as to cover and thatch their huts and to keep them dry. The minister of a parish not far off, not knowing of the other, sent them also about two bushels of wheat and half a bushel of white peas.

They were very thankful, to be sure, for this relief, and particularly the straw was a very great comfort to them; for though the ingenious carpenter had made frames for them to lie in like troughs, and filled them with leaves of trees, and such things as they could get, and had cut all their tent-cloth out to make them coverlids, yet they lay damp, and hard, and unwholesome till this straw came, which was to them like feather-beds, and, as John said, more welcome than feather-beds would have been at another time.

This gentleman and the minister having thus begun, and given an example of charity to these wanderers, others quickly followed, and they received every day some benevolence or other from the people, but chiefly from the gentlemen who dwelt in the country round about. Some sent them chairs, stools, tables, and such household things as they gave notice they wanted; some sent them blankets, rugs, and coverlids, some earthenware, and some kitchen ware for ordering their food.

Encouraged by this good usage, their carpenter in a few days built them a large shed or house with rafters, and a roof in form, and an upper floor, in which they lodged warm, for the weather began to be damp and cold in the beginning of September. But this house, being very well thatched, and the sides and roof made very thick, kept out the cold well enough. He made, also, an earthen wall at one end with a chimney in it, and another of the company, with a vast deal of trouble and pains, made a funnel to the chimney to carry out the smoke.

Here they lived comfortably, though coarsely, till the beginning of September, when they had the bad news to hear, whether true or not, that the plague, which was very hot at Waltham Abbey on one side, and at Romford and Brentwood on the other side, was also come to Epping, to Woodford, and to most of the towns upon the Forest, and which, as they said, was brought down among them chiefly by the higglers, and such people as went to and from London with provisions.

If this was true, it was an evident contradiction to that report which was afterwards spread all over England, but which, as I have said, I cannot confirm of my own knowledge, namely, that the market-people carrying provisions to the city never got the infection, or carried it back into the country, both which, I have been assured, has been false.

It might be that they were preserved even beyond expectation, though not to a miracle, that abundance went and came and were not touched, and that was much for the encouragement of the poor people of London, who had been completely miserable if the people that brought provisions to the markets had not been many times wonderfully preserved, or at least more preserved than could be reasonably expected.

But now these new inmates began to be disturbed more effectually, for the towns about them were really infected, and they began to be afraid to trust one another so much as to go abroad for such things as they wanted, and this pinched them very hard, for now they had little or nothing but what the charitable gentlemen of the country supplied them with. But, for their encouragement, it happened that other gentlemen in the country, who had not sent them anything before, began to hear of them and supply them, and one sent them a large pig, that is to say, a porker, another two sheep, and another sent them a calf. In short, they had meat enough, and sometimes had cheese and milk, and all such things. They were chiefly put to it for bread, for when the gentlemen sent them corn they had nowhere to bake it or to grind it. This made them eat the first two bushel of wheat that was sent them in parched corn, as the Israelites of old did, without grinding or making bread of it.

At last they found means to carry their corn to a wind-mill near Woodford, where they had it ground, and after-wards the biscuit-baker made a hearth so hollow and dry that he could bake biscuit-cakes tolerably well; and thus they came into a condition to live without any assistance or supplies from the towns; and it was well they did, for the country was soon after fully infected, and about 120 were said to have died of the distemper in the villages near them, which was a terrible thing to them.

On this they called a new council, and now the towns had no need to be afraid they should settle near them; but, on the contrary, several families of the poorer sort of the inhabitants quitted their houses and built huts in the forest after the same manner as they had done. But it was observed that several of these poor people that had so removed had the sickness even in their huts or booths; the reason of which was plain, namely, not because they removed into the air, but, (1) because they did not re-move time enough; that is to say, not till, by openly con-versing with the other people their neighbours, they had the distemper upon them, or (as may be said) among them, and so carried it about them whither they went. Or (2) because they were not careful enough, after they were safely removed out of the towns, not to come in again and mingle with the diseased people.

But be it which of these it will, when our travellers began to perceive that the plague was not only in the towns, but even in the tents and huts on the forest near them, they began then not only to be afraid, but to think of decamping and removing; for had they stayed they would have been in manifest danger of their lives.

It is not to be wondered that they were greatly afflicted at being obliged to quit the place where they had been so kindly received, and where they had been treated with so much humanity and charity; but necessity and the hazard of life, which they came out so far to preserve, prevailed with them, and they saw no remedy. John, however, thought of a remedy for their present misfortune, namely, that he would first acquaint that gentleman who was their principal benefactor with the distress they were in, and to crave his assistance and advice.

The good, charitable gentleman encouraged them to quit the place, for fear they should be cut off from any retreat at all by the violence of the distemper; but whither they should go, that he found very hard to direct them to. At last John asked of him whether he, being a justice of the peace, would give them certificates of health to other justices whom they might come before, that so, whatever might be their lot, they might not be repulsed now they had been also so long from London. This his worship immediately granted, and gave them proper letters of health, and from thence they were at liberty to travel whither they pleased.

Accordingly they had a full certificate of health, intimating that they had resided in a village in the county of Essex so long that, being examined and scrutinised sufficiently, and having been retired from all conversation for above forty days, without any appearance of sickness, they were therefore certainly concluded to be sound men, and might be safely entertained anywhere, having at last removed rather for fear of the plague, which was come into such a town, rather than for having any signal of infection upon them, or upon any belonging to them.

With this certificate they removed, though with great reluctance; and John inclining not to go far from home, they moved towards the marshes on the side of Waltham. But here they found a man who, it seems, kept a weir or stop upon the river, made to raise the water for the barges which go up and down the river, and he terrified them with dismal stories of the sickness having been spread into all the towns on the river, and near the river, on the side of Middlesex and Hertfordshire; that is to say, into Waltham, Waltham Cross, Enfield, and Ware, and all the towns on the road, that they were afraid to go that way, though it seems the man imposed upon them, for that the thing was not really true.

However, it terrified them, and they resolved to move across the forest towards Romford and Brentwood; but they heard that there were numbers of people fled out of London that way, who lay up and down in the forest called Hainault Forest, reaching near Romford, and who, having no subsistence or habitation, not only lived oddly and suffered great extremities in the woods and fields for want of relief, but were said to be made so desperate by those extremities as that they offered many violences to the county, robbed and plundered, and killed cattle, and the like; that others, building huts and hovels by the road-side, begged, and that with an importunity next door to demanding relief; so that the county was very uneasy, and had been obliged to take some of them up.

This, in the first place, intimated to them that they would be sure to find the charity and kindness of the county, which they had found here where they were before, hardened and shut up against them; and that, on the other hand, they would be questioned wherever they came, and would be in danger of violence from others in like cases as themselves.

Upon all these considerations John, their captain, in all their names, went back to their good friend and benefactor, who had relieved them before, and laying their case truly before him, humbly asked his advice; and he as kindly advised them to take up their old quarters again, or if not, to remove but a little farther out of the road, and directed them to a proper place for them; and as they really wanted some house rather than huts to shelter them at that time of the year, it growing on towards Michaelmas, they found an old decayed house, which had been formerly some cottage or little habitation, but was so out of repair as scarce habitable, and by the consent of a farmer to whose farm it belonged, they got leave to make what use of it they could.

The ingenious joiner and all the rest, by his directions, went to work with it, and in a very few days made it capable to shelter them all in case of bad weather, and in which there was an old chimney and an old oven, though both lying in ruins; yet they made them both fit for use, and raising additions, sheds, and lean-tos on every side, they soon made the house capable to hold them all.

They chiefly wanted boards to make window-shutters, floors, doors, and several other things; but as the gentlemen above favoured them, and the country was by that means made easy with them, and, above all, that they were known to be all sound and in good health, everybody helped them with what they could spare.

Here they encamped for good and all, and resolved to remove no more. They saw plainly how terribly alarmed that county was everywhere at anybody that came from London, and that they should have no admittance anywhere but with the utmost difficulty, at least no friendly reception and assistance, as they had received here.

Now, although they received great assistance and encouragement from the country gentlemen and from the people round about them, yet they were put to great straits, for the weather grew cold and wet in October and November, and they had not been used to so much hardship; so that they got colds in their limbs and distempers, but never had the infection; and thus about December they came home to the city again.

I give this story thus at large, principally to give an account what became of the great numbers of people which immediately appeared in the city as soon as the sickness abated; for, as I have said, great numbers of those that were able and had retreats in the country fled to those retreats. So, when it was increased to such a frightful extremity as I have related, the middling people who had not friends fled to all parts of the country where they could get shelter, as well those that had money to relieve themselves as those that had not. Those that had money always fled farthest, because they were able to subsist themselves; but those who were empty suffered, as I have said, great hardships, and were often driven by necessity to relieve their wants at the expense of the country. By that means the country was made very uneasy at them, and sometimes took them up, though even then they scarce knew what to do with them, and were always very backward to punish them, but often, too, they forced them from place to place, till they were obliged to come back again to London.

I have, since my knowing this story of John and his brother, inquired and found that there were a great many of the poor disconsolate people, as above, fled into the country every way, and some of them got little sheds, and barns, and outhouses to live in, where they could obtain so much kindness of the country, and especially where they had any the least satisfactory account to give of themselves, and particularly that they did not come out of London too late. But others, and that in great numbers, built themselves little huts and retreats in the fields and woods, and lived like hermits in holes and caves, or any place they could find, and where, we may be sure, they suffered great extremities, such that many of them were obliged to come back again whatever the danger was; and so those little huts were often found empty, and the country people supposed the inhabitants lay dead in them of the plague, and would not go near them for fear, no, not in a great while; nor is it unlikely but that some of the unhappy wanderers might die so all alone, even sometimes for want of help, as particularly in one tent or hut was found a man dead, and on the gate of a field just by was cut with his knife, in uneven letters, the following words, by which it may be supposed the other man escaped, or that, one dying first, the other buried him as well as he could:—

"O mIsErY!
We BoTH ShaLL DyE,
WoE, WoE."

I have given an account already of what I found to have been the case down the river among the seafaring men; how the ships lay in the offing, as it's called, in rows or lines astern of one another, quite down from the Pool as far as I could see. I have been told that they lay in the same manner quite down the river as low as Gravesend, and some far beyond, even everywhere, or in every place where they could ride with safety as to wind and weather; nor did I ever hear that the plague reached to any of the people on board those ships, except such as lay up in the Pool, or as high as Deptford Reach, although the people went frequently on shore to the country towns and villages, and farmers' houses, to buy fresh provisions, fowls, pigs, calves, and the like for their supply.

Likewise I found that the watermen on the river above the bridge found means to convey themselves away up the river as far as they could go, and that they had, many of them, their whole families in their boats, covered with tilts and bales, as they call them, and furnished with straw within for their lodging, and that they lay thus all along by the shore in the marshes, some of them setting up little tents with their sails, and so lying under them on shore in the day, and going into their boats at night; and in this manner, as I have heard, the river-sides were lined with boats and people as long as they had anything to subsist on, or could get anything of the country; and, indeed, the country people, as well gentlemen as others, on these and all other occasions, were very forward to relieve them, but they were by no means willing to receive them into their towns and houses, and for that we cannot blame them.

There was one unhappy citizen, within my knowledge, who had been visited in a dreadful manner, so that his wife and all his children were dead, and himself and two servants only left, with an elderly woman, a near relation, who had nursed those that were dead as well as she could. This disconsolate man goes to a village near the town, though not within the bills of mortality, and finding an empty house there, inquires out the owner, and took the house. After a few days he got a cart and loaded it with goods, and carries them down to the house; the people of the village opposed his driving the cart along, but with some arguings and some force, the men that drove the cart along got through the street up to the door of the house. There the constable resisted them again, and would not let them be brought in. The man caused the goods to be unloaden and laid at the door, and sent the cart away; upon which they carried the man before a justice of peace; that is to say, they commanded him to go, which he did. The justice ordered him to cause the cart to fetch away the goods again, which he refused to do; upon which the justice ordered the constable to pursue the carters and fetch them back, and make them reload the goods and carry them away, or to set them in the stocks till they came for further orders; and if they could not find them, nor the man would not consent to take them away, they should cause them to be drawn with hooks from the house-door and burned in the street. The poor distressed man upon this fetched the goods again, but with grievous cries and lamentations at the hardship of his case. But there was no remedy; self-preservation obliged the people to those severities, which they would not otherwise have been concerned in. Whether this poor man lived or died I cannot tell, but it was reported that he had the plague upon him at that time; and perhaps the people might report that to justify their usage of him; but it was not unlikely that either he or his goods, or both, were dangerous, when his whole family had been dead of the distemper so little a while before.

I know that the inhabitants of the towns adjacent to London were much blamed for cruelty to the poor people that ran from the contagion in their distress, and many very severe things were done, as may be seen from what has been said; but I cannot but say also that, where there was room for charity and assistance to the people, without apparent danger to themselves, they were willing enough to help and relieve them. But as every town were indeed judges in their own case, so the poor people who ran abroad in their extremities were often ill-used and driven back again into the town; and this caused infinite exclamations and outcries against the country towns, and made the clamour very popular.

And yet, more or less, maugre all the caution, there was not a town of any note within ten (or, I believe, twenty) miles of the city but what was more or less infected and had some died among them. I have heard the accounts of several, such as they were reckoned up, as follows:—

In Enfield	32	.	In Deptford	. . .	623
" Hornsey	58	.	" Greenwich	. .	231
" Newington	17	.	" Eltham and Lusum	.	85
" Tottenham	42	.	" Croydon	. . .	61
" Edmonton	19	.	" Brentwood	. .	70
" Barnet and Hadleigh.	43	.	" Romford	. . .	109
" St. Albans	121	.	" Barking Abbot	. .	200
" Watford	45	.	" Brentford	. . .	432
" Uxbridge	117	.	" Kingston	. . .	122
" Hertford	90	.	" Staines	. . .	82
" Ware	160	.	" Chertsey	. . .	18
" Hoddesdon	30	.	" Windsor	. . .	103
" Waltham Abbey	23	.			
" Epping	26	.		*Cum aliis.*	

Another thing might render the country more strict with respect to the citizens, and especially with respect to the poor, and this was what I hinted at before, namely, that there was a seeming propensity or a wicked inclination in those that were infected to infect others.

There had been great debates among our physicians as to the reason of this. Some will have it to be in the nature of the disease, and that it impresses every one that is seized upon by it with a kind of a rage, and a hatred against their own kind, as if there was a malignity not only in the distemper to communicate itself, but in the very nature of man, prompting him with evil will or an evil eye, that, as they say in the case of a mad dog, who, though the gentlest creature before of any of his kind, yet then will fly upon and bite any one that comes next him, and those as soon as any who had been most observed by him before.

Others placed it to the account of the corruption of human nature, who cannot bear to see itself more miserable than others of its own species, and has a kind of involuntary wish that all men were as unhappy or in as bad a condition as itself.

Others say it was only a kind of desperation, not knowing or regarding what they did, and consequently unconcerned at the danger or safety, not only of anybody near them, but even of themselves also. And indeed when men are once come to a condition to abandon themselves, and be unconcerned for the safety or at the danger of themselves, it cannot be so much wondered that they should be careless of the safety of other people.

But I choose to give this grave debate a quite different turn, and answer it or resolve it all by saying that I do not grant the fact. On the contrary, I say that the thing is not really so, but that it was a general complaint raised by the people inhabiting the outlying villages against the citizens to justify, or at least excuse, those hardships and severities so much talked of, and in which complaints both sides may be said to have injured one another; that is to say, the citizens pressing to be received and harboured in time of distress, and with the plague upon them, complain of the cruelty and injustice of the country people in being refused entrance and forced back again with their goods and families; and the inhabitants, finding themselves so imposed upon, and the citizens breaking in as it were upon them whether they would or no, complain that when they were infected they were not only regardless of others, but even willing to infect them; neither of which were really true, that is to say, in the colours they were described in.

It is true there is something to be said for the frequent alarms which were given to the country of the resolution of the people of London to come out by force, not only for relief, but to plunder and rob; that they ran about the streets with the distemper upon them without any control; and that no care was taken to shut up houses, and confine the sick people from infecting others; whereas, to do the Londoners justice, they never practised such things, except in such particular cases as I have mentioned above, and such like. On the other hand, everything was managed with so much care, and such excellent order was observed in the whole city and suburbs by the care of the Lord Mayor and aldermen, and by the justices of the peace, church-wardens, &c., in the out-parts, that London may be a pattern to all the cities in the world for the good government and the excellent order that was everywhere kept, even in the time of the most violent infection, and when the people were in the utmost consternation and distress. But of this I shall speak by itself.

One thing, it is to be observed, was owing principally to the prudence of the magistrates, and ought to be mentioned to their honour, viz., the moderation which they used in the great and difficult work of shutting up of houses. It is true, as I have mentioned, that the shutting up of houses was a great subject of discontent, and I may say indeed the only subject of discontent among the people at that time; for the confining the sound in the same house with the sick was counted very terrible, and the complaints of people so confined were very grievous. They were heard into the very streets, and they were sometimes such that called for resentment, though oftener for compassion. They had no way to converse with any

of their friends but out at their windows, where they
would make such piteous lamentations as often moved
the hearts of those they talked with, and of others who,
passing by, heard their story; and as those complaints
oftentimes reproached the severity, and sometimes the
insolence, of the watchmen placed at their doors, those
watchmen would answer saucily enough, and perhaps be
apt to affront the people who were in the street talking
to the said families; for which, or for their ill-treatment of
the families, I think seven or eight of them in several
places were killed; I know not whether I should say
murdered or not, because I cannot enter into the particular cases. It is true the watchmen were on their duty,
and acting in the post where they were placed by a lawful authority; and killing any public legal officer in the
execution of his office is always, in the language of the
law, called murder. But as they were not authorised by
the magistrates' instructions, or by the power they acted
under, to be injurious or abusive, either to the people
who were under their observation, or to any that concerned themselves for them; so when they did so, they
might be said to act themselves, not their office; to act as
private persons, not as persons employed; and consequently, if they brought mischief upon themselves by
such an undue behaviour, that mischief was upon their
own heads; and indeed they had so much the hearty
curses of the people, whether they deserved it or not, that
whatever befell them nobody pitied them, and everybody
was apt to say they deserved it, whatever it was. Nor do
I remember that anybody was ever punished, at least to
any considerable degree, for whatever was done to the
watchmen that guarded their houses.

What variety of stratagems were used to escape and
get out of houses thus shut up, by which the watchmen
were deceived or overpowered, and that the people got

away, I have taken notice of already, and shall say no more to that. But I say the magistrates did moderate and ease families upon many occasions in this case, and particularly in that of taking away, or suffering to be removed, the sick persons out of such houses when they were willing to be removed either to a pest-house or other places, and sometimes giving the well persons in the family so shut up leave to remove upon information given that they were well, and that they would confine themselves in such houses where they went so long as should be required of them. The concern, also, of the magistrates for the supplying such poor families as were infected—I say, supplying them with necessaries, as well physic as food—was very great, and in which they did not content themselves with giving the necessary orders to the officers appointed, but the aldermen in person, and on horseback, frequently rode to such houses and caused the people to be asked at their windows whether they were duly attended or not; also, whether they wanted anything that was necessary, and if the officers had constantly carried their messages and fetched them such things as they wanted or not. And if they answered in the affirmative, all was well; but if they complained that they were ill supplied, and that the officer did not do his duty, or did not treat them civilly, they (the officers) were generally removed, and others placed in their stead.

It is true such complaint might be unjust, and if the officer had such arguments to use as would convince the magistrate that he was right, and that the people had injured him, he was continued and they reproved. But this part could not well bear a particular inquiry, for the parties could very ill be well heard and answered in the street from the windows, as was the case then. The magistrates, therefore generally chose to favour the people and remove the man, as what seemed to be the least wrong and of the least ill consequence; seeing if the watchman was injured, yet they could easily make him amends by giving him another post of the like nature; but if the family was injured, there was no satisfaction could be made to them, the damage perhaps being irreparable, as it concerned their lives.

A great variety of these cases frequently happened between the watchmen and the poor people shut up, besides those I formerly mentioned about escaping. Sometimes the watchmen were absent, sometimes drunk, sometimes asleep when the people wanted them, and such never failed to be punished severely, as indeed they deserved.

But after all that was or could be done in these cases, the shutting up of houses, so as to confine those that were well with those that were sick, had very great inconveniences in it, and some that were very tragical, and which merited to have been considered if there had been room for it. But it was authorised by a law, it had the public good in view as the end chiefly aimed at, and all the private injuries that were done by the putting it in execution must be put to the account of the public benefit.

It is doubtful to this day whether, in the whole, it contributed anything to the stop of the infection, and, indeed, I cannot say it did, for nothing could run with greater fury and rage than the infection did when it was in its chief violence, though the houses infected were shut up as exactly and as effectually as it was possible. Certain it is that if all the infected persons were effectually shut in, no sound person could have been infected by them, because they could not have come near them. But the case was this, and I shall only touch it here, namely, that the infection was propagated insensibly, and by such persons as were not visibly infected, who neither knew whom they infected or who they were infected by.

A house in Whitechapel was shut up for the sake of one infected maid, who had only spots, not the tokens come out upon her, and recovered; yet these people obtained no liberty to stir, neither for air or exercise forty days. Want of breath, fear, anger, vexation, and all the other griefs attending such an injurious treatment cast the mistress of the family into a fever, and visitors came into the house and said it was the plague, though the physicians declared it was not. However, the family were obliged to begin their quarantine anew on the report of the visitor or examiner, though their former quarantine wanted but a few days of being finished. This oppressed them so with anger and grief, and, as before, straitened them also so much as to room, and for want of breathing and free air, that most of the family fell sick, one of one distemper, one of another, chiefly scorbutic ailments; only one a violent colic; till, after several prolongings of their confinement, some or other of those that came in with the visitors to inspect the persons that were ill, in hopes of releasing them, brought the distemper with them and infected the whole house, and all or most of them died, not of the plague as really upon them before, but of the plague that those people brought them, who should have been careful to have protected them from it. And this was a thing which frequently happened, and was, indeed, one of the worst consequences of shutting houses up.

I had about this time a little hardship put upon me, which I was at first greatly afflicted at, and very much disturbed about, though, as it proved, it did not expose me to any disaster; and this was being appointed by the alderman of Portsoken Ward one of the examiners of the houses in the precinct where I lived. We had a large parish, and had no less than eighteen examiners, as the order called us; the people called us visitors. I endeavoured with all my might to be excused from such an employment, and used many arguments with the alderman's deputy to be excused; particularly I alleged that I was against shutting up houses at all, and that it would be very hard to oblige me to be an instrument in that which was against my judgment, and which I did verily believe would not answer the end it was intended for; but all the abatement I could get was only, that whereas the officer was appointed by my Lord Mayor to continue two months, I should be obliged to hold it but three weeks, on condition nevertheless that I could then get some other sufficient housekeeper to serve the rest of the time for me, which was, in short, but a very small favour, it being very difficult to get any man to accept of such an employment, that was fit to be entrusted with it.

It is true that shutting up of houses had one effect, which I am sensible was of moment, namely, it confined the distempered people, who would otherwise have been both very troublesome and very dangerous in their running about streets with the distemper upon them, which, when they were delirious, they would have done in a most frightful manner, and as indeed they began to do at first very much, till they were thus restrained; nay, so very open they were that the poor would go about and beg at people's doors, and say they had the plague upon them, and beg rags for their sores, or both, or anything that delirious nature happened to think of.

A poor, unhappy gentlewoman, a substantial citizen's wife, was (if the story be true) murdered by one of these creatures in Aldersgate Street, or that way. He was going along the street, raving mad, to be sure, and singing; the people only said he was drunk, but he himself said he had the plague upon him, which, it seems, was true;

and meeting this gentlewoman, he would kiss her. She
was terribly frighted, as he was only a rude fellow, and
she ran from him, but the street being very thin of people, there was nobody near enough to help her. When
she saw he would overtake her, she turned and gave him
a thrust so forcibly, he being but weak, and pushed him
down backward. But very unhappily, she being so near,
he caught hold of her, and pulled her down also, and
getting up first, mastered her, and kissed her; and which
was worst of all, when he had done, told her he had the
plague, and why should not she have it as well as he? She
was frighted enough before, being also young with child;
but when she heard him say he had the plague, she
screamed out and fell down into a swoon, or in a fit,
which, though she recovered a little, yet killed her in a
very few days, and I never heard whether she had the
plague or no.

Another infected person came and knocked at the door
of a citizen's house where they knew him very well; the
servant let him in, and being told the master of the house
was above, he ran up, and came into the room to them
as the whole family was at supper. They began to rise up,
a little surprised, not knowing what the matter was, but
he bid them sit still, he only came to take his leave of
them. They asked him, "Why, Mr——, where are you
going?" "Going?" says he; "I have got the sickness, and
shall die to-morrow night." 'T is easy to believe, though
not to describe, the consternation they were all in. The
women and the man's daughters, which were but little
girls, were frighted almost to death, and got up, one running out at one door and one at another, some downstairs
and some upstairs, and getting together as well as they
could, locked themselves into their chambers, and
screamed out at the window for help, as if they had been
frighted out of their wits. The master, more composed

than they, though both frighted and provoked, was going to lay hands on him and throw him downstairs, being in a passion, but then, considering a little the condition of the man and the danger of touching him, horror seized his mind, and he stood still like one astonished. The poor distempered man all this while, being as well diseased in his brain as in his body, stood still like one amazed. At length he turns round: "Ay!" says he, with all the seeming calmness imaginable, "is it so with you all? Are you all disturbed at me? Why, then I'll e'en go home and die there." And so he goes immediately downstairs. The servant that had let him in goes down after him with a candle, but was afraid to go past him and open the door, so he stood on the stairs to see what he would do. The man went and opened the door, and went out and flung the door after him. It was some while before the family recovered the fright, but as no ill consequence attended, they have had occasion since to speak of it (you may be sure) with great satisfaction. Though the man was gone, it was some time, nay, as I heard, some days before they recovered themselves of the hurry they were in; nor did they go up and down the house with any assurance till they had burnt a great variety of fumes and perfumes in all the rooms, and made a great many smokes of pitch, of gunpowder, and of sulphur, all separately shifted, and washed their clothes, and the like. As to the poor man, whether he lived or died I don't remember.

It is most certain that, if by the shutting up of houses the sick had not been confined, multitudes who, in the height of their fever, were delirious and distracted would have been continually running up and down the streets; and even as it was a very great number did so, and offered all sorts of violence to those they met, even just as a mad dog runs on and bites at every one he meets; nor can I doubt but that, should one of those infected, diseased creatures have bitten any man or woman while the frenzy of the distemper was upon them, they, I mean the person so wounded, would as certainly have been incurably infected as one that was sick before, and had the tokens upon him.

I heard of one infected creature who, running out of his bed in his shirt in the anguish and agony of his swellings, of which he had three upon him, got his shoes on and went to put on his coat; but the nurse resisting, and snatching the coat from him, he threw her down, ran over her, ran downstairs and into the street, directly to the Thames in his shirt, the nurse running after him, and calling to the watch to stop him; but the watchman, frighted at the man, and afraid to touch him, let him go on; upon which he ran down to the Stillyard stairs, threw away his shirt, and plunged into the Thames, and, being a good swimmer, swam quite over the river; and the tide being coming in, as they call it, that is, running westward, he reached the land not till he came about the Falcon stairs, where landing, and finding no people there, it being in the night, he ran about the streets there, naked as he was, for a good while, when, it being by that time high water, he takes the river again, and swam back to the Stillyard, landed, ran up the streets again to his own house, knocking at the door, went up the stairs and into his bed again; and that this terrible experiment cured him of the plague, that is to say, that the violent motion of his arms and legs stretched the parts where the swellings he had upon him were, that is to say, under his arms and his groin, and caused them to ripen and break, and that the cold of the water abated the fever in his blood.

I have only to add that I do not relate this any more than some of the other, as a fact within my own knowledge, so as that I can vouch the truth of them, and especially that of the man being cured by the extravagant adventure, which I confess I do not think very possible; but it may serve to confirm the many desperate things which the distressed people falling into deliriums, and what we call light headedness, were frequently run upon at that time, and how infinitely more such there would have been if such people had not been confined by the shutting up of houses; and this I take to be the best, if not the only good thing which was performed by that severe method.

On the other hand, the complaints and the murmurings were very bitter against the thing itself. It would pierce the hearts of all that came by to hear the piteous cries of those infected people, who, being thus out of their understandings by the violence of their pain, or the heat of their blood, were either shut in or perhaps tied in their beds and chairs, to prevent their doing themselves hurt, and who would make a dreadful outcry at their being confined, and at their being not permitted to die at large, as they called it, and as they would have done before.

This running of distempered people about the streets was very dismal, and the magistrates did their utmost to prevent it; but as it was generally in the night and always sudden when such attempts were made, the officers could not be at hand to prevent it; and even when any got out in the day, the officers appointed did not care to meddle with them, because, as they were all grievously infected, to be sure, when they were come to that height, so they were more than ordinarily infectious, and it was one of the most dangerous things that could be to touch them. On the other hand, they generally ran on, not knowing what they did, till they dropped down stark dead, or till they had exhausted their spirits so as that they would fall and then die in perhaps half-an-hour or an hour; and, which was most piteous to hear, they were sure to come to themselves entirely in that half-hour or hour, and then to make most grievous and piercing cries and lamentations in the deep, afflicting sense of the condition they were in. This was much of it before the order for shutting up of houses were strictly put in execution, for at first the watchmen were not so vigorous and severe as they were afterward in the keeping the people in; that is to say, before they were, I mean some of them, severely punished for their neglect, failing in their duty, and letting people who were under their care slip away, or conniving at their going abroad, whether sick or well. But after they saw the officers appointed to examine into their conduct were resolved to have them do their duty or be punished for the omission, they were more exact, and the people were strictly restrained; which was a thing they took so ill and bore so impatiently that their discontents can hardly be described. But there was an absolute necessity for it, that must be confessed, unless some other measures had been timely entered upon, and it was too late for that.

Had not this particular of the sick being restrained as above been our case at that time, London would have been the most dreadful place that ever was in the world; there would, for aught I know, have as many people died in the streets as died in their houses; for when the distemper was at its height it generally made them raving and delirious, and when they were so they would never be persuaded to keep in their beds but by force; and many who were not tied threw themselves out of windows, when they found they could not get leave to go out of their doors.

It was for want of people conversing one with another, in this time of calamity, that it was impossible any particular person could come at the knowledge of all the extraordinary cases that occurred in different families;

and particularly I believe it was never known to this day how many people in their deliriums drowned themselves in the Thames, and in the river which runs from the marshes by Hackney, which we generally called Ware River, or Hackney River. As to those which were set down in the weekly bill, they were indeed few; nor could it be known of any of those whether they drowned themselves by accident or not. But I believe I might reckon up more who, within the compass of my knowledge or observation, really drowned themselves in that year than are put down in the bill of all put together, for many of the bodies were never found who yet were known to be lost; and the like in other methods of self-destruction. There was also one man in or about White-cross Street burned himself to death in his bed; some said it was done by himself, others that it was by the treachery of the nurse that attended him; but that he had the plague upon him was agreed by all.

It was a merciful disposition of Providence also, and which I have many times thought of at that time, that no fires, or no considerable ones at least, happened in the city during that year, which, if it had been otherwise, would have been very dreadful; and either the people must have let them alone unquenched, or have come together in great crowds and throngs, unconcerned at the danger of the infection, not concerned at the houses they went into, at the goods they handled, or at the persons or the people they came among. But so it was, that excepting that in Cripplegate parish, and two or three little eruptions of fires, which were presently extinguished, there was no disaster of that kind happened in the whole year. They told us a story of a house in a place called Swan Alley, passing from Goswell Street, near the end of Old Street, into St. John Street, that a family was infected there in so terrible a manner that every one of the house died. The last person lay dead on the floor, and, as it is supposed, had laid herself all along to die just before the fire; the fire, it seems, had fallen from its place, being of wood, and had taken hold of the boards and the joists they lay on, and burnt as far as just to the body, but had not taken hold of the dead body, though she had little more than her shift on, and had gone out of itself, not hurting the rest of the house, though it was a slight timber house. How true this might be I do not determine, but the city being to suffer severely the next year by fire, this year it felt very little of that calamity.

Indeed, considering the deliriums which the agony threw people into, and how I have mentioned in their madness, when they were alone, they did many desperate things, it was very strange there were no more disasters of that kind.

It has been frequently asked me, and I cannot say that I ever knew how to give a direct answer to it, how it came to pass that so many infected people appeared abroad in the streets at the same time that the houses which were infected were so vigilantly searched, and all of them shut up and guarded as they were.

I confess I know not what answer to give to this, unless it be this, that in so great and populous a city as this is it was impossible to discover every house that was infected as soon as it was so, or to shut up all the houses that were infected; so that people had the liberty of going about the streets, even where they pleased, unless they were known to belong to such-and-such infected houses.

It is true that, as several physicians told my Lord Mayor, the fury of the contagion was such at some particular times, and people sickened so fast and died so soon, that it was impossible, and indeed to no purpose, to go about to inquire who was sick and who was well, or to shut them up with such exactness as the thing re-

quired, almost every house in a whole street being infected, and in many places every person in some of the
houses; and that which was still worse, by the time that
the houses were known to be infected, most of the persons infected would be stone dead, and the rest run away
for fear of being shut up; so that it was to very small
purpose to call them infected houses and shut them up,
the infection having ravaged and taken its leave of the
house before it was really known that the family was any
way touched.

This might be sufficient to convince any reasonable person, that as it was not in the power of the magistrates, or
of any human methods of policy, to prevent the spreading
the infection, so that this way of shutting up of houses
was perfectly insufficient for that end. Indeed it seemed
to have no manner of public good in it, equal or propor-
tionable to the grievous burden that it was to the particular families that were so shut up; and, as far as I was
employed by the public in directing that severity, I frequently found occasion to see that it was incapable of
answering the end. For example, as I was desired, as a
visitor or examiner, to inquire into the particulars of several families which were infected, we scarce came to any
house where the plague had visibly appeared in the family but that some of the family were fled and gone. The
magistrates would resent this, and charge the examiners
with being remiss in their examination or inspection. But
by that means houses were long infected before it was
known. Now, as I was in this dangerous office but half
the appointed time, which was two months, it was long
enough to inform myself that we were no way capable
of coming at the knowledge of the true state of any family but by inquiring at the door or of the neighbours. As
for going into every house to search, that was a part no
authority would offer to impose on the inhabitants, or

any citizen would undertake, for it would have been exposing us to certain infection and death, and to the ruin of our own families, as well as of ourselves; nor would any citizen of probity, and that could be depended upon, have stayed in the town, if they had been made liable to such a severity.

Seeing then that we could come at the certainty of things by no method but that of inquiry of the neighbours or of the family, and on that we could not justly depend, it was not possible but that the uncertainty of this matter would remain as above.

It is true masters of families were bound by the order to give notice to the examiner of the place wherein he lived, within two hours after he should discover it, of any person being sick in his house, that is to say, having signs of the infection, but they found so many ways to evade this and excuse their negligence that they seldom gave that notice till they had taken measures to have every one escape out of the house who had a mind to escape, whether they were sick or sound; and while this was so, it is easy to see that the shutting up of houses was no way to be depended upon as a sufficient method for putting a stop to the infection, because, as I have said elsewhere, many of those that so went out of those infected houses had the plague really upon them, though they might really think themselves sound. And some of these were the people that walked the streets till they fell down dead, not that they were suddenly struck with the distemper as with a bullet that killed with the stroke, but that they really had the infection in their blood long before; only, that as it preyed secretly on the vitals, it appeared not till it seized the heart with a mortal power, and the patient died in a moment, as with a sudden fainting or an apoplectic fit.

I know that some even of our physicians thought for a

time that those people that so died in the streets were seized but that moment they fell, as if they had been touched by a stroke from heaven, as men are killed by a flash of lightning, but they found reason to alter their opinion afterwards; for upon examining the bodies of such after they were dead, they always either had tokens upon them or other evident proofs of the distemper having been longer upon them than they had otherwise expected.

This often was the reason that, as I have said, we that were examiners were not able to come at the knowledge of the infection being entered into a house till it was too late to shut it up, and sometimes not till the people that were left were all dead. In Petticoat Lane two houses together were infected, and several people sick; but the distemper was so well concealed, the examiner, who was my neighbour, got no knowledge of it till notice was sent him that the people were all dead, and that the carts should call there to fetch them away. The two heads of the families concerted their measures, and so ordered ⁺heir matters as that when the examiner was in the neighbourhood they appeared generally at a time, and answered, that is, lied, for one another, or got some of the neighbourhood to say they were all in health, and, perhaps, knew no better, till, death making it impossible to keep it any longer as a secret, the dead-carts were called in the night to both the houses, and so it became public. But when the examiner ordered the constable to shut up the houses there was nobody left in them but three people, two in one house, and one in the other, just dying, and a nurse in each house, who acknowledged that they had buried five before, that the houses had been infected nine or ten days, and that for all the rest of the two families, which were many, they were gone, some sick, some well, or whether sick or well could not be known.

In like manner, at another house in the same lane, a man having his family infected, but very unwilling to be shut up, when he could conceal it no longer, shut up himself; that is to say, he set the great red cross upon his door, with the words, "Lord have mercy upon us," and so deluded the examiner, who supposed it had been done by the constable, by order of the other examiner, for there were two examiners to every district or precinct. By this means he had free egress and regress into his house again, and out of it, as he pleased, notwithstanding it was infected, till at length his stratagem was found out, and then he, with the sound part of his servants and family, made off and escaped, so they were not shut up at all.

These things made it very hard, if not impossible, as I have said, to prevent the spreading of an infection by the shutting up of houses, unless the people would think the shutting of their houses no grievance, and be so willing to have it done as that they would give notice duly and faithfully to the magistrates of their being infected, as soon as it was known by themselves; but as that cannot be expected from them, and the examiners cannot be supposed, as above, to go into their houses to visit and search, all the good of shutting up houses will be defeated, and few houses will be shut up in time, except those of the poor, who cannot conceal it, and of some people who will be discovered by the terror and consternation which the thing put them into.

I got myself discharged of the dangerous office I was in as soon as I could get another admitted, whom I had obtained for a little money to accept of it; and so, instead of serving the two months, which was directed, I was not above three weeks in it; and a great while too, considering it was in the month of August, at which time the distemper began to rage with great violence at our end of the town.

In the execution of this office I could not refrain speaking my opinion among my neighbours as to this shutting up the people in their houses; in which we saw most evidently the severities that were used, though grievous in themselves, had also this particular objection against them, namely, that they did not answer the end, as I have said, but that the distempered people went day by day about the streets; and it was our united opinion that a method to have removed the sound from the sick, in case of a particular house being visited, would have been much more reasonable on many accounts, leaving nobody with the sick persons but such as should, on such occasion, request to stay and declare themselves content to be shut up with them.

Our scheme for removing those that were sound from those that were sick was only in such houses as were infected, and confining the sick was no confinement; those that could not stir would not complain while they were in their senses, and while they had the power of judging. Indeed, when they came to be delirious and light-headed, then they would cry out of the cruelty of being confined; but for the removal of those that were well, we thought it highly reasonable and just, for their own sakes, they should be removed from the sick, and that, for other people's safety, they should keep retired for a while, to see that they were sound, and might not infect others; and we thought twenty or thirty days enough for this.

Now, certainly, if houses had been provided on purpose for those that were sound to perform this demi-quarantine in, they would have much less reason to think themselves injured in such a restraint than in being confined with infected people in the houses where they lived.

It is here, however, to be observed that after the funerals became so many that people could not toll the bell, mourn or weep, or wear black for one another, as they did before; no, nor so much as make coffins for those that died; so after a while the fury of the infection appeared to be so increased that, in short, they shut up no houses at all. It seemed enough that all the remedies of that kind had been used till they were found fruitless, and that the plague spread itself with an irresistible fury; so that as the fire the succeeding year spread itself, and burned with such violence that the citizens, in despair, gave over their endeavours to extinguish it, so in the plague it came at last to such violence that the people sat still looking at one another, and seemed quite abandoned to despair; whole streets seemed to be desolated, and not to be shut up only, but to be emptied of their inhabitants; doors were left open, windows stood shattering with the wind in empty houses for want of people to shut them. In a word, people began to give up themselves to their fears, and to think that all regulations and methods were in vain, and that there was nothing to be hoped for but an universal desolation; and it was even in the height of this general despair that it pleased God to stay His hand, and to slacken the fury of the contagion in such a manner as was even surprising, like its beginning, and demonstrated it to be His own particular hand, and that above, if not without the agency of means, as I shall take notice of in its proper place.

But I must still speak of the plague as in its height, raging even to desolation, and the people under the most dreadful consternation, even, as I have said, to despair. It is hardly credible to what excesses the passions of men carried them in this extremity of the distemper, and this part, I think, was as moving as the rest. What could affect a man in his full power of reflection, and what could make deeper impressions on the soul, than to see a man almost naked, and got out of his house, or perhaps out of his bed, into the street, come out of Harrow Alley, a populous conjunction or collection of alleys, courts, and passages in the Butcher Row in Whitechapel,—I say, what could be more affecting than to see this poor man come out into the open street, run dancing and singing, and making a thousand antic gestures, with five or six women and children running after him, crying and calling upon him for the Lord's sake, to come back, and entreating the help of others to bring him back, but all in vain, nobody daring to lay a hand upon him or to come near him?

This was a most grievous and afflicting thing to me, who saw it all from my own windows; for all this while the poor afflicted man was, as I observed it, even then in the utmost agony of pain, having, as they said, two swellings upon him, which could not be brought to break or to suppurate; but, by laying strong caustics on them, the surgeons had, it seems, hopes to break them, which caustics were then upon him, burning his flesh as with a hot iron. I cannot say what became of this poor man, but I think he continued roving about in that manner till he fell down and died.

No wonder the aspect of the city itself was frightful. The usual concourse of people in the streets, and which used to be supplied from our end of the town, was abated. The Exchange was not kept shut, indeed, but it was no more frequented. The fires were lost; they had been almost extinguished for some days by a very smart and hasty rain. But that was not all; some of the physicians insisted that they were not only no benefit, but injurious to the health of people. This they made a loud clamor about, and complained to the Lord Mayor about it. On the other hand, others of the same faculty, and eminent too, opposed them, and gave their reasons why the fires were, and must be, useful to assuage the violence of the distemper. I cannot give a full account of their arguments on both sides; only this I remember, that they cavilled very much with one another. Some were for fires, but that they must be made of wood and not coal, and of particular sorts of wood too, such as fir in particular, or cedar, because of the strong effluvia of turpentine; others were for coal and not wood, because of the sulphur and bitumen; and others were for neither one or other. Upon the whole, the Lord Mayor ordered no more fires, and especially on this account, namely, that the plague was so fierce that they saw evidently it defied all means, and rather seemed to increase than decrease upon any application to check and abate it; and yet this amazement of the magistrates proceeded rather from want of being able to apply any means successfully than from any unwillingness either to expose themselves or undertake the care and weight of business; for, to do them justice, they neither spared their pains or their persons. But nothing answered; the infection raged, and the people were now frighted and terrified to the last degree, so that, as I may say, they gave themselves up, and, as I mentioned above, abandoned themselves to their despair.

But let me observe here, that when I say the people abandoned themselves to despair, I do not mean to what men call a religious despair, or a despair of their eternal state, but I mean a despair of their being able to escape the infection or to outlive the plague, which, they saw, was so raging and so irresistible in its force, that indeed few people that were touched with it in its height, about August and September, escaped; and, which is very particular, contrary to its ordinary operation in June and July, and the beginning of August, when, as I have observed, many were infected, and continued so many days, and then went off, after having had the poison in their blood a long time; but now, on the contrary, most of the people who were taken during the two last weeks in

August, and in the three first weeks in September, generally died in two or three days at furthest, and many the
very same day they were taken; whether the dog-days,
or, as our astrologers pretended to express themselves,
the influence of the dog-star had that malignant effect,
or all those who had the seeds of infection before in them
brought it up to a maturity at that time altogether, I
know not; but this was the time when it was reported,
that above 3000 people died in one night; and they that
would have us believe they more critically observed it
pretend to say that they all died within the space of two
hours, viz., between the hours of one and three in the
morning.

As to the suddenness of people's dying at this time,
more than before, there were innumerable instances of
it, and I could name several in my neighbourhood. One
family without the Bars, and not far from me, were all
seemingly well on the Monday, being ten in family. That
evening one maid and one apprentice were taken ill, and
died the next morning, when the other apprentice and
two children were touched, whereof one died the same
evening, and the other two on Wednesday. In a word, by
Saturday at noon the master, mistress, four children, and
four servants were all gone, and the house left entirely
empty, except an ancient woman who came in to take
charge of the goods for the master of the family's brother,
who lived not far off, and who had not been sick.

Many houses were then left desolate, all the people
being carried away dead; and especially in an alley
farther on the same side beyond the Bars, going in at the
sign of Moses and Aaron, there were several houses together, which, they said, had not one person left alive in
them, and some that died last in several of those houses
were left a little too long before they were fetched out to
be buried; the reason of which was not, as some have

written, very untruly, that the living were not sufficient
to bury the dead, but that the mortality was so great in
the yard or alley that there was nobody left to give notice
to the buriers or sextons that there were any dead bodies
there to be buried. It was said, how true I know not, that
some of those bodies were so much corrupted and so
rotten that it was with difficulty they were carried; and
as the carts could not come any nearer than to the Alley
Gate in the High Street, it was so much the more difficult
to bring them along; but I am not certain how many
bodies were then left. I am sure that ordinarily it was
not so.

As I have mentioned how the people were brought
into a condition to despair of life and abandon themselves, so this very thing had a strange effect among us
for three or four weeks; that is, it made them bold and
venturous, they were no more shy of one another, or restrained within doors, but went anywhere and everywhere, and began to converse. One would say to another,
"I do not ask you how you are, or say how I am; it is certain we shall all go; so 't is no matter who is sick or who
is sound;" and so they ran desperately into any place or
any company.

As it brought the people into public company, so it was
surprising how it brought them to crowd into the
churches. They inquired no more into whom they sat near
to or far from, what offensive smells they met with, or
what condition the people seemed to be in, but looking
upon themselves all as so many dead corpses, they come
to the churches without the least caution, and crowded
together, as if their lives were of no consequence compared to the work which they came about there. Indeed,
the zeal which they showed in coming, and the earnestness and affection they showed in their attention to what
they heard, made it manifest what a value people would

all put upon the worship of God if they thought every day they attended at the church that it would be their last.

Nor was it without other strange effects, for it took away all manner of prejudice at or scruple about the person whom they found in the pulpit when they came to the churches. It cannot be doubted but that many of the ministers of the parish churches were cut off, among others, in so common and dreadful a calamity; and others had not courage enough to stand it, but removed into the country as they found means for escape. As then some parish churches were quite vacant and forsaken, the people made no scruple of desiring such Dissenters as had been a few years before deprived of their livings by virtue of the Act of Parliament called the Act of Uniformity to preach in the churches; nor did the church ministers in that case make any difficulty of accepting their assistance; so that many of those whom they called silenced ministers had their mouths opened on this occasion and preached publicly to the people.

Here we may observe, and I hope it will not be amiss to take notice of it, that a near view of death would soon reconcile men of good principles one to another, and that it is chiefly owing to our easy situation in life and our putting these things far from us that our breaches are fomented, ill blood continued, prejudices, breach of charity and of Christian union, so much kept and so far carried on among us as it is. Another plague year would reconcile all these differences; a close conversing with death, or with diseases that threaten death, would scum off the gall from our tempers, remove the animosities among us, and bring us to see with differing eyes than those which we looked on things with before. As the people who had been used to join with the Church were reconciled at this time with the admitting the Dissenters to preach to them, so the Dissenters, who with an un-common prejudice had broken off from the communion of the Church of England, were now content to come to their parish churches, and to conform to the worship which they did not approve of before; but as the terror of the infection abated, those things all returned again to their less desirable channel, and to the course they were in before.

I mention this but historically. I have no mind to enter into arguments to move either or both sides to a more charitable compliance one with another. I do not see that it is probable such a discourse would be either suitable or successful; the breaches seem rather to widen, and tend to a widening further, than to closing, and who am I that I should think myself able to influence either one side or other? But this I may repeat again, that 't is evident death will reconcile us all; on the other side the grave we shall be all brethren again. In heaven, whither I hope we may come from all parties and persuasions, we shall find neither prejudice or scruple; there we shall be of one principle and of one opinion. Why we cannot be content to go hand in hand to the place where we shall join heart and hand without the least hesitation, and with the most complete harmony and affection,—I say, why we cannot do so here I can say nothing to, neither shall I say anything more of it but that it remains to be la-mented.

I could dwell a great while upon the calamities of this dreadful time, and go on to describe the objects that ap-peared among us every day, the dreadful extravagancies which the distraction of sick people drove them into; how the streets began now to be fuller of frightful objects, and families to be made even a terror to themselves. But after I have told you, as I have above, that one man, being tied in his bed, and finding no other way to deliver himself, set the bed on fire with his candle, which unhappily stood within his reach, and burnt himself in his bed; and how another, by the insufferable torment he bore, danced and sung naked in the streets, not knowing one ecstasy from another; I say, after I have mentioned these things, what can be added more? What can be said to represent the misery of these times more lively to the reader, or to give him a more perfect idea of a complicated distress?

I must acknowledge that this time was terrible, that I was sometimes at the end of all my resolutions, and that I had not the courage that I had at the beginning. As the extremity brought other people abroad, it drove me home, and except having made my voyage down to Blackwall and Greenwich, as I have related, which was an excursion, I kept afterwards very much within doors, as I had for about a fortnight before. I have said already that I repented several times that I had ventured to stay in town, and had not gone away with my brother and his family, but it was too late for that now; and after I had retreated and stayed within doors a good while before my impatience led me abroad, then they called me, as I have said, to an ugly and dangerous office, which brought me out again; but as that was expired while the height of the distemper lasted, I retired again, and continued close ten or twelve days more, during which many dismal spectacles represented themselves in my view, out of my own windows and in our own street, as that particularly from Harrow Alley, of the poor outrageous creature which danced and sung in his agony; and many others there were. Scarce a day or night passed over but some dismal thing or other happened at the end of that Harrow Alley, which was a place full of poor people, most of them belonging to the butchers, or to employments depending upon the butchery.

Sometimes heaps and throngs of people would burst

out of the alley, most of them women, making a dreadful clamour, mixed or compounded of screeches, cryings, and calling one another, that we could not conceive what to make of it. Almost all the dead part of the night the dead-cart stood at the end of that alley, for if it went in it could not well turn again, and could go in but a little way. There, I say, it stood to receive dead bodies, and as the churchyard was but a little way off, if it went away full it would soon be back again. It is impossible to describe the most horrible cries and noise the poor people would make at their bringing the dead bodies of their children and friends out of the cart, and by the number one would have thought there had been none left behind, or that there were people enough for a small city living in those places. Several times they cried "Murder," sometimes "Fire;" but it was easy to perceive it was all distraction, and the complaints of distressed and distempered people.

I believe it was everywhere thus at that time, for the plague raged for six or seven weeks beyond all that I have expressed, and came even to such a height that, in the extremity, they began to break into that excellent order of which I have spoken so much in behalf of the magistrates, namely, that no dead bodies were seen in the streets or burials in the daytime, for there was a necessity in this extremity to bear with its being otherwise for a little while.

One thing I cannot omit here, and indeed I thought it was extraordinary, at least it seemed a remarkable hand of Divine justice, viz., that all the predictors, astrologers, fortune-tellers, and what they called cunning-men, conjurers, and the like; calculators of nativities and dreamers of dreams, and such people, were gone and vanished; not one of them was to be found. I am verily persuaded that a great number of them fell in the heat of the calamity, having ventured to stay upon the prospect of getting great estates; and indeed their gain was but too great for a time, through the madness and folly of the people. But now they were silent; many of them went to their long home, not able to foretell their own fate or to calculate their own nativities. Some have been critical enough to say that every one of them died. I dare not affirm that; but this I must own, that I never heard of one of them that ever appeared after the calamity was over.

But to return to my particular observations during this dreadful part of the visitation. I am now come, as I have said, to the month of September, which was the most dreadful of its kind, I believe, that ever London saw; for, by all the accounts which I have seen of the preceding visitations which have been in London, nothing has been like it, the number in the weekly bill amounting to almost 40,000 from the 22nd of August to the 26th of September, being but five weeks. The particulars of the bills are as follows, viz.:—

From August the 22nd to the 29th	7496
" " 29th " 5th September . . .	8252
" September the 5th " 12th " . . .	7690
" " 12th " 19th " . . .	8297
" " 19th " 26th " . . .	6460
	38,195

This was a prodigious number of itself, but if I should add the reasons which I have to believe that this account was deficient, and how deficient it was, you would, with me, make no scruple to believe that there died above ten thousand a week for all those weeks, one week with another, and a proportion for several weeks both before and after. The confusion among the people, especially within the city at that time, was inexpressible. The terror was so great at last that the courage of the people appointed to carry away the dead began to fail them; nay, several of them died, although they had the distemper before and were recovered, and some of them dropped down when they have been carrying the bodies even at the pit side, and just ready to throw them in; and this confusion was greater in the city, because they had flattered themselves with hopes of escaping, and thought the bitterness of death was past. One cart, they told us, going up Shoreditch was forsaken of the drivers, or being left to one man to drive, he died in the street, and the horses going on, overthrew the cart, and left the bodies, some thrown out here, some there, in a dismal manner. Another cart was, it seems, found in the great pit in Finsbury Fields, the driver being dead, or having been gone and abandoned it, and the horses running too near it, the cart fell in and drew the horses in also. It was suggested that the driver was thrown in with it, and that the cart fell upon him, by reason his whip was seen to be in the pit among the bodies; but that, I suppose, could not be certain.

In our parish of Aldgate the dead-carts were several times, as I have heard, found standing at the churchyard gate full of dead bodies, but neither bellman or driver or any one else with it; neither in these or many other cases did they know what bodies they had in their cart, for sometimes they were let down with ropes out of balconies and out of windows, and sometimes the bearers brought them to the cart, sometimes other people; nor, as the men themselves said, did they trouble themselves to keep any account of the numbers.

The vigilance of the magistrates was now put to the utmost trial, and, it must be confessed, can never be enough acknowledged on this occasion also; whatever expense or trouble they were at, two things were never neglected in the city or suburbs either—

1. Provisions were always to be had in full plenty, and

the price not much raised neither, hardly worth speaking.

2. No dead bodies lay unburied or uncovered; and if one walked from one end of the city to another, no funeral or sign of it was to be seen in the daytime, except a little, as I have said above, in the three first weeks in September.

This last article perhaps will hardly be believed when some accounts which others have published since that shall be seen, wherein they say that the dead lay unburied, which I am assured was utterly false; at least, if it had been anywhere so, it must have been in houses where the living were gone from the dead, having found means, as I have observed, to escape, and where no notice was given to the officers. All which amounts to nothing at all in the case in hand; for this I am positive in, having myself been employed a little in the direction of that part in the parish in which I lived, and where as great a desolation was made in proportion to the number of inhabitants as was anywhere;—I say, I am sure that there were no dead bodies remained unburied; that is to say, none that the proper officers knew of; none for want of people to carry them off, and buriers to put them into the ground and cover them; and this is sufficient to the argument; for what might lie in houses and holes, as in Moses and Aaron Alley, is nothing; for it is most certain they were buried as soon as they were found. As to the first article, namely, of provisions, the scarcity or dearness, though I have mentioned it before, and shall speak of it again, yet I must observe here—

1. The price of bread in particular was not much raised; for in the beginning of the year, viz., in the first week in March, the penny wheaten loaf was ten ounces and a half; and in the height of the contagion it was to be had at nine ounces and a half, and never dearer, no, not all that season. And about the beginning of Novem-

ber it was sold ten ounces and a half again; the like of which, I believe, was never heard of in any city, under so dreadful a visitation, before.

2. Neither was there (which I wondered much at) any want of bakers or ovens kept open to supply the people with bread; but this was indeed alleged by some families, viz., that their maid-servants, going to the bakehouses with their dough to be baked, which was then the custom, sometimes came home with the sickness, that is to say, the plague upon them.

In all this dreadful visitation there were, as I have said before, but two pest-houses made use of, viz., one in the fields beyond Old Street and one in Westminster; neither was there any compulsion used in carrying people thither. Indeed there was no need of compulsion in the case, for there were thousands of poor distressed people who, having no help, or conveniences, or supplies but of charity, would have been very glad to have been carried thither and been taken care of, which, indeed, was the only thing that I think was wanting in the whole public management of the city, seeing nobody was here allowed to be brought to the pest-house but where money was given, or security for money, either at their introducing or upon their being cured and sent out, for very many were sent out again whole; and very good physicians were appointed to those places, so that many people did very well there, of which I shall make mention again. The principal sort of people sent thither were, as I have said, servants who got the distemper by going of errands to fetch necessaries to the families where they lived, and who in that case, if they came home sick, were removed to preserve the rest of the house; and they were so well looked after that, in all the time of the visitation, that there was but 156 buried in all at the London pest-house, and 159 at that of Westminster.

By having more pest-houses I am far from meaning a forcing all people into such places. Had the shutting up of houses been omitted and the sick hurried out of their dwellings to pest-houses, as some proposed, it seems, at that time as well as since, it would certainly have been much worse than it was. The very removing the sick would have been a spreading of the infection, and the rather because that removing could not effectually clear the house where the sick person was of the distemper, and the rest of the family, being then left at liberty, would certainly spread it among others.

The methods also in private families, which would have been universally used to have concealed the distemper, and to have concealed the persons being sick, would have been such that the distemper would sometimes have seized a whole family before any visitors or examiners could have known of it. On the other hand, the prodigious numbers which would have been sick at a time would have exceeded all the capacity of public pest-houses to receive them, or of public officers to discover and remove them.

This was well considered in those days, and I have heard them talk of it often. The magistrates had enough to do to bring people to submit to having their houses shut up, and many ways they deceived the watchmen and got out, as I have observed. But that difficulty made it apparent that they would have found it impracticable to have gone the other way to work, for they could never have forced the sick people out of their beds and out of their dwellings. It must not have been my Lord Mayor's officers, but an army of officers that must have attempted it; and the people, on the other hand, would have been enraged and desperate, and would have killed those that should have offered to have meddled with them or with their children and relations, whatever had befallen them for it; so that they would have made the people, who, as it was, were in the most terrible distraction imaginable, —I say, they would have made them stark mad; whereas the magistrates found it proper on several accounts to treat them with lenity and compassion, and not with violence and terror, such as dragging the sick out of their houses, or obliging them to remove themselves, would have been.

This leads me again to mention the time when the plague first began, that is to say, when it became certain that it would spread over the whole town, when, as I have said, the better sort of people first took the alarm, and began to hurry themselves out of town. It was true, as I observed in its place, that the throng was so great, and the coaches, horses, waggons, and carts were so many, driving and dragging the people away, that it looked as if all the city was running away; and had any regulations been published that had been terrifying at that time, especially such as would pretend to dispose of the people otherwise than they would dispose of them-selves, it would have put both the city and suburbs into the utmost confusion.

But the magistrates wisely caused the people to be encouraged, made very good bye-laws for the regulating the citizens, keeping good order in the streets, and mak-ing everything as eligible as possible to all sorts of people.

In the first place, the Lord Mayor and the sheriffs, the Court of Aldermen, and a certain number of the Common Council men, or their deputies, came to a resolution and published it, viz., that they would not quit the city them-selves, but that they would be always at hand for the pre-serving good order in every place and for the doing jus-tice on all occasions; as also for the distributing the public charity to the poor; and, in a word, for the doing the duty and discharging the trust reposed in them by the citizens to the utmost of their power.

In pursuance of these orders, the Lord Mayor, sheriffs, &c., held councils every day more or less, for making such dispositions as they found needful for preserving the civil peace; and though they used the people with all possible gentleness and clemency, yet all manner of presumptuous rogues, such as thieves, housebreakers, plunderers of the dead or of the sick, were duly punished, and several declarations were continually published by the Lord Mayor and Court of Aldermen against such.

Also all constables and churchwardens were enjoined to stay in the city upon severe penalties, or to depute such able and sufficient housekeepers as the deputy aldermen or Common Council men of the precinct should approve, and for whom they should give security; and also security in case of mortality, that they would forthwith constitute other constables in their stead.

These things re-established the minds of the people very much, especially in the first of their fright, when they talked of making so universal a flight that the city would have been in danger of being entirely deserted of its inhabitants, except the poor, and the country of being plundered and laid waste by the multitude. Nor were the magistrates deficient in performing their part as boldly as they promised it; for my Lord Mayor and the sheriffs were continually in the streets, and at places of the greatest danger, and though they did not care for having too great a resort of people crowding about them, yet in emergent cases they never denied the people access to them, and heard with patience all their grievances and complaints. My Lord Mayor had a low gallery built on purpose in his hall, where he stood a little removed from the crowd when any complaint came to be heard, that he might appear with as much safety as possible.

Likewise the proper officers, called my Lord Mayor's officers, constantly attended in their turns, as they were in waiting; and if any of them were sick or infected, as some of them were, others were instantly employed to fill up and officiate in their places, till it was known whether the other should live or die.

In like manner the sheriffs and aldermen did in their several stations and wards, where they were placed by office, and the sheriffs' officers or sergeants were appointed to receive orders from the respective aldermen in their turn, so that justice was executed in all cases without interruption. In the next place, it was one of their particular cares to see the orders for the freedom of the markets observed, and in this part either the Lord Mayor or one or both of the sheriffs were every market-day on horseback to see their orders executed, and to see that the country people had all possible encouragement and freedom in their coming to the markets and going back again, and that no nuisances or frightful objects should be seen in the streets to terrify them or make them unwilling to come. Also the bakers were taken under particular order, and the Master of the Bakers' Company was, with his court of assistants, directed to see the order of my Lord Mayor for their regulation put in execution, and the due assize of bread, which was weekly appointed by my Lord Mayor, observed, and all the bakers were obliged to keep their ovens going constantly, on pain of losing the privileges of a freeman of the city of London.

By this means bread was always to be had in plenty, and as cheap as usual, as I said above; and provisions were never wanting in the markets, even to such a degree that I often wondered at it, and reproached myself with being so timorous and cautious in stirring abroad, when the country people came freely and boldly to market, as if there had been no manner of infection in the city, or danger of catching it.

It was indeed one admirable piece of conduct in the said magistrates that the streets were kept constantly clear, and free from all manner of frightful objects, dead bodies, or any such things as were indecent or unpleasant, unless where anybody fell down suddenly or died in the streets, as I have said above, and these were generally covered with some cloth or blanket, or removed into the next churchyard, till night. All the needful works that carried terror with them, that were both dismal and dangerous, were done in the night; if any diseased bodies were removed, or dead bodies buried, or infected clothes burnt, it was done in the night; and all the bodies which were thrown into the great pits in the several churchyards or burying-grounds, as has been observed, were so removed in the night, and everything was covered and closed before day. So that in the daytime there was not the least signal of the calamity to be seen or heard of, except what was to be observed from the emptiness of the streets, and sometimes from the passionate outcries and lamentations of the people, out at their windows, and from the numbers of houses and shops shut up.

Nor was the silence and emptiness of the streets so much in the city as in the out-parts, except just at one particular time, when, as I have mentioned, the plague came east and spread over all the city. It was indeed a merciful disposition of God, that as the plague began at one end of the town first, as has been observed at large, so it proceeded progressively to other parts, and did not come on this way, or eastward, till it had spent its fury in the west part of the town; and so, as it came on one way, it abated another. For example, it began at St

Giles's and the Westminster end of the town, and it was in its height in all that part by about the middle of July, viz., in St. Giles-in-the-Fields, St. Andrew's, Holborn, St. Clement Danes, St. Martin-in-the-Fields, and in Westminster. The latter end of July it decreased in those parishes; and coming east, it increased prodigiously in Cripplegate, St. Sepulchre's, St. James's, Clerkenwell, and St. Bride's and Aldersgate. While it was in all these parishes, the city and all the parishes of the Southwark side of the water, and all Stepney, Whitechapel, Aldgate, Wapping and Ratcliff, were very little touched, so that people went about their business unconcerned, carried on their trades, kept open their shops, and conversed freely with one another in all the city, the east and north-east suburbs, and in Southwark, almost as if the plague had not been among us.

Even when the north and north-west suburbs were fully infected, viz., Cripplegate, Clerkenwell, Bishopsgate, and Shoreditch, yet still all the rest were tolerably well. For example, from 25th July to 1st August the bill stood thus of all diseases:—

St. Giles, Cripplegate	554
St. Sepulchre	250
Clerkenwell	103
Bishopsgate	116
Shoreditch	110
Stepney parish	127
Aldgate	92
Whitechapel	104
All the ninety-seven parishes within the walls	228
All the parishes in Southwark	205
Total	1889

So that, in short, there died more that week in the two parishes of Cripplegate and St. Sepulchre by forty-eight

than in all the city, all the east suburbs, and all the Southwark parishes put together. This caused the reputation of
the city's health to continue all over England, and especially in the counties and markets adjacent, from whence
our supply of provisions chiefly came, even much longer
than that health itself continued; for when the people
came into the streets from the country by Shoreditch and
Bishopsgate, or by Old Street and Smithfield, they would
see the out-streets empty and the houses and shops shut,
and the few people that were stirring there walk in the
middle of the streets. But when they came within the
city, there things looked better, and the markets and
shops were open, and the people walking about the
streets as usual, though not quite so many; and this continued till the latter end of August and the beginning of
September.

But then the case altered quite; the distemper abated
in the west and north-west parishes, and the weight of
the infection lay on the city and the eastern suburbs, and
the Southwark side, and this in a frightful manner.

Then, indeed, the city began to look dismal, shops to
be shut, and the streets desolate. In the High Street, indeed, necessity made people stir abroad on many occasions; and there would be in the middle of the day a
pretty many people, but in the mornings and evenings
scarce any to be seen, even there, no, not in Cornhill and
Cheapside.

These observations of mine were abundantly confirmed
by the weekly bills of mortality for those weeks, an ab-
stract of which, as they respect the parishes which I have
mentioned, and as they make the calculations I speak of
very evident, take as follows.

The weekly bill, which makes out this decrease of the
burials in the west and north side of the city, stands
thus:—

From the 12th of September to the 19th—

St. Giles, Cripplegate	456
St. Giles-in-the-Fields.	140
Clerkenwell	77
St. Sepulchre	214
St. Leonard, Shoreditch	183
Stepney parish.	716
Aldgate	623
Whitechapel	532
In the ninety-seven parishes within the walls .	1493
In the eight parishes on Southwark side . . .	1636
Total	6070

Here is a strange change of things indeed, and a sad change it was, and had it held for two months more than it did, very few people would have been left alive. But then such, I say, was the merciful disposition of God, that when it was thus the west and north part, which had been so dreadfully visited at first, grew, as you see, much better; and as the people disappeared here, they began to look abroad again there; and the next week or two altered it still more; that is, more to the encouragement of the other part of the town. For example:—

From the 19th of September to the 26th—

St. Giles, Cripplegate	277
St. Giles-in-the-Fields.	119
Clerkenwell	76
St. Sepulchre	193
St. Leonard, Shoreditch	146
Stepney parish.	616
Aldgate	496
Whitechapel	346
In the ninety-seven parishes within the walls .	1268
In the eight parishes on Southwark side . . .	1390
Total	4927

From the 26th of September to the 3rd of October—

St. Giles, Cripplegate	196
St. Giles-in-the-Fields	95
Clerkenwell	48
St. Sepulchre	137
St. Leonard, Shoreditch	128
Stepney parish.	674
Aldgate	372
Whitechapel	328
In the ninety-seven parishes within the walls .	1149
In the eight parishes on Southwark side . . .	1201
Total	4328

And now the misery of the city, and of the said east and south parts, was complete indeed; for, as you see, the weight of the distemper lay upon those parts, that is to say, the city, the eight parishes over the river, with the parishes of Aldgate, Whitechapel, and Stepney; and this was the time that the bills came up to such a monstrous height as that I mentioned before, and that eight or nine, and, as I believe, ten or twelve thousand a week, died; for it is my settled opinion that they never could come at any just account of the numbers, for the reasons which I have given already.

Nay, one of the most eminent physicians, who has since published in Latin an account of those times, and of his observations, says that in one week there died twelve thousand people, and that particularly there died four thousand in one night; though I do not remember that there ever was any such particular night so remarkably fatal as that such a number died in it. However, all this confirms what I have said above of the uncertainty of the bills of mortality, &c., of which I shall say more hereafter.

And here let me take leave to enter again, though it may seem a repetition of circumstances, into a description of the miserable condition of the city itself, and of

those parts where I lived at this particular time. The city
and those other parts, notwithstanding the great numbers
of people that were gone into the country, was vastly full
of people, and perhaps the fuller because people had for
a long time a strong belief that the plague would not
come into the city, nor into Southwark, no, nor into
Wapping or Ratcliff at all; nay, such was the assurance
of the people on that head that many removed from the
suburbs on the west and north sides, into those eastern
and south sides as for safety, and, as I verily believe,
carried the plague amongst them there, perhaps sooner
than they would otherwise have had it.

Here also I ought to leave a further remark for the use
of posterity, concerning the manner of people's infecting
one another; namely, that it was not the sick people only
from whom the plague was immediately received by
others that were sound, but the well. To explain myself,
by the sick people I mean those who were known to be
sick, had taken their beds, had been under cure, or had
swellings and tumours upon them, and the like; these
everybody could beware of; they were either in their beds
or in such condition as could not be concealed.

By the well I mean such as had received the contagion,
and had it really upon them, and in their blood, yet did
not show the consequences of it in their countenances;
nay, even were not sensible of it themselves, as many
were not for several days. These breathed death in every
place, and upon everybody who came near them; nay,
their very clothes retained the infection, their hands
would infect the things they touched, especially if they
were warm and sweaty, and they were generally apt to
sweat too.

Now it was impossible to know these people, nor did
they sometimes, as I have said, know themselves to be
infected. These were the people that so often dropped

down and fainted in the streets; for oftentimes they would go about the streets to the last, till on a sudden they would sweat, grow faint, sit down at a door and die. It is true, finding themselves thus, they would struggle hard to get home to their own doors, or at other times would be just able to go into their houses and die instantly; other times they would go about till they had the very tokens come out upon them, and yet not know it, and would die in an hour or two after they came home, but be well as long as they were abroad. These were the dangerous people; these were the people of whom the well people ought to have been afraid; but then, on the other side, it was impossible to know them.

And this is the reason why it is impossible in a visitation to prevent the spreading of the plague by the utmost human vigilance, viz., that it is impossible to know the infected people from the sound, or that the infected people should perfectly know themselves. I knew a man who conversed freely in London all the season of the plague in 1665, and kept about him an antidote or cordial, on purpose to take when he thought himself in any danger, and he had such a rule to know or have warning of the danger by as indeed I never met with before or since. How far it may be depended on I know not. He had a wound in his leg, and whenever he came among any people that were not sound, and the infection began to affect him, he said he could know it by that signal, viz., that his wound in his leg would smart, and look pale and white; so as soon as ever he felt it smart it was time for him to withdraw, or to take care of himself, taking his drink, which he always carried about him for that purpose. Now it seems he found his wound would smart many times when he was in company with such who thought themselves to be sound, and who appeared so to one another; but he would presently rise up and say publicly, "Friends here is somebody in the room that has the plague," and so would immediately break up the company. This was indeed a faithful monitor to all people that the plague is not to be avoided by those that converse promiscuously in a town infected, and people have it when they know it not, and that they likewise give it to others when they know not that they have it themselves; and in this case shutting up the well or removing the sick will not do it, unless they can go back and shut up all those that the sick had conversed with, even before they knew themselves to be sick, and none knows how far to carry that back, or where to stop; for none knows when, or where, or how they may have received the infection, or from whom.

This I take to be the reason which makes so many people talk of the air being corrupted and infected, and that they need not be cautious of whom they converse with, for that the contagion was in the air. I have seen them in strange agitations and surprises on this account. "I have never come near any infected body," says the disturbed person; "I have conversed with none but sound, healthy people, and yet I have gotten the distemper!" "I am sure I am struck from Heaven," says another, and he falls to the serious part. Again, the first goes on exclaiming, "I have come near no infection or any infected person; I am sure it is in the air. We draw in death when we breathe, and therefore 't is the hand of God; there is no withstanding it." And this at last made many people, being hardened to the danger, grow less concerned at it, and less cautious towards the latter end of the time, and when it was come to its height, than they were at first. Then, with a kind of a Turkish predestinarianism, they would say, if it pleased God to strike them, it was all one whether they went abroad or stayed at home; they could not escape it, and therefore they went boldly about, even into infected houses and infected company; visited sick people; and, in short, lay in the beds with their wives or relations when they were infected. And what was the consequence, but the same that is the consequence in Turkey, and in those countries where they do those things, namely, that they were infected too, and died by hundreds and thousands?

I would be far from lessening the awe of the judgments of God and the reverence to His providence, which ought always to be on our minds on such occasions as these. Doubtless the visitation itself is a stroke from Heaven upon a city, or country, or nation where it falls; a messenger of His vengeance, and a loud call to that nation, or country, or city to humiliation and repentance, according to that of the prophet Jeremiah (xviii. 7, 8): "At what instant I shall speak concerning a nation, and concerning a kingdom, to pluck up, and to pull down, and to destroy it; if that nation, against whom I have pronounced, turn from their evil, I will repent of the evil that I thought to do unto them." Now to prompt due impressions of the awe of God on the minds of men on such occasions, and not to lessen them, it is that I have left those minutes upon record.

I say, therefore, I reflect upon no man for putting the reason of those things upon the immediate hand of God, and the appointment and direction of His providence; nay, on the contrary, there were many wonderful deliverances of persons from infection, and deliverances of persons when infected, which intimate singular and remarkable providence in the particular instances to which they refer, and I esteem my own deliverance to be one next to miraculous, and do record it with thankfulness.

But when I am speaking of the plague as a distemper arising from natural causes, we must consider it as it was really propagated by natural means; nor is it at all the less a judgment for its being under the conduct of human causes and effects; for, as the Divine Power has formed the whole scheme of nature and maintains nature in its course, so the same Power thinks fit to let His own actings with men, whether of mercy or judgment, to go on in the ordinary course of natural causes, and He is pleased to act by those natural causes as the ordinary means, excepting and reserving to Himself nevertheless a power to act in a supernatural way when He sees occasion. Now 't is evident that in the case of an infection there is no apparent extraordinary occasion for supernatural operation, but the ordinary course of things appears sufficiently armed, and made capable of all the effects that Heaven usually directs by a contagion. Among these causes and effects, this of the secret conveyance of infection, imperceptible and unavoidable, is more than sufficient to execute the fierceness of Divine vengeance, without putting it upon supernaturals and miracle.

The acute penetrating nature of the disease itself was such, and the infection was received so imperceptibly, that the most exact caution could not secure us while in the place. But I must be allowed to believe—and I have so many examples fresh in my memory to convince me of it, that I think none can resist their evidence—I say, I must be allowed to believe that no one in this whole nation ever received the sickness or infection but who received it in the ordinary way of infection from somebody, or the clothes, or touch, or stench of somebody that was infected before.

The manner of its coming first to London proves this also, viz., by goods brought over from Holland, and brought thither from the Levant, the first breaking of it out in a house in Long Acre where those goods were carried and first opened, its spreading from that house to other houses by the visible unwary conversing with those who were sick, and the infecting the parish officers who were employed about the persons dead, and the like. These are known authorities for this great foundation point, that it went on and proceeded from person to person and from house to house, and no otherwise. In the first house that was infected there died four persons. A neighbour, hearing the mistress of the first house was sick, went to visit her, and went home and gave the distemper to her family, and died, and all her household. A minister, called to pray with the first sick person in the second house, was said to sicken immediately, and die with several more in his house. Then the physicians began to consider, for they did not at first dream of a general contagion. But the physicians being sent to inspect the bodies, they assured the people that it was neither more or less than the plague, with all its terrifying particulars, and that it threatened an universal infection, so many people having already conversed with the sick or distempered, and having, as might be supposed, received infection from them, that it would be impossible to put a stop to it.

Here the opinion of the physicians agreed with my observation afterwards, namely, that the danger was spreading insensibly, for the sick could infect none but those that came within reach of the sick person, but that one man who may have really received the infection and knows it not, but goes abroad and about as a sound person, may give the plague to a thousand people, and they to greater numbers in proportion, and neither the person giving the infection or the persons receiving it know anything of it, and perhaps not feel the effects of it for several days after.

For example, many persons in the time of this visitation never perceived that they were infected till they found, to their unspeakable surprise, the tokens come out upon them; after which they seldom lived six hours, for those spots they called the tokens were really gangrene spots, or mortified flesh in small knobs as broad as a little silver penny, and hard as a piece of callus or horn; so that, when the disease was come up to that length, there was nothing could follow but certain death, and yet, as I said, they knew nothing of their being infected, nor found themselves so much as out of order, till those mortal marks were upon them. But everybody must allow that they were infected in a high degree before, and must have been so some time, and consequently their breath, their sweat, their very clothes, were contagious for many days before.

This occasioned a vast variety of cases, which physicians would have much more opportunity to remember than I; but some came within the compass of my observation or hearing, of which I shall name a few.

A certain citizen who had lived safe and untouched till the month of September, when the weight of the distemper lay more in the city than it had done before, was mighty cheerful, and something too bold, as I think it was, in his talk of how secure he was, how cautious he had been, and how he had never come near any sick body. Says another citizen, a neighbour of his, to him one day, "Do not be too confident, Mr ——; it is hard to say who is sick and who is well, for we see men alive and well to outward appearance one hour, and dead the next." "That is true," says the first man, for he was not a man presumptuously secure, but had escaped a long while, and men, as I said above, especially in the city, began to be over-easy upon that score. "That is true," says he; "I do not think myself secure, but I hope I have not been in company with any person that there has been any danger in." "No?" says his neighbour. "Was not you at the Bull Head Tavern in Gracechurch Street with Mr.

—— the night before last?" "Yes," says the first, "I was; but there was nobody there that we had any reason to think dangerous." Upon which his neighbour said no more, being unwilling to surprise him; but this made him more inquisitive, and as his neighbour appeared backward, he was the more impatient, and in a kind of warmth says he aloud, "Why, he is not dead, is he?" Upon which his neighbour still was silent, but cast up his eyes and said something to himself; at which the first citizen turned pale, and said no more but this, "Then I am a dead man too," and went home immediately and sent for a neighbouring apothecary to give him something preventive, for he had not yet found himself ill; but the apothecary, opening his breast, fetched a sigh, and said no more but this, "Look up to God;" and the man died in a few hours.

Now let any man judge from a case like this if it is possible for the regulations of magistrates, either by shutting up the sick or removing them, to stop an infection which spreads itself from man to man, even while they are perfectly well and insensible of its approach, and may be so for many days.

It may be proper to ask here how long it may be supposed men might have the seeds of the contagion in them before it discovered itself in this fatal manner, and how long they might go about seemingly whole, and yet be contagious to all those that came near them. I believe the most experienced physicians cannot answer this question directly any more than I can; and something an ordinary observer may take notice of, which may pass their observation. The opinion of physicians abroad seems to be that it may lie dormant in the spirits, or in the blood-vessels, a very considerable time. Why else do they exact a quarantine of those who come into their harbours and ports from suspected places? Forty days is, one would think, too long for nature to struggle with such an enemy as this, and not conquer it or yield to it. But I could not think, by my own observation, that they can be infected so as to be contagious to others above fifteen or sixteen days at furthest; and on that score it was, that when a house was shut up in the city, and any one had died of the plague, but nobody appeared to be ill in the family for sixteen or eighteen days after, they were not so strict but that they would connive at their going privately abroad; nor would people be much afraid of them afterward, but rather think they were fortified the better, having not been vulnerable when the enemy was in their own house; but we sometimes found it had lain much longer concealed.

Upon the foot of all these observations I must say, that though Providence seemed to direct my conduct to be otherwise, yet it is my opinion, and I must leave it as a prescription, viz., that the best physic against the plague is to run away from it. I know people encourage themselves by saying God is able to keep us in the midst of danger, and able to overtake us when we think ourselves out of danger; and this kept thousands in the town, whose carcasses went into the great pits by cartloads, and who, if they had fled from the danger, had, I believe, been safe from the disaster; at least 't is probable they had been safe.

And were this very fundamental only duly considered by the people on any future occasion of this or the like nature, I am persuaded it would put them upon quite different measures for managing the people from those that they took in 1665, or than any that have been taken abroad that I have heard of. In a word, they would consider of separating the people into smaller bodies, and removing them in time farther from one another, and not let such a contagion as this, which is indeed chiefly dangerous to collected bodies of people, find a million of people in a body together, as was very near the case before, and would certainly be the case if it should ever appear again.

The plague, like a great fire, if a few houses only are contiguous where it happens, can only burn a few houses; or if it begins in a single, or, as we call it, a lone house, can only burn that lone house where it begins. But if it begins in a close-built town or city and gets a head, there its fury increases, it rages over the whole place, and consumes all it can reach.

I could propose many schemes on the foot of which the government of this city, if ever they should be under the apprehensions of such another enemy (God forbid they should), might ease themselves of the greatest part of the dangerous people that belong to them; I mean such as the begging, starving, labouring poor, and among them chiefly those who, in case of a siege, are called the useless mouths, who being then prudently and to their own advantage disposed of, and the wealthy inhabitants disposing of themselves, and of their servants and children, the city and its adjacent parts would be so effectually evacuated that there would not be above a tenth part of its people left together for the disease to take hold upon. But suppose them to be a fifth part, and that two hundred and fifty thousand people were left, and if it did seize upon them, they would, by their living so much at large, be much better prepared to defend themselves against the infection, and be less liable to the effects of it than if the same number of people lived close together in one smaller city, such as Dublin or Amsterdam, or the like.

It is true hundreds, yea, thousands of families fled away at this last plague, but then, of them, many fled too late, and not only died in their flight, but carried the distemper with them into the countries where they went, and infected those whom they went among for safety; which confounded the thing, and made that be a propagation of the distemper which was the best means to prevent it; and this too is an evidence of it, and brings me back to what I only hinted at before, but must speak more fully to here, namely, that men went about apparently well many days after they had the taint of the disease in their vitals, and after their spirits were so seized as that they could never escape it, and that all the while they did so they were dangerous to others; I say, this proves that so it was; for such people infected the very towns they went through, as well as the families they went among; and it was by that means that almost all the great towns in England had the distemper among them, more or less, and always they would tell you such a Londoner or such a Londoner brought it down.

It must not be omitted that when I speak of those people who were really thus dangerous, I suppose them to be utterly ignorant of their own condition; for if they really knew their circumstances to be such as indeed they were, they must have been a kind of wilful murderers if they would have gone abroad among healthy people, and it would have verified indeed the suggestion which I mentioned above, and which I thought seemed untrue, viz., that the infected people were utterly careless as to giving the infection to others, and rather forward to do it than not; and I believe it was partly from this very thing that they raised that suggestion, which I hope was not really true in fact.

I confess no particular case is sufficient to prove a general, but I could name several people within the knowledge of some of their neighbours and families yet living, who showed the contrary to an extreme. One man, a master of a family in my neighbourhood, having had the

distemper, he thought he had it given him by a poor
workman whom he employed, and whom he went to his
house to see, or went for some work that he wanted to
have finished, and he had some apprehensions even while
he was at the poor workman's door, but did not discover
it fully; but the next day it discovered itself, and he was
taken very ill, upon which he immediately caused himself to be carried into an outbuilding which he had in
his yard, and where there was a chamber over a work-
house, the man being a brazier. Here he lay, and here he
died, and would be tended by none of his neighbours,
but by a nurse from abroad; and would not suffer his
wife, nor children, nor servants to come up into the room,
lest they should be infected, but sent them his blessing
and prayers for them by the nurse, who spoke it to them
at a distance, and all this for fear of giving them the
distemper, without which he knew, as they were kept up,
they could not have it.

And here I must observe also that the plague, as I suppose all distempers do, operated in a different manner on
differing constitutions; some were immediately overwhelmed with it, and it came to violent fevers, vomitings, insufferable headaches, pains in the back, and so
up to ravings and ragings with those pains; others with
swellings and tumours in the neck or groin, or armpits,
which till they could be broke put them into insufferable
agonies and torment; while others, as I have observed,
were silently infected, the fever preying upon their spirits insensibly, and they seeing little of it till they fell into
swooning, and faintings, and death without pain.

I am not physician enough to enter into the particular
reasons and manner of these differing effects of one and
the same distemper, and of its differing operation in several bodies; nor is it my business here to record the observations which I really made, because the doctors them-

selves have done that part much more effectually than I can do, and because my opinion may in some things differ from theirs. I am only relating what I know, or have heard, or believe of the particular cases, and what fell within the compass of my view, and the different nature of the infection, as it appeared in the particular cases which I have related; but this may be added too, that though the former sort of those cases, namely, those openly visited, were the worst for themselves as to pain —I mean those that had such fevers, vomitings, headaches, pains, and swellings, because they died in such a dreadful manner—yet the latter had the worst state of the disease; for in the former they frequently recovered, especially if the swellings broke, but the latter was inevitable death; no cure, no help could be possible, nothing could follow but death.

And it was worse also to others, because, as above, it secretly, and unperceived by others, or by themselves, communicated death to those they conversed with, the penetrating poison insinuating itself into their blood in a manner which it is impossible to describe, or indeed conceive.

This infecting and being infected without so much as its being known to either person is evident from two sorts of cases which frequently happened at that time; and there is hardly anybody living who was in London during the infection but must have known several of the cases of both sorts.

1. Fathers and mothers have gone about as if they had been well, and have believed themselves to be so, till they have insensibly infected and been the destruction of their whole families, which they would have been far from doing if they had the least apprehensions of their being unsound and dangerous themselves. A family, whose story I have heard, was thus infected by the fa-

ther; and the distemper began to appear upon some of them even before he found it upon himself. But searching more narrowly, it appeared he had been affected some time, and as soon as he found that his family had been poisoned by himself he went distracted, and would have laid violent hands upon himself, but was kept from that by those who looked to him, and in a few days died.

2. The other particular is, that many people having been well to the best of their own judgment, or by the best observation which they could make of themselves for several days, and only finding a decay of appetite, or a light sickness upon their stomachs; nay, some whose appetite has been strong, and even craving, and only a light pain in their heads, have sent for physicians to know what ailed them, and have been found, to their great surprise, at the brink of death, the tokens upon them, or the plague grown up to an incurable height.

It was very sad to reflect how such a person as this last mentioned above had been a walking destroyer perhaps for a week or a fortnight before that; how he had ruined those that he would have hazarded his life to save, and had been breathing death upon them, even perhaps in his tender kissing and embracings of his own children. Yet thus certainly it was, and often has been, and I could give many particular cases where it has been so. If then the blow is thus insensibly striking; if the arrow flies thus unseen, and cannot be discovered, to what purpose are all the schemes for shutting up or removing the sick people? Those schemes cannot take place but upon those that appear to be sick, or to be infected; whereas there are among them at the same time thousands of people who seem to be well, but are all that while carrying death with them into all companies which they come into.

This frequently puzzled our physicians, and especially

the apothecaries and surgeons, who knew not how to discover the sick from the sound; they all allowed that it was really so, that many people had the plague in their very blood, and preying upon their spirits, and were in themselves but walking putrefied carcasses, whose breath was infectious and their sweat poison, and yet were as well to look on as other people, and even knew it not themselves; I say, they all allowed that it was really true in fact, but they knew not how to propose a discovery.

My friend Dr. Heath was of opinion that it might be known by the smell of their breath; but then, as he said, who durst smell to that breath for his information? since, to know it, he must draw the stench of the plague up into his own brain, in order to distinguish the smell! I have heard it was the opinion of others that it might be distinguished by the party's breathing upon a piece of glass, where, the breath condensing, there might living creatures be seen by a microscope, of strange, monstrous, and frightful shapes, such as dragons, snakes, serpents, and devils, horrible to behold. But this I very much question the truth of, and we had no microscopes at that time, as I remember, to make the experiment with.

It was the opinion also of another learned man, that the breath of such a person would poison and instantly kill a bird; not only a small bird, but even a cock or hen, and that, if it did not immediately kill the latter, it would cause them to be roupy, as they call it; particularly that if they had laid any eggs at any time, they would be all rotten. But those are opinions which I never found supported by any experiments, or heard of others that had seen it; so I leave them as I find them, only with this remark, namely, that I think the probabilities are very strong for them.

Some have proposed that such persons should breathe hard upon warm water, and that they would leave an un-

usual scum upon it, or upon several other things, especially such as are of a glutinous substance and are apt to
receive a scum and support it.

But from the whole I found that the nature of this contagion was such that it was impossible to discover it at
all, or to prevent its spreading from one to another by
any human skill.

Here was indeed one difficulty which I could never
thoroughly get over to this time, and which there is but
one way of answering that I know of, and it is this, viz.,
the first person that died of the plague was on December 20, or thereabouts, 1664, and in or about Long Acre;
whence the first person had the infection was generally
said to be, from a parcel of silks imported from Holland,
and first opened in that house.

But after this we heard no more of any person dying of
the plague, or of the distemper being in that place, till
the 9th of February, which was about seven weeks after,
and then one more was buried out of the same house.
Then it was hushed, and we were perfectly easy as to the
public for a great while; for there were no more entered
in the weekly bill to be dead of the plague till the 22nd
of April, when there was two more buried, not out of the
same house, but out of the same street; and, as near as I
can remember, it was out of the next house to the first.
This was nine weeks asunder, and after this we had no
more till a fortnight, and then it broke out in several
streets, and spread every way. Now the question seems to
lie thus: Where lay the seeds of the infection all this
while? How came it to stop so long, and not stop any
longer? Either the distemper did not come immediately
by contagion from body to body, or if it did, then a body
may be capable to continue infected without the disease
discovering itself many days, nay, weeks together; even

not a quarantine of days only, but soixantine; not only forty days, but sixty days or longer.

It is true there was, as I observed at first, and is well known to many yet living, a very cold winter and a long frost, which continued three months, and this, the doctors say, might check the infection; but then the learned must allow me to say, that if, according to their notion, the disease was, as I may say, only frozen up, it would, like a frozen river, have returned to its usual force and current when it thawed, whereas the principal recess of this infection, which was from February to April, was after the frost was broken and the weather mild and warm.

But there is another way of solving all this difficulty, which I think my own remembrance of the thing will supply; and that is, the fact is not granted, namely, that there died none in those long intervals, viz., from the 20th of December to the 9th of February, and from thence to the 22nd of April. The weekly bills are the only evidence on the other side, and those bills were not of credit enough, at least with me, to support an hypothesis or determine a question of such importance as this; for it was our received opinion at that time, and I believe upon very good grounds, that the fraud lay in the parish officers, searchers, and persons appointed to give account of the dead, and what diseases they died of; and as people were very loth at first to have the neighbours believe their houses were infected, so they gave money to procure, or otherwise procured, the dead persons to be returned as dying of other distempers; and this I know was practised afterwards in many places, I believe I might say in all places where the distemper came, as will be seen by the vast increase of the numbers placed in the weekly bills under other articles of diseases during the

time of the infection. For example, in the months of July
and August, when the plague was coming on to its highest pitch, it was very ordinary to have from a thousand
to twelve hundred, nay, to almost fifteen hundred a week
of other distempers. Not that the numbers of those distempers were really increased to such a degree, but the
great number of families and houses where really the infection was, obtained the favour to have their dead be
returned of other distempers, to prevent the shutting up
their houses. For example:—

Dead of other diseases beside the plague—

From the 18th July to the 25th	. . . .	942
" 25th July " 1st August	. . . . .	1004
" 1st August " 8th	. . . . . .	1213
" 8th " 15th	. . . . . .	1439
" 15th " 22nd	. . . . . .	1331
" 22nd " 29th	. . . . . .	1394
" 29th " 5th September	. . . .	1264
" 5th September to the 12th	. . . . .	1056
" 12th " 19th	. . . . . .	1132
" 19th " 26th	. . . . . .	927

Now it was not doubted but the greatest part of these,
or a great part of them, were dead of the plague, but the
officers were prevailed with to return them as above, and
the numbers of some particular articles of distempers discovered it as follows:—

	Aug. 1 to 8.	Aug. 8 to 15.	Aug. 15 to 22.	Aug. 22 to 29.	Aug. 29 to Sept. 5.	Sept. 5 to 12	Sept. 12 to 19	Sept. 19 to 26.
Fever	314	353	348	383	364	332	309	268
Spotted Fever .	174	190	166	165	157	97	101	65
Surfeit . . .	85	87	74	99	68	45	49	36
Teeth	90	113	111	133	138	128	121	112
	663	743	699	780	727	602	580	481

There were several other articles which bore a proportion to these, and which, it is easy to perceive, were increased on the same account, as aged, consumptions, vomitings, imposthumes, gripes, and the like, many of which were not doubted to be infected people; but as it was of the utmost consequence to families not to be known to be infected, if it was possible to avoid it, so they took all the measures they could to have it not believed, and if any died in their houses, to get them returned to the examiners, and by the searchers, as having died of other distempers.

This, I say, will account for the long interval which, as I have said, was between the dying of the first persons that were returned in the bill to be dead of the plague and the time when the distemper spread openly and could not be concealed.

Besides, the weekly bills themselves at that time evidently discover this truth; for, while there was no mention of the plague, and no increase after it had been mentioned, yet it was apparent that there was an increase of those distempers which bordered nearest upon it; for example, there were eight, twelve, seventeen of the spotted fever in a week, when there were none, or but very few, of the plague; whereas before, one, three, or four were the ordinary weekly numbers of that distemper. Likewise, as I observed before, the burials increased weekly in that particular parish and the parishes adjacent more than in any other parish, although there were none set down of the plague; all which tell us, that the infection was handed on, and the succession of the distemper really preserved, though it seemed to us at that time to be ceased, and to come again in a manner surprising.

It might be, also, that the infection might remain in other parts of the same parcel of goods which at first it came in, and which might not be perhaps opened, or at

least not fully, or in the clothes of the first infected person; for I cannot think that anybody could be seized with
the contagion in a fatal and mortal degree for nine weeks
together, and support his state of health so well as even
not to discover it to themselves; yet if it were so, the
argument is the stronger in favour of what I am saying,
namely, that the infection is retained in bodies apparently well, and conveyed from them to those they converse with, while it is known to neither the one nor the
other.

Great were the confusions at that time upon this very
account, and when people began to be convinced that
the infection was received in this surprising manner from
persons apparently well, they began to be exceeding shy
and jealous of every one that came near them. Once, on
a public day, whether a Sabbath-day or not I do not remember, in Aldgate Church, in a pew full of people, on a
sudden one fancied she smelt an ill smell. Immediately
she fancies the plague was in the pew, whispers her notion or suspicion to the next, then rises and goes out of
the pew. It immediately took with the next, and so to
them all; and every one of them, and of the two or three
adjoining pews, got up and went out of the church, nobody knowing what it was offended them, or from whom.

This immediately filled everybody's mouths with one
preparation or other, such as the old women directed, and
some perhaps as physicians directed, in order to prevent
infection by the breath of others, insomuch that if we
came to go into a church when it was anything full of
people, there would be such a mixture of smells at the
entrance that it was much more strong, though perhaps
not so wholesome, than if you were going into an apothecary's or druggist's shop. In a word, the whole church
was like a smelling-bottle; in one corner it was all perfumes; in another, aromatics, balsamics, and variety of

drugs and herbs; in another, salts and spirits, as every one was furnished for their own preservation. Yet I observed that after people were possessed, as I have said, with the belief, or rather assurance, of the infection being thus carried on by persons apparently in health, the churches and meeting-houses were much thinner of people than at other times before that they used to be. For this is to be said of the people of London, that during the whole time of the pestilence the churches or meetings were never wholly shut up, nor did the people decline coming out to the public worship of God, except only in some parishes when the violence of the distemper was more particularly in that parish at that time, and even then no longer than it continued to be so.

Indeed nothing was more strange than to see with what courage the people went to the public service of God even at that time, when they were afraid to stir out of their own houses upon any other occasion; this, I mean, before the time of desperation, which I have mentioned already. This was a proof of the exceeding populousness of the city at the time of the infection, notwithstanding the great numbers that were gone into the country at the first alarm, and that fled out into the forests and woods when they were further terrified with the extraordinary increase of it. For when we came to see the crowds and throngs of people which appeared on the Sabbath-days at the churches, and especially in those parts of the town where the plague was abated, or where it was not yet come to its height, it was amazing. But of this I shall speak again presently. I return in the meantime to the article of infecting one another at first, before people came to right notions of the infection, and of infecting one another. People were only shy of those that were really sick, a man with a cap upon his head, or with clothes round his neck, which was the case of those that had swellings there. Such was indeed frightful; but when we saw a gentleman dressed, with his band on and his gloves in his hand, his hat upon his head, and his hair combed, of such we had not the least apprehensions, and people conversed a great while freely, especially with their neighbours and such as they knew. But when the physicians assured us that the danger was as well from the sound, that is, the seemingly sound, as the sick, and that those people who thought themselves entirely free were oftentimes the most fatal, and that it came to be generally understood that people were sensible of it, and of the reason of it; then, I say, they began to be jealous of everybody, and a vast number of people locked themselves up, so as not to come abroad into any company at all, nor suffer any that had been abroad in promiscuous company to come into their houses, or near them, at least not so near them as to be within the reach of their breath or of any smell from them; and when they were obliged to converse at a distance with strangers, they would always have preservatives in their mouths and about their clothes to repel and keep off the infection.

It must be acknowledged that when people began to use these cautions they were less exposed to danger, and the infection did not break into such houses so furiously as it did into others before; and thousands of families were preserved, speaking with due reserve to the direction of Divine Providence, by that means.

But it was impossible to beat anything into the heads of the poor. They went on with the usual impetuosity of their tempers, full of outcries and lamentations when taken, but madly careless of themselves, foolhardy and obstinate, while they were well. Where they could get employment they pushed into any kind of business, the most dangerous and the most liable to infection; and if they were spoken to, their answer would be, "I must trust to God for that; if I am taken, then I am provided for, and there is an end of me," and the like. Or thus, "Why, what must I do? I can't starve. I had as good have the plague as perish for want. I have no work; what could I do? I must do this or beg." Suppose it was burying the dead, or attending the sick, or watching infected houses, which were all terrible hazards; but their tale was generally the same. It is true, necessity was a very justifiable, warrantable plea, and nothing could be better; but their way of talk was much the same where the necessities were not the same. This adventurous conduct of the poor was that which brought the plague among them in a most furious manner, and this, joined to the distress of their circumstances when taken, was the reason why they died so by heaps; for I cannot say I could observe one jot of better husbandry among them, I mean the labouring poor, while they were all well and getting money than there was before, but as lavish, as extravagant, and as thoughtless for to-morrow as ever; so that when they came to be taken sick they were immediately in the utmost distress, as well for want as for sickness, as well for lack of food as lack of health.

This misery of the poor I had many occasions to be an eye-witness of, and sometimes also of the charitable assistance that some pious people daily gave to such, sending them relief and supplies both of food, physic, and other help, as they found they wanted; and indeed it is a debt of justice due to the temper of the people of that day to take notice here, that not only great sums, very great sums of money were charitably sent to the Lord Mayor and aldermen for the assistance and support of the poor distempered people, but abundance of private people daily distributed large sums of money for their relief, and sent people about to inquire into the condition of particular distressed and visited families, and relieved them; nay, some pious ladies were so transported with zeal in so good a work, and so confident in the protection of Providence in discharge of the great duty of charity, that they went about in person distributing alms to the poor, and even visiting poor families, though sick and infected, in their very houses, appointing nurses to attend those that wanted attending, and ordering apothecaries and surgeons, the first to supply them with drugs or plaisters, and such things as they wanted; and the last to lance and dress the swellings and tumours, where such were wanting; giving their blessing to the poor in substantial relief to them, as well as hearty prayers for them.

I will not understake to say, as some do, that none of those charitable people were suffered to fall under the calamity itself; but this I may say, that I never knew any one of them that miscarried, which I mention for the encouragement of others in case of the like distress; and doubtless, if they that give to the poor lend to the Lord, and He will repay them, those that hazard their lives to give to the poor, and to comfort and assist the poor in such a misery as this, may hope to be protected in the work.

Nor was this charity so extraordinary eminent only in a few, but (for I cannot lightly quit this point) the charity of the rich, as well in the city and suburbs as from the country, was so great that, in a word, a prodigious number of people who must otherwise inevitably have perished for want as well as sickness were supported and subsisted by it; and though I could never, nor I believe any one else, come to a full knowledge of what was so contributed, yet I do believe that, as I heard one say that was a critical observer of that part, there was not only many thousand pounds contributed, but many hundred thousand pounds, to the relief of the poor of this distressed, afflicted city; nay, one man affirmed to me that he could reckon up above one hundred thousand pounds a week, which was distributed by the church wardens at the several parish vestries by the Lord Mayor and aldermen in the several wards and precincts, and by the particular direction of the court and of the justices respectively in the parts where they resided, over and above the private charity distributed by pious hands in the manner I speak of; and this continued for many weeks together.

I confess this is a very great sum; but if it be true that there was distributed in the parish of Cripplegate only, £17,800 in one week to the relief of the poor, as I heard reported, and which I really believe was true, the other may not be improbable.

It was doubtless to be reckoned among the many signal good providences which attended this great city, and of which there were many other worth recording,—I say, this was a very remarkable one, that it pleased God thus to move the hearts of the people in all parts of the kingdom so cheerfully to contribute to the relief and support of the poor at London, the good consequences of which were felt many ways, and particularly in preserving the lives and recovering the health of so many thousands, and keeping so many thousands of families from perishing and starving.

And now I am talking of the merciful disposition of Providence in this time of calamity, I cannot but mention again, though I have spoken several times of it already on other accounts, I mean that of the progression of the distemper; how it began at one end of the town, and proceeded gradually and slowly from one part to another, and like a dark cloud that passes over our heads, which, as it thickens and overcasts the air at one end, clears up at the other end; so, while the plague went on raging from west to east, as it went forwards east, it abated in the west, by which means those parts of the town which were not seized, or who were left, and where it had spent its fury, were (as it were) spared to help and assist the other; whereas, had the distemper spread itself over the whole city and suburbs at once, raging in all places alike, as it has done since in some places abroad, the whole body of the people must have been overwhelmed, and there would have died twenty thousand a day, as they say there did at Naples; nor would the people have been able to have helped or assisted one another.

For it must be observed that where the plague was in its full force, there indeed the people were very miserable, and the consternation was inexpressible. But a little before it reached even to that place, or presently after it was gone, they were quite another sort of people; and I cannot but acknowledge that there was too much of that common temper of mankind to be found among us all at that time, namely, to forget the deliverance when the danger is past. But I shall come to speak of that part again.

It must not be forgot here to take some notice of the state of trade during the time of this common calamity, and this with respect to foreign trade, as also to our home trade.

As to foreign trade, there needs little to be said. The trading nations of Europe were all afraid of us; no port of France, or Holland, or Spain, or Italy would admit our ships or correspond with us; indeed we stood on ill terms with the Dutch, and were in a furious war with them, but though in a bad condition to fight abroad, who had such dreadful enemies to struggle with at home.

Our merchants were accordingly at a full stop; their ships could go nowhere, that is to say, to no place abroad; their manufactures and merchandise, that is to say, of our growth, would not be touched abroad. They were as much afraid of our goods as they were of our people; and indeed they had reason, for our woollen manufactures are as retentive of infection as human bodies, and if packed up by persons infected, would receive the infection, and be as dangerous to touch as a man would be that was infected; and therefore, when any English vessel arrived in foreign countries, if they did take the goods on shore, they always caused the bales to be opened and aired in places appointed for that purpose. But from London they would not suffer them to come into port, much less to unlade their goods, upon any terms whatever; and this strictness was especially used with them in Spain and Italy. In Turkey, and the islands of the Arches indeed, as they are called, as well those belonging to the Turks as to the Venetians, they were not so very rigid. In the first there was no obstruction at all; and four ships which were then in the river loading for Italy, that is, for Leghorn and Naples, being denied product, as they call it, went on to Turkey, and were freely admitted to unlade their cargo without any difficulty, only that when they arrived there, some of their cargo was not fit for sale in that country, and other parts of it being consigned to merchants at Leghorn, the captains of the ships had no right nor any orders to dispose of the goods; so that great inconveniences followed to the merchants. But this was nothing but what the necessity of affairs required, and the merchants at Leghorn and Naples having notice given them, sent again from thence to take care of the effects, which were particularly consigned to those ports, and to bring back in other ships such as were improper for the markets at Smyrna and Scanderoon.

The inconveniences in Spain and Portugal were still greater, for they would by no means suffer our ships, especially those from London, to come into any of their ports, much less to unlade. There was a report that one of our ships having by stealth delivered her cargo, among which was some bales of English cloth, cotton, kerseys, and such-like goods, the Spaniards caused all the goods to be burned, and punished the men with death who were concerned in carrying them on shore. This, I believe, was in part true, though I do not affirm it; but it is not at all unlikely, seeing the danger was really very great, the infection being so violent in London.

I heard, likewise, that the plague was carried into those countries by some of our ships, and particularly to the port of Faro, in the kingdom of Algarve, belonging to the King of Portugal, and that several persons died of it there, but it was not confirmed.

On the other hand, though the Spaniards and Portuguese were so shy of us, it is most certain that the plague, as has been said, keeping at first much at that end of the town next Westminster, the merchandising part of the town, such as the city and the water-side, was perfectly sound till at least the beginning of July, and the ships in the river till the beginning of August; for to the 1st of July there had died but seven within the whole city, and but sixty within the liberties, but one in all the parishes of Stepney, Aldgate, and Whitechapel, and but two in all the eight parishes of Southwark. But it was the same thing abroad, for the bad news was gone over the whole world that the city of London was infected with the plague, and there was no inquiring there how the infection proceeded, or at which part of the town it was begun or was reached to.

Besides, after it began to spread it increased so fast, and the bills grew so high all on a sudden, that it was to no purpose to lessen the report of it, or endeavour to make the people abroad think it better than it was; the account which the weekly bills gave in was sufficient; and that there died two thousand to three or four thousand a week was sufficient to alarm the whole trading part of the world, and the following time being so dreadful also in the very city itself put the whole world, I say, upon their guard against it.

You may be sure, also, that the report of these things lost nothing in the carriage. The plague was itself very terrible, and the distress of the people very great, as you may observe of what I have said. But the rumour was infinitely greater, and it must not be wondered that our friends abroad, as my brother's correspondents in particular were told there, namely, in Portugal and Italy, where he chiefly traded, [said] that in London there died twenty thousand in a week; that the dead bodies lay unburied by heaps; that the living were not sufficient to bury the dead or the sound to look after the sick; that all the kingdom was infected likewise, so that it was an universal malady, such as was never heard of in those parts of the world; and they could hardly believe us when we gave them an account how things really were, and how there was not above one-tenth part of the people dead; that there was 500,000 left that lived all the time in the town; that now the people began to walk the streets again, and those who were fled to return, there was no miss of the usual throng of people in the streets, except as every family might miss their relations and neighbours, and the like. I say they could not believe these things; and if inquiry were now to be made in Naples, or in other cities on the coast of Italy, they would tell you that there was a dreadful infection in London so many years ago, in which, as above, there died twenty thousand in a week, &c., just as we have had it reported in London that there was a plague in the city of Naples in the year 1656, in which there died 20,000 people in a day, of which I have had very good satisfaction that it was utterly false.

But these extravagant reports were very prejudicial to

our trade, as well as unjust and injurious in themselves, for it was a long time after the plague was quite over before our trade could recover itself in those parts of the world; and the Flemings and Dutch, but especially the last, made very great advantages of it, having all the market to themselves, and even buying our manufactures in several parts of England where the plague was not, and carrying them to Holland and Flanders, and from thence transporting them to Spain and to Italy, as if they had been of their own making.

But they were detected sometimes and punished, that is to say, their goods confiscated, and ships also; for if it was true that our manufactures as well as our people were infected, and that it was dangerous to touch or to open and receive the smell of them, then those people ran the hazard by that clandestine trade, not only of carrying the contagion into their own country, but also of infecting the nations to whom they traded with those goods, which, considering how many lives might be lost in consequence of such an action, must be a trade that no men of conscience could suffer themselves to be concerned in.

I do not take upon me to say that any harm was done, I mean of that kind, by those people. But I doubt I need not make any such proviso in the case of our own country; for either by our people of London, or by the commerce which made their conversing with all sorts of people in every county and of every considerable town necessary, I say, by this means the plague was first or last spread all over the kingdom, as well in London as in all the cities and great towns, especially in the trading manufacturing towns and seaports; so that, first or last, all the considerable places in England were visited more or less, and the kingdom of Ireland in some places, but not so universally. How it fared with the people in Scotland I had no opportunity to inquire.

It is to be observed that while the plague continued so violent in London, the outports, as they are called, enjoyed a very great trade, especially to the adjacent countries and to our own plantations. For example, the towns of Colchester, Yarmouth, and Hull, on that side of England, exported to Holland and Hamburg the manufactures of the adjacent counties for several months after the trade with London was, as it were, entirely shut up; likewise the cities of Bristol and Exeter, with the port of Plymouth, had the like advantage to Spain, to the Canaries, to Guinea, and to the West Indies, and particularly to Ireland; but as the plague spread itself every way after it had been in London to such a degree as it was in August and September, so all, or most of those cities and towns, were infected first or last, and then trade was, as it were, under a general embargo, or at a full stop, as I shall observe further when I speak of our home trade.

One thing, however, must be observed, that as to ships coming in from abroad, as many you may be sure did, some who were out in all parts of the world a considerable while before, and some who when they went out knew nothing of an infection, or at least of one so terrible; these came up the river boldly, and delivered their cargoes as they were obliged to do, except just in the two months of August and September, when the weight of the infection lying, as I may say, all below Bridge, nobody durst appear in business for a while. But as this continued but for a few weeks, the homeward-bound ships, especially such whose cargoes were not liable to spoil, came to an anchor for a time, short of the Pool,[1] or freshwater part of the river, even as low as the river Medway, where several of them ran in, and others lay at the Nore, and in the Hope below Gravesend. So that by

---

[1] *That part of the river where the ships lie up when they come home is called the Pool, and takes in all the river on both sides of the water, from the Tower to Cuckold's Point and Limehouse.*

the latter end of October there was a very great fleet of homeward-bound ships to come up, such as the like had not been known for many years.

Two particular trades were carried on by water-carriage all the while of the infection, and that with little or no interruption, very much to the advantage and comfort of the poor distressed people of the city, and those were the coasting trade for corn and the Newcastle trade for coals.

The first of these was particularly carried on by small vessels from the port of Hull and other places on the Humber, by which great quantities of corn were brought in from Yorkshire and Lincolnshire. The other part of this corn-trade was from Lynn, in Norfolk, from Wells and Burnham, and from Yarmouth, all in the same county; and the third branch was from the river Medway, and from Milton, Feversham, Margate, and Sandwich, and all the other little places and ports round the coast of Kent and Essex.

There was also a very good trade from the coast of Suffolk with corn, butter, and cheese; these vessels kept a constant course of trade, and without interruption came up to that market known still by the name of Bear Key, where they supplied the city plentifully with corn when land-carriage began to fail, and when the people began to be sick of coming from many places in the country.

This also was, much of it, owing to the prudence and conduct of the Lord Mayor, who took such care to keep the masters and seamen from danger when they came up, causing their corn to be bought off at any time they wanted a market (which, however, was very seldom), and causing the corn-factors immediately to unlade and deliver the vessels loaden with corn, that they had very little occasion to come out of their ships or vessels, the money being always carried on board to them, and put into a pail of vinegar before it was carried.

The second trade was that of coals from Newcastle-upon-Tyne, without which the city would have been greatly distressed; for not in the streets only, but in private houses and families, great quantities of coals were then burnt, even all the summer long, and when the weather was hottest, which was done by the advice of the physicians. Some indeed opposed it, and insisted that to keep the houses and rooms hot was a means to propagate the distemper, which was a fermentation and heat already in the blood; that it was known to spread and increase in hot weather, and abate in cold; and therefore they alleged that all contagious distempers are the worse for heat, because the contagion was nourished and gained strength in hot weather, and was, as it were, propagated in heat.

Others said they granted that heat in the climate might propagate infection, as sultry, hot weather fills the air with vermin and nourishes innumerable numbers and kinds of venomous creatures, which breed in our food, in the plants, and even in our bodies, by the very stench of which infection may be propagated; also, that heat in the air, or heat of weather, as we ordinarily call it, makes bodies relax and faint, exhausts the spirits, opens the pores, and makes us more apt to receive infection, or any evil influence, be it from noxious pestilential vapours, or any other thing in the air; but that the heat of fire, and especially of coal fires kept in our houses, or near us, had a quite different operation, the heat being not of the same kind, but quick and fierce, tending not to nourish but to consume and dissipate all those noxious fumes which the other kind of heat rather exhaled and stagnated than separated and burnt up. Besides, it was alleged that the sulphurous and nitrous particles that are often found to be in the coal, with that bituminous substance which burns, are all assisting to clear and purge the air, and render it wholesome and safe to breathe in, after the noxious particles, as above, are dispersed and burnt up.

The latter opinion prevailed at that time, and, as I must confess, I think with good reason, and the experience of the citizens confirmed it, many houses which had constant fires kept in the rooms having never been infected at all; and I must join my experience to it, for I found the keeping good fires kept our rooms sweet and wholesome, and I do verily believe made our whole family so, more than would otherwise have been.

But I return to the coals as a trade. It was with no little difficulty that this trade was kept open, and particularly because, as we were in an open war with the Dutch at that time, the Dutch capers at first took a great many of our collier-ships, which made the rest cautious, and made them to stay to come in fleets together. But after some time the capers were either afraid to take them, or their masters, the States, were afraid they should, and forbade them, lest the plague should be among them, which made them fare the better.

For the security of these northern traders, the coal-ships were ordered by my Lord Mayor not to come up into the Pool above a certain number at a time, and ordered lighters and other vessels, such as the wood-mongers, that is, the wharf-keepers or coal-sellers, furnished, to go down and take out the coals as low as Deptford and Greenwich, and some farther down.

Others delivered great quantities of coals in particular places, where the ships could come to the shore, as at Greenwich, Blackwall, and other places, in vast heaps, as if to be kept for sale, but were then fetched away, after the ships which brought them were gone, so that the seamen had no communication with the river-men, nor so much as came near one another.

Yet all this caution could not effectually prevent the distemper getting among the colliery, that is to say, among the ships, by which a great many seamen died of it; and that which was still worse was, that they carried it down to Ipswich and Yarmouth, to Newcastle-upon-Tyne, and other places on the coast, where, especially at Newcastle and at Sunderland, it carried off a great number of people.

The making so many fires, as above, did indeed consume an unusual quantity of coals; and that upon one or two stops of the ships coming up, whether by contrary weather or by the interruption of enemies I do not remember, but the price of coals was exceeding dear, even as high as £4 a chalder; but it soon abated when the ships came in, and as afterwards they had a freer passage, the price was very reasonable all the rest of that year.

The public fires which were made on these occasions, as I have calculated it, must necessarily have cost the city about 200 chalders of coals a week, if they had continued, which was indeed a very great quantity; but as it was thought necessary, nothing was spared. However, as some of the physicians cried them down, they were not kept alight above four or five days. The fires were ordered thus:—

One at the Custom House, one at Billingsgate, one at Queenhithe, and one at the Three Cranes; one in Blackfriars, and one at the gate of Bridewell; one at the corner of Leadenhall Street and Gracechurch; one at the north and one at the south gate of the Royal Exchange; one at Guild Hall, and one at Blackwell Hall gate; one at the Lord Mayor's door in St. Helen's, one at the west entrance into St. Paul's, and one at the entrance into Bow Church. I do not remember whether there was any at the city gates, but one at the Bridge-foot there was, just by St. Magnus Church.

I know some have quarrelled since that at the experiment, and said that there died the more people because of those fires; but I am persuaded those that say so offer no evidence to prove it, neither can I believe it on any account whatever.

It remains to give some account of the state of trade at home in England during this dreadful time, and particularly as it relates to the manufactures and the trade in the city. At the first breaking out of the infection there was, as it is easy to suppose, a very great fright among the people, and consequently a general stop of trade, except in provisions and necessaries of life; and even in those things, as there was a vast number of people fled and a very great number always sick, besides the number which died, so there could not be above two-thirds, if above one-half, of the consumption of provisions in the city as used to be.

It pleased God to send a very plentiful year of corn and fruit, but not of hay or grass, by which means bread was cheap, by reason of the plenty of corn. Flesh was cheap, by reason of the scarcity of grass; but butter and cheese were dear, for the same reason, and hay in the market just beyond Whitechapel Bars was sold at £4 per load. But that affected not the poor. There was a most excessive plenty of all sorts of fruit, such as apples, pears, plums, cherries, grapes, and they were the cheaper because of the want of people; but this made the poor eat them to excess, and this brought them into fluxes, griping of the guts, surfeits, and the like, which often precipitated them into the plague.

But to come to matters of trade. First, foreign exportation being stopped or at least very much interrupted and rendered difficult, a general stop of all those manufactures followed of course which were usually brought for exportation; and though sometimes merchants abroad were importunate for goods, yet little was sent, the passages being so generally stopped that the English ships would not be admitted, as is said already, into their port.

This put a stop to the manufactures that were for exportation in most parts of England, except in some outports; and even that was soon stopped, for they all had the plague in their turn. But though this was felt all over England, yet, what was still worse, all intercourse of trade for home consumption of manufactures, especially those which usually circulated through the Londoners' hands, was stopped at once, the trade of the city being stopped.

All kinds of handicrafts in the city, &c., tradesmen and mechanics, were, as I have said before, out of employ, and this occasioned the putting off and dismissing an innumerable number of journeymen and workmen of all sorts, seeing nothing was done relating to such trades but what might be said to be absolutely necessary.

This caused the multitude of single people in London to be unprovided for, as also of families whose living depended upon the labour of the heads of those families; I say, this reduced them to extreme misery; and I must confess it is for the honour of the city of London, and will be for many ages, as long as this is to be spoken of, that they were able to supply with charitable provision the wants of so many thousands of those as afterwards fell sick and were distressed, so that it may be safely averred that nobody perished for want, at least that the magistrates had any notice given them of.

This stagnation of our manufacturing trade in the country would have put the people there to much greater difficulties, but that the master-workmen, clothiers and others, to the uttermost of their stocks and strength, kept on making their goods to keep the poor at work, believing that as soon as the sickness should abate they would have a quick demand in proportion to the decay of their trade at that time. But as none but those masters that were rich could do thus, and that many were poor and not able, the manufacturing trade in England suffered greatly, and the poor were pinched all over England by the calamity of the city of London only.

It is true that the next year made them full amends by another terrible calamity upon the city; so that the city by one calamity impoverished and weakened the country, and by another calamity, even terrible too of its kind, enriched the country and made them again amends; for an infinite quantity of household stuff, wearing apparel, and other things, besides whole warehouses filled with merchandise and manufactures, such as come from all parts of England, were consumed in the fire of London the next year after this terrible visitation. It is incredible what a trade this made all over the whole kingdom, to make good the want and to supply that loss; so that, in short, all the manufacturing hands in the nation were set on work, and were little enough for several years to supply the market and answer the demands. All foreign markets also were empty of our goods by the stop which had been occasioned by the plague, and before an open trade was allowed again; and the prodigious demand at home falling in, joined to make a quick vent for all sorts of goods; so that there never was known such a trade all over England for the time as was in the first seven years after the plague, and after the fire of London.

It remains now that I should say something of the merciful part of this terrible judgment. The last week in September, the plague being come to its crisis, its fury began to assuage. I remember my friend Dr. Heath, coming to see me the week before, told me he was sure that the violence of it would assuage in a few days; but when I saw the weekly bill of that week, which was the highest of the whole year, being 8297 of all diseases, I upbraided him with it, and asked him what he had made his judgment from. His answer, however, was not so much to seek as I thought it would have been. "Look you," says he, "by the number which are at this time sick and infected, there should have been twenty thousand dead the last week instead of eight thousand, if the inveterate mortal contagion had been as it was two weeks ago; for then it ordinarily killed in two or three days, now not under eight or ten; and then not above one in five recovered, whereas I have observed that now not above two in five miscarry. And, observe it from me, the next bill will decrease, and you will see many more people recover than used to do; for though a vast multitude are now everywhere infected, and as many every day fall sick, yet there will not so many die as there did, for the malignity of the distemper is abated;" adding that he began now to hope, nay, more than hope, that the infection had passed its crisis and was going off; and accordingly so it was, for the next week being, as I said, the last in September, the bill decreased almost two thousand.

It is true the plague was still at a frightful height, and the next bill was no less than 6460, and the next to that, 5720; but still my friend's observation was just, and it did appear the people did recover faster and more in number than they used to do; and indeed, if it had not been so, what had been the condition of the city of London? For, according to my friend, there were not fewer than 60,000 people at that time infected, whereof, as above, 20,477 died, and near 40,000 recovered; whereas, had it been as it was before, 50,000 of that number would very probably have died, if not more, and 50,000 more would have sickened; for, in a word, the whole mass of people began to sicken, and it looked as if none would escape.

But this remark of my friend's appeared more evident in a few weeks more, for the decrease went on, and another week in October it decreased 1843, so that the number dead of the plague was but 2665; and the next week, it decreased 1413 more, and yet it was seen plainly that there was abundance of people sick, nay, abundance more than ordinary, and abundance fell sick every day, but (as above) the malignity of the disease abated.

Such is the precipitant disposition of our people (whether it is so or not all over the world, that's none of my particular business to inquire), but I saw it apparently here, that as upon the first fright of the infection, they shunned one another, and fled from one another's houses and from the city with an unaccountable and, as I thought, unnecessary fright, so now, upon this notion spreading, viz., that the distemper was not so catching as formerly, and that if it was catched it was not so mortal, and seeing abundance of people who really fell sick recover again daily, they took to such a precipitant courage, and grew so entirely regardless of themselves and of the infection, that they made no more of the plague than of an ordinary fever, nor indeed so much. They not only went boldly into company with those who had tumours and carbuncles upon them that were running, and consequently contagious, but ate and drank with them, nay, into their houses to visit them, and even, as I was told, into their very chambers where they lay sick.

This I could not see rational. My friend Dr. Heath allowed, and it was plain to experience, that the distemper was as catching as ever, and as many fell sick, but only he alleged that so many of those that fell sick did not die; but I think that while many did die, and that at best the distemper itself was very terrible, the sores and swellings very tormenting, and the danger of death not left out of the circumstance of sickness, though not so frequent as before; all those things, together with the exceeding tediousness of the cure, the loathsomeness of the disease, and many other articles, were enough to de-ter any man living from a dangerous mixture with the sick people, and make them as anxious almost to avoid the infection as before.

Nay, there was another thing which made the mere catching of the distemper frightful, and that was the terrible burning of the caustics which the surgeons laid on the swellings to bring them to break and to run, without which the danger of death was very great, even to the last. Also, the insufferable torment of the swellings, which, though it might not make people raving and distracted, as they were before, and as I have given several instances of already, yet they put the patient to inexpressible torment; and those that fell into it, though they did escape with life, yet they made bitter complaints of those that had told them there was no danger, and sadly repented their rashness and folly in venturing to run into the reach of it.

Nor did this unwary conduct of the people end here, for a great many that thus cast off their cautions suffered more deeply still, and though many escaped, yet many died; and at least it had this public mischief attending it, that it made the decrease of burials slower than it would otherwise have been. For as this notion ran like lightning through the city, and people's heads were possessed with it, even as soon as the first great decrease in the bills appeared, we found that the two next bills did not decrease in proportion; the reason I take to be the people's running so rashly into danger, giving up all their former cautions and care, and all the shyness which they used to practise, depending that the sickness would not reach them, or that if it did, they should not die.

The physicians opposed this thoughtless humour of the people with all their might, and gave out printed directions, spreading them all over the city and suburbs, advising the people to continue reserved, and to use still the utmost caution in their ordinary conduct, notwith-standing the decrease of the distemper, terrifying them with the danger of bringing a relapse upon the whole city, and telling them how such a relapse might be more fatal and dangerous than the whole visitation that had been already; with many arguments and reasons to ex-plain and prove that part to them, and which are too long to repeat here.

But it was all to no purpose; the audacious creatures were so possessed with the first joy and so surprised with the satisfaction of seeing a vast decrease in the weekly bills, that they were impenetrable by any new terrors, and would not be persuaded but that the bitterness of death was past; and it was to no more purpose to talk to them than to an east wind; but they opened shops, went about streets, did business, and conversed with anybody that came in their way to converse with, whether with business or without, neither inquiring of their health or so much as being apprehensive of any danger from them, though they knew them not to be sound.

This imprudent, rash conduct cost a great many their lives who had with great care and caution shut them-selves up and kept retired, as it were, from all mankind, and had by that means, under God's providence, been preserved through all the heat of that infection.

This rash and foolish conduct, I say, of the people went so far that the ministers took notice to them of it at last, and laid before them both the folly and danger of it; and this checked it a little, so that they grew more cautious. But it had another effect, which they could not check; for as the first rumour had spread not over the city only, but into the country, it had the like effect, and the people were so tired with being so long from London, and so eager to come back, that they flocked to town without fear or forecast, and began to show themselves in the streets, as if all the danger was over. It was indeed surprising to see it, for though there died still from 1000 to 1800 a week, yet the people flocked to town as if all had been well.

The consequence of this was, that the bills increased again 400 the very first week in November; and if I might believe the physicians, there was above 3000 fell sick that week, most of them newcomers, too.

One John Cock, a barber in St. Martin's-le-Grand, was an eminent example of this; I mean of the hasty return of the people when the plague was abated. This John Cock had left the town with his whole family, and locked up his house, and was gone in the country, as many others did; and finding the plague so decreased in November that there died but 905 per week of all diseases, he ventured home again. He had in his family ten persons; that is to say, himself and wife, five children, two apprentices, and a maid-servant. He had not been returned to his house above a week, and began to open his shop and carry on his trade, but the distemper broke out in his family, and within about five days they all died, except one; that is to say, himself, his wife, all his five children, and his two apprentices; and only the maid remained alive.

But the mercy of God was greater to the rest than we had reason to expect; for the malignity, as I have said, of the distemper was spent, the contagion was exhausted, and also the winter weather came on apace, and the air was clear and cold, with some sharp frosts; and this increasing still, most of those that had fallen sick recovered, and the health of the city began to return. There were indeed some returns of the distemper even in the month of December, and the bills increased near a hundred; but it went off again, and so in a short while things began to return to their own channel. And wonderful it was to see how populous the city was again all on a sudden, so that a stranger could not miss the numbers that were lost. Neither was there any miss of the inhabitants as to their dwellings, few or no empty houses were to be seen, or if there were some, there was no want of tenants for them.

I wish I could say that as the city had a new face, so the manners of the people had a new appearance. I doubt not but there were many that retained a sincere sense of their deliverance, and that were heartily thankful to that Sovereign Hand that had protected them in so dangerous a time; it would be very uncharitable to judge otherwise in a city so populous, and where the people were so devout as they were here in the time of the visitation itself; but except what of this was to be found in particular families and faces, it must be acknowledged that the general practice of the people was just as it was before, and very little difference was to be seen.

Some, indeed, said things were worse; that the morals of the people declined from this very time; that the people, hardened by the danger they had been in, like seamen after a storm is over, were more wicked and more stupid, more bold and hardened, in their vices and immoralities than they were before; but I will not carry it so far neither. It would take up a history of no small length to give a particular of all the gradations by which the course of things in this city came to be restored again, and to run in their own channel as they did before.

Some parts of England were now infected as violently as London had been; the cities of Norwich, Peterborough, Lincoln, Colchester, and other places were now visited; and the magistrates of London began to set rules for our conduct as to corresponding with those cities. It is true we could not pretend to forbid their people coming to London, because it was impossible to know them asunder, so, after many consultations, the Lord Mayor and

Court of Aldermen were obliged to drop it. All they could do was to warn and caution the people not to entertain in their houses or converse with any people who they knew came from such infected places.

But they might as well have talked to the air, for the people of London thought themselves so plague-free now that they were past all admonitions; they seemed to depend upon it that the air was restored, and that the air was like a man that had had the small-pox, not capable of being infected again. This revived that notion that the infection was all in the air, that there was no such thing as contagion from the sick people to the sound; and so strongly did this whimsy prevail among people that they ran all together promiscuously, sick and well. Not the Mahometans, who, prepossessed with the principle of predestination, value nothing of contagion, let it be in what it will, could be more obstinate than the people of London; they that were perfectly sound, and came out of the wholesome air, as we call it, into the city, made nothing of going into the same houses and chambers, nay, even into the same beds, with those that had the distemper upon them, and were not recovered.

Some, indeed, paid for their audacious boldness with the price of their lives; an infinite number fell sick, and the physicians had more work than ever, only with this difference, that more of their patients recovered; that is to say, they generally recovered, but certainly there were more people infected and fell sick now, when there did not die above a thousand or twelve hundred in a week, than there was when there died five or six thousand a week, so entirely negligent were the people at that time in the great and dangerous case of health and infection, and so ill were they able to take or accept of the advice of those who cautioned them for their good.

The people being thus returned, as it were, in general,

it was very strange to find, that in their inquiring after their friends, some whole families were so entirely swept away that there was no remembrance of them left, neither was anybody to be found to possess or show any title to that little they had left; for in such cases what was to be found was generally embezzled and purloined, some gone one way, some another.

It was said such abandoned effects came to the king, as the universal heir, upon which we are told, and I suppose it was in part true, that the king granted all such, as deodands, to the Lord Mayor and Court of Aldermen of London, to be applied to the use of the poor, of whom there were very many. For it is to be observed, that though the occasions of relief and the objects of distress were very many more in the time of the violence of the plague than now after all was over, yet the distress of the poor was more now a great deal than it was then, because all the sluices of general charity were now shut. People supposed the main occasion to be over, and so stopped their hands; whereas particular objects were still very moving, and the distress of those that were poor was very great indeed.

Though the health of the city was now very much restored, yet foreign trade did not begin to stir, neither would foreigners admit our ships into their ports for a great while. As for the Dutch, the misunderstandings between our court and them had broken out into a war the year before, so that our trade that way was wholly interrupted; but Spain and Portugal, Italy and Barbary, as also Hamburg and all the ports in the Baltic, these were all shy of us a great while, and would not restore trade with us for many months.

The distemper sweeping away such multitudes, as I have observed, many if not all the out-parishes were obliged to make new burying-grounds, besides that I have mentioned in Bunhill Fields, some of which were continued, and remain in use to this day. But others were left off, and which, I confess, I mention with some reflection, being converted into other uses or built upon afterwards, the dead bodies were disturbed, abused, dug up again, some even before the flesh of them was perished from the bones, and removed like dung or rubbish to other places. Some of those which came within the reach of my observation are as follow:

1. A piece of ground beyond Goswell Street, near Mount Mill, being some of the remains of the old lines or fortifications of the city, where abundance were buried promiscuously from the parishes of Aldersgate, Clerkenwell, and even out of the city. This ground, as I take it, was since made a physic garden, and after that has been built upon.

2. A piece of ground just over the Black Ditch, as it was then called, at the end of Holloway Lane, in Shoreditch parish. It has been since made a yard for keeping hogs, and for other ordinary uses, but is quite out of use as a burying-ground.

3. The upper end of Hand Alley, in Bishopsgate Street, which was then a green field, and was taken in particularly for Bishopsgate parish, though many of the carts out of the city brought their dead thither also, particularly out of the parish of St. Allhallows on the Wall. This place I cannot mention without much regret. It was, as I remember, about two or three years after the plague was ceased that Sir Robert Clayton came to be possesed of the ground. It was reported, how true I know not, that it fell to the king for want of heirs, all those who had any right to it being carried off by the pestilence, and that Sir Robert Clayton obtained a grant of it from King Charles II. But however he came by it, certain it is the ground was let out to build on, or built upon, by his

order. The first house built upon it was a large fair house, still standing, which faces the street or way now called Hand Alley, which, though called an alley, is as wide as a street. The houses in the same row with that house northward are built on the very same ground where the poor people were buried, and the bodies, on opening the ground for the foundations, were dug up, some of them remaining so plain to be seen that the women's skulls were distinguished by their long hair, and of others the flesh was not quite perished; so that the people began to exclaim loudly against it, and some suggested that it might endanger a return of the contagion; after which the bones and bodies, as fast as they came at them, were carried to another part of the same ground and thrown all together into a deep pit, dug on purpose, which now is to be known in that it is not built on, but is a passage to another house at the upper end of Rose Alley, just against the door of a meeting-house, which has been built there many years since; and the ground is palisadoed off from the rest of the passage, in a little square; there lies the bones and remains of near two thousand bodies, carried by the dead carts to their grave in tha· one year.

4. Besides this, there was a piece of ground in Moorfields, by the going into the street which is now called Old Bethlem, which was enlarged much, though not wholly taken in on the same occasion.

[*N. B.*—The author of this journal lies buried in that very ground, being at his own desire, his sister having been buried there a few years before.]

5. Stepney parish, extending itself from the east part of London to the north, even to the very edge of Shoreditch Churchyard, had a piece of ground taken in to bury their dead close to the said churchyard, and which for that very reason was left open, and is since, I suppose, taken

into the same churchyard. And they had also two other burying-places in Spitalfields, one where since a chapel or tabernacle has been built for ease to this great parish, and another in Petticoat Lane.

There were no less than five other grounds made use of for the parish of Stepney at that time, one where now stands the parish church of St. Paul, Shadwell, and the other where now stands the parish church of St. John's at Wapping, both which had not the names of parishes at that time, but were belonging to Stepney parish.

I could name many more, but these coming within my particular knowledge, the circumstance, I thought, made it of use to record them. From the whole, it may be observed that they were obliged in this time of distress to take in new burying-grounds in most of the out-parishes for laying the prodigious numbers of people which died in so short a space of time; but why care was not taken to keep those places separate from ordinary uses, that so the bodies might rest undisturbed, that I cannot answer for, and must confess I think it was wrong. Who were to blame I know not.

I should have mentioned that the Quakers had at that time also a burying-ground set apart to their use, and which they still make use of; and they had also a particular dead-cart to fetch their dead from their houses; and the famous Solomon Eagle, who, as I mentioned before, had predicted the plague as a judgment, and ran naked through the streets, telling the people that it was come upon them to punish them for their sins, had his own wife died the very next day of the plague, and was carried, one of the first in the Quakers' dead-cart, to their new burying-ground.

I might have thronged this account with many more remarkable things which occurred in the time of the infection, and particularly what passed between the Lord

Mayor and the Court, which was then at Oxford, and what directions were from time to time received from the Government for their conduct on this critical occasion. But really the Court concerned themselves so little, and that little they did was of so small import, that I do not see it of much moment to mention any part of it here, except that of appointing a monthly fast in the city and the sending the royal charity to the relief of the poor, both which I have mentioned before.

Great was the reproach thrown on those physicians who left their patients during the sickness, and now they came to town again nobody cared to employ them. They were called deserters, and frequently bills were set up upon their doors and written, "Here is a doctor to be let," so that several of those physicians were fain for a while to sit still and look about them, or at least remove their dwellings, and set up in new places and among new acquaintance. The like was the case with the clergy, whom the people were indeed very abusive to, writing verses and scandalous reflections upon them, setting upon the church-door, "Here is a pulpit to be let," or sometimes, "to be sold," which was worse.

It was not the least of our misfortunes, that with our infection, when it ceased, there did not cease the spirit of strife and contention, slander and reproach, which was really the great troubler of the nation's peace before. It was said to be the remains of the old animosities, which had so lately involved us all in blood and disorder. But as the late Act of Indemnity had laid asleep the quarrel itself, so the Government had recommended family and personal peace upon all occasions to the whole nation.

But it could not be obtained, and particularly after the ceasing of the plague in London, when any one that had seen the condition which the people had been in, and how they caressed one another at that time, promised to have more charity for the future, and to raise no more reproaches; I say, any one that had seen them then would have thought they would have come together with another spirit at last. But, I say, it could not be obtained. The quarrel remained; the Church and the Presbyterians were incompatible. As soon as the plague was removed, the Dissenting ousted ministers who had supplied the pulpits which were deserted by the incumbents retired; they could expect no other but that they should immediately fall upon them and harass them with their penal laws, accept their preaching while they were sick, and persecute them as soon as they were recovered again; this even we that were of the Church thought was very hard, and could by no means approve of it.

But it was the Government, and we could say nothing to hinder it; we could only say it was not our doing, and we could not answer for it.

On the other hand, the Dissenters reproaching those ministers of the Church with going away and deserting their charge, abandoning the people in their danger, and when they had most need of comfort, and the like, this we could by no means approve, for all men have not the same faith and the same courage, and the Scripture commands us to judge the most favourably and according to charity.

A plague is a formidable enemy, and is armed with terrors that every man is not sufficiently fortified to resist or prepared to stand the shock against. It is very certain that a great many of the clergy who were in circumstances to do it withdrew and fled for the safety of their lives; but 't is true also that a great many of them stayed, and many of them fell in the calamity and in the discharge of their duty.

It is true some of the Dissenting turned-out ministers stayed, and their courage is to be commended and highly valued, but these were not abundance; it cannot be said that they all stayed, and that none retired into the country, any more than it can be said of the Church clergy that they all went away. Neither did all those that went away go without substituting curates and others in their places, to do the offices needful and to visit the sick, as far as it was practicable; so that, upon the whole, an allowance of charity might have been made on both sides, and we should have considered that such a time as this of 1665 is not to be paralleled in history, and that it is not the stoutest courage that will always support men in such cases. I had not said this, but had rather chosen to record the courage and religious zeal of those of both sides, who did hazard themselves for the service of the poor people in their distress, without remembering that any failed in their duty on either side. But the want of temper among us has made the contrary to this necessary, some that stayed not only boasting too much of themselves, but reviling those that fled, branding them with cowardice, deserting their flocks, and acting the part of the hireling, and the like. I recommend it to the charity of all good people to look back and reflect duly upon the terrors of the time, and whoever does so will see that it is not an ordinary strength that could support it. It was not like appearing in the head of an army or charging a body of horse in the field, but it was charging Death itself on his pale horse; to stay was indeed to die, and it could be esteemed nothing less, especially as things appeared at the latter end of August and the beginning of September, and as there was reason to expect them at that time; for no man expected, and I dare say believed, that the distemper would take so sudden a turn as it did, and fall immediately 2000 in a week, when there was such a prodigious number of people sick at that time as it was known there was; and then it was that many shifted away that had stayed most of the time before.

Besides, if God gave strength to some more than to others, was it to boast of their ability to abide the stroke, and upbraid those that had not the same gift and support, or ought not they rather to have been humble and thankful if they were rendered more useful than their brethren?

I think it ought to be recorded to the honour of such men, as well clergy as physicians, surgeons, apothecaries, magistrates, and officers of every kind, as also all useful people who ventured their lives in discharge of their duty, as most certainly all such as stayed did to the last degree, and several of all these kinds did not only venture but lose their lives on that sad occasion.

I was once making a list of all such, I mean of all those professions and employments who thus died, as I call it, in the way of their duty; but it was impossible for a private man to come at a certainty in the particulars. I only remember that there died sixteen clergymen, two aldermen, five physicians, thirteen surgeons, within the city and liberties before the beginning of September. But this being, as I said before, the great crisis and extremity of the infection, it can be no complete list. As to inferior people, I think there died six-and-forty constables and head-boroughs in the two parishes of Stepney and White-chapel; but I could not carry my list on, for when the violent rage of the distemper in September came upon us, it drove us out of all measures. Men did then no more die by tale and by number. They might put out a weekly bill, and call them seven or eight thousand, or what they pleased; 't is certain they died by heaps, and were buried by heaps, that is to say, without account. And if I might believe some people, who were more abroad and more conversant with those things than I—though I was public enough for one that had no more business to do than I had,—I say, if I may believe them, there was not many less buried those first three weeks in September than 20,000 per week. However the others aver the truth of it, yet I rather choose to keep to the public account; seven and eight thousand per week is enough to make good all that I have said of the terror of those times; and it is much to the satisfaction of me that write, as well as those that read, to be able to say that everything is set down with moderation, and rather within compass than beyond it.

Upon all these accounts, I say, I could wish, when we were recovered, our conduct had been more distinguished for charity and kindness in remembrance of the past calamity, and not so much a valuing ourselves upon our boldness in staying, as if all men were cowards that fly from the hand of God, or that those who stay do not sometimes owe their courage to their ignorance and despising the hand of their Maker, which is a criminal kind of desperation, and not a true courage.

I cannot but leave it upon record that the civil officers, such as constables, head-boroughs, Lord Mayor's and sheriffs'-men, as also parish-officers, whose business it was to take charge of the poor, did their duties in general with as much courage as any, and perhaps with more, because their work was attended with more hazards, and lay more among the poor, who were more subject to be infected, and in the most pitiful plight when they were taken with the infection. But then it must be added to that a great number of them died; indeed it was scarce possible it should be otherwise.

I have not said one word here about the physic or preparations that we ordinarily made use of on this terrible occasion—I mean we that went frequently abroad up and down street, as I did; much of this was talked of in the books and bills of our quack doctors, of whom I have said enough already. It may, however, be added, that the College of Physicians were daily publishing several preparations, which they had considered of in the process of their practice, and which being to be had in print, I avoid repeating them for that reason.

On thing I could not help observing, what befell one of the quacks, who published that he had a most excellent preservative against the plague, which whoever kept about them should never be infected or liable to infection. This man, who, we may reasonably suppose, did not go abroad without some of this excellent preservative in his pocket, yet was taken by the distemper, and carried off in two or three days.

I am not of the number of the physic-haters or physic-despisers; on the contrary, I have often mentioned the regard I had to the dictates of my particular friend Dr. Heath; but yet I must acknowledge I made use of little or nothing, except, as I have observed, to keep a preparation of strong scent to have ready, in case I met with anything of offensive smells, or went too near any burying-place or dead body.

Neither did I do, what I know some did, keep the spirits always high and hot with cordials and wine, and such things, and which, as I observed, one learned physician used himself so much to as that he could not leave them off when the infection was quite gone, and so became a sot for all his life after.

I remember my friend the doctor used to say that there was a certain set of drugs and preparations which were all certainly good and useful in the case of an infection, out of which, or with which, physicians might make an infinite variety of medicines, as the ringers of bells make several hundred different rounds of music by the changing and order of sound but in six bells, and that all these preparations shall be really very good: "Therefore," said he, "I do not wonder that so vast a throng of medicines is offered in the present calamity, and almost every physician prescribes or prepares a different thing, as his judgment or experience guides him; but," says my friend, "let all the prescriptions of all the physicians in London be examined, and it will be found that they are all compounded of the same things, with such variations only as the particular fancy of the doctor leads him to; so that," says he, "every man, judging a little of his own constitution and manner of his living, and circumstances of his being infected, may direct his own medicines out of the ordinary drugs and preparations. Only that," says he, "some recommend one thing as most sovereign, and some another. Some," says he, "think that *pill. ruff.*, which is called itself the antipestilential pill, is the best preparation that can be made; others think that Venice treacle is sufficient of itself to resist the contagion; and I," says he, "think as both these think, viz., that the last is good to take beforehand to prevent it, and the last, if touched, to expel it." According to this opinion, I several times took Venice treacle, and a sound sweat upon it, and thought myself as well fortified against the infection as any one could be fortified by the power of physic.

As for quackery and mountebanks, of which the town was so full, I listened to none of them, and have observed often since, with some wonder, that for two years after the plague I scarcely saw or heard of one of them about town. Some fancied they were all swept away in the infection to a man, and were for calling it a particular mark of God's vengeance upon them for leading the poor people into the pit of destruction, merely for the lucre of a little money they got by them; but I cannot go that length neither. That abundance of them died is certain; many of them came within the reach of my own knowledge; but that all of them were swept off I must question. I believe rather they fled into the country, and tried their practices upon the people there, who were in apprehension of the infection before it came among them.

This, however, is certain, not a man of them appeared for a great while in or about London. There were, indeed, several doctors who published bills recommending their several physical preparations for cleansing the body, as they call it, after the plague, and needful, as they said, for such people to take who had been visited and had been cured; whereas, I must own, I believe that it was the opinion of the most eminent physicians at that time that the plague was itself a sufficient purge, and that those who escaped the infection needed no physic to cleanse their bodies of any other things, the running sores, the tumours, &c., which were broke and kept open by the directions of the physicians, having sufficiently cleansed them; and that all other distempers, and causes of distempers, were effectually carried off that way; and as the physicians gave this as their opinions wherever they came, the quacks got little business.

There were, indeed, several little hurries which happened after the decrease of the plague, and which, whether they were contrived to fright and disorder the people, as some imagined, I cannot say, but sometimes we were told the plague would return by such a time; and the famous Solomon Eagle, the naked Quaker I have mentioned, prophesied evil tidings every day; and several others telling us that London had not been sufficiently scourged, and that sorer and severer strokes were yet behind. Had they stopped there, or had they descended to particulars, and told us that the city should the next year be destroyed by fire, then, indeed, when we had seen it come to pass, we should not have been to blame to have paid more than a common respect to their prophetic spirits; at least we should have wondered at them, and have been more serious in our inquiries after the meaning of it, and whence they had the foreknowledge. But as they generally told us of a relapse into the plague, we have had no concern since that about them; yet by those frequent clamours, we were all kept with some kind of apprehensions constantly upon us; and if any died suddenly, or if the spotted fevers at any time increased, we were presently alarmed; much more if the number of the plague increased, for to the end of the year there were always between 200 and 300 of the plague. On any of these occasions, I say, we were alarmed anew.

Those who remember the city of London before the fire must remember that there was then no such place as that we now call Newgate Market, but that in the middle of the street which is now called Blowbladder Street, and which had its name from the butchers, who used to kill and dress their sheep there (and who, it seems, had a custom to blow up their meat with pipes to make it look thicker and fatter than it was, and were punished there for it by the Lord Mayor); I say, from the end of the street towards Newgate there stood two long rows of shambles for the selling meat.

It was in those shambles that two persons falling down dead, as they were buying meat, gave rise to a rumour that the meat was all infected, which, though it might affright the people, and spoiled the market for two or three days, yet it appeared plainly afterwards that there was nothing of truth in the suggestion. But nobody can account for the possession of fear when it takes hold of the mind.

However, it pleased God, by the continuing of the winter weather, so to restore the health of the city that by February following we reckoned the distemper quite ceased, and then we were not so easily frighted again.

There was still a question among the learned, and at

first perplexed the people a little, and that was in what manner to purge the house and goods where the plague had been, and how to render them habitable again, which had been left empty during the time of the plague. Abundance of perfumes and preparations were prescribed by physicians, some of one kind and some of another, in which the people who listened to them put themselves to a great, and indeed, in my opinion, to an unnecessary expense; and the poorer people, who only set open their windows night and day, burned brimstone, pitch, and gunpowder, and such things in their rooms, did as well as the best; nay, the eager people, who, as I said above, came home in haste and at all hazards, found little or no inconvenience in their houses, nor in the goods, and did little or nothing to them.

However, in general, prudent, cautious people did enter into some measures for airing and sweetening their houses, and burned perfumes, incense, benjamin, rosin, and sulphur, in their rooms close shut up, and then let the air carry it all out with a blast of gunpowder; others caused large fires to be made all day and all night for several days and nights; by the same token that two or three were pleased to set their houses on fire, and so effectually sweetened them by burning them down to the ground; as particularly one at Ratcliff, one in Holborn, and one at Westminster; besides two or three that were set on fire, but the fire was happily got out again before it went far enough to burn down the houses; and one citizen's servant, I think it was in Thames Street, carried so much gunpowder into his master's house, for clearing it of the infection, and managed it so foolishly, that he blew up part of the roof of the house. But the time was not fully come that the city was to be purged by fire, nor was it far off; for within nine months more I saw it all lying in ashes; when, as some of our quacking philosophers pretend, the seeds of the plague were entirely destroyed, and not before; a notion too ridiculous to speak of here, since, had the seeds of the plague remained in the houses, not to be destroyed but by fire, how has it been that they have not since broken out, seeing all those buildings in the suburbs and liberties, all in the great parishes of Stepney, Whitechapel, Aldgate, Bishopsgate, Shoreditch, Cripplegate, and St. Giles, where the fire never came, and where the plague raged with the greatest violence, remain still in the same condition they were in before?

But to leave these things just as I found them, it was certain that those people who were more than ordinarily cautious of their health, did take particular directions for what they called seasoning of their houses, and abundance of costly things were consumed on that account, which I cannot but say not only seasoned those houses, as they desired, but filled the air with very grateful and wholesome smells, which others had the share of the benefit of as well as those who were at the expenses of them.

And yet after all, though the poor came to town very precipitantly, as I have said, yet I must say the rich made no such haste. The men of business, indeed, came up, but many of them did not bring their families to town till the spring came on, and that they saw reason to depend upon it that the plague would not return.

The Court, indeed, came up soon after Christmas, but the nobility and gentry, except such as depended upon and had employment under the administration, did not come so soon.

I should have taken notice here, that notwithstanding the violence of the plague in London and in other places, yet it was very observable that it was never on board the fleet, and yet for some time there was a strange press in the river, and even in the streets, for seamen to man the fleet. But it was in the beginning of the year, when the plague was scarce begun, and not at all come down to that part of the city where they usually press for seamen; and though a war with the Dutch was not at all grateful to the people at that time, and the seamen went with a kind of reluctancy into the service, and many complained of being dragged into it by force, yet it proved in the event a happy violence to several of them, who had probably perished in the general calamity, and who, after the summer service was over, though they had cause to lament the desolation of their families, who—when they came back, were many of them in their graves—yet they had room to be thankful that they were carried out of the reach of it, though so much against their wills. We indeed had a hot war with the Dutch that year, and one very great engagement at sea, in which the Dutch were worsted, but we lost a great many men and some ships. But, as I observed, the plague was not in the fleet, and when they came to lay up the ships in the river the violent part of it began to abate.

I would be glad if I could close the account of this melancholy year with some particular examples historically; I mean of the thankfulness to God, our preserver, for our being delivered from this dreadful calamity. Certainly the circumstance of the deliverance, as well as the terrible enemy we were delivered from, called upon the whole nation for it. The circumstances of the deliverance were indeed very remarkable, as I have in part mentioned already, and particularly the dreadful condition which we were all in, when we were, to the surprise of the whole town, made joyful with the hope of a stop of the infection.

Nothing but the immediate finger of God, nothing but omnipotent power, could have done it. The contagion despised all medicine; death raged in every corner; and had it gone on as it did then, a few weeks more would have cleared the town of all, and everything that had a soul. Men everywhere began to despair; every heart failed them for fear; people were made desperate through the anguish of their souls, and the terrors of death sat in the very faces and countenances of the people.

In that very moment, when we might very well say, "Vain was the help of man,"—I say, in that very moment it pleased God, with a most agreeable surprise, to cause the fury of it to abate, even of itself; and the malignity declining, as I have said, though infinite numbers were sick, yet fewer died, and the very first week's bill decreased 1843; a vast number indeed!

It is impossible to express the change that appeared in the very countenances of the people that Thursday morning when the weekly bill came out. It might have been perceived in their countenances that a secret surprise and smile of joy sat on everybody's face. They shook one another by the hands in the streets, who would hardly go on the same side of the way with one another before. Where the streets were not too broad, they would open their windows and call from one house to another, and ask how they did, and if they had heard the good news that the plague was abated. Some would return, when they said good news, and ask, "What good news?" and when they answered that the plague was abated and the bills decreased almost 2000, they would cry out, "God be praised," and would weep aloud for joy, telling them they had heard nothing of it; and such was the joy of the people that it was, as it were, life to them from the grave. I could almost set down as many extravagant things done in the excess of their joy as of their grief; but that would be to lessen the value of it.

I must confess myself to have been very much dejected

just before this happened; for the prodigious number that were taken sick the week or two before, besides those that died, was such, and the lamentations were so great everywhere, that a man must have seemed to have acted even against his reason if he had so much as expected to escape; and as there was hardly a house but mine in all my neighbourhood but what was infected, so had it gone on it would not have been long that there would have been any more neighbours to be infected. Indeed it is hardly credible what dreadful havoc the last three weeks had made, for if I might believe the person whose calculations I always found very well grounded, there were not less than 30,000 people dead and near 100,000 fallen sick in the three weeks I speak of; for the number that sickened was surprising, indeed it was astonishing, and those whose courage upheld them all the time before, sank under it now.

In the middle of their distress, when the condition of the city of London was so truly calamitous, just then it pleased God, as it were, by His immediate hand to disarm this enemy; the poison was taken out of the sting. It was wonderful; even the physicians themselves were surprised at it. Wherever they visited they found their patients better; either they had sweated kindly, or the tumours were broke, or the carbuncles went down, and the inflammations round them changed colour, or the fever was gone, or the violent headache was assuaged, or some good symptom was in the case; so that in a few days everybody was recovering, whole families that were infected and down, that had ministers praying with them, and expected death every hour, were revived and healed, and none died at all out of them.

Nor was this by any new medicine found out, or new method of cure discovered, or by any experience in the operation which the physicians or surgeons attained to;

but it was evidently from the secret invisible hand of Him that had at first sent this disease as a judgment upon us; and let the atheistic part of mankind call my saying what they please, it is no enthusiasm; it was acknowledged at that time by all mankind. The disease was enervated and its malignity spent; and let it proceed from whencesoever it will, let the philosophers search for reasons in nature to account for it by, and labour as much as they will to lessen the debt they owe to their Maker, those physicians who had the least share of religion in them were obliged to acknowledge that it was all supernatural, that it was extraordinary, and that no account could be given of it.

If I should say that this is a visible summons to us all to thankfulness, especially we that were under the terror of its increase, perhaps it may be thought by some, after the sense of the thing was over, an officious canting of religious things, preaching a sermon instead of writing a history, making myself a teacher instead of giving my observations of things; and this restrains me very much from going on here, as I might otherwise do. But if ten lepers were healed, and but one returned to give thanks, I desire to be as that one, and to be thankful for myself.

Nor will I deny but there were abundance of people who, to all appearance, were very thankful at that time; for their mouths were stopped, even the mouths of those whose hearts were not extraordinary long affected with it. But the impression was so strong at that time that it could not be resisted, no, not by the worst of the people.

It was a common thing to meet people in the street that were strangers, and that we knew nothing at all of, expressing their surprise. Going one day through Aldgate, and a pretty many people being passing and repassing, there comes a man out of the end of the Minories, and looking a little up the street and down, he throws his hands abroad, "Lord, what an alteration is here! Why, last week I came along here, and hardly anybody was to be seen." Another man, I heard him, adds to his words, " 'T is all wonderful; 't is all a dream." "Blessed be God," says a third man, "and let us give thanks to Him, for 't is all His own doing, human help and human skill was at an end." These were all strangers to one another. But such salutations as these were frequent in the street every day; and in spite of a loose behaviour, the very common people went along the streets giving God thanks for their deliverance.

It was now, as I said before, the people had cast off all apprehensions, and that too fast; indeed we were no more afraid now to pass by a man with a white cap upon his head, or with a cloth wrapt round his neck, or with his leg limping, occasioned by the sores in his groin, all which were frightful to the last degree but the week before. But now the street was full of them, and these poor recovering creatures, give them their due, appeared very sensible of their unexpected deliverance; and I should wrong them very much if I should not acknowledge that I believe many of them were really thankful. But I must own, that for the generality of the people, it might too justly be said of them as was said of the children of Israel, after their being delivered from the host of Pharaoh, when they passed the Red Sea, and looked back, and saw the Egyptians overwhelmed in the water, viz., that they sang His praise, but they soon forgot His works.

I can go no farther here. I should be counted censorious, and perhaps unjust, if I should enter into the unpleasing work of reflecting, whatever cause there was for it, upon the unthankfulness and return of all manner of wickedness among us, which I was so much an eyewitness of myself. I shall conclude the account of this calamitous year therefore with a coarse but sincere stanza

of my own, which I placed at the end of my ordinary
memorandums the same year they were written:—

A dreadful plague in London was
In the year sixty-five,
Which swept an hundred thousand souls
Away; yet I alive!

H. T.

MODERN LIBRARY GIANTS

A series of sturdily bound and handsomely printed, full-sized library editions of books formerly available only in expensive sets. These volumes contain from 600 to 1,400 pages each.

THE MODERN LIBRARY GIANTS REPRESENT A SELECTION OF THE WORLD'S GREATEST BOOKS